Gift of the
Phoenix

Donna Cook

Enjoy the journey!

Donna Cook

Published by Penrose House Press, LLC
United States of America
www.penrosehousepress.com

www.giftofthephoenix.com

ISBN 978-0-9882089-0-2

Printed in the United States of America

Acknowledgements

My sincere thanks to those who made this novel possible.

Elyse Martin, editor extraordinaire and stalwart friend. This book would not be here without you.

Elizabeth Mulleneaux, the most loyal cheerleader a writer could hope for and President of the official fan club.

All my amazing readers, some of whom knew me before and some of whom didn't; the final product is much improved because of you: Brad Boren, Staci Boren, Julie Boyer, Ian Crittendon, Maryann Cook, Carly Griffitts, Ketsy Hendershott, Krystal Hillsman, Ashley Lee, Becca Martin, Kyle Martin, Rachel McAvoy, Paul Moreno, Allison Nielsen, Lauren Ray, and Marjory Steele. If I have inadvertently omitted anyone, please accept my apologies, blame my poor record-keeping, and know your voice made a difference. Thank you.

Michael Arbon, Vicki Armstrong, Staci Boren, Blake Cook, Evan Grainger, Lim Lai Hock, Lynn Bennett, Michael A. Johnson, Janet Little, Rachel McAvoy, June Paxton, Freddie and Moira Proctor, Pollyanna Rondeau, Patrick L. Rowley, Brian Rushing, and Margaret M. St. John for their generosity and support of the novel. Modern-day patrons and rock stars, every last one.

My mother, Barbara, the first to believe in me.

My father, Donald, for igniting my love of reading at a tender age.

My sons John, Benjamin, and Christopher, who inspired the tale of three heroes and gave their mother unfailing enthusiasm and support.

Kira (the book blurb Queen), Sheahan, and Annika, daughters of my heart.

My wonderful husband and creative soul mate, Kevin, for the awe-inspiring cover illustration, for never letting me forget I am a writer, and for giving me joy every, single day.

To Elyse
for helping me bring the Phoenix to life

and

To Kevin
for bringing it back from the dead.

PART 1

The Gathering

Prologue

When the flame that had been burning for the last 1,074 years fell to a wisp and winked out of existence, the seven men and women ringing the altar knew they were about to witness something rare. They did not know they were about to witness something devastating. They stood in the center of an upper room, hewn out of rock in a time before time, circled by windows open in every direction to the sky beyond. A chill air crept in, past the circle of cloaked figures, and into the void left by the flame.

Nashua cradled the glass orb in her hands, longing to dry her palms. The Head of the Order gave Nashua a warning glance, as if she needed one. Not the slightest movement could deviate from the ceremony. She knew that. She took a breath and forced her hands to still. *Just don't drop it,* she thought.

The man opposite Nashua, his cloak a ghost of color in the darkness, held his orb over the coals on the altar. He rotated it until the opening in the top faced down. "Relessa."

A puff of ash fell from his orb and settled on the coals. Just as it should.

He turned his orb upright and placed it on the stone tablet in front of him. Around the circle the ceremony progressed, through each Order member until it came to Nashua. *My turn.* She raised the orb, walking her fingers along its surface, rotating it, praising her steady hands. "Relessa." The ash released to the coals below. Relieved, she set it on the tablet in front of her.

The two remaining members of the Order of Ceinoth returned their ash, ending with the Head of the Order. The Head raised her hands, the sleeves of her cloak sliding down her arms, and spoke with the rhythm of a drum: "Eta retune. Eta retune. Eta retune." She lowered her arms. They were only minutes away.

3

All were silent. Except for the last light of day, all was dark.

The coals burst into life, illuminating the cloaked members of the Order and the round room in which they stood. The flames roared toward them. Each flinched but the blaze halted and they recovered once it was clear the fire would not leap its bounds. Nashua could see now why the altar of coals was so large. This was not the minute flame she was accustomed to seeing. The fire dominated the whole of the altar. The entire room was aglow. She fought the need to draw back from the heat.

All awareness in the room turned to Nashua. The Head of the Order met her eyes. Suppressing her nerves, Nashua focused and withdrew into herself. Her vision withdrew too until all she saw was the Eternal Flame in front of her. The song began within her. The magic, too. The pewter horn around her neck warmed and reverberated with magical power. She sang the Song of Calling with more than just her voice. The magic carried the song across the entire land to every soul in it. She felt immersed in power, her body pulsating with the pewter horn. When the last note left her and the song died away the magic went with it and she was only Nashua again, aware of all around her. She felt mournful. She would never sing that way again.

The Rock of Light fell to silence; only the crackling of the flames remained. The pendant of the Head of the Order, silver flames surrounded by a braided band of ribbon, glinted in the light. Time slipped and Nashua had the odd feeling of eternity pausing and claiming this one moment.

The Head led the group around the altar to their final position facing the Pillar. Nashua felt the warmth from the Eternal Flame blazing behind them. Raised in front of them, the cup-shaped Pillar of Receiving stood waiting. Beyond was the window facing in the direction of the Realm of the Phoenix, and now, at last, Nashua could look for herself.

She stared openmouthed at the sight before her. A veil of darkness swept over the land, approaching them, concealing what she was looking for. It rushed forward until it completely surrounded the Rock of Light in darkness. The Great Darkness was everywhere. The only light anywhere in the land was now inside this tower, coming from the Eternal Flame behind them, brought to life when the Phoenix had resurrected itself in the Realm.

Now, after its journey from the Realm to the Rock of Light, cloaked in darkness along the way, the Phoenix emerged before them.

The Glorious Bird.

Nashua saw now why the Phoenix was so called. Its feathers were so brilliant they appeared still to be aflame. Its eyes shone and danced as if made of glowing embers. The bird filled the window as it flew in and dwarfed the members standing weak-kneed in front of it. The wind from its wings beat back Nashua's hair and cloak. Nashua felt as much heat from the Phoenix as she did from its flame behind her.

The Phoenix hovered over the pillar between it and the Order members. In its claws was a massive egg of ash. The Phoenix set the egg on the pillar. The Head of the Order bowed. The other members followed and Nashua heard the bird flying away. When they straightened, the bird was already in the distance, the darkness retreating with it, leaving only the first moonlight in its wake. A rare event indeed.

Nashua's eyes leapt to something else. The egg of ash was glowing. *Was this supposed to happen?* She snuck a glance at the Head of the Order. As the ceremony demanded, the Head had started toward the pillar, but she looked like someone trying not to appear alarmed. Nashua looked back at the egg. A ball of light emerged from it, expanding past it. Nashua resisted the urge to retreat as the ball of light came nearer to where they all stood. She looked at the other members. Decorum was fading. Each member was turning to the Head of the Order for guidance. *This is not supposed to happen.*

The Head signaled for them to stay in their places but she was no longer moving forward herself. The light touched the Head of the Order and they all jumped as she cried out in pain and leapt backwards.

Nashua turned back to the light.

She could not look away now even if she wanted to. All down the line, Order members jerked back as if they had been burned. As the light pressed on Nashua she felt no pain. She was bound in place by

5

delicious warmth. All around her was the dome of light, pulsating in a rainbow of colors. She was in there alone.

In front of her were the pillar and the egg of ash.

She felt an urge to pick it up. She dared not. That was the job of the Head of the Order.

The light grew brighter, as if urging her on. She squinted against it but kept her eyes fixed on the egg. She stood a moment longer, then made her decision. She approached the pillar and climbed the steps. She hesitated. The prompting to act intensified. She reached up, cupped the egg in both hands, and brought it down to her. It was heavier than she imagined, with the texture of porous stone.

Suddenly, it crumbled. Nashua's heart leapt into her throat. Her hands fumbled to contain what was inside, dropping to her knees in her efforts to salvage it. The egg of ash was more than just ash this time. In fact, there was barely any ash at all and what little there was, Nashua realized with horror, was strewn on her gown and the floor around her.

Before she could think any more, Nashua started speaking. It wasn't her voice. It was low, melodious, sorrowful, powerful.

As each word passed out of her mouth, the Order members standing outside the ball of light listened with astonishment, which soon ascended to horror. When the light finally withdrew the Order members could only stare, a chill rooting them to the spot. Nashua knelt in the center, holding more than ash and shaking like she would never stop.

One

1,203 years later.

The old woman looked like a piece of fruit left to rot in the sun. Corren watched her cross the grounds of Tower Hall South, home to a clandestine group of wizards and their pupils. Unknown visitors were uncommon, but she drew his attention for more reasons than that. He had been extracting finger root with a single word, *enbiree*, and collecting it in a woolen bag. The appearance of this woman caused him to stop mid movement. He stood under a hickory tree, the bag lying forgotten at his feet.

She drew near, her brittle hair yellowed in the sun. Now he noticed her eyes. One was brown, the other blue. He found it uncomfortable to look at her, as if he were staring impolitely at her oddity, but neither could he look away. She shuffled under the canopy of the tree, her frame darkened by shadow, and stopped. She was here for him, a fact he somehow knew the moment he saw her.

"Corren of Landsdowne," she said.

Just as this stranger's presence was out of the ordinary, so too was this greeting. It had been years since he was "Corren of Landsdowne." No one from that village would know to look for him here.

Memories flashed through his mind: Corren watching Mother Taiven collapse in front of Tower Hall South on their way home to Landsdowne... wizards and witches swarming around her body and ushering him inside their stone halls... the echoing of their voices as he heard phrases like "what do we do with him?" and "who would take on an eight-year-old boy?" Even now, Corren was amazed at how sharply he could recall the memory of himself, orphaned for the second time in his life, huddled on a narrow bed in an empty room, not knowing what would become of him, not yet knowing it was

Aradia who would save him. It was a turning point in his childhood. Aradia had knelt by his bed—her long silvery hair and powerful presence a contrast to her young age—and asked him "will you allow me to care for you?" He knew at that moment that nothing could harm him if she decided to keep him safe. So he stayed. Magic had permeated every aspect of his life since then, a skill that came so natural to him it felt akin to fate. Even before he was of age, Aradia selected him to be one of her apprentices. Despite his promise to himself that he would find his parents someday, in the thirteen years following Mother Taiven's death, he never did make it back.

So why was this woman calling him "Corren of Landsdowne"?

"You know me?" he asked, unable to tame his eagerness.

The woman nodded. "Once. Long ago."

He took a step forward. She was too aged to be his mother, but perhaps... "Are you my grandmother?"

Her strange eyes saddened. "No, boy. I bring you news of a different sort."

Her answer stung and he realized the yearning for his family had never lessened—it had only been buried. He regretted his rashness. It was not like him to be so unguarded. "What news?" he asked, trying to recover a sense of formality.

She did not reply, only stretched out her frail hand. Shining in her palm was a red stone. "Take it," she said. As if there were nothing else he could have done, he did.

It was rectangular, nearly as long as his hand and half as wide, coming to a soft point at both ends. Its scarlet color was captivating. He wrapped his fingers around its smooth surface and everything fled from his consciousness. All he knew was the stone and himself holding it. A jolt raced up his arm. As abruptly as it came the feeling fled. He opened his hand. The stone looked harmless enough, but his palm tingled and heart pounded. Something inside him was different. Something he did not know had been sleeping, started to awake.

"Show it to no one," the old woman said, and he startled. Her voice pulled him back into the world. "*Tell* it to no one," she said. "Come see me in a month, exactly."

"What is it?" He did not mean to whisper.

8

She did not answer, only gave him directions to her home... in Landsdowne.

"How do you know me? Who are you?"

She was already turning to leave. "You will know more than you want to soon enough." She left the shadow of the tree and slowly crossed the grass with the concentrated walk of the elderly. He watched her only for a moment, his vision drawn to the stone. He felt as if part of him were sliding into its depths. He closed his fist around the stone and held it protectively to his chest.

He knew he should embrace caution. Unknown magic could be dangerous, deadly even. He watched the old woman disappear around a building. He feared neither the woman nor the stone. Did that make him a fool? He began to consider how, in a month's time, he would sneak away to Landsdowne, without Aradia knowing the reason why.

Nicolai had never been this close to a wizard before. It was almost enough to distract him from recent events. Almost.

It was a strange thing to see a wizard pulling water from Nicolai's own well. He was clearly parched, for he filled his cup with the ladle and drank it down in nearly one gulp. Travelling long, no doubt. Nicolai wanted to ask why a wizard couldn't just conjure up some water, but decided against it.

"I should've brought more water," the wizard said. "I wasn't expecting such a long journey today."

"Help yourself," Nicolai said and extended his hand. "I'm Nicolai of Knobby Tree."

He shook it wearily. "Corren of Tower Hall South."

Corren the wizard was tall, nearly as tall as Nicolai, and held himself with the surety of someone who took self-confidence for granted, though Nicolai sensed no air of superiority either. His sharp features and dark hair added to his rather serious countenance, but all this was softened by his clear blue eyes and polite manner. He wore a cloak of fine linen, tightly woven, soft from the looks of it.

He was not the first traveler to make use of their well, though certainly the most interesting. Their well was situated not far from the

9

road leading from Stonebridge to South Caedmonia. The road ran along his family's homestead on one side, neighbors to the west bordered another, and the other two sides were hemmed in by the Wilds. Nicolai's family had farmed their land in the shadow of the Wilds for ten generations. Local farmers of Knobby Tree thought it an unfortunate plot: cursed for its location. It was so undesirable that even if Nicolai's family wanted to sell no one would buy it. Nicolai thought this foolish considering the fact that their soil was known to be fertile (at least in recent years), but this was not enough to dispel the fear of generations. Nicolai's father was never much bothered by the presence of the Wilds, but when Nicolai was a child his mother sent him out to play with the admonition not to go into the trees.

Corren sighed and wiped his brow. It was a warm autumn day, but Nicolai preferred it to working in the summer heat. It mattered less now that the harvest was finally over. "Traveling long?" Nicolai asked.

"Well, I thought I was going to... to a meeting in Landsdowne, but as soon as I got there I was sent straight back out. Now I'm going to Stonebridge just to fetch a pot for a little old lady." The wizard glanced at Nicolai and shrugged as if to say he wasn't bothered by it.

Nicolai knew better. He smiled. "Elders can be demanding that way."

"I suppose." Corren took another drink, tipping his head back to empty the cup, and set the ladle on the rim of the well.

"If you've a flask I'll fill it for you."

"I was going to ask. Thank you."

Corren and Nicolai grabbed the ladle at the same time, pulled away together, and inadvertently knocked it down the center of the well. Nicolai dove for it, catching the end of the handle with the tips of his fingers before grabbing it with his other hand.

"That was close," he said, depositing it into the bucket. His stomach smarted from where he had crushed it against the well. Corren was staring in astonishment, not at Nicolai, but at his shirt. Nicolai followed his gaze with a glance and his heart tightened. His necklace had come out and the yellow stone attached to it glinted in the sun. Nicolai shoved it back under his shirt, his heart pounding in his ears.

Corren was filling his water flask as if nothing had happened at all. Nicolai thought he saw the wizard's hands shaking.

"Well," Corren said, glancing at him without quite meeting his eyes. "I thank you for your hospitality. I'd best be on my way."

Nicolai nodded a farewell. Corren had noticed the stone, there was no doubt about that, and Nicolai questioned the wisdom of wearing it. *But what else am I to do with this thing?*

Nicolai felt sure he would be seeing Corren again, and his sense of foreboding only increased when the wizard headed not for Stonebridge, but back the way he'd come.

The day the woman visited Nicolai, he had been clearing the ditch in the west field. Rain had clogged it with debris and the water broke a groove through the side of the trench. She came along the edge of the corn stalks that stood well over her head: the last corn days away from harvesting. He first thought she was a stranger to the area and likely lost. He wondered how someone so feeble looking came to be traveling alone. Perhaps she wasn't lost but had a companion who was hurt and needed help. He tried to anticipate her reason for being there, but by the time she was next to him he found himself waiting for her to speak. Something about this woman stilled him. It may have been her eyes, the one brown and one blue making it difficult to know which one to look at. Still, something else caused him to look at her as if he already knew she had been coming.

"You are Nicolai," she said, not as a question.

He cocked his head. "Do I know you?"

"Hmm," she said, "I suppose the answer to that is 'no.' But I know *you*, and I'm here to give you what is yours."

She held out a hand, her skin mottled with sun spots. In her palm was a stone. It was such a luminous yellow he squinted to look at it. She held it out, but he did not take it.

"That is not mine," he said, wondering how she could think it was.

"It belongs to you," she said nodding.

"I think you've made a mistake."

"I'm sure I haven't." She took his hand.

11

"But I've never seen..." She placed the stone in his palm, released him, and his words died in his mouth. It was cool to the touch as a gem is cool, but he realized at once this was no mere gem. There was something else within it, something he could not see, but could feel. His fingers curled inward, the stone cradled in his hand. When his grasp was complete, a sensation ignited in his palm, shot up his arm, and caused him to jerk in surprise. He gaped at her.

She leaned in, her eyes holding his. "It is yours."

Despite her admonition to keep the stone a secret, he had no intention of hiding such a thing from his father. After she had gone, he went toward his father working in the north field. Nicolai began with a walk but after a few steps burst into a run.

Nicolai stood over his father by nearly a head. Nicolai told him what happened, still holding the stone and catching his breath.

Graham furrowed his brows at the stone, which Nicolai held close as if afraid something was going to happen to it. "How did she know your name?"

"I don't know. She never told me hers, now I think of it."

"You didn't ask?"

Nicolai thought back on the conversation. It had been peculiar, like a dream, or something that happened without his feet quite on the ground. "No."

Graham looked around, scanning for her. There was only the field, the house, the road. "Why would a stranger give you something so valuable?" he asked. "Do you think it was stolen?"

Nicolai dropped his eyes to the stone. He felt part of him sinking into its center, while the rest of him stood rooted to the earth. The stone pulled at Nicolai. If he should have been alarmed by this, he wasn't. The old woman had said it was his. Against all reason Nicolai believed her. "No," he said. "I don't think it's stolen."

Nicolai felt an urge to leave and tightened his fingers around the stone.

"Nicolai? What's wrong?"

Nicolai shook his head. He felt he needed to run, but his mind fought against it. He told himself to calm down. Why did he feel fear?

Graham looked at Nicolai in concern. His eyes dropped to the stone, and he pressed his lips together. "I... don't know... if you should keep that."

It took all Nicolai's will to fight the urge to run from his father. Perhaps he *should* fear the stone. Perhaps there was dark magic in it. What else would bring on such emotion? But Nicolai didn't fear the stone. He feared his father. His father who he loved, his father who had never harmed him. Still, he needed to run. Escape. But Nicolai would not allow his feet to do it. He would not run from his father.

His face must have betrayed something of this.

"What's wrong?" Graham asked. "What is it?" He leaned in and Nicolai flinched back.

Graham straightened in surprise.

Nicolai brought the stone up, pressed it to his chest with both hands. His father's eyes locked on it.

"Drop the stone, son."

"No." His voice sounded far away but was firm. He had to run. Flee. Run *now*. He felt these thoughts would crush him if he did not obey. His father's eyes were on the stone; his face resolute. Nicolai saw as if in slow motion, Graham's hand rising, his aim on the stone.

Nicolai let go his will.

Time caught up in a rush. His legs reacted but it was too late. His father's hand was already there. Nicolai jerked away in a panic, his arm flinging back and his father lunging after it. The two men stumbled, Nicolai backward and Graham ramming into Nicolai's chest as he stretched for the stone, both their eyes on it, the impact and uncertain footing bringing them to the ground. Nicolai lost the advantage of height.

As Nicolai hit the ground he saw his father's hand close around his own, and around the stone. A yellow light flashed out of the stone and Nicolai clenched his eyes shut. His father crashed on top of him, not moving. Nicolai jerked the stone away and the light withdrew.

Graham felt like dead weight. Nicolai, panting, held him and rolled him onto the ground. He feared his father had hit his head and hoped he had only passed out. Still seeing flashes from the light, Nicolai blinked his eyes furiously, pulling himself up to kneel next to his

13

father. That was when his sight cleared and he saw his father's face: his mouth hung open, his eyes staring at nothing.

Everything around Nicolai pressed in on him, turning to blackness. The screams he heard, he would later learn, belonged to his mother who had come out to the field. But to his ears and to his stricken mind her screams were nonexistent, indistinguishable from his own. Every part of him cried out as he clutched his father to his chest. He had not passed out.

The stone had killed him.

Two

To say the old woman lived in Landsdowne was not quite accurate. She lived past the boundary of the village with no signs leading to her location, not even a path snaking through the oak and elm that grew here. Driven by the knowledge of a second stone, Corren made his way as swiftly as the aches in his legs would allow. He had only a few landmarks to lead the way south—a tree stump, a creek bed, a ridge—until finally he reached his destination. The break in the trees offered a view of the Cliffs of the Realm which, some twenty miles south of here, reared into the sky. The rock surface gave the appearance of protrusions here and there but this was illusion. As if polished by a great hand, the Cliffs were smooth and harder than any known material. A reminder of powers greater than man and wizard alike.

Though drawn to this sight, Corren turned his attention to a cabin on the other side of the clearing: a structure so vine-covered it seemed just another outgrowth of the forest. He crossed the clearing and knocked on the front door. It was the second time he had knocked on the woman's door that day. When she had answered that morning, he scarcely had the opportunity to speak before she pressed two coins into his hand and insisted he travel to Stonebridge to buy her a pot. For some reason she had been difficult to argue with, but he was prepared for that now. He was not going to be sent away again without answers.

This time she did not open the door. "Come in, Corren."

He stepped inside. A bed ran along the wall to his right. Opposite him stood a loom in one corner, a rocking chair in the other, and between the two a wooden chest. The old woman sat to his left at a table under the only window. Crowded behind her was an alcove serving as kitchen with its stove, worktable, and shelving. The only decoration hung above the chest, a tapestry so aged it looked ready to disintegrate... like the old woman who owned it.

"Where's my pot?"

"I'll get your pot later," he said.

"Don't bother," she said, picking up a cup of tea. "I didn't need it anyway."

He looked at her in exasperation. She stirred her tea with a pewter spoon. From her neck hung a small horn of the same pewter, rimmed with red jewels, which she had worn when she came to the Tower, too. He'd had enough. "Tell me what this stone is."

She drank her tea, leaving only the dregs. He didn't say a word lest it should remind her of a measure of barley she needed from Moran or Welton or some such place. His legs throbbed from a day's walking and he fumed to know it had all been for a pot she didn't even need. She set her cup on the table and looked at him. "You never made it to Stonebridge, did you?"

"I... no. On the way to Stonebridge, just after the Wilds, there's a farm and..." he paused. She waited, as if she knew what he was going to say. Heart beating, he sat down at the table. "The owner has a stone like mine."

She raised her eyebrows. "Except?"

"Except it's yellow," he said, his anger draining away as he leaned forward. "Is that why you sent me? To see him?"

A smile flickered over her face.

"Why?" Corren asked. "Who is he?"

Before she could answer, she glanced out the window, her brows coming together. "Did you hear that?"

Suppressing his irritation at another delay, Corren listened. A breeze rushed through the forest, rustling leaves somewhere far from them, but nearby everything was still. "I don't hear anything."

She sat, her eyes searching. He felt sympathy for this woman, living alone without anyone to look after her, fearful of the sounds of her own world.

"I'm sure it was nothing," he said. As soon as he finished his sentence he heard something too: a crunch of leaves and a scraping on the ground.

She stood, backing away from the window. "Did you tell anyone you were coming?" She spoke in a whisper.

"No."

"Did anyone follow you?"

"Why would anyone follow me?"

She was backing into the corner, squeezing between the wall and the rocking chair, her eyes not leaving the window. "If someone is here... we must... we can't be seen."

Corren approached her with his hand raised. "It's alright. No one is—" He heard it again. It was faint, but growing louder. The sound was measured, like the footsteps of someone trying not to be heard.

"Are you in trouble?" he asked, his voice lowered now. "Is someone after you?"

She shook her head and put her finger to her lips.

Feeling unsettled, Corren reprimanded himself for allowing her fear to affect him. Deciding it was a traveler happening past, he walked to the door to see who it was. "No!" she hissed and he stopped, his hand on the handle.

The footsteps were getting closer. He felt certain it wasn't just one pair of feet walking. The footsteps stopped.

Corren and the old woman hovered in their places. He stole to the window. The flap was pulled up and a breeze slipped through the opening, chilling his brow and neck where he was perspiring. Corren edged around the sill, scanning the trees.

A hand rushed through the opening and seized him around the neck, pinning him against the wall. The old woman screamed and Corren clawed at the muscular arm choking him, but it hardly budged. A broad face came through the window and the man it belonged to grinned at Corren. His nose angled in the center, like it had been broken once. He caught sight of the old woman and said, "There's the one we want."

The door slammed against the bed and a bald man entered. He wore plain trousers and a tunic like any man might, but held a knife with a broad, curved blade. He eyed her, advancing on her. "Are you sure?"

"She has the horn," the other said, nodding to her necklace. Her hand went to it, her eyes on the knife.

Pinpricks of light jabbed at Corren's vision and his chest burned from lack of air. He fumbled on the table, his blood pounding. He felt the cup and with a surge of determination, smashed it into the face of the man in the window, shattering it into knife-like pieces. The man released him and disappeared hollering. Corren gasped for breath, coughing as the bald man lunged at him, swinging the knife. Corren stumbled to the right, grabbing the man's wrists to keep the knife away, his legs getting caught up on the end of the bed. He crashed into the wall. He croaked out an unintelligible word and coughed again, struggling against the man, his heart racing.

The first man charged through the door, blood running down his face. The bald man broke free from Corren's grasp and raised the knife.

"Forcio reva!" Corren yelled hoarsely.

Both men flew backwards.

The bald one slammed against the wall, knocking the chair and chest both. The other man crashed against the stove, roared with pain, and crumpled to the floor. Corren hurried away from the wall. The bald one recovered, his eyes locked on Corren as he lunged the tip of the blade toward Corren's chest.

"Lazien!" Corren shouted, driven by fear more than thought. The man halted and clutched his arms to his chest, the knife clattering to the floor and he dropping to the ground with it, crippled by the heat Corren sent through his body. The man cried out, writhing on the floor until, a moment later, he fell unconscious. Corren had never seen the effects of that spell on a man before. It frightened him as much as anything else.

He heard a cry. Corren spun to see the other man holding the woman in front of him with one arm. His other hand grasped her jaw, the tips of his fingers pressing wells into her skin. He glared at Corren, blood running into the crevices of his broken nose. "Don't try anything," he warned, "or I'll break her neck."

She gave a whimper and closed her eyes. For a moment the two men stared at one another, Corren's blood pounding through him.

18

"Tevala!" he shouted, raising his arm. The man's arms flung away and Corren lunged forward to pull the woman toward him. The man roared, reaching after her, but as Corren caught her, he yelled "Lazien!" once more. The man doubled over and collapsed to the floor, his face contorting with screams until he, like his companion, fell still.

Panting, Corren and the old woman stared at the men on the floor. Their presence seemed to consume the entire room. Corren struggled to comprehend what just happened, his body pricking. The old woman was shaking. "Are you alright?" he asked.

She nodded, but did not speak, her eyes staying on the man who had seized her.

"Who are these men? Why are they after you?"

She shook her head. "I don't know. I don't know how... anyone found me." Her eyes were wide, her breathing rapid. "I have to tell you quickly... before it's too late."

"Look, please...sit down," Corren said, trying to calm her, though he did not feel calm either. "Tell me what's going on." She had not moved and was still trembling. Afraid she was about to collapse, Corren took her by both shoulders and guided her back to her chair. "Here, sit. It's alright."

Circling the table to his own seat, his legs began to shake as he stepped over the man on the floor. When Corren saw the knife not far from where the bald man had fallen, he retrieved it even though he knew the man would not wake for hours. Corren sat. "Wh... Why are these men after you?"

"I..." She stopped, closed her eyes, took a breath. Littered on the table were shards of her cup. One still had specks of moist tea leaf clinging to it. The woman's hands were clasped together and Corren put his hand over hers. She seized it. Taken aback, he waited in silence. Her breathing settled; her grip on his hand eased. She squeezed his hand once more before releasing it. "Thank you, Corren."

When she opened her eyes he was not disturbed by their oddity, but found them instead to have their own beauty.

19

"There is much to tell," she said. "Where to begin?"

He took a breath. "Why don't you begin, by telling me your name?"

Corren felt it must be approaching midnight, though he could not say for certain. He had traveled as far away from Nashua's cabin as his exhaustion would allow before collapsing into a depression under an elm tree. It was not safe to stay at the cabin, even for the night, but neither did he have the strength to travel back to Tower Hall South. He was grateful Aradia was away on another trip. She would learn of his absence eventually, but he was glad he did not have to think of how to explain it to her now. He had enough troubling him.

Despite his fatigue, his mind would not rest. He wondered if the men who had attacked them were awake yet. Nashua had warned Corren about them. "They were after me," she had said. "They didn't know about you. If you let them go, they'll take news of you."

"What are you suggesting?"

"You must decide."

Corren was not about to kill anybody, no matter who they were. Neither could he keep them captive for months on end. He had decided on a memory charm. They would awake with no memory of him, confused and alone in Nashua's cabin.

Alone, because Nashua was no longer there either.

Not far from her cabin, Nashua lay in a deep, unmarked grave. As soon as she had delivered her message to Corren, the force that had kept her alive for the last twelve centuries no longer sustained her. She completed her task and was free from her burden.

There was a new burden now, one for Corren to bear.

He would not do so alone.

Three

When Nicolai was six years old, he discovered a secret.

His mother and father were picking beans in the east field, as he had been, most of the day in the heat. He longed for shade or a place to lie down. Little by little he slowed as his parents advanced ahead of him. The bags at their waists gaped open for more beans. More and more. Always more and never finished, or so it felt to Nicolai. His father noticed him dragging behind. "Go find a lucky clover," he said over his shoulder. "It'll give us a good harvest."

Nicolai did not hesitate. He knelt and slipped the strap off his shoulder, the bag sagging on the ground, and ran for the clover fields at the edge of the forest. "Don't go into the trees," his mother called. He didn't stop running until he was in the line of shadow next to the woods, the clover spread out like a blanket under his feet. An escape from the sun was one reason he'd taken his father's challenge so eagerly, but the other reason was quite different.

He felt there was something magical about these forests, the Wilds they were called. If they were wild, they were also beautiful, at least in Nicolai's mind. Wherever he was, he would often find himself gazing in their direction. Even at night he would kneel on his bed, chin resting on the windowsill, so he could see their shadows in the distance. Though still a child, Nicolai recognized there was something more to his love of the Wilds than perhaps he understood. He was right.

Today he would find out why.

Crawling on all fours, feeling hidden from the world, Nicolai decided going into the trees just a *little* way would be okay so long as he found a lucky clover and brought a good harvest. A good harvest meant meat in the winter, dried fruits in the cellar and—his mother had promised—a woolen jacket. He had outgrown his current one two winters ago.

Initially, these were the thoughts he used to justify himself. They drove him past the first trees (with a flutter in his stomach), on past the second line of trees, and the third. The clover had almost gone now, replaced by leaves and twigs. He stood up. The forest was quiet.

He looked back through the trees at the slivers of field still visible. He had gone too far. He should not go any farther.

He looked ahead of him into the forest, its depths veiled by a maze of branches and tall trunks. He could not turn back either.

He took a step forward when it happened. He became aware of a sensation unlike any he'd experienced before. Something seemed to wrap around him. Or was it through him? Everything was still, except that as he looked around it seemed everything was vibrating, or maybe humming, just under the surface. Just as he was.

Though surprised by this, he didn't run home as some may have done. He didn't want it to stop, in fact wanted more of it. Surely it came from somewhere and Nicolai thought he could sense where. He began to follow it. Into the trees he went. The further in he got, the less it felt like a vibration and the more it felt like a glowing energy.

He knew he was drawing close and his steps quickened. As if materializing out of the hill itself, a tall man with mossy robes and long wild hair appeared so near to Nicolai he stumbled in his efforts to avoid colliding with him.

He should've felt afraid, leery perhaps, surprised at the least. He felt none of those things, only the glow coming from the slender man in front of him. The man neither smiled nor scowled, but studied him.

Nicolai studied him back. His eyes were the deepest green Nicolai had ever seen. He had certainly never seen *eyes* that shade before.

"You are too young," the man said.

Nicolai had the impression the conversation was over before it had even begun.

Something tugged at his awareness. It was distracting as he was trying to formulate a question to ask this man, something that would explain who he was or what Nicolai was feeling. Whatever was tugging at his mind escalated to a full jerk: "Nicolai!" The man's lips did not move.

"How did you know my name?" he asked. The man smiled.

"Nicolai!" he heard again. It wasn't the man who spoke: his mother was calling him. He cocked his head in recognition, but did not take his eyes from the man. "I want to stay."

"Nicolai!" He heard the panic in her voice.

"Go child," he said. His voice soothed him as much as the warm feeling did. "Come back when it is time."

He felt the glow within him fading, as if he were being sent away. He did not want to go. "Who are you?"

The man considered him.

"I won't tell," Nicolai promised. Unlike the promises children sometimes make without real intent, Nicolai meant what he said.

The man nodded. "I am Salerno." Nicolai smiled. He felt he had been given something precious. "Now go."

Nicolai took a few steps toward his mother's voice, then turned back. "Are you..." Nicolai stopped, but made himself finish, "...human?"

Salerno's eyebrows shot up. Nicolai feared he insulted him. Salerno's voice was majestic in his reply. "I am a faerie." Nicolai's heart soared. A faerie! A faerie had talked to *him*, a human! Not just talked to him, but told him to come back!

Nicolai longed to ask when but the energy was sliding back into a vibration now. He knew Salerno would not answer.

Nicolai ran through the forest in a blur toward the sound of his mother calling for him. As he came into her view she reached through the trees toward him, but would not go in.

The stone hung around Nicolai's neck, ever present in his mind. He sat at the table eating porridge and hearthstone biscuits. His mother sat opposite him, silence between them. His father's place at the head of the table was empty. In fact, the house felt empty. The original two-room structure was built over three hundred years ago and had, over time, gained a kitchen, a second bedroom, a porch, and a loft upstairs

23

where Nicolai slept. Behind them was the sitting area with the fireplace and mantle added by Nicolai's grandfather. This house had passed from generation to generation for years. Nicolai had never before considered just what that must have meant to the people who lived here. This home had seen many deaths.

Nicolai forced himself to take another bite of porridge. After a morning full of chores his body needed the nourishment, but eating felt a chore. There was no sign of the woman. The wizard who visited their well the day before had not returned. Nicolai regretted letting Corren go without questioning him. While his reaction to the stone *could* have been surprise at seeing something of worth in such a place and on such a man, Nicolai didn't think so. Corren knew something. Nicolai considered going to Tower Hall South to ask for him, but what if the woman came while he was gone? He didn't want to risk missing her. He felt trapped and this waiting was becoming unbearable.

His mother set her spoon on the table and leaned forward on her elbows. She finally came to say whatever had been on her mind all during breakfast. Nicolai tensed in anticipation. Like his father, his mother Reeghan was of small build. Her face gave the impression of a stern woman, an impression magnified by her exacting and straightforward personality, but people who knew her knew better. She rarely spoke harshly. Not a day in Nicolai's life had passed without an embrace from his mother. Or a smile. Until recently. "We need to plant in the north field."

Nicolai said nothing at first. No matter how bad things ever got in the past, his father never took a field out of fallow. It compromised the soil and thus, their future. It was a short-sided solution.

"The field must rest if it is to endure."

"It is the only way we can pay for the labor to help harvest."

The accusation was slight but it was there. Nicolai could not keep up with the work alone. He was to blame for their situation and they both knew it.

"Elorna knows where to find laborers," she said.

Nicolai tore off a piece of biscuit and pinched it between his fingers. "If we find someone to work for room and board and a share of the crop, we won't need to plant the north field."

"We'll have no share of the crop to spare, especially if prices are down at market again," she said. "To pay for another man we must plant more crops."

Nicolai felt she was trying to convince herself as well as him. "You know we can't do that."

Reeghan leaned closer. "If we don't plant then we must..." She bit her lip and glanced at his shirt, the stone concealed beneath it. "You must sell it."

He looked at her, the answer to her suggestion immediate and firm in his eyes.

She withdrew her hands and put them on her lap. "Then what are we to do, Nicolai? What must we do?"

Take it back, he thought. *I wish I could take it back.*

"We'll have a good crop," he said. "It will be enough."

They heard footsteps on the porch and Nicolai stood at once. By the time there was a knock, he was already at the door. He had hoped for the old woman but was not disappointed to see Corren instead, conspicuous in his wizard's cloak. They looked at one another a moment, each understanding what this encounter was going to be about.

The wizard spoke first. "I wonder if I might have a word with you about that stone?"

Reeghan jumped up from the table and the bench crashed to its side behind her. "No!"

Nicolai stared at her. "Mother..."

She rushed to the door. "You get away from us! Leave us alone!"

Corren stepped back, eyes wide, and Nicolai held his mother at her shoulders trying to restrain her. "Please stop."

"Go!" she screeched at Corren. She shoved the door closed and fumbled with the bolt.

"What are you doing?" Nicolai had never seen her like this before.

"You must destroy it," she said, her face reddening as she fought her tears. "I beg you. Destroy that thing before it destroys us all." She pressed her fingers to her mouth.

Nicolai put his hand on her shoulder and she flinched away from him. Her eyes darted to his shirt. He withdrew his hand. He wanted to ease her grieving, remove her fear, be comforted himself, but she would not let him. "I'm not going to hurt you." *Please stop looking at me like you're afraid of me.*

"But your father..."

"It was the stone," Nicolai said. "I didn't..."

"Then get rid of it!"

He jerked back.

"Bury it! Throw it in the river. The well. Anything! Why do you keep it?"

"I don't know!" He turned away from her. The stone pressed against his chest and he didn't understand it. He wore the stone to keep others safe from it, but also... to keep the stone safe from others, and he had no idea why. He was tired of not knowing what this was.

Nicolai turned to the door, his mind decided. He took hold of the latch and Reeghan grabbed his arm. Her touch was not reassuring. "Don't. Please. We know nothing of this man. He could be evil too, like the stone he seeks. Let him be gone. Let him be gone and we can be rid of it."

Nicolai did not remove his hand from the latch. She may be right; the stone could be evil. Destroying it might be the logical thing to do, but for some reason, he could not do it.

It was time to find out why.

Corren lingered in the yard of Nicolai's farmhouse, unsure of what to do next. Should he wait for Nicolai to be alone outside and approach him then? Should he try at the door again, perhaps force his way into the house if necessary? He wasn't sure he could lord over them that way, but there wasn't time to waste either. Caught by indecision, he lingered. That turned out to be enough.

When Nicolai stepped out of the house, the sound of the woman pleading came out after him. Nicolai pulled the door closed, cutting off her cries. He stepped out of the shade of the porch and into the light. He was muscular and tan from a life of labor in the sun, wearing the pants and tunic of a farmer. This fact struck Corren differently today than it had the day before.

He approached Corren now, his feet crunching on the dirt. "What do you know about this stone?" he asked. He spoke in the same mild tone Corren heard him use yesterday, only now with an undertow of determination in his voice.

Corren felt the weight of what he knew pressing on him. Nicolai would feel it soon, too. "That is a question not quickly answered," he said. "I do have answers for you."

Nicolai didn't respond, only waited. A breeze picked up and rushed by them, Corren's cloak rustling, Nicolai's hair pushed by the wind. Neither man released their gaze from the other.

Corren considered telling Nicolai what he wanted to know—he knew what it was to wait—but he remembered what Nashua had told him. He was the Gatherer. He had to trust his feelings on how to do it. He thought of the red stone in his bag. Nicolai's yellow stone. And the other. "There's someone else who needs to hear this, too. I think you both should hear it together."

"My mother won't listen," Nicolai said.

Corren shook his head. "I don't mean her."

"Then who?"

Corren hesitated. "Prince Marcellus."

Four

The pounding of horses' hooves echoed through the street and could be heard rolling down the hill through nearly all of Stonebridge. Down below, on the docks by the sea, it would be a sound like thunder, but here in the upper reaches of the city, the ground shook and the citizens lining Victory Way cheered the returning army and their prince at its head. Prince Marcellus led his knights through the gates of the grounds. Instead of going past the castle and to the stables on the left, as he normally would have done, he dismounted at the entrance. The knights filed past him, the hammering of the hooves beating in his chest. A page and a squire both rushed to him.

"Inform the king of my arrival," Marcellus said before the page reached him.

The boy stopped on his heels, bowed, said "Yes, your Highness," and went back the way he'd come.

"You'll have to take him for me today," Marcellus said, handing the reins to his squire. Marcellus preferred to care for Kedron himself, but other demands sometimes rendered this impossible. "Mind the hooves," he said.

"Yes, your Majesty."

He gave his steed a pat on the neck before allowing the squire to lead him away.

There was a line of citizens seeping out the side entrance of the castle, out the gates, and down the street. For two days following each full moon, the king heard the petitions of his subjects, but that was still a week away. Marcellus guessed the damage he saw along the southern coast of Stonebridge as he rode into the city was the reason for their presence here today.

He ascended the steps and the sentinels bowed and pulled open the doors to let him in. The arched windows surrounding the doors flooded the entryway with light. Mahogany sideboards, placed at intervals along the walls, held marble vases overflowing with flowers. Overhead a series of chandeliers bloomed in wrought iron and kept the entrance glowing even in the deep hours of night.

The page Marcellus sent upon his arrival must have delivered his message. Before reaching the Throne Room, Marcellus was met by King Clement himself. The king was a robust man bestowed with broad shoulders and an even broader smile, framed by a snowy, white beard. Atop his hair, beset with gray, sat the simple crown he preferred for those times when crowns were called for. Even when no crown adorned his father's head, Marcellus always saw him the same: the epitome of what a king should be.

"You have succeeded against the outlaws," Clement said with a smile, "with more speed than even I expected."

"They were unorganized and short on determination," Marcellus said. "The journey wearied me more than the fight."

"You never tire."

"You look worn, Father. Have you been hearing them all day?"

"They've been waiting since dawn, but I've only been able to hear them for the last hour. There was an earthquake under the sea last night and much damage was done in the southern quarter."

The southern quarter was an area of Stonebridge consisting of wooden buildings and aging docks, making it more susceptible to damage than the stone buildings in the central and northern part of the city's coastline. Marcellus thought of the citizens waiting outside the castle doors and his heart went out to them. He accepted the fact that even the greatest of kings could not protect their people from the ravages of nature, but his acceptance did not make him like it any more.

"Most areas only have water damage to contend with," the king continued, "and citizens are already cleaning. Some lost a significant portion of their goods or supplies, so we are assisting with that. The south quarter gives me the most concern. We've set up shelter in the Guild Hall and Quinn's knights are helping citizens repair the damage and distribute food."

"I'll send Orin's men to help."

"The three southernmost docks were damaged as well."

Marcellus bowed his head. "I'll see to it." He took note of the pallor of the king's skin and did not care for it. The worry Marcellus carried on behalf of his father came out from its hiding place and rose to the surface. "You should rest," Marcellus said.

The king shook his head, as Marcellus knew he would. "There is no time for resting. I've just been informed that the emissaries from Sakkara have nearly arrived. We must prepare to receive them."

"What emissaries?"

"One of the princes of Sakkara has been slain," Clement said. "I received an advance message from King Jareth several days ago, though he did not offer many details. He sent his oldest son, Prince Akren, along with Princess Praea to meet with us. I believe they are coming to ask for our assistance."

"Assistance with what?"

"That I do not know."

The carriage came to the rim of a valley and Princess Praea of Sakkara laid eyes on their destination at last. The valley was several miles across, sloping up on either side and swathed through the middle by a river. Dotted throughout were homesteads and hedged-off fields. The other side of the valley climbed into a hill until it presented Stonebridge on its crest like a gift. Despite Praea's exhaustion, she couldn't help but be awed by the sight of the City of Cities. It was the most prosperous of any kingdom and so secured by its knights that no armies had ever approached within miles of its city walls. Now that Praea set eyes on them, she didn't think anything could breech them anyway. Even from this distance the walls of the city were formidable. The walls surrounding the castle, perched on the summit overlooking the city, seemed even more forbidding. Even if an enemy could get to it, Stonebridge was well protected. It was for this reason that Praea and her brother had come.

Praea stretched her legs in front of her, careful not to crowd her brother Akren who was still sleeping. His hair stuck out in odd directions and his head rested against the frame of the carriage. This assault on his appearance was lessened by the profile of his face, as princely as a statue. Praea decided to let him rest until they were closer. It had been a difficult journey.

After they crossed the valley and passed through the city's south gate, Praea watched the shoreline far below with eagerness, for Stonebridge was legendary for more than one reason. It was home to the Bridge of a Thousand Ages. She saw it now, stretching into the sea before dead ending into nothing. The Bridge, it was said, hovered over the water with no visible support. The archway at its entrance was rumored to be magically protected so no person could step foot on the Bridge itself. In Sakkara, where most people had never seen the Bridge themselves, these tales were considered exaggerated, though Praea knew them to be true enough. Though she had desired to see the Bridge herself, it was not what she desired most. She leaned over her brother and looked to the south. There it was. Down the coast, beyond the outer reaches of the city, a structure shot up from the ground in imitation of a lighthouse. This was no lighthouse. It was the Rock of Light. Shining from within its head was a point of light. Praea shivered. Her eyes were upon the Eternal Flame at last. The carriage made a turn, began the ascent up the street, and the vision of the Eternal Flame was swept from her view.

Praea sighed and nudged her brother awake. As he groaned and saw to his appearance, she steeled herself for the purpose of their visit. She had spent the last several days turning her grief into a rock of determination. No matter what it took, this trip would not be in vain.

They soon exited the carriage in front of the castle that stood at the head of the grounds like a guard. A full five stories high with its towers rising yet higher, it was well equipped as a fortress. The arrow holes on the towers were wisely placed and battlements ran along its top in the event the city's walls—then the walls to the castle grounds—should be breeched. Despite its practicality, the castle lacked nothing in splendor. Carvings adorned the ledges of arched windows. The grand stair was flanked on either side by pillars topped by gold orbs, symbols of royal power glittering in the sun.

King Clement and Prince Marcellus, the personifications of such power, were no less distinctive. Praea had never seen the Prince

31

before, but she remembered seeing King Clement once, long ago when she was a girl, while he was visiting her father at their castle in Dahlia. He wore the marks of age even then. The years since that time had not passed him by unnoticed. Despite the imprint the years left on him, the king exuded vitality. The prince stood at the king's side, looking as immovable as the walls protecting their city. His hair was so dark it was nearly black. His eyes were such a brilliant blue they were startling to behold. His overall persona was so commanding that Praea had no trouble imagining the fear he must instill in his enemies even before drawing his sword. Though he was gracious and in no way threatening, Praea thought the citizens of Caedmonia had done well to dub him Marcellus the Protector.

Following introductions and greetings, King Clement inquired about their desires, meaning their lodging needs. Praea said they desired no more than to meet with the king and prince without delay. She ignored the glare of her brother and the raised eyebrows of Prince Marcellus, and instead focused on the face of the king.

He smiled. "Of course, Princess."

"It is not necessary to rush the king so," Akren said. "We see you are busy with your subjects, your Grace. We do not mean to demand your attention at the moment of our arrival."

The king waved a hand. "This is a serious matter and urgent, I'm sure, to the heart of you both. Let us not waste any more time. Please follow me."

The king led them through the entrance hall and to a room of the castle where they settled themselves around a mahogany table. Diagonal shafts of light shone in through two high windows and placed their marks on the table's surface.

The king expressed his sorrow upon hearing the news of their brother's death, and asked what had happened.

"Prince Rowan had been encamped with a number of our troops along the northern border," Akren began, his face drawn tight with anger.

"In the Wedge?" the king asked. Though Sakkarans did not generally refer to it in those terms, Praea understood King Clement to be asking for clarification. The Wedge was a strip of land along

Sakkara's northern border to which Norrland claimed a right, but it was under Sakkaran control, and peopled by Sakkaran citizens. Norrland had asked for the land on more than one occasion over the years. Recently their requests had turned to demands. Praea's blood ran hot as she considered their recent tactic.

Akren nodded in the affirmative and continued. "During the night, in a manner that is still not clear to us, a Norrland knight infiltrated the camp and murdered him in his sleep." Akren's voice trembled.

"Did anyone see the attacker?" King Clement asked, his face solemn.

Akren shook his head. "No. But the sword he left in my brother's chest bore the Norrland crest." The image of this pierced Praea, but her mind held to the matter at hand and closed it away.

King Clement and Prince Marcellus exchanged glances. "The sword was left in his body?" Marcellus asked.

Akren nodded. "His things had been gone through as well."

"Was anything taken?"

"Not that we can tell."

Prince Marcellus furrowed his brows. He was known not just for his strength but for his military strategy. Praea's father had expressed his gratitude more than once that Caedmonia and her prince were their allies. "Why would a knight abandon his sword?" he now asked.

This was met with silence. Praea did not like the doubt she saw in the prince's eyes. Her country needed his help. Norrland had decided to take Sakkaran land by force; Praea had no doubt of that. If they had any hope of resisting they needed Caedmonia. That meant Prince Marcellus had to believe it, too.

"We know what Norrland is trying to do," Akren now said. "For many months they have allowed their border areas to attack our villages unchecked. Our communications with them lead us to one conclusion: they want Sakkara. My father is weary of talking with them. He will not relent to their demands. With this act of murder they have incited us to war, a war they know we cannot win."

"If they were going to leave a signature, why not simply attack you?" Marcellus asked.

"I dare say they want to appear the innocent victim of *our* attack so as not to draw the attention of *you*."

Marcellus furrowed his brows again and Praea leaned in. "They know they would not win if you joined our side," she said. "They want to steal our land and pay no penalties for it."

"They do not think the murder of a Prince of Sakkara will make them appear guilty?" the king asked.

"They deny it," Akren said. "They claim it was the act of their border rebels and not that of their troops. We have endured enough of their lies to know better."

The king stroked his white beard with his hand. Praea thought she saw it shake, but he put it under the table and leaned back in his chair.

Praea pressed on. "The time has come for Sakkara to defend herself."

"I think you agree, Princess," the king said, "war should be avoided if possible."

War was inevitable. Praea only wanted the assurance they had come for. "Will Caedmonia stand by us if war should come?"

"Is war coming to you, or are you going to it?"

Praea sat back in shock and the king smiled. "You have suffered a great loss, and Caedmonia grieves with you. You always have a friend and ally here. We will approach this situation with wisdom. We will meet with Norrland and find out what they intend. Were these rebel groups or the kingdom itself?"

"The kingdom will never admit to anything," she said.

"That may be, Princess, but the arrival of joint envoys from Caedmonia and Sakkara may be all it takes for them to rethink their intentions, whatever those may be. We will send a letter to King Gunderic of Norrland, requesting reception of envoys at Messina. He has always been accommodating to us and we can presume his assent. We will bring along enough troops to make a point without appearing to threaten. Prince Marcellus has met with them before and I'm sure his presence there on your behalf will be enough to discourage any... boldness."

Akren nodded. "We thank you for your graciousness, King Clement."

Praea tried to calm her emotions. This was not the reaction she had been hoping for. Prince Marcellus seemed to sense this. He leaned forward to her. "What recourse do you wish to see, my Lady?"

Praea forced her voice to be steady. "Justice."

Marcellus considered her, his blue eyes piercing in his examination of her. "They'll not injure your kingdom again," Marcellus said, "or they'll have it." Praea felt a chill. If anyone could make good on that promise, it was the prince in front of her.

King Clement's face was slightly ashen and Marcellus knew he was pushing himself too far. Following the meeting, Marcellus walked with his father back to the Throne Room. As they walked, several high officials were summoned, given an assignment, and dismissed. By the time they reached the antechamber off the Throne Room, Marcellus had the most crucial items under control. The antechamber was a small room, lit by only a few wall lanterns and furnished with a pair of lounges. A page stood by the far door leading to the throne. Marcellus and his father stopped a distance away so they could speak privately.

"I could have used your energy and efficiency yesterday," Clement said.

"Is there anything else that needs to be done immediately?"

Clement shook his head with an undercurrent of weariness no one but Marcellus would have noticed. The king rubbed one shaking hand with another before catching himself and clasping his hands behind his back. Marcellus remembered seeing his hand shake in the meeting with Akren and Praea. His condition was getting worse.

"I've kept my citizens waiting long enough," Clement said. He turned toward the door to the throne.

"If it pleases your Grace, I have a request of the king."

Clement smiled. "Ask of your king and your request shall be granted."

"I wish for my king to rest."

Clement's smile faded and he shook his head. "You worry too much. There aren't many more."

"The line is out the gates. Allow me to hear them awhile. I'll pass the judgment of Clement the Beloved."

"Not Marcellus the Fierce?"

Marcellus smiled. He had been a fiery youth, often difficult for his tutors and caretakers to control, so his father had dubbed him Marcellus the Fierce. He had not yet tired of teasing Marcellus about it. "I believe the title is Marcellus the Protector."

"They don't know you like I do," the king said with a grin.

"You're changing the subject," Marcellus said. "Please rest."

"Some will only want to see the king. I do not wish to disappoint them."

Marcellus knew that what he did not wish was to be too ill to take care of his citizens the way he would like. He put his hand on his father's shoulder. "Most will be happy enough to have their requests granted. Rest here in the antechamber and I'll send for you if someone insists on the king."

Clement put his hand on Marcellus' cheek. "A king is meant to take care of his subjects."

"A son is meant to take care of his father."

Clement sighed, weariness pulling on his face. "I see you intend to badger me until I agree. I *could* use refreshment. Send for me if there is a need."

"Of course," Marcellus said, relieved his father relented. He signaled to the page. "Attend to him."

The page bowed and approached the king as Marcellus went to the throne.

Five

Corren led them past the south gate market in Stonebridge, venturing into territory that was new to Nicolai. He and his father never had time to do more than travel to the market, conduct their business, and go home. Nicolai and Corren walked along a street that ran parallel to the city's east wall and up to the castle, which dominated the northeastern corner of the city. To their left, the buildings fell away down the city's hill. Nicolai's first view of the sea came unobstructed and sudden. Nicolai had never seen such a large body of water in one place, could almost not comprehend it even though it stood as evidence before his very eyes. The horizon seemed to stretch away and kiss the sky at some impossible point in the distance.

"You coming?" Corren was several paces ahead of Nicolai, watching him. Nicolai had stopped without realizing it.

He nodded and Corren led the way once more, but Nicolai's eyes were on the sea, sparing just enough glances at the road in front of him to prevent colliding with Corren's back.

A line of people along the interior side of the city's wall drew his attention away from the sea. The line led up through the gates to the castle. Corren glanced at the people as he passed but did not slow. Nicolai met the eyes of a man with reddened, weathered skin and stopped to ask what was going on. The man pointed to the docks.

"A great wave crashed all along the shore yesterday evening," he said. Nicolai looked. Corren too, for he had stopped as well, though he seemed impatient about it. From this vantage point, Nicolai did not see any damage at first. As he looked farther south he saw debris floating by the shoreline far below. "I work for a trader on the south dock," the man said, "and the only thing left of the building is part of a wall." Other people in line began to tune into the conversation,

37

including a woman in a gray dress. A wide-eyed girl with brown ringlets clung to her skirt.

Corren looked ahead to the castle and took a step toward it but Nicolai did not follow this clue. "What caused the wave?" Nicolai asked the man. "A storm?"

"No storm," a man further down said. "It was an earthquake under the waters." He nodded his head as if to remove any doubt of his knowledge of things. "I've seen it before. That is not the worst of it." His eyes narrowed and he leaned in. "Have you ever seen the waters swallow an island?"

"What?" Nicolai asked.

He pointed to what Nicolai knew to be the Pearl and Crescent Islands, only a few miles out from the coast. They were uninhabitable rock for the most part, notable only because one island was shaped like a crescent moon while the other circular shaped island sat within its gulf. Only Nicolai didn't see two islands. He saw only the crescent-shaped island.

"What happened?" Nicolai asked.

"I'll tell you what happened. The Pearl is gone! Sank right into the sea it did!"

Nicolai tried to imagine an island in the cove of Crescent Island's bay, then tried to imagine that island sinking into the sea.

"My brother says a monster ate it!" the little girl said.

Her mother hushed her. "Don't listen to his tales."

"It was an earthquake," the first man said kindly, bending his reddened face down to her. He put his hands together and slid them back and forth. "The earth shook under the water and made the water come sloshing up over the edge. Just like shaking a cup." She looked at him skeptically. Nicolai gathered she thought a monster sounded more credible.

"It wasn't a monster," said a frail voice. They all looked around to see a withered woman resting on a bench next to the wall. "It wasn't an earthquake either. What took that island was the same thing that made it."

Something about her manner silenced the group. The girl looked at the ocean and nestled deeper into her mother's skirts.

"What was that?" Nicolai asked.

She looked at him. "Black magic."

No one said anything for a moment. The sounds of the city and the people surrounded them, but they were quiet. There were a few nervous glances in Corren's direction. Corren watched the woman with what Nicolai thought a carefully neutral expression.

"Wasn't no black magic," the older man said, though Nicolai thought him unconvinced himself.

The woman raised her brows, giving her a haunted look. "Oh no? No one talks about it anymore. The tales aren't told anymore. Forgotten. But I know. I've heard them since I was no bigger than this one here." She stuck a finger in the direction of the little girl, who disappeared behind her mother.

The woman went back to staring into the distance. They each returned to their own thoughts, shifting away from each other to indicate there would be no more discussion.

Corren pulled on Nicolai's sleeve and they went on their way. Nicolai heard the mother murmuring to the little girl. "It was only an earthquake, honey. Nothing to be afraid of."

They walked through the gates, following the line to the side entrance of a castle so far removed from Nicolai's world that it reminded him of the position in which he now found himself. Before he left home, his mother had admitted he was an adult and she could not forbid him from going. She gave him food and a few coins for his journey and made one thing clear: he was not to return until the stone was destroyed.

Corren had been alarmed by this. "You're not going to destroy it are you?"

"How can I answer that," Nicolai had said, "when you haven't yet told me what it is?"

Nicolai didn't know if he could bring himself to destroy it. He didn't know if he could neglect his responsibilities at home either. He had enough money for a night at an inn, and he took note of a few as they had made their way through the city, but after that? His choices between keeping and destroying it were equally reprehensible. As he and Corren approached the sentinel at the side door, open for the line of people leading into it, Nicolai once again put the matter out of his mind. He would make his choice when he had more information. There was no sense weighing a decision until then.

"We seek audience with Prince Marcellus," Corren told the sentinel.

A sword hung from the guard's left hip. "Get in line," he said.

"We seek the prince, not the king."

"The prince is hearing requests right now."

Corren pressed on. "We wish a private audience."

The sentinel raised one eyebrow. He looked sideways at Nicolai, then eyed Corren. "Then get in line," he said, "and request it."

A dwindling line of people stood waiting in the Throne Room, the arches of the ceiling soaring two stories above them. A mural spread over the wall behind the throne, depicting a countryside at dawn, the mountains in the background illuminated by the sun's rays. None of this detracted from, but rather led the eye to, the throne, accented with gold inlay and upon which sat Prince Marcellus. Sitting here was a duty Marcellus did not take lightly. King Clement the Beloved had a gift for discerning the needs of his citizens even when, especially when, those needs went unspoken. Marcellus had not the same gift— he and his father both knew it—so when his father entrusted him with hearing the needs of the citizens Marcellus felt that trust. With each person who approached the throne he would often ask himself, *What would my father do?*

He had heard over two score requests in this frame of mind when two young men, one in a fine cloak and the other simply dressed, approached the throne and bowed. "I am Corren of Tower Hall South," the cloaked one said. This was answered by whispers from the people in line and Marcellus himself studied the man closer.

"I am Nicolai of Knobby Tree," the other said.

An odd pairing, Marcellus thought. "What is your request?"

"We wish to meet with the prince privately," Corren said, "if it pleases your Majesty."

After making such a presumptuous request the wizard looked at him boldly, as one would expect a wizard to do. The other, who Marcellus assumed to be a farmer from his appearance, had no arrogance in his eyes, but as Marcellus scrutinized him the man did not look away either. Marcellus kept a benevolent expression. "Many citizens wait in line behind you. It would not be prudent to take time for a private meeting. Rest assured, you can make your request here."

"We wish nothing from the king's storehouse."

Marcellus raised his brows. He considered again the man's cloak. "Then what is the purpose of your errand?"

Corren seemed to be thinking. "Your Highness, this is for your ears only."

Marcellus had no intention of granting such a request. If he met privately with everyone who desired it he would not have time for much else. He refused to call his father from resting either. If these men knew anything that required a private meeting, he would know who they were already. Perhaps they were embarrassed by whatever needs they had, but sitting on the throne of Clement the Beloved was not enough for him to grant everything asked of him.

"Confess your needs or be dismissed."

The guards shifted into readiness. The line shuffled as people jockeyed for a better view of the promised drama.

"We have information for you, regarding," and here the wizard lowered his voice, "a certain stone."

Marcellus maintained his posture but felt his color drain. They could not mean what he thought they meant. "The treasury is full of many valuable jewels," he said. "I know of no stone I should desire."

The wizard did not respond, only kept his gaze firm. This did not concern the treasury. Marcellus already knew that.

The assembly stilled and the room waited in silence with them. Marcellus looked at the guards who awaited any command.

He rose from the throne. "I am sure the king will be happy to meet with his people once more," he said, "while I excuse myself with these good citizens."

Six

Corren and Nicolai followed the prince and his two guards down the deserted hallway. Marcellus opened a door and gestured Corren and Nicolai into a small room, instructing the guards to wait outside. Before he closed the door behind him Corren heard him say, "No one enters."

The room had a secluded feel. The walls were covered with dark, wood panels. A single bronzed plate dominated the center of one wall. The only furnishing was a table constructed of rich wood and circled by low-backed chairs, one on each side. Corren sat on one of these with the prince opposite him and Nicolai to his left. Now that they were here at last, Corren felt a wave of apprehension.

"You have my attention," Marcellus said. "Though you are not who I was expecting."

"An old woman?"

Marcellus nodded and Nicolai leaned forward.

"I'm afraid she has passed," he said. Nicolai sat back in alarm. "But she told me what we need to know."

"Which is what?" the prince asked.

Corren took a deep breath, trying to decide the best way to begin. "Your Highness, what do you know about the Phoenix?"

Marcellus furrowed his brows. He was even more daunting up close than he had been on the throne. "It's a bird," he said with the shrug of one shoulder. "Said to live in the Realm of the Phoenix on the other side of the Cliffs."

"Yes," Corren said, being careful not to show offense at this description of the Phoenix. "The Phoenix is a powerful magical creature and highly intelligent. Its power goes well beyond that of any wizard." Corren knew this did not convey what the Phoenix truly was. Some of the greatest magical advancements came after someone felt

42

they learned a new principle or technique from the Phoenix. These rare moments were so altering that the effects were felt for hundreds of years afterward, causing every wizard Corren knew to regard the Phoenix with a kind of reverence. For the wizards in the Order, especially, who they were and what they did they owed to the Phoenix.

"The Phoenix is the only one of its kind," Corren continued, "and has existed for longer than recorded time. No one knows quite how old it is."

The expression of the prince was not overtly dismissive, but Corren saw the doubt on his face. Nicolai showed no sign of questioning what he was hearing.

"Every 600 to 1,400 years the Phoenix goes through a long process of death and rebirth. As part of this process it builds itself a pyre in the top of a large *detanae* tree, a tree unique to the Realm. Atop this pyre it dies, bursts into flame, and resurrects itself from the ashes. Many people know at least something of this, but very few know that when the Phoenix is reborn it rolls this ash into an egg and brings it to the Rock of Light as a gift to the Order of Ceinoth."

Nicolai put one arm on the table. "Is that when the Great Darkness comes?"

"Yes. The cloak of darkness is not so much to protect the Phoenix as it is to conceal what it carries. The Phoenix is well protected by its own magic. That is... it usually is."

"Some songs say that wizards call the Great Darkness upon the land as a curse, bringing death and sickness in its wake," Nicolai said. "Many people fear it, and the wizards who bring it. Other songs say, and this my father believed, that the Great Darkness comes so the great light can come. The Eternal Flame burns brightest after the darkness leaves and, for a time, brings good fortune to all those who look upon it."

"What do you say?" Corren asked.

"I do not know, but I have no fear of it."

"It is all superstition," Marcellus said. "There are deaths and people falling ill every day. It is only when the Great Darkness comes that they have something besides the unfairness of life to blame it on."

43

"You are correct," Corren said. Marcellus seemed surprised to hear him say it. "The Great Darkness brings neither fortune nor sorrow. It conceals ash, our sacred magic."

The corner of Marcellus' mouth went up a little. He seemed to soften. "This is what you needed a private audience to tell me?"

This was said without sternness and Corren took encouragement from it. "No, your Highness. The last time the Phoenix came to the Rock of Light it didn't bring ash, or at least, not very much of it. It brought three stones."

From his traveling bag, Corren retrieved a bundle of silk and set it on the table. He slid the silk away to reveal the fiercely-colored red stone. Even when he was not holding it, it called to him, touching his core. Though he had kept the stone hidden since Nashua had given it to him, he had pulled it out in every private moment since then, feeling his soul drawn into it. Corren pulled his eyes away with difficulty and looked at Nicolai.

Nicolai's gaze was locked on the stone with astonishment. "And yours," Corren said gesturing to him.

Nicolai did not move at first. Finally he pulled out his necklace exposing the brilliant, yellow stone encased in an iron casing on the end of a chain. Except for the color, the two stones were identical. Corren felt again what he felt the first time he saw Nicolai's stone: a warm sensation spreading through his body. It was not as compelling a feeling as he had for his own stone but there was a connection nonetheless.

Marcellus had been very still since the appearance of Corren's stone. He studied both the stones and the men in front of him.

Nicolai tucked his necklace back into his shirt and Corren nodded to Marcellus. "Your stone, I believe, is blue."

Nicolai glanced at Marcellus, who made no reply, only watched as Corren rewrapped his stone and slipped it in his bag. Corren pulled out a scroll and unrolled it. It was brittle parchment and seemed inclined to crumble to dust, but it held. "Along with the stones," Corren said, "the Phoenix delivered a prophecy. This is the record of it." Corren assumed that as a farmer Nicolai would not be able to read and the prince would be more trained in warfare and diplomacy than letters, leaving such matters to his scribes. So, Corren took a steadying breath and began to read:

> The Glorious Bird in ashes and stone will die.
> The Cunning One obtains the sacred magic by stealth.
> Unable to revive, the Phoenix of All Ages will perish.
> From the forbidden union, three defenders will be born.
>
> Red brother of flame, the Gatherer, the Seeker,
> Must ensure the Great Readying, and prepare to exchange.
> Blue brother must cross through light and extinguish darkness.
> Yellow brother must pierce evil and preserve life.
>
> Each stone has secrets only its bearer can unlock.
> All four elements must provide their singular powers.
> Only the Three as one can prevent this thievery.
> If they fail, evil will swallow the land, never to be restrained.

Corren let the scroll roll itself back up, guiding it with his hands, its parchment crackling at the effort. He placed it on the table and the silence settled around them like a shroud. Nicolai stared at it, his thoughts indiscernible.

Marcellus was armed with a frown and Corren's apprehension made a reappearance. "What is meant by *that?*" Marcellus asked.

"I am Red Brother. You are Blue Brother. Nicolai is Yellow Brother. The Phoenix is in danger and we're meant to protect it." Corren felt a slip of cold fear as he thought of the consequences if they failed.

Before he could explain further, Nicolai sat back, his brows pinched together. "What are you saying? We're brothers? Actual brothers?"

"Yes. You and I were taken away when we all were born."

"Taken away from where?" Marcellus asked, straightening. This had a considerable effect on his frame. Corren had the sudden, unpleasant vision of Marcellus drawing a sword.

45

"From here. The castle." Corren tried to gather his thoughts. There was so much to explain. He opened his mouth, but Marcellus' eyes had narrowed.

"Why didn't the woman tell me this when she gave me the stone weeks ago?"

"She said I'm the Gatherer. I assume it fell to me to tell you of this because I'm the oldest."

"Ah." Marcellus stood, his face hard. "Now I see." He took three steps toward the door and Corren exchanged a glance with Nicolai. Marcellus swung it open. "Guards!" his voice boomed, and Corren startled as the two guards came through the door. "Arrest these men." They drew their swords, the metal scraping against their scabbards.

"What?!" Corren said standing, backing away.

"On charges of high treason," Marcellus said louder, eyeing him. "The penalty of which is death."

"No," Corren said.

"You will await trial by the king."

"Your Highness, we did nothing wrong," Nicolai said, standing himself now, taking a step away from the advancing guards.

"Don't do this," Corren said. He held Marcellus' gaze but the prince's eyes were unyielding.

"The king will hear you in court." He snatched the scroll from the table and left, closing the door behind him.

Seven

Corren's mind worked as the guards advanced. Unnerved by the twist of events, his heart beat in his ears. The last thing he wanted was an altercation with the king's guards, but he would not allow them to take him away either. "I do not wish to harm you," Corren said, backing toward the wall. "Bring the prince back."

The guard closest to him narrowed his eyes and raised his sword to the base of Corren's neck. "Tie them up," he said to the other guard. There was no opportunity for this order to be obeyed.

Corren said an incantation and the tip of the blade at his neck swung away, resisting the hold of its owner. The guard's eyes widened, following its path. He blinked then locked his eyes on Corren and seized him by the arm.

Corren felt the pressure of his grip tingling down to his fingers. "Surgio arlet!"

The guard jerked his hand away, falling back a step. He stared at his fist and clenched it in pain. The spell had been small, restrained, but it did what Corren wanted.

"Bring the prince back," he repeated.

"Evil wizard!" the second guard said, rushing past his companion, his sword raised. Corren recoiled, shouted "Cinerata!" and the sword glowed red. The guard flung it out of his hand, shouting. The red hot sword clanged to the floor. Both guards fell into a retreat. Nicolai took a step back too, staring at Corren in astonishment.

The door slammed open and Marcellus burst through it, a broadsword already drawn. He scanned the scene: the guards and Nicolai alike hovering at the edges of the room; the sword—now back to its normal color—lying on the floor.

Marcellus met Corren's eyes and raised his sword in warning. "You *will* go peacefully."

Corren raised his hands. "I do not wish to fight. I only want you to hear what I have to say."

"You are in no position to wish for anything," Marcellus said. "These guards may be afraid of your magic tricks, but not I."

With that statement Corren understood something: the prince was an unbeliever. "What can it harm you to listen?"

"Nothing you say will persuade me. You are not who you say you are."

Corren needed some way to reverse Marcellus' resistance. He needed to prove who they really were. He could think of only one way to do that. "Are you willing to ask the king?"

Marcellus did not answer. He did not move. The tip of his sword held steady and his face gave nothing away. The guards looked at Marcellus, eyes wide at the events happening in front of them. They all waited. Corren held his tongue. Marcellus lowered his sword, but his face remained fierce. He drew near until he was only a hand's breadth from Corren's face. Corren could not help but feel the power of Caedmonia's warrior prince.

"You will follow my commands to the letter," Marcellus said lowly. "I will let the king decide whether or not he wishes to see you." Here he lowered his voice even more, so no one but Corren could hear. "If you even *attempt* to harm my father," he said, "I will gut you."

Marcellus set a full six guards around the wizard and the farmer with a warning to all that when he returned he had better find things as he left them. If he discovered any more of his knights cowering in a corner, he was not going to be happy.

The Throne Room was empty at last and so the king was in his office. This room consisted of a sitting area in the front and a heavy desk in the rear where the king now sat. Along one wall stretched the fireplace and on the opposite wall hung a map of the kingdom and the territories surrounding its borders. Behind the desk several glass-paned doors led to an expansive balcony, opening to a view of the city and the sea beyond.

Evening was falling. The darkening sky felt foreboding as Marcellus approached his father and handed him the scroll. "We have an interesting situation," Marcellus said. He noticed his own hand trembling and realized he was afraid of what he might find out. The wizard Corren was too confident the king would know something. Marcellus clenched his hands and his will alike. These men were liars. He was only here to confirm that.

The king unrolled the parchment, the light from the lamp on the corner of the king's desk revealing its many creases. "What is this?"

"Part of a plot to usurp the throne, I believe, though a poor one. It's supposedly an ancient prophecy that says I have two brothers from a forbidden union. It says together we're all meant to save the Phoenix and the world from utter destruction."

The king blinked, incredulous. "That's quite a tale." Marcellus felt a wave of relief he did not expect, since he had not even acknowledged to himself his own worry. It was clear the king was as disbelieving of this as Marcellus was.

"Indeed," Marcellus said.

"How did you hear of this?"

"Two men, the ones claiming to be my brothers, were in the line for requests. A wizard from Tower Hall South and a man from Knobby Tree. A farmer, or so he appears. At first I waited to see what their motive was. Then the wizard claimed to be my *older* brother."

"Ah." The king sat back.

"They are in confinement in the Plate Room."

Clement rubbed his snowy beard with a tremulous hand. "Quite bold they were, to do this in the Throne Room."

"No, Sire. They wished to see me alone."

The king raised his brows and studied Marcellus for a moment. Marcellus knew that look. He long ago learned how to keep his composure under it, but he had never learned how to subdue the nervousness that always went with it. There was nothing to do but wait. His father stood and paced to the open doors behind him. The air was still. So was the king. He turned and faced Marcellus. "Why, my son, did you grant them private audience?"

Ah. Of course. Marcellus paused as he considered his reply. Keeping a secret from his father was one thing, and that had been bad enough, but he could not lie when asked directly. He longed to look down at his feet or at the gash on the corner of the desk left from the time he had first swung a sword and, surprised by its weight, took out a chunk of the wood. Marcellus forced himself to look his father in the eye and not hide like a child.

"A few weeks ago I was given a stone," he said, "and told to keep it hidden with the assurance that more information would be forthcoming. These men claimed to know what it was. My intrigue caused me to grant their request. They each have a similar stone, it turns out. I'm sorry, Father. I should've told you. It was an elaborate plot, obviously." He decided to keep his feelings about his stone (not to mention theirs) to himself. He felt enough the fool.

"Who gave you the stone?"

"An old woman. I... don't know her name."

The king raised his brows once more. It was unlike Marcellus not to obtain such basic information, though no one could be more surprised than Marcellus himself when he realized how little he knew once she was gone. He didn't think to question Corren and Nicolai further, either. He realized now he should have gotten more information before arresting them. Everything about this situation had him off balance. He was ready for it to be over. "She is with them?" the king asked.

"No. They claim she died, but they must be protecting her. We need to find her if she has part in this."

"We cannot collect all the old women of the city. Perhaps a name would be helpful." It was a gentle jab.

"Yes. She will not be hard to distinguish however. She had one blue eye and one brown."

Clement took a step back. He had a look of astonishment Marcellus did not like.

"Father?" The king did not answer and Marcellus took a step toward him. "Father?"

Clement's hand came up to his neck. "A horn? Did she have a horn around her neck? Rimmed in red jewels?"

These words hung in the air. A rare kind of fear and uncertainty took hold of Marcellus. *How does he know that? How does he know?* Marcellus felt outside of himself. Something was wrong, but he couldn't grab hold of what it was. "Did... she come see you, too?" Maybe that's all it was. The old woman came to see the king too, that was all. Surely.

The king gestured to the scroll. "Read that to me."

No, he thought. *I don't need to read it. You need to send these men away.* Marcellus read it. The simple task of forming words felt clumsy. *These ridiculous words. They're not true.*

When he finished he looked at his father who had turned toward the city with a gaze that saw not what was in front of him, but something in his own mind.

"Bring them to me," said the king. "Tell no one of this."

Marcellus dropped his arms to his side, the parchment loosely in his hand. "They're not my brothers." Clement furrowed his brows together. Marcellus wanted to shake him. "Are they?"

Clement looked at him with sorrowful eyes. "I don't know, my son."

Marcellus shook his head. What did that mean? How could the king not know? How was that possible?

Before he could think anymore, the king said, "Bring them in."

Eight

One of the few times King Clement said anything to Marcellus about his mother, it had been precious little. The king had just returned from a battle in the west and was in the stables with Marcellus, then a seven-year-old boy. His father sat on a crate, still filthy and tired from his long journey, describing the events of his battle. He left nothing out for he knew Marcellus longed for every detail. Marcellus was tending to the king's warhorse, Edred—something he had never before been permitted to do. There in that private space, with straw crunching underneath his feet and the comforting smell of the horse, Marcellus listened enraptured.

When he removed the bridle and reins and struggled to pull down the saddle, the king asked, "Do you need help?"

"Go on," he grunted. "I can do it."

He did do it. As he listened to his father, Marcellus fed and watered the horse and set to grooming him, the coat glistening under the care of the brush, the horse's skin twitching in appreciation. He admired the build of the horse as he went—the largest in the king's stables by almost a hand. When he finished scraping the hooves and the king was done talking, the time for inspection arrived.

Marcellus watched as his father examined his work, lingering on the hooves.

Clement looked at Marcellus. "Well done, my son."

Marcellus puffed out his chest, beaming.

"Let's allow him to rest now, shall we?" Clement said, patting his horse on the flanks. They turned not to the left toward the castle as Marcellus expected, but rather to the right, farther along the stables. Marcellus did not know where they were going, but he would follow his father anywhere. He took his father's hand as they passed stall after stall.

"Are you being diligent in your studies?" Clement asked.

"Yes, Sire."

"Sir Preston informs me you read very well."

"We've been reading about the Athelstan Wars."

"Have you now? What did you make of them?"

"I thought King Athelstan to be foolish at first. Even I could see he was weak along the river. I would have attacked him there too if it had been me."

"It set things back for him didn't it? Did Sir Preston teach you this?"

"No. He grew angry with me for criticizing him. He said King Athelstan's counter offensive was brilliant and he was a great hero."

"So he was."

"Yes," Marcellus said. "But even heroes make mistakes. Can I not learn from them?"

"I hope you shall. One day *you* will be the defender of this kingdom. You are right to learn whenever a lesson presents itself."

They had walked to the end of the stables and stopped. "I want to learn from you," Marcellus said. "When can I go with you to fight?"

Clement laughed. "Not for many years."

"Sir Preston said you're the greatest king Caedmonia has had in many generations."

"Well, what else is he going to say to the king's son?"

Marcellus thought about that. "Yes. Maybe. But I've heard stories about you. I think Sir Preston is right. I can only think of one foolish thing you've done."

The king raised his brows, a smile tugging at his lips. "What was that?"

"Not expanding the naval fleet quick enough. We were lucky Hathmirr did not attack us on our shoreline. For two years they had far more sea power than we did. They could have breached us here."

He nodded, "Very good."

Marcellus considered him. "You weren't really thinking about it, were you?" The smile faded from his father's face. "Your heart wasn't in it then."

Clement spoke quietly. "The kingdom was in mourning."

Marcellus hesitated, but his desire to ask overcame the fear his father would put him off once again. "What was my mother like?"

For a long while, he did not answer. Marcellus watched him struggle to keep a calm face. He was trying not to weep. At last he said, "She was the most glorious queen ever to grace the throne. Her glory is now in you." Clement cleared his throat and straightened. "But we are forgetting the purpose of our walk."

Marcellus wanted to press him. He wanted to know what his mother was *like*. He wanted to know the sound of her voice and the way she walked and what made her laugh. He wanted to *know* her. These were things that were lost forever, things no one could tell him, and certainly nothing his father would ever bring himself to say. He couldn't understand why his father would never talk about her.

"What is the purpose of our walk?" It was what he was supposed to say.

Clement put a hand on his shoulder. "You should not be sad. Today is a day of gladness." With that he swept his arm toward the stall behind him.

"Edred's colt," Marcellus said. Though he was not really a colt anymore.

"Quite grown now," Clement said. "How do you think he'll fare?"

Marcellus suspected, as anyone might, that the offspring of his father's warhorse would fare quite well, but he stepped forward to examine him anyway. He couldn't help but smile as he took stock of the horse's build, examined his hooves and teeth. "He'll be magnificent. He's magnificent now."

"Worthy of a prince?"

Marcellus gaped at his father, who laughed. "I expect you to care for him yourself. It will be many years before I grant you a squire."

He ran to his father and embraced him. "Oh Father! Thank you!" His father hugged him back. Marcellus reached up on tiptoe and kissed him on the cheek. "I'll take excellent care of him, Father. He'll be beautifully groomed—day and night!"

"He's already been broken, but you're to stay within the castle grounds with him, understood? No wandering."

"Yes, Sire."

54

"Good boy. Let's see you saddle him up."

A knight came by as Marcellus heaved the saddle on the horse with some difficulty. It was lighter than his father's had been, but still, going up was a lot harder than pulling down. "A boy of seven is too young," the knight said.

"Not this boy," Clement said.

Marcellus mounted the horse, who at first had danced away skittishly before Marcellus had him under control. His father was beaming at him. Marcellus knew if he were able to do things at a younger age then most, his father was the reason. Even at a distance, he could feel his father's arms supporting him.

Marcellus entered the Plate Room and dismissed his knights. They filed out, avoiding any questioning glances. Corren and Nicolai looked at him, waiting. Marcellus felt he was losing something, felt that something was being pulled from his grasp, but he didn't know what that something was. All he knew was he did not want to bring these men to his father. He wanted them to leave.

He did not always get what he wanted.

"Follow me," Marcellus said.

Nicolai followed Marcellus and Corren deeper into the bowels of the castle than he ever imagined he would go. Up the steps they went, down a corridor and finally to a pair of doors. Before they went through, the prince said, to Corren more than to Nicolai, "You will bow and wait for your king to address you."

The king stood waiting for them, hands clasped behind his back, in a sitting area with two couches and several plush chairs. Along one wall was a fireplace massive enough to heat the entire room. In it a fire raged. A log popped and caved in on itself, the flames leaping in reply.

Marcellus bowed to the king. "Your Grace, I present Corren of Tower Hall South and Nicolai of Knobby Tree."

Corren and Nicolai each bowed too, and waited.

King Clement said nothing. His face wore an expression of wonderment and confusion. Nicolai, who had been resisting Corren's assertion about who they were, looked now at the king and knew it to be true. The king's face had a shocking resemblance to Nicolai's own. The shape was the same: the same forehead, same nose, same eyes, except for the color. Nicolai's were a light green. The king's eyes were a soft blue and when Nicolai looked at Corren's eyes he discovered the same blue in *them*. It was the only resemblance he saw between Corren and the king. It was all he needed.

Nicolai turned cold and felt the world—or rather *his* world—fall out from underneath him.

The king spoke. "I am curious," he said haltingly, though with authority, "as to your upbringing."

Nicolai listened as Corren explained how he had been orphaned and eventually reared at Tower Hall South (a story he had shared with Nicolai during their journey to Stonebridge just that morning). Nicolai only said he was raised on a farm on the edges of Knobby Tree. "If I was an orphan, nothing was said to me about it."

The king nodded at this. "An uncomfortable thing to consider at this point, I imagine."

Corren and Marcellus glanced at Nicolai as if this thought had not yet occurred to them. Nicolai kept his eyes on the king. "Yes, Sire."

Clement the Beloved acknowledged this with a nod. He addressed himself to Corren. "I understand you believe there is a prophecy claiming, among other things, that I have two sons I did not know about. While others may question my fidelity, I know it for myself. My wife bore one son," he gestured to Marcellus. "She never bore another. How could two more sons be possible?" The king said this without accusation.

"Your grace," Corren began, "the woman who gave me the prophecy... her name was Nashua."

The king blanched. It was his only reaction but Nicolai didn't miss it.

"She took Nicolai and me upon our birth in order to hide our identities. Three sons were born to you that day, not one."

56

The king said nothing for a moment. The three young men watched him in anticipation. At last, it was Marcellus who spoke. "Sire?"

The king startled out of his thoughts, then gave a troubled smile. "Why don't we sit?"

They settled down—in chairs so soft Nicolai's body ached with the reprieve—and he had a sense of unreality. The king sat to his right, Corren the wizard to his left, the prince opposite him. He was in most unlikely company.

"When Queen Elana was with child..." The king halted. He knit his thick brows together, his face struggling to contain the emotion he did not want to release. Nicolai noticed Marcellus watching in earnest. He looked as poised as ever, but Nicolai thought he saw something else underneath: vulnerability firmly restrained. Nicolai felt compassion toward him.

King Clement composed himself. "When we learned she was expecting I left it to her to select a midwife. I trusted her judgment and so I was... unprepared... for her choice." The king looked at Corren, who seemed to be waiting for something he knew was coming. Nicolai thought he could guess what it might be. "It was Nashua."

"Nashua was the midwife?" Marcellus asked, incredulous.

"Yes. It troubled me. I knew nothing about her. *No one* knew anything about her. She was quite aged and I feared she would drop the baby. I really didn't see how she could be a help. I confess... Elana and I quarreled about it a bit." It seemed to trouble him to say this and he rushed out the next sentence. "Do not misunderstand me. We were happy. We had waited many years for this, *many* years, and she finally had what she had long wanted, as did I. But I worried about her health. I wanted..." He stopped. "Well, no need for me to say who won the argument. The day came, Nashua was summoned, and I waited. In this very room, in fact." Clement sat for a moment, his face darkening. He swallowed hard and went on. "A page came to the door and told me the midwife was requesting a physician. I was prepared for that. I had a physician waiting in another room of the castle. I sent the page to fetch him and went to Elana's room.

"I was almost there when... I heard an amazing sound." He stopped, smiling at the memory of it. "It was a baby's cry. *Our* baby's cry." He looked at Corren, then Nicolai. The sorrow on the king's face reached deep into Nicolai's heart as the king held his eyes. "But," and he spoke now with a great deal of effort, "it sounded like it was coming from behind me, farther down the hall. I heard it again, this time from Elana's room in front of me. I thought it was just an echo. The odd play of sound we sometimes get among these stone halls." He leaned forward, anxious now. "Wouldn't you think the same? How could I know?"

No one answered. The king went on.

"So in I went, and I found you," this to Marcellus now, "wrapped in a blanket next to Elana on her bed." His faced pulled down with the weight of his thoughts. Nicolai suddenly knew he didn't want to hear the rest. "It was a terrible sight. She was bleeding to death. I knew it the moment I saw her." Clement brought a trembling hand to his forehead before putting it back in his lap.

Marcellus looked pale.

"Elana was alone. Nashua was gone. The cry I heard behind me must have been her taking the two of you away. The physician came, but there was nothing to be done." Clement looked down, fighting the tears in his eyes. "She asked to hold you," he said to Marcellus. "As she did I held her and she said the last thing she would ever say." The king was silent so long that Nicolai thought he wasn't going to tell them what it was.

Marcellus looked stricken. His voice broke as he asked, "What was that?"

The king smiled, tears escaping his eyes and leaving wet trails down his cheeks. He spoke in a whisper. "She said, 'It was worth it.'"

Nine

As Corren listened to Clement tell the story of their birth and flight, something inside him shifted. He had been so overwhelmed by the prophecy and all its implications that he failed to register one fact: this was his father. He looked at Nicolai and Marcellus, somber in the aftermath of what they had heard. These were his brothers. He had sought out his family and found them, along with a great deal more. Corren knew he needed to focus on the task at hand—he still had so much to tell them—but he could not seem to recover from the fact that he was sitting here with his family. After so many years of wondering, of feeling there was a shroud in his heart woven with mystery and pain, after all he had been through, here they were. He looked at his father and saw his own eyes looking back at him. He wasn't alone in the world. He was connected to someone else. His father. His father sat right in front of him. For the first time in his life, Corren felt whole, not realizing until then just how much he had been broken.

Marcellus leaned in toward Clement, his expression pained, looking as if he wished he could speak to him privately. "What about... the forbidden union?"

The king considered Marcellus, then turned to Corren. "Do *you* know what that is?" It was obvious the king knew, but only wanted to know if Corren did, too.

Corren sat back, surprised. "No."

He nodded. "It's just as well."

Corren exchanged glances with Nicolai, but Marcellus kept an eye on their father. "What is it?" he asked.

"It is in the past, where it will stay."

Marcellus gripped Clement's arm. "Are you my father?"

Clement startled, then smiled. "Oh yes, my son." He put his hand on Marcellus' cheek. Corren watched that tender display with longing. "It was nothing like that."

Marcellus exhaled shakily and sat back, working to regain his composure.

Clement's eyes lingered on Marcellus for a moment, then he regarded each of them in turn. "Three sons." Corren looked between the king and Nicolai and saw the same kind face on each, Nicolai's pale green eyes and young age the only thing to distinguish them. Clement's countenance grew dark. "How could she take you from us? Why would she steal you?"

"Well," Corren said slowly, "she didn't *quite* steal us."

"What do you mean?"

"Perhaps you'll understand better if I start at the beginning." Corren told the king what he already told Marcellus and Nicolai about the Phoenix regenerating every several hundred years and bringing its ash to the Rock of Light as a gift to the Order of Ceinoth. He explained that the Order of Ceinoth was an organization consisting of seven people, each representing a different group known as a branch of the Order. Each branch was distinguished by their own brand of magic and their own (secretive) ways of utilizing the ash, which was potent indeed.

"You are part of this Order?" Clement asked.

Corren nodded. "I am an apprentice to Aradia, Head of the Wysard branch and also the current Head of the Order. We are based at Tower Hall South and are better known because we take on so many students."

"Also for your powerful wizards," Nicolai said.

Corren noticed that both Nicolai and Clement were studying him with odd expressions. He decided it was a strange mix of admiration, curiosity, and caution. Marcellus' expression, however, was much easier to dissect: skepticism.

Corren nodded. "Yes. But it is because we are such a large branch that our presence is so visible."

"Visible?" Marcellus asked. "You must be one of the most secretive groups in Caedmonia."

Corren smiled. "The fact that you know where to find us at all is what makes us more visible. Five other branches are located in Caedmonia as well, and one in Sakkara, but even I don't know where they all are. I know at least two are here in Stonebridge, including Nashua's branch, the Cantori branch. They are charged with standing watch over the Eternal Flame that resides in the Rock of Light."

"They're the ones who keep it stoked," Marcellus said.

"No. They watch it. It burns all on its own." Marcellus looked doubtful and Corren shrugged. "It is connected to the Phoenix. Douse it in water if you like; it will burn on as long as the Phoenix lives. In fact, it is by watching this flame that we know when the Phoenix is preparing to regenerate. It is how the Order knows to gather together when the Phoenix is bringing the ash. I only know a little about the ceremony that occurs, but I do know that usually it is the Head who receives the ash on behalf of the Order. However for some reason the Phoenix chose Nashua last time. Only she could retrieve the stones, and it was through her mouth that the prophecy was spoken."

The king shook his head. "I don't understand. When did this happen? I thought the Phoenix regenerated over a millennium ago."

"1,203 years ago."

"But..." and this from Nicolai, "I thought you were saying Nashua was there."

"She was there."

Their reaction to this was similar to what Corren's had been: no small amount of disbelief. All he could do was acknowledge it with a shrug and go on. "The Phoenix gave Nashua the stones, the prophecy, and one thing more. The head of Nashua's branch wears a pewter horn necklace, which I suspect they enchant with the ash to aid in the singing of their songs. The Phoenix embedded red stones into her horn. At first, no one knew why. This was just one of the mysteries the Order was debating after the arrival of the prophecy. Everything that had happened was so unprecedented. No one knew what it all meant or what was to be done. Truth be told, they understood very little. They knew three brothers would be born, but Nashua said no one even considered the possibility that we would come all at once.

61

They talked mainly about *when* they thought we would come, which they correctly deduced to be close to the time the Phoenix would regenerate. Even that left a wide window of time. The shortest recorded life span of the Phoenix is 642 years and the longest is 1,473 years. There was a lot of debate about what to do with the stones until the time came to deliver them, and they were at a complete loss to know how to find the Three once we were born.

"The Order guards many secrets of the Phoenix, but there are some things passed down only from Head to Head. They considered making the prophecy one of them. In the end, they decided the entire Order would be responsible for preserving the prophecy through the centuries. Nashua, however, felt it shouldn't be passed down at all. Since she did not yet know she would live as long as she did, she didn't feel she could disagree with them. After a few more days of the Order debating what it all meant, Nashua felt she needed to leave. She left the Order to go into hiding." This had surprised Corren. It was difficult to become a member of the Order, needing not just skill, but approval of the existing members. There was even a Test of Virtue, the nature of which was hidden, to make sure that the secrets of the Order of Ceinoth stayed in safe hands. It was so difficult to get in that members were not likely to want to leave. Nashua was the only member to leave for a reason other than death.

"When Nashua first had the feeling to go into hiding," Corren continued, "she said it felt as if it wasn't even her idea. That was her first clue to the nature of the stones in her horn. Years... centuries... passed and she lingered on. She felt the horn had granted her long life so she could deliver the stones herself, and she was right about that. Yet other than that, all that time, she had no idea what she was to do. She was just biding her time. She spent those years moving from place to place. Apparently people start talking when the old woman in the village never dies.

"About 21 years ago she again had thoughts that she felt came not from her, but from the horn. She said she knew then that it was guiding her.

"For several months she knew what she needed to do, even if she didn't know why." Corren and the king locked eyes for a moment and

62

Corren felt he was talking to just him. "She knew when we were conceived. She knew for the moment her job was to hide us away in a safe place until the time came for her to deliver the stones. She said she felt strongly that our identities must be guarded, presumably to protect us from whoever is also after the Phoenix."

Corren stopped, still looking at the king. "She said it was a difficult thing to do. Who would want to deprive a mother of her child? And she was depriving her of two." The king looked down and Corren glanced at his brothers. "It was for this reason she decided to share the prophecy with the queen."

Clement jerked up. "She knew?"

Corren nodded. "Nashua decided she could not steal two babies. She wanted the queen to agree on her own that this must be done. The queen thought about it for a few weeks, then agreed. She would allow Nashua to take the oldest, red brother, and the youngest, yellow brother." The king stared in amazement. "When the time came and Nashua saw the queen was in danger, she did not want to leave. She wanted to help, even though she knew there was nothing she could do. Nashua does not have healing magic; her magic is different. Still, she wanted to stay. She didn't want to leave her alone. It was the queen who insisted she go, knowing Nashua had to leave with us without being seen. That is what she did.

"After she took us away," Corren said, "the horn was silent again for many years, up until about a month ago. The time had come at last. She delivered the stones and then met with me, yesterday in fact, to tell me what I have just told you. This completed her tasks. She died as soon as we were finished talking, and the horn went with her."

"What do you mean, the horn went with her?" Marcellus asked.

"It disintegrated," Corren said. "Into ash."

Ten

After several minutes of silence, Corren saw Nicolai open his mouth to speak, seem to reconsider, and close it again.

"Speak freely, my son," Clement said.

Marcellus looked up at that.

Nicolai looked stunned as well and shook his head. "It was nothing, your Grace."

"I have a question," Corren said, but this was directed at Marcellus. "Why did you arrest us?"

Marcellus seemed to be controlling his expression, his face indiscernible. "You said you were the oldest brother."

"So?"

Marcellus narrowed his eyes. Clement interjected, "That would make you heir to the throne."

The king said this without emotion, surveying Corren with what felt like uncomfortable precision. Nicolai looked at Corren in amazement... or was it apprehension?

A draft of air rushed through the open doors of the balcony, disturbing papers on the desk, dousing Corren's body with a chill that went beyond just the wind. Marcellus stood to close the doors, looking grateful for a reason to move.

Corren watched him shut each door with a definitive thud. "I... I'm not after the throne," he heard himself say.

"That's not how it works," said the king. He turned to Nicolai and Corren was grateful he was not expected to reply. "I believe you had something to say."

Marcellus came back to the group and would not look at Corren. Corren did not want him to.

"Well..." Nicolai shifted in his seat, his eyes still on Corren, his face reflecting the previous topic. "Why would anyone want to harm the

Phoenix? What good does that do them?"

"The point isn't so much to harm," Corren said, latching onto the subject change, feeling odd but trying to act normal. "You could seize its magic, take it for yourself. That is no small amount of power a person would have. The Phoenix would be destroyed, *you* would be immortal, and you could do whatever you wanted and there wouldn't be anyone anywhere who could stop you." Corren's words hung in the air but Marcellus' expression did not change. "You do not want such magic in the wrong hands," Corren said. "No person, no *kingdom* would be safe. If someone stole the power of the Phoenix not even the Order could do anything about it."

This was met with silence. Corren again felt the weight of what they were being asked to do. In addition to his uncertainty about how to do it, he feared what their world would become if they failed.

"Anyone that thirsty for power would be no friend to the crown," Clement said. "What kind of enemy might that be?"

"I don't know, but whoever is after the Phoenix is going to be powerful already, there's no question about that. There is one thing I think we do know. The Order thought, and I agree, that if someone were going to try and harm the Phoenix, it would be as it is dying right before it resurrects itself. That is the only time the Phoenix is vulnerable. That time is not far off."

"How do you know?" Nicolai asked.

"As the Phoenix goes through its life cycle, it goes through several distinct changes. The Eternal Flame reflects this and goes through changes itself, including extinguishing itself when the Phoenix dies. There are five changes in the flame. The Cantori branch of the Order watches the flame and sings a song to announce each change.

"The First Song, the Song of Cresting, sounds approximately half way through the life of the Phoenix. That one sounded 547 years ago. The rest of the songs are nearer to the end of the Phoenix's life, and get more and more predictable. While the timing of the First Song can vary by centuries, the timing of the Second Song, which sounded several months ago, varies only by as long as one year. The progression through each successive stage gets quicker.

"The next Song can sound at any time, but it may be as far as nine months away. That's my hope. The longer the better. We need as much time as we can get. Once we hear it, however, we'll only have a month before the Phoenix regenerates. Seven weeks at best."

"Seven weeks to do what?" Marcellus asked, an edge in his voice.

"I'm not sure," Corren said, carefully meeting his eye, "but I think the first thing we need to do is determine what these stones do."

"How do you propose to do that?" Clement asked.

"I think we need to put them all together..."

"No," Nicolai said so sharply they all looked at him in surprise. "Why not?"

Nicolai's jaw was set. "We need to be careful with these stones. I don't think they should be touching anything."

Marcellus stood up and paced to the doors. Corren watched him go, then leaned forward to Nicolai, puzzled by his reaction. "We need to find out what they do. There wasn't much Nashua could tell me about either the prophecy or the stones other than speculation by Order members. She thinks we are the ones who need to figure out what to do next and I think she's right."

"What's to figure out?" Nicolai asked. "It sounds like the stones are going to tell us what to do, like Nashua's horn."

"I'm not so sure. If that were the case, what's the point of the prophecy? And why doesn't the prophecy mention Nashua's stones? I think they are different. Even if the stones are going to give us some guidance, the prophecy sounds to me like there is something we must do on our own. I think putting the stones together will help."

Nicolai shook his head again.

"Is any of this really necessary?" Marcellus asked this in a tone that pulled all eyes to him while prohibiting a response. He stood tall and imposing, the dark sky visible through the panes of glass behind him. "Think what you want about this prophecy affair, but I say you've neglected something rather important."

"What's that?" Corren asked, trying not to let Marcellus raise his defenses or admit how intimidating he found Marcellus to be.

"Even if someone wanted to get to the Phoenix, there is no way they would be able to do it. There are only two ways said to lead to the Realm of the Phoenix, right?"

Corren nodded. "The Bridge of a Thousand Ages and the Cliffs of the Realm."

"Exactly. The Cliffs of the Realm are higher than any known mountain, the sides of which are so smooth they are impossible to traverse."

"Yes, but..."

"The Bridge goes to some supposed gateway so mysterious no one knows how to get through it. Correct?"

"Granted, but..."

"Has anybody *ever* gotten past these things?"

"Not that I know of," Corren said, his voice tightening, "however..."

"When the Phoenix comes *here*," Marcellus said forcefully, "it's supposedly cloaked in darkness so thick that a fire right in front of you could not penetrate it. Even if you *could* see the Phoenix, its magic is supposed to be so powerful no one can hurt it."

"It's vulnerable *in the Realm*," Corren said. "Right before it dies it's open to attack."

"Nobody can get to it there!" Marcellus clasped his hands behind his back, his eyes luminous and firm. "Am I right?"

Corren could only clench his jaw.

"I thought as much. Though I'd like to spend my time protecting the *untouchable* Glorious Bird, my priority will be helping a kingdom *without* the benefit of magical protection. I'm traveling to the border in two days and would like to prepare and get some rest. If you'll excuse me."

Marcellus swept pass them, as unstoppable as a storm, and left the room. Corren turned and stared at the king, and Nicolai with him.

Clement looked after Marcellus, concerned. He glanced at Corren and Nicolai. "That's why I call him Marcellus the Fierce. He can be a bit stubborn at times."

"Yes," Corren said. "I've noticed."

Clement smiled. "He has a good heart, even if you haven't seen it yet."

Corren sighed, disarmed by Clement's sincerity. Their father's affection for Marcellus was evident. "We need to figure out what to

67

do," Corren said. "I don't think we can do this without him."

"Give him some time," Clement said. "This has been a lot to take in, for everyone. Why don't we retire for the evening and meet again tomorrow?" The king stood and they each stood with him. "It's getting late, too late to travel. The castle is open to both of you. You're welcome to stay here."

"Your Highness is most gracious," Corren said, glancing at Nicolai, thinking of his need for a place to stay. "But we should be careful not to raise too much suspicion."

Clement nodded. "Your true identities will stay between us for now. I will arrange for you to be the king's guest. I know how to give orders that are not questioned. That status is open ended. You may come and go as you please."

They were shown to rooms by a page in a uniform. Corren disappeared into one and Nicolai entered the next, his mind in a haze. The page shut the door, and Nicolai stood alone in the center. He was aware of a rug under his feet, a bed with linens, a slender window, and a fireplace with a fire already ignited in its belly. The room was cold, the heat from the fire not yet warming the place where Nicolai stood.

Nicolai took out his stone.

It glinted in the firelight, a stunning yellow, cool in his hands, deep at its core. Nicolai remembered a line from the prophecy: *Each stone has secrets only its bearer can unlock.* Given what his stone had already done, did he want to know its power? If they were meant to stop this Cunning One, just what was he going to be asked to do? Part of him slid into the stone's depths, and Nicolai could not resist it.

A knock at the door prompted Nicolai to tuck his stone back under his shirt. He opened the door to reveal Corren. "At least now you have a place to stay," Corren said.

Nicolai had the feeling Corren did not come to his door to say that. "I'm not going to impose myself on the king. It's too late to go to an inn tonight."

Corren smiled and nodded as if he did not really hear what Nicolai had said. "I'm going on the Bridge," he said.

Nicolai widened his eyes. "The Bridge of a Thousand Ages?"

Corren nodded.

"You can't get on it," Nicolai said.

"That might be true." He paused. "Or it might not."

Though Nicolai sensed his worry, he also knew his decision was firm. They looked at each other a moment.

"Are you coming?" Corren asked.

Praea sat in a room in the guest quarters of the castle, not wanting to get ready for bed despite the lateness of the hour. Her mind would not settle down. Though she knew getting into bed would cause her weariness to take over and allow her to sleep, Praea had no desire for it. The events of the last days tumbled around in her mind. She kept landing on the assurances of Prince Marcellus. He seemed both sincere and capable, and she found herself clinging to that with all her strength.

A knock at the door startled her and she opened it to reveal a page with a message. He handed it to her and she noticed the seal. Her heartbeat quickened.

"Does my Lady desire a scribe?"

"That won't be necessary. Thank you."

The page bowed and left and she latched the door.

Praea read the message once, sighed, then read it again. She walked to the fireplace and tossed the parchment into the flames. The fire took it quickly, transforming it into charred and curling fragments. She waited longer than she needed to, until the last of it collapsed into the embers. She went to her trunk. She lifted the lid to reveal underclothes, the sachet filled with lavender, and the box with her brushes and pins.

She ignored these and withdrew a slender rod tucked inside the trunk, using it to pry off one of the boards under the lid. From the nook this revealed, she removed a small bag drawn up with a tie. She set this on her lap, the maroon velvet stark against her pale dress. She replaced the board, closed the lid, and carried the bag with her as she went to the canopy bed and sat down.

She removed its contents: a deceptively delicate-looking necklace. The chain was of the perfect length, designed so the glass ball on the end of the necklace would rest at the base of her neck.

She looked at it a long time, stalling. Like a soapy bubble, the clear glass reflected suggestions of color. Finally she secured it around her neck, the ball nudging against the tender place assigned to it.

This simple act took the last of her energy and weariness pressed over her. She curled on the bed and fell asleep in an instant.

Marcellus had to get out of there.

He didn't know which he wanted to escape more, cryptic messages from some bird or the appearance of two brothers. More specifically, an older brother. There was only one place on the grounds free from interruption. If ever he needed to flee to it, it was now.

At the northwestern corner of the grounds, there was an area nestled away from everything else, contained by its own walls and accessible only by a gate, which Marcellus now entered and locked. Within was a piece of forest not consumed by the grounds, but rather embraced within them. He passed through aged oak, aspen, and fragrant pine as the ground sloped downward. This change in elevation, along with the shelter of the trees, rendered him invisible from any other vantage point on the castle grounds, including the towers. A break in the trees brought him to his destination: a vast, natural spring. At one end stairs had been carved into the rock and led down into the pool. The water's surface never quite stilled, moved by whatever underground spring fed it.

Marcellus deposited his clothes on a bench near the water's edge, descended the steps, and dove under the surface. The water was cool and ran over him like silk. The moon gave a little light, not like those dark nights when he swam anyway, using memory to avoid the rocks that lurked under the surface. Tonight, however, Marcellus' obstacles were clear.

He swam the distance to the other side, then came up and shook the hair out of his face. He turned and pushed off from the edge. The sound of the water was heightened in the quiet of the night. He floated along the surface on his back, the stars above staggering.

Generally he would be pacified by such a beautiful night sky, but at the moment the heavens seemed empty and cold, uninterested in anything that might be troubling him. What did any of it matter? Was there any feeling in the universe for a prince in danger of losing his life's purpose? Had there been any sorrow in those skies when his mother had bled to death 21 years ago?

Marcellus felt his heart contract. He had so wanted to hear about his mother. When his father finally said more than a sentence about her it was too grisly to bear. Her last words rung in his mind: *It was worth it.* Was it?

He dove below the surface and swam down as far as he dared. The spring was deep, and the undercurrent strong. He never swam to the bottom on his own.

He came back up to breathe, disappointed he didn't find the dolphins on his first pass. He didn't want to be alone. Something swam past his legs, and he smiled.

He dove again and this time saw two dolphins circling him. The familiar sensation of being with them surrounded him. It was a feeling he both enjoyed and resisted. When they were near him, he felt a shimmering change within him. Inevitably he had the thought that he could stay underwater indefinitely, with no need for air or breath. That was the part that scared him. It was an illogical thought and he didn't like how his mind persisted with it, even tempted him to test it. He never would.

He grabbed the fin of the nearest dolphin, smooth and firm, and sped through the water as they pulled him along. He let go near the surface, drew breath into his lungs, then grabbed hold as they swirled around him. A smooth body brushed against his bare skin. They pulled him along the bottom, his grip tightening against the strong currents.

Marcellus stayed until he was too tired to remain any longer, too tired to feel the weight of his heart. He patted the side of the dolphin he was holding and it came to the surface. He climbed the marble steps, weary, and heard them leap out over the water. He turned just in time to see them dive back down and disappear.

71

Eleven

Lanterns lined the deserted street next to the docks and Corren and Nicolai passed in and out of their discs of light. Merchant ships sat in the water, creaking as they swayed. As the two hurried along, the docks tethered with merchant ships gave way to those with smaller sailing vessels. After that, the docks wedged nearer to the Bridge were thick with little fishing boats, bobbing and knocking against each other.

The street gave way to a plaza, into which other streets fed. By day this was a bustling thoroughfare, but now the only inhabitants were a wizard, a farmer, and the furtive light of the moon. It was just as well, for here stood the archway at the entrance to the Bridge of a Thousand Ages, and Corren did not want to be disturbed.

"What are we looking for?" Nicolai asked.

Corren bent near the stone blocks, sensing the magic barrier placed over them. "Weaknesses," he said. Unlike the low walls leading away from the archway, there was no moss darkening the stone, no discoloration from sun or wind or sea salt. It was unmarred, magically guarded from anything—or anybody—with a mind to touch it.

This magic had not always been there, at least according to Nashua though she did not know for sure. Until the sounding of the First Song several hundred years ago, the Bridge was unprotected by the Order. Following the song came rumors of an attempt to get through the Gateway at the end of the Bridge. Shortly after that the rumors began of the Bridge shocking people, or worse. Nashua assumed the Order placed some sort of enchantment upon it to keep people away. Being a member of the Wysard branch, Corren could confirm the Order protected the Bridge, though he had never heard of anyone trying to get on. Looking at the archway he saw the enchantment placed upon it was ancient magic. Weak magic.

Corren furrowed his brows. Had the prophecy been lost? Did the Order not know what danger the Phoenix was in? That didn't seem likely. Perhaps there were more protections nearer to the Gateway. There was only one way to find out. "Keep an eye open," he said to Nicolai.

"What are you going to do?"

"I think I can break through this." Corren crept his hand toward the archway, his arm tingling as he approached it, his senses discerning the different elements in the magical shield. He was nearly touching it. "Anyone coming?" he asked without slowing or looking around.

"No."

"Good."

He channeled his thoughts, said an incantation, and touched the stone. A ripple of energy spread out from his fingers, visibly running over the archway and down the Bridge in waves. It shot back toward him unexpectedly and he tried to remove his hand from the stone but he was too slow. The rebound made contact and pain ripped through his arm, sending him stumbling backwards. He clenched his hand into a fist, his fingers throbbing in bright stabs of pain.

"Corren!"

Corren pinched his eyes closed. He felt Nicolai grab his hand, but he could not unclench it.

"Let me see it."

He let Nicolai open his fingers, at which point he looked down himself. The skin was glossy and red from the boils on his fingertips. Nicolai grabbed the bag at his waist and dug through it. Corren tried to clear his mind, to set aside the pain and focus. As firmly as he could he said, "Katath."

The boils fled first, then the pain. Within seconds all that was left was reddened tender skin. Corren exhaled and flexed his fingers. If he had worked the spell properly his skin would have shown no signs of past injury, but healing had never been Corren's strong point. He had some sort of block, according to Aradia. It wasn't the best healing but at least his fingers weren't throbbing anymore.

He looked at Nicolai who was holding a bit of wood and staring in amazement at Corren's hands.

"What's that?" Corren asked, pointing.

Nicolai glanced at the wood in his hand like he forgot it was there. "Alder bark."

Corren smiled. "Thanks, but those boils were caused by magic. Herbs wouldn't have helped." Nicolai put it back inside his bag, free from offense. "I didn't know you were an herbalist," Corren said.

Nicolai shrugged. "I know a little." He gestured to the Bridge. "It seems to be protected alright."

Corren shook his head and flexed his hand again, his fingertips still hot. "No, it isn't. Now I *know* how to get through."

"You're not doing it again?"

"Not the same thing, no. I have another idea. Though a staff would make this a lot easier."

Corren studied the Bridge again, double checking his theory before he gave it another go.

Nicolai was eyeing him. "I really don't think you should."

Corren looked around. The plaza was deserted, though the moon lent more light than he would have preferred. He looked at the Rock of Light far down the shoreline, the Eternal Flame steady within it. If anyone were looking they certainly could not see him from there. At least, he hoped not. Sneaking away from Tower Hall South had been one thing, but going on the Bridge was another matter. The consequences could be severe. But Marcellus had been right about there being only two ways to get into the Realm. As far as Corren was concerned the Cliffs were impassable. That meant if someone was going to get into the Realm, they'd be going through the Gateway to do it. Which meant Corren and his brothers had to find out exactly what that Gateway was. There would never be a better time than now.

He turned back to the archway. "Alright. No point waiting."

This time he used both hands and a different incantation, which he had to bellow. There was a risk someone would hear it, but he needed the power. Again, a rippling energy flew out from his hands, shooting down the length of the Bridge, the bulk of which was concealed in darkness. The residue of the spell turned red and hovered over the stones like a mist, then vanished.

Corren stood, satisfied. "There."

They both jumped when a spark from the end of the Bridge arched low in the air before disappearing.

Nicolai looked around quickly, then back at Corren, concerned.

"Alright," Corren admitted. "I didn't know that was going to happen. But look." He walked through the archway, stepping onto the Bridge. "We can get through now."

"So can anyone else."

"If I could figure that out, anyone who poses a threat to the Phoenix could do it. That was old magic. Our real concern is the Gateway."

"We're going on the Bridge?"

"All the way to the end. And just in case someone saw that, we'd better be quick."

Twelve

The low walls made for an open view as they traveled over the moonlit sea on a bridge supported not by pillars but by some unseen power. Corren was in a hurry to get away from the city and out of sight. Nicolai felt no cause to argue. He kept turning back to make sure no one was coming to investigate the spark, but when the shoreline disappeared in darkness it looked as uninhabited as when they'd left. He kept an even pace with Corren. The Bridge was a silvery outline in the moonlight. Nicolai felt wrapped in a silence every bit as substantial as sound. The water passing beneath them had nothing to lap against to declare its presence. Even their footsteps and the occasional hushed conversation could not dispel the quiet that seemed to be everywhere.

They traveled on.

After a time, the shadow of Crescent Island reared out from the sea, its companion Pearl Island lost in the depths of the water. As they drew closer, Nicolai could see the water crashing along the island's shoreline, glimpses of white foam breaking through the darkness. The island was not far. Nicolai thought the end of the Bridge must be drawing near.

When the end became visible it was uncertain at first, as if only a mirage, but the closer they got the more real it appeared. Their pace quickened, as if they were reaching a harbor of safety.

"When you woke this morning," Corren said, "did you think you'd find yourself here by day's end, a prince in the middle of the Bridge of a Thousand Ages?"

"I'm no prince."

"By birthright you are," Corren said, looking at him to make his point.

Nicolai considered him. "Heir to the throne, huh?"

76

Corren looked away. Shrugged. "Seems unlikely." Nicolai thought he heard something else in Corren's voice: desire.

At last they reached the end. The end of the Bridge curved into a large circle, the center of which opened to the water underneath. Corren walked up to the wall surrounding the opening and leaned over, Nicolai following his lead. The sea churned far below.

"This is the Gateway?" Corren said.

"I'm pretty sure if you go through that, the only place you'll end up is the bottom of the ocean."

"I think you're right," Corren said, but he kept looking.

Nicolai stepped back and that was when he saw it. Several feet higher than their line of sight and hovering in midair above the opening in the Bridge, was a small ring of metal. Nicolai felt a chill. "Corren."

Corren looked at Nicolai, then followed his gaze to the ring. After a moment's pause, he said, "This is it."

Nicolai knew that but that didn't keep him from feeling surprised. He thought the Gateway would be different, not this floating ring of metal. "I don't see how anyone could get through that."

"Well," Corren said, circling the perimeter of the wall, his eyes never leaving the ring, "you don't walk through it, do you?"

"You get through magically?"

Corren had stopped next to Nicolai's other side, a look of concentration on his face. "Yes."

"Do you know how to do it?"

Corren hoisted himself onto the wall. Nicolai had to stop himself from grabbing him. "No," Corren said, high atop a wall even higher above the sea. The ring was at eye level now. "I don't know how." He stretched out his hand, but did not touch the ring though it was well within reach. "Vilioray."

Corren kept his hand outstretched. Nothing happened that Nicolai could see.

"Hmm," Corren said, brows furrowed.

"Are you trying to get through?"

"No. I'm trying to learn its properties so I can see where it might be weak, but several of them are hidden." Corren began circling the ring again, slowly sidestepping his way around the wall. He would say a word, wait, say a word again. Nicolai saw no change in the ring as Corren uttered these words. Whatever was happening, Corren seemed to understand it.

At last Corren climbed down from the wall, and Nicolai relaxed. "I don't know," Corren said. "This has a lot of unique qualities. Getting through would be complicated. A spell *might* do it, or more likely a powerful potion could breech it."

"Do you think you could get through?"

"No." Corren rubbed his forehead. "We don't need to get through. We only need to make sure no one else does. Though..." He pressed his lips together and shook his head. "I admit I'd like to get through. How often I've wished to have lived in the time before the Cliffs and the Bridge, when the Realm was open to almost anyone who wanted to go. So I could lay eyes on the Phoenix myself." He turned to Nicolai. "Just to *see* it with my own eyes."

Nicolai had that feeling of being caught in someone else's passion, but his confusion about something Corren said overpowered it. "What do you mean, before the Cliffs and the Bridge? They've always been here."

Corren looked at him in surprise. "No... I thought everyone knew that story."

"I didn't know," Nicolai said.

"I see." He seemed taken aback. "They appeared the last time the Phoenix came. Before that, the Realm was more accessible, though not many people ventured there. Mainly it was members of the Order and sometimes their apprentices going there to study the Phoenix. It's how we know so much about it. We can't do that anymore though," he said glancing at the ring. "This Gateway is well defended. That explains why the defense at the entrance was so weak. It must be to keep citizens away."

Nicolai thought about this and tried to fit all the pieces together. "Then why did the Phoenix bring the stones?"

Corren shrugged, his brows furrowed like he was trying to discover the reason, too. "I don't know the reason, but I..." Corren stopped, his mouth parted. "Wait... a... minute," he said. He dug in his bag and brought out a bundle Nicolai recognized.

As Corren uncovered his stone, gentle warmth engulfed Nicolai. It was subtle—nothing like the draw of his own stone—but unmistakable. He had felt it the first time he saw Corren's stone, too.

"What if?" Corren said, and held the stone up toward the ring.

Nicolai drew a sharp breath. The stone looked like it would fit into the ring. Fit perfectly, in fact.

Corren glanced at him, eyes alight.

Nicolai nodded. "Go on."

Corren lifted himself onto the wall again and stood. He held out his stone and Nicolai's heart began to pound. He clutched the edge of the rough wall, watched Corren take his stone to the ring, slide it in, and let go.

It rested there.

Nothing happened.

Corren glanced down at Nicolai, who raised his eyebrows.

Corren looked back to the ring. "Perhaps a little farther." He pushed slowly but firmly on the top of the stone.

It slipped free of the ring, past Corren's grasping hand, plummeting to the sea.

Nicolai lunged down and caught it smartly but he went too far. His footing gave way. His legs flew up and he dropped headlong toward the water in a dizzying spin. His hand scraped against the inner side of the wall as he fumbled for the ledge, then the wall disappeared and the water rushed up toward him... and stopped.

He hovered over the water, just cleared of the wall. As he hung upside down he saw the underside of the Bridge stretching away from him. The chain around his neck slackened, the stone under his shirt slid and he grabbed it before it could go any farther. He heard a word far above him. Quick as he had fallen he was reversing direction, back through the center of the circle, the world tumbling in an impossible way before he found himself sitting on the Bridge at Corren's feet.

Corren knelt down. "Are you alright?"

"What on earth?"

"I'm sorry," he said. "I've never used that spell on a person before."

When the world stopped rocking Nicolai became aware of two things: his heart pounding and Corren's stone clasped in his hand. He had grabbed it on instinct. If he had had time to give it any forethought, he would have let it fall to the sea. But he didn't let it fall. As it was, Corren's stone sat in his hand and Nicolai held it, unharmed.

He handed it back to Corren, who held it close. Nicolai's eyes were still on the stone, his mind still working it out. Maybe only the Three could touch the stones. Maybe...

Nicolai swallowed hard. He thought about the stones in Nashua's horn telling her what to do and remembered what happened right before his father grabbed his stone. Nicolai had been guided too, only he hadn't listened. A wave of nausea hit him. If he had run like the stone told him to, if he had not resisted, maybe his father would still be alive.

Corren dipped his head to get Nicolai to look him in the eye. "What's wrong? Are you hurt?"

Nicolai waved his hand, shook his head. "No. It's only... I touched your stone, but my father... I mean, my father who raised me. He tried to take the stone from me." Corren's eyes widened. "To protect me. But when he touched it..." His throat tightened.

Corren sat back on his heels. He knew something. Nicolai could see that. "Did he... survive?"

Nicolai's could only shake his head. It was his fault. All his fault.

Corren closed his eyes and sighed. "I'm sorry." They sat there for a moment. Nicolai wished he could hear the water. It was too quiet.

"Our stones are protected," Corren said. "They cannot be stolen or taken from us. You could touch my stone because you saved it for me, not for yourself. Your father... he must have meant to keep it from you."

"He thought the stone was hurting me," Nicolai said, his voice rising. "He wasn't a thief."

Corren rushed to reassure him. "I'm sure he was only doing what he thought was best."

Nicolai nodded, looking down, wishing for something else to talk or think about.

Corren withdrew his gaze, seeming to understand Nicolai's thoughts, and examined his stone. Nicolai fought against his grief in private. "The Realm has a similar protection," Corren said. "Before the Cliffs appeared, you could enter the Realm safely as long as you meant no harm. Those who entered with less than honorable intentions would... wither to death."

"*Wither to death?*" Nicolai said, so horrified by the suggestion it moved him to stand. He turned and looked at the Gateway, floating in the dark, and frustration emerged. "Even if someone did get through the Gateway, what chance would they have?"

Nicolai could feel Corren watching him, studying him. Corren stood too and turned his attention to the Gateway. "You would have to know how to get through *and* how to magically protect yourself once you're there." Corren turned back to Nicolai and leaned against the wall. "Normally, I wouldn't consider it a possibility, but the Phoenix needs help beyond its own protection or the prophecy would not have come. We have to assume someone is going to know how to get to the Phoenix and that means getting to it in the Realm. Our job is to stop whoever that is."

"Are these stones really going to be any more effective than Cliffs and a Gateway and whatever it is that withers people to death?"

Corren put his stone away and stood facing Nicolai, his face resolute. "I don't know what the stones are for. But the Phoenix brought them for a reason."

Thirteen

They headed back down the Bridge in silence. Corren had been stunned to hear about the death of the man Nicolai considered to be his father. Thoughts of that swirled in his mind along with questions about the Gateway. How would someone break through that ring? It would take advanced magic, that much was certain. Corren doubted he could figure out how to get through, but that didn't stop the nagging feeling a vulnerability was there. If the Gateway couldn't be broached, why would the Phoenix bring the stones? But what were they supposed to do that the Phoenix couldn't do already? Corren's mind returned again to the Phoenix dying, its one moment of weakness. In that moment, unable to protect itself, the Phoenix would need defenders.

If only he knew how they were to do it.

His thoughts were interrupted by a sound that made both he and Nicolai stop short. It sounded like a rumble, far away, but he couldn't tell which direction it came from. "What is that?"

Nicolai took a step forward, peering down the Bridge. "Someone's coming."

Corren looked down the Bridge and saw shapes in the darkness. He heard horses' hooves rumbling along the stone bridge and heading their way. "There's more than one."

He and Nicolai exchanged glances and darted back toward the Gateway. "Don't let..." Corren began, but his voice seized in his throat and his arms bound to his side. He lost his balance and fell forward, twisting and landing on his shoulder, skidding to a stop. He saw Nicolai collapse too, unable to use his arms either.

Whoever was coming had bound them magically, both hand and voice.

The clopping sound echoed on the stone as four horses came into view. Dismounting off of each were men in long black cloaks. It was the Guard. The Guardian branch of the Order of Ceinoth was charged with keeping dark wizards out of certain areas, which kept them mostly far north of here. Corren realized now that the spark he saw when he broke the barrier to the Bridge must have sent an alert.

They gathered around. The nearest one bent over Corren, heavily browed and stern faced, clutching his staff. "This one's a wizard."

"Not this one," Corren heard another say, referring to Nicolai.

"Are you from the Citadel of Zeverai?" the Guard member in front of him asked. Corren shook his head no.

The man narrowed his eyes. "We'll see, won't we? Stand up," he said. "You have a lot to answer for."

The Guard lifted Corren and Nicolai to their feet and shoved them in the direction of shore. Corren's mind was working. How was he going to get out of this?

At the end of the Bridge another group of the Guard waited, among them a man Corren recognized. Kennard, Head of the Guardian branch, was a broad-chested, bald man with dark skin and darker eyes, which now widened in shock. "I know this one." He waved a hand as he said an incantation and Corren felt his ability to speak return. "What are you doing here?"

Corren sighed with relief. "I'm sorry. I can explain."

"Does Aradia know you're here?"

Corren shook his head. "She doesn't know I'm in Stonebridge. She's traveling but I don't know where."

"What are you doing on the Bridge?"

"I only wanted to see what was at the end of it." Corren regretted it the second he said it.

Kennard rolled his eyes. Corren kept his face as sheepish as he could. Now that he gave his excuse he'd have to stick to it. He wished he had thought of something better.

"Do you have no sense?" Kennard said.

"I know I shouldn't have but I wanted to see it for myself. I wondered what it looked like because no one could tell me exactly." Corren knew he was rambling like a child but now that he had started he couldn't seem to stop. "I know I shouldn't have broken through

83

the enchantment but I know it's more for keeping the citizens off anyway." Kennard raised his brows. "I didn't think there would be any harm. We were coming back on our own, ask them." Corren gestured to the Guard members who had found them on the Bridge.

Kennard sighed and rubbed his brow. "Your curiosity has gotten you into trouble before."

Corren saw Nicolai glance at him but Corren ignored it.

"The Bridge, Corren? Didn't the enchantment on it at least give you pause? Why don't you break into the Rock of Light next?" He held his hands up in warning. "I'm not serious. Don't do that."

"I wouldn't," Corren said, shaking his head.

"But the Bridge is alright?" Kennard sighed. "What next with you?"

Corren didn't answer. Despite Kennard's words, Corren could see he was softening and didn't want to say anything to ruin it.

Kennard's eyes landed on Nicolai as if he had just noticed him. "You're not from Tower Hall South."

"No, sir. I'm a farmer. Nicolai of Knobby Tree."

"Well Nicolai of Knobby Tree, I don't know how you came to be with Corren, but you might want to go your own way if you're not fond of trouble."

Corren thought that was a little harsh. He hadn't been in trouble in years and even in his youth he was largely obedient even if his curiosity *had* gotten the best of him at times. Corren was in no position to argue, however, so he stayed silent.

Kennard fixed Corren with a stern look. "You're not a child anymore Corren. You can't expect people to humor you forever. If it was anything else I'd only give you a warning, but this is the Bridge of a Thousand Ages. I'll have to report this to Aradia when she returns from her trip. She can decide what to do with you."

Corren would have pleaded with him not to but he knew it was no use. "Yes, sir. I am sorry."

"Alright then," he said with a scowl. "You can go."

Corren and Nicolai hurried away. Before they ducked around a building Corren looked over his shoulder to see Kennard and the Guard members pointing their staffs at the Bridge, restoring the protective enchantment.

Fourteen

Marcellus had spent the day preparing for what was sure to be a delicate meeting with Norrland, during which the fate of three nations and their fighting men would be decided. The thought of that didn't give him near as much trouble as the thought of meeting again with his brothers.

His brothers. If he felt any fondness for them—for the simple reason that they too were his mother's sons—he felt too guarded to let those feelings loose. They had brought in their wake news of a foolish prophecy, a threat to his right to the throne, and, though he felt like a child admitting it to himself, competition for his father's affection.

Marcellus stood by the open balcony doors in the king's office, waiting for Corren and Nicolai to arrive. The wind was restless, bearer of the storm visible away in the west, its mountainous clouds swaggering over the sea. As the ill wind advanced ships fled to shore, seeking safe harbor.

"I don't think you've sat down once today." His father stood next to him. "You should rest while you have the chance."

"There's work to be done," he said more tersely than he meant to. "I don't have time to rest and I'm not keen on wasting my time waiting for them."

This was followed by a moment of thick silence.

"I asked them to arrive later so we could talk first," Clement said. "I know this has been difficult for you..."

"Not at all," Marcellus said, though he avoided looking at his father and stared out at the city instead. The tops of the buildings were familiar but he did not really see them. Not today.

"Marcellus..."

"I can handle it."

His father paused before walking back to his desk. Marcellus knew his father well enough to know he was not finished talking, so Marcellus stayed where he was to maintain his resolve.

He knew how to maintain resolve. In Marcellus' relatively young life, he had fought with the sword many times. When faced with battle, if he felt any fear he had long ago learned how to channel that into resoluteness and acute concentration. He had a keen eye for opportunities in battle, knew how to find an enemy's weakness and penetrate it. Despite the reputation he had earned himself by the battles that he *did* fight, he was too sensible to rush into war when other options were available. Sometimes avoiding battle was the wise thing to do, whether by diplomacy or careful use of spies. He had done it more times than he had fought. But never had he avoided a battle simply due to fear. He had never run simply to save his own life, nor would he ever. He had never run from any burden or responsibility placed upon him, and those burdens and responsibilities were many.

For this reason, the feelings he had now were foreign and unwelcome. If he had it within himself to run out of the room and avoid this convoluted mess of heirs and prophecies, he would do it. But it was not within himself. He only knew how to stand and fight.

A knock at the door echoed through the room. Neither man moved. "My son," Clement said. "I know not your thoughts. But I wish to reassure you of my love and regard for you. Despite anything that happens, that will never change."

Nicolai had the impression of walking into a private moment. The king, his father he reminded himself, greeted them warmly. Marcellus was reserved but polite, his agitation of the previous night gone, at least for now. They settled into a tentative group once more. Corren gave a report of their trip to the Bridge the night before and the trouble they landed in. Nicolai still didn't know how that was going to play out. When he had asked Corren what was going to happen, he could only say, with no small amount of concern, that he didn't know.

"You think there's a weakness in the Gateway?" the king asked.

Corren nodded. "There must be."

"What do you do about that?"

"I don't know yet. I think what we need to do now is put these stones together." Corren glanced at Nicolai when he said this. Nicolai's hesitation must have been apparent. "It's safe Nicolai. No one is trying to take it from you."

"What are you talking about?" Marcellus asked.

Corren had discreetly left out any mention of Nicolai's father, but he told them about it now as sensitively as Nicolai could've wished. Nicolai listened with a kind of internal resistance, holding his grief away. Clement and Marcellus both regarded Nicolai with compassion.

Corren moved away from the subject, for which Nicolai was grateful, by explaining the protective nature of their stones. Clement considered this information thoughtfully. "Perhaps you each should keep your stones close, for the sake of others who might accidentally come across it."

"That's why I made the necklace," Nicolai said.

"Can you make two more?" Corren asked.

"If you wish."

Corren bent down and took his stone out of his bag but did not unwrap it. "We need to put these stones together."

Nicolai still felt leery but Corren knew more about magic than anyone else. They had to trust him. He took his stone out of its iron clasp and held it on his lap. He felt it pulling at him. He kept his eyes on Corren.

Corren looked at Marcellus expectantly.

"Now?" Marcellus asked.

"Why not?"

"What is putting them together going to do? They're just stones."

Nicolai puzzled at this, almost took offense. *Just stones?* "Your Highness, you don't really believe that, do you?"

Marcellus looked at him and Nicolai met his gaze without threat or disrespect. He had no animosity toward Marcellus, a prince he had long felt Caedmonia fortunate to have. He really just wanted to understand. What exactly was the prince resisting?

Marcellus seemed to sense this. His eyes yielded, softened. "Marcellus is fine," he said. He stood and headed for the door. "Wait here."

Marcellus returned with an ornately carved wooden box, which he placed on his father's desk. With both hands he tilted up the lid. There sat his stone, sole possessor of the box's velvety interior. It was a stunning blue, both beautiful and alarming. Marcellus had stolen glances at it more times than he would ever admit. Each time he felt a part of himself journey to the center of it. He felt the same way now as he held it in his palm. He pinched his eyes closed and forced himself to look elsewhere.

With it securely in his hand, he turned to Corren and Nicolai. They stood near him, waiting.

Corren held his scarlet stone out and Marcellus did not look at it, tried not to feel anything from it. *Just stones,* he told himself firmly. *Nothing's going to happen.* Marcellus touched the tip of his stone to Corren's. They each looked at Nicolai.

Nicolai raised his stone, a luminous yellow, and brought it toward them. As it neared the others, Marcellus felt pulled by the trembling space between them. Time seemed to pause as the gap slowly closed. His heart jolted, the stones touched, and his grip on the stone compulsively tightened. All three stones went alight, each in their own color, blinding and raw. A ball of light emerged in the center, swirling and raging like a tempest. It expanded in a dizzying rush past their hands, their arms, colliding with their chests. Marcellus, Corren, and Nicolai each arched backwards, yelling in pain, and Marcellus felt searing heat tear through his body. The pain was all he knew. His surroundings vanished. Then quick as it came the pain was gone and he was on his back, panting.

He rolled over, pulled himself up to his knees, dizzy and shaking. His father was at his side. "Are you alright?"

Marcellus grunted. He realized he was kneeling where the desk used to be. He glanced around and saw Corren and Nicolai extracting themselves from the floor, too. Not only the desk but several chairs were far removed from their original locations. Everything near where they had been standing had been shoved back several feet from the sheer force of whatever energy had erupted from the stones. Marcellus looked at the stone still in his hand.

It appeared unchanged.

He stood, the dizziness waning.

"Are you hurt?" his father asked.

He shook his head, wiping sweat from his brow.

"Sit, my son."

Marcellus began to walk unsteadily. "I'd rather walk."

Corren rose weakly, leaning against a chair for support. He looked pale. "Sit before you faint," the king instructed and Corren obeyed.

"What happened?" Nicolai asked. He stood solidly, eyeing his stone with a mixture of concern and revulsion. He alone seemed recovered. "Is this evil?" he asked quietly. He put it back in the casing and let it fall against his chest as he turned to face Corren. "You don't know what you're dealing with."

"I thought something like this might happen," Corren said, breathlessly. "I wasn't sure but... I certainly did not expect such force."

Marcellus made his way to the fireplace, his strength slowly returning. He gripped the mantle and took a deep, steadying breath. The warmth from the flames soaked into him. Reassured him. The stones and the light and the pain flashed through his mind and he closed his eyes.

"These stones are unique, aren't they?" Nicolai asked. "How could you know that was going to happen?"

"Well, I didn't know for sure. I just suspected it. Nashua told me that the Order made a few speculations about the prophecy before she left. One of these had to do with the Great Readying. They thought the stones needed to come together in order to seal their magic."

"What do you mean, seal the magic?"

Corren seemed to be catching his breath but still looked a little clammy. "The more powerful the magic, the more complicated the process to complete the magic. Obviously anything coming from the Phoenix is going to be powerful and could have come already fully ready. But the Order didn't think so. The Order thought the magic could not be completed, made ready, until the stones were in the hands of the proper bearers. They thought whatever powers the stones held would be delivered to their bearers at that time."

"If its power is weak knees I think I'm better off on my own," Marcellus said.

Nicolai regarded them. "I feel alright."

They looked at him.

"I mean... I felt weak at first, but only for a moment. Why are you two... why did it affect you differently?"

Marcellus didn't know what to say to that. He felt better each passing minute but he wasn't used to being so weakened. "Where does it say all this about the Readying again?" he asked, mainly as a diversion from Nicolai's question.

"It's actually in three places in the prophecy. The first is: 'Red brother of flame, the Gatherer, the Seeker, must ensure the Great Readying, and prepare to exchange.' "

"Alright."

"Later, there is a line that says, 'Each stone has secrets only its bearer can unlock.' Then later it says 'only the Three as one can prevent this thievery.' "

Marcellus was incredulous. "The Order decided the stones needed to come together... from *that?*" He felt an underlying sense of frustration and awe. How could the Order glean such meaning from a prophecy Marcellus felt to be so cryptic?

Corren said, "I think they were right." He examined his stone. His color was improving and he sat up straighter. "Are your stones warm?"

Marcellus released the mantle, standing more solidly on his own two feet. He looked at his stone. In the midst of everything else he hadn't noticed the gentle warmth coming from it. "Actually, yes."

"And yours?" Corren asked Nicolai.

Nicolai nodded. "Yes. It's not... pulling me in anymore either."

"Nor mine," Corren said, with a regrettable tone. He turned to Marcellus. "Is yours?"

Marcellus looked at his stone. The reflection from the fire danced on its edges. He felt nothing. For the first time since the stone came to him, it was quiet. Still. *Maybe,* Marcellus thought, *waiting.* At that

90

moment, he realized something was different, not just with the stone but within himself. He could no longer deny. He could no longer turn away. What just happened with the stones was no trick. Whatever was happening here, it was real. He kept his eyes on his stone, still beautiful, still mysterious, still his. "No," he answered. He looked at Corren as he said this, even though his answer was also admitting he *had* felt something before. Even though by answering as he did, it meant he had changed his mind about some things.

But only some things. The matter of heirs would be dealt with in its own time.

"The stones are warm," Corren said. "They've been made ready."

"Made ready to do what?" Nicolai asked.

Corren had no answer for this.

In silence, they slowly began putting the room back together, uprighting chairs, shoving the desk back into place, picking up small objects that had flown off its surface. As they did this, Nicolai looked thoughtful. "In between all those lines in the prophecy it also says, 'All four elements must provide their singular powers.' That doesn't seem to apply to the stones being made ready."

"You have a good memory," Corren said. Nicolai shrugged, setting a silver quill stand on the desk. "The Order wasn't sure what the four elements refer to, but most thought it refers to a potion that has equal balance of all four elements."

"How is that a potion?" Marcellus asked.

"Many complex potions demand attention to the elemental balance. Simple potions may lean heavily on one element. Say, bark of a willow, for earth. If you aren't creating a simple potion, if you want something of significant power, all the elements need to be in there. Usually perfectly balanced. It is this balance that gives it such power. So the four elements referred to in the prophecy may be referring to a potion."

"Maybe so," Nicolai said. "But right after that it says 'only the Three as one can prevent this thievery.' I'm just saying that line doesn't seem to be talking about the Great Readying. Why can't that line be talking about the three of us and not the stones?"

"I think it does both," Corren said. "Often prophecies carry layers of meaning."

"Layers of annoyance," Marcellus said. "Why doesn't it just say what it means?"

"Because," Corren said seriously, "prophecies have a way of becoming clear to those who need to know, while remaining obscure to those who aren't meant to know."

They sat down again, the room restored. Marcellus rubbed his forehead in frustration. "So who isn't meant to know? Who is our enemy?" *Who was the reason for all this?*

"That we don't know," Corren said. "I think we can use some deductive reasoning to help us figure that out."

"And what is your deductive reasoning?"

"Well, the Realm is magically protected so it stands to reason it's going to be someone who knows how to do magic. Someone with a high degree of skill. The most skillful wizards and witches outside of the Order reside in the Citadel of Zeverai."

"I've never heard of them." Marcellus said.

"They're in Norrland," Corren said. Marcellus exchanged significant glances with his father. Norrland was coming up a lot lately.

"I think we should consider them first because they are rather known for their... *questionable* techniques," Corren said.

"What? Like black magic?" Nicolai asked.

"You could put it that way. The Order prefers they stay in their own land. They insist on it, in fact."

Marcellus furrowed his brows. "How do they do that?"

"I suppose the same way you make sure Norrland stays in their own land."

Marcellus thought about this. Perhaps the Citadel of Zeverai had not just the ability, but the motivation to strike at something held so dear by the Order. Perhaps they wanted a share of the Order's power. He looked at his father and smiled wryly. Politics among wizards was not so different from politics among nations.

"Perhaps," his father said to Marcellus, in a strategic tone of voice Marcellus had heard many times before, "we should see what we can find out about this Citadel."

Marcellus nodded. "I'll take care of that on my trip. We have some spies I think we can use." He glanced at Corren and Nicolai. "I'll see what I can find out and we'll talk about it when I return."

"If you're going somewhere we should go with you," Corren said.

"I can't take you on a march and I'm not staying here."

Corren seemed hesitant. "I really think we need to stick together."

Marcellus struggled to keep his irritation at this at bay. Brother or no, prince or no, Corren had no business making demands that affected things that went beyond him. "Corren, do you expect me to put the needs of the kingdom and our allies on hold for the next nine months?"

"Well, no, but..."

"Good. Tomorrow, I'm going to the border and while I'm there I'll find out what I can about the Citadel. You learn what you can here. When I get back, we'll talk about it."

Corren nodded reluctantly. He obviously wanted to argue, but didn't. "How long will you be gone?"

"I'll try to be back in two weeks."

Corren had an uneasy sense of foreboding, but he knew he could not get Marcellus to stay. He had hoped they could make good use of the time while Aradia was gone. Once she returned, he did not know how he would be able to hide his activities from her. He didn't even know how long she would be gone. When she had left a few days ago she said she would be gone "awhile." For her that meant at least two weeks. Sometimes it meant as long as two months. Corren could only hope that would be the case this time as well.

Meanwhile, the king had invited him and Nicolai to stay at the castle, obvious in his desire to simply get to know them better. For Corren, this was reason enough. He felt grateful to be able to accept since he needed a place to work on this in secrecy. That would be impossible at the Tower. For Nicolai's part, however, he was apparently prepared to spend his time at an inn rather than accept board from the king. Seeing this, Corren slyly let it slip to the king that Nicolai had been forbidden by his mother to return home until the stone was destroyed. Nicolai was none too happy about Corren's indiscretion, but the outcome was still what Corren had wanted. Two of the Three would be together, which was the best they could do until Marcellus returned.

So it was that they took up residence as the king's guests in a castle that otherwise would have been their home, while Marcellus was ready to head for the border, alone, bringing him that much nearer to the Citadel of Zeverai.

Fifteen

Even though Nicolai was supposedly a prince and therefore entitled to stay at the castle, according to Corren and the king anyway, his identity as a farmer felt more genuine. The idea of dining in the Great Hall with royalty, nobles, knights, and key men of the city, as if he had some claim with them... that was what felt the masquerade. Since he thought it important Marcellus have his necklace before he left in the morning, Nicolai spent the rest of the afternoon and evening in the castle's smithy forging the casings and links for both necklaces. It was a relief to do something physical and he didn't mind the ready excuse to avoid dinner in the castle either. Late in the evening he returned to the guest quarters appointed to him and found a fire lit, a warm bath in the center of the room, and a tray of food on the table. He felt no right to any of it. Only grime and hunger permitted him to indulge.

That night sleep eluded him. He left the room seeking some form of respite and found it atop one of the castle's high towers open to the night sky. The night air chilled him, making the warmth of his stone that much more noticeable. He looked over the parapets to the west. From this angle he saw the bottom edge of the city slipping down to the bay, the ships at port little dark boulders on the water. The Bridge drew away from shore, near it the curved shape of Crescent Island just discernible. Nicolai tried to imagine how it looked before Pearl Island was swallowed by an earthquake. Or a monster, depending on which tale you chose to believe. Beyond this the water fled to the edge of the world, a sparkling strip of moonlight on its surface the only thing making it feel near.

He wandered to the other side of the tower. From there he saw the Wilds, a dark mass on the other side of the valley, their outline so faint he almost couldn't see it. The comfort they brought him was fleeting. He had never been so far from them. They looked strangely diminished. Forbidden and foreign. Just like the place he was now.

Nicolai looked away.

He could not see the eastern portion of the grounds with its various outbuildings, including the smithy where he had been earlier that evening. What he saw instead was the western and northern sections of the grounds. To the west were the stables and expansive training arenas for the king's knights. To the north were the royal gardens spreading clear to the outer wall. On the other side of this wall, supposedly, was a narrow band of trees that came to an abrupt halt at the edge of the Great Gorge. Nicolai had never seen the Gorge, nor could he see it now, but he knew it was there. The strategic location of the castle on a hill, one side of it guarded by the Gorge, was just one more reason Stonebridge was a difficult city to attack.

At the far end of the gardens, swathed in blue moonlight, was a solitary tree. The outer wall ran along one side of it. Open courtyard surrounded its other sides. It was a grand tree, its wide spread impressive even from this height. It was here that something unexpected caught Nicolai's attention.

A shadowy figure crossed the courtyard, hidden by a long, hooded cloak. It was a woman, Nicolai decided, reacting on instinct but also judging by her slight build. The figure disappeared under the canopy of the tree. The grounds were deceptively quiet then, as if nothing out of the ordinary could be found.

Nicolai waited a brief moment, then descended the tower.

By the time he made his way to the gardens and approached the tree, an oak he saw now, whoever had been there was gone. All he saw were the tree and the bushes lining the wall. He slowed his steps, disappointed. It was a truly magnificent old oak. As he slipped under its massive canopy, he could feel its ancient years almost tangibly seeping from the bark. He looked up and heard a rustling overhead. Branches dipped violently and leaves clamored in protest. Nicolai heard something that sounded like wings, only louder. He darted out from under the tree and scanned the empty sky. He still heard the noise, softer now, but saw nothing. Then, silence.

96

He heard the sound of a branch cracking. He spun toward it. It did not come from the tree; it came from the ground by the bushes. He rushed over and bent low, searching. He saw a glimmer and met the eye of someone who then stood, surprised but unafraid. He straightened, his eyes fixed on the cloaked woman who now stood in front of him. Nicolai registered this must have been the figure he saw from the tower, but his mind, heart, and body were overtaken with different thoughts entirely. Whoever she was, her mere presence stunned him. She looked at him too, saying nothing, only meeting his eyes in a way that felt at once familiar, deep, and staggering. He felt as if he knew her somehow, felt an astonishing connection with her, but he had never seen her before. She was heartbreakingly beautiful.

"What are you doing out here?" he asked. It seemed the most logical thing to say. He could not possibly say what he was truly thinking, though he felt she somehow knew what that was anyway.

"Only..." Her voice penetrated him. He did not know he could feel such delight simply by hearing a person speak. "I was... only... out for a walk."

She did not want to tell him what she was doing, he thought, but did not want to lie either. "Well," he said smiling. "A midnight stroll through the bushes perhaps."

She smiled then too, and his heart felt it. With difficulty, she began to step over the bushes. He reached out his hand to help her and she took it with a gentle smile. He steadied her as she climbed over the hedge toward him, but his awareness kept coming back to her hand in his. When she stood in front of him, he thought she waited longer than necessary before releasing him. "Thank you."

They lingered under the shelter of the tree, cocooned by shadow and moonlight, pulsing with the discovery of something new that had yet to be named. "I suppose," she said, "we shouldn't be out here." She was right, it wasn't appropriate, but he felt she wanted to stay as much as he did.

"I'll escort you back to the castle," he said, and offered her his arm as if it were the most natural thing he could do.

She nodded her assent and slipped her arm through his.

They walked slowly through the winding, terraced garden, eyes on the delicately lit path in front of them, on each other, then retreating to the path again. Their silence was light. Alluring. They offered tentative smiles, unable to speak—either of the tender draw between them or anything else. They passed under the gentle reach of tree after tree, moonlight winking through here and there. Nicolai could hear the soft tapping of her shoes on the flagstone pathway. He felt awakened by her.

The door to the castle came much too soon.

They stopped and she slowly withdrew her arm. They both knew they should not go inside this way. "Thank you."

She smiled and for some reason they each laughed a little.

He opened the door for her. As she went through she looked back over her shoulder at him. It wasn't until the door was closing that his senses caught up with him and he yanked it open, poking his head in after her. "I'm Nicolai," he said, more eagerly than he meant to.

She turned, her features striking and new to him in the flickering light of the torches on the walls. Before she started walking away again she said, "I am Praea."

Sixteen

"Why am I always the last to know?" Theo asked.

Marcellus looked at his childhood friend. He was a ruddy, heavily-muscled man with an energetic, almost irreverent nature that had been only slightly subdued by adulthood. Marcellus liked him anyway. He was his only friend growing up, probably the only person unperturbed by the fact that Marcellus was also the prince. He was able to bring out a side of Marcellus no one else could. A few years ago Marcellus made him a commander of one of the southern battalions. What he lacked in military strategy he made up for with gusto and an ability to persuade men into devoted obedience. They were marching out of the city gate with a force five hundred strong, the sun still only a suggestion of pale gold on the eastern horizon, the earth dark but awakening. The damp air had a hint of the cooler weather the coming months would bring. "What do you mean?" Marcellus asked.

"You have meetings with two mysterious guests and your closest friend doesn't know a thing about it?" Theo said with a look of mock offense on his face.

Marcellus thought of his stone warm against his chest, hidden from view. He smiled lightly but this news disturbed him. Who else was talking about this? "How do you know about those meetings?"

Theo laughed. "When the prince grants private audience, that's news. What are they doing here?"

Marcellus kept his expression unrevealing. "They're the king's guests."

"*Why* are they the king's guests?"

Marcellus was familiar with Theo's dogged persistence and knew how to handle it. He looked at him pointedly. "Because the king invited them."

Theo sighed with mock exasperation. "Fine," he said. "Keep your secrets." Marcellus smiled, knowing Theo wasn't really bothered. They began the descent into the valley, the river a sleeping shadow down its belly. The horses' hooves rumbled lowly on the grassy hillside. Theo ran a broad hand through his unruly hair, tints of red emblazoned by the rising sun. His amused smile told Marcellus he wasn't done with his jesting. "Are you at least going to tell me about the princess?"

"What about her?"

"Don't try to tell me your father isn't attempting to arrange *that* match. He's running out of options. You can't turn them all down, you know."

Marcellus laughed. "Stop harassing me. You're getting to be as bad as he is. The envoys from Sakkara are strictly matters of state, of which you are well aware."

Theo glanced dismissively at Prince Akren who was a short distance away from them, leading his small unit of guards from Sakkara. Theo turned back to Marcellus, undeterred. "Caedmonian heirs aren't matters of state? The king is getting old. He wants grandsons."

"He's not getting old," Marcellus said, in a tone that was light but that communicated to his friend nonetheless that he was done talking about it.

And he doesn't need more heirs.

They came to the river in affable silence—both understanding it to be a mere lull in their verbal duels. Marcellus would allow himself the luxury of such distractions for now. Soon enough he would be balancing the fate of both Norrland and Sakkara. Since he felt he knew how to handle that situation, it was the prophecy and the Citadel of Zeverai that truly dominated his thoughts.

He could not even guess where that path would lead him.

Marcellus was off to the border, Corren was off to Tower Hall South for the day to arrange an extended leave of absence and smuggle out supplies of some sort, and Nicolai had plans of his own.

He left the castle at dawn and got himself some food in the city, not wanting to impose himself on the king any more than necessary. This tendency was not lost on Corren. "Eat in the Great Hall," he said. "The king wants you there. You are his son."

"Maybe he doesn't want another son."

Corren had seemed disturbed by this suggestion. Nicolai softened it with a shrug, but he did not withdraw his words, nor did he join Corren in the Great Hall to discover what aromatic delights it apparently held. Now, leaving the city gates, he finished off the last of his rye bread and, with his final bronze coin in his pocket, settled into a steady gait down the road. It felt good to be walking, to be doing anything other than sitting around wondering what the next several months would hold. He inhaled the crisp morning air, free from the heavy smells of the city. His mind began to clear for the first time since leaving home with Corren two days ago. Only two days. It felt a much bigger gap than that, a gap impossible to cross or to close, and on the other side... his former life. One he wasn't sure he could leave.

The walk was not a short one and gave him plenty of time to till around what he had learned of his stone, his brothers (a whole new family when he had no problems with the old one), and a prophecy that placed a distinct burden on his shoulders with no clear way to meet it. It was a murky, bewildering mix of thoughts. The one light in it all, strangely, was his memory of Praea. He heard her speak, saw her face, felt her hand in his, remembered all he had felt last night and took pleasure in reliving it. His rational mind regretted letting her go without knowing how to find her. Did she live at the castle or was she a guest, as he was? Would she be gone before he had a chance to meet her again? His mind fretted over these things somewhat, but his heart had the better of it. He felt a distinct calmness, a certainty that they would meet again.

He took a circuitous route to his destination, avoiding his own home and mother as he did so. He did not want to see her until he knew what he wanted to say. She would not speak to him anyway as long as he had the stone. She had made that much clear and in such a manner that he knew time would not cause her to change her mind. It made no difference. At least not at this point. He skirted the fields and kept out of sight, but he had no choice but to come very near to the farm.

After all, there was only one way to reach Salerno.

Long ago Nicolai learned how to find Salerno without being summoned first. Many times after that first encounter as a child, Nicolai had gone back into the woods trying to find the faerie king, always without success. It wasn't until he was twelve years old that Salerno summoned Nicolai again and taught him how to find Salerno on his own. At this point Nicolai began what he could only term his training, learning secrets and magic unique to faeries. Since he was not a faerie himself, he could not do everything they could do. But he learned much, under the condition that he would never reveal the source of his knowledge, nor teach their secrets to anyone else. Why he was allowed or why he was chosen, he still didn't know.

He entered the Wilds and felt wrapped in their familiarity. Nicolai walked through the trees and along the path that would not be readily apparent to anyone who did not already know it was there. It was a path he felt and remembered more than saw. The ground sloped upward. He followed its subtle incline until he came to the side of an abrupt hill. It was the same hill where he had first seen Salerno. An ordinary-looking hill, in most respects. Few, if any, other humans had ever set eyes on it, kept away by one thing or another.

But Nicolai was not kept away. He spoke in the ancient, magic language of faeries:

Ανοίξτε στον καθαρό στην καρδιά.
Γη, αποκαλύψτε την καρδιά διαβίωσής δική σου.

Open to the pure in heart.
Oh earth, reveal thy living heart.

The hill grumbled, shrugged, earth moving a bit here and a bit there until the first slim opening appeared, announced by a shaft of soft, green light. The opening stretched, yawned, and the light brightened. Nicolai squinted. The earth quieted. He stepped forward into the light so dazzling it was all he could see, but he knew the way. As he heard the earth closing behind him the light softened and he saw the grassy tunnel before him. He removed his shoes and walked on the lush grass down the tunnel to the Grand Cavern.

Gaping before him, the Grand Cavern opened up the heart of this immense hill underneath which the faeries hid. A soft, glowing light hovered in the air, almost glittering as it did so. This light was borne not of the sun but of the will of the faeries, giving life and nourishment to the things growing here under the earth. Those things were many. Thick vines, evergreen and often flowering with tiny bursts of white or yellow, covered the walls of the cavern. Where the vines weren't growing, round protrusions poked out from the rock, like little shelves or planters. From these sprang every variety of flower to be found above the earth as well as several that could only be found below: hollitas, buzzing buttons, trumpet bells, and pinas hanging down, vine-like, to the floor. Living harmoniously with hollyhocks, many-petaled roses, and graceful lilies were purple yewlies, kitonas, and tiny, orange hivebears with berries that tasted like honey. The center of the Grand Cavern offered a magnificent sparkling pool. Winding off from this, in several directions, were narrow streams of glistening water working their way down the various caverns leading to the hundreds of nooks and caves that made up this, the realm of the earth faeries: Amon Tunde.

Several faeries were lounging by the water or in the water, or else nestled together in groups talking quietly. The faeries themselves were no less varied than the growing things found here. While distinctly similar to humans, some were wild-looking, like a gnarled branch, with untamed hair and eyes of purple or flaming orange, like the blooming flowers around them. Some wore their hair short and layered like so many leaves. Others had long hair, smooth like flowing water, with soft brown eyes the color of the earth and a calm and steady countenance, nothing to distinguish their appearance from that of a human. The faeries passed over grass, rock, and water alike in bare feet, but they wore robes of russet or honey-colored silk, or soft *undanna* cloth (a unique fabric made from the fibrous petals of faerie whip flowers), or draped in emerald cloaks of moss. They seemed to blend easily with the earth and all natural things in it, for the two were bound as one, the faeries giving life to the earth as it in turn gave

103

life to them... and their magic. This was a sacred place. A place for faeries and light and things that grow, but not a place—most would agree—for a human.

All looked in Nicolai's direction when he entered. He received the usual mixed reception. Some faces were warm and friendly, others disdaining but at least no longer aggressive, finally resigned to his occasional presence here. Not everyone agreed with Salerno that Nicolai should be allowed in Amon Tunde, much less taught their ways. Since Salerno was king of the earth faeries, there wasn't much to be done.

Salerno stood waiting for him in front of the pool, as he always did. Despite his wild appearance, Salerno always had a calming influence on Nicolai. He greeted him now by enveloping him in that same soothing presence Nicolai had felt the first day he met him, and by saying his name: "Nicolai."

Nicolai bowed. Salerno smiled and gestured behind him and they began to walk. It always started thus. They took the central tunnel leading off the Grand Cavern and followed it deeper into the forest, though far under its surface, the light and sweet-smelling air made possible by the presence of the earth faeries. This was the only passageway that didn't have other passageways breaking off from it. It led to the Royal Cavern and throne of Salerno.

"You come seeking advice?" Salerno asked after they had walked a time in silence.

"That is one thing." Advice would be difficult to seek since Nicolai could not explain exactly what was going on, feeling this was a secret that needed to stay guarded even from Salerno. He did explain, however, that he felt torn between two obligations. On the one hand, he felt he needed to help some "friends" in the city, but he had responsibilities to the farm and to his mother.

"You must follow your heart," Salerno said with his soothing voice.

"Who will help on the farm?"

"You reveal your heart already." It was true. He knew what he had to do.

"What about my mother?"

"Are you concerned about her?"

104

"Of course."

"If you are willing to leave your mother in order to help your friends, it must be important. Let her hire one more hand than planned until you are able to return."

"But the crops," Nicolai said.

Salerno stopped and faced Nicolai. The long tunnel stretched away in either direction. They were alone. "You have just finished your harvest, and you are worried about the next? How long will you be away?"

Such a simple question, Nicolai thought. There was only one simple answer. "I don't know."

Salerno raised one arched eyebrow, his intense green eyes alight. "A secret even from me? I sense it is not the only one."

Nicolai smiled. "No."

Salerno nodded easily. One thing Nicolai could say about the faeries, their ways were different. A human may have pressed him for information, but Salerno respected Nicolai's thoughts and feelings as his own. "If you are away," Salerno said, "I will make sure the crop is abundant. There will be no shortage."

Nicolai exhaled, relieved. Salerno's assistance was the main reason for Nicolai's visit. "Thank you for helping," he said.

Salerno tilted his head and looked at Nicolai with unflinching directness. "Something is calling to you," he said. "I see it in your heart, even as you resist it. You do not yet know who you really are." Nicolai wanted to look away, wanted to, as Salerno said, resist what he was hearing. Salerno's words had a way of resonating within him, whether he wanted them to or not. "Your true character is a mystery even to yourself, but you will soon discover it." Salerno smiled mildly. "Do not be afraid of what you find."

Not far from the Sakkaran and Norrland border, Prince Hugh, youngest prince of Sakkara, found himself in a dank, confined room he took to be a hut. Rope cut across his chest and arms, binding him to the chair. The four men who held him captive watched him with various degrees of anger and frustration.

Not for the first time, the man nearest him struck him hard across the face with the back of his hand. It was armored and this time the blow was delivered without restraint. The impact nearly caused Hugh to pass out again. His cheek burned. His skull throbbed. He tasted blood and felt a ragged sliver of tooth on his tongue. He bent his head and spit weakly, the red-tinged drool hanging from his lip before finally dropping. The floor, and the muddy boots of the man standing on it, went into and out of focus.

"I'm not going to ask you again," the man hissed in his ear. "You have not even begun to see what I will do to you if you continue to resist."

"I...told you..." Hugh gasped. The room spun rapidly and he heaved his head upright, his back and chest aching at the effort. He closed his eyes, willing the room to still. "I don't know... what you're talking..." This time the blow was so hard it knocked him to his side, the chair he was bound to falling with him. The impact blew through his entire body. A ripping pain exploded behind his eyes and screamed through his neck and shoulders. He heard the roar of fury from his captor as if from a great distance.

"Maybe he doesn't have it," someone said.

"He has it!" his attacker said furiously. "If we fail to get this one, you won't live to tell the tale, I can tell you that for sure. Do you want to go back empty handed again?"

"No."

"Then get him up."

Hugh felt his head jerk, the room spin, the ropes cut into him. He realized his chair had been abruptly set on its feet. His attacker's face swept in front of him. Hugh struggled to bring the wide face into focus. Blackness swept over his vision, all except a few shapes that may have been eyes or a nose or a mouth with a dark voice.

"Now," the dark voice said, swimming to him through a wide, black sea. "Tell me where to find that stone."

Seventeen

Corren drove the cart up to the Bridge of a Thousand Ages, pulled the horse to a stop, and dismounted. He had borrowed the cart from the king and had taken it to Tower Hall South that morning in order to smuggle out his books, cauldrons, scales, and anything else he thought he might need. He'd left his office nearly bare, locked to prevent anyone from seeing it in such a questionable state. He'd given his lead students instructions to carry them through the next few weeks. When they'd asked about the reason for his leave he'd put them off easily (being an apprentice had certain advantages). He would be able to do no such thing with Aradia. He still didn't know how he was going to keep such a secret from her and was grateful to have at least a few weeks to think about it.

The square in front of the Bridge of a Thousand Ages was teeming with people, carts, and horses. It was not quiet as it had been two nights ago, but boisterous with shouts, conversations, hooves clopping, and wheels bumping over the cobblestone. People were busy, too busy to notice one cart and driver out of many. Corren stretched as if he had only stopped to work out the aches and pains of a long journey, wandering farther away from the horse and nearer to the entrance without actually looking at it. He nonchalantly scanned the crowd. He saw women with baskets, men unloading crates from carts, people of all sorts coming in and out of the various shipping warehouses common here. He saw no cloaks, at least none of the sort he was concerned about. No one appeared to be watching him. He turned and looked out over the boats with their masts and sails, over the water, and finally, at the Bridge itself. It reached away from shore, its shadow darkening the water below.

Releasing his concerns about the crowd around him, Corren focused his concentration on the archway. He held out his hand, slowly inched nearer, and hovered it within a hair's breadth of the surface. He closed his eyes. The stone was so ancient he could feel the weight of its many years as he likewise felt the magic protecting it. He sensed the magic's energy, mentally picking it apart with a precision borne of both practice and instinct. He opened his eyes, dropped his hands, and took a step back. The barrier was markedly different from what he had found the other night. It was more advanced. More powerful. More than sufficient protection.

At least for most.

Corren examined the spell again, just to be sure he hadn't been hasty in his assessment of it. He came to the same conclusion as before and his heart sank. He was reasonably sure he could break through this barrier as well. It was only a hunch. He could only be certain with a staff, for breaking this spell would surely require a staff, but he was as convinced as he could be without actually doing it. Corren had an unusual gift for magic and he knew it, but as tempting as it was to think he saw a weakness in this barrier no one else would, he could not believe it. Talented or not, Corren did not flatter himself to think he was the most powerful wizard in existence. That meant if he could break through this enchantment, someone else could as well. Someone with intentions quite different from his own.

He climbed onto the cart, the wooden seat creaking underneath him. He led the horse away from the Bridge and up the road to the castle. Even though he knew the Order would have plans to protect the Phoenix he was not aware of, he could not help but feel, now more than before, that whatever the Order was doing it would not be enough. Like the prophecy said, it would be up to Corren and his brothers to keep the Realm of the Phoenix safe from intrusion. If only he knew how they were meant to do it.

When Nicolai returned to Stonebridge that night, Corren coerced him to go to the Great Hall for dinner. As Corren passed through the wide double doors, however, Nicolai held back. Praea was coming down the hallway, looking radiant in a pale yellow dress. She was even more beautiful by day, fair, with eyes a crystalline blue and honey-colored hair hanging past her shoulders. She walked with a gentle yet confident composure Nicolai found to be an intriguing mix. His reaction to her was immediate, strong, and welcome. She had seen him too, and offered a delicate smile.

With a wonderful commotion in his heart, he slowly approached. They met and stopped a few feet from the doors, tentative and expectant. "I thought I might see you again," he said. "That is, I'd hoped I would." Perhaps he should exercise more prudence, but he only said what he honestly felt. It seemed so natural to say it.

She smiled. "It's good to see you too, Nicolai."

The pleased look on her face gave him encouragement and he smiled, too. He felt a certain intimacy with her, like there was no one else in the world but just they two. She felt familiar to him, as if they had somehow known each other all along. He reminded himself this was only their second meeting. He knew not even the simplest things about her. "Do you live here in the castle?" he asked.

She hesitated and gave a smile he could not interpret. The question seemed to please her, though he didn't know why. "No. I am from Sakkara and a little out of sorts in your city. Where I'm from the countryside is a much more comfortable walk away."

He understood how she felt, for he missed the countryside, too. He was about to say this when another thought struck him and took precedence over any other. "You are going back then? To Sakkara?" Her smile faded a little and she seemed reluctant to answer. He was just as reluctant to hear it. "Not too soon I hope," he said.

A blush rose to her cheeks but the width of her smile increased.

The sound of footsteps drew their attention and they both looked down the hall. An advisor Nicolai had been introduced to earlier was walking toward them, made eye contact, and nodded. Nicolai and Praea looked at one another, more self-conscious now, their intimacy intruded upon. "Are you going to the Great Hall?" Nicolai asked while they waited for the advisor to approach.

"I am," she said.

The advisor came close and addressed them. "Ah, Princess Praea," he said with a bow. "I see you've met the king's honored guest."

Nicolai's heart contracted. *Princess?* He took note of her dress: the satin material, the delicately embroidered bodice. Still modest for a princess, but far above his own station, *clearly* above his station. How could he not have noticed before? He had been so enamored of her he couldn't see the obvious.

"We have not been formally introduced," she said.

He wanted to cringe, hide, run all during the advisor's introduction, she as Princess Praea of Sakkara, and he, Nicolai, as a common farmer from Knobby Tree. Whether or not that were actually true was beside the point; he dressed the part, and felt it, too. More importantly, it was all she would see in him: a farmer. Only a farmer. Never before had he been ashamed to think of himself as such.

"You must tell me how you came to be the honored guest of such a noble king," she said, with the same heartbreaking smile she had worn all along, which he knew now he must have misinterpreted. How could he have been so foolish as to think her interested in him? She was only being polite, stately, nothing more.

He remembered the things he had said to her and felt his cheeks getting warm. He straightened and bowed. "Please excuse me, my Lady," he said, "but I must be getting inside."

He could not look at her, did not want to look at the advisor, and hastily retreated to the Great Hall, his heart pounding and complaining against the disappointment. More than disappointment.

Corren was at his side, taking him by the elbow. "There you are. I feared you had escaped. Come, our seats are over here."

Corren led him through the length of the Great Hall, a grand and open space with all the magnificence of the rest of the castle. Many people milled about, a large number of them the king's knights, greeting one another and making their way to their seats. Nicolai saw a merchant who owned half the booths at the main gate. Nicolai's family sold him the better part of their harvest every year. There were several other important citizens from the city here as well. From their easy manner Nicolai gathered this wasn't their first visit. Nicolai furrowed his brows as he took in every evidence of nobility. Elaborate tapestries lined one entire wall, their scenes portraying country life as quaint and somehow virtuous, though Nicolai doubted anyone here found it virtuous enough to actually want such a life themselves. He passed one long table after another, and began to see it all through covetous eyes. The tables were of thick wood, each painstakingly carved with the smallest details and upon which lay an astonishing variety of food: glistening, roasted fowl; pale wedges of cheese; silver bowls full of fruit so exotic he couldn't identify them all; crystal glass goblets presenting their contents like an endowment to the worthy. Nicolai had been struck by the fine atmosphere of the castle from the moment he entered it, it wasn't that he hadn't noticed, but he had not been overwhelmed with the desire to live here. Now, however, he felt differently. This way of life was thrust into the regrettable realm of what he wished had been, of what could have been... *like her.*

Nicolai took hold of himself and took a deep, resolute breath. *Be grateful for what you have.* That was what his father would say.

Nicolai wanted to be. He truly did. He ached with shame and regret anyway.

They came to the frontmost table where sat the king, who was delighted to see Nicolai in the Great Hall at last. "Ah, Nicolai! You please me greatly with your presence." They settled down with the king and he enthusiastically encouraged them to fill their plates. "You must not forget the tartlets," he said. "They are a castle specialty."

Nicolai took hearty portions as instructed, not wanting to be rude. He found himself checking the door and at last saw Praea come in. She scanned the room looking for something and his heartbeat quickened. Her eyes lighted on Nicolai's and stopped, as if she found what she sought. He looked away to Corren, who had already engaged the king in conversation. Nicolai was content to let them talk, not in the mood to do so himself. Clement, however, eagerly sought to draw Nicolai into their discussion. Nicolai tried to please him, for the king was kind and easy to like, but still, something in Nicolai held back. It was more than just his mellow mood. It seemed somehow disrespectful to his father's memory to bond with Clement too easily.

Praea had found a seat at a table halfway down the room. Looking at her only made him want her all the more, but he could not keep himself from doing it. She met his eyes and there was a powerful pause before he could bring himself to look away.

Determined to control himself, he focused on his meal. This did nothing to ease his painful awareness of the differences between her world and his. The meat was delicately prepared, covered with a tangy orange glaze. The bread was not dark and heavy (like any bread Nicolai had ever had), but pale and light; it seemed to dissolve without effort in his mouth. The strawberries were flawless. The wine was light and sweet. There was not a pot of stew or plate of biscuits in sight.

In his efforts to keep his eyes away from Praea, he noticed several people in the hall who seemed aware of the king's enthusiasm for his guests. They were obvious topics of discussion. Nicolai worried the king was too openly interested in them. It was sure to raise questions.

"You are not the only citizens here," the king said when Nicolai quietly raised his concerns. "Each night this hall is filled with people from the city."

"But not farmers, your Grace."

The king smiled and nodded. "Not usually, this is true. Merchants and Guild members are more common here. From time to time, those who have done me a service, no matter who they may be, are welcomed in this way as well." Clement tore off a piece of bread and put it in his mouth with a tremulous hand. Nicolai remembered seeing it shake before.

"What was our service?" Nicolai asked.

"That detail is confidential isn't it?" the king said with a wink.

"Excuse me, your Grace." At the sound of Praea's voice, Nicolai looked up in surprise. He was even more surprised to see her looking at him quite deliberately, a gentle smile on her face. He longed to look at her. She seemed so genuine, yet he knew she could not feel for him as he felt for her. He smiled politely, but it took all his will power to turn to Corren while she talked with the king.

"I'm sorry to disturb you," he heard her say.

"Not at all, my Lady. Are your needs being attended to?"

"Yes, my Lord."

"I hope you know you are welcome to join us here. I would be delighted to visit with you again."

"Thank you, my Lord." Her voice drew Nicolai's eyes to her, against his will. She was so beautiful. "I am enjoying meeting the people of Caedmonia," she said.

The king seemed pleased by her answer. She looked at Nicolai again, this time with a hint of sadness in her eyes. He had a passing thought that she was disappointed in his behavior to her, that she felt as miserable as he did. He dismissed this as folly.

"That is well, my Lady," Clement said. "What can I do for you?"

"I only wished to know when we may expect messengers from my brother and Prince Marcellus."

"It is not quite a three day journey. I expect Prince Marcellus will send a messenger once he arrives and again as there is news. You will be the first to know when word is received."

"Thank you, your Majesty."

Nicolai watched her leave, longing for her. He leaned in to the king. "Why is the princess here?" As the king explained her brother's murder, Nicolai's heart broke for her. He saw her leave the room and wanted to follow her, to talk to her, to comfort her. He knew he had no right to do any of it, and stayed where he was.

Praea sat alone in her room, another letter held loosely in her hand. Her mind had wandered, yet again, from the disturbing contents of the letter to Nicolai. Her heart quickened at the thought of him and she wondered at herself. She could not explain her immediate draw to him. More than physical attraction for a man, this was something else, something deeper. How could she explain it, even to herself? She barely knew him. Knew him not at all, in fact. Yet, neither could she deny what she felt. He didn't feel like a stranger. He felt like a memory.

She recalled the look on his face when they were introduced that evening and it saddened her. At first, she thought his behavior at dinner meant he was not interested in her. She feared she had misunderstood him. Once she could escape the Great Hall, once she was alone, she was able to consider it further and thought she knew what was bothering him. Obviously his status as a farmer was a worry to him, though it bothered her not at all. She decided when next she saw him, she would put his mind at ease.

She looked at the letter. "The time has come. You now have everything you need. I do not doubt you. Do not doubt yourself."

She pondered this, and feared it—not for the first time. *What if I'm the wrong one?* If that were true, it was too late now. Despite her own will, the damage had been done. There was no point delaying further. She walked to the fireplace and tossed the letter in, where it burned with exquisite ease.

Eighteen

The next day, the king informed Corren and Nicolai that he had his own ideas about how they would pass the time waiting for Marcellus to return.

It was a clear morning. Clement, Corren, and Nicolai talked alone as they strolled under a covered stone walkway on the west side of the castle. The knights' training grounds were some distance away and this was what drew Nicolai's attention. The open arena used for battle training was busy with knights and squires practicing their sparring. Nearby was a small, open shelter protecting a tempting rack packed with swords and spears. To the left of this were the stables and easily the largest collection of horses Nicolai had ever seen or heard of. Past the arena and stables were an archery range, a gated run for the horses, the armory, and—lining the far wall of the castle grounds—barracks for the battalions assigned to Stonebridge. The whole area was a massive, sprawling complex that took up fully half of the castle grounds and was—by day—the most fraught with activity.

"You want us to do what, Sire?" Corren asked.

The king leaned in, his customary smile surrounded by snowy white beard. "It is not necessary to address me so formally in private, my son."

Corren, normally so composed, was clearly touched and a smile softened his highly-defined features. "Thank you, Father."

Clement smiled broadly. "Marcellus thought it would be a good idea if you were trained in weapons. Two weeks isn't much time, but it's a start."

Nicolai (momentarily concerned that he, too, might be expected to start addressing the king as 'Father') perked up at the king's suggestion. "Do you mean with swords, Sire?"

Nicolai's formality in addressing the king was evident to all, but so too was his sudden enthusiasm and Clement chuckled easily. "I knew any son of mine would be eager to get his hands on a sword."

"Actually," Corren said slowly, his smile wilting, "there were some things I wanted to look up in the books I brought from the Tower. It may take most of the day." Nicolai and Clement exchanged glances. "Perhaps tomorrow," Corren went on. "Or the day after." Corren was, apparently, one son who wanted nothing to do with getting his hands on a sword. They came to an uneasy stop.

"As you wish, my son," the king said. Corren bowed and retreated back to the castle, leaving Clement and Nicolai to watch after him. "Well," Clement said. He turned to Nicolai. "Let me take you to Knight Whittaker. He is a fine instructor and has agreed to teach you." They began to walk again, emerging from the shelter of the shade and venturing onto the sun-drenched grass.

"Won't he wonder why he is instructing me?"

"I'm sure he won't even consider it. He teaches many people, more than a few at my personal request."

Nicolai's worry was rooted in something else. He decided he had no choice but to verbalize it. "Sire, there are certain... resemblances between us."

The king nodded. "Yes. I noticed that the first I saw you. You are a version of myself in my younger years, though much better looking." They both smiled at the jest. Clement went on, more serious in tone. "The likenesses are not glaring if you do not know to look for them. People will see what they expect to see. They will not be looking for similarities between a farmer and a king." He said this gently, and put his hand on Nicolai's elbow. "They will be blind enough to the prince in you."

Nicolai looked away uncomfortably, thinking no one could be more blind to that fact than he was himself.

As they neared the arena, the sight of knights engaged in strenuous swordplay rejuvenated him. Clashing metal, glinting swords, decisive movements. Nicolai imagined himself in the shoes of every knight he saw. Clement introduced him to Knight Whittaker. Nicolai's enthusiasm deflated slightly at the sight of him. He was broad in the chest and shoulders, had arms twice as thick as Nicolai's, and stood a good head taller, no small feat considering Nicolai was a tall man himself. The king left them alone and Nicolai remained resolute. He was, for some reason, meant to defend the Phoenix. Since he doubted that would involve running the enemy down with a plow, this was his chance to learn to do something useful.

Nicolai noticed the knights fought with real swords but the young squires were being instructed with wooden ones—toys they seemed— and this was what Knight Whittaker handed him. It was roughly carved and rather unexciting. Nicolai looked at the real swords on the nearby rack, disappointed. "I'd hate to accidentally run you through," Whittaker said with a laugh, taking a wooden sword in his own hand. "We begin with stances."

They worked on different stances, footwork, and moves for the next few hours before doing anything that could remotely be termed sparring. Once the sparring began, however, Nicolai discovered his gratitude for wooden swords. His arms, ribs, and chest throbbed with the bruises developing from the blunt impact of Whittaker's weapon. The huge knight's method of teaching was unyielding and, in Nicolai's opinion, loud. He had a fondness for yelling that Nicolai found more than off-putting. "To the left, left, LEFT!" he would say. Or, "Bring that sword round like you mean it. AGAIN!"

They practiced only a few prescribed strokes at a time, over and over and over again until he felt he could do it in his sleep. As the afternoon wore on, he became so bored and exhausted he nearly *was* doing it in his sleep. Whittaker solved this problem by rapping him on the head and shouting, "Wake up boy!" This ignited something in Nicolai he didn't know he had and he executed his next move with such anger, strength, and speed that he earned Whittaker's first words of praise. "Ah! There's a man in you after all!"

By the time they left off for the day, well after lunch and not far from dinner, Nicolai was sore, tired, and raging with the foreign desire of taking Whittaker's head off with his sword. *Perhaps this is how they motivate men to battle,* Nicolai thought as he grimaced his way back to the castle. *Provoke them until they're ready to kill.*

৪ ৪ ৪

"Everything is well, I trust?" Clement asked. "I did not see you at dinner."

After recovering from his workout that day, Nicolai had come to the king's office to see him privately. "Knight Whittaker was kind enough to work with me for most the day," Nicolai said. "I had a late lunch and wasn't hungry for dinner."

Clement smiled knowingly. "He is a strict task master. His methods have proven highly effective, particularly when working with less experienced men."

"Yes, Sire. Thank you." Nicolai bowed his head slightly in acknowledgement. "I've come to see if I might be able to repay you for your kindness."

"I expect no payment, my son."

"I mean about your hands."

Taken aback, the king looked at his hands. They trembled stubbornly. Clement smiled and shrugged. "The best physicians have been at my disposal. There is nothing they can do. It continues to get worse."

Nicolai waited a moment out of respect for the king's high opinion of his physicians, then said, "Will you allow me to try?"

Clement smiled. "If it pleases you."

"I intend for it to please you, Sire."

The king sat at his couch and Nicolai joined him, putting the shoulder bag he had brought with him on the floor. The king watched quietly as Nicolai removed the needed items from his bag and began crushing herbs and seeds in a wooden bowl. He carefully cupped his hands to conceal the technique he learned from the faeries to extract the most potent healing properties from the seeds.

"I was quite spry in my day," the king said lightly. "Before Marcellus the Protector came along, it was King Clement who secured the kingdom."

Nicolai smiled. "I'm sure, your Majesty."

"I've turned a great deal over to Marcellus in recent years. He is quite capable. He long has had the spirit of a king." Clement's expression faltered. "Of course now..."

Nicolai could guess the king's thoughts: there was more than one heir now. Nicolai did not want to broach the subject. It was not his decision to make, though if it were he would feel more comfortable with Caedmonia in the hands of a prince who had already proven himself. Nicolai liked Corren, but what did he know about ruling a kingdom?

Nicolai got up and walked to the washstand to add water to the mixture. Dipping his fingers into the bowl, he worked the moist and lumpy concoction into a smooth paste. When he sat down, he found the king watching him tenderly. "I hope your stay here is comfortable."

"Yes, Sire."

There was a long pause. Nicolai felt sure the king was about to insist he call him 'Father.' To his relief, the king only smiled faintly and said, "You have everything you need?"

"Yes, Sire." Nicolai could feel the weight of his formality. He did not doubt the king felt it as well.

Clement nodded solemnly, "That is good, my son."

They were quiet for a moment, stilled by all that had gone unspoken. This was when Nicolai understood something. Clement's desire to embrace Nicolai as a son was not just on the surface, not just a sense of obligation or propriety. His desire for Nicolai was only that of a loving father. Genuine. Deep. And, as Nicolai resisted, painful.

The realization of this penetrated Nicolai. Something within him started to give.

He took a small amount of paste onto his fingers. "I'm going to put this on the back of your neck," he said quietly. He rubbed it into the base, just below the hairline. His father's skin was soft and aged, one of the few tangible evidences of the long years that his regal demeanor could not undo.

Clement looked doubtful, surely questioning Nicolai's reason for putting the paste on his neck when he believed the problem to be in his hands.

Nicolai sat back. "How is it now?"

Clement raised his hands. They were steady. He looked at them in amazement, as if waiting for the shaking to start. It didn't.

Satisfied, Nicolai rose to the washstand where he rinsed his hands. He returned to the couch and began packing his bag. Clement continued to stare at his hands.

"You healed me."

"No. I don't think there is a way to do that, but this will keep your symptoms at bay for a while. Hopefully a long while." Nicolai paused, then said as gently as he could. "Eventually, the shaking will return." Nicolai gave him a large leaf folded with the remaining paste. "Put this on when you begin to shake again. I'll make more when you run out."

"Thank you, Nicolai." Clement offered a smile. Nicolai returned it. As Nicolai turned to leave, Clement said, "Have you had a chance to explore the castle?"

"Just a little," Nicolai said, growing warm at the memory of the garden. "I don't want to go where I shouldn't."

His father shrugged. "Private rooms are easy enough to spot. They're either guarded or locked." He smiled encouragingly. "Enjoy yourself. I invite you."

Nineteen

The hour was late when the knock came on Nicolai's door. He rushed to it, driven by the thought that it might be Praea. He knew it was foolish, but the hope blossomed anyway. He swung open the door to reveal Corren laden with two oversized books. Nicolai suppressed his disappointment with difficulty.

"Do you have a moment?" Corren asked. He adjusted his hold under the weight of the books. "It's not too late is it?"

"Not at all," Nicolai said. "Come in."

Corren walked to the chair under the window and deposited the books on the little table next to it with a substantial thud. They were leather bound and, although in good repair, ancient looking. The leather had grown dark, nearly black in places. Only the edges of the spine held hints of a former, lighter brown. "I think I know what to do about the Gateway," Corren said, opening the top book. He leaned over its pages and Nicolai followed, the strong, musty smell of old books hitting him. "I want to hide an element on it."

Nicolai furrowed his brows. "Hide an element?"

"Here," Corren said. "Sit down. I'll tell you what I mean."

Nicolai and Corren sat in chairs opposite each other. "Everything in existence, everything you can see along with some things you cannot, is made up of different elements. This is true whether it is a natural object like a flower, or a created object like a clay pot or the Gateway."

Nicolai was familiar with this concept. He knew, for example, that the chicory flower consisted of more than twenty different elements, though he no doubt called them by different names than Corren did. Nicolai said none of this, however, and let Corren continue.

"Magic involves not just the ability to *sense* these elements—which is an inborn trait—but also the ability to control and manipulate them. That is what takes skill, practice, and years to master.

"Now," he said, "the Gateway is an extremely complicated magical object, obviously. To get through it you would need either a spell or a potion or, I suspect, some combination of the two. Each method has advantages and I think you would need to harness the advantages of both in order to control that Gateway."

Corren discussed the advantages and disadvantages of spells versus potions. He continued in this vein for another minute, his eyes lighting up as he talked about something he obviously loved. Nicolai found his enthusiasm contagious even though he didn't understand everything Corren said. He discussed the difference between conjuring spells and transformative spells and energizing spells. He explained the different kinds of potions: liquid potions and potions that reduced to creams or pastes or even powders. Nicolai lost the thread of the conversation completely when Corren started talking about *why* you might want a powder instead of a paste, and Corren seemed to catch himself then.

"Well, to my point. It doesn't matter whether this 'Cunning One' is going to use a spell or a potion, so for the sake of discussion let's say it will be a spell. That spell, like all spells, will draw on and manipulate elements to achieve a certain result. In this case, opening the Gateway in order to get into the Realm. Because of the nature of the ring, a spell would have to be designed *specifically* to get through it. You couldn't use just any breeching spell, even a powerful one. That's because every element in that Gateway has been linked together and cannot be broken if you want the Gateway to work. This is a really simplified way of talking about it, but basically what that means is you have to manipulate *all* the elements at the *same time* or it won't work." Corren paused and raised his eyebrows in question.

Nicolai nodded that he understood.

"Alright," Corren continued, flipping through the pages of the book again, "what I want to do is conceal a new element on the Gateway that the Cunning One won't expect. The *manner* of attack won't matter. Spell or potion, it won't matter because there will be a hidden element that throws everything off. Do you see?"

"So however someone tries to get through the Gateway, it won't work?"

122

"Exactly," Corren said. "Here it is." He pointed to a page full of words Nicolai couldn't read, but there was a black and white illustration of an elm leaf. "This is a potion of concealment. It's very advanced and very effective. Even a spell designed to reveal properties of an object will not reveal anything hidden by this potion, provided you hide the right kind of element."

Nicolai sat back in his chair. "How do you know what the right kind of element is?"

"It's all a matter of understanding how these elements will react together. That's not really a concern," he said, moving the book to the side and revealing the one underneath, this with red gilded lettering on the cover. "My concern is that every element you can conceal with this potion requires a staff to manipulate." He opened the second book and found his place. This time there was no illustration, only undecipherable words. "Unless, of course, I use this one. It's a fiery element that is very strong. The Concealment Potion will be able to hide it and it should be strong enough to render an attack ineffective."

"You don't need a staff for it?"

"Normally this *would* need a staff to make, but since it mainly involves manipulating fire, I can do it. I don't know why, but I've always been able to do anything with fire."

"What do you mean? What can you do?"

"Well, whatever I want." Nicolai saw no conceit in Corren as he said this. It was a simple statement of fact as if it were something he took for granted, like the ability to walk. Corren sat back. "Even though there are literally thousands of elements, they all fall into one of four larger categories. Earth, water, fire, and air." Corren stopped, sighed. "Even that is too simplified. When we talk about the four elements, we're talking about different kinds of powers you can draw on. Sometimes the power of fire is drawn upon by the very simple procedure of heating a potion over flame until it reaches a certain temperature. Other times the element of fire is drawn from an object with fiery elements, like we've been discussing. Fire elements can be found in dragon scales, certain gems, a few plants. Like that. Other times the powers associated with the element of fire are *created* by

123

accelerating the energy within an object or a person to *create* more heat. You always need a staff to create fire like this. Usually, anyway."

"So what part can you do?"

Corren held his eyes, hesitating. Color rose to his cheeks. "All of it." He seemed reluctant to say this.

Nicolai furrowed his brows.

Corren held out his hand, far out to his left. He said "Sfe ere" and a ball of flame ignited in the palm of his hand for the briefest moment before snapping back out of existence. Black smoke curled up into the air, thinning out and dissipating. Corren's skin was untouched. Unmarred. He looked back to Nicolai and shrugged, but he seemed to be struggling to conceal his own pleasure at what he had done.

Nicolai realized his mouth was hanging open and promptly shut it. "How many other wizards can do that?"

Corren shook his head, looked back to the book. "Without a staff? None that I know of."

If Nicolai had had any doubt in his mind before, one thing was certainly clear to him now. Corren was no ordinary wizard.

"Anyway," Corren said, scratching his brow lightly with his finger. "There's still the matter of getting back on the Bridge. We'll need to think more about that. But as far as protecting the Gateway, I think this will work." Corren took a deep breath and looked at Nicolai. "So that's my plan. We conceal an element. What do you think?"

Nicolai sat back in his chair. It was a lot of information to take in. He held onto it all as best as he could and thought about things for a while. Corren let him think uninterrupted. Nicolai remembered their trip to the Bridge and what Corren had said then as well. "When you were examining the ring and talking about properties," Nicolai asked, "is that the same thing as elements?"

Corren shrugged. "Close enough. A *property* is what you can make an element *do*. It's a fine distinction. Why do you ask?"

"Because you said something about hidden properties."

"Yes. I believe I found them all, though."

"So you got around whatever magic was hiding the properties?"

Corren smiled and Nicolai thought he knew what he was getting at. Nicolai went ahead with it. "How do we know the Cunning One can't

124

find this element you want to hide and just work it into the spell meant to open the Gateway?"

Corren nodded. "That's a good question."

"I hope you have a good answer."

Corren laughed. "I think I do. I know how to uncover the elements hidden on the Gateway because of the way they were hidden. If there were anything hidden in the way I'm suggesting we use, I wouldn't know *what* was hidden, though I would be able to tell *something* was there if I looked long and hard enough. If there were some secret element on the Gateway, I think I would know it even if I couldn't identify it. The methods of hiding the elements are not what make the Gateway so effective. The brilliance lies elsewhere. It is in the way these elements were sealed together. Their properties work off of each other in a manner I've never seen or even heard of before. Honestly, it would take me centuries to puzzle it out."

"So how is the Cunning One going to be able to do it?"

"I wish I knew. But the threat is real or there would have been no need for a prophecy."

"Do you think the Cunning One will be able to find your hidden element?"

Corren sighed. "The possibility is remote, though no more remote than getting through that Gateway to begin with, I suppose. But there is something else we can work to our advantage. Time. Any spell, or potion for that matter, that can break through that Gateway is going to take days if not weeks to create. Any examination of the ring and its elements will happen well before an actual attack is planned. If we hide the element shortly before the Phoenix regenerates, hopefully it won't be discovered. Someone would have to suspect the ring's elements have changed in order to bother hunting for anything new. We wait for the Songs and use time to our advantage."

Nicolai sighed and nodded. "It sounds like a smart plan." Nicolai meant it sincerely, but his words came out a little deflated. He realized at that moment that he had just one nagging doubt.

Corren closed the book carefully, the pages coming together with a soft thud. "But?"

Nicolai smiled. "I think there's something else we should be thinking about in the meantime."

"What's that?"

"The stones."

Corren furrowed his brows and sat back in the chair. "Hmm," he said and it was all he could say for they were interrupted by another knock at the door.

This time Nicolai opened it to reveal a page, perhaps thirteen years old, in his tidy red and gold uniform. His stance was rigid and well-practiced, but he had an unmistakably sleepy look. "Nicolai of Knobby Tree?" he asked. His voice squeaked a little on the word 'Knobby.'

Nicolai smiled. "Yes."

"A message for you, sir."

He handed Nicolai a crisp letter. It was sharply folded and bound by a red seal, the shape of a flame in the seal's center. "Do you wish me to send for a scribe, sir?" the page asked.

"I can read it if you like," Corren said, coming to look at the note.

Nicolai nodded his agreement. The only person he knew who would be writing him was Marcellus. Whatever he had to say should probably stay between the three of them.

"Are you Master Corren of Tower Hall South?" the page asked, but Corren's eyes were wide and fixed on the seal of the letter.

"I am," he answered in a wary voice.

"I have one for you too, sir."

The young boy held it out—the same parchment with the same red-flamed seal—and Corren took it with trepidation. "Thank you," he said, in a dry voice.

Nicolai realized these letters were not from Marcellus. He held his tongue until the page was gone and the door shut. "What?"

Corren didn't answer, only broke the wax seal and began to read:

Master Corren, apprentice of the Wysard branch of the Order of Ceinoth at Tower Hall South. You are hereby summoned to the Cloister in Stonebridge to answer charges of blatant misconduct and willful trespassing on forbidden ground. Please present yourself on the fifth day of the month of Rujan, at the ninth hour. Sincerely, Aradia, Head of the Wysard branch and Head of the Order of Ceinoth.

Corren looked at Nicolai, his pale face full of dread. Nicolai felt a little of that dread himself. "That's the day after tomorrow," Nicolai said, handing Corren his letter to read. "I thought you said she'd be gone for a while."

Corren made a sort of groan then closed his eyes. "She must have been at the Cloister. I don't know." He took a breath, opened Nicolai's letter, and read aloud:

Nicolai of Knobby Tree. Your presence is requested at the Cloister in Stonebridge regarding your recent attendance on the Bridge of a Thousand Ages. Please arrive on the fifth day of the month of Rujan, at the ninth hour, to answer questions pertaining to this incident. With regards, Aradia, Head of the Order of Ceinoth.

Corren looked up. "Yours doesn't sound so bad." He handed the letter back to Nicolai. "That's good." He said it in such a dull voice that he offered little consolation to Nicolai.

He watched Corren amble his way to the chair and fall—rather than sit—into it. "She can't arrest us or anything can she?"

"She can't do anything near as bad to you as what she's going to do to me," Corren said. "*You* don't need to worry." He pinched his eyes closed. "She's going to kill me."

"Not really?" Nicolai asked, alarmed. He imagined Corren in his long wizard's cloak going to the gallows and somehow it didn't seem to fit. What would the punishment be for a wizard who, with a word, could send the noose up in flames?

Corren smiled humorlessly. "No, but my career is in her hands. More than that, I was hoping to get my staff soon." He groaned and closed his eyes again. "This really complicates things."

Nicolai went to the bed and sat, the letter in his hands. Corren's eyes were still closed. He already looked condemned. "If you want a staff so badly, why don't you already have one?"

Corren opened his eyes, sighed, then launched into his explanation. "Forging a staff is no small matter," he said. "Many wizards never do it. But without a staff your abilities and powers are limited. With a staff, especially if you make it well, your power more than doubles. Triples maybe. Normally, an apprentice waits five or six years before forging his own staff, sometimes longer. Aradia told me before she left I was only a few months away, and frankly I was counting on it." He got up, let out a frustrated sigh, and paced to the door.

"How long have you been an apprentice?"

"Three years."

Nicolai raised his eyebrows. Corren distractedly ran a hand through his dark hair. "Has an apprentice ever forged a staff so quickly before?"

Corren cast him a sideways glance. He turned and paced back toward the window. "I don't know that it's ever happened before, but I need a staff to get on the Bridge. I can't break through their new spell without one. But now..." He stopped at the window and looked out to the blackness. "I was hoping for more time to figure out how to deal with Aradia." He grew still, his solemn face reflected in the glass.

Nicolai understood these letters represented a problem, but he sensed something else bothering Corren. Something he was working up to. Nicolai stayed silent and let him come to it on his own.

"Aradia's going to ask questions," he finally said.

"Yes," Nicolai said, waiting for the rest.

"She's going to want to know what I was doing out there."

Nicolai set his letter on the bed, the flaps of the parchment open slightly. "So tell her the same story," he said. "You have a history of being too curious, don't you?"

Corren bristled visibly at this. "When I was a kid, sure. But it's been a long time since I..." he stopped himself and waved his hand dismissively. "You know, never mind. Aradia is going to be a lot more suspicious than Kennard was. She's no fool."

"What do you suggest, then?"

Corren stared out the window. Nicolai felt Corren was going to say what was troubling him at last. He turned and faced Nicolai, resolute. "I think we need to tell her the truth."

Nicolai stood abruptly. "What?"

"It's the Order's job to protect the secrets of the Phoenix. She's the Head. We don't know what they've learned about the prophecy over the last 1,200 years. What if they already know something and can help us? We could use their cooperation."

Nicolai was shaking his head. "We're not supposed to tell anyone. Nashua was clear about that. It was the Order Nashua was hiding from."

"No. Nashua didn't know what she was hiding from. Her task was to deliver the stones and the prophecy and she did that. The reason for her secrecy could've passed by now."

"You have no way of knowing that. What if it hasn't?"

"Listen, Aradia is probably the most knowledgeable and powerful witch the Order has ever seen. She is the youngest person ever to become Head of the Order. Is it an accident that she is my sage? She could be a significant asset. Even if she doesn't know what we need to do, it can't hurt to ask her."

"No, Corren. I told my father even though I shouldn't have and look what happened." It caused Nicolai pain to say this out loud, but his concern over Corren's suggestion overruled it.

"We told the king and that turned out fine," Corren said.

"It's too soon to know how that will turn out, and we only told him to avoid being hung for treason. We didn't have much choice."

"This could be just as serious."

"She's going to hang you?"

"No, but..."

"Corren, I say we guard this secret as we were instructed. Nashua specifically told us to keep it between us. Aradia doesn't have a stone; she doesn't need to know."

Corren was quiet for a moment. He seemed only to be formulating his next argument.

Nicolai beat him to it, not willing to concede. His voice was firm. "The prophecy says only *we* can figure out what our stones do. Aradia can't help with that." Corren sighed and sat back down. Nicolai could see he was relenting. "In any case, this is not the kind of decision we should make without Marcellus."

"Well," Corren said, rubbing his brow, "I can't argue with that."

But the fact that he still disagreed was clear. Nicolai felt it would not just be unwise to tell other people who they were, but dangerous. As he saw Corren sitting there, willing to agree yet unpersuaded, Nicolai felt he needed to go a step further. "You won't tell Aradia until we can talk to Marcellus about it?"

"No."

"Are you giving me your word?"

Corren looked at him sharply, apparently unprepared for that. He hesitated.

Nicolai waited.

Finally Corren nodded and said, "I give you my word."

Twenty

Marcellus was not expecting what awaited him at the border.

Two and a half days after leaving Stonebridge, Marcellus and his company were in the northeastern corner of Caedmonia, with Norrland not far to the north and the Sakkaran border just over the ridge to the east. They had made good time, leaving plenty of daylight to set up camp. He and Prince Akren rode ahead of the company with a few of Marcellus' commanders as they scouted out possible areas for their encampment. Marcellus wanted to put the bulk of his troops convenient to both borders in the event a rapid deployment was necessary, though he considered this unlikely. In a few days, he would take a smaller unit with him and Prince Akren to the meeting in Messina with Norrland's king, Gunderic.

He had met with Gunderic diplomatically before and knew how to handle him, but if Norrland really was behind this he would have to be careful. He was not seeking a confession, nor expecting one unless Norrland decided to declare open war. A confession was not imperative. In all likelihood, the murderer would never be caught, unfortunate as that was. The main goal of the meeting was to prevent any more hostility. Marcellus believed the strategy he developed would be effective and was confident he could settle the matter across the table.

Marcellus knew the border area well and so knew before leaving Stonebridge where he wanted his troops to settle. He now assessed the site to confirm it, pleased to see his memory had not failed him.

"There," he said, pointing. The woods were to the rear and the east, and the hill gave a good vantage point, as well as the strategic advantage of height. He indicated where he wanted the various battalions placed, where the rear camp with its kitchens and supplies should be, and where the lookouts should be raised.

"Ho there!" Donnelly said. They looked in the direction Marcellus' senior commander was pointing. A lone rider came speeding over the ridge separating Caedmonia from Sakkara, racing toward them.

Marcellus and his commanders gathered instinctively in a line, though he felt no threat. "It's one of yours, isn't it?" he asked Prince Akren.

Akren, who Marcellus had found to be rather aloof, leaned forward, his long face ever composed, and narrowed his eyes. Sakkara's green and yellow colors on the rider's tunic were visible now. Akren bolted his horse toward the rider. The others followed at a full run. They pulled up just short of Akren, who had met the rider half way. He was a Sakkaran messenger and panting, an aura of alarm about him.

"Your Majesty." He seemed surprised to see his prince, understandable since he would not have known Akren would be there. The messenger briefly looked at the others in the assembly, nodding his head in greeting as he did so. "I didn't expect you, your Highness. The commander heard the troops," he nodded to the Caedmonian troops beyond, "and he wanted me to deliver a message to send for you. Since you are here..." he broke off, concerned.

"Is Norrland attacking?" Akren asked.

The messenger shook his head. "Your majesty... we found..."

"What is it?" Akren said, growing impatient.

"I'm sorry, your Majesty. It's Prince Hugh."

Marcellus looked sharply at Akren, who had blanched. He seemed unable to react. "Where?" Marcellus asked the messenger.

"Not far, your Highness," he said pointing. "Over the ridge."

"Take us there."

They followed the messenger over the ridge to a unit of Sakkaran troops gathered around a small cluster of trees, which seemed to be drawing their attention. Once he drew near, Marcellus saw what they were looking at. He immediately regretted Akren's presence here.

Hanging by the neck from a thick branch of an oak, was what Marcellus took to be Prince Hugh, though it was his dress that identified him as the prince more than his face. He had been severely beaten and was swollen beyond recognition. Large patches of blackened blood stained his clothing.

Akren dismounted and lumbered forward, gaping at the sight. The troops nearby shuffled back a few steps. Akren could not speak. His face wrenched together, his lips trembling and working as if straining for a scream. His light skin turned an angry, tormented red.

Marcellus looked away from Akren's face, finding the grisly scene of Hugh an easier sight to bear than the anguish now emanating from the last remaining prince of Sakkara. He noticed something he had not seen before. Hugh's ears were missing. It was the final piece of evidence to confirm Marcellus' hunch: Hugh had been tortured.

At this moment, Akren collapsed to his knees and found his voice. His wail tore through the air, echoed through the hills, and ripped through the hearts of all men present.

Before the sun set, Marcellus sent a fast-riding messenger to Stonebridge. If he rode well, he'd be there by tomorrow night. He was carrying a message Marcellus had drafted to his father, informing him of the situation and asking for reinforcements. If this was Norrland's doing, they would be sure to pull out everything they had after this. Marcellus thought he had better do the same. He also sent word to King Jareth of Sakkara, since Akren was in no condition to do it himself. Akren had gone through the emotions of grief and rage with alarming starkness. It was all Marcellus could do to keep Akren from blindly leading his bewildered troops into battle right then. Marcellus coaxed him into taking some strong ale, shortly after which he was able to retire Akren to a tent deep within Caedmonian ranks. This had been difficult; Akren wanted to camp with his troops. Marcellus understood this desire, but their numbers were too few. He feared the next target would be Akren himself. Marcellus would not trust the Sakkaran knights to guard their prince until he knew how the last had been taken. The circumstances of his capture were still unclear.

Now, as night fell, Marcellus lay in bed unable to sleep, his mind brooding over the peculiarities of the situation. There was much to consider. What Marcellus returned to most was Prince Hugh and his missing ears. He had clearly been tortured.

The question remained: tortured for what?

133

Twenty-One

When Nicolai had suggested to Corren the night before that they keep in mind the role of the stones, what he did *not* mean was for them to deliberately attempt to "unlock" their stones' secrets. Yet that was what Corren spent the first part of the day trying to do. Nicolai flatly refused to tamper with his own stone, but curiosity kept him watching while Corren tried to bring forth the secrets of his. They were in Corren's room, which had a distinctly darker feel than Nicolai's did. The bedding and upholstery were all in deep shades of maroon, brown, and red and even the mantle around the fireplace was a dark hickory. Nicolai sat on the lounge, watching as Corren stood in the center of the room and examined his stone. For the most part, it remained stubbornly silent about what secrets or powers it may hold. After a time Corren finally uttered an incantation that got a reaction: a pain in his hand so sudden and severe he dropped the crimson stone on the rug. He healed himself—much as he had healed the blisters from the magic guarding the Bridge—and persisted on.

Leaving the stone on the floor, looking more wary now, Corren sent an incantation to it that way. The spell rebounded and shot at him in a flaming, crackling arch. He dove to the floor and the fire flew over his head, just missing him. The tapestry on the wall behind him had not been so fortunate, however, and threatened to go up in flames completely until Corren said a spell that snuffed them out like blowing out a candle. Whiffs of smoke curled up to the ceiling and the rank smell of burnt tapestry filled the room. Corren slowly straightened, watching it and panting.

It was at this point that Nicolai decided he'd rather be with Knight Whittaker.

Nicolai ventured through the training grounds at the time appointed for their next session, occasionally stretching the sore muscles he'd woken up with. The arena was busy again. Nicolai watched the knights fighting, this time paying closer attention to their movements. He saw the long thrusts and short jabs Whittaker taught him and recognized the way the knights held their swords to block. Only they wouldn't just block. They'd turn a block into a counterattack that they would turn into a defensive stance, transitioning from one to the next in one seamless movement. Now knowing a little of what went into that kind of skill, Nicolai had new appreciation for it. Today he wasted no time with fantasies. Today he watched and learned.

As he approached the rear of the training grounds, closer to the barracks, he kept an eye out for Whittaker, but didn't see him anywhere. Nicolai's search led him to the armory. Here, he stopped short at the door. The space wasn't terribly wide, and the ceiling was low, but the room was astonishingly deep; Nicolai became aware of his mouth hanging open. He shut it and slowly walked into the room. Row after row of wooden shelves and racks offered up breastplates, shields, broadswords, two-handed swords, pikes, longbows, crossbows, axes, maces. Nicolai had never seen such an array of weaponry, and in such awe-commanding numbers.

He ventured down a middle row, letting his fingers graze the cool metal of the shields, the ribbed handles of the pikes. A pile of interesting-looking daggers was too tempting to resist. He stopped to pick one up. It was relatively light and compact and fit snugly in Nicolai's hand. The handle was only slightly longer than the grip of his fist. The blade was the same length as the handle. It narrowed to a deathly point. Nicolai decided it looked more like a spearhead than a dagger.

"It's a throwing spear." Nicolai turned abruptly and saw Whittaker's massive frame filling up the aisle. "When you're approaching your enemy in the line, you throw a few of these before they get into range. The idea is to knock down some men before you need your sword."

Nicolai examined the throwing spear again. He had never seen one before, but he liked the feel of it in his hand. "Can I try it?"

Whittaker regarded him, then gathered up a handful of spears. "Take some and let's go." On his way down the aisle, Whittaker retrieved a shield, too. Once they were outside he showed Nicolai how to hold the spears in his shield hand and throw with the other.

"You want to get rid of all your spears before the enemy gets in range," he explained. "At that point, you'll want your sword. Here, this is how you hold it. HERE! That's right." He pointed at a stack of hay against the wooden barricade of the archery range. "Hit the center if you can. NOW!"

Nicolai took aim and threw the spear. The weight of the handle reacted in a way he didn't expect. It missed the stack of hay completely.

"Maybe we should go back to swords," Whittaker said, but did not move.

Nicolai took aim again, this time with a better feel for it. He hit the hay almost in the center and impulsively looked at Whittaker with delight. He saw the look of surprise on Whittaker's face, right before he removed it. "Don't get overly excited. Let's see if you can do it again."

The next three Nicolai threw didn't hit shy of center: they hit dead on. He did not bother to conceal his pleasure. Even Whittaker looked slightly less stern than usual. Nicolai spent the next few hours practicing, increasing the difficulty level at a steady pace, first by running while throwing, then by charging the hay while on horseback and throwing to the target that way. This took considerably more practice, but after several tries he had it. His aim wasn't always on center, but mostly it was, and always close enough to be deadly. He felt he had been throwing spears all his life.

"Alright," Whittaker said at last. "Enough is enough. Your first line of defense is solid." Nicolai accepted this for the compliment it was, even if it was offered with a scowl. "Let's get back to those swords. That's where the battle is won." Nicolai was ready to get back to that too, determined to learn all Whittaker was willing to teach him. "Now get a sword from the rack," Whittaker said. "Go, go, GO!"

Praea knew the earliest she would hear anything from her brother and Prince Marcellus would be late tomorrow, and more likely not for a few more days. She was finding the wait difficult to bear up with patience. Still, she hoped for good news. In spite of her inherent mistrust of Norrland, she felt relatively confident that they would not be so bold as to bring Caedmonia into a war, too. She did not doubt Prince Marcellus' ability to make that consequence plain to them. Her brother Rowan's murderer may never be found, but at least Sakkara was protected. As she walked through the beautiful gardens of the castle grounds, she tried to let go of her desire for revenge. She had to think about what was best for her country and she reminded herself that war was costly.

The sky overhead began to darken, sliding into an ashen blue. It was nearly dusk. By this time tomorrow, she would be fulfilling the command received in her last message. If she could.

Praea took a deep breath and pushed the thought out of her mind. She tried to focus instead on the amazing variety of flowers and trees abundant in the garden, with its many terraces and levels. The garden was stunning in its beauty and a welcome diversion. She thought of the last time she had come here, late at night, when it was too dark to appreciate its splendor. Instantly her mind flew to Nicolai, though she found her thoughts were never very far from him to begin with. She had been watching for him, but hadn't found him yet. She hadn't seen him in the castle, nor had she seen him in the Great Hall at dinner. She began to fear he was back in Knobby Tree tending his farm.

A view of several terraces below her opened up as she walked around a curve in the path. On the ground level, sitting on a stone bench next to a weeping willow in full bloom, was Nicolai.

Her entire body reacted to the sight of him and she stopped automatically.

There was a flower bud in a nearby planter, which he was absently stroking with long smooth strokes from the base to the tip. She was mesmerized by his movement, puzzled by it, until she realized with astonishment that he was making it bloom. Within a matter of seconds, a brilliantly colored orange poppy blossomed wide and wondrous. Nicolai looked on as if it were something he had done a hundred times before. His thoughts seemed far from here, the poppy a mere distraction.

Praea followed the pathway down to him. The walkways tended to meander and maze through the garden, and he came in and out of her view. Each time he was blocked from her sight, she feared the next time she would see the bench, he would be gone. At last, she came around a bend in the path and saw the willow, the orange poppy, and Nicolai, who apparently heard her approach. He turned toward her, and stood.

Nicolai's heart began to pound the moment he saw her. She approached tentatively, offering him a nervous smile. "Hello Nicolai."

The sound of her saying his name was bittersweet. It gave him more joy than he thought he had a right to. "M'lady," he said, and bowed a little, as he thought he should. He told himself if he had any sense at all he would leave, but her presence was too sweet. He did not want to leave her company yet. That was not the only thing. He had worried about her and needed to know she was alright. "I was sorry to hear about your brother," he said. A dark shadow passed over her face. He resisted the urge to reach out and console her. "I recently lost my father," he said gently. "I know it's difficult."

"I'm sorry," she said, and she seemed genuinely concerned. She even took a step closer to him. "Are you alright?"

He nodded. "And you?" He did not ask the way a stranger asks, out of courtesy. He asked as a friend asks, and she answered in kind.

"I miss him," she said. Her voice trembled very slightly.

Again, he had to stop himself from taking her hand. Part of him felt she would welcome his touch, but he knew that couldn't be. He would not offend her by taking liberties. "Were you close, my Lady?"

She nodded and a slow smile lightened her expression. "When I was little we used to climb the apple trees together," she said. "Rowan was older and could climb quite high. He knew no fear. When I was brave enough, he would help me get as high as he was. Too high, usually. I was lucky I never fell, but he helped me keep my balance and I felt safe with him. He could never fall, or so I believed." She paused,

138

remembering. Her smile was so light and free now, he could imagine her as a curly-headed girl scampering up through the branches. "We'd eat an apple and spread the seeds out on our laps," she said, fanning her hands out in front of her, "and make a wish on every one." She puzzled her expression at him, but still wore a smile. "I haven't thought of that in years."

"That's a nice memory," he said, smiling too. A moment passed and their gaze seemed to settle into something new, their expressions growing more serious. She looked so deeply into his eyes and he into hers that he felt as if his soul was laid bare before her. He looked away to settle himself.

After a moment, she said, "I saw you from above." She pointed one slender hand at the orange poppy, so recently coaxed into a bloom. A delicate silver bracelet hung from her wrist. "I was admiring your handiwork."

He felt a sudden panic. "Handiwork, my Lady?"

"I saw you make it to... didn't you...?" His concern must have been obvious to her, for she looked distressed herself.

"Er..."

"I'm sorry," she said. "I thought..." She stopped and gathered herself. She took a deep breath. At the sight of her discomfort, his panic fled and his heart softened. He considered simply telling her how he did what he did. It was then that he knew he was letting himself get too close. *She does not think of me that way,* he thought firmly. He decided he needed to save himself this torture and leave. "Are you a wizard?"

He shook his head and took a step back. A flower from the branch of the willow tree behind him slid against his ear and he brushed it away. "I'm just a farmer, my Lady," he said. That statement carried more weight than it ever had before. She looked sober and he gathered she understood his meaning perfectly.

"Please," she said, her voice feeling tender to him. "Call me Praea." But he knew it could never be Praea, not for him.

He took another step back, avoiding her eyes with difficulty, surrounded by his longing for her. "It would not be proper my Lady." He said it so softly, he wondered if she had even heard it.

139

She took a step toward him and whispered, "Can you not say it?"

His skin heating up, he looked at her. He longed to reach for her. She came closer then, intimately close, and he did not back away. He couldn't. He didn't want to. He wanted to believe that what he saw on her face was what he hoped for. She put her hand on his arm, her eyes holding his, and any doubt he had about her feelings for him fled in that moment. He released his resistance in a rush, and his heart began to pound. She took another step, only half a step, for that was all the room there was between them. Her gown rustled lightly and he could smell the lavender in her hair. Every part of him quickened, her presence almost tangibly engulfing him. He forgot who he was—who she was—and as she came closer still he could feel her before they touched, could feel himself leaning down to meet her in spite of everything. Their lips met and everything around him fled away. He was charged by her presence in him, every part of him caught up by her. In that gentle kiss he was lost to her from that moment on.

They pulled apart slowly. "Say it," she whispered.

They heard footsteps approaching and jerked apart. The intruder was near. Praea held his eyes and said again, "Say it."

How can I help but love her? Nicolai thought. "Praea," he said gently, and she smiled.

The footsteps belonged to a messenger summoning Praea to the king. Nicolai lingered in the garden awhile, but Praea did not immediately return. As the last light of day fled Nicolai left too, feeling foolish to wait in the dark. He had no desire to go back to his room, even though it grew late enough to do so. He decided to take advantage of Clement's invitation to explore. Of course, his main reason for wanting to do so had more to do with another chance at meeting Praea than with the castle itself. He grew warm every time he thought of her kiss. After enough guards and attendants gave him an odd look as he passed, he realized he was walking around with a permanent smile on his face. He hardly cared.

Nicolai's exploration of the castle led him to a room (tucked away at the end of a deserted hallway) that made him momentarily forget his search for Praea. The furnishings in the room were sparse and beautifully simple, certainly plain compared to the other furnishings he'd seen in the castle. The walls were what he found to be so extraordinary. Covered from ceiling to floor, the walls had been painted with trees. He was completely surrounded by them. He almost felt like he was standing in his fields at home looking at the Wilds.

Then it struck him. These *were* the Wilds.

There were slight differences, almost as if this had been painted 50 years ago before certain trees he was familiar with had fully grown and before the saplings he knew now had come into being. His eyes scanned the room, working slowly from left to right. He was more and more sure of it the farther he moved along. He was looking at the Wilds. Nicolai smiled and wondered who in the castle loved the Wilds as much as he did.

His smile evaporated, though, when he saw what was on the rear wall. Painted in between some of the trees was a distant, pale green light. Nicolai knew those trees well. He knew that path well. He stepped closer, not believing it. Yet here it was. There was no mistaking it. The light on the mural could not have been there on accident.

It led straight to the hidden location of Salerno.

Twenty-Two

The situation at the border had changed drastically. Someone was after the Sakkaran royals with a degree of malevolence Marcellus had only read about, never personally witnessed. It called for a new strategy.

It had been a gray and misty morning, but as the sun rose in the sky its heat burned off the last remnants of haze. The Caedmonian camp dominated the crest of a broad and flat-topped hill, allowing for a generous view of the surrounding area. To their rear, deeper into Caedmonia, were patches of forest, often broken by meadows and valleys, which eventually led to the barrier marked by the Wilds. To the north of camp and across a wide basin began the tree line that marked Norrland territory. Beyond this was the bare and open land of Norrland. Marcellus surveyed this on his way to the commanders' meeting tent; he saw nothing to cause him worry. His worries lay elsewhere.

The commanders' meeting tent was large enough to accommodate the men gathered. That was its one luxury. Marcellus believed swift and efficient troops packed light and so his commanders gathered around the large plank of wood that normally served as a wagon cover —this supported by crates of food. In the corner was a large chest, which was all the room they had for anything else they might need for their meetings. When Marcellus entered the commanders rose, bowed, and, when Marcellus indicated they should do so, sat again.

Chief of Marcellus' commanders was Donnelly. Like most the commanders, he was older than Marcellus, but Donnelly was considerably so, having served as a commander under Clement since before Marcellus was born. He had a wide, broad face, thick eyebrows, and a large, fleshy nose. Donnelly was keen and sharp as a leader and Marcellus relied upon him more than any of the others.

Theo sat next to him, his red hair working its wild way to his shoulders. His normally jovial countenance was serious, matching that of the other half dozen commanders present.

Marcellus greeted them all with a simple, "Men," and they got right to business. The first item on the agenda was a message he received that morning from King Gunderic of Norrland. Prince Akren arrived as they were discussing this.

All present stood. "Prince Akren, I did not know you were up," Marcellus said. He had checked on the prince earlier and found him still sleeping. After the trauma of the night before, Marcellus was not desirous to wake him. "I trust you are being attended to?"

Akren dismissed this with a wave of his hand. His eyes were heavy and his skin drawn, but his appearance was neat and he held himself regally. "I've come to meet with you."

"Of course. Please sit down. We were discussing a message from King Gunderic."

Donnelly was on Marcellus' left, but the officer on Marcellus' right rose to offer his seat to the Sakkaran prince. Akren sat, and the others with him. He looked around at the commanders.

"Do you wish to meet with me privately?" Marcellus asked.

"That won't be necessary," he said, turning to Marcellus and nodding to the parchment in front of him. "What did Gunderic say?"

Marcellus read the message wherein the King of Norrland consented to the meeting in Messina as Marcellus knew he would, but requested it be pushed back a few days. He said he had suspicions of a rebellion within one of his own troops near the Sakkaran border and was coming, with more troops, to investigate.

Akren's astonishment at this flashed in an instant. "We're not going to sit here and wait for them to attack us?"

Marcellus sat back, surprised by his reaction. Gunderic's request for a few more days was not out of line. While the mention of more troops was concerning, and certainly not something to overlook, he did not think it warranted undue alarm. "Gunderic knows I am here on your behalf," Marcellus said. "I do not think he would invite war with me."

"He is setting us up. He does not wish to meet. He wishes to fight and wants only time to bring more troops." He was not as wildly emotional as he had been the night before, but his distrust of Norrland was heated and resolute.

The commanders around the table studied Akren, sizing him up. This was not the sort of prince they were used to, though Marcellus suspected everyone here understood Akren was under pressure of an intensely personal nature. Marcellus responded calmly. "We cannot forbid him from moving troops within his own country. We'll send scouts out," he nodded at Theo, who nodded in return, understanding the implied command, "and keep an eye on their movements. I have already requested reinforcements from Stonebridge, feeling it prudent after yesterday's events. We will not be outnumbered. Meanwhile, we will find out in Messina if the rebels are getting as out of hand as it seems and if Norrland truly wants to get them under control."

"*Always* they blame their actions on the rebels," Akren said, his voice rising. "Now he is saying the movements of his own troops are under control of the rebels, just to avoid accountability."

Marcellus thought this accusation perhaps a little unjust. He knew the rebels genuinely gave Norrland trouble, hiding in the northern section of the Duncraig Mountains and gaining the sympathies of Norrlanders in their region who harbored them and made their work easier. However, Marcellus also knew Norrland to be persistent in its claims to the strip along the border region, so appropriately termed the Wedge. So Akren's distrust of King Gunderic was not unwarranted.

"What is the point of this meeting if we cannot believe anything they say?" Akren continued. "It is not enough to 'discourage boldness' as your good King Clement seems to think." Donnelly shifted in his seat. Marcellus knew he wanted to speak in defense of his king, but Marcellus communicated with a look that he wished to handle this himself. It was an unspoken message to all his commanders and they held their tongues. "It is too late for *discouragement*," Akren said forcefully. "The time for action has come. It is Norrland who is at fault. What more proof do you need?"

"What proof do you have?"

Akren's eyes widened in surprise. "Who else would be doing this?"

"I do not pretend to know what Norrland is thinking. It may very well be that what they intend is war. I believe the wise thing is to wait until we meet with them. I still find it odd that a sword with the Norrland crest on it was deliberately left in your brother's body only for them to deny involvement later. Maybe the rebels are setting them up. Maybe not. We still do not know for sure."

"Fight one and fight them both. They are one in the same as far as I'm concerned."

"Not as far as I'm concerned."

Akren sat back angrily at this, but Marcellus held up his hand.

"You have every reason to mistrust them. Norrland has given you much grief over a strip of land that, in my opinion, rightly belongs to your country."

"Norrland does not see it that way, nor do their 'rebels.' Both believe the land is theirs and act accordingly. Why should I distinguish between the two when both are working toward the same end?"

"Because their tactics have been very different. Norrland may pester you with requests for negotiations and attempts to prove the land is theirs, but they have done so peacefully. The rebels make no secret about their intent to take it from you by force. The violence along the border continues to increase and this may be the most recent of it. My communications with Gunderic lead me to believe they are actively trying to prevent this activity. The truth of this remains to be seen. Meanwhile, I am not willing to war against an innocent nation."

Akren narrowed his eyes. His jaw clenched and his whole demeanor stiffened. Yet, he said nothing. Marcellus waited. He would not try to guess what was on his mind. Akren would have to say it himself. The commanders around the table sat in uneasy silence. "Whose side are you on?" Akren asked.

"Yours." Marcellus said it with firmness and without hesitation.

Akren felt the force of his answer. His face relented, his shoulders dropping ever so slightly. "Even with two Sakkaran princes slain, you still take no action." His words were bold, but his tone was resigned and it softened their delivery considerably. "Do you expect me to do nothing?" He looked defeated and discouraged, the sorrow in him returning with the abating of his anger. Marcellus grieved for him. He hoped never to know that kind of loss.

"No," Marcellus said quietly. "I expect you to be wise."

Akren looked at the table, sober and still. "I will not let my brothers' deaths go unavenged."

"Nor should you. But make sure your sword falls upon the proper neck."

Akren sighed and ran a hand through his hair. He sat up straighter and looked at Marcellus with regained composure. "Do you have a plan for the meeting?"

"I do," Marcellus said. "I realize King Gunderic will not allow Sakkaran troops over his border, even in pursuit of rebels. We both know he will not budge on this, but if the rebels truly are getting out of hand he is going to need some assistance. If you agree, I am prepared to lend troops to help. Since I am a neutral party, I will suggest you each agree to allow my troops free movement over the border when in pursuit of rebel units."

"Will Gunderic see you as a neutral party when you agree the land is ours?"

"He realizes our opinion on the matter, but Caedmonia has never interfered in the disagreement. Gunderic knows this and respects it. If he is not in alignment with the rebels, I believe I can persuade him to let me do this. If he refuses, then we will know the truth behind his intentions."

"He may refuse simply on point of honor and how can you argue with that? You cannot force him to allow your troops in his land."

"No. I do not intend to force him. I intend to find out his true alliances. The situation is grave. He will understand that. I will make it clear we are looking for more than his word on which to place our trust."

Akren leaned back in his chair, lacing his fingers in front of him and pondering the suggestion.

"I do not expect an answer now," Marcellus said. "We have time. Think about this and we will talk again when you are ready." Akren

146

nodded in agreement. "Meanwhile, there is another matter to consider."

"Which is?"

"Your safety and the manner in which these murders occurred to begin with." Marcellus saw Akren tense again, but went on. "I do not think an attempt will be made on you while you are in my camp..."

"I do not intend to stay in your camp."

Marcellus raised his brows. Out of the corner of his eye he saw his commanders exchanging glances. Marcellus studied Akren's face. He seemed determined, not because his emotions were ruling him, but for another reason. Marcellus believed he knew what was behind it, but felt obligated to dissuade him anyway. He addressed the matter carefully. "Prince Akren, according to your men, your brother Hugh was taken without anyone seeing it happen."

"It was in the middle of the night. Most men would have been sleeping."

"Not your watchmen. The knights at the posts were doubled up, a precaution they decided to take after Rowan's murder. Yet no one saw anything."

"What are you trying to say?"

"Either you have watchmen who are not doing their jobs, or they are deliberately looking the other way."

This was met with silence. Akren did not answer.

"I'm sure you have considered this," Marcellus said. One of the pitfalls of nobility was the ever-present possibility of spies among you. Akren would not be a stranger to this concept.

"All the watchmen spies?" Akren finally said. "What is the likelihood of that?"

"Not all," Marcellus said. "If a prince is being smuggled out of camp with no witnesses, it must be a small group to go undetected. A small group only needs a small way in. Many watchmen would see an enemy troop advancing, but half a dozen men or less would only need the eyes at one post to turn in the other direction to get in. Half a dozen is more than enough to overpower a sleeping prince who should be safe in his own camp. But he was not safe. And neither are you."

"You think I should hide from my own men?"

147

"No. I think you should stay here until the meeting with King Gunderic. It is what you were planning on anyway."

"That was before I found my troops here. How would it look if I did not stay with them? I would look afraid, unable to command my own troops. No. I will stay in my own camp."

Marcellus felt no need to press further. He respected Akren's decision. It was what Marcellus would do himself if in the same situation, and he had already considered this as a possibility. Still, the presence of spies could not be ignored, and he had a plan—if Akren would agree—to help sniff them out. "Perhaps there is an alternative," Marcellus said. "Prince Rowan was murdered in his tent, an event I cannot protect you from unless you are here, though I do not think that is a likely fate for you. You said Rowan's belongings were searched. Someone is after something, or perhaps some information. Do you know what that might be?"

Akren shook his head wearily. "No."

"Well, my guess is their search of Rowan's tent did not yield what they wanted, and so they went after Hugh next. Their tactic changed. Instead of killing him right away, they took him away first so they could torture him for what they wanted."

"What do they want?"

"I have no way of knowing that," Marcellus said.

"Nor I. I can think of nothing Norrland, or anyone else, would want so badly. Other than land."

"Did Hugh have the authority to grant it?"

"No. But he had the power to persuade the king."

Marcellus nodded thoughtfully. "If this was really about granting land, even a prince held hostage would give an enemy more leverage than a prince dead. I do not think that was it. In any case, we do not know if their torture gave them what they wanted or not. If they didn't get what they were looking for, it is likely they will try to take you away next. If they did get what they want, the next step may be open war."

"The fact that Norrland is bringing more troops to the area suggests this as a possibility."

Marcellus nodded. "It does. If that is the case, the reinforcement troops I've already sent for will be most welcome." Marcellus did not want to revisit their discussion of Norrland. He wanted to focus on the enemy within Sakkara's ranks. "If the attackers did *not* get what they wanted, you will be their next target. We cannot guard against foul play within your camp. If you insist on staying there, that matter will be fully in your own hands. What we *can* do is place small units of Caedmonian knights around your camp to keep an eye out for intruders. We can use units small enough to hide in the ground cover and stay far enough away to avoid detection by your watchmen. Both attacks occurred at night, so we only need to watch at that time. We will watch for small groups attempting to enter your camp. If we see anyone suspicious, we can lay hold of them for questioning. There may be no attempt on your life, especially in the next few days and with our troops so nearby. I think it is worth the extra protection at least until we meet with Gunderic." Akren looked thoughtful. "Do you agree to this?"

"Where would you place your units?"

Marcellus instructed Theo to retrieve a map of the border area from the chest. As he spread it on the table, each man rose to look at it closer. Together with the commanders, they discussed possible locations, settling details on the number of units and the size of those units.

"We will need to be flexible about the locations," Commander Donnelly said, leaning on the table with his broad arms, eyes under his thick eyebrows studying the map. "This map does not show what kind of ground cover there is."

"I agree," Marcellus said. "As long as we have one unit covering each of the Sakkaran lookouts, we should be able to see what we need to see. Scout it out tonight and we'll discuss it again in the morning."

As the last of the details firmed up, the group slowly settled around the table, quiet and pondering the tasks appointed them. Marcellus considered Akren. His eyes were on the map, sharp and focused. He was more of the man Marcellus had first met in Stonebridge. "Are you comfortable with this?" Marcellus asked.

Akren nodded. "Yes. Thank you. It will help."

149

"It is the best we can do."

"Meanwhile, I will try to discover the traitors from within."

Marcellus nodded. "Be careful who you ask to help with that. Given the nature of what has occurred, your spies may be deeper in than you think." Akren nodded, and Marcellus would not take the liberty of saying more, for how Akren handled his own men was none of Marcellus' affair. He would give advice if asked for it, but he would not interfere. He could only hope Akren would keep his investigation as quiet as he could. If the traitors caught wind of it, it could cause them to go underground. And splinters should not be allowed to fester.

Twenty-Three

On the southern edge of Stonebridge, a slender stretch of land poked out into the sea. At the end of this rocky and wave-beaten outcropping was a tall tower-like rock formation better known as the Rock of Light. The great openings all around the top, from which shone the Eternal Flame, had a strange rhythmic symmetry, even with the irregular edges of the windows themselves. Fashioned from the same rough stone, the interior circular stairway led from the entrance at the bottom straight to the tower's upper chamber and its stone altars. These things were an inherent part of the structure and not shaped by any human hands. This incomprehensible monument was said to have been created solely by the magic of the Phoenix at the beginning of time, eons before the first wizard would ever discover it and the Eternal Flame burning within, before its purpose came to be fully understood, before there ever was a group of witches and wizards worthy to receive the ash, before the Order of Ceinoth ever came to be. The Rock of Light had always been there. If there came a time when the Order of Ceinoth did not exist, the Rock of Light and its flame would go on.

Built right next to the Rock of Light was the Cloister. A small, round building of stone like a little footstool jutting out of the base of the tower, the Cloister was built by the Order of Ceinoth over 12,000 years ago. Few were permitted to enter the Cloister or the entrance to the Rock of Light that they guarded, except for the Order members themselves. It was to this tiny and forbidding enclave that Corren and Nicolai now approached.

Corren raised a fist to knock on the simple wooden door, but it swung open even before he touched it. There stood Aradia, cloaked in the heavy white robe of the Order, her silken hair, nearly silver in color, falling the length of her back. The pendant worn by the Head of the Order (a braided band of ribbon encircling a silver flame) hung around her neck, but the clasp of her cloak was the purple star of her branch, the Wysard branch. Aradia's graceful face, still healthy and young, formed into a welcoming expression and she extended a slender hand to Nicolai.

"You must be Nicolai of Knobby Tree," she said. "Thank you for coming." Nicolai nodded and she turned to Corren. She looked neither welcoming, nor stern. Only disappointed. Corren found it difficult to maintain eye contact with her. "Master Corren," she said simply.

"Sage Aradia."

She gestured them inside and closed the door behind them. The lighting was poor; only one torch burned in a holder on the wall. It took a moment for Corren's eyes to adjust to the darkness. They were in a small entryway with another door opposite them leading further into the Cloister. It was closed and Corren doubted he would be privileged to see what lay beyond it. He was further in the Cloister than he ever would have expected to be without being a member of the Order. He only wished the circumstances were such that he could enjoy it.

There were four small chairs, lightly upholstered in velvet, on either side of the inner doorway. Aradia motioned them to sit down. She sat opposite them, leaning forward with a serious expression. Corren gathered she had business to attend to here that had caused her to meet with them in this way. He could not imagine it meant anything good if her business was so important that she could not leave, and yet Corren's actions were serious enough to cause her to take time out for it instead of waiting for a more convenient time.

Aradia looked at Corren directly for what felt a long time. He waited, his body temperature rising incrementally the longer the waiting went on, until he could feel beads of sweat developing on his forehead and under his arms. It was not the first time he had come under such scrutiny from her. Aradia was known for her bald, silent examinations of people, situations, and magic alike. Some suggested it was her unique form of divination, though Aradia herself once confessed to him she merely had an aptitude for using her

152

observations to discern hidden truths. That thought held little comfort for Corren now. "I confess, Corren," she began softly, at last, "I am not quite sure where to begin." Corren shifted slightly. "Kennard informs me you are as thoughtlessly curious as you ever were, but this goes far beyond curiosity."

"It was foolishness," Corren said lowly.

She raised her eyebrows and sat back in her chair. "Indeed."

She glanced at Nicolai then back at Corren. "So you were with this young gentleman from Knobby Tree, on the Bridge of a Thousand Ages, when all along I believed you to be at Tower Hall South. Please explain how this came to be."

Corren was not pleased with having to lie to her. He fought the urge to simply tell her the truth. But he was not the only one with a stone and he had to respect Nicolai's wishes, at least until he could speak with Marcellus, too. He had given his word. "I met Nicolai on my journey to Stonebridge," he began, the lie already well practiced in his mind. "He was on his way to the city to conduct business there and during the journey we became friends."

"Why were you going to Stonebridge?"

Corren hesitated. "You know I've been wondering about my parents."

Aradia's expression softened in understanding, but she sighed all the same.

"I know you told me to put it behind me. But..."

"I understand how you must feel Corren." She looked briefly at Nicolai, then continued gently. "This has always been your biggest hurdle. These distracting thoughts cripple you."

He nodded, trying not to show relief that she was not questioning the truthfulness of his tale. So far.

She fixed him with a compassionate but firm expression. "You must trust me. The chances of you finding your parents are slim, even assuming they're still alive. You have too much work to do to allow this to stop you." She looked at him intently. "I must say, I thought we had moved past this."

"I'm sorry. You were right. I *have* felt off center, and I'm sure this is the reason." He was silent and she considered him. He knew this would not be enough, that more questions were coming, but he sat silently hoping she would dismiss him with a warning anyway.

"And the Bridge?" she finally prompted. The edge in her voice told him he should have offered this explanation without forcing her to request it again.

Corren was genuinely pained by what he was about to say next. "I was curious," he said, "but I also..." He really wished Nicolai was not here to hear this. "I suppose I was flattered by Nicolai's admiration of my ability to do magic. I... I wanted to show him what I could do."

Her annoyance was evident now. "You were showing off." It was a statement, not a question.

Corren looked down and nodded. He felt as embarrassed as if it were actually true, mainly because, he reluctantly admitted to himself, it was a perfectly believable story. She knew him well, knew his history well, and despite all he had done in recent years to overcome certain vanities, he was now forced to claim he had suffered a severe relapse. Since he could not tell her the truth, he had no choice. What other tale would she believe?

"You are much too old for this kind of childish behavior," she said in a stern and exasperated tone. Her reaction affected him deeper than he was prepared for. She believed his tale—and he found he didn't like it. "Did your judgment truly not overrule such an impulse? I entrust you with far too much if this is still how you will choose to behave."

He shook his head, heartbroken she was thinking such things of him. "I'm sorry."

"How am I to make you my Successor when you persist in your childish follies?"

Corren could not hide his reaction to that. Aradia had never discussed Successors with him, nor had he ever mentioned it to her, but he had long hoped for this rare honor. In the deepest corners of his heart he had aspired to it, long before he had even been able to admit his own ambition to himself. To succeed her and be a member of the Order, to know the secrets of the Phoenix, to have the kind of knowledge and power and opportunity associated with such a position... he could think of nothing greater. Nothing he wanted more.

She was watching him closely, as she ever did. For some reason, she looked slightly amused.

"Sage Aradia," he said, leaning to her earnestly. "I am sorry. You do not need to mistrust me."

"You are saying I can trust you?"

"Yes."

She leaned forward, considering him. "Only time will tell if that is true."

He nodded. "Yes."

She nodded, too. "I am glad we understand one another." She sat back, clasping her hands together on her lap, resuming her intense scrutiny of him. Corren noticed even Nicolai squirming in his seat. Finally, her expression relaxed. "Alright little one," she said, using a phrase she favored from his youth whenever he was in trouble. "I have one final question for you."

"Yes?" He didn't want any more questions. He wanted to know his fate so he could go on his miserable way.

"How on earth did you come to be a guest at the king's castle?"

Her obvious incredulousness almost caused him to laugh. It was the tone of voice he was most familiar with, the one she used most often with him. One that only faintly veiled her pride in him. It was the same tone of voice she used when she asked how he had managed to master a complex spell after only a few attempts, or how he came to put together a potion no one had ever tried before with stunning results. With this one question, Aradia communicated her fondness for him, even in the midst of his glaring stupidity.

It gave him a comforting kind of reassurance. Maybe she would be merciful after all. This time answering her question was a little easier, though still a lie, perhaps because he felt more certain that he would be believed. And less embarrassed by the tale. "In the course of my search for my parents, I made acquaintance with one of the king's commanders. When I told him I was an apprentice at Tower Hall South, he thought the king would be interested in seeing me. As it turns out, the king is quite fascinated with the goings on at the Tower.

He invited me to stay because, I believe, he wanted to learn more. Since I needed a place to lodge anyway, I accepted. We talked at length about students and apprentices and many of the fundamentals of magic. He had many questions."

"Our existence has often threatened the royalty of nations because they do not understand us," Aradia said, her mood somewhat lighter now. "Did you ease his mind?"

"I believe so," Corren said, feeling increasingly relaxed himself. "He was quite a gracious host."

She smiled. "I'm sure. And so you were a guest of the great King Clement. The apprentices will have even more reason to envy you now."

Aradia turned to Nicolai. "You are from Knobby Tree?"

He seemed startled to be the object of her full attention. "I am."

"May I inquire why you were made a guest of the king as well?"

Nicolai hesitated. "I performed a small service for him."

Aradia smiled kindly then. "No 'small service' would warrant such an honor from such a king. Perhaps you can teach your new friend Corren here a few things of humility."

Corren blinked with the sting and she looked at him knowingly. She stood and they stood too, following her lead. Corren's heart lifted. Was he truly only getting away with a warning? Though, a warning from Aradia was unlike a warning from any other. Still, here they were ready to leave and she had made no mention of any kind of suspension or, more importantly, of his staff. "Well, dear Corren, I think I understand well enough what happened. You couldn't have picked a worse time, though. The Order is quite sensitive to trespassing of this nature, particularly now." Corren and Nicolai exchanged the briefest of glances at this. She was referring to the prophecy; Corren was sure of it. For the first time he realized they could have been viewed as people fulfilling the prophecy by trying to attack the Phoenix, not protect it. Corren flushed at the thought of the trouble he nearly got himself into. As soon as she dismissed them, he planned on getting as far out of sight of the Cloister as he could.

"What's done is done, bad timing or no," she said.

Corren waited expectantly.

"Well," she said. "Let's be done with this." She turned toward the door, not the one leading to the outside and Corren's expected reprieve, but rather toward the one leading deeper into the Cloister. She opened it and walked through ahead of them, gesturing Corren and Nicolai to follow her. Together they stepped over the threshold and Corren froze at the sight in front of him. Perched on a raised platform and situated in a semicircle at the head of the circular room were seven high-backed chairs. Aradia walked regally to the chair in the center and sat down. Three cloaked members of the Order sat to her left, two sat to her right. The only empty chair was at the end of the line, a crescent moon embroidered into the seat back. All eyes and faces were set strictly on him. Corren's legs would not work. He was drenched in cold fear and could not think what to do. Nicolai nudged him in the back, which prompted Corren's legs to obey and carry him unwittingly to the center of the room where he stopped, sick with dread.

Corren recognized two members aside from Aradia: Kennard, the Head of the Guardian branch who had salvaged him from his fate a few nights ago, even if only temporarily; and Bellamy, the Head of the Layrin branch in Sakkara and Aradia's old friend. Corren had never seen the other members before, a woman and two men. With that strangeness their stern faces seemed twice as daunting.

"Corren of Tower Hall South," Aradia began, "has been charged with blatant misconduct and willful trespassing on forbidden ground. Are you said person?"

Corren startled. "Yes."

"Nicolai of Knobby Tree, who is not a member of any branch of the Order and so not subject to our authority, has been requested to appear as witness. Are you said person?"

Nicolai answered in the affirmative. Aradia turned to Kennard. "Sage Kennard, please present the Order with your knowledge of this incident."

Corren frantically searched his memory for any tale, any story, any whisper-thin rumor of an apprentice being brought to trial by the Order. He could think of none. He had no idea what to expect and was still reeling with the realization of just how serious the situation was.

He listened with ringing ears as Kennard explained what happened that night. This was followed by Aradia questioning Nicolai, who quite believably offered the same explanation Corren had given just moments before. He was suddenly exquisitely grateful Aradia had spoken with them first. Nicolai even added his own apology for "encouraging Corren" to take him on the Bridge.

Corren related again what he had told Aradia, struggling to keep the shaking out of his voice.

Aradia turned to Kennard. "Do you have any more questions for Corren about the events of that evening?"

"No," he said. "I have questions for him about the following day."

Corren felt a chill drop through his body. Aradia hesitated for the briefest moment, a hardness on her face in a flash before it was gone. "Proceed," she said calmly.

Kennard turned to Corren whose mind had gone horribly blank.

"Why were you at the Bridge the next day?"

In Corren's panic, time seemed to slow. He did the only thing he could think to do. Stall. "I'm sorry?"

"After we found you on the Bridge, I decided to have members of the Guard patrol the entrance. You were seen there."

"Did he attempt to get back on the Bridge?" Aradia asked.

"No," Corren said a little too forcefully. "I had merely stopped there to rest." He inwardly cursed this pathetic answer, but could not think what else to say.

"You stopped there to rest?" Kennard asked incredulously.

"I did not try to get on. I did nothing wrong."

"Why would you stop there, of all places?"

"Am I not allowed even near the entrance?"

"That would be advisable," this from Aradia, who had narrowed her eyes slightly.

Corren sighed. "I know I shouldn't have gone on the Bridge, but even at the time, I did not know it was... quite this serious. I did not mean to be the cause for so much worry. I am truly sorry to have caused you all so much concern. I will do whatever you want... I will

158

stay as far away from the Bridge as you want. I will not bring you any more grief."

All were silent awhile following this. Corren felt more at their mercy than at any time preceding this, because his explanations were finished and his answers were now living independent of him. The question of whether they would save him or seal his fate still dodged away unanswered and he no longer had any influence on the outcome. He did not know their thoughts, did not know if he should have said something differently or said more or *not* have said something. He wanted this to be over. He wanted to know what his fate would be, and yet was afraid to know.

The woman Corren did not know leaned forward slightly and glanced at Aradia.

"Sage Kai'Enna," Aradia said. "You may address the accused."

Corren turned his attention to Kai'Enna as respectfully as he could. She was a beak-nosed woman with gray hair and keen eyes. Judging by appearance, she was the eldest member present. She had been studying him carefully all through his testimony. "You are considered to be an unusually skilled wizard, do I understand correctly?"

Corren blinked uncertainly. "Some have said as much to me, yes."

She cocked her head at him. "Is this false humility on your part? You had no hesitation, apparently, about stripping down ancient barriers to a Bridge you knew to be forbidden to you. Curiosity alone would not drive a person to do this, neither would the lust for praise from those around you," she said, this with a look toward Nicolai. "Only arrogant pride would drive such an act. That combined with high levels of skill can lead one down dangerous roads indeed." Corren looked to Aradia for assistance, but she sat as formally as she had all along. "It is my suggestion, Sage Aradia," but though Kai'Enna addressed Aradia, she did not remove her eyes from Corren, "that the Order take this fact into consideration when deciding upon the consequences, in addition to the *timing* of this incident, which may not be as coincidental as some would hope."

"Sage Aradia, if I may," Kennard said. She nodded and he continued. "While the need for caution is apparent, that does not justify punishment for a crime which was not committed. We must

159

deal with the issue at hand and not bring additional speculation into it."

"We must deal," one of the men now said forcefully, "with that which we have been charged to protect." He was a thinning, harsh-looking man with dry, sagging skin and hair as black as coal.

"Sage Merhat," Aradia said to him. "We must not let fear cloud our judgment or we may be blinded to the real enemy and unintentionally give a vulnerable opening."

"How do we know that our enemy isn't *him*," Merhat said jabbing a finger in Corren's direction. "Both of them for that matter." Nicolai flinched at this.

Aradia raised her hand. "Our conversation is bordering on the edge of indiscretion. We have discussed this matter already. I do not wish to do so again in present company."

Merhat sat back obediently, eyes glaring at Corren.

Aradia turned her attention back to Corren, but addressed the Order at large. "What is the will of the Order regarding the testimony presented? Sage Kai'Enna?"

Kai'Enna pursed her lips, a deep thoughtfulness in her eyes. Corren could no longer look. He looked instead at the tip of Aradia's shoe poking out from underneath her white cloak, the heavy fabric puddling around it. "Suspension," he heard Kai'Enna say.

He closed his eyes, the image of the shoe still floating behind his lids. *This can't be happening.* There would be no staff any time soon if he were suspended.

"Sage Bellamy?"

"Probation."

Corren's heart beat painfully.

"Sage Merhat?"

"Expulsion."

Corren looked up sharply. Expulsion was a fate he had not even considered. He would be forced to leave the Tower permanently, forbidden to use the magic he had learned there. Corren turned to Aradia desperately, shaking his head no in pleading. She looked at him unwaveringly. He could not read her expression. "Sage Kennard?"

Kennard hesitated. Corren turned his pleading eyes to him. Corren dared not speak, though if he thought it would help he would drop to his knees and beg. "Probation."

"Sage Solesmay?" This last member of the Order had been silent through the entire proceeding. His sole contribution to the matter rang through the room like a reverberating gong: "Expulsion."

Two for probation. Two for expulsion. Corren never thought he'd find himself wishing to be placed on probation, but that was exactly his wish now. All eyes turned to Aradia. She was silent for what seemed an excruciatingly long time. Corren felt sealed to the floor, certain he would be unable to move if asked to do so.

At last, Aradia spoke: "As you all know, my responsibilities for Corren are twofold. He is both my apprentice, and my charge. I have cared for him from a young age and know his character better than anyone. I appreciate knowing the will of the Order before offering you my thoughts, because I want to fully understand what I am asking of you."

She exhaled resolutely. "If there is too much arrogance here, as Kai'Enna has suggested, the fault for that may partially be mine. As I have confided on more than one occasion, I have a tendency to indulge the young man you see before you. That tendency has not been fueled by his skill, but rather by his nature. Has he struggled in the past to subdue his weaknesses, to control his curiosity and rein in his pride? Yes. Have not we all struggled with weaknesses to one degree or another? I am sure we have. Corren is not perfect, and the current situation illustrates this more than any other. But by and large he has mastered these weaknesses, even with this recent lapse in judgment, and has made great strides. He is a forthright and moral young man. He strives to a higher state of self-awareness and self-perfection, not out of lust for praise, but out of a sincere desire to be a good person. This has been my judgment of him over these last many years. I now ask the Order to take my opinion of him into consideration. Unless you, my peers, esteem me to be a poor judge of character, than I encourage you to take this incident for what I believe it is: an act full of foolishness yet devoid of malice or ill will. I request

161

the Order to allow me, as Corren's sage, to deal with my apprentice within the authority of my own branch. What say you?"

Corren desired even more to tell her the truth now, for the simple reason of being worthy of the praise she had just given him. Whether for the right reason or not, nothing changed the fact that he had spent his entire defense lying to everybody. And she had just defended him.

Kai'Enna was the first to speak. "Yea."

"Yea," Corren heard again.

One "yea" after another swept over him in a wave of guilty relief.

Aradia nodded in solemn approval. "Nicolai of Knobby Tree, we thank you for your testimony. May those in your village have joy in your return. Corren of Tower Hall South, you are released to your sage. Fellow members of the Order of Ceinoth... we depart until duty and desire bid us return."

Twenty-Four

The letter had instructed Praea to meet in the woods. She went through the eastern gate of the city and made her way back up the steep hill to the forest. She reached the top slightly winded, for she had dallied too long at the castle and had to rush to make up time. Behind her was the high stone wall of the castle grounds, on the other side of which were the gardens. She moved into the safe covering of the trees. Here, finally, she slowed her pace, ears alert for the call.

It was quiet, almost peaceful. She brought her hand to her necklace and felt the cool glass ball nestling against the base of her neck. Stomach fluttering, she lowered her hand and looked up. The branches of oak, aspen, and elm mingled here. Beyond them all was open sky awaiting the cloak of darkness. Praea watched and listened. At first she heard nothing but the wind slipping through branches and the scurrying of some small animal unseen. She heard something behind her that was not of the forest, and not what she was expecting. She spun and saw a flash of black disappear behind a large tree a stone's throw away.

Her senses pricked, her eyes not moving from the spot. Heart pounding, she took a step back. Dry leaves underfoot protested more loudly than she wanted now. She took another crackling step, then gasped. A gnarled, menacing face surrounded by a black cowl appeared around the tree trunk, leering at her.

Without pausing to think Praea turned and ran deeper into the woods, away from the man she heard chasing her. She darted in between trees, ducking under low hanging branches, her arms stinging with their scrapes as she pushed them away. She quickly glanced back and saw not one but two men in black, closing in on her. Praea blindly crashed through the woods, her footsteps conjuring up a bewildering sound of crunching leaves that mingled with the shouts of the men who were drawing nearer with each step she took. A wasted, narrow branch, leafless and knotted failed to yield when she shoved at it, and its tip cut across her cheek and neck as she flew by. Her bracelet snagged on the branch and broke free. She halted automatically—for her brother gave her that bracelet—and almost went back for it before coming to her senses. One of her pursuers rushed through the trees behind her. She screamed and ran, horror gripping her as he reached her arm and snagged it with his fingertips. She fled just barely out of his grasp.

A thick growth of trees blocked the way in front of her. She veered to her right and the ground dipped sharply beneath her. She slid down an incline, gaining speed, her feet giving way. She crashed onto her back, still sliding. Her arm reached out for something to grab on to and in that instant the ground beneath her disappeared.

Time slowed as she arched out, almost felt as if she were floating, frozen in midair. She plunged rapidly, saw the river glittering far below. Panic engulfed her, her own scream deafening in her ears. The water rushed up to her, closer and closer, the wind screeching past her.

When she thought of the only thing she could do to save herself, a fresh wave of horror hit her. She had to do it alone. She said the incantation as she had been taught, but doubt and terror swallowed it. *It's not working... Oh, Nicolai...* Something transformed in her. Her will burst forth like fire igniting. Heat radiated from the ball around her neck then fanned out through her body in a rush. Her flash of astonished relief fled in an instant: she had slowed, but it was too late.

Praea hit the water, then plummeted into blackness.

With Marcellus at the border and Corren taken by Aradia to some mysterious destination, Nicolai found himself the lone man in Stonebridge. What Corren's punishment was going to be or how long he would be gone, Nicolai didn't know. Where he himself should go or what he should do next, he knew just as little. What he needed was advice. He could not expect Salerno to help without fully disclosing the details of his situation, so that was not an option. His mother was

164

just as out of reach. If he wanted advice, there was only one person left. The king. But for some reason, he hesitated.

Seeking his own counsel instead, Nicolai spent the afternoon at the shipping docks, watching little fishing boats and many-oared long boats and high-sailed merchant vessels pulling into and out of the bay. The air was rank with the smell of fish and salt water. The people working here were too busy to bother with a stranger sitting out of the way on the low breaker wall.

As he sorted through all that had happened over the last few days, clear answers eluded him. He frequently found his thoughts going in circles. More than once his mind wandered back to his fields at home and the preparations needed for the coming winter, wondering if they were getting done. Other times, more frequently, his mind would stray to Praea and his heart would tighten as he lingered with her in his mind. Sometimes he merely watched the clouds moving in, a thick, dark mass with the promise of rain, and he would think of nothing at all. Always the question of the prophecy and what to do next would return, the weight in the pit of his stomach returning with it.

His stone lay warm against his chest, both a burden and an odd kind of comfort. There was something about this stone only he could figure out. Something only he could do. So why didn't he know what that was?

Nicolai sat until dusk. As the light began to fade and the air grew chill from the clouds now overhead, it hit him how much time he had wasted with nothing to show for it. An uncommon occurrence to be sure. He decided he at least needed to get back and tell Clement the outcome of their trip to the Order that morning. Once in the castle, his empty stomach first propelled him into the Great Hall. He didn't see Clement there (or Praea, disappointingly) so he sought him out in his office. There Nicolai found him surrounded by several knights, Knight Whittaker one among them. Nicolai hesitated at the door. The page had said he could come in, but he expected Clement to be alone.

His father caught his eye and gestured for him to come in but did not stop in his conversation with Knight Whittaker. "If she is to be found," Clement was saying soberly, "it will most likely be by scouts to the north, but I want our bases covered."

"Yes, your Highness," Whittaker answered. "I will send units in all directions."

The king turned to another knight in the room. "Commander Quinn, you and Orin will reinforce our position at the border. Send word to Prince Marcellus tonight and prepare to depart morning after next."

"Yes, Sire."

The tone of Clement's voice combined with Marcellus needing reinforcement at the border made it impossible for Nicolai not to interrupt. "Excuse me, Sire," he said, bowing. "Is something wrong?"

The knights in the room did not seem to appreciate the interruption. Clement turned to Nicolai without the slightest hint of annoyance. "We've just received word from Prince Marcellus. Another prince of Sakkara has been slain along the border." Nicolai's heart tightened and he thought of Praea. "We do not expect open war, but we need to be sure our numbers are sufficient to discourage it." He gestured a dismissal to his commander and all the knights except Whittaker began filing out, some casting curious glances at Nicolai. "At the moment," Clement continued, "I'm more concerned about Princess Praea. I've just been informed she is missing."

"What?!" Nicolai blurted.

Whittaker addressed the king, but looked at Nicolai pointedly. "Anything else before I go, Sire?"

Nicolai barely heard this. His senses heightened to an alarming degree and he felt his own blood rushing through his veins. His mind tightened around one thought: Praea. Nothing else mattered. "Where?" he asked Whittaker. "Where was she seen last?"

Whittaker looked at the king in exasperation. Clement's expression clearly indicated he expected him to answer the question. Whittaker sighed and turned to Nicolai. "At the east gate near the woods," he said. "She was seen leaving but not returning."

"Let me help. I can track her."

Whittaker looked taken aback and openly dismissive. "My men are on it already. They leave at first light."

"You're waiting till morning?"

166

"We're already searching the city," Whittaker said, his voice rising, though not as much as it did on the training grounds. "If she is outside the city gates it will have to wait until daybreak."

"I can track her!"

"I'm not taking along anyone who is only going to slow us down!" Whittaker stubbornly turned to the king. "Anything else, Sire?"

"No," Clement said regally. "You may go." Whittaker left the room with one last glare at Nicolai, but he was too preoccupied to care. He turned to Clement in desperation. Since there was still a page in the room, Nicolai kept up the formalities, but he did it in a rush. "Your grace, pray forgive my boldness."

"What do you desire, Nicolai?"

"A horse."

Clement looked after Whittaker, no doubt guessing Nicolai's intentions.

"I'll return it," Nicolai said urgently.

Clement looked at Nicolai then with an expression he had seen before, though not coming from the man in front of him. It was a look of pride, a slight gleam of it in Clement's eye. He gestured to the page and said. "Of course. Anything you need."

Nicolai bowed. "Thank you, your Majesty."

Clement watched them as they hurried out the door. "You're welcome, my son."

Nicolai's determination to find her was the only thing keeping his panic at bay. Once outside the east gate, he dismounted the horse and held the torch he had brought with him down low, lighting the dirt road with a flickering glow, shadows darting away.

"We're closing the gates," someone called above him. He waved them off. There were many footprints overlapping and hiding one another, several of which, *many* of which, could have been hers. He scanned the area with difficulty, forming a semicircle from one end of the gate to the other. That was where he found it. Leading up along the city wall was one single set of footprints. They were small like a woman's. And they weren't going anywhere a woman would normally go alone. They were going to the woods.

With the sound of the city gates rattling to a close behind him, Nicolai mounted and pushed the horse into a gallop up the hill. What otherwise would have been a well-lit night under the full moon was near darkness instead. The clouds above were a perfect shroud. Nicolai rode past the end of the city wall to the forest and dismounted again to find the tracks. He found them, and with the torch as his guide, followed them to the entrance of the forest. Here he discovered two new sets of footprints, larger ones, heading into the forest, too.

His heart stopped and his panic found new urgency. Leaving the horse, he broke into a run, eyes flashing from the ground in front of him to the darkened trees and back again. "Praea!" Branches reared up out of the dark and Nicolai pushed them away as he passed. "Praea!"

Pausing to make sure he was still going in the right direction, Nicolai checked the trail. He still saw multiple tracks, all widely spaced to indicate they had been running as well. A flicker of silver caught his eye. He came to an abrupt halt and bent hastily to the ground. In the darkness, Nicolai almost missed it. Pinching a delicate chain between his thumb and forefinger, he lifted the bracelet he remembered seeing Praea wear.

"PRAEA!"

He ran again, holding the torch low in front of him, firm on her tracks. These turned sharply and he turned sharply with them. His feet gave way and he was sliding. He released the torch and scrambled for a foot hold, arms reaching out, hands open wide, groping for something to hold on to as he picked up speed. He felt the ground dip violently just as he caught hold of a thick branch and tightened his grip desperately. It halted his fall, but his feet were no longer touching the ground. He looked down and saw the torch slide over the edge and diminish as it fell far below him.

Heart pounding in his ears, Nicolai swung his feet back, reaching for ground. He hit nothing on his first pass, caught a toe hold on his second try, and pushed down firmly. He arched his body up and found ground for his other foot.

168

Gripping the branch, he slowly hooked hand over hand, muscles straining, until he was over solid earth and finally on his way back up the blackened incline, using trees as supports and guides. Once at the top he sat down weakly, muscles throbbing. He looked back into the blackness the way he had just come.

He didn't have his torch, but he didn't need it. He knew what he saw right before he lost his footing. Praea's footprints had careened into a slide as well, only he was here... and she wasn't.

Twenty-Five

When Corren and Aradia first left the Cloister, she had made it clear that there would be no discussion and no delays. He had only been able to look back over his shoulder at Nicolai with a helpless glance. He didn't know where they were going or what was going to happen once they got there. They walked through Stonebridge and headed not for the south gate and the road to Tower Hall South, as Corren had anticipated, but rather toward the east gate. They passed through the gate's busy market and afterward walked the wide dirt road that cut through the southern edge of Ravenswood forest. They occasionally stepped to the side of the road, making room for the merchants on their way to and from Stonebridge, their carts loaded with goods and kicking up dust. After a time, the forest petered out and a broad meadow spread a healthy distance away from them before ending at the town of Sheehan.

Situated on the rim of Kilona Lake, Sheehan had sprung up on the western side of the Eridanos dam over fifty years ago when the dam had been completed. The dam was a massive stone structure that accomplished more than turning Kilona Valley into Kilona Lake. The dam tamed the Big Winding River's yearly floods and provided a reliable irrigation system to the farms that dotted the wide valley between Stonebridge and the Wilds. When the Eridanos dam was built, three mills were built into it too, each powered by the massive water wheels that notched across the top of the dam in neat succession, their dull roar heard even on the edges of town. Corren had never known Aradia to come here before, though she rarely shared the itinerary of her trips with him and could have been here many times.

The midafternoon sun was high and warm and Corren was grateful when they stopped at an inn on the edge of Sheehan for food. The inn was cool and dark and the ale refreshing. They did not speak and Corren had long ago given up trying to engage Aradia in conversation; when he had tried to thank her once they had left the Cloister, she had only said "You may think me merciful, but I do not intend to go easy on you."

"What will my punishment be?" he had asked. She did not reply. Little had been said since then.

They finished their meal, which consisted of broiled trout from the lake and steamed vegetables. The asparagus had been tough and rubbery, but Corren ate it anyway. He was tired, worn as much by the ordeal of the circumstances as he was by the journey. He was ready to rest and wondered if the beds at the inn were soft. Aradia rose. "Time to be off." He realized Sheehan had been only a stop.

He followed her out the door. When they passed through the town and began working their way north along the rim of the lake, he looked back at it with longing. He could see along the length of the dam, the tops of the water wheels barely visible with their slow, steady turning, but he faced forward again to follow Aradia on their slow, steady march. He could not think of another town or village near here and began to fear that the distance she was putting between him and Nicolai and the Bridge was going to be too great. At this point he didn't dare protest. He followed obediently, pondering what to do.

They walked for the rest of the day, Kilona Lake to their right, the foothills of the diminutive range of the Carnelian Mountains on their left. When the sun had just dipped under the horizon and the sky was beginning to fade, they reached the river that snaked through the mountains before feeding into the northern tip of the lake. They crossed this at a broad and rocky shallow of the river. Near the bank Corren missed a step and landed up to his ankles in the cold, rushing water. He reached the other side in dripping shoes, muttering under his breath, and said a spell to evaporate the moisture with controlled heat, leaving his feet warm and dry. Aradia glanced back at this but did not slow. They continued walking as darkness steadily slipped over them. Corren had decided she meant to walk him straight through the night when their destination became known: a lone wooden cottage perched not far from the bank of the lake, its heart as dark as the sky above, empty perhaps, maybe even abandoned.

Aradia approached the darkened threshold and dropped her hand over the length of the door, saying her distinctive unlocking spell. She opened it without knocking. Corren followed her inside, hovering in the weak slice of silvery light let in by the open door. She pointed her staff at a huge oil lamp hanging from the ceiling. "Igneth," she said. As light flooded the cottage, he saw it was not empty or abandoned. It was her home.

The front room was simply furnished, with a long couch that looked to be used for a bed and a few small tables cluttered with books, parchments, hourglasses. Corren could see the kitchen at one end, better stocked for potion making than for preparing food; he noticed she had several different cauldrons for just that reason. Her ornately carved apothecary box sat on the wooden worktable next to several jars and boxes of all sizes, filled with potion ingredients he was sure. Bunches of dried flowers and herbs hung from the rafters and the entire room was filled with their thick aroma. There were two doors leading off the main room but they were closed and Aradia did not invite him to see them.

She provided him with hard bread, dried fruits, and cold, clear water from her pump. Following this, they wearily bedded down for the night, she on the couch and he on a soft mat placed on the opposite side of the room. His muscles ached. They had been going uphill almost the entire journey, sometimes only gently, sometimes rather steeply, but it had been a constant climb nonetheless. He looked over at Aradia. Her eyes were closed and her long, silvery hair fell over the pillow, the ends curling over the edge and dipping toward the floor. He glanced at the lantern and said "Egeth," extinguishing the light. "Goodnight Aradia."

"Sleep well Corren," she said with no edge or harshness in her voice. "Tomorrow we begin."

When Commander Donnelly received the order to pick his best men for the operation in Sakkara, Prince Marcellus had placed particular emphasis on the word *best*. Donnelly took this to heart. This was a tricky operation. Risky. Requiring not just skilled knights, but intelligent ones as well. Donnelly understood this. He shifted his weight, got into a more comfortable position, and resumed his surveillance of the Sakkaran lookout assigned to him. It was late and the moon was high, casting sufficient light for Donnelly and his knights to do their job. As he thought of the knights he'd selected for this operation, he reminded himself, again, that sometimes risks were necessary to get the job done. The thought did not give him as much comfort as he sought. He had an odd sense of foreboding. Even with that, he knew he would not undo his decision. The last prince of Sakkara needed all the protection he could get. In order to give him that protection, more than a few Caedmonian men were putting their lives on the line.

And one woman.

Corren awoke at first light. His mind picked up his surge of thoughts from the night before as if he had never left them. The sweet smell of flowers hanging from the rafters overhead lingered in the air. He looked over at Aradia and saw she was still sleeping. He stretched out his aches before rolling up the mat and going into the kitchen to prepare breakfast, grateful for any activity that would take his mind off things, even if only a little bit. By the time Aradia awoke, he had a warm porridge prepared.

He served it to her silently. She smiled knowingly. "You look like a man humbled and tormented by his own folly." He caught her tone, casual and light, but could not bring himself to smile.

"So," she said. "This is day two of my lessons to you about self-control and obedience."

"Day two?"

"Oh dear. Did you not learn anything yesterday?"

This time he did smile.

"I thought so," she said. "Your punishment will serve two purposes. The first is, hopefully, to train your brain to exercise more caution. The best way to do that is to have lots of unhappy consequences to ponder from the *last* lapse in judgment. The second purpose will conveniently ease *my* burden, which these days is quite heavy. Being the Head of the Order at the time of regeneration is both exhilarating and exhausting. I can't even tell you all I have to do. In this way the timing of your foolishness is a benefit instead of a problem, and your punishment will help me immensely. So here it is. I need a Sevenfold Alcalic Base brewed."

Corren blinked.

She looked at him calmly. "You do remember how to do that?"

"Of course, but... that's it? We're going to brew a potion?"

She smiled and shook her head. "Did I say we? You are going to brew this potion while I get some work done."

"Ah." The Sevenfold Alcalic Base was a monster of a potion. Even brewing it with an assistant or two made for laborious work. Brewing it alone... but it was better than being expelled from the Tower and Corren wasn't about to complain. From her light manner, Corren was even hoping this might be all the punishment she was planning. The potion took three days to brew. He could be back in Stonebridge in five. It was five days he'd rather not lose, but there was little he could do about it. At this point, being back before Marcellus returned was the best he could hope for.

They sat there quietly finishing their breakfast. Aradia looked perfectly relaxed, but Corren's mind would not still. He did not know even half the responsibilities of the Head of the Order and it was possible that her preparations were for something perfectly normal, but he couldn't help but wonder if the Order was preparing to defend the Phoenix. Just as he was. Could he really sit here and not ask her? So much more could be accomplished if they were working together instead of wasting so much time with secrecy. He was convinced it was the right thing to do, but one thing prevented him. He had given Nicolai his word. Nicolai had not asked for it lightly, nor had Corren given it lightly.

As he thought of this, Corren knew he could not break his promise. Resigned to this fact, Corren began to wonder if he could obtain the information he sought another way. No options came immediately to

174

mind. As he pondered the events of the last many days, Corren thought he may have found an opening. "Can I ask you a question?"

"I'm sure you can," she said.

"When I went on the bridge, one of the Guard members asked me if I was from the Citadel of Zeverai. Why would he ask me that?"

She furrowed her brows at him. After a long pause she said, "That's an interesting question for you to ask."

"I thought it was an interesting question for *him* to ask."

She nodded, her brows still furrowed, her head moving up and down slowly as if she were doing a great deal of thinking. "I'm afraid, Corren, that is not a question I can answer."

"You can't answer because you don't know or because you don't want to tell me?"

She smiled wryly. "Ever the curious one."

"I'm not trying to pry," he said defensively.

She laughed. "You're not in trouble for asking a question."

"Do you know why he asked me that?"

She considered him, serious now. He waited, trying to control the urge to ask her again. Just when she looked about to reply, something interrupted her and she paused, her mouth partially open.

A glorious, haunting, illuminating song filled the air. They locked eyes in comprehension as the notes swelled with a power and sweetness that filled Corren's entire body, reaching down into the most tender parts of his soul and causing him to tremble and his skin to tingle. The song seemed to be living in him and in everything around him. The last note held for a long time, fading ever so slowly. For a time he could not tell if he could still hear it or only hear the memory of it. Then all was silent.

"Already," Aradia said breathlessly, clearly affected by its power as well. "So soon."

Corren knew what that was. The Third Song. The Song of Preparing. The song that could have taken another nine months to sound, that he *wanted* to take another nine months to sound, but which was sounding now. Time was now short. It was only four weeks, seven at the most, until the Fourth Song, and only hours after that until the Fifth and final Song and the Phoenix's regeneration. The

Phoenix's one moment of vulnerability was possibly only a month away, and here he was by Kilona Lake, Marcellus was at the border of Norrland, and Nicolai was either in Stonebridge or Knobby Tree and Corren didn't even know which. He closed his eyes briefly. Some Gatherer he turned out to be.

He looked at Aradia and saw the excitement on her face. Under different circumstances, he realized, he would be feeling it, too. He smiled and tried to match her enthusiasm.

They both stood together. "This could have happened yesterday and saved me a journey," she said, but she was still smiling. "I have to go back to the Cloister for the Strengthening Ceremonies. I'll find a ride or rent a carriage in Sheehan. You'll be alright here by yourself won't you?" She was already gathering her traveling cloak and staff.

"Yes, but... I'm staying?"

She stopped and looked at him seriously. She seemed to be thinking. "I need this base as soon as possible," she said finally. "It cannot wait." *Why?* he longed to ask. "I'm tempted to feel I need to babysit you, but..." She stepped closer to him. "I do hope this matter with the Bridge is the last such thing we see from you."

"Yes."

"I do not think I've misjudged your character. You won't give me a reason to regret what I did for you yesterday, will you?"

He shook his head. He hoped not.

"Because if you should fail me again, there will be no more chances."

He swallowed. "I understand."

She smiled and put a warm hand on his shoulder. "Good. Begin immediately. We'll talk more when I return."

She went into another room that he could see was her office. She lifted a pouch off the desk and secured it around her waist. She looked around briefly then came out and locked the door behind her with a word. "You should have everything you need," she said at the open front door, glancing at the stores in her kitchen. "Do not delay. The potion must be perfectly brewed."

"I can manage it."

She smiled. "I know you can. I'll see you in three days."

176

Twenty-Six

Nicolai wandered in the base of the gorge, his steps heavy and off-balance, his mind too distraught to handle even the simple task of walking. He led the horse with the reins held loosely in one hand and Praea's bracelet tucked in the other. He estimated he was below the drop off he had almost gone over the night before. He looked at the cliffs above and shuddered. Could anyone survive a fall like that? Determined, he scanned the muddy and rocky bank of the river. He saw a few bird tracks and the winding lines of water snakes, but nothing else. No footprints. Nothing. *Maybe a little farther.* That's what he told himself as he continued down river with still no signs. *A little farther. Just a little farther.* He kept his eyes on the ground, over the water, across the shore. Never up to the cliff and its impossible height.

The sheer cliffs retreated away from both sides of the river. Aged aspen, oak, and elm claimed the space made available. The Great Gorge widened the nearer he came to the sea, trees thickening to his left, dropping back and overtaking the bend that followed the coastline. *This is too far.*

He stopped. His mind was buzzing. He looked at the water rushing by, mentally following the churning water into its depths where the current would be strong. He closed his eyes.

A haunting echo sang through the canyon. The Third Song. It was sweet, bright, powerful, unbearable. In his already vulnerable state he felt tears stinging his eyes as the song penetrated him. When the vibrant, shuddering song faded away, Nicolai was left in his sorrow, sharp and raw. It washed over him with all the force of the river that raged beside him. He fought it with all the willpower he had, because giving in to it would mean giving up, and he was not willing to do that. Not yet.

In order to take hold of himself, his mind clung to the distraction of the song, which brought with it random thoughts about the prophecy, the Phoenix, the stone around his neck. "Now what?" He rubbed his forehead, trying to focus. He couldn't remember exactly what Corren had said about the songs and how much time that gave them now. He only remembered Corren was hoping this song wouldn't sound for many months. Yet, here it was. Surely there was something Nicolai should be doing, but he still didn't know what. What could he do? He couldn't do anything. Without a clear plan of action, the hold these thoughts had on him slipped away and his fear for Praea returned full force. He had to find her.

Then, through the trees to his left, Nicolai thought he heard a voice but then it was gone. He wasn't sure he had heard it at all. His heart began to pound and he willed it to calm so he could hear better. Was it a voice or a trick of sound? All of a sudden, in what had before been a still and quiet morning, he heard nothing but sound. Water rushed behind him. The tops of the trees swayed slowly in a persistent wind, the leaves rustling lowly. Nicolai didn't move, not wanting to add even the crunch of his feet along the shore to the noise around him. He didn't want to miss anything.

Then he heard it again, a female voice. Very faint. And crying.

"Praea?" he called, dropping the reins and tearing into a run. Breaking past branches and tree trunks, vaulting over a fallen log, Nicolai could hear it clearer now. "Praea!"

Nicolai crashed through a bush and skidded to a halt. A girl of around ten or eleven crouched on the ground in front of him, crying, cradling her ankle and rocking back and forth. She startled at his sudden appearance and shrank back from him.

His heart plummeted. *No, no, no, no.* He had been so certain he had finally found Praea that he looked around as if somehow she would still be there. There was nothing. No one. Only the little girl in front of him. *Praea.* This time the wave of grief that swept over him forced him to slump against a nearby tree. He looked back to the child and vaguely registered the frightened look on her face. He struggled to settle himself enough to attempt a shaky smile, trying to reassure her. "Are you hurt?" he heard himself ask.

"My ankle..." the little girl said, still watching him fearfully.

Automatically, numbly, he walked over and knelt down. She jerked back. "I'm not going to hurt you," he said.

She cautiously removed her hands to reveal a cut and some swelling. "I tripped," she said pointing timidly to a branch nearby, "and cut myself on the wood."

"Sprained your ankle, too." He carefully put Praea's bracelet in his bag, reluctant to let it go, feeling somehow it was like giving up. He tried not to think of it that way and began pulling out what he needed.

"I heard a strange song," she said.

He looked at her briefly. "Yes."

She was silent while he used faerie magic to crush and bind the oblong leaf of feverwort. He covered his hand to conceal what he was doing and hide the brief flash of light that sparked between his fingers.

"Were you the one who sang it?" she asked quietly.

"No."

He placed the salve of feverwort and honeysuckle on her cut and wrapped her ankle with torn cloth from his bag. Minor scrapes and flaking skin covered the palms of her hands where she'd caught herself going down. It was nothing needing attention. He helped her stand. When she tested her leg she was able to put her full weight on it. She looked at him in amazement.

"Are you far from home?" he asked.

She shook her head and pointed through the woods. Through the trees he saw a longhouse in a nearby clearing. He nodded and sighed, relieved she was safe and his responsibility to her was over. It was too much. He turned to leave.

"Wait," she said. He turned back heavily. "We need a healer," she said quickly. "At home. We found..." she paused.

"A woman?" he asked, his heart leaping.

She shook her head. "A bird."

For the second time, Nicolai's heart sank. He had to get out of here.

"Please, we don't know what's wrong with it."

179

He hesitated, and he rarely hesitated at a plea for help, but to turn further away from Praea, even if there were no hope—he didn't know if he could do it.

The little girl clasped her hands in front of her chest. "Please, I don't want the bird to die."

He saw in his mind's eye again the shore of the river with no tracks leading out of it, the cliffs high above the water... much too high above. He looked at the little girl in front of him with a need, a real need however small, and not a vain hope.

Reluctantly, he took a step toward the girl and she bounded ahead, leading the way. He followed her, but he left his heart behind him.

Nicolai followed the little girl across the clearing and toward the house nestled against the base of the cliff, her brown hair flying out behind her as she ran. She led him around the back of the simple wood-paneled home. What he saw there caused him to come to a halt.

Trembling on the ground under an apple tree was the most extraordinary creature he'd ever seen. Indeed it looked like a bird, one could say it *was* a bird, but that would not be quite accurate. His mind wrestled to grasp what he was seeing. "It can't be." It was about five feet tall, with shimmering golden feathers and a delicately beautiful head with a tall, silver plume. The talons looked powerful and large enough to grab a man around his thighs. The magnificent beauty of it took his breath away.

The bird gave a terrible, violent shudder and Nicolai took a step back. Were his eyes playing a trick on him?

He looked at the girl in astonishment and she looked up at him imploringly.

"Did I just see...?" Nicolai asked, turning back to the bird. "Did...but that's impossible." The bird shuddered again and he knew with certainty what he saw. He rushed over and knelt. "They're a myth," he said to himself. *Aren't they?*

The bird shuddered again and the form was even clearer this time. Each time it shuddered, it would transform into another shape before transforming back into a bird. The shape was that of a woman. Now he knew it wasn't a bird. It was a Tulaga.

Nicolai turned to the girl. "Where did you say you found her?"

"Down by the river," she said. "I thought it had drowned. My father helped me bring it back here."

"Bring *her* back here," Nicolai said looking into the Tulaga's eyes. They were glassy and glazed. Something was wrong and he had no idea what it was. "It's like the magic is—"

Then it happened. The radiant face of the Tulaga as a bird shuddered. For the briefest moment, he saw her face with a long scratch trailing across her cheek. His heart started beating rapidly, his mind a confusing whirlwind of thoughts.

"Praea..." his hands started shaking. *How?* He had that same feeling of wonder like the day he met a faerie in the forest. Now that feeling was mixed with horror because she was hurt and he had no idea how to help her. She looked at him mournfully before shuddering again and closing her eyes in pain.

Frantically he dropped his bag on the ground and began pulling out its contents. "What's wrong? What's wrong?" He held up a sprig of pine, considering, then set it down, deciding against it. Something was wrong with her *magic*. What was he going to do about *that*?

His chest was burning. He felt as if he were tearing apart. Here she was, right in front of him, and he couldn't help her. He looked at the pile of herbs and seeds and nuts in front of him and made a decision. Something was better than nothing. He started crushing a lavender seed and glanced up at the girl. "I need water," he said.

She had backed away and was staring at him in alarm, like when he had crashed in on her through the woods. "Water," he said firmly.

She raised a trembling hand and Nicolai looked in the direction she was pointing, straight down to his own chest. Glowing around the neck of his tunic was a yellow light. He realized his chest was burning for a different reason than he had first thought. He slipped his necklace out of his shirt and squinted at the light that shone brightly from his stone. Far beyond the steady warmth he had grown used to ever since they had put their three stones together, this was so hot he felt the warmth creeping up his arm. But it did not burn.

181

A thought came to him clearly, almost as if it were not his own. In fact, looking at the stone, he was sure it wasn't his thought at all.

It was a horrifying suggestion.

He looked at the trembling golden bird. *Praea*. How could he risk it? Yet the thought pressed on him. Slowly he removed the stone from the necklace, letting the empty casing fall back against his chest. He looked at Praea. He didn't think he could do it. He remembered the consequences the last time he disobeyed the stone, but this was different. What would happen when it touched her?

The thought grew more insistent. Reluctantly, he held the stone over her chest. The shimmering golden feathers gave way to her bodice then caved into feathers again. The sense of urgency increased to an almost unbearable level and he knew he should not fight it.

He looked at the stone.

He looked at Praea's face as it materialized and transformed into the delicate face of a bird.

He looked at the stone again.

"Don't take her from me," he said and in one swift movement pressed the stone against her chest with both hands. A burning heat seared down his arms and raced through his body. He closed his eyes against the blinding light bursting from the stone. He was thrown, landing on his back. The heat and light were gone in an instant.

The stone no longer in his hand, he looked frantically to his right and saw it land on the grass a few feet from him. He clambered after it and snatched it up.

The glittering golden bird was gone. Praea was on her side, gingerly pulling herself into a sit, a bewildered look on her pale face. He crawled to her, dazed himself. "Are you hurt?" he asked, clasping his stone into the casing and tucking it away. The terror of what he had just done still lingered. He watched her anxiously.

The scratch on her face shrank to a thin, white line then vanished completely. The color returned to her face. She was healing right in front of him. She straightened and her eyes focused on him. "Nicolai?" Her voice was strong and clear.

Exhaling, his tension and worry drained in a rush and he slouched over. "Oh, thank you."

182

Twenty-Seven

"What happened?" Praea asked, looking around in confusion. Her eyes grew wide. She looked at Nicolai in horror. He could only look at her with relief.

She scrambled to her feet and away from the house toward the river, with the girl still looking at them aghast. Nicolai quickly gathered his bag together and followed. "Praea," he called. She disappeared into the trees and he ran to catch up to her. He wasn't about to lose her twice. He caught hold of her elbow. "Wait."

She stopped but would not turn. He gently turned her toward him and she looked up at him in anguish. "No one's supposed to know," she said. "*No* one."

He shook his head. "But why?"

She glanced back at the longhouse, still visible through the trees. She started walking again, this time allowing him to walk with her. They emerged at the river, the sound of the water distinctly less ominous now that she was safe. The horse had wandered slightly downstream where it was taking a drink. Finally she asked, "How much do you know about Tulaga?"

"Only that they are women who transform into golden birds. I thought they were a myth."

"Such has been the opinion for many centuries now. It was not always that way. Tulaga used to be much more numerous, long ago, but..." she stopped abruptly. She seemed to be debating whether or not to go on. "Nicolai," she said turning to him. "The nature of this... it's a secret so highly guarded my father doesn't even know."

Her father didn't know? he thought. *How was that possible?*

She put her hand to her forehead and closed her eyes. She looked past him to the other side of the river and the great, rearing cliff, as if looking for an answer. Or perhaps an escape. When she started kneading her hands in worry, he stepped closer to her, took her hands in his and squeezed them. "I understand I'm not meant to know," he said. "You don't have to explain anything and I won't tell anyone what I saw. I give you my word."

She searched his eyes and again he felt that connection, absolutely startling in its starkness. He didn't look away this time, both unsettled and thrilled by it. He smiled to reassure her that he didn't intend to pressure her.

"Thank you," she said finally, the panic gone.

She took a deep breath and they continued to make their way downstream. To his surprise, she began again.

"Long ago Tulaga were well known, and well loved, among the people. We have a unique kind of magic, beyond the ability merely to transform. It can be a great service in ways other magic cannot." She fell silent, thoughtful. "It was a different time then."

"What happened?"

"Well, Tulaga rely upon..." she glanced at him as they approached the horse. He patted it on the flanks and gathered the reins. "We rely upon Phoenix ash."

Nicolai gaped at her. "Phoenix ash?"

"It is what makes our magic and our transformations possible. The ash, combined with certain abilities in those chosen to be Tulaga, make it possible to be who we are. Without the ash, we would not exist."

Stunned, he clicked his tongue at the horse and they began walking again, the animal trailing behind. "Then... you're in the Order of Ceinoth?"

"We are the Eala branch of the Order. Many centuries ago the ash became scarce. Very scarce." Her voice was filled with regret. "It became necessary to conserve. No one ever knows how long it will be until the Phoenix rises again, bringing its ash with it. So the Tulaga planned and stretched and hoped it wouldn't take too long."

The wind picked up and rushed past them. Nicolai thought of the stones and knew they were the reason the ash was scarce. Who else had been affected by this?

"Ever since, there have been only two Tulaga at any given time. At the most. A sage and an apprentice. I am the apprentice."

"Your sage is in the Order?" She nodded and Nicolai realized he knew who it was. She must have been Kai'Enna, the only woman besides Aradia present at the Cloister yesterday.

"When the sage dies," Praea continued, "the apprentice takes her place in the Order and sets about finding a successor. It is risky, but it was the only way there could even be a hope of enough ash to last to the next regeneration. It was the only thing we could do to prevent our extinction."

They had come to the point where the river drained into the sea and they stopped, watching the vast horizon. Nicolai felt fresh awe at the sight of it. Like so many things in his life right now, it was infinitely bigger than he was. A lone seagull soared over the sea, wings spread wide as it scanned the water below.

"It has been a burden," she said, "not just because I am one of only two, but because the last of our ash is now gone."

"It's gone?"

She held up her necklace, the tiny glass ball sparkling between her fingers. "I have the last of it right here."

Nicolai leaned in to see a tiny speck, which he took to be the ash, suspended in the center of the ball. "There's no more ash? Anywhere?"

"As far as I know, the other branches still have their ash. This is the last of ours. When the Phoenix brings its ash, it is carefully divided between the branches of the Order. It is completely their charge after that. Last time there was only a fraction of the usual amount, not even as much as one branch would have normally received."

"Do you know why there was so little?" he asked, a little nervous of her answer, as if by being a bearer of one of the stones he carried some responsibility for her situation.

She shook her head. "No, but I know there was a lot of debate about what to do. Everyone's magical secrets were in jeopardy, not just ours. Finally they decided to divide the ash evenly, as they had always done, and hope for the best. To avoid any future conflict each branch entered into an agreement to ensure no one would ask another branch for additional ash. It was the only fair solution."

"They wouldn't really let the Tulaga go extinct?"

"They would. Around 400 years ago another branch ran out of ash and their magic has been lost as a result. The Order had to split the Wysard branch into two so they didn't lose the magical balance of seven branches. That was when the Guard became their own branch."

Nicolai shook his head. "I can't believe no one was willing to share their ash."

"Even if they were willing, they wouldn't have been able to do it. The contract was magical and cannot be broken without terrible consequences. If you run out, there's really nothing to be done." She shrugged and looked out to sea.

"So the last of the ash for the Tulaga has come to you."

She nodded slowly, her golden hair illuminated by the late morning sun, her gentle face full of many emotions: regret, acceptance, strength. All at once. Even in the midst of everything, he felt such peace and joy in her presence. He had nearly lost her, and here she was. He resisted the sudden urge to pull her into an elated embrace. As he watched her, he promised himself he would do everything in his power to make sure he never lost her again.

"I was progressing in my training well—quite well," she said, "until I learned I would be the last one. That presented a bit of a hurdle to me. What if I couldn't do it, if I was the wrong one? It would be wasted. Over."

"What do you mean, wrong one?"

"Becoming a Tulaga is extremely difficult. Sometimes a sage chooses wrong and has to select another apprentice."

"Wouldn't she then get the ash?"

Praea shook her head. "Each Tulaga has a glass necklace specifically prepared for her. It's sealed to her, in a manner of speaking. Part of the process, which is quite complicated, connects the ash to its specific wearer. Once the ash is in the necklace, there is no going back. If she cannot transform, the ash is lost. It wouldn't work for anyone else. We have not often lost ash this way, but it has happened. The risk is always real. The thought of taking the last of the ash... it wasn't a responsibility I asked for. Or wanted. I lost my confidence and even asked Kai'Enna to choose someone else. But she refused. She said she had faith in me."

Like him, Praea had been placed with a heavy burden to which she had not aspired. "But you succeeded."

"I suppose I did. This was the first time I attempted it."

He raised his eyebrows. Had she done her transformation incorrectly, causing something to go wrong? "So is that why you were..." he searched for the word to describe what he saw when he found her.

She shook her head, seeming to understand what he was asking. She told him about the men chasing her, about falling off the cliff. He instinctively stepped closer to her, as if to protect her from danger. "The only thing I could think to do to save myself was transform, even though I'd never done it before. It wasn't working at first. I did everything right, I know I did, except... fear can hold back certain kinds of magic. I was beyond fear, but then..." she stopped and looked down. "I thought about..." She smiled weakly, blushing. "I thought about you Nicolai, and something happened to me. I knew I could do it."

His legs slackened. She looked at him, vulnerable in her admission and he aching with the knowledge of it.

"I began the transformation," she said softly, dropping her eyes again, but she seemed to be talking for lack of knowing what else to do, as if to postpone his reaction to what she had said. As if she feared his rejection. How could he feel anything other than amazement and gratitude that she felt that way for him? "It was enough to slow me down," she said, but he had stepped close to her, talking hold of her hand. "But I wasn't able to finish transforming and I hit the water. I was... stuck."

She looked at him finally, and when their eyes met he felt it in his chest. "Weak," she said quietly, her eyes imploring. Tender. His heart ached more than he thought possible. "Then I was by that house," she whispered, "and you were there..." he pulled her closer. He kissed her and this time neither one of them hesitated. He held her close to him, cupping her chin in his hand. Then his relief that she was safe

187

overwhelmed him and he held her tightly and felt her embrace tighten, too.

He didn't know how long they stayed that way, but when they pulled apart he kept her near. He rested his forehead on hers and ran the back of his fingers along her soft cheek. It was in that sweet moment that Nicolai remembered something horrible and the smile slid off his face. She registered it immediately.

"What's wrong?"

He straightened and they separated, but he kept her hand in his. She watched him with apprehension. "I have something to tell you," he said. He paused, dreading it. "It's about your brother."

As he found the words to tell her about her brother Hugh, the second of her brothers slain within a month, her eyes widened and her hands flew up to her mouth. She started shaking her head, her hands still covering her mouth, her face frozen in an expression of horror.

"I'm so sorry," he said.

She began pacing in random directions, her face becoming firm, her eyes looking at the ground, but not appearing to see it. She was still shaking her head.

"Praea..."

"I need to get to Dahlia. I shouldn't be here. I need to get home."

He nodded, eager to do anything to help. "Let's get back to the castle and..."

"No," she said, coming to a halt. "I can't wait the five days it would take to travel with the royal escort."

"How else?"

"I'll fly."

Nicolai hesitated. "Can you fly all that way?"

"I don't know, but it's the fastest way." She looked determined, stubborn even.

"I don't think you should go so far on your own. Someone's after you, too. What will you do when you have to stop? What if someone sees you?"

"I can't wait five days, Nicolai," she said. "I can't make that journey again. Not again..." her voice broke. "I can't just sit and think...

188

about..." she was struggling not to cry. "And this time without even Akren. I need..." she shook her head, frustrated, still fighting to keep it in and Nicolai could see she was losing the battle. "My father must be..." she stopped, a great gasp escaping her, and Nicolai pulled her to him.

She let him hold her, her grief tearing free in terrible sobs. She clung to him and he held her tightly. He felt her every shudder, felt the warm moisture of her tears seeping through his tunic.

He held her a long time until her sobs finally faded away, until she merely rested against him, still and sober. He let her be the first to pull away. He stayed silent while she wiped the tears from her reddened cheeks.

She took a shallow, shaky breath, then looked at him, calmer now. "I'm not going back in that carriage. I'm going to fly."

"That is not a safe way to travel."

She paused. "No."

Nicolai considered things. He wanted to make sure she was safe. He thought he knew how to do it, but could he go so far away now that the Third Song had sounded? That obligation was just as real and, though he slightly resented it, laid even more claim on him.

He looked at Praea's face, felt a fresh surge of his love for her, and knew there was only one thing he could do. "I can get you there in half that time." *A little more than two days there,* he thought, *and two days back. I may even be back before Marcellus. I can't do anything before then anyway.*

She shook her head. "That's impossible."

"Going on horseback is faster than going by carriage."

"That's still a good four days if you don't want to kill the horse."

"Not if we go through the Wilds."

She raised her eyebrows. "I'd be safer on my own."

"I can get you through safely. You won't have to go all the way around them and you won't have to be on your own either. No one goes in there. If someone is after you, you'll be safe there." Though with the climb out of the Gorge still ahead of them, he knew it would take most the rest of the day just to get to the safety of the Wilds.

"No one goes in there because no one ever comes out."

189

He smiled and shook his head. "I've been in the Wilds many times." Her eyes widened. "I can get you through."

She furrowed her brows. "You can make flowers bloom, you can find lost Tulaga at the bottom of a gorge, and now the Wilds? Who *are* you?"

He smiled softly. "I'm just a farmer." He brushed her hair off her shoulder and rested his hand there. "Will you come with me?" She considered him a moment, her eyes penetrating in her analysis of him and no part of him resisted this. He only waited, trusting her to know he meant what he said.

Finally she nodded. "I will."

Twenty-Eight

The Third Song did not escape the notice of the third brother. Marcellus had been in the middle of the encampment walking to the kitchen tent for breakfast when it sounded. By the time it was over, he realized he had stopped walking. He was not the only one. The camp had stilled to listen to it, compelled to do so. Once it faded away and the only song left was that of the wind, the men took to speculating, wondering what it had been. Most seemed not to know and began discussing something similar they had heard many months ago. Others spoke of the Phoenix, debating which of its tales were legend and which were fact. Marcellus, forcing his legs to propel him through the crowd, registered all this on the periphery of his thoughts. He spoke to no one. He had too many thoughts of his own, none of which could be shared with any man here.

With all that had happened since his arrival at the border, Marcellus had almost forgotten about the prophecy. Corren and Nicolai and the joining of the stones seemed far away, long ago somehow. It had faded in his mind. Like a dream. He had grown used to the steady warmth of the stone against his chest and largely ignored it. Now it was an uncomfortable reminder. A new weight of responsibility seemed to settle around him. While Marcellus did not remember exactly how much time was left them now that the song had sounded, he knew it wasn't long. He surveyed the camp knowing there was still so much to do here. There had been no attempt on Prince Akren's life last night but that made no guarantee about the nights to come. There was still the meeting in Messina to contend with as well. So much depended on the outcome of that meeting, which still wasn't for another three days. Marcellus began to consider different scenarios resulting from that meeting and to calculate the time each would require before he could go home again. As he thought of the delay before his return to Stonebridge, his unease grew, as if waiting was not something he should do. Neither could he leave. Even if he did leave, what exactly was he supposed to do once he was home?

This uncertainty, this completely unfamiliar realm... it was more than unsettling. The song brought with it a sense of urgency. But urgency to do what? He did not know and he did not like not knowing. They needed Corren to guide them in this.

Marcellus liked that fact even less.

He remembered then what he had told Corren he would do here. Marcellus had nearly forgotten, or perhaps purposely put it out of his mind. Regardless of the reason, he was grateful he now had something concrete to do.

He sought out one of his men. With most of the camp heading to the kitchen for breakfast he was not hard to find. Marcellus directed him behind the kitchen tents to talk privately. The hearty smell of gravy wafted through the fabric and they could hear the sound of the men talking inside. Marcellus urged the man, one of his more skilled spies, a few more steps away, out of earshot of the men in the tent. "I have an assignment for you," Marcellus said, keeping his voice low. "It stays between us. Not even the commanders know of this."

"Yes, your Highness." The man's heavily-lidded eyes gave him a rather lethargic expression. It concealed his tactical intelligence and was just one of the things that made him useful as a spy. He had the look of a witless grunt, acted the part well, and thus encouraged the enemy to consider him too stupid to be dangerous.

"Are you aware of the Citadel of Zeverai?" Marcellus asked.

The spy looked slightly taken aback. There was a sudden clang from the kitchen. The man startled at it but Marcellus didn't flinch. He was watching the spy carefully. He looked back to Marcellus and nodded. "Yes."

"Where is it located?" Marcellus asked.

"Do you know of the Gray Boulder Foothills in Norrland?"

"Yes."

"They are in the southernmost tip of those."

"Then it is not far," Marcellus said.

"No, your Majesty."

"What do you know of them?"

"Only that they are dark wizards. The knights fear them. We used to hear of their battles with other wizards, but we haven't heard of any in a long time."

Marcellus thought about this. "Would you say they've been unusually quiet?"

"I suppose you could put it that way."

"Would *you* put it that way?"

The man looked away, thinking. He turned back to Marcellus. "I really don't know enough about them to say."

Marcellus nodded. *Good answer.* "I would like more information about their activities, and quickly. Can you arrange that?"

The man raised his eyebrows at this, his large eyes wide, hesitating at the unusual request. "I'm not sure how I would infiltrate them. They are wizards, not knights."

"We do not have time to infiltrate them but you can ask around about them. Observe their comings and goings."

"It might be difficult."

"I will pay you appropriately for the increase of your troubles," Marcellus said, for the loyalty of spies must be won in many ways. Though he realized it may take a wizard to spy on wizards and wondered, too late, if he should've brought Corren along after all. For the time being, however, this was the best Marcellus could do. "Do what you can. I want to see you again in five days' time."

Nicolai knew Praea's attackers could be anywhere. As they traveled out of the Gorge and into the town of Sheehan, Nicolai kept this threat firmly in mind. Using his last bronze coin they bought a few rations before Nicolai escorted her through the city with haste. Keeping her close, Nicolai checked those they passed for anyone who struck him as suspicious. If a man seemed to look at Praea too long Nicolai would put his arm around her shoulder, give the stranger a hard glare, and ask under his breath, "Is that one of the men?" "No," was always the answer, and always Nicolai would relax slightly only to grow tense again as they moved on. Even after they were free from Sheehan's limits and made their way down the hill leading away from the city, Nicolai kept his eyes open and his senses alert. The dam was a towering presence on their left, the water rushing from the three wheels along the top like waterfalls. He carefully scanned the trees on their right until, half way down the hill, they gave way to a view of Stonebridge's city walls. The Big Winding River cut its way through the valley's green basin. They had to go south before they found a crossing shallow enough for the horse. The horse splashed through and they headed north again. Nicolai urged the horse on, eager to get Praea out of the open valley. It was dusk when they entered the shadowy canopy of the Wilds at last and Nicolai relaxed for the first time since leaving the Gorge.

He dismounted the horse, slowing their pace to allow the mare a needed rest. Praea rode wearily atop. Even though he felt she was safe now he pressed on a little farther, preferring not to make camp until they were inside the borders of Amon Tunde. They had not gone far when Nicolai felt it: a change in the ground, a very slight vibration he had learned to detect through training from the faeries. This was the beginning of Amon Tunde. Above ground the forest looked no different, but the earth faeries dwelt below. Nicolai exhaled and allowed himself a tired smile. He felt like he was coming home.

Then something happened that Nicolai did not anticipate. One of the faerie sentinels appeared, blocking their way and causing Praea to gasp and Nicolai to bring the horse to a halt. Nicolai knew this faerie as Keck, but did not call him by name. "We're just passing through," Nicolai said.

Keck had short, spiked hair and blue eyes in a shade less common among faeries but, thankfully, natural to humans. Praea surely would've asked awkward questions if his eyes had been yellow or orange. He wore a long, brown cloak the mottled color of tree bark. It appeared as a common woolen cloak, however Nicolai knew it to be made of a unique material enchanted to blend into the surroundings when desired. Keck could pull up the hood and make himself invisible to passersby until he decided to make himself known. "She may not pass," Keck said, pointing to Praea.

Nicolai urged the horse to the left, attempting to circle the faerie. "She's with me," he said.

Keck stepped directly in front of him and Nicolai stopped again. Keck looked at him levelly. He was firm, threatening even.

"I'll be right back," Nicolai told Praea in a reassuring voice, indicating to Keck that he wanted to speak to him privately. They walked some distance away, but Keck kept a close eye on Praea. She watched him anxiously as well. "I'm escorting her to Sakkara," Nicolai said in a hushed voice. "It's important we get there quickly. I will not go south." He meant the Hidden Door, of course, but even though Praea was out of earshot, he still felt the need to speak discreetly.

"She cannot pass."

"But she's with me."

Keck shook his head no.

Nicolai glanced at Praea and back to the faerie. "Tell Salerno..."

"It is on Salerno's orders that I am acting." Nicolai stared in disbelief. "You can go farther north," Keck said. "But I wouldn't recommend it."

Nicolai had not been expecting this. He tried to think of an argument that would help him, but there was no point. If Salerno was ordering this there was nothing to be done. Nicolai looked at Keck in resignation and asked the question he already knew the answer to, needing to hear it anyway. "Salerno knows I am with her?"

"Of course."

Nicolai nodded. He left Keck and returned to Praea, weighing their options.

Praea looked at him expectantly, her face pale with fatigue but the uncertainty of the situation prompting a renewal of her energy. "Who is that man?"

Nicolai could not answer that question without either breaking an oath or telling a lie, so he decided not to answer at all. "We'll need to go further north," he said.

She furrowed her brows. She had not missed his avoidance tactic, but did not press him. "How far?"

"A way," he acknowledged. "It will probably be another day's worth of traveling by the time we go north and back south again on the other side of the Wilds. It will still be quicker than going around the forest on the southern road."

Her disappointment was evident. "You wish to go around the forest to the north? That will add more than a day."

"No, not that far. We would just be crossing through the Wilds a little north of here." He wouldn't go into Amon Tunde if Salerno forbid it, but Salerno could not stop them from skirting its borders. They could stay on its outer edge and hope that would offer some protection.

Praea looked at the faerie who had not moved from where he had met privately with Nicolai, and was still eyeing them diligently. "We'll be safe?"

Nicolai hesitated. "I admit it is an area I'm not as familiar with and there are rumors of dangers there that do not exist here, but I can tell you many of the supposed dangers of the Wilds are only myths."

She bent down and said low enough that only he could hear, half teasing and half serious. "Like Tulaga?"

He smiled nervously. "Let's hope not." She raised her eyebrows and Nicolai sighed. As much as he wanted to be reassuring, Praea needed to understand the situation they were now in. "Truthfully, at this point, all our options could be dangerous," he said. "If we go to the south, I think we'd be too close to the main road, the only road leading to Sakkara and a likely place for someone to look for you. If we stay in the Wilds and go north there *are* some unknowns, but I still believe I can get us through safely. I would much rather deal with the forest than with assassins."

She glanced at the faerie anxiously.

"I'm sorry Praea. I know this is not what I promised you."

She looked at him gently.

"What do you want to do?" he asked her. He watched her carefully, her weariness returning as she considered things. He would not push her. Whatever her decision, he would do his best to keep her safe.

"I could still fly," she said and he prepared to protest, but she continued. "Even that carries risks. We'll go together. We'll go north."

❧ ❧ ❧

Nicolai led the horse on foot, back in the direction they had just come. The light was fading quickly now. Praea's physical and emotional exhaustion overtook her. The shock of seeing another man in the forest, the disappointment of a longer journey, it all added to what had already been a wrenching day. She was too exhausted to even think much about it. Her body ached, begging for relief. She caught herself swaying as she struggled to stay awake.

They had not gone far when Nicolai brought the horse to a stop. He turned to her and extended his hand so she could dismount. She put her hand in his and slid off unsteadily. "Why are we stopping?"

"You need to rest," he said.

"There is light still left."

"Not for traveling. It's been a long day." She allowed him to lead her to a broad tree with a thick and gnarled trunk, its massive canopy overhead. "Are we far enough away from that man?"

He nodded. "Don't worry. We'll be safe here tonight."

She sat on the ground and leaned against the tree gratefully, closing her eyes. The earth was hard and a knot stuck into her back, but now that she had stopped she could not muster the energy to move away from it. She thought she could sleep right where she was and not move all night. She felt a sudden warmth and opened her eyes to see Nicolai laying his cloak over her, leaving him only in a short-sleeved tunic. "Your hands are cold," he said simply. As he walked away she put her nose to the edge of the cloak, breathed in his smell. She watched him clear brush away from a relatively flat area under the shelter of the tree. His arms were lean and strong, tanned brown from years of laboring over the earth. He looked tired, but certainly not fatigued as she was. He started to build a small fire, Praea watching in silence. Once a decent blaze was going she moved closer to draw on its warmth. They ate bread and dried venison from their rations, sitting close, watching the fire flicker and tease the air above it. She wanted to stay sitting next to him, but with her stomach satisfied she could resist sleep no longer. She settled on her side on the ground, gave him one last smile, and fell instantly asleep.

Nicolai, too, lay down but stayed awake for a time after that. He was too reluctant to pull his gaze away from Praea's sleeping face.

197

Twenty-Nine

Corren was almost a full day into brewing the potion when he made a startling discovery.

Though the day was wearing out and the light in the cottage grew dim, Corren had not yet lit a lantern. He was too distracted. He added a pinch of powdered tortoise shell to the potion, waited ten counts, added another pinch. He set the remaining powder on the table and grabbed a finger-length stick of burnt hickory. He held it above the potion, said "Kursh," and watched as the hickory turned to dust and settled on the surface of the swirling potion. For twenty minutes this went on as he added one ingredient after another in quick succession.

The stirring began again. The Sevenfold Alcalic Base was complicated and sensitive, requiring almost constant stirring at certain stages. He had to keep his eye on several different hourglasses to ensure he stirred, added, and rested at precisely the right times. He had ruined this particular potion more than once as a student thanks to being off by only a minute at one stage or another. It was the first time he had brewed it without an assistant and sorely wished he had one now. The muscles in his arm burned. He switched to stirring with the other, careful not to slow the movement of the spoon. He watched the hourglass. Four minutes later, he stopped stirring, relieved.

He turned the hourglass back over and stretched. He rubbed his arms firmly, working his way to his neck and shoulders, groaning as he did so. During the last four hours of brewing, the potion had required constant attention. Now he had only 15 minutes while the potion rested before he had to add the next ingredient and begin stirring again. This was only the first day, too. The potion took three days to brew. What had looked like a mild punishment at first was now beginning to border on torture. He felt like a student all over again.

He wandered out of the kitchen and collapsed on the couch. He sat in the near dark for five full minutes before he finally looked at the lantern, said "Igneth," and began wondering, yet again, what Aradia and the Order knew about the prophecy. He considered a line in the prophecy—*All four elements must provide their singular powers*—and how the Order, at least in Nashua's time, believed that line had to do with a potion. What if Aradia and the current Order understood what it was? What if this base had something to do with it? His hope that time here was not being wasted but rather serving to defend the Phoenix was the only thing keeping him here. That and the fear of Aradia's wrath.

Corren craned his head and checked the hourglass on the table. Five minutes to go. He peeled himself from the couch, groaned, and shuffled to the work table. He looked for the sarcena nectar he would need to add next. He didn't see it and his heartbeat quickened. If she had been here, Aradia would have chastised him for not double checking that all his ingredients were together beforehand. She would have been right to do so. If he had to go hunting for this one ingredient and didn't find it in time, the day's work would be wasted and he'd have to start all over again. He frantically scanned the table again and cursed.

His weariness vanished; he searched the shelves in a barely controlled panic. He could not find the bottle. He began again with a more thorough search, worried now she might not have it at all. He looked at the tiny hourglass on the table. Three minutes. In desperation, he looked even in unlikely places: big jars, earthen pots, wooden boxes common for leaves and other raw herbs, not for a liquid like he now needed. "Ivy, lemon balm, stripped dog fern," he mumbled, his hands touching each container, checking them off. "Belladonna, trout gills, laurel oil, anise, garlic." Corren retrieved a lone oak box from a high shelf and hastily opened the lid to check its contents. He froze, the potion forgotten.

Inside was a gold leaf. Not gold the way leaves turn gold in the fall, but a pure, luminous gold. He held the box, not wanting to move, a chill running up his neck. He slowly placed the box on the table, the leaf shining at him. When he picked up the leaf, the sensation of

199

holding it seemed to linger just under his skin. It was soft and supple. It seemed still to be living. "What is this?" He had never seen anything like it, nor heard of anything like it.

He stared at it, his body still, the large leaf nearly covering his open hand. His eyes wandered as he tried to think where this leaf could've come from. *The Mountains of Vitra perhaps,* he thought as he distractedly watched the sand falling steadily through the hourglass. *Or maybe it came from Aglan. There are unusual trees known to exist in that forest.* He frowned. *But golden trees?*

Corren registered what he was seeing. The hourglass! He hastily set the leaf down and frantically resumed his search, bottles clinking, boxes scraping, and finally, *finally,* finding the tiny bottle of nectar tucked behind a large ceramic jug. He magically withdrew three and a half drops, sending them arching through the air and into the cauldron just as the sand stopped falling through the hourglass. Heart beating hard, he stirred, rotating the next hourglass with his free hand. He closed his eyes and exhaled, his nerves settling down. This time, as Corren stirred he did not notice the stiffness in his body. Instead, he looked at the tip of the golden leaf still visible in the open wooden box.

What is it, he asked himself again. *Where did Aradia get it?* What he really wanted to know was why she had it.

As Donnelly guarded his post near a Sakkaran lookout for the second night in a row, he wearily thought to himself that he should have put Janus in charge, stayed behind, and got some sleep. That was pushing it, though. It had been risky enough bringing her along at all. Usually when Donnelly's troops traveled with the prince, Janus stayed behind to avoid detection. The prince's knowledge of a woman in his army, secretly at that, would surely result in the dismissal of them both. At best. Once this clandestine operation on behalf of Sakkara came into play, however, Donnelly was exceedingly glad she was here. Prince Marcellus said to pick the best men for the job and she was the best Donnelly had. As a side benefit, it lessened the odds the prince would see her around camp since this assignment meant she would spend most the day sleeping. It had been plenty risky to bring her along on the march, something they had never done before. Janus had never liked staying behind but this time, for some reason, she insisted on coming. There was simply no arguing with her when her mind was set.

Not that Donnelly didn't try. "It'll be boring for you," he had tried to assure her. "Just a diplomatic mission. Lots of sitting around doing nothing."

She wasn't listening. They had avoided getting caught for so long now (much longer than Donnelly had thought possible), he felt Janus had grown too confident. Like the day of reckoning would never come. "I'm going with you. Stop trying to talk me out of it."

He knew by her tone alone that the battle was lost. Donnelly felt a fatherly affection for Janus, but times like these she was more like a rebellious teenage daughter. Stubborn and uncontrollable. Of course, it didn't help matters that she wasn't often wrong. Still he knew her luck in avoiding the prince would not hold out forever. What would she do then?

"He's going to see you," Donnelly said. He tried to say this with a do-what-you-want-it's-your-own-neck sort of voice, but he knew very well that he would suffer the consequences, too.

"Don't worry," she said. "I'll lie low." Donnelly laughed at this. "I know how to behave myself," she said defensively, though with a smile.

"For your sake, let's hope so."

"I'm pretty adept at staying out of trouble."

"You mean avoiding the consequences of the trouble you cause."

He was teasing her and she smiled. "Relax, Donnelly. When have you ever regretted taking me on?"

He didn't bother to answer that one. He had never regretted it, but it wasn't like he had ever had a choice.

Thirty

The next morning Praea and Nicolai left at first light, heading north. Though her body was stiff from sleeping on the ground she felt rested physically, calm and resolute emotionally. For the most part she drew on the same strength that had seen her through the first several days following Rowan's death. Only once, while she and Nicolai were riding, did a wave of grief hit her so unexpectedly that she had to nestle her cheek against Nicolai's back, unable to resist her tears. She did not wish to talk about it. Perhaps Nicolai understood this, for when she tightened her hold around his waist he simply held her hand and squeezed it. Other than this, she felt almost normal, happy even. She knew Nicolai was no small part of the reason. He was noticeably more relaxed this day than he had been the day before. He seemed to think the Wilds was the safest place for her to be. Though she never thought she'd willingly find herself here, she couldn't deny that she felt safe.

Sometimes they went at a good pace, allowing the horse to trot when the terrain was not too rough. Other times they walked. Praea noticed Nicolai had a tendency to dismount the horse frequently, much more often than was required for the horse to rest. By midday, she had taken to dismounting and walking with him, expecting by then that he would be on foot for a time. This behavior prompted her to consider certain questions she had about him. She puzzled at his sudden and unexplained changes in course, a slight veer to the left or right when Praea could see no reason for them. When she questioned him about this, he only said, "This is the way." And so, sometimes they rode, but more often they walked. She replayed the events of the previous night and their encounter with the woodsman. It bothered her a bit that she still didn't understand the necessity of this detour. Despite her questions, she trusted him. More than that, her feelings for him were powerful. As they talked together her affection for him only increased.

The climb in elevation had been slow and steady since entering the Wilds. As they continued north they began to see the occasional pine among the oak and aspen. They were in a relatively flat area now, a good place to allow the horse to run, yet they were walking, following some uneven route only Nicolai understood. "Perhaps we should mount," she said, prepared to ask for an explanation if he wanted to continue walking. Nicolai's eyes fixed on the ground in front of him. He frowned as if he saw something concerning. He stopped, putting his hand on her arm to halt her.

Her heart responded nervously. "What is it?"

He stared at a spot on the ground. Praea began watching, too. Slowly, Nicolai crouched down and grabbed a nearby stick. He put his finger to his mouth and gestured her to follow him. He gingerly walked forward, being careful not to make sound, keeping one hand protectively on her arm and holding the stick with the other. He crouched down—she with him—and he pointed at dry maple leaves strewn on the ground. They rustled gently in the wind.

"I don't see…" she began, but she realized something. There *was* no wind.

Her eyes fixed on the moving leaves. Was something underneath them? She felt to step back, but he said, "Look closer," a slow smile tugging the corner of his mouth. He pointed and moved his finger in a large circle just above the leaves.

A little uneasy, she did look closer. The more she looked the more her eyes began to play tricks on her. What were only stems began to look like brittle little hands and what was just broken bits of leaf looked almost like a tiny body, with leafy arms, legs, back, and a tucked down head. Then she realized there were many of these leafy bodies forming the quivering circle Nicolai had just pointed out. "What—?"

One of the broken bits of leaf shifted, revealed a pointed little face peeking at her, and ducked down again.

Praea gasped and jerked back. Nicolai laughed gently. "They can't hurt you as long as you stay out of the circle. But we need to let them

203

know what we think of their mischief. Watch." He stood and backed up a few steps. She was only too happy to follow. He took the stick and flung it into the middle of the circle. At once a cacophony of high-pitched squeals pierced the air, prompting Praea to cover her ears. A score of tiny, leaf-like beings scattered in every direction, scurrying across the ground on two feet, scampering up trees. When three came straight for her she leapt out of the way as they went running past. Soon the chaos of sound died away and the ground became still again as the last of them disappeared from sight.

Praea looked in shock at Nicolai who was laughing good-naturedly. She began to laugh too as she said, "What on earth?"

"I'm sorry they startled you. I forgot what a shock they can be if you're not used to them."

"What are they?"

"Pixies. Devilish things really. But they're only a danger if you don't know to look for them. They form circles in the path of travelers, hunters, whoever they can. Once their victim steps in the circle, the pixies dance and make the person to dance, too."

Praea laughed at the thought of a hunter dancing in a pixie circle. "That doesn't sound dangerous. It sounds comical." It made her want to see one of the pixies again. All of a sudden they seemed cute.

"The problem is the pixies won't let you go until you're so exhausted you literally fall down dead." Praea's smile froze and her eyes widened. "Most disappearances in the Wilds can be attributed to pixies."

She felt a sudden chill. "That's terrible," she said, looking around quickly. "They can circle us while we're standing here? What about when we're sleeping?"

"No. They have to make the circle and create their spell first. You would have to step inside it. Fortunately for us, they have a hard time keeping still, so as long as we watch for them, we'll be fine. If I scared them enough, we won't see any again for a while."

Praea kept a keen eye out for moving leaves after that. The more they talked and traveled the more she relaxed and forgot about the pixies. Pine trees were growing more numerous now, the oak and maples nearly gone (and their dried leaves on the ground with them), but several trembling aspen persisted here and there. Often a green and sun-drenched meadow dotted their way, red and orange coralroots brightening the earth with their fall blooms. It was quiet and peaceful and made Praea think of the green hills surrounding Dahlia. "It's really pretty here."

Nicolai smiled. "Yes."

"People talk about the Wilds like they're so terrible and dangerous, but they're so beautiful."

"There are things people don't understand about the Wilds, so they fear it, as perhaps they should, but their fear colors what they see so they miss the beauty completely."

Praea sensed he was talking about more than he was really saying. "What don't they understand?"

Nicolai laughed and said lightly. "Well, for one thing, they don't know enough about pixies."

She waited for more but it was all he said and she could not restrain her disappointment in this. What was he keeping from her?

He stopped at some bushes Praea had never seen before with dark green leaves and deep maroon berries. He smiled and picked a few.

"What are they?" she asked, though it was not the question she wanted to ask.

"Thickleberries." He ate one to show they were edible then handed her the rest before picking more.

She tentatively placed one in her mouth. She chewed more eagerly, pleased by the sweet and tangy taste. She picked more herself now, but her nagging questions would not leave her alone. As they walked close together, cupping berries in their hands, she thought about the last few days. She found a question she thought he would answer. "Nicolai?"

"Hmm?"

"There's something I don't understand. When you found me before, after I fell, how did you help me? I went from feeling so weak I thought I was dying to feeling stronger and healthier than I ever have before. What did you do to me?"

He tensed immediately, though he looked like he was trying to hide it. They skirted around a massive fallen log, mossy and brittle. The

205

horse jumped it neatly, hooves thumping the ground as it landed. "I don't understand what happened myself," he said, but he was avoiding her eyes. Her heart sank. "I'm just grateful you're okay."

Praea stopped.

Nicolai stopped, too. He gave her a nervous smile.

Slowly, she brought her hand up and placed it on his chest, resting it there. He stilled, watching her face. His breathing was shallow. Hers as well, unable to resist what touching him did to her. She ran her fingers over the material—felt the firmness of his chest underneath—up to his neck. She slipped her finger under the chain just visible above the rim of his tunic. She began lifting the chain, wanting to see again what was at the end of it, wanting to confirm in her mind what she had only caught a glimpse of before he had hastily tucked it out of sight. She lifted her hand a finger's breadth, the chain draped heavily over it, when he realized what she was doing. His eyes widened and his hand came up in a blur, clasping her wrist against his chest. They each froze.

She narrowed her eyes.

He closed his eyes briefly, then looked at her with an earnest expression. "You must not ever do that again. It is dangerous."

"How can it be? It healed me didn't it?"

He lowered her arm, shifting her hand to rest inside his.

"Nicolai?"

He looked away from her. "It has done harm, too."

"Like what?"

He would not speak, only shook his head.

She took her hand away and he looked at her in surprise, understanding the gesture. "What is it?" she demanded.

"No. I cannot tell you that."

All her doubts came rushing to the surface. What was he hiding? Was she being foolish to trust a man she hardly knew, her feelings for him blinding her to reason? She could stay silent no more. "The way you cannot tell me who that man was last night or why, exactly, we're taking this detour?"

He furrowed his brows, considering her for a moment.

206

She regretted her tone, but could not retract her words. She wanted answers.

"Do you mistrust me?" he asked. It was not an accusation or a diversion. He genuinely wanted to know.

"No. I... of course I trust you." She answered this automatically, truthfully, realizing herself the depth of her trust in him as she said it. It did nothing to lessen her frustration. What she really wanted was for him to trust *her*. As she had trusted him.

"You are entitled to ask questions," he said, softly. "I'm afraid I cannot answer this one." He looked genuinely regretful. "Praea, I would not keep something from you without good reason."

She knew he spoke honestly, but she wished him to confide in her. This desire pressed on her. She found herself crossing her arms, wanting him to know she was upset, wanting him to be moved by it, to relent. "You keep a lot of secrets Nicolai."

He straightened. He saw what she was doing and she immediately regretted her attempt to coerce him. "Yes," he said firmly. "I do. And since learning you are a Tulaga I will be keeping one more."

He gathered up the reins and walked on.

Marcellus stood alone in the meeting tent, leaning over the table and examining a map. It was a map of the Sakkaran camp and its environs, drawn only that morning with the aid of Prince Akren and Marcellus' commanders who had kept watch over the camp the previous two nights. No attempts had been made on Akren's life. No leads on possible traitors had been found. What they did have was information about the lay of the land, including clusters of trees, short ridges, and tall grass. All of this information had been drawn in charcoal on a large piece of parchment. There were notes about estimated distances between various landmarks and watch posts, for nothing was really to scale. Marcellus evaluated the Sakkaran location again. All in all, it was a terrible place for an encampment and Marcellus thought they would do better to move the entire camp about half a league to the southeast. This suggestion was rejected by Akren, knowing they would be moving in a matter of days anyway. So it was that Marcellus came to brood over the various weaknesses of their location, checking and rechecking that the Caedmonian units had all those weaknesses covered.

Dusk was rushing in, along with the wind that had been steadily increasing all day. Marcellus stood to light the lanterns then returned to the map, this time running his finger along this ridge and that grove, in his mind ticking off the units covering each. His finger rested on a wide valley. His eyes scanned the map again, mentally adjusting the noted distances. He looked back at the place marked by his finger. "We need another unit."

A shadow passed over his hand. Theo entered the tent, his red hair sticking up in tufts where it had been blown by the wind.

"Just in time," Marcellus said. "Have the commanders left for the Sakkaran camp yet?"

"I don't think so."

"Bring them to me."

Theo, always adept at reading Marcellus' tone, left immediately, without the slightest smart remark. Minutes later he returned with all but one commander in tow. A gust of wind came in too and Marcellus pinned the rustling map to the table with his hands. The lantern above swung on its hook. "Where's Donnelly?"

"Already gone, your Highness." This from a commander named Slade. The door flap closed and the air stilled, but the fabric of the tent puffed and snapped in the wind.

"Too far ahead to catch?" Marcellus asked

"No."

"Good. We'll be adding another unit." Marcellus dropped his finger on the map. "Here." The commanders leaned over the table, checking the location. "Catch up to Donnelly before he gets there and make sure he knows. We don't want him and his men thinking our new unit is the enemy."

"Yes, your Highness."

"Quickly. I'll send the other unit shortly." They filed out obediently. Theo lingered behind. Marcellus surveyed the map again. He felt better, the nagging feeling that he had been missing something finally gone.

"Who will head the new unit?" Theo asked. He was trying to conceal his hope but Marcellus heard it in his voice. Marcellus pretended not to notice to spare Theo's pride. Theo had his strengths, and Marcellus used those strengths to his best advantage, but strategy was not Theo's strong point. Marcellus needed someone who could think on his feet.

"Tonight, it will be me," Marcellus said. "I want to evaluate conditions myself. Tomorrow I'll make a permanent assignment. We only have a few more nights of this." He rolled up the map and put it in the trunk. When he stood he saw Theo's disappointment. Marcellus clapped him on the shoulder as they left the tent together, the wind rushing around them. "You'll be first in command while I'm gone."

"Yes, Prince," Theo said, only slightly appeased by Marcellus' offering. To command sleeping troops for one night was not much and they both knew it.

Wanting to lift his friend's spirits, Marcellus smiled wryly and slugged him on the arm. "Try to keep the revelry to a minimum."

"Maybe you should just stay here then," Theo said, but he smiled just the same.

There were no large canopy trees for Nicolai and Praea to seek shelter under this night. All around were only tall, spindly pines, the ground dotted with pine cones. He and Praea found a small clearing in which to bed down for the night. Though they spoke as gently to each other as they ever did, Praea had been unusually quiet, hurt by his comment to her. Nicolai decided not to intrude on her thoughts. He was not angry with her, and believed she understood this, but neither would he be pressured to tell her about the stone or anything else he could not divulge without breaking a confidence. Since there was nothing more he could say about it, only she could decide where that would leave them.

He cleared a small area for the fire, sweeping the ground bare of pine needles and mulch, gathering some in a pile to use for tinder. Praea collected wood and together they started to build a cone of sticks. Abruptly she stopped and turned to him, placing her hand on his arm. "I'm sorry, Nicolai." She looked more sorrowful than he would wish her to be. "I had no right to push you."

He took her hand. "Praea, I do trust you. It isn't that..."

She shook her head. "You don't have to explain. I just..." She paused, then leaned in more earnestly, looking at him directly. "You are one of only three people who know who I really am Nicolai. I don't regret that. I trust you." She smiled. "You obviously know how to keep a secret."

He smiled as well, brought her hand up, and placed a kiss on it.

Still smiling, she brushed her fingertips along his cheek and they returned to building the fire, suddenly a much more enjoyable task. As Nicolai pulled out his flint and steel, he thought again of what Praea had said. Three people knew who she was. Kai'Enna was one. He was second. Who was the third? He asked her about this tentatively, wondering if it were too much to ask something so confidential after what had happened. She answered readily.

"The Head of the Order always knows who the apprentice is." A spark caught on the dried pine needles they were using as tinder. Nicolai quickly leaned in and blew to encourage it. "It is a fortunate thing, too," Praea went on, settling on the ground and watching him. "When my father grew apprehensive about this apprenticeship that he knew so little about, Kai'Enna tried to ease his mind, but to no avail. Finally Aradia came to Dahlia herself, vouched for my safety, and assured him he didn't need to worry. He never interfered with my training after that. I don't know how she did it, but I'm grateful to her. She didn't have to do that for me."

"I'm sure she is as anxious for your survival as you are."

Praea nodded thoughtfully. The pine needles were burning nicely now. He added some tinder and sat back, satisfied. Praea placed their bag of rations at his side and moved closer to him. Together they watched the fire and ate bread, some venison, and the last of the thickleberries they had gathered earlier.

They began to talk about small things, like the way thickleberries tickled the tongue when you first put them in your mouth. This led to talking about anything and everything that came to mind. He told her

210

about his upbringing in Knobby Tree and the sternness of his mother who would, nevertheless, sit by his side without leaving whenever he was sick and slip him an extra muffin whenever there was one to spare. He told of his father and the gentle way he taught him to work hard without complaining, while still delighting Nicolai with stories and filling him with the feeling that happiness could be found in your heart no matter what else lay around you. He talked about the pain of losing his father and she talked of the torment of losing her two brothers and they talked about the terrible starkness of death in general and wept together.

She told him of Sakkara and its gentle green hills and misty mornings. She told him about the modesty of Dahlia compared to Stonebridge, including the castle, but how she loved her city and the way she could walk the streets freely and speak with her people often. Many of the citizens she had come to regard as friends, including the woman who sold soft woolen tunics and her husband who made fine leather boots. They talked about the funny shape of pine cones and the hypnotic flicker of flames.

At one point they tried to lie down and go to sleep, but instead of sleeping they talked about the beauty of a star-ridden sky. He told her the stories about the constellations he knew: Rukhs and the Two-Headed Cow, Skylark the Valiant, and Loria Keeper of the Night. She laughed delightedly at some of these. That was when he stopped watching the sky and started watching her face. This did not escape her notice and she turned to him first with a questioning glance, then with a tender expression. Then they talked for a long time without speaking, only looking at one another and running fingertips along the other's hands and shoulders and cheeks. They kissed and laughed and kissed some more and curled up together under the stars until at last they slept, eyes tired and voices dry and hearts light with joy from the last happy night they would have in a very long time.

Thirty-One

Marcellus and the five men he brought with him slowly advanced around a long and narrow stretch of trees leading in the direction of the Sakkaran camp. The moon, full just two nights ago, cast a pale blue tint over the earth. The wind pulled stealthily over the land like a whisper before picking up to a gust, exploding into a violent gale, then dying back down to a deceptive calm before beginning again. Each time the wind pushed through in this way, the treetops above answered with a roar and the high grass in the valley to Marcellus' right would flatten and dip in shuddering waves across the land. The trees opposite the valley moaned in reply.

His unit settled into a position that allowed a view of the valley as well as a view of the Sakkaran lookout between here and the camp. The lookout was a small, raised platform with a simple railing running around the sides. The two watchmen stood at the ready, unaware that they, themselves, were under scrutiny. They moved slowly as they surveyed the surrounding area. If Marcellus descended into the valley and out of the cover of the trees, they would be able to see him as well, but he had no intention of moving without cause.

With the light from the harvest moon as strong as it was, Marcellus thought it unlikely an attack would occur tonight. Such stealth would work better on a darker night. Though whoever the attackers were, they may be feeling emboldened by the confidence of past success or be motivated for some other reason to attack the last prince swiftly. In any case, the risk to Akren was great enough to justify precaution.

The light made it easy for Marcellus to survey the area though, able to take visual stock of perhaps one-fifth of the area surrounding the Sakkaran camp. It was his main purpose for coming tonight. He made a mental note of where Slade's unit would be (across the valley hidden in a band of trees). Beyond that was yet another group of trees, much darker in the distance, and beyond that would be another Sakkaran lookout. This was far away, hidden from Marcellus' view. He only knew of its existence because of the map. Another Caedmonian unit kept an eye on those Sakkaran guards. In the opposite direction of Marcellus was an open field, across from which was a small group of trees where Donnelly's unit kept watch on the same lookout Marcellus and Slade could see.

So it went, around the encampment, with one or two units keeping an eye on each Sakkaran watch point. This was the only lookout with three Caedmonian units covering it (now that Marcellus was here). Now that he *was* here, he was glad he decided to add the extra coverage. The positions of the valleys and trees in this particular area gave too many routes of attack—or escape—for only two Caedmonian units to cover. The valley was wide, still difficult for so few men to protect, but since they needed to stay out of sight of the Sakkaran guards this was the best they could do. Marcellus looked again at the raised platform and the two men atop. He wondered if they be friend or foe. He realized he may never truly know.

Donnelly's unit kept their eyes alternately on the Sakkaran guards and the hilly but narrow valley nearby. It was colder tonight than it had been the previous night, owing to the wind. Donnelly had his unit spread out along the tree line (Janus at the far end) not too far to communicate with each other in the event of an emergency but far enough apart to keep a better eye on the area. He tried to stay alert but after two uneventful nights in this location, his mind seemed to be expecting another and he found himself less aware than he should be. He stood slowly and stretched his arms and legs. He was still strong, still quick, but his bones creaked a little more than they used to and his muscles protested at things he didn't use to mind. He had the thought, not for the first time, that he was getting too old for this. Stubbornness caused him to reject this notion and he straightened, took a deep invigorating breath, and forced his mind into fresh alertness. He scanned the area with sharp, keen eyes.

Just in time.

Marcellus' visual scans of the valley became slow and rhythmic, careful to watch for a shifting shadow, however small. He would begin at the platform, with its two men pacing, and run his eyes over the valley, up and down, working his way west, paying extra attention to the tree line opposite him or the dips and hills in the tall grass. He lost count of how many times he had done this. On this particular pass his eyes halted for some reason farther down the valley, just before he would have looked back to the Sakkaran guards again.

He focused on the area that caught his attention. He saw nothing. His mind worked to analyze the flash that had caused his eyes to still in the first place. Likely it was only a shudder in the grass or perhaps a small animal. Still, his eyes would not be moved from the spot.

He held his breath, waiting. The wind rushed through, the grass and trees trembled, and his eyes laid hold of something moving that didn't seem right. He snapped his fingers. Out of the corner of his eye he saw the knight down the line look toward him. Marcellus kept his eyes on the spot and pointed to it with a sharp jab of his finger. The knight turned and watched, too.

The wind was steady now and there was no more roaring. Just incessant movement. Marcellus wished it would stop. A few feet away from where he had been watching he saw something else, just for a blink. It was a rounded shape, appearing and disappearing in the grass. His heart began to pound. His eyes had not seen enough to confirm what his instincts told him, so he rose slightly from his crouch. He took a few slow, hunched steps forward, willing it to manifest itself.

Then it did.

Two shapes he saw this time, again a few feet away from the last sighting. Whatever it was, it was moving. And toward the Sakkaran camp. Marcellus took his eyes from the area for the first time since he first spotted it and looked immediately to the platform. It was empty. He stood abruptly and scanned the area around the lookout. He saw no one. *Where are they?*

214

Eyes flashing now between the platform and the area with the moving shapes, Marcellus signaled his men to gather to him. They came as quickly as they could without making too much noise. "See it?" Marcellus whispered to the knight nearest him, and the knight nodded. Everyone had their sights on it now. The shapes were dividing, becoming more distinct, more numerous as they drew closer. As they came even with where Marcellus and his men stood, a good distance away in the middle of the broad valley, he could discern them quite clearly. Six men.

"Will Slade's men see them?" the knight asked. Slade was opposite the valley and slightly to the south. The six men Marcellus was watching were in between the two Caedmonian units, but due to the size of the valley, still a healthy distance from each.

"They'd better if they'd like to keep their jobs," Marcellus said.

The attackers were as close as they were going to get to Marcellus' position. He sensed his knights eager to move. "Not yet," Marcellus said. "We'll hedge them in."

"If the others see them."

"They couldn't possibly miss if they're watching at all. We attack from the rear, try to close off an escape." Marcellus regretted the wide valley even more now. The enemy had many escape routes. His only advantage against them was the element of surprise.

"Where are the watchmen?" the knight asked.

"I don't know," Marcellus said. "They either went to their camp or fled to the north, on the other side of these trees."

"Donnelly's unit will have them in sight."

"Let's hope so. Those are two watchmen we'll want to talk to."

Donnelly's unit was in a dead run. The watchmen had abandoned their platform and when they saw Donnelly's men approaching, fled. They were heading down into the hilly valley, away from camp, far away from any other Caedmonian units. It would be up to Donnelly's unit to stop them. He ran with a speed borne only of desire, knowing they needed to catch them quickly to prevent escape. The watchmen ahead would disappear and reappear as they ran down into the dips

215

and up over the hills. Donnelly's legs burned, his sword banged against his thighs, and still the gap was increasing. But just for him. Two of his knights were ahead of him in the chase, pulling away. Donnelly saw the watchmen and his knights disappear down the other side of a hill. Next Donnelly heard shouts, hollers, and thuds. When he reached the top he saw the scuffle on the ground. *Got 'em!* By the time he reached the group, his knights were raising to a stand, their swords pointing to the man on the ground. He was panting, his arms up in the air in surrender.

Donnelly came to a halt, the knights who had been running behind him coming to a stop too. "Where's the other one?" Donnelly asked, looking around frantically. He saw nothing, no one. The knights looked too. Donnelly ran to the top of the next hill. "Where's the other one?!" He looked back at his knights surrounding the captured watchman and took stock.

"Wait a minute," he said. "Where's Janus?"

When Marcellus saw slight movement descending into the valley opposite them, he knew Slade's unit had begun their approach on the enemy. Marcellus signaled his men to move. They moved swiftly, quietly, not wanting to be found out just yet. They had barely descended the hill, however, when the loud crack of a branch breaking drew everyone's attention down the line. A knight must have slipped or tripped for there was still some kind of commotion.

Angry, Marcellus looked back to the enemy in a hurry and saw they had all broke into a run. Marcellus ordered a charge, his body driven to action by a sudden rush of energy and urgency. Their quarry had run in the direction of Slade's unit initially, obviously not seeing them at first.

Marcellus heard a man shouting orders, saw him pointing, and the group of six men divided into two, running toward their two best escape routes. The group nearest Marcellus consisted of three men, including the one who had given the order to disperse. This was the group Marcellus gave orders to zero in on.

He ran in a direction that he hoped would cut them off, pushing himself to move faster, his heart pounding in his chest, his body pulsing with determination, his mind analyzing the ever changing situation. The three men were aware of him and countered his approach with a switch in direction which he matched.

The distance closed between him and the enemy, but his own knights fell behind as he outran them. The nearer he came, the more alone he was. As he came close enough to draw his sword— which he did with a ringing sound that was swallowed by the wind—he knew that if they decided to turn and fight, it would be three against one.

The man nearest him turned in defense as his fellows ran on. Marcellus did not slow, only slashed his sword across the man's shoulder before he had a chance to swing. The man hollered and fell to the ground as Marcellus passed.

Marcellus ran on, trusting his knights in the rear to detain the man who had fallen. The enemy who had given the order, the leader Marcellus surmised, was in front. *That's the one I want.*

On the leader's tail was the second man and fast approaching them both was Marcellus who shifted his sword to his left hand, pulled a dagger from his belt, and flung it sharply. The nearest man went down yelling, the dagger lodged in his thigh.

Still flying over ground, Marcellus leapt over the man, in hot pursuit of the enemy he wanted most. He was almost there. The leader spun and slashed his sword with such unexpected speed that Marcellus almost didn't block it.

Sparks flew as their blades collided and the two men circled around each other, trying to tame the momentum of their run. The leader swung his blade at Marcellus again, but this he anticipated. He brought his blade up, braced himself.

As the two swords met Marcellus forced his blade in a fierce circle around that of the other, gaining the leverage he sought. He yanked his sword to the left and pulled his opponent's sword free of his grasp.

Shock and alarm registered on the man's face as he stumbled to reach after his sword. Marcellus lunged at him. He purposely kept his aim off, intending only to further force his opponent off balance and send him to ground. It worked.

The leader dodged, fell on his back, sliding, and looked up in time to find the tip of Marcellus' sword at the base of his neck. The two men froze. As Marcellus' knights came up around him, the leader closed his eyes in resignation.

Donnelly led his knights and their sole captive back to the still empty platform and down the other valley guarded on one side by Slade's unit and on the other by the new unit added by the prince. He didn't know who was heading that one, but they were nearest. He sought them to find out if they had seen anything unusual. He did not know where the last watchman had disappeared to, Janus either. While Donnelly feared the worst could have happened, he could not imagine a single man taking Janus down.

Once he rounded the line of trees, he saw two groups of men in the valley. He halted. One group was near to him, the other much further away. Both were moving toward the other and not at a concerning speed. They were too far for him to know for sure who these people were so he sent out the call only Caedmonian knights would know to answer. When the answer came he continued his advance with swiftness, proceeding to the nearest group who had halted when they heard his call.

It turned out to be Slade's unit, or rather some of them, with two men in captivity. Slade was not with them. The knights present explained what had happened, saying there were six attackers advancing on the Sakkaran camp. Three came toward Slade's unit and three went in another direction, pursued by the unit led by the prince.

"The prince?!"

"We heard him giving the orders to chase."

Donnelly looked around instinctively, now glad Janus was nowhere to be seen.

"The three that came toward our unit split off again," the knight continued. "We split as well and caught these two, but I don't know what happened to the other one. Commander Slade went after him."

Donnelly began explaining what had happened with the Sakkaran watchmen. As he was talking, the other Caedmonian unit was nearing and sure enough, Donnelly saw Prince Marcellus among them.

"What happened to the other watchman?" the knight asked Donnelly. Before he could respond, the question was answered for him.

"He's right here."

Donnelly spun toward the sound of Janus' voice. There she was, her bow slung easily over her shoulder, leading along the missing watchman. An arrow protruded from the man's calf, making it difficult for him to walk and impossible to run away. Donnelly's relief at seeing Janus safe and the last watchman captured, quickly turned to panic. She did not know the prince was here.

"He tried to get away from me," she said, oblivious to Donnelly shaking his head no, willing her to hush, "but I got in a shot."

Donnelly stole a glance at the prince and saw immediately that it was too late. Marcellus was approaching rapidly, his eyes locked on Janus in disbelief.

"It was a bad shot," the watchman growled.

"Says who?" she said indignantly. "I got you exactly where I wanted you." She came up to Donnelly and leaned in with a grin. "Dead men tell no tales." But the last word trailed away, her brows furrowed together. Her eyes widened and she spun to find herself eye to eye with the prince.

She glanced at Donnelly in a panic, but there was nothing he could say. The day of reckoning had come at last. She hastily bowed her head. "Your Highness."

Prince Marcellus looked from Janus to Donnelly in astonishment. He looked to the surrounding men, all of whom had stilled uncomfortably. The prince's eyes narrowed. He apparently deduced by their lack of surprise that everyone here already knew of the presence of a woman in the king's army. Everyone but the prince.

"What," Marcellus began lowly, his eyes firmly on Donnelly, intense and fierce, "is this woman doing here?"

"Capturing a traitor who otherwise would have escaped," she said.

Shut up, Janus. Shut up.

219

Marcellus turned to her sharply. "I did not ask the question of you and when you are addressing your prince you would do well to remember it."

Donnelly internally cringed at this. Marcellus was not one to demand formalities (he always received them without asking anyway) and Donnelly knew the prince had made that statement not out of pride but out of fury. This was going to be as bad as he feared.

Janus immediately bowed her head. "I meant no disrespect, your Highness."

Marcellus turned back to Donnelly. Another knight ran up. "Your Highness, you need to see this." The knight turned back toward the way he had come, watching the prince, eager for him to follow.

Marcellus leaned in to Donnelly. "I'm not through with you." He glanced at Janus. "Either of you."

Marcellus followed the knight. With a worried glance at each other, Donnelly and Janus followed, too.

They were led to the last of the missing attackers, lying on the ground, severely wounded and barely breathing. Not far from him lay Commander Slade in a pool of his own blood. He was already dead.

Thirty-Two

The attacker found with Slade was so badly injured that he never made it back to camp alive. That left seven prisoners for Marcellus to deal with. Not to mention the woman.

Marcellus was up at first light, his body still groggy from the short amount of sleep, but his mind alert with all he had to do. With the rising sun, he sent a messenger to the Sakkaran camp to summon Prince Akren. Marcellus thought he should probably wait for Akren to arrive before questioning the prisoners, but found it difficult to resist the urge to do it himself. He did not know how effective Akren's methods would be and wanted to avoid mistakes. Still, he thought the most appropriate thing he could do was prime the prisoners for questioning and wait. Ideally, Donnelly would be the man he would send for that task. He was Marcellus' most skilled commander in that area—his most skilled commander period—which only made this whole issue with the woman more difficult to understand. Marcellus didn't know what was behind it but he was ready to find out.

When he left his tent, the camp was starting to stir. Many men were out and about, a few wandering toward the kitchen though it was still a little too early for breakfast. On his way to Donnelly's tent, Marcellus scanned around for the woman. After a fair bit of looking he found her some distance away, walking purposefully with a handful of knights following her. She was relatively young, around Marcellus' age, with dark brown hair she wore in a long, thick braid reaching all the way to her waist, making no attempt to conceal her gender. She had a bow and quiver slung over her shoulder. Marcellus moved nearer, not sure yet if he wanted to summon her or just observe.

"Hold up, Janus," said the knight nearest her, increasing his pace to keep up.

221

"Not now, Flanagan." She looked distracted, worried. Marcellus didn't gather it was about the men following her. They did not appear to be threatening her in any way. Marcellus slowed his pace, following them unawares.

"Ah, you've finally met your match, have you?" Flanagan said, in a friendly, jesting way. Janus rolled her eyes and didn't slow.

"Later."

"I never thought I'd see the day," he said. He stopped, amused, and called after her. "Janus is *scared*." Flanagan leaned forward on this last word, apparently knowing the effect it would have on her, for she stopped and spun. Marcellus stopped too, staying close to a tent and out of sight.

"Of *you?*" she said.

Flanagan laughed, pleased with his results. "Then why won't you duel me?"

"Because I..." she said forcefully, but she stopped herself. She looked around at the knights watching, then back to Flanagan. She smiled, her posture relaxing. "I don't know if it's worth my time."

Flanagan nodded and gestured her to go on.

She rolled her eyes and said, "What do I get if I win?"

The excitement of the group increased noticeably. Marcellus was under the impression he was watching some sort of ritual. He was too curious to stop it.

"What do you want?" Flanagan asked.

Janus shrugged, looked to be casting about for something. "Your meats ration," she said finally, as if it made no difference to her.

"Only that? Are you trying to keep your girlish figure?" The men laughed. Marcellus saw nothing wrong with her figure. Indeed, though she was of fair height for a woman, she looked much too delicate to be of any use as a knight. She tossed her bow and quiver to the side. "Your meats ration *for a week*," she said, pulling a sword from a fellow knight.

Flanagan hesitated. More than anything, that got Marcellus' attention. Why was this knight, who was easily twice her size, hesitating?

222

"No? Don't challenge me only to change your mind." She put on an air of exasperation, but her half-smile gave her true feelings away.

"Now Flanagan's scared," another knight taunted.

"Alright," he said, holding out his hand to the crowd. "Alright, agreed. Meats ration for one week."

There was an expectant pause. Janus raised one eyebrow at him. "And you Flanagan? What do *you* want?"

Everyone laughed and he smiled sheepishly.

She rolled her eyes again, but she was clearly amused. "Do none of you have any originality?" She put her hand on her hip and gestured to him with the sword. "Alright then, but you have to say it."

He smiled boldly and raised his sword. "My prize," he said loudly, "will be a kiss."

They all whooped and hollered. Marcellus groaned. Janus shook her finger mockingly. "I know you don't dare ask for more."

The crowd laughed but Flanagan just shook his head. "Are you ready?"

She raised her sword, the crowd hushed, and Marcellus found himself holding his breath. Janus and Flanagan circled each other slowly, sizing each other up, waiting for someone to make a move. It was a ridiculous match, this huge knight against a woman. She wore an amused grin but he was all seriousness. Just when Marcellus thought he should stop it before she got hurt, Flanagan made the first move. It was nothing spectacular—the usual opening move—and she blocked it easily. This was followed by more moves that were routine enough, but Marcellus was impressed to see her managing it. She didn't look to have strength enough to wield a blade. A small crowd gathered and Marcellus had to adjust his position to keep them in his sights.

Flanagan attacked her with a frightening lunge and Marcellus jerked forward as if to stop it himself. She matched it with such startling speed that Marcellus froze and raised his brows. Flanagan was attempting to recover but using her speed to work his size against him, she got him off balance. The next thing Marcellus knew it was over. Her sword was pointing at the tip of Flanagan's neck and they each froze. She had won.

223

The men cheered and Marcellus slowly crossed his arms in front of his chest, considering things.

"I hope breakfast is soon," she said, tossing the borrowed sword back to its owner who caught it smartly. "I'm starving."

Out of the corner of his eye, Marcellus saw Donnelly tentatively approaching. Marcellus kept his eyes ahead, watching Janus and Flanagan shake hands good-naturedly. When Marcellus finally looked to Donnelly he was watching the scene with a kind of dread. "You should know," Marcellus began, "I do not believe sparring for a kiss is the kind of distraction my men need."

Donnelly blushed, an amusing sight on this bulky man. "Please, your Highness. I doubt anyone would really kiss her even if they won. They have too much respect for her. It's all lighthearted now."

Marcellus faced Donnelly fully, arms still crossed. "What do you mean 'now'?"

"Well," Donnelly looked around. "Admittedly when she first came on there was a bit of... some of the men..." He looked pained. "They were a little..."

"Forward?"

Donnelly nodded. "She said they'd have to beat her in a duel if they wanted to... well... but she's an archer so they thought she was just playing hard to get. After a while, when no one could beat her and after they saw her in a battle, things changed. She became just one of the men."

"Except for the sparring for kisses."

Donnelly sighed. "I swear it's not a problem, your Highness."

Marcellus was incredulous. "What's the story here? Do you love this woman?"

"What?" He sounded mortified.

"She's young for you but she's an attractive woman." Marcellus said this a little defensively. Was it such a ridiculous suggestion?

Donnelly blinked unexpectedly at this. "No, your Highness. You know I'm loyal to my wife."

"I should hope so." Neither man spoke for a moment. "No one has beaten her?"

"No, your Highness."

224

"How many have tried?"

"More than I've kept track of." Donnelly looked at Marcellus apologetically. "I'm sorry I kept this from you, your Majesty. I have no good explanation to offer except to say I once judged her to be a good asset and she has proven my judgment correct. I know that doesn't excuse my deception. I am willing to submit myself to the consequences."

Marcellus considered Donnelly. He had served most of his time under the king with a long history of loyalty. Marcellus even considered him a friend. "Have you kept any other secrets from me?"

"No, your Highness. I would not have kept this one if I felt it would place you or the king or Caedmonia in any danger. I would forgo my life before that."

"Yet there are knights in my army who knew you were deceiving me."

Donnelly lowered his eyes and nodded. He truly looked regretful. "The men honor you. They only held their tongues out of fondness for her. When I took her on, I made it clear I would not mention her presence to you, but I would not lie about it if asked either. Neither did I instruct anyone else to keep the secret. They did it on their own. I admit, I did not think it would last more than a few weeks."

"How long has she been with you?"

Donnelly hesitated. "A number of years, your Highness."

Years? Marcellus looked to where Janus had been. She and the men were gone. He looked back at Donnelly. "What fate do you think you deserve for your crime?"

"I will accept whatever punishment you give me, your Highness."

"I am sure you will." Marcellus let this statement fall with force, for it would be the most powerful consequence Donnelly would face. He waited a moment. "You still have not answered the question I asked you."

Donnelly nodded. He looked at Marcellus with the strength and resolution Marcellus had always respected in him. "To be relieved of my position, your Highness."

Some may think this a soft punishment for deceiving the crown, but Marcellus knew Donnelly would consider this a fate worse than death.

He would be disgraced, without means to support himself, and stripped of his life's purpose.

"I see," Marcellus said. "I shall take that into advisement. Meanwhile, we have seven prisoners taking up room in seven tents. Keep them isolated, but ready them for questioning. Prince Akren will arrive shortly, I am sure, and we will want to find out what they know."

Donnelly looked at him, stunned. "Your Highness?"

Marcellus gave Donnelly a half smile. "You know I dislike repeating my commands. Get going."

Donnelly smiled too, unable to conceal his relief. "Yes, your Majesty. Thank you." He turned to leave but halted, his relief turning now to concern. "But... Janus?"

There was an expectant pause as Marcellus tried to ascertain the right thing to do. He had never before encountered such a situation. "I make no allowances for weakness," Marcellus finally said. "I expect her to carry her weight."

Donnelly nodded. "That and more, your Highness."

Marcellus nodded, too. "Off with you then." Donnelly smiled and left, Marcellus watching him go.

A woman in his army. And Marcellus allowing it.

He hardly knew himself.

Marcellus expected Prince Akren to arrive much sooner than he did but the prince did not come until noon. He had spent the morning gathering information about the two watchmen, information he now planned to take into his interrogation of them. He wanted to meet with them first but Marcellus was eager to get to the attackers, particularly their leader. Marcellus suggested they divide their efforts and meet together later. He was glad not to have to press too hard for this. Akren readily agreed. Marcellus walked toward the tent where the leader was being held captive. As he approached, Donnelly exited the tent and stopped when he saw Marcellus nearing.

"Is the prisoner ready?" Marcellus asked without stopping.

"Yes, your Highness."

"Good." Marcellus reached for the tent flap and Donnelly started speaking urgently.

"You should know I assigned some knights from my unit to help." Donnelly seemed uneasy, obviously still on edge from their last conversation.

"With seven prisoners I would expect no less," Marcellus said, turning back to the tent. "Come with me."

He opened the flap, stepped inside, and saw why Donnelly was nervous. Sitting on the floor at the opposite side of the tent was the leader, leaning against a stack of crates, his hands tied behind his back. Nearby were two of Donnelly's men. Or rather, one man and one woman.

The knight and Janus both bowed when Marcellus entered, but Marcellus looked back over his shoulder to glare at Donnelly. Donnelly offered a guilty shrug.

Not wanting any distractions from the prisoner's point of view however, Marcellus continued on as he normally would. He passed Janus and the knight, nodding to each slightly, meeting her eyes for the briefest moment, then turned to the prisoner.

Marcellus stood without speaking, his hands behind his back, watching the prisoner with a firm gaze. On Marcellus' opposite side Donnelly held back, waiting.

The prisoner looked at Marcellus defiantly at first but after a time, when Marcellus neither moved nor spoke, the man's unease grew and he looked away. Marcellus kept still, eyeing the man calmly. The man began to fidget looking everywhere but at Marcellus. Marcellus used his instincts to help him know how long he could go on this way and leave the man feeling vulnerable and willing to cooperate without going on too long and triggering a defensive mechanism and stubborn silence.

Finally he spoke, "What are you after?"

"The princes of Sakkara." He said it with a strong voice. Marcellus could see why he was the leader. Still, there was weakness underneath and Marcellus did not fail to detect it.

"No," Marcellus said. "What are you after?"

The man narrowed his eyes and looked at the faces in the room. Marcellus noticed he looked at each person with no small amount of trepidation, including the woman, which told Marcellus that at least Donnelly's knights had done their job. "I don't know what you're talking about," he said.

"I'm sure you do."

The man looked down at the ground and said again, "I don't know what you're talking about."

Marcellus walked to a nearby crate, upon which was the man's sword. Marcellus unsheathed it slowly. The metal scraped and rang, long and ominous. Marcellus let the sound die away before turning back to the prisoner. He made a show of examining the blade, which was dull in a few places, nicked in others. Still deadly enough. Running his hand across the hilt, Marcellus glanced at the prisoner. The man startled and looked away. "No Norrland crest on this one," Marcellus said.

"Why would there be?" he said roughly, but he would not look at Marcellus. Marcellus was gaining the advantage.

Marcellus placed the tip of the sword on the earthen floor. "You searched the tent of Prince Rowan and found nothing. You tortured Prince Hugh for something."

"That was for pleasure," he said darkly.

Marcellus made no reaction to this remark and said levelly, "Tell me what you're after."

"You'll just kill me anyway."

"Rich of *you* to insult *my* honor, murderous dog." The man said nothing, fuming. Marcellus saw his prisoner's rage was growing in his helpless situation. Marcellus pressed him. "Executions for murder are swift. Since you are useless to me, you'll hang before the sun sets as Prince Akren watches on."

The man faced Marcellus then, his eyes wild with hate. "Too bad you weren't next! It would've been a pleasure to slit your throat in the dark of night!"

In a flash, Janus had her bow and arrow drawn, aimed at the man's face. Her movements had been so quick Marcellus only saw them in a blur. Her eyes were alight, angry. The knights in the room looked at her in shock, the prisoner in open fear, but Marcellus managed to keep his poise. He held up his hand and Janus reluctantly lowered her bow, the stunning anger in her eyes slowly ebbing away. He looked at her a moment longer than he normally would have, taking in her intensity, not sure what to make of it.

Marcellus looked away and crouched in front of the trembling prisoner. Death was easier to face from a distance, and she had just brought his fear of it to the fore. Marcellus intended to take full advantage of this, unexpected though it was. He noticed a small hole in the crate near the man's head and surmised Janus had already let her arrow fly once at the man. Marcellus knew she had missed him on purpose.

The prisoner noticed what Marcellus was looking at and Marcellus met his eye. "I'm not near as kind as she is," he said lowly. "You tell me what you're after."

The man, shaken, could not look at Marcellus. "What if I do?"

"You may find prison less offensive than the grave."

The man closed his eyes. "It matters not to me."

Marcellus waited.

The man shrugged, his eyes still closed in resignation. "A stone," he said quietly. "It was a stone." Icy dread dropped through Marcellus' body. *He can't mean what I think he means.* Marcellus stood and paced away. The terrible dread followed him. This movement, this pacing away from the prisoner and stopping, was a signal to Donnelly to take over. Marcellus listened, his back turned, his mind working.

"What kind of stone?" Donnelly now asked.

"Just... a stone."

"What? A diamond?"

"I don't know. I was only told each prince has a stone and if I asked about it they would know what it was."

Each prince has a stone? Marcellus thought. *What's going on here?*

"Why not just raid the treasury?" Janus asked. "Who carries a stone of enough value to be worth all this trouble?"

Marcellus felt its warmth against his chest. He resisted the urge to put his hand over it, protect it.

229

"I don't know. We were supposed to get the stone and kill the prince."

Marcellus turned at this, but it was Donnelly who spoke. "You were going to kill him even after getting the stone? Did you get stones from the first two?"

"No."

A sudden almost uncontrollable anger overtook him and Marcellus rushed up to the man with fierce urgency. He got in the man's face and the man cringed away. "Who wants it?" Marcellus demanded, his voice frightening even to his own ears.

"I don't know."

"You're lying and I don't spare the necks of liars!"

"No!" The man shook his head, eyes wide with terror. "I don't know who. I was hired by a man in Treton who took the job from someone else, but he didn't tell me who."

Marcellus could see he was telling the truth. He straightened, breathing hard, and tempered his rage with difficulty. "Well then, he'll be who we talk to next won't he?"

Thirty-Three

It was when they stopped for lunch that Praea discovered the lake.

They had been traveling in a northeasterly direction for most of the morning and had stopped by a group of thickleberry bushes, deciding to collect as many as they could because the bushes were becoming more sparse and the berries would help stretch their rations. In the same spirit, Nicolai was searching nearby for signs of game. He was a short distance away from her when Praea came to the edge of a clearing with a massive lake lying in the center. She called to Nicolai to come see, but did so without removing her eyes from the lake, mesmerized. It seemed to be bathed in moonlight. "Isn't that incredible?" she asked when she felt Nicolai at her side. The water was clear as cut glass, motionless, illuminating the blue light of a moon though the sun had fully risen, though she felt its warmth even now on her skin.

"What?" Nicolai asked.

"I've never seen anything like that."

"What are you looking at?" He reached up and put his hand in the air, leaned in like he was looking at something very near to him. He bent his fingers curiously.

"What..." she started to ask. She heard a noise. Like his fingers were scraping something she couldn't see. It sounded like tree bark.

She reached out quickly, not trusting her own eyes, and felt nothing. He seized her arm and pulled it back. "How...? You went right through it!"

"Through what?"

"The tree."

"I don't see a tree. I only see the lake."

"What lake?" He looked around, eyes searching, brows furrowed.

Praea stared at the lake in dread. "It... It's right in front of us." It was right there. Still and calm as death. Nicolai turned and began scanning the area, as if afraid someone were near. Praea, however, knew there was no one. Only the lake. She took two steps toward it, into the moonlight and felt cool, as if night had descended over her.

She looked back to Nicolai. He was gone. A shiver ran through her, but not from the cold.

"Nicolai?"

She took a step back in his direction. She heard a whispering sound behind her and spun around, heart pumping madly. She saw nothing... no one... but the whispering continued. The hairs stood on her neck and she looked around. Everywhere she turned the whispering seemed to chase her, like it was coming from nowhere and everywhere at the same time. She couldn't understand the words. They blurred and twisted together, like several voices talking at once but she couldn't understand what any of them were saying.

On the right side of the lake, still far from where she stood, she saw a woman coming out of the trees, cloaked in deep blue and carrying a lantern. Another woman came behind her, and another. A line of women emerged, walking solemnly toward the water with its knife-like edge, perhaps a dozen women in all. The whispering became louder, surrounding her, bombarding her, a confusion of sound.

Amidst it all, one word became recognizable: *Praea.*

Her heart stopped. The woman at the head of the line turned her head and looked in Praea's direction—right at her it felt. The whispering swelled to a roar and she heard it again. It came from the woman looking at her: *Praea.*

Praea stumbled back frantically, blindly, until she was in the glaring sun again and felt someone against her back, grabbing her arms. She screamed.

"Praea!" It was Nicolai. He spun her and she saw Nicolai looking at her in wild alarm. She had backed right into him.

"What happened? Where did you go?" Panting, she looked over her shoulder. She could still see the lake, but the women were gone. The whispering was gone. A lock of her hair had come loose and fallen over her eyes. She brushed it back with trembling fingers. "The lake," was all Praea could say.

Nicolai rubbed her arm in concern. "There is no lake there."

"There *is*."

"Alright," he said. "Alright. We're getting you out of here." He started going toward the right, but Praea pulled on him.

"No! Not that way. The women are over there."

"What women?"

"I can't see them anymore, but I know they're there. We have to go around. This way." She started walking to the left, not caring how much it would add to their journey to go around the lake in this direction. She wanted to avoid going anywhere near where she had seen the women emerge from the trees.

Nicolai led the horse, looking around. "It's an illusion," he said. "No one's here."

"It's not an illusion." But she looked around too.

"Something's not right," he said.

"Let's just hurry."

They mounted the horse and headed north again. This time she was the one holding the reins since Nicolai could not see the lake she knew they needed to avoid.

"How far north?" Nicolai asked.

"It's a big lake," she said and urged the horse into a trot. They traveled in silence. Praea only slowed the horse when the terrain demanded it.

"I don't like this Praea. This is too far. We shouldn't be going so far away."

"So far away from what?"

He did not answer and she pushed the horse on. She did not stop until they had gone far enough north that she could no longer see the lake through the trees. There was a stream nearby and they stopped to allow the horse to drink. Nicolai quickly filled their flasks, eager to move on. "Can you still see it?" he asked.

"No."

"Can we go east now?"

Praea nodded. *What happened? Why couldn't Nicolai see it? And my name. I heard my name.* She kept glancing in the direction of the lake. Nicolai watched her helplessly.

"Someone put a spell on you. We need to keep going." He brought the horse to her.

"There's no spell on me," she said. "There's a spell on the lake."

A rustling caused them both to turn. They looked over a stretch of trees not much different from all the other trees they had passed on their journey that day. There was no noise. No movement. Nothing to cause alarm.

Except that they *were* alarmed.

"Get on the horse," Nicolai said quietly, not wanting to take his eyes from the trees. Praea pulled herself up, the saddle creaking. He heard the rustling again. The horse's ears pricked. This time Nicolai saw something, too. The underbrush beneath a tall pine not far away had moved before becoming still again. This was different from pixie movement. It was larger, more erratic, and much, much quicker.

Nicolai made to take the horse's reins but the underbrush moved again, now swirling around them in a rapid arc. The horse reared in alarm and Praea threw her arms around the horse's neck, trying to stay on. When the movement finally stopped, Nicolai saw what it was. The horse bolted away out of Nicolai's reach. He looked back to the creature that was now only a stone's throw away.

It was the size of a wolf—and Nicolai would have gladly placed a wolf in its place—but this was a nintu, its black, watery eyes looking right at Nicolai. Crouched on all fours, the nintu's legs were short, its stocky body sparsely covered in wiry fur and slung low over the ground. A low sound hissed through the air as its wide, flat face split open to reveal a double row of jagged, sharp teeth. Perched on top of its round head were bat-like ears, with a tuft of coarse hair at the tip of each. What made the nintu truly deadly was its claws, raking at the ground. Silvery and razor-sharp, they looked like the long metal blades of scythes. If the nintu got hold of him, it could shred skin, muscle, and bone with equal ease.

234

Nicolai heard the stomping of hooves, some distance away, as Praea fought to get the horse under control. He did not take his eyes from the nintu but in a blink it bolted. Nicolai barely had time to leap out of the way, claws slashing the air beneath him as he did so. He spun and faced the nintu where it had stopped a short distance away, its fierce mouth open and ready, claws glinting and piercing the ground under it. Nicolai heard the rustling of leaves off to his right. A second creature was approaching. Heart pounding, Nicolai pulled his hunting knife from his belt. "Hurry, Praea!"

He caught a glimpse of the second nintu racing toward his side. He heard the pounding of the horse coming at full gallop. The first nintu in front of him gave a low, gravelly growl. This nintu sprung toward him but Nicolai pulled back and flung the knife so hard he heard it cutting through the air. His aim was sure. The knife lodged in the creature's chest, propelling it onto its back.

The horse came tearing into view, Praea bringing it to an abrupt halt as the second nintu appeared, then swerved off in a different direction, startled by the appearance of the horse.

"Get on!" Praea said, reaching to him. The horse was dancing and threatening to run again. Nicolai scrambled on as the creature came up on their left. Nicolai clung to Praea as the horse bolted into a wild run.

Looking back, Nicolai saw the blur of the nintu racing up behind. And gaining. They darted through the trees, more than once ducking under low-hanging branches. He caught a glimpse of a small cave and had the sudden, unpleasant thought of nintus swarming out of it. Nearly on them now, the creature leapt and swung its scythe-like claws so near the horse that it reared wildly. Nicolai and Praea both slid off backwards, crashing on their backs. The horse bolted again and the creature tore after it.

They scrambled to their feet, panting, straightening in time to see the nintu charging toward them. Nicolai saw a broken branch lying on the ground and dove for it while Praea bolted in the opposite direction. It was she who the nintu followed. It sprang up and caught its claws on her skirt as it trailed behind her. She shrieked and spun and the creature circled around with her, the material ripping. Nicolai had the terrifying vision of the nintu severing her leg in two.

"Get off!" Nicolai roared and swung the branch at the beast as it came round. Nicolai hit it dead on, but not before its back claws, glinting darkly, stretched out behind it and sliced through the inside of Nicolai's calf.

Nicolai roared again, searing pain shooting up his body. He stumbled into Praea who caught him around the chest. The nintu went flying from the blow, dropping into a roll on the ground.

Gripping the branch like a spear, Nicolai glanced at his leg just long enough to confirm it was still there. He locked his sight on the creature, white pinpricks of light dancing on the edge of his vision.

The nintu rolled off its back and onto its feet, facing away from them. Nicolai took several lunging, painful steps toward it. The nintu shook its head as if trying to shake off a daze as Nicolai raised the branch. He brought down the tip with all his strength, piercing the sharp edge through the nintu's body, pinning it to the ground. The nintu screeched as it clawed at the ground. Nicolai's leg burned, sharp pain cutting clear to his shoulders. "AARRRR!" Still he held the branch fast as the creature slowed its clawing, shuddered, and at last fell still.

Nicolai let go of the branch, stumbled, and collapsed to the ground, clutching his blood-soaked leg.

Praea was at his side in an instant. "Let me see." She pried his hands away and dark blood ran thick. Across the inside of his calf, a gash the length of his hand gaped open. It looked deep. Much too deep.

Praea tore a strip of fabric from her dress and began wrapping it just below his knee. Nicolai removed his water flask from his belt, brought it over the wound and poured, groaning as he quickly and firmly spread open the skin so he could see better. Praea gasped. Pain swept over him in a nauseating wave. He let go. He saw what he needed to see. The nintu had cut into the bone.

"Oh, Nicolai." She urgently tightened the binding. The blood slowed, but did not stop. She pressed her hands firmly to the wound, blood seeping through her fingers.

With shaking hands he grabbed his bag and dumped its contents onto the ground. His hands were dark with blood and he wiped them on his pants, removing the blood as best he could. He looked first for henbane, but he didn't have any and knew there wouldn't be any around. He put a gisem leaf under his tongue instead. It would be too mild to do much good, but he did it anyway. He stiffly gathered elm leaf, hazelnut, knotgrass, yarrow, while waves of pain rolled over him.

"What do you want me to do?" she asked as he crushed the elm leaf and tore the knotgrass. Her arms trembled slightly from putting so much pressure on a wound that would not staunch its flow.

"In a minute," he said, acutely aware he was losing too much blood.

"Nicolai," she said. She looked at his shirt. "Use it."

He looked down at his tunic, underneath which was the stone. It was warm, as it always was, but not lit. He shook his head. "I can't..." He wanted to say more, wanted to explain that he had no control over this stone and what it did or did not do.

"But..."

He only shook his head again, trying to clear it, trying to focus.

She stopped, sighed. "Alright."

He used magic to crush the hazelnut into fine powder. Though he cupped his hands, hid it as best as he could, the light sparked between his fingers. Praea jerked back in surprise. "Cup your hands," he said.

She removed her hands from his leg and a fresh surge of blood released from the wound. She wiped her hands on her dress and cupped them. He placed the mixture in her palms and grabbed the water flask. "Try not to let the water through." As he poured, some of the water seeped through and she tightened her fingers together.

"Sorry," she said.

"You're fine." He added more water, worked the mixture into a paste, then magically extracted the fluid from the yarrow stem, its substance glittering and sparkling. He worked that in as well.

Praea looked at him.

He scooped the finished ointment onto the tip of his fingers and hovered with it over the wound. Blood continued to seep out of it. As he thought about what needed to be done, his heart began to pound and a wave of nausea hit him. He knew he could not do it correctly, not to himself. He put the paste back in her hand. "I need you to do this," he said. Her eyes widened. "Rub it far in," and her face went pale. "Cover the bone. Make sure you get it in the bone."

"Nicolai..."

"You must..." he said, feeling distinctly lightheaded now. "I can't do it to myself."

She pressed her lips together and nodded.

He closed his eyes.

When she plunged her fingers into his wound and pressed against the bone, he could not restrain his scream. He felt the blood drain from his face and chest. The pain exploded over him.

"It's almost over," she said. "It's almost over," she said again and again, and all he knew was the pain and her words. He clung to them. *It's almost over. It's almost over.*

Then it *was* over. His body sagged and she clung to him, kissing his cheek, "I'm sorry. I'm so sorry." He was sweating, shaking, but Nicolai could feel the ointment working. The pain was slowly abating, receding in sluggish, reluctant waves. Praea released him and put her hand on his back. "You should..." she began, but her eyes had caught sight of the wound. She stared at it in open awe.

Nicolai looked, too. The flow of blood stopped first. The wound began to close, constricting and thinning until it sealed together. When a thick, dark, shiny scab formed, Nicolai leaned forward to examine it. The wound had been deep and healing would take time to complete. This was good enough for now.

He sighed with relief. "Thank you."

Praea looked stunned. "How can you not be a wizard? Are you part of the Order?"

He shook his head. "No. Nothing like that." He put his hand to her cheek, smiled wearily. She knew by this he would say no more. She sighed, but did not press him.

Nicolai looked around, fully aware of their surroundings for the first time. The nintu was not far away, the spear-like branch still protruding from its back. Beyond that Nicolai saw four blackened trees.

238

Blackened. Not charred, not burned, just black. Even the leaves were in place on their branches, each black and frail as parchment.

The blackened trees flanked each side of a long corridor of trees that were still alive and not black, but dark and evil-looking, sparsely flaked with leaves, their twisted and gnarled trunks and branches clearly visible. Their tops arched together unnaturally, leading away from where Nicolai and Praea sat.

Or was it leading toward them?

He looked behind him. The earth drew up into a great mound with a large cave in its center, the entrance he had seen earlier facing them. There must have been openings in the top of the cave because faint columns of sunlight shone down from above and dimly illuminated the interior. In his haste amidst the chaos of the chase, Nicolai had thought this was the nintu's den.

He knew now he had been wrong.

Thirty-Four

Since Corren had made a promise to Nicolai he couldn't break, that left him only one option. The gold leaf continued to nag at him. Aradia knew something, she had to. That was no ordinary leaf and defending the Phoenix was no ordinary task. But after two days of pondering Corren kept returning to the same questions without finding any answers. Of course that could have been because he wasn't exactly thinking clearly—he had not been this tired in years—but thinking clearly or not he wouldn't be able to find his answers without more information.

He had already combed through the rest of Aradia's stores but didn't find anything else unusual. In the final minutes of a long stretch of monotonous stirring he found himself looking at her locked office door. He knew he shouldn't snoop, especially after the trouble he was already in, but the situation was desperate. At least, he *felt* desperate. It was the last day of brewing and Aradia would likely be back this afternoon or evening. Any chance he had to find more information would be gone.

He checked the hourglass. Two minutes to go.

His eyes burned. He rubbed them, sighing. How he wanted to just sleep. His muscles and joints ached whether he moved them or not. Even his scalp ached. He had forgotten what true exhaustion felt like. The top of the hourglass drained its contents at last. Corren stopped stirring, turned the next wretched hourglass, and collapsed on a nearby stool. He leaned his head on the cool, wooden worktable.

He chanced to close his eyes.

A sudden feeling of falling caused him to jerk upright. He looked at the hourglass. Five minutes had passed in a breath. Corren dragged himself to his feet, went to the pump, and splashed cold water on his face and neck. He shocked at the chill. He took a cold drink but his mind was on the warmth of his stone.

Corren looked at the office door again and wondered how she had locked it.

It was shockingly easy for Corren to break into Aradia's office. Upon reflection it made sense given no one knew she was here and she probably trusted him not to snoop. That thought alone almost caused him to shut the door and mind his own business. Almost.

Around the perimeter of the small room were trunks and shelves crammed with nearly every type of magical aide a person could want. Corren stopped to covet her collection of mortars and pestles, some of porous stone, some marble, others granite, ash, oak, elm. The various materials were useful when needing to achieve subtle variations of effect from different herbs. Corren thought he could poke through her shelves all day, but he was not here to indulge his fantasies.

In the center of the room, Aradia's desk was piled with bound volumes, stacks of parchment, and a few scrolls. Corren hoped to find some answers here. He had brought the hourglass with him and gingerly set it on her desk next to a large feather quill. Corren flipped through the left stack of books: herbologies and incantation encyclopedias used for creating custom-designed spells. Nothing out of the ordinary. Nothing helpful. He moved to the stack of books on the right. Opening the cover on the first book, the leather binding worn and fraying, he read the title page:

"Magick from the Isle of Iona
(Lake of the Moon)
Dianese branch of the Order of Ceinoth."

Corren straightened in surprise. To confirm what he just read, he carefully flipped through the delicate pages. "Wait a minute." He checked the next book, then went through the other volumes. Unsettled, he closed the last book and adjusted the stack to look as if it had not been moved. He sat staring at it, hands on his knees. His mind went back to events that occurred many months ago, shortly after the Second Song had sounded. Aradia had ordered a search of every apprentice and student, not just at Tower Hall South, but throughout every branch of the Order. "What's going on?" he had asked her.

"Each of the seven branches keep their own secrets, Corren," she had said, and he nodded. He already knew that. "Highly sensitive material has been stolen from each branch."

"From *each?*" he asked. It was unheard of for such things to occur.

She nodded, angry. "I don't know how or who did it, but I guarantee I'm going to find out." After a few months of interrogations and searches, however, the issue had died down and Corren forgot all about it, until now. Because now the stolen material was on Aradia's desk, right in front of him.

She must have found who did it. This is what he told himself. Perhaps the thief is who is after the Phoenix. Corren furrowed his brows. Perhaps. He continued searching her desk, focusing on the stacks of parchment, looking—indeed hoping—for any mention of the Citadel of Zeverai. He had a distinct feeling of unease.

What he found next did nothing to settle his mind.

The hourglass was nearly out of time. Shaken, Corren had no choice but to leave and carefully lock the door behind him.

Corren was so distracted that he nearly ruined the whole potion by adding the seed from an anise star without first splitting it into two. He could not stop thinking about what he found in Aradia's office, not to mention what he found in the second room leading off the living room, which he had likewise broken into. Not that he didn't have an explanation for it all. The explanation was easy. Obvious even.

So why couldn't he shake the feeling something was not quite right?

He went through the last hour of brewing in a stupor. When the three days of nothing but potion brewing had finally passed, he felt only mildly relieved. He placed the last bottle of the potion on a shelf and looked around him. The cauldron was clean. All supplies and tools were neatly put away. He simply stood in the kitchen, looking at nothing, thinking the impossible. He knew what he wanted to do, but he didn't dare. Even for him, it was too much, too drastic, too risky.

"Foolhardy," he said out loud. He heard no conviction when he said it. He realized there was no point seeking out information if he wasn't going to act on it.

Corren looked at her office door again. Aradia would be back any time now. He would have to hurry.

Once in her office Corren moved quickly, alert to the sound of anyone approaching, his blood rushing with sudden urgency, a fresh burst of energy lighting his movements and his mind. He picked up the parchment he had found earlier, the one that gave him a chill even now. He held it in his hand as he looked for a blank sheet to write on. It took a minute but he found one he thought was a match. He held the blank parchment to the document he had taken from Aradia's desk.

"Perfect."

He set the blank parchment on the only clear area of her desk, grabbed the quill, and studied the original document carefully. It was in Aradia's familiar handwriting, long and graceful. The parchment was relatively new. If he did it right, she may never know the difference. His student days came back to him and the hours he spent each day copying manuscripts. To entertain himself, he had often tried to mimic the hand of the original document. He had gotten so good at it that the copy and the original were sometimes impossible to tell apart. He hoped now that he still knew how to do that, that he wasn't too tired to do it well.

Corren studied the spacing of the lines and letters, double checking the sizing using his finger. Carefully as he could without taking too much time, he began to make a copy. Checking against the original frequently—amazed his hand was steady while the rest of him shook— he came to the crucial point halfway down the parchment and hesitated.

This alone could give it away.

He put the quill back in the ink well so the tip would not drip as he considered things. Why was he doing this? Aradia would have no mercy for such deception. Maybe he should just tell her about the stones and the prophecy. She could tell him what was going on and everything would be clear. But he no longer wanted to tell her, and if he weren't going to tell her this was the only opportunity he would have for action. But if Aradia found out...

Corren ran through everything in his mind once more. *Just in case,* he told himself. *It's just to be safe.*

He grabbed the quill and looked at the phrase on the original:

"*Turn to the west.*"

On the copy, he carefully wrote down the words:

"*Turn to the east.*"

Quickly as he dared, he finished copying the rest. He compared the two. The forgery was an exact duplicate down to every detail—except one. He put the copy on Aradia's desk where it belonged and left her office, locking it behind him, with the original in his hands.

Corren heard a carriage approach and come to a halt, the horse snorting and the harness jangling. This was followed by gravelly footsteps on the path outside. He rushed to hide the parchment in his cloak and pulled down the cauldron only to act like he was putting it away again when Aradia walked in the door.

"Just finished?" she asked him, smiling.

He nodded and thought he should try to look normal. He settled on looking exhausted. That, at least, required no pretending.

She asked for the bottled potion and he handed it to her. She carefully put a drop of the potion on a wooden slab and bent down to examine it, her silver hair falling down in a shiny sheet. She sniffed, tasted it, and sniffed again before finally standing and pronouncing it perfectly brewed. "As usual," she said with her familiar pride.

Immediately, Corren rebuked himself. What had he been thinking? How could he do this to her? He felt guilty, did he *look* guilty? Why

244

was he just staring at her? What would he normally be saying? "How was it?" he asked.

She removed her cloak and hung it on a hook on the wall. "We're living in historic times, Corren. Do you realize how many Order members live their whole lives to see a thing like this and never get to see it?" Her eyes glistened with excitement.

His mind was spinning. If he had any sense at all he'd show her the parchment and beg the forgiveness of someone obviously driven mad by three days of brewing the Sevenfold Alcalic Base without an assistant.

"As much as I'd like to tell you about it, you'll have to forgive me if I make you wait. There is one thing I need you to do, and swiftly."

"I want to talk to you," he said.

She cocked her head. "You look so serious. Are you still thinking about the Citadel of Zeverai? I told you there is no more I can say," she said firmly. "You understand as Head of the Order I guard many secrets."

He nodded numbly. *Of course she did.*

"Time is of the essence," she said, gently now. "I need you to do this quickly. Then you'll have time to rest, I promise."

She went into the kitchen and began gathering food. "Bring your bag," she instructed. He did as he was told. She filled his bag with food while telling him he was to travel to Sheehan and wait there for a package for her. "It wasn't there when I left this morning and I don't have time to wait. It could come at any time or it may still be a few days. Go to the inn and sleep but make sure they bring you the package as soon as it is delivered. Come straight back. Understand?"

He nodded. *Tell her, just tell her.*

"I would send you with the carriage but I will need it." She looked at him sympathetically. "I know you're exhausted, but I need you to fly. There's no time to lose."

He left obediently, not knowing exactly how to tell her what he had done and dreading the look of disappointment and shock he would see on her face when he did.

ஐ ஐ ஐ

245

From the doorway, Aradia watched Corren leave, all tired eyes and dragging feet but obedient nonetheless. He was her best pupil, no question about that. Given the time frame she was working in she was glad she had made the decision to bring him on as an assistant. There was too much to do alone.

When Corren was out of sight she sent out a nightingale call and went back inside. She went into her office, took two steps inside and froze.

She looked around. Everything looked as she had left it. There was something else.

She extended her left hand in front of her, palm up, fingers tightly together. She slowly circled her other hand around it. Methodically, she reached in each direction with her right hand in a cupped shape, said "essena kapta," and pulled down on top of her other hand as if gathering something and collecting it in her hand.

Finished with this, she brought both hands in front of her, to eye level, and briskly rubbed them together. "Div ayde." She kept her eye on her hands, watching carefully. After a few seconds, she pulled her hands closer still. "Revilio." She blew on them. Wisps of gray smoke swirled out from between her hands before dissipating. This she had expected. She continued to blow until the gray matter was gone.

When she carefully opened her hands she saw what she had feared: a little brown mass that looked like a grain of rice. Pursing her lips together, she picked it up and looked at it. She knew what it meant, but put it in her mouth to confirm it.

She heard footsteps and turned to see a man at the door. "Did anyone see you coming?" she asked.

"No."

"Good. What is your report?"

When he told her, her eyes widened and she felt a chill. Actually felt a chill. This physical reaction was almost as shocking to her as the message itself. She pulled herself together. "Are you sure?" The man repeated the information. She questioned him, hunting for flaws, but no mistake had been made. In fact everything was, at last, terribly clear.

Aradia swallowed hard. "Retrieve Corren."

Praea and Nicolai lingered at the entrance of the cave, taking it all in. No one was inside but Praea saw that had not always been the case. In the center of the almost perfectly round cave, a large circle was painted on the floor in red. Five stone pillars reaching to waist height were evenly spaced around the edge of the circle. Holes in the ceiling of the cave directed a shaft of light onto the top of each pillar. A series of murals covered the right side of the cave. Nicolai and Praea moved to take a closer look. When Praea saw the first mural, her hands flew to her mouth and she gasped. *Rowan.* A man in Sakkaran armor with a prince's crown on his head lay on the ground. A sword with the Norrland crest on the hilt was embedded into his chest. Her brother's face, crudely drawn, contorted in pains of death, brought to her eyes an image even worse than her nightmares had been.

Not wanting to see more yet not able to stop, Praea looked to the next picture. A woman, a woman with long golden hair, plummeted over the edge of a cliff. Images, memories, flashed through Praea's mind.

"What is this?" Nicolai said, putting his arm firmly around her shoulder. She thought she had never heard anger in his voice before now.

Her heart pounded as if she were falling this very minute. For an instant, she no longer saw what was in front of her; her mind's eye replayed her plunge to the river. The memory of hitting the water was so powerful she felt the memory of the impact, and closed her eyes.

As if pulled against her will, she proceeded to the next picture. It displayed a bloody corpse, crown on his head, hanging from a tree. Nicolai had not told her how Hugh had died because he did not know, but Praea understood this picture just revealed it to her. Now her horror turned to anger. *Who is doing this?* Three slashes of color— red, blue, yellow—underlined the painting and below these a word: *Seezth.* Praea registered that she had seen this before, under Rowan's picture. She looked back at that mural to confirm her memory. There it was, the three colors and the word.

Nicolai pointed to the word with a strange urgency. "This word. What does it say?"

"Seezth."

"What does that mean?"

"I don't know. It's a wizard word. A spell."

The colors and the word were not under her picture, but they were under the next: this a crowned figure, long and lean, laying on the ground with his neck slit open, blood pooling all around. *Akren!* Praea's trembling hands covered her neck. *No.* "He can't be."

Nicolai stepped ahead to the next picture. She followed. She stared at it for what felt a long time, afraid to know its significance, not understanding the connection.

It was the Bridge of a Thousand Ages, retreating into the distance. At its end was a gigantic blue ball of light. Praea couldn't explain why, but this picture frightened her more than anything she had seen so far. In the next mural a cloaked figure faced away from them, facing toward the Phoenix, huge and glorious and awe-provoking even in the painting. A terrible black mark grew in the center of its chest where two rays of light were hitting it, one white, one violet. The lights came from the cloaked figure, whether from a staff or not, Praea could not tell. *That's impossible,* she thought. *It couldn't be done.*

Nicolai and Praea moved together to the last scene at the back of the cave, directly opposite the entrance. Larger than all of the others, it commanded such a huge space they had to step back in order to see it clearly.

A woman cloaked in fiery red feathers, arms outstretched with a staff in one hand, rose above the ground. She was surrounded by a red glow, a look of triumph on her face, the Phoenix blackened and dead on the ground beneath her feet.

"No," Nicolai said.

Praea stepped in closer, leaned in, eyes wide, her entire body prickling. *It can't be.* She could deny the roughly drawn face, deny the long silvery hair. There was no mistaking the familiar pendant: a braided band of ribbon encircling the silver flame. Praea felt the color drain from her face and whispered, "Aradia."

Thirty-Five

Once free from the constraints of the cabin and far enough away from Aradia that his guilt was less immediate, Corren made a decision. He wasn't going back. If he had to suffer the consequences for it later, then so be it. He still planned to go to the inn and sleep—for he desperately needed it—but after that he would head for the castle in search of Nicolai. If Marcellus wasn't back, they would head to the border to get him. Together, the Three could decide what to do next. He only hoped too much time had not been lost.

The sun sank low in the sky. Corren moved wearily along, tempted to find a tree to sleep under right then. He wondered what was in Aradia's package. He was considering whether or not to wait in Sheehan for it in order to find out when he heard a noise behind him. He turned toward it. Two men were approaching. One was stumpy, his bald head reflecting the orange light from the setting sun. The other was towering, thick-armed and wearing a false smile under a crooked, broken nose. Corren knew these men. They were the men who had attacked Nashua at her cabin, who had tried killing him to get to her, whose memories he erased so they would not remember him. And they were coming straight for him.

Corren turned to face them but took a step backwards as they approached. The bald one said, "Are you Corren?"

Corren raised his hand. "Stay away from me."

They startled and slowed their pace but did not stop. The man with a broken nose raised his dark eyebrows. "Now why would you say a thing like that?" He gave a signal to his partner, a short jab of the finger to his left. They split apart, walking toward either side of him.

"I'm warning you," Corren said.

If someone gave a signal, Corren didn't see it. They both lunged at him at once. "Privatia essa!" Corren shouted. The short one flew backwards, skidded across the ground, and hit his bald head on the trunk of an oak. The other smashed his fist into Corren's eye and Corren stumbled back, reeling. Blindly, he said another incantation, hoping his aim would be good. He heard the man fall and, blinking rapidly, Corren focused on his attacker who was now sprawled on the ground in front of him. The man began stirring but Corren said "surgia tal" and he stopped moving, unconscious.

Panting, Corren glanced at the bald man. He, too, was unconscious. Corren's eye throbbed. He was too stunned to say the spell to heal it. What were these men doing here?

Corren's legs went limp and he collapsed to the ground, his arms bound magically to his sides. He could not open his mouth. With dread, Corren realized someone else was here.

He heard footsteps behind him, the slow, steady pace of someone approaching with supreme confidence. Corren could not turn. He could not speak. He could only wait.

The crunching of gravel grew louder. Ominous. Right behind him. Now coming around to his front.

He saw the shoe poking out of the cloak first and his heart stopped as Aradia knelt in front of him. He felt a strange mixture of relief and fear. His mind was reeling. *Why is she binding me?*

"This is what I like about you, Corren," she said easily. "Look what you can do and you don't even have a staff yet." She gently placed her hand on his throbbing eye. "Ayalla," she said. The pain fled in an instant, his injury healed, but she did not look at him. She stood, faced the men on the ground, and waved her staff. "Revia madi."

The men began to stir. Aradia waited in silence. Corren watched, his mind working, resisting his own thoughts. *It can't be what I think. It can't be what I think.* The man with the broken nose groaned and pulled himself into a sit. He caught sight of Aradia. Fear overtook his countenance as he leapt to his feet. When the bald man saw Aradia he followed in short order. They gave Corren but a glance, only stood watching Aradia warily.

She raised her arm and said "eket!" as she slashed her finger in the air in front of her. Bloody gashes tore open on each of their cheeks and they clapped their hands to their wounds, their faces cringing in pain. Corren's heart began pumping madly, painfully fast.

"I expect you to do your jobs without my assistance," she said.

She said it in such a calm voice, the voice he had always known, that his mind found it impossible to bring together what he was seeing. *No, no, no. This is impossible.*

"Fetch the carriage," she said. The men took off in a dead run, still clutching their cheeks, blood staining their fingers.

Corren stared at her in disbelief, his mind a torrent of questions and emotions so confusing he could not even identify them.

She turned to him. She raised her hand. If he could've moved he would've cringed but she only said "relessa," and his bonds were loosed. "Get up," she said.

He scrambled to his feet and stumbled backward but she did not move at all, only watched him calmly.

"It's you," he said, unable to contain himself. "You're the one after the Phoenix."

"Yes," she said simply.

"But..." Corren said, shocked she had actually said it, the impact real and unavoidable now that she confirmed it. "How... how..."

"How did I deceive you?" she prompted, as if they were discussing something as ordinary as conjuring spells. "Deceive so many?" but now she smiled in a way he'd never seen before. His blood chilled. "I have talents of which even *you* were not aware, Corren. Perhaps you will allow me to explain them to you, though it is truly self-indulgent for me to do so. I have been the object of admiration by so many, yourself included, and yet *no one* knows my greatest talent. I confess it will be satisfying to share it at last."

The sound of the carriage approaching drew her attention. "Good," she said. "This will be much more comfortable." She watched it silently. He watched her. He wanted to run. She gave him a sideways glance and an amused smile, but the warning in it was clear. He stayed where he was.

The carriage drew to a stop, the brown and white horse tucking its head as the bald man pulled up sharply on the reins. The other man jumped down from the seat and opened the door with a blood-stained hand. Aradia gestured to it. "Shall we?"

Corren ran through all the incantations he knew, frantically searching for one that would help him. *But against her?* Even if he could bring himself to attack her, he knew he couldn't defeat her. At this moment he only wanted to get away.

She laughed lightly. "Come now, Corren. We both know you wouldn't stand a chance." Her smile evaporated. "Get in."

He hesitated. He didn't want to get in but the hardness in her eyes affected him as never before. He climbed into the carriage, which dipped with his weight. She climbed in after him, settling herself opposite. "Where was I? Ah, yes. My story.

"When I was a little girl, before my father sent me away to the Tower, a traveling minstrel came through Stonebridge and I snuck away to see the performance. I had never seen such a thing before and my first reaction was open-mouthed wonder. During the play, two performers in particular caught my attention.

"One actress was so unconvincing in her performance that I found my thoughts wandering. I watched the other players and wondered about their lives and even noticed those in the audience more than I paid attention to her. In short, Corren, I was bored.

"But when the *other* actress played her part," and here Aradia leaned in almost in childlike excitement, a cascade of silver hair falling over her shoulder. "I immediately lost myself in her world. I *believed* her when she cried in anguish. I *longed* for her to obtain her desires, entirely forgetting that it was all make believe. All I saw was her. All I believed was her story. Long after the show was over I still felt the effects of her powerful spell." Aradia sat back. "My first taste of *magic*." A slow, familiar smile graced her face. Corren couldn't reconcile the smiling woman in front of him with what had unfolded. Perhaps there was something else, something he was missing. Perhaps there was some reasonable explanation. He desperately wanted that to be true. He clung to that hope, his heart painfully awaiting confirmation.

"I began to ponder the difference between the two performances," Aradia went on. "What made one so insufferable, and one so utterly...

illusionary? Finally, I came to a conclusion, and I think you'll agree that this was quite clever reasoning for a girl as young as I was. The more powerful performance was made possible, I decided, because the actress had to *believe it herself,* even if only for that moment. One cannot be angry and offer a smile and hope to conceal ones anger. Your expression would be too hard, and your eyes would certainly give you away. If you are angry, and wish not to reveal that fact, then for a moment you must not just *pretend* to be happy, but make yourself believe it. If there is just cause to be angry, it will come back at a more appropriate time," and here Aradia offered an amused smile. "Meanwhile, no one *else* need know about it.

"I decided to experiment with this, practice if you will. At first my efforts mainly involved feigning sickness to get out of chores. I was a difficult child, often in trouble, and this was just one example of my short sightedness. To use knowledge like that for something as petty as avoiding chores, well..." she waved her slender hand lazily. "At least it gave me the chance to improve my performance. My parents really were terrible and offered little motivation for me to do any better. I stayed in this mode until the moment I left them.

"Tower Hall South, however," she said, her eyes glinting, "presented me with possibilities I had never before imagined. Magic, for me, was effortless, natural, not to mention satisfyingly *powerful.* I finally found my place in the world, away from the ordinary and mundane. I knew I wanted to be Head of the Order within my first week of being there. I studied those in power, and imitated them. I learned to act appropriately benevolent, just, calm-tempered... all of it. I began using what my parents termed a 'strong will' for something more worthwhile. For a reward as insignificant as dessert after dinner (the carrot on the stick my parents usually offered me) I could not quite manage a consistent performance.

"But for Head of the Order? For the most powerful position anywhere, even more powerful than a queen? For that Corren," she said, raising her eyebrows, "I could do just about anything."

His shock and revulsion were evident now. She watched him, apparently pleased by this. "People praise my brilliance," she said, "when really, they have no idea."

253

He shook his head. When he spoke his voice trembled with anger. "I gave you my trust."

"You didn't give me your trust," she said simply. "I took it."

"You're supposed to *protect* the Phoenix," he said, his voice rising. "Protect it!"

She shrugged one shoulder, showing no reaction to his growing anger. "The Order cannot protect it forever. What better way to preserve its magic than to take it for myself? Others have tried to take it before and it is only a matter of time before somebody succeeds. Should it be someone unworthy? Does it not stand to reason that it should belong to the most powerful member of the Order for the last thousand years? Who better to wield the power of the Phoenix than Aradia? It has always been my fate." Her expression changed then, became sober. "You," she said quietly, "are a surprise however. One of the Three, under my own nose."

His eyes flew wide and he held his breath. She smiled. "You need to work on your acting, Corren."

He narrowed his eyes.

"I had thought the Three were the princes of Sakkara," she said, "but now I know better."

"It was *you*? We thought Norrland..."

"An obvious scapegoat. But from the start I wondered if something had gone wrong. The first prince's death was inevitable, bound by magic he had no strength to resist, but the stone eluded me and I did not know why. I thought perhaps the magic I used had been too vague to be effective because I did not know which color stone each one had."

It took all Corren's self-control not to cover his stone with his hand, not to reveal it, suddenly more concerned about the stone than he was about himself.

"When the second prince failed to deliver the stone, even under torture, well, then I knew something was wrong. He died as he was destined to, but still I was empty handed."

Two? She's killed two?

"Meanwhile, there were a few unanswered questions about you. Not that I imagined the two were connected. Your story about the Bridge never sat right with me, however, and I set about discovering the truth." She smiled faintly. "Even on the rare occasion I make a mistake, it all sorts out eventually. Fate always works to my advantage. I make sure of that."

Corren was shaking his head. "Aradia... you murdered them. Two of their household are dead because of you."

"Three. Soon to be four."

"But... if it isn't them why kill another?"

"I cannot change what is already in motion." She furrowed her brows. "Well, I could, but it's an awful lot of work and I'm a little pressed for time."

Corren's anger snapped and burst forth in a rage. "HOW COULD YOU DO THAT?!" The carriage echoed with his shouts, reverberated in his own soul. He had never yelled at her before, never dared, never even wanted to, but now he wanted to scream, shake her, make her stop, purge her from whatever evil stained her, make her as she was before, as he had thought she was.

She did not react, but considered him carefully. "There may be things you don't know about me, but there is little I don't know about you. You thirst for power just as much as I do. You are convinced I am in the wrong, yet you refuse to see that if you were capable of taking the power of the Phoenix to yourself, you would do it."

"No, I wouldn't."

"Yes, you would." She smiled knowingly. "I saw it in your eyes when I hinted you would be my successor. Not that I have any need of one. I may not have ever said it before, but it was unspoken between us. You, the most prized, the most skilled, the most favored of all my apprentices. You were the top of the heap and you knew it. And when I said it out loud, confirmed your deepest ambition, there was a powerful hunger in your eyes. You *craved* it."

Corren swallowed hard.

"What would you have done, I wonder, if you thought someone *else* were in line ahead of you?" She leaned in, her eyes sharp. "You would not stoop to murder for something like that. But if you knew how to obtain the ultimate power... endless power and an endless life in which to wield it... you would not let anything stop you." Corren's

255

skin prickled. "And neither will I." She sat back and looked at him soberly. "I'm only doing what is necessary to ensure my success. I *could* spare your life," and he thought he saw a flash of regret in her eyes before it was gone. "I could choose one of the others. Only all together do you pose any threat to me." She shook her head. "There is no margin for error here. And as you know, Corren, I believe in being thorough."

Her words lingered as she now looked at him without emotion and any hesitation he had at defending himself was gone. "Bla—"

"Bindari," she said, cutting off his incantation. His magical binding returned and if he could have roared in frustration he would have.

She looked away from him, opened the door to the carriage, and stepped out. The man with the crooked nose waited, the gash on his cheek raw and terrible. "Tie him up and be sure to bind his mouth," she said. "Take him to the cave. I'll meet you there." She turned and looked at Corren directly. "This one I need to handle myself."

Thirty-Six

Nicolai and Praea left the cave and traveled through the Wilds with fresh haste but they were no longer headed for Dahlia. They traveled due north for as long as the sun was up to give them their bearings. At nightfall they were forced to make camp or risk becoming lost in an area of the Wilds Nicolai simply didn't know. It had been nearly dusk when they left the cave so they had not gone far. "How much farther to the border, do you think?" Praea asked.

Nicolai shook his head. "A day. Half a day maybe. I don't know."

She did not respond to this and little else was said. Her concern was for Akren and it seemed to take all her energy to hope he was still alive.

Nicolai feared for Akren too, but that was not all. Nicolai had plenty of time during the long, dark hours of the night—for this night they kept watch—to ponder what connection Praea's brothers had in all this, to hope Marcellus would still be at the border when they arrived, and to worry about Corren. Did Aradia know who he was? Would she spare him if she did? Nicolai clung to the hope that somehow, *somehow* Corren was alright and they could get to him before anything terrible happened.

Corren's hands were bound behind his back, his legs tied at his knees and ankles, and his mouth tightly covered with black cloth. He lay on the floor of the carriage, having fallen when it had lurched sharply. With no way to brace his fall he had slammed against the edge of the seat opposite him. His chest still throbbed from the impact. He managed to arrange himself on his side after that, wedged tightly against the base of the seat to brace against movement. His shoulder ached from the pressure of his awkward position but he was too tired to do anything about it. He had a vague notion that delirium was setting in. Though his survival instincts helped in his fight to stay alert, his exhaustion prevailed and he slipped in and out of sleep, often jolting awake with a feeling of terror or confusion or both.

The sun set and with it darkness swallowed him inside and out. The pale light of the moon seemed not to reach him. It was not enough.

There was no resisting now.

His mind wanted to deny all he had learned about Aradia. His heart wanted to deny it, too. Her words ran through his mind soft as silk and black as death. Persistent and merciless, they sank into him. There was no undoing them, no fleeing from them. No destroying them. She changed every memory he ever had of her. They had each one been smeared. It both angered and saddened him. He had loved her. How could he not have seen this in her?

The carriage came to a jarring halt. Corren tensed, his eyes wide, his heart pounding so hard he felt the reverberations throughout his body. The carriage shook as the men dismounted. Aradia's last words came to him. *Take him to the cave. This one I need to handle myself.* He saw again the way she looked at him when she said it and he briefly closed his eyes against it. Where was he? What was she going to do? He heard the men talking. He strained to listen and it became clear. They were only stopping for the night.

Corren unclenched his body and began to shake mildly, his hair drenched in sweat. At length his body quieted and in the aftermath of his fear, discomfort took over. The muscles in his back and thighs burned. His desire to stretch was so strong he lengthened himself as much as he could and tightened his muscles over and over in a frustrating attempt at relief. He finally relented, aching. His stomach ached as well and he thought it must have been from hunger though he had no desire for food. Not that it mattered. He heard them say they were too afraid to unbind his mouth and would not be feeding him anyway.

At long last, he slept. He dreamt of Aradia plunging a Norrland sword into his chest and he woke with a start. Darkness pressed on his eyes for a long time before he fell into another feverish dream, this one with Aradia at the Gateway. The waves of the sea churned and

258

heaved all around, but he heard no sound, only a soft buzzing in his own mind. She had one hand on the Gateway and another stretched out to him, white and pale in the darkness. She smiled. "Come, Corren. Rule with me. You know you want to."

That moment stilled and thinned as he decided what to do. Rule with her or not? Take her hand or no?

Then the Bridge began to give way and sink slowly, inevitably into the sea. He could not move his legs or arms to save himself and Aradia watched him, expressionless, as the water engulfed first his feet, his legs, chest, mouth, nose.

Corren startled awake, and wept.

Nicolai and Praea were on the move at first light. They pushed the horse hard, eating their rapidly dwindling rations atop his back and stopping only for water. Nicolai's leg was still sore and needed more ointment but he did not want to take the time to make it. By late morning they emerged from the shelter of the Wilds at last, the sun painfully dazzling after the shadows of the forest. They descended into a deep valley, flanked on its northern edge by more trees. They could either go around these to the right or proceed down the middle of a broad pass through the woods ahead and to their left. "Which way?" Nicolai asked.

A low, rumbling sound drew their attention. Nicolai pulled the horse to a stop. The noise sounded familiar.

"What is that?" Praea asked.

Nicolai recognized the sound now. "Troops." It came from the west and they followed it cautiously. The thunder of sound intensified. As the mass of men and horses became visible over the horizon, their banners became visible, too.

"Caedmonian knights," Praea breathed out, relieved.

Nicolai kicked the horse into a run and Praea's grip around his waist tightened. A small unit broke away from the troops and rode up to meet them. As they drew near, Nicolai saw a face he knew. Knight Whittaker looked at them first in confusion and, once he realized who they were, amazement.

"Princess Praea!" he said in his commanding voice. "You're safe." He looked at their torn and dirty clothes, Nicolai's gruesome scab visible through his ripped pants. "Are either of you hurt?"

"No, sir," Nicolai said.

"How on earth did you find her?"

"I looked, sir."

Whittaker raised his eyebrows.

"Where are Prince Marcellus and Prince Akren?" Praea asked.

"We are headed for their encampment now."

"And Prince Akren, he is safe?"

"I do not know, my Lady. We have come from Stonebridge."

"Is the encampment far from here?"

"No. Not far."

"We must get there right away."

Whittaker's brows were still knitted together in confusion at the situation, but he nodded his head. "We will take you there, my Lady."

Janus was sitting on an upturned crate trimming the fletching on her arrows when a general stir among the troops began to go up. She stood, the arrow in one hand, her knife in the other. She followed the direction of what appeared to be curiosity seekers. She heard someone say "It's the Princess of Sakkara," and another, "Who's that with her?"

No one seemed to know the answer to that question. Janus made her way through the crowd to find out for herself. When she saw the Princess of Sakkara, looking frightfully worn, and her mysterious rider, Janus halted in astonishment. She did not know who this man was either.

But she knew whose son he was.

Nicolai and Praea reached the encampment shortly after noon, disappointed to find Marcellus and Akren gone to Messina. Since her brother was seen alive and well just that morning Praea was partially comforted. The princes were expected back before evening. A commander named Donnelly arranged quarters for them to clean up and provided Nicolai with a clean change of clothes. "We have no dresses here, my Lady," Donnelly said, "but we have a woman we can send to Messina to obtain clothes for you. It is not far from here. Dresses there will not be as fine as you are used to, I am afraid, but it is the best we can do."

"That is very kind, commander. Thank you."

Once Nicolai bathed, changed, and ate the warm stew and cornbread from the kitchen, he went to Praea's tent to check on her. He did not intend to enter it, not wanting to compromise her in the eyes of others, but she was fraught with worry for Akren and asked Nicolai to wait. Her plea was so tender and vulnerable that he had no desire to refuse her. He was, in fact, grateful for a reason to stay. With the tent flap left open, they waited together through the long hours of the afternoon with Nicolai emerging frequently to find Commander Donnelly and inquire after Marcellus and Akren. Praea, still awaiting a change of clothes, preferred to stay in her tent.

The dress, it turned out, returned from Messina before the princes did, brought by a lady who, to Nicolai's surprise was obviously a knight. Even more surprising was the look she gave him, deep and curious, penetrating and personal. She left without a word, however. Shaken, Nicolai left Praea alone to bathe and change.

The sun was low in the sky, the western horizon ablaze with oranges, yellows, and reds, when Commander Donnelly finally came and said, "They have returned."

Praea caught sight of a few hundred troops making their way across the valley toward the encampment. Instead of going to the meeting tent as Donnelly had indicated, she headed straight for them. Nicolai thought she was moving with as much speed as she could and still carry herself in the manner of a princess, but as she descended into the valley with Nicolai and Donnelly behind her, and as the faces of the men became clear, she picked up the hem of her simple blue dress and broke into a run. Her fair hair flew out behind her, having been released of her braids long ago.

The troops came to a halt as Marcellus and Akren dismounted, coming toward her with haste and concern. It wasn't until Praea enveloped her brother in a relieved embrace that Marcellus looked to Nicolai in confusion.

"You're safe," Praea said as Nicolai and Donnelly approached. "I'm so glad you're safe."

"Praea," Akren said, holding her by the shoulders and pulling her away so he could see her face. "Pull yourself together. What happened? What are you doing here?"

In a trembling voice Praea explained what they had found in the cave. Nicolai watched Marcellus carefully. When she got to the part about the Bridge, the Phoenix, and Aradia, Marcellus gave Nicolai a significant look.

"Wait," Akren said. "Where is this cave?"

"In the Wilds," she said. "A little more than half a day from here."

"Why on earth were you in the Wilds?"

"Well," and here Praea hesitated. Nicolai understood her difficulty. How to explain the turn of events that led them into the Wilds without also explaining how she managed to survive a fall down the Great Gorge? "I wanted to get home and it was faster that way." Akren furrowed his brows, as if he thought that were no kind of explanation at all, but she continued. "I had heard about dear Hugh." She looked down. Her hands were clasped regally in front of her, but her knuckles were white as she struggled to subdue her emotion. Nicolai found it difficult not to be able to comfort her but he was forced to restrain himself. To act the farmer again.

Akren was caught off guard by her sudden emotion, blinking back tears himself but looking around at the others self-consciously. "Perhaps we should finish this conversation in private."

Akren and Praea began walking back to the camp, Donnelly following, and Marcellus gave a signal to his troops to continue on. He did not move himself and Nicolai stood by him, waiting. The troops passed by, the deep trembling in the ground rising through Nicolai's legs. Not one knight looked at their prince but Nicolai could sense their curiosity. Marcellus had the air of a commander inspecting his troops in formation—though Nicolai knew better—and they had the air of men intending to impress. When the last man passed,

Marcellus turned to Nicolai and Nicolai faced him plainly. "Where," Marcellus asked, "is Corren?"

Corren passed another night tied up in the carriage and they were off again at daybreak. He could not imagine where they were taking him and dared not think what Aradia had planned that would justify such a long journey.

Having slept some he was no longer fatigued, though he was thirsty and hungry. His hunger had passed the peak of mind-numbing pain and finally subdued to a dull and steady ache. However, the rest of his body more than made up for any lack of pain in his stomach. The long duration of being bound and his inability to change positions had led his muscles to frequently cramp in painful spasms. Terrible as this was, it was not the pain that concerned Corren the most. If ever he were loosed, he wanted to be able to move with decision and force, for his mind had gone through a stark change. He had shed the heavy cloak of grief and currently churned in a feral rage. Blind fury like nothing he had ever experienced before tore through him like fire. Wild. Uncontrollable. And hungry for release.

He no longer needed anyone to unbind his mouth.

Let them free his arms and he would kill Aradia with his bare hands.

Thirty-Seven

The carriage had been moving at a fast clip ever since their departure that morning, but now, at midday, it was starting to slow. Corren heard his captors saying, "There it is," and "I wonder if she's here yet."

Corren alerted his senses. His body tensed. A cramp in his shoulders that had come and gone all day flared up and he struggled to ignore it because he had to be ready. He had to watch for any sliver of opportunity. Through the window he saw nothing but tall pine trees passing by. He jerked and rolled onto his back, put his feet flat on the floor, and grimaced at the pain this caused in his shoulders. He arched his back to relive some of the pressure, but kept his feet where they were.

Someone sped past the window, the sound of hooves thundering by. The sharp sound of a blade being unsheathed was followed by a yell from the front of the carriage.

They came to a sudden stop and he slid roughly forward, slamming against the base of the seat. He heard men shouting, horses neighing, steel clanging, his own heart pounding. He looked to the window, saw nothing, no one. He worked his way onto his back again. Then the din of noises fell ominously silent.

The carriage shook as the driver dismounted from the bench and Corren's skin pricked horribly when he heard the sound of feet landing on the ground. Corren lifted his feet, ready to kick. The driver was approaching. A shadow cast itself through the window and the door opened. Corren thrust his legs at the man who appeared but he had been too quick and stepped back out of the way.

"Whoa, whoa, whoa." Corren knew that voice and registered who it was just as Marcellus stuck his head around the door. "It's me."

Corren closed his eyes and dropped his head in a rush of relief.

Marcellus reached in and heaved Corren into a sit, letting Corren's legs hang out the door. Corren groaned as his muscles protested the sudden movement.

Nicolai came running from the front of the carriage, Princess Praea and a handful of knights trailing behind. "Are you alright?" Nicolai asked as Marcellus pulled off the gag.

Corren tried to speak, but was too hoarse. He nodded, clearing his throat.

Marcellus started untying the ropes around Corren's hands and Corren leaned forward so he could reach better. "Did Aradia do this?" Marcellus asked.

"How—" Corren's voice cracked and he cleared his throat again. Nicolai pulled a water flask from his belt and put it to Corren's lips. Then Corren forgot his bonds and the pain and all his questions and only knew the incredible, cool taste of the water in his mouth. He closed his eyes and drank deeply. He drank long past the point when he would normally stop, drank until the flask was empty and he was left relieved but still wishing for more. "Thank you," he said.

Nicolai nodded, knelt, and started loosing the rope around Corren's ankles. "How long have you been like this?"

"It'll be two days at sunset," Corren said, his voice hoarse.

"What?!"

Corren shook his head. "How did you find out about Aradia?"

Marcellus gave a humorless laugh. "There's something you need to see."

Corren's arms were free at last and his muscles burned as he moved them. The back of his arm seized in a cramp and he clutched it with his other hand. "Eteta," he said through gritted teeth. The cramp relented only a bit, for internal injuries were particularly difficult for him to heal, but it was enough. Enough to take the edge off. He carefully stretched his arms, twisted his torso, and, once the bonds around his knees were loosed, gingerly extended his legs. He let out a long, loud sigh.

Nicolai stood. "You should walk."

"Where are we?" Corren asked. "How did you find me?"

Marcellus and Nicolai exchanged glances as Corren stood. "Come with us," Marcellus said. "We'll explain." Marcellus led him past the front of the carriage and the princess started to follow but Marcellus held up his finger. "Just a moment, my Lady."

She stopped, surprised, and Corren looked back at her inquisitively as Marcellus and Nicolai led him along. Corren just now realized the curiosity of her presence. She stayed behind as instructed but was clearly reluctant and kept her eyes on them. "I don't know why she insisted on coming in the first place," Marcellus said lowly.

"Because she wanted to know what was happening," Nicolai said.

Near Praea was the bald man, slumped on the driver's bench, eyes gaping blankly and his cheek still bearing Aradia's mark.

"She's only put herself in more danger," Marcellus continued angrily.

"I'm not disagreeing with you," Nicolai said. "I would have rather she stayed behind as well."

Looking around for the man with the broken nose, Corren saw him on the other side of the carriage, both his tunic and the ground dark with his blood. Corren faced forward again, his legs gaining strength as he walked. "How did you find me?" Corren repeated.

"We weren't trying to find you," Nicolai said. "Not yet anyway. We came to this cave of Aradia's so we could have knights standing guard. Then we were going to go to Tower Hall South to look for you."

"We heard your carriage approaching and hid, expecting to ambush Aradia," Marcellus said, "but I saw you through the window. Or at least, I was pretty sure it was you."

"But... wait a minute." Corren stopped walking. "Did you say a cave?"

"Yes." Nicolai pointed. "Over there."

Up ahead was a mound of earth that looked to be a cave, the entrance guarded by two knights, but Corren could tell right away it was more than that. He thought he understood now why Aradia brought him here. He turned to Marcellus and Nicolai, urgent now. "Aradia's still coming," he said. "She was going to meet us here."

"We have the road watched," Marcellus said.

"No, no. She won't be coming that way."

"Then how—?"

A deafening boom echoed through the trees and they ducked instinctively. "There!" Nicolai said.

Standing at the entrance to the cave was Aradia, silver hair falling over her gray cloak, spiraling staff in hand, and not one he had seen her use before. Around her the two Caedmonian knights lay on the ground morbidly still. Corren's heart leapt into his throat. What did she do to them?

Aradia locked eyes with Corren—and his skin shuddered—before looking swiftly to Marcellus and Nicolai. Then Corren saw something on her face he had never seen before. Fear. But quickly it was gone and she smiled a terrible smile.

Marcellus drew his sword and Corren raised his hand. Before he could say the incantation however, she stepped back neatly, disappearing inside the cave.

"She's trapped," Marcellus said, springing into a run.

"No," Corren said running too, "she's not."

They ran into the cave, first Marcellus, then Nicolai, then Corren gangling after them, in time to see Aradia disappear from the middle of a red circle painted on the floor. A burst of energy blew past Corren's ear and a shimmering mass, slightly transparent, filled the entryway behind them. Through it Corren could see Praea and the others running toward the cave. "Don't!" He yelled at them. "Don't touch it!" They stopped and he heard their shouting as if through water. "Stay away!" he said.

He took a step back. "Dismannath!"

Nothing happened.

"Abri!" The mass brightened momentarily, but stayed in place. Praea and the knights backed far away. Corren furrowed his brows.

A wave of dizziness swept over him and he struggled to stay upright. Turning he saw a luminous ball of red light floating in the center of the circle. Marcellus staggered a step and Nicolai, who was closest to the circle, fell to his knees. "Get away!" Corren shouted and Nicolai started crawling to where Marcellus and Corren were huddled near

267

the doorway. The walls of the cave glowed red in the reflected light and Corren saw flashes of images on the walls.

"What is that?" Marcellus said. "What is it?"

"It's a *cimota*, but I've never seen one that big before. It's taking our energy." Corren's legs started trembling as he grew weaker and he fell against the wall seeking support. The ball of light grew bigger as it drew on their strength. The cave was vibrating and rumbling as if the *cimota* were drawing in the very walls.

"We need to get out of here," Marcellus said, eyes flashing, and he thrust his sword through the shield blocking the door. He pulled back on the hilt and saw nothing but a stump, for the blade had completely disintegrated. Marcellus widened his eyes in horror.

"Pennitrett," Corren said, but the door remained blocked. *Think.* "En terri! Katath! Come on!" Corren said one incantation after another but words were thick and heavy in his mouth now and he wasn't sure what he was saying anymore.

Marcellus slid to the floor.

Corren tried to think of another incantation, but his mind had gone blank. He couldn't think what to do next.

He saw the red. Glowing like fire. He saw five circles of white light above him. Were they holes in the ceiling? Lights coming from somewhere else? He couldn't tell. They seemed to be floating and circling above him. But when had he fallen to the floor? Corren looked at Marcellus and Nicolai, their faces weak and pallid.

We're going to die, he thought.

Corren felt cold everywhere, everywhere but his chest. There his stone still felt warm. Alive. Then it hit him. *The stones.* Had he said it out loud? He fumbled for his stone, fingers awkward and trembling. "Stones," he said, but he couldn't hear his own voice. "Stones." The stone came free from the clasp and Corren stretched out his arm with it cradled in his palm. Blackness was closing in on him. He gasped for air. "Together."

৪৩ ৪৩ ৪৩

Huddled on his knees, Nicolai saw it, red like everything else but distinct and breathtaking. Corren's stone. Nicolai's stone was already in his hand, the yellow intense and untarnished by the red light. As he stretched out his hand, as the tip of his stone neared Corren's, he saw Marcellus' blue stone coming in, too.

Nicolai's arm was tingling. It took all his strength to reach his stone toward the others. His vision pinched to black but in the center he saw the three stones touching—red, blue, yellow—and erupt in both light and power.

Then everything went black.

Nicolai opened his eyes weakly. Above him he saw the roof of the cave and the archway of the door glowing red and next to that, stunning blue sky. The force of the blast had flipped him on his back and, he assumed, broke through whatever had been blocking the doorway because now the only thing blocking the door was him. To his right was his stone and he snatched it up and tucked it away. A powerful surge of energy was rising in him. He felt his mind clearing and his strength returning. It was the same surge of healing energy he had felt the first time the three stones had been joined together.

A deafening rumble plowed through the air and Nicolai felt it in the ground, too. He looked to his left. Corren and Marcellus were still on the floor, unconscious, their stones on the ground next to them. The red ball had expanded clear to the stone pillars at the edge of the circle and was audibly pulsating. *Thump. Thump. Thump.* The walls were shaking violently now, bits crumbling to the ground, which in turn answered with a puff of dust. The ball was already affecting him again, his muscles weakening.

Nicolai scrambled to Corren and Marcellus, scooped up their stones, put them in his pocket, and grabbed their wrists. A mass of rock from the ceiling crashed next to Marcellus' head, smaller pieces breaking off and skating across the floor. "Come on!" Nicolai said tugging, slowly dragging them each by one arm. A deafening crack sounded in his ear and he saw a massive split race up the wall. He gave another huge tug and they lurched toward him. "Come on!"

Praea came beside him, grabbing Corren's arms. Nicolai let go of Corren and used both hands for Marcellus. Praea going first, they shuffled backwards, Marcellus and Corren scraping along the ground. Finally Corren was clear. Nicolai had Marcellus as far out as his chest when a terrifying roar came from the cave. The walls gave way and Nicolai heaved backward with an urgent rush of energy, pulling Marcellus free as the interior of the cave collapsed, dust and rubble bursting out of the entrance.

Nicolai fell backwards with the blast, landing on his back with a shuddering thud that reverberated through his skull. Dust clouded the air, choked his lungs, and he started coughing. There was a confusion of noise as the knights came up running and shouting. When the dust cleared Nicolai saw Corren on the ground next to him, slowly rousing, and Praea pulling herself into a sit. Marcellus was at his feet, eyes blinking open. Nicolai looked to the cave. It was nothing but rubble.

Aradia stood in front of the circle through which she had escaped. The red light leading from the tip of her staff to the center of the circle shuddered and disappeared. The vision provided by the *cimota* disappeared too.

"NO!"

She raced to the center of the red circle in disbelief. The *cimota* destroyed the cave as she knew it would, but the Three had escaped. And the stones had been around their necks the entire time. Aradia wanted to rage at the loss but would not allow it. This created new complications and she could not waste time on pointless emotions. *Would not!* She forced herself to focus and her breathing to still.

She walked out of the small and simple room and closed the door. To her left was the office Corren had broken into just two days ago. To her right was the kitchen, the bottle of the potion he had brewed still waiting for her on the shelf. Any affection she may have once felt toward her apprentice was gone, replaced by white hot hatred, but even this emotion she forced herself to tuck away. As she proceeded to her office she concentrated on one peculiarity. She saw them there again in her mind: the Three and Praea.

270

Aradia's trip to see Praea's father was what had led her to believe the princes of Sakkara were the Three. Was it mere coincidence that a person like Praea would have three brothers? It had explained so much. When Aradia found out she was wrong about the princes, she assumed she must have been wrong about Praea, too. Now she wasn't so sure. And why was Praea still alive when she was supposed to be dead? There was only one explanation for that. Kai'Enna must have given her the ash, despite Aradia's suggestion not to. Well, Aradia had more pressing matters to deal with now.

She walked to her desk and sat down. She considered it all again, everything she had learned since becoming Head of the Order, everything she had learned since the sounding of the Second Song, all of the information she had gained through stealth and persuasion, all the secrets she had uncovered. She drew on all her knowledge to puzzle out what had happened.

She placed her hand on the stack of stolen books, her long fingers absently rubbing the rough binding. She closed her eyes. Then it hit her. Aradia had only been partially wrong.

She stood. New circumstances called for a new plan, and she already knew what that was going to be. She knew what she had to do and she knew exactly where she was going. Now that she knew who her targets were, she would not fail.

Thirty-Eight

Corren drifted past one blackened tree, then another. He paused in front of the archway of trees, their nearly bare canopies entwined overhead and leading away from where he stood. He pondered this for a while, then moved on to the next blackened tree, then the last. Here he stopped. He lifted his hand, put it to the wood, resisted the sensation of revulsion on his skin. He closed his eyes, feeling what he suspected, and feared.

Pulling his hand away, he opened his eyes.

These were the trees Aradia used to make the new staff he saw in her hand and he had previously found in the room in her cabin with the magical red circle leading to the cave. The staff felt dark even then, there was no denying that, but he did not want to believe it was hers. The reason it felt dark was now clear to him. She had called upon powers that used nature against itself, that created evil and unnatural results. Powerful results. She did this not once or twice (for two segments of wood for one staff was a difficult task few could manage), but she did this four times. Four segments of wood. He could hardly fathom it. And she did not take a suitable branch, as was normally done. She removed the core, killing the tree in the process, and she did it without leaving so much as a seam. Her old staff was notoriously powerful. He resisted thinking about what this one could do.

Corren closed his eyes. "How on earth are we going to defeat her?"

Nicolai and Praea went into the trees a short distance, just enough to be out of earshot. For safety reasons, they had to stay in sight of the others.

"Marcellus has arranged for the guards to escort you home in the carriage." Her eyes widened in protest, but he continued. "There were

272

rations and blankets and other supplies found in the trunk on the back. They'll need to restock once in Dahlia before they can come back..."

She was shaking her head no.

He stopped. "What?" he asked gently.

"Aradia did this, Nicolai. *Aradia.*"

"I know."

"This is far too personal for me to do nothing."

"And what do you think you're going to do?" Nicolai asked.

She shook her head. "I don't know, but I have to do something."

After seeing her insistence on coming to the border in the first place, Nicolai was prepared for this resistance. He had had no opportunity to dissuade her before, so this time he asked Marcellus to let him speak with her privately. "Why would she listen to you?" Marcellus had asked, but Nicolai gave no answer, only walked over to Praea and pulled her aside. "You know Aradia is powerful," he said now. "Those knights didn't stand a chance against her. What chance do you think you would have?"

She didn't answer.

"Please trust me," Nicolai said. "Everything that can be done is being done. Bringing you along would only slow things down and give us one more person to guard."

She looked sharply to Marcellus and Corren and back at Nicolai. "*You're* going?"

"Yes."

"Why are *you* going?"

"Praea..." he considered things for a moment. "There are certain questions you have ... certain things you've seen ... I have to ask you not to speak to anybody about them."

She narrowed her eyes. "What's going on?" He shook his head but she leaned in. "Nicolai, if you know something about this I have a right to know. This is my family."

"You and your family are not targets anymore."

"How can you possibly know that?" She was asking in frustration and he hated being the source of that.

"I'm sorry. I really am. But I can't tell you. I trust you, it isn't that. If I thought I could safely tell you... if I could somehow know it wouldn't put you in more danger..."

"More than I'm already in?"

"Yes," he said firmly.

Her expression relented, sorrow fighting for a place with her frustration. He longed to take her in his arms, to comfort her. He wanted to keep her safe and resented the fact that the only way to do that was by sending her away. All he wanted was to just stay with her and let the rest of the world vanish around them. She looked at him with deep directness. This link between them no longer startled him. He allowed himself to sink into the warmth of it and for a moment the world *did* vanish, and they stood alone. If there was anything he was hoping for, anything he wished to have if they somehow managed to come out of all this unscathed: it was her. And he knew she knew it.

"Please," he said. "Go with the carriage."

The company finally headed out and they reached the edge of the woods as the sun first brushed the horizon. There they split. Praea and her escort turned toward Sakkara and Nicolai watched the carriage go. He caught a glimpse of her. They locked eyes one last time, then the carriage rounded a turn and she was gone.

He turned toward the border with a mixture of relief and regret. Marcellus had been observing him. Nicolai noticed this but made no comment. Likewise, Marcellus asked no questions. In their mutual exhaustion, they rode along in silence, the Three going in one direction, and Praea in the other.

PART II

The Labyrinth

One

When Corren was 16 years old, Aradia took him on a journey to the Layrin branch of the Order in Sakkara. He was to assist her as a traveling aide but also to have a unique opportunity to learn about a different branch. This, she said, would support him in his growth. "If you are to be appointed an apprentice," she said, "you must strive to learn as much as you can, to go beyond that of your peers."

He hung on her every word, trying to glean as much knowledge as he could about what to do to become her apprentice. Newly appointed to Head of the Wysard branch, it would still be four more years before the current Head of the Order would die and Aradia take his place. She had appointed two apprentices so far but she often hinted that they were disappointments to her, though she never said so directly. "Who will be worthy to carry on my legacy?" she had asked him.

I hope to be, he had thought, though he didn't dare verbalize it.

They reached Tower Hall North well after dark, following the light from the lanterns hung around its main entrance to guide them on their last stretch of the road. "They are expecting me," she said.

A man in a long robe of undyed wool opened the heavy iron door. He was an older man—in his fifties Corren would later learn—though he didn't look it, and had a smooth, round face and dark eyes that glittered when he smiled. Corren liked him immediately. "Aradia," he said with a smile. "At last."

"Bellamy," she said, smiling warmly and they embraced. She introduced Bellamy, Head of the Layrin branch, to Corren and they were ushered inside.

Following Bellamy down a narrow hallway, Corren saw he wore his long dark hair, with hints of gray, in a twisting spiral down his back. The walls were mostly unadorned, as were many of the unpainted

277

wooden doors they passed, the only exception being the regular appearance of the mysterious magical symbols crafted by the Layrin branch. The symbols were all similar to one another—with interlocking patterns, fluid and perfectly balanced—yet so intricate that no two were exactly alike. These were carved into doors or shaped out of iron and hung on the walls. Corren noticed one of these symbols on Bellamy's hand, white, flat, shining like a scar and in clear contrast to his deep olive skin. Corren nearly missed the fact that the same symbol was subtly carved in black on the top of Bellamy's ebony staff.

He led them into a square dining hall and they sat down at one end of a dark wooden table, one table of many, in the otherwise unoccupied room. Bellamy went through an open door at the far end; he returned shortly carrying an unusual dish with a likewise unusual smell, at once spicy and sweet. Casually as he could Corren poked at it with his fork, trying without success to determine the ingredients. It looked like a stew and pie combination gone bad. Even their bread was curious, pressed flat and poked with several holes. Unused to such fare, Corren proceeded with caution. He discovered he liked it, particularly the bread with its tangy flavor, and ate ravenously. "His adolescent appetite is hard to appease," Aradia said good-naturedly. Bellamy chuckled. Corren, unoffended, paid this no heed. They talked of times and people foreign to Corren, but he found their conversation fascinating anyway. Once his stomach was full, however, a warm sleepiness took over; he had a hard time staying focused on what they were saying. At one point he jerked his head up, not having realized he was falling asleep. Aradia and Bellamy both looked at him with amusement. "I'd better get my young charge to bed," she said.

The next day they ate breakfast in a considerably noisier dining hall, surrounded by members of the Layrin branch of the Order, every last one of whom was male. If Aradia felt uncomfortable or out of place surrounded by men, she didn't show it. Afterwards, they went straight to the Tower's vast library where they would spend nearly every waking hour of the next three days. Aradia had come to this library for her own reasons; Corren was not privy to them. His job was to keep her supplied with ink and parchment, along with anything else she needed, and copy the occasional passage out of a book, though she did most of her copying herself. Otherwise, he was free to examine the volumes. This he did eagerly.

It didn't take Corren long to discover the most interesting shelves. Interesting, he decided, because they were strictly off limits. Along half of the back wall were shelves shielded by locked wooden cupboard doors. The top of each door had an opening that was lined with vertical wooden dowels. Corren peered through these in order to see the contents better. Though significantly veiled in the darkness of the cupboard, Corren could see the books were finely bound with embossed lettering down the spines. He strained to read the titles.

Enchanted Hedges, one read. *Centering, Visions, and Interpr...* was all he could see on another, the rest of the title obscured in darkness, though he was certain the last word was "Interpretations."

"Tempting, isn't it?"

Corren jumped at the sound of Aradia's voice. She was smiling down at him.

"Do you need ink?" Corren asked.

"No. Only checking to be sure you're not getting into trouble. It looks like it's a good thing I did."

"I was just looking," Corren said, feeling distinctly guilty now.

"Knowledge is one of the two great temptations to an intelligent mind, Corren." She nodded toward the encased books. "What person of any mental merit would not want to know what secrets these books hold?"

He looked back at the cases and hungered for them even more than he had before her arrival. What secrets *did* they hold? His eyes lighted, not for the first time, on the silver lettering of a slender volume. *Raegheri* was all it said. Corren had no idea what that might be and so this title, even more than the others, tugged at his curiosity.

"You must learn to keep yourself in check, however," Aradia now said. She smiled and looked around the library. "There is a whole room here waiting for you. You don't need to thirst only for the water that is forbidden."

She began to walk back to her table. Had he been seeking only the forbidden? He began to wonder.

"What is the other great temptation to an intelligent mind?" he asked.

She turned and fixed him with a serious gaze. "Power."

He spent the next three days settled at a small table, crowded by sizeable stacks of books. By the time their last morning in the library had come and gone, he had a pleasant bundle of notes, though nothing compared to that of Aradia's.

That afternoon, Corren accompanied Aradia and Bellamy through the lawns on the Tower's grounds. This was the first opportunity Corren had had to really take in their surroundings. Tower Hall North was situated on a slight rise on the edge of Whelan, an unassuming community full of squat, stone, round buildings with chimneys poking through the center of their peaked roofs. Rich green hills surrounded the area, kept lush by the near constant mist in the air and well appreciated by the many flocks of sheep Corren saw grazing on the distant hillsides.

Unlike the grounds of Tower Hall South, which was practically overrun with its trees and gardens, the grounds of Tower Hall North were as plain and unadorned as the interior of the buildings. Corren followed Aradia and Bellamy through the wide open area, blanketed with thick green grass and dotted with the occasional clover. Aside from the beautiful view of the town and hillsides, there was only one item of interest Corren saw here. It dominated the entire rear area of the complex. When the party came to a stop, Corren surveyed what was in front of him with more than mere curiosity.

Growing within a round depression of earth was a sprawling, circular Labyrinth. Mounds of dirt formed the base of the walls and were topped by green hedges tall enough to conceal whoever might be bold enough to enter it. Mist hung in the entryway. The leaves of the hedges were such a dark green they looked waxy. Even from a distance Corren felt the magic seeping from them.

"You are sure of this?" Bellamy asked Aradia. "It is never easy to witness the secrets of the Labyrinth."

Aradia looked on with calm determination. "That is because too many fear their future," she said, "instead of embracing their destinies."

Corren held his breath. Aradia had explained the Labyrinth was one of the great magical secrets of the Layrin branch. They enchanted and tended its hedges with techniques known only to them. No doubt Phoenix ash was a part of it. The purpose of the Labyrinth, she explained, was to delve into the darkest part of your mind and heart, and (sometimes) thrust you forward to the blackest moment of your future.

"Why would you want to see that?" Corren had asked, horrified.

"The Layrin believe such unflinching self-examination leads to perfection, their ultimate goal. But it is difficult to endure, so not all their members partake of it."

"And why do you want to do it?"

Here Aradia smiled. "Because the Labyrinth also unveils the pathway to your greatest success. But too few people see it that way. They are so frightened by the obstacles in their way they cannot see them for what they really are." Aradia paused and Corren found himself leaning in. "A map to your greatest destiny," she said.

He smiled. "I want to know my destiny."

She laughed easily. "You are much too young for the rigors of the Labyrinth. A person unprepared for such a journey is almost always crippled by it. And that is not even taking into account the final concern."

"Which is what?"

"Unfortunately Corren, not everyone has a great destiny waiting for them. The vast majority of people live lives of disappointing mediocrity, and that is if they are lucky enough to escape outright failure. Sorrow is at the end of many a road. When that becomes foreknowledge in a person's life... well, it would be enough to break anyone, wouldn't it?"

Bellamy had been holding the same stance ever since Aradia had entered the Labyrinth: his eyes closed, his arms stretched out in front

281

of him, unintelligible incantations coming out as hoarse whispers, the symbols etched into his staff and hand each glowing white. They were waiting for Aradia to journey to the center, receive her vision, and journey back out. The Labyrinth looked no different than it had before, but it felt different. Though touched only by the outer boundary of its magic, Corren felt wrapped in its power. What would it be like to step inside? According to Bellamy, not everyone made it to the center where the magic was its most potent. Fear drove them back before they made it all the way. Corren could see why. Just standing at the perimeter was knee buckling.

His awe for its powers increased, but his desires for it increased too. *My greatest destiny,* he thought. Corren agreed with Aradia. The Labyrinth was a tool worth using. While she may be right that some people are destined to end their lives in failure, Corren did not believe he was one of them. As he and Bellamy awaited Aradia's return, Corren tried to imagine what he would see if he went into the Labyrinth. What would be so terrible to face? He could not begin to guess. But pondering the fantasy of his greatest destiny was not difficult at all. Head of the Order. Brilliant wizard. Aradia's heir.

At long last, Aradia emerged, mist trailing after her for the briefest moment before curling back into the hedges. The glowing scar faded and Bellamy lowered his arms. Aradia walked up to him and they embraced. She said nothing, however, as the three of them headed back to the Tower.

Corren studied her face. She did not look disturbed. Sober, perhaps, but ultimately calm and confident as she ever was. *What did she see?* he wondered. *Did she like what she saw?* Finally she acknowledged his inquisitiveness, which he was making no effort to hide, and answered his questions without saying a word.

Aradia cast him a sideways glance, and winked.

Two

Corren woke up sweating and disoriented. The tendrils of his dream entwined with his thoughts and he did not at first remember where he was. Sun shone through the fabric of the tent. He lay on a stiff straw mat. Corren looked to his right and saw his shoes with a thin layer of dust ringing the edge of the soles. His bag and traveling cloak sat next to these. To his left was another straw mat, empty, and at his feet the tent flap hung closed. The air was stifling. Corren sat up, wiping the sweat from his brow and along his hairline.

The last few days came back to him in a rush of memories: brewing the potion, breaking into the office, a haunting conversation with Aradia, the carriage ride, the cave, the stones. Corren closed his eyes. He remembered now where he was: on the border of Caedmonia and Norrland, encamped with over a thousand Caedmonian troops. His dream brought back a previously fond memory that now felt black and heavy.

He pulled on his shoes, stood, and stretched the aches out of his body. Corren stepped gratefully into the relatively cooler air of the outdoors, the soft breeze refreshing him. The sun was high overhead. The general noise of the encampment blurred the distinct sounds of men talking and feet walking and came to him more as an overall hum. A handful of knights passed by, their conversation temporarily faltering at the sight of him, their eyes questioning. They walked on and Corren was content to let them do so. He did not wish to speak to anyone. He stretched one last time, then turned to his left and began his search for Marcellus and Nicolai.

It had been a long day. The Three sat in Marcellus' tent, tired, stiff, and full from the dinner they had just eaten (the second meal they had taken there that day). Marcellus rubbed his eyes; they were scratchy from fatigue.

Nicolai pulled himself up from a semi-lounging position to snatch another slice of bread off the wooden tray on the table. He dipped the slice in the shallow bowl of olive oil and took a bite as he leaned back in the chair again. They were gathered around the squat, round table rather loosely, having edged their chairs away slightly over the course of the day to accommodate themselves as they stretched their legs out before them. Outside, the sounds of the troops occasionally wafted in through the tent fabric, muffled sounding, for the canvas of the tent was thick, double-layered, and not well-suited for eavesdropping. The sitting area was situated comfortably on one end of the tent and Marcellus' feather-down mattress presented itself invitingly on the other. After so many hours of talking, planning, discussing, and debating, Marcellus was more than ready to retire. But not yet. They weren't done yet.

The prophecy—with its desperately brittle parchment—lay open on the table next to a bowl of skeletal grape vines. On these, only a few grapes remained, too small and sour to eat. While developing their strategy against Aradia, the Three had delved into the prophecy and its veiled messages as much as they could. Some of it seemed clear enough, but the rest was hopelessly cryptic, at least in Marcellus' mind. Nevertheless, Corren was convinced his plan about hiding an element on the Gateway to thwart any attack was proven the correct way to go.

The first reason for this was because it seemed logical within the rules of magic; the second reason was because Corren believed the prophecy predicted it. "*All four elements must provide their singular powers,*" he had read from the prophecy. "The Concealment Potion I want to brew is perfectly balanced with all four elements, air, earth, water, and fire. That's pretty rare, and is what gives it such power. This has to be what we're supposed to do. This will work." That was what Corren had said. Nicolai seemed to agree. Marcellus could find no reason not to. He had questioned Corren about this plan as much as he could within his limited understanding, but there was no escaping the fact that they all had to trust Corren's knowledge of the situation. What else could they do?

Corren's plan was this: create what Corren referred to as a "fiery element," and brew a Concealment Potion that would allow him to hide the element on the Gateway. "No matter how Aradia attacks the Gateway," Corren said, "she'll be using magic specifically crafted to break through the elements in that ring. Our hidden element will throw her off and keep her out. The Phoenix will be safe." Corren and Nicolai described the Gateway as a metallic-type ring and Marcellus could not visualize Corren's plan at all. Was he going to pour the potion on there? Rub it on like a paste? Apparently even that process was magical, as Corren explained when Marcellus asked him about it. "I'll use a spell to very *carefully* coat the ring with the potion," Corren said. "It will need to touch the entire surface of the ring evenly and simultaneously or else the ring will reject it. I'll apply it in a thin layer, so the potion should dry quickly and it will dry clear."

This process required a staff, apparently, and Corren planned on making one when he went to Tower Hall North in the morning. He didn't want to wait until they returned to Stonebridge to warn the Order about Aradia and thought the Head of the branch at Tower Hall North could alert the other members quickly. Nicolai was going with him so he could describe exactly what was in the cave. Marcellus' travel itinerary was still up for debate.

So this was the "hidden element" plan, as Corren called it. He also called it their first line of defense. Marcellus considered their first line of defense to be the several hundred troops they would place around the entrance to the Bridge. Hunting Aradia down, while appealing, was not practical; she could be anywhere by now. However, they knew she was going to be at the Bridge sometime near when the Phoenix regenerated, the paintings on the cave walls had made that much clear at least. The obvious thing in Marcellus' mind was simply to meet her there. For reasons which still mystified Marcellus, Corren had debated just how helpful hundreds of well-armed, well-trained soldiers were going to be.

"I trust even a witch can't survive a blade through the heart," Marcellus had said, not bothering to hide his irritation.

"The reach of her staff is a lot longer than the reach of your sword," Corren said. "She won't need to get anywhere near you to strike."

"That's what archers are for," Marcellus said, exasperated at having to state the obvious. "She can't fend us all off at once."

"We'll see," was Corren's reply. Marcellus looked at him in disbelief. Here was a man who had so little faith in the king's army, yet he was supposed to be heir to the throne. This, Marcellus knew, was the heart of his frustration during their entire conversation. If the situation were different, if Corren had been anyone other than the eldest brother, Marcellus would have welcomed his knowledge. Marcellus utilized expert advisors all the time, considering them invaluable. There was no denying the fact that it wasn't military might that saved them in the cave (Marcellus still had the hilt of his melted sword to prove it); Aradia's magic had been defeated by magic. That was something Marcellus knew nothing about, despite the fact that one of the stones was hanging around his own neck.

That brought up another matter. What on earth was his stone supposed to do? Corren thought maybe the stones had already fulfilled their roles. "Without them, Aradia surely would have conquered us in that cave," he had said.

No question there.

But what about Nicolai's stone? It was during their discussion of the cave that Nicolai's stone came into the conversation. Corren was explaining what the pictures on the inside of the cave were—*Incanurals*—and how these were actually complicated, advanced spells intended to force a future outcome. "Tricky magic," Corren had said a little gravely, "even for Aradia thankfully." The magic had worked on the first two Sakkaran princes, but not on the last. It had been a military intervention that thwarted the spell on Akren, Marcellus was keen to point out. This wasn't all about magic. This witch wasn't invincible. If a little covert operation could stop her spell from slitting Akren's throat open, then why couldn't a couple of units at the Bridge stop her too?

That was as far as they got into that debate, for this was when Nicolai said Akren wasn't the only one to escape Aradia's magic.

Princess Praea had too. Nicolai found her injured at the bottom of the Great Gorge.

"She fell off the cliff?" Corren had asked. "Like in the painting?"

"How could she survive that?" Marcellus asked.

"She must have hit the water just right," Nicolai said. Though Marcellus judged Nicolai to be a man of impeccable honesty, this statement seemed to be hiding more than it revealed. Nicolai went on to describe how his stone lit, became incredibly hot yet without burning his skin, and healed her almost instantly when he placed it on her chest.

Corren declared it a healing stone. "That could be useful," he said.

Nicolai didn't seem so sure. "Well, I agree that's what it does, but I'm pretty sure I can't control it. It lit for its own reasons."

Why would it light for her, though? Marcellus wondered. Corren voiced the same opinion. "I see no reason why it would light for her," he said. "I think you just need to learn how to control it."

Nicolai disagreed with this in that soft but firm way that was so like their father, saying he felt certain the stone had a mind of its own. "But," he conceded, "I've never really *tried* to control it. Maybe I need to."

Marcellus wondered at his own stone again. It sat against his chest, warm, elusive, silent. What could it do? Marcellus didn't know and didn't have any idea how to discover this. The prophecy was of little help. *Blue brother must cross through light and extinguish darkness.* That, apparently, was the Phoenix's idea of telling him what to do. Corren had asked Marcellus what he thought it meant. This was Marcellus' reply: "I haven't the first idea. If the Phoenix wanted to be helpful, it could have been a little more specific. Like how *many* troops it wants guarding the Bridge. That would have been valuable."

"I really don't think it matters," Corren said.

"How can you say that?"

"She's powerful, Marcellus. More powerful than I think you realize."

"If she's so powerful, then why did she run when she saw us yesterday?"

"Did she run or did she lure us? She knew what she was doing."

287

Marcellus had no argument for that. No good one anyway. There was no disputing what Aradia did in that cave.

Corren softened his earnestness when he saw his point had been taken. "I do think we have one advantage over her," he said. "This line in the prophecy." He tapped the parchment with his finger. "*Only the Three as one can prevent this thievery.* I think Aradia is taking that literally. When we were in the carriage, she said to me that only all together do we pose a threat to her. I think if it had been just any three people standing outside that cave, she would have simply attacked us. Probably successfully. But she fears this line of the prophecy. I think that's why she lured us in the cave the way she did."

Marcellus thought this to be a huge advantage. If you know what your enemy fears, and press it upon them without pressing too hard and triggering wild, intense self-defense, you can play them into your hand. Marcellus began pondering how they could use Aradia's fear against her. This was the kind of strategy he excelled at. He kept his musings to himself for the moment; he didn't want to reveal his thoughts until he knew better himself what he wanted to do. Meanwhile, this he could say for certain: when Aradia came to the Bridge, his troops would be ready. "And damn her if she can get past them," he said.

That was when the porter had brought in their food, the aroma from the roast duck coming in a few moments ahead of him. By unspoken consent they halted their discussion in favor of a quiet dinner. It was a welcome respite, and now that the meal had ended, no one seemed in a rush to pick up their conversation again. At length, Marcellus took the lead in this. He was ready for bed.

"If you two go to Tower Hall North while I stay here and prepare the troops," Marcellus began, "we can be ready to depart for Stonebridge by the time you return. That will be quicker than if I go with you."

Marcellus and Nicolai each watched Corren for a response. They had debated this once already, without resolution. Corren was reluctant to have them split up again. This seemed an emotional reaction more than anything in Marcellus' view, for Tower Hall North was only about half a day's journey from here. Even factoring in time for Corren to make a staff, he would be back in just two days. In two days Marcellus could be ready to march home with the troops they needed. He planned on bringing home more men than originally planned so they could protect the Bridge without pulling from units already stationed in the city and weakening her defenses. "If I go with you," Marcellus said again, "it will only delay things."

Corren was eager to get back to Stonebridge and start working on the Concealment Potion; Marcellus' reminder about saving time was obviously tempting to him. Nicolai must have sensed this, for he leaned in now and said, "I agree with Marcellus. We'll be back in two days and can head back to Stonebridge. Together."

"Alright," Corren nodded. "Agreed."

"It's settled then," Marcellus said standing. He went to a large trunk in the corner and from this retrieved two swords in their scabbards. He handed one to Nicolai, who lit up and took it eagerly. Marcellus held out the second one to Corren, who only looked at it. "Just in case," Marcellus said. Nicolai was already standing, unsheathing his sword with a distinct ringing sound. He swung it about, testing its weight and balance, thrusting and parrying with open air. Marcellus couldn't help but observe this with amusement. Maybe they were related after all.

"This isn't quite the weapon I had in mind," Corren said, still not taking the sword.

"You'd rather a bow?"

Corren shook his head. "I'd rather a staff."

Marcellus considered him. "Well, since you don't have a staff you'd better take the sword. You can't journey to Tower Hall North unarmed."

"I'm not exactly defenseless," Corren said firmly.

Marcellus set the sword in his empty chair, annoyed. "Suit yourself. I'll take you to the quartermaster. He'll outfit you with horses and whatever you need." Marcellus headed for the tent flap and heard them following after him. Before he reached the door, Corren spoke again.

"Wait..."

Marcellus stopped and turned. He and Nicolai watched Corren, who appeared to be searching for words.

"I never thanked the two of you," Corren said. He seemed both sincere and vulnerable in saying it. "For saving me, I mean. So, thank you."

Marcellus and Nicolai exchanged glances. "We were lucky to happen upon you," Nicolai said with a shrug.

"Well," Corren said, and here he looked directly at Marcellus. "I thank you just the same."

It was in that precise moment that Marcellus understood something. It surprised him to realize that he would've genuinely liked Corren, if only the circumstances were different.

If only.

Janus watched this most unlikely trio exit the prince's tent with a disbelief that oscillated with fascination. Their connection to one another was unmistakable. She was close enough to be sure. Yet she couldn't believe it. How could it be that she did not know of this? How was any of this possible? She watched them numbly, her mind reeling. She needed more information and for that she needed to go south. Unfortunately Donnelly was sending her and her battalion into the Wedge to help with the Norrland rebel problem. She had no idea how long it would be before she could come back.

Janus followed the three brothers with a kind of longing, staying far enough back to avoid detection or suspicion. She wanted answers, and she would get them. For now, Janus could only wait and watch and wonder: *how many are there?*

Three

Many hours before this, Praea had been riding in her carriage—or rather, Aradia's carriage—along with half a dozen guards provided for her by Prince Marcellus. According to Nicolai, she should return to Dahlia, wait safely in the castle, and let others deal with the situation at hand.

The situation at hand had changed.

When she first journeyed to Caedmonia, she believed Norrland was goading them into war, in a most despicable way. Since war was fought by kings and knights, and she was neither, she had thought that going to Caedmonia to request an alliance was the best she could do for her kingdom. And for her brother.

Now, however, things had become even more personal. This was not about war. This was about... what? *Why?* she asked herself again. *Why would Aradia do this?*

At first, when she thought about the paintings in the cave, she could not think beyond the haunting images of her brothers (and herself) frozen in the moment of death. But now, she kept returning to the final images: Aradia hitting the Phoenix with a spell, Aradia rising in dark, fiery glory as the Phoenix lay dead at her feet. Praea repressed a shudder. Aradia was going to steal the power of the Phoenix, that much was clear, but Praea could not imagine how she could be successful in such a thing. And what did that have to do with her? With her brothers? What did Nicolai have to do with all this? What was this strange alliance between him, Prince Marcellus, and Corren? Wasn't Corren one of Aradia's apprentices?

Praea shifted uncomfortably in her seat. She had no answers to any of these questions. Dark masses and shadows floated past, the daunting manifestation of the woods in darkness. They were to travel all night on the well-established road to Dahlia. Prince Marcellus had made it clear to his knights that they should make haste; she knew they would not stop at Tower Hall North even if she asked. Once in Dahlia she would be delivered to her father, who would likely keep her within the castle grounds. For her safety.

Would he let her pay a visit to Tower Hall North and warn the Order there? Would she have to simply send a message? Would they believe her if she did? She would not have believed it herself if she had not seen it with her own eyes. Aradia. The Head of the Order. It was unheard of.

This was no longer in the realm of kings and princes and knights, a war fought among men. This was in her realm. The realm of the Order. She was as duty-bound as anyone else—maybe more so—to do something about this.

The carriage bounced over a few ruts in the road, causing her full bladder to complain. Praea knocked on the carriage door and leaned out to the driver. He looked back to her. "My Lady?"

"May we stop for a moment? I need to visit the trees."

He nodded; she sat back and waited for the carriage to stop. A knight opened the door for her and offered her his hand so she could exit comfortably. She picked her way through the darkness to the looming shadows of the trees.

The knights surrounding the carriage of Princess Praea stood at attention, eyes scanning the darkness for any signs of movement, ears keen for any menacing sounds. Princess Praea had concealed herself discreetly behind a tree, and they waited tensely, anxious to keep moving.

More minutes than seemed appropriate passed. Knight Reid, head of this company, looked at the others with him. The knight on his left met his eyes and shrugged at Reid's unspoken question. Reid waited a few more minutes, not wanting to intrude, then finally called out, "My Lady?"

This was answered by silence, other than the distant roaring of wind through trees far from where they stood.

Reid took a few steps forward, his senses heightened even more. "My Lady? Princess Praea?"

No answer.

He gestured for a knight to join him and they marched purposefully in the direction the princess had gone. They would spend the next several hours looking for her, but they would not find her. This was because she was currently in the form of a great, glittering bird, flying due east in a direct course for Tower Hall North.

Since Praea's identity as a Tulaga was still a secret, she had to hide her necklace and present herself to the Head of the Layrin branch simply as the Princess of Sakkara: a most unusual visitor indeed, particularly when wearing a plain peasant's dress. Bellamy had welcomed her to Tower Hall North curiously, but warmly, and granted her a private meeting. He sent for food and drink and settled himself opposite her attentively.

She explained what had happened to her brothers, how she herself had been chased (leaving out a few revealing details), and how she and Nicolai had come upon the cave. She described what she had seen there, concluding with the disturbing image of Aradia killing the Phoenix. Throughout her telling, Bellamy's friendly countenance had morphed from concern to curiosity and now, to denial.

A young man in a plain cloak of undyed wool brought in a tray of food and drink. They paused discreetly. Bellamy nodded in thanks to the young man and he left them alone again.

"Now Princess," Bellamy said. "I know Aradia personally. I have for years. Perhaps someone painted her image as you say, though I don't know why they would do so. But I can vouch for her character myself. You must be mistaken."

"Allow me to finish," she said. She related their journey to the border and subsequent return with Prince Marcellus, who also had a chance to inspect the cave. "Shortly after we left the cave, we heard a carriage arriving. Inside was one of her apprentices, Corren." At this Bellamy straightened. "He was tied up inside and guarded by men we assume were working for Aradia."

"What would cause you to make such an assumption? What did they have to say about it?"

"We were not able to ask them," Praea said, "because they perished in the fight to free Corren."

"Then how can..."

"My assumption, as you say, was confirmed when Aradia herself showed up, from inside the cave we had just seen to be empty."

"She came through the circle?" Bellamy asked.

"Yes. When she did that she killed the two knights we had left guarding the entrance."

Bellamy flinched as if burned. "Were they attacking her?"

"No."

Bellamy furrowed his brows.

She went on, before he could interrupt again, to describe Aradia's ensuing retreat and attempt to kill those who had followed her into the cave. When Praea finished, she allowed all she had said to sink in. Bellamy looked in utter disbelief.

"To be a person in her position....what you suggest is extremely unlikely. You do realize she is Head of the Order of Ceinoth?"

Praea nodded.

"The Order of Ceinoth is charged with the protection of the secrets of the Phoenix," he said, as if making a case. "To even become a member of the Order, one must undergo rigorous scrutiny by current Order members."

"Yes, I know."

"This is even truer for the Head. Aradia is entrusted with more secrets than anyone."

"Then who better to know its weaknesses?"

Bellamy blinked at this. He seemed unable to accept what he had heard.

Praea leaned forward. "I realize I am only one person telling you what I saw, but I am not the only one. Contact the others, if you must, and they will tell you the same thing. Do you have some other explanation for what we saw?"

He said nothing, a little taken aback at first. He thought about her question. She did not press him for an answer. After a time he sighed, rubbed his eyes with his hands, and when he spoke next it was with a distinctly deflated tone in his voice. "No. I have no other explanation. It is ... it is so unbelievable."

"I think you need to alert the other members of the Order," Praea said. "Aradia is still out there. Who knows what she'll do next."

"What do *you* think she'll do?" he asked.

Praea clasped her hands together on her lap and shook her head. "I fear to know the answer to that."

Aradia knelt in a small clearing of her own making, deep in the bowels of the forest. In front of her, a small cauldron hung over an open fire so high the tips of the flames licked the rim of the cast iron bowl. Inside, the concoction boiled uproariously. Aradia watched, perfectly still, excitement awakening in her breast. She saw no need to subdue this.

Finally, it was time.

She took her staff in one hand, grabbed the bottle next to her with the other and stood. As she walked up to the pot her face flushed and her skin almost burned from the heat. She uncorked the bottle (forbidding herself emotion at the memory that it had been Corren who prepared this for her) and poured the entire contents into the cauldron.

Bright white flames shot twenty feet into the air, the cauldron groaning in protest. Aradia took one swift step back and aimed her staff at the top of the white flame, her mind sharply focused on her task. "Deseritta yi obay! Deseritta yi obay! DESERITTA YI OBAY!"

The flames quivered, their height maintained, their heat almost unbearable, their properties now under Aradia's command.

Aradia kept her staff firmly pointed at the flames and from her robes she removed a glass sphere, cleverly crafted to be hollow on the inside but without leaving an opening on the outside. The sphere was not empty, however. Its contents were invisible to the naked eye, but Aradia knew what was there. She held it high in front of her, its rainbow of colors swirling in the reflection of the fire.

Aradia began the rhythmic chant of an incantation. The trees surrounding the clearing shuddered as if bent back by an unknown wind. The pillar of white flame dipped at its tip. Aradia strengthened her voice, continuing the chant, every part of her body pulsating. The top of the flame now dove down toward her outstretched hand clutching the sphere. When the flame first touched the sphere and entered it, a flash of light flew out in each direction, blowing Aradia's hair and robe. She did not flinch. Her voice rose, almost as if echoing outside herself, as she guided the white flame into the sphere, capturing it there.

The pillar of flame was gone. The cauldron was empty. The night was dark and still, all except for the last light of the sphere absorbing into itself, slowly sinking into darkness.

Aradia was breathing deeply, her heart pounding, as she brought the sphere closer, marveling at it. She felt a mixture of triumph and longing. She had just accomplished what no other witch or wizard had ever done: where were the adoring masses? No one anywhere knew that she had just burst the bounds of known magic. Even this was only the beginning.

Soon enough, she told herself. *Soon enough my glory will be revealed for all to admire.* She could wait until then, for above all else Aradia was a patient woman. She placed the sphere back in her pocket and left the clearing one step closer to her goal than she had been when she entered it.

Four

When Corren and Nicolai arrived at Tower Hall North, Corren was shocked to learn the princess had already been and gone. Nicolai looked positively alarmed by this. "Did Princess Praea go to Dahlia?" he asked urgently.

Bellamy shook his head, eyeing Nicolai curiously. "She did not tell me where she was going." He turned and gestured for them to follow. "I would like to hear your version of things, if you please."

"Of course."

Bellamy looked much as Corren remembered him, his long, dark hair in a twisted braid down his back. He led them into his office, a plain room with only a desk, a few chairs, and one enormous Layrin symbol painted in black on the rear wall. They settled quickly. Nicolai confirmed Praea's story, though he still seemed flustered, then Corren told of his experience. He found it particularly difficult to relate what Aradia had said in the carriage.

Bellamy's countenance grew dark. "I will send word to the Order and alert the Guard. I'll request a meeting at the Cloister, though I don't really have the authority to do so."

"How do we know other Order members aren't a part of this too?" Nicolai asked.

"Has anything led you to that conclusion?" Bellamy asked.

"No, but it is something I've thought about."

Corren spoke up. "The men Aradia had working for her weren't magical, which makes me think she was trying to do all this as far out of sight of the Order as she could."

"I agree," Bellamy said. "In any case, they need to be warned. You realize the Order may want to speak with you."

"We're heading back to Stonebridge," Corren said, "so we'll be close. You can reach us at the castle."

Bellamy nodded. "You leave today?"

"Actually, I was hoping we might leave tomorrow."

"Of course. You can rest yourselves here."

"Well, I was thinking I could spend the time forging a staff."

Bellamy raised his brows.

"How long have you been an apprentice?"

"Three years."

"Quite soon to be forging your own staff, don't you think? And you were young for an apprentice to begin with."

"Aradia thought I was ready and quite frankly, I'm not keen to travel on without one."

"*Aradia* thought you were ready?"

Corren smiled wryly at the irony. "Yes, I know. But she was not wrong. I already know how I'm going to do it."

Bellamy rested his elbows on the arms of his chair and brought the tips of his fingers together in a little tent. "Hmm," he said. The white scar of his symbol shone on his olive skin. "You've selected your wood?"

Corren nodded.

"Seed of influence? Everything?"

"Yes."

Bellamy continued to scrutinize Corren. "I still think you are too young."

"I'm sure I don't need your permission," Corren said as respectfully as he could. "I'm only asking for a place to do it."

Bellamy raised his brows and he and Corren studied each other. Nicolai looked between them uncomfortably. "It is true, you are not in my branch and so I do not really have any authority over you. But since you find yourself without a sage, I feel some responsibility for you. It would be reckless of me not to discourage you."

Corren had an idea; his heartbeat quickened as he thought of it. "I understand. Perhaps you would feel more comfortable if I demonstrated my readiness."

"How would you do that?"

"The Labyrinth."

Bellamy smiled slightly and rested his hands in his lap. "You have long desired to go in the Labyrinth, not understanding what effect it would have on you."

While it was true that Corren had wanted to enter the Labyrinth ever since seeing Aradia go through it, his motivation for wanting to do so now went beyond mere curiosity. The Labyrinth showed a person's greatest destiny, and surely there would be nothing greater in Corren's destiny than defending the Phoenix. Maybe the Labyrinth would help him know how to do it. "I am no longer a child," Corren said. "You cannot deny that."

Bellamy looked solemn. "No. You are not a child. And as such you are responsible for the consequences of your own choices, even reckless ones."

Corren resisted the urge to offer a retort. Instead, he sat in silence.

"You are free to make your own decisions," Bellamy said, studying his hands. "You may stay here while you forge your staff. I won't interfere." He looked at Corren directly now. "But you do not need to go through the Labyrinth."

"I would like to go."

Bellamy sighed. "It is not to be entered into lightly."

Corren remembered what Aradia had said about it, that not everyone has a great destiny for the Labyrinth to reveal: *Sorrow is at the end of many a road. When that becomes foreknowledge in a person's life, it is enough to break anyone.* Corren set aside the unease these words brought.

"I understand," Corren said. "I am ready. Are you going to forbid me?"

Bellamy sat still for a long time, the massive symbol unique to his branch looming behind him. Corren did not rush his answer. Finally Bellamy stood. "You may enter."

Corren stood at the entrance to the Labyrinth. Bellamy and Nicolai were both behind him. Bellamy must have begun his incantation for Corren could feel the magical energy of the Labyrinth seeping toward him with fresh power. The hedges felt to be vibrating, though they looked perfectly still. A translucent mist swirled gravely in the interior. Corren curled his hands into fists, inhaled deeply, then let his breath out slowly, relaxing his fingers as he did so.

Bellamy's instructions had been simple: follow the path to the center and back again. "Do not worry if you cannot make it all the way," he had said.

Corren remembered his reason for doing this, swallowed his doubt, and stepped into the Labyrinth. His skin tingled as the mist surrounded him. The silence was palpable; he felt that even if he had uttered a word he would not have been able to hear it. The narrow pathway curved around the perimeter of the Labyrinth and Corren followed it. The hedges with their dark, waxy leaves towered on either side as his bare feet fell on soft grass, cold and dewy. He could not hear his footsteps. He pressed on, for much longer than it seemed he should have, but at last he saw the first turn, which would lead him circling in the opposite direction, one layer closer to the center.

Corren turned the corner and a vision exploded before his eyes. He saw the Mountains of Vitra as if from a distance. A pinpoint of light, fiery orange, lit for just a second on the slope of one of the mountain peaks, then was gone.

Corren blinked and the vision left him. The hedges were restored to his view, curving now to the right, beckoning him on. He had not consciously come to a stop, but once he realized he had done so he continued on. What he saw was not as much a vision as it was a memory, though one he had long forgotten. As a child, when he was still under the care of Mother Taiven in Landsdowne, he would walk the path behind their house, follow it to the lake, and sit and gaze at the Mountains of Vitra. He had often wished he could leave his life behind and escape into them where it was safe and solitary, absent of loss and pain. This was what he thought as a child. His adult mind recognized this fantasy as folly, but his heart still remembered the feeling, that hopeful longing for escape. One night, in a fit of childish fury, Corren had snuck out intending to do just that. Escape. Disappear from one world and reinvent himself in a new one. Naturally, reality and fear took over and he never got past the lake.

That was the night he first saw the pinpoint of light, the same light he saw in his vision just now. After seeing it that first night, he stole away as frequently as he dared to see if he could catch it again. Sometimes he would wait for a long time and never see it. Other times it would appear in a wink so quick he sometimes wondered if he had imagined it. When he did see it, it was always in the same place. Always the same color. The color of fire.

Corren wondered why the Labyrinth would retrieve this memory. He felt disappointed. He wanted the Labyrinth to show him his greatest destiny. The pathway to success. His future, not his past.

As he approached the next turn he slowed slightly, turned expectantly, and again a vision brought him to an involuntary halt.

He stood on a rocky ledge, facing the sheer wall of mountain. Materializing on the stone in a rush of fire was an archway, carved into the side of the mountain. Fiery lettering in a language he could not read dashed over the top of the archway as if being written by an unseen hand. The archway and wording alike burned for a moment, then they were gone, the mountain bare and cold again.

The vision vanished, leaving Corren unsettled. This was no memory. He had never seen that archway before. He moved forward, having to force himself to do so, disturbed not so much by what he saw, but by how he felt. He did not know why, but a distinct feeling of dread had settled into him. He tried to shed it as he followed the path, curving more tightly now. As he approached the next turn he stopped prematurely. Stunned by his own behavior, he shook himself and marched around the turn.

A wide lake of fire appeared before him, churning and boiling like liquid lava, in a deep underground cavern. Three slender pieces of wood, tentatively sealed together, were in his grasp. Corren gripped this, the beginnings of a staff, in his right hand and held it over the fire below. Flames slowly reached up, curling around the wood and his hand alike. The wood began to twist and mold together, bonded by the claw-like grasp of the fire but not burned by it.

When the vision left Corren this time, he was drenched in sweat. He had never seen anything like that. He had never heard of any such method of forging a staff. He could not explain why, but for some reason what he saw terrified him. He resisted this, reprimanding himself. His fight against this irrational fear did him no good. It clung to him anyway. He made himself go on.

His steps down the pathway seemed ineffective. He was moving along, he knew he was, had to be, but the path seemed to stretch away from him. Was it delusion? Was it magic? He could not tell, only willed himself to put one foot in front of the other until after what felt an impossibly long time, the turn ahead materialized.

It took all his willpower to keep walking. He could not stop. He knew if he did he would not be able to go on. His heart beat painfully as he made the turn.

In this vision he held the partially completed staff with its now twisted shaft in one hand. In the other hand he held his scarlet stone. He knew he was saying an incantation but the words floated to his ears slow and distorted and he could not make them out. Slowly, he brought his hands closer together, the stone and the tip of the staff nearing each other. They almost touched and he let go of the stone but it did not fall. It hovered there, as if of its own accord. The tip of the staff spun and turned, opening for the stone that now entered into it. The wood twisted, then stilled, the stone encased in its tip, the deep red still visible between the curving pieces of wood: like bare roots wrapped around a stone of blood.

Corren shivered, his arms wrapped around himself, his feet not moving, his eyes wide. The vision was gone. He wanted to go back. He did not want to see any more. These visions engulfed him in a terror he did not understand. He did not know if he could take another one.

He stood for a long time, the tall hedges seeming to press in on him. He had no sense of time. Then, alarmingly, no sense of place. A feeling of disconnectedness struck him. He knew neither himself nor where he was and feared he was flying away from the earth. The hedges seemed to come and go, like an illusion. The ground too. Even when he saw the earth beneath him, saw his feet on the ground, he could not feel it. What he felt and saw more than anything was himself floating, spinning, his arms and legs flailing as if trying to get anchored to something, anything. It was like swimming in air. Was he propelling up, down, forwards, backwards? He could not tell. A flash of his own feet on the ground appeared and he wondered if he were actually doing none of it, really just standing there, then the vision of reality or unreality was gone and he was back in the air again, unbound to anything that could keep him in his own world.

"Illumay."

That was the word.

Except it sounded like this "Illl...UUUMMM...aayyyy......" It resonated with the same power he felt in the hedges of the Labyrinth. Corren wondered if it came from somewhere else because it sounded not like his voice and it was not a word he had ever known. But his lips moved to form the word and he knew it meant *deliverance*. When it was over he was lying on his back in the middle of the path on solid ground while the hedges flew up on either side before giving way to clear, blue sky.

Corren sat, slowly, knelt, achingly, then stood. He tried to focus on the aches in his body; they were comforting compared to the fear that seemed to reside everywhere else. It was not enough. He felt the fear and followed the path of the Labyrinth severely curving to his left.

Corren walked because he would not be defeated. He knew before he saw it that he was approaching the center. He walked, then the turn. He walked just close enough to the turn to see the center of the Labyrinth. Before he entered it, he froze.

The center was circular in shape, empty, silent, as well lit by the sun as every other part of the Labyrinth had been but in Corren's mind it was shadowed by darkness. The hedges swirled around in a blur, as if to enter would be like slipping into a vortex. He knew, instinctively he knew, he was about to discover the reason for his terror. Like plunging into icy water, moving too rapidly to allow a second thought, Corren took one step, two, three, into the heart of the Labyrinth. The vision opened before his eyes.

Corren held the staff. The spiraling wood glistened, the red stone in its tip cold and dark. The stone went alight, blinding, startling, stark, and powerful. Corren lifted his staff high, stone alight, and stretched out his arm as far as he could. The stone made contact with something—he knew not what—and darkness rushed over him, as quick and immediate as a candle snuffed out. He saw himself lying on the ground, his face unnatural, his eyes blank as hollow glass.

Corren stumbled back from the center of the Labyrinth and collapsed to the ground. The hedges were no longer swirling and the center of the Labyrinth was as it had been before, empty but no longer silent, for the reverberation of a scream he did not remember making echoed in his ears. It seemed to go on and on and he wished desperately that it would stop. He stared at the center of the Labyrinth in horror but his eyes and his mind saw only the memory of the final vision. The vision of his own death.

Five

Nicolai woke the next morning to find Corren out of bed. They had been given a small room in the tower with two narrow beds and not much else. Though the beds were comfortable enough, Nicolai had not slept well due to his concern for Corren; he had come out of the Labyrinth insisting all was well but pale as death. Each time Nicolai awoke during the night, Corren was lying on his bed, eyes wide, staring at the ceiling. He would not talk.

Now the weak light of dawn filtered through the small, round window and Nicolai sat up to look through it. This side of the Tower faced the Wilds, much less feared in this area for the simple reason that the dangers of the Wilds lurked elsewhere. The ground sloped up severely from the buildings to the line of trees. It was here that Nicolai saw Corren, sitting on the ground alone.

Nicolai dressed quickly. When he reached Corren he had not moved, only sat staring at the tree in front of him. Nicolai came almost right next to him, leaves crunching under foot, before Corren noticed his presence and startled. Though his color was back, his normally sharp features looked gaunt. Corren offered a smile, but it was only a mask.

"Did you sleep at all?" Nicolai asked, brushing away a few twigs and sitting down too.

Corren let the smile fall. He looked back to the tree. "Some."

"Have you forged your staff yet?"

"No."

Nicolai wanted to ask him what was wrong, what he had seen in the Labyrinth, but he knew Corren would not tell him. Instead he asked, "Are we still heading back to the encampment today?"

"As soon as I make my staff." Corren looked at his lap where his hands were cupped together. He opened them and Nicolai saw he was holding a walnut. "This was going to be my seed of influence."

Nicolai had no idea what that meant, but Corren explained. "Every staff is unique to the wizard who crafts it," he said, and his voice was almost normal. "It's up to the wizard to select a wood depending on the properties he wants his staff to have." It was as if something in him shifted. He spoke as if he explained the technicalities of staff making every day and found the normalcy reassuring. Only the dark circles under his eyes remained to show anything had been wrong.

Nicolai was not sure if he was comforted by Corren's apparent return to self or not.

"Then you need to carefully select a tree," he continued, gesturing to the tree in front of him. It was a sturdy oak probably a good thirty years old, one of the few in this forest heavily dominated by pine. "It should be healthy, have good retention properties, and have a suitable branch, like that one." He pointed and Nicolai saw a thick branch high above them. "Then you choose a seed of influence. It can be something small like a sunflower seed, or something like this walnut. The size is not as important as its properties. Of course, you add properties to it. Then you bind the seed within the tip of your staff and magically link them all together. It's amazing how powerful such a thing can be, what it can help you do."

A flash of concern crossed Corren's face.

"There are literally thousands of combinations, each with its own strengths and weaknesses." He played with the walnut, rolling it between his fingers. "You have to be aware of your own abilities and forge a staff that suits you. Your sage will sometimes guide you, but it's better to have a full understanding of the possibilities and make those decisions on your own." He frowned at the walnut, his hands quiet now.

"It sounds complicated," Nicolai said. "You're sure you want to do this now?"

"I need a staff," Corren said. "I can't exactly..." but his voice trailed away.

Nicolai decided to give him a nudge, encourage him to say whatever was on his mind. He leaned in. "Corren..."

"I came to forge a staff and that's what I'm going to do," Corren said straightening. "Then we can go."

Nicolai considered him. Corren obviously had his mind made up. Nicolai wasn't going to make him talk if he didn't want to. "I'll leave you to it then. Let me know when you're ready." He made to get up but Corren clutched his arm.

Nicolai froze. Corren let go and shrugged. "You can stay... if you want."

He sounded hopeful, maybe desperate. Nicolai understood. "I'll stay."

Corren exhaled, smiling weakly. "Well then."

It turned out to be a long process. Corren began by removing the branch from the tree. He did this without touching it, saying one incantation after another. The branch spun in midair, slowly at first, then rapidly. The little twigs that had branched off from it pulled in slowly and joined the wood of the main shaft, melding into one smooth line as it rotated. Finally Corren's incantations ended, the staff stopped spinning, and he reached up and grabbed it before it fell to the earth.

He was panting as if he had just sprinted up hill. When Nicolai expressed his amazement at what he had done, Corren only knelt and said, "That was the easy part."

Corren laid out a strip of cowhide. On this he arranged the walnut and several other herbs. His incantations began again. He touched nothing but leaves crumbled, stems split, granules emerged from the very earth. All these things combined together and spun as one solid mass in the air. Corren's concentration was unfaltering. He spoke almost constantly. His eyes never left what was in front of him. Nicolai could see it was taking all his energy to work this magic.

The walnut split open to receive the spinning mass of herbs. It sealed itself shut again; everything merged together. The walnut was smoothed and enlarged from the magic it had just endured. Nicolai thought he could hear a low humming sound. Corren finally used his hands to touch the walnut, plucking it out of the air. With his other hand he picked up his staff. He rose, holding both in front of him.

A minute went by before Nicolai realized something was wrong. Corren stood there, not moving, not speaking, not even breathing it seemed. Nicolai could not read Corren's face. Holding the staff and walnut in front of him, Corren scowled at it. Or was he concentrating? Corren's face flared in anger.

"ULTIMAH WYSARD BINDARI MAJJICKA!" he roared, and clapped the walnut and staff together. A flash of light flew out in every direction and Nicolai felt a hot rush of wind tear by.

Nicolai blinked the spots from his eyes. Corren held his staff, the walnut now concealed within its tip. He was still scowling, only looking at Nicolai now. "There's nothing wrong with this staff," he said, and marched off to Tower Hall North without waiting for Nicolai to follow.

Corren secured the saddle bag to the horse. Nicolai was bidding Bellamy farewell, thanking him for the hospitality. Bellamy received this warmly. "You are welcome here anytime, Nicolai," he said.

All Corren could think about when he saw Bellamy was the Labyrinth. Since he had decided to forget about the Labyrinth, the sooner they left Bellamy's presence the happier Corren would be.

Nicolai mounted his horse and Bellamy turned to Corren with a smile, but also with soberness in his eyes. Corren gripped his staff defensively.

"Thank you, Bellamy," Corren said. "We will see you in Stonebridge."

Bellamy leaned in. Corren's pulse quickened and he pulled his staff close to him. Bellamy spoke lowly, so only Corren could hear. "The journey in confronts us," he said gently. "The journey out enlightens us."

Corren did not look at him. "Yes," he said. "I know."

Six

Donnelly was wearing an expression of guilt and embarrassment with which Marcellus was becoming far too familiar.

It was midafternoon, and clear skies promised good weather for the departure of the troops in the morning. He and Donnelly walked through the rear encampment, making their way from one armory to the next, checking that their weapon stores were adequate for the troops heading into the Wedge.

Marcellus had left Donnelly in charge of the troops during his journey into the Wilds, including not just the daily management of over a thousand men—no small task in itself—but also preparing the troops for their missions into the Wedge and assigning someone from his own battalion to temporarily take his place as commander. When Marcellus returned to the encampment, far sooner than anticipated, Donnelly had rightly assumed he would go back to being commander of his battalion.

Originally, that was Marcellus' plan as well, but who knew what the next few weeks would bring? Upon reflection, he decided to take Donnelly back to Stonebridge as his right-hand man. Marcellus needed someone he could put in charge at a moment's notice in case he was otherwise occupied. Since Marcellus needed extra men to return with him to Stonebridge, he would bring Donnelly's battalion with its temporary commander and use them to guard the Bridge. The Wedge was no place for a battalion with a green commander anyway. It all worked out perfectly.

Except for one thing. Now that Marcellus had decided to keep the temporary commander in place, at least for the next several weeks, he wanted to meet him. That was when Marcellus asked who the commander was. That was when Donnelly's face went slack and his mouth parted ever so slightly. That was when Marcellus knew.

"It's Janus, isn't it?"

Donnelly's nod in the affirmative was barely discernible.

Marcellus came to a halt. "What are you thinking? A female knight is one thing, but a commander?"

"Your Highness, with you gone I needed someone I could trust to..."

Marcellus did not want to hear it and held up his hand, cutting Donnelly off. "I understand she's an asset. I see her skills. You can keep her, that's fine. But let's not be unreasonable. The men are not going to take orders from a woman."

"They have already, your Highness." It was not Donnelly who said it. Marcellus turned to find Janus standing within arm's reach. She bowed her head and faced him calmly, awaiting his reply.

Marcellus, quite frankly, did not know what to make of her. She addressed him respectfully, but with a confidence that suggested familiarity. Something about her manner threw him off, though not enough to cause him to lose control of the conversation. "You have been a temporary commander over a stationary battalion for a mere four days," he said. "I do not believe that demonstrates the willingness of hundreds of men to obey your orders in battle."

"No, it wouldn't," she said. "I have led my fellow soldiers in battle already. They answered my commands without question or hesitation."

While Marcellus controlled his indignation at this statement, he did not bother to conceal it. It was Donnelly he addressed. "What," he said levelly, "was *she* doing commanding *your* battalion?"

Donnelly threw Janus an exasperated glance and sighed. He faced Marcellus like a man doomed to fate, but a man who would face it head on nonetheless. Though this was a quality of strength Marcellus had always admired in him, it did little to curb Marcellus' displeasure. "This was during the West Sea Battle last year," Donnelly began. "When the pirates attacked the city in larger numbers than we expected, it was Janus' idea to split the battalion and cut them off in the rear. I made the decision to put her in charge of the flank on the south." He glanced at Janus. "Truthfully, I'd do it again. She was a key figure in our capture of that ship. The men thought so, too."

310

Marcellus looked to Janus. "That was *your* idea?"

"Yes, your Majesty. I remembered Maher's battle at Blue Cove and thought a similar strategy would help us."

Marcellus could not stop himself from staring at her in amazement. This battle had taken place over 400 years ago. "How did you come to know anything of Maher's battle?"

"I'm interested in military strategy," she said simply.

Marcellus glanced at Donnelly, who raised his eyebrows as if to say, *See?*

Marcellus looked back at Janus. She met his eyes unflinchingly, though without arrogance. He straightened and clasped his hands behind his back. "Are you familiar with the Athelstan Wars?"

A smile teased at the corner of her mouth. "Yes, your Highness."

"What is your analysis of King Athelstan's attack in the first battle?"

She looked at Donnelly in delighted disbelief. Marcellus would soon discover the reason for this. Janus began her answer in earnest. "Well, he should have protected the river better. I don't know what made him neglect it. He would have gotten much farther on his first pass were it not for that."

Marcellus knew firsthand how blasphemous this answer was considered to be by many and did not expect her to offer it. He was brought back, for the second time in recent weeks, to his conversation with his father as a child. Marcellus had made the same judgment about Athelstan's first attack, despite his teacher's protests, and he had been right. Just as she was.

"He was still brilliant," Janus said, holding out her hand as if mortified he might think she considered the famous king to be anything less. "His counterattack was swift and hit the enemy in a place they did not expect. Conquering Baker's Field gave him a reliable base of operations for the first campaign, not to mention a secure road for supply trains."

Marcellus listened as Janus continued on her views of the succeeding battles, excitement growing in her eyes, her manner becoming more animated, as if she could not stop her own passion. It was not her enthusiasm that struck Marcellus most curiously, though he had certainly not expected it. It was the nature of her analysis. She

311

was sharp, knowledgeable, insightful. He had never heard a woman talk like that before and few (if any) of his commanders could have made such a skillful assessment.

When she finally finished speaking, Marcellus said nothing. Only stared at her. He was aware of the many sounds surrounding them: the men talking in a group some distance away and the tents billowing out with a snap in the gentle breeze, the snorting of a horse in the stalls not far from where they stood, the clap of a crate being stacked on top of another. Noise all around, but he had never felt so still and silent in all his life.

She furrowed her brow at him. "You don't agree?"

His hands were still clasped behind his back and he squeezed them together. He shifted his weight slightly from one foot to the other. Those two movements brought him back to himself and he cleared his throat with a little cough. "I would say," he said, "that I *do* agree."

A smile spread across her lips and Marcellus felt compelled to retreat his gaze to Donnelly when she did this. Donnelly waited with a meek expression indicating he would accept any change of heart from his prince without comment. "I do not believe we have been properly introduced. From whence do you hail, Janus?"

She glanced abruptly at Donnelly before bowing and saying "Janus of Moran, your Majesty."

"Janus of Moran, this is a temporary assignment." Her dark brown eyes lit with excitement again. "Within two months Donnelly will return to his post as your commander. In the meantime, you and your men"—and he felt it odd to say such a thing to a woman—"will return to Stonebridge for training and city security."

The joy that had been on her face shifted just under the surface and her smile faltered. "Stonebridge, your Highness? I thought we were marching into the Wedge."

"I have need of an additional battalion in Stonebridge. Is there a problem?"

She blinked. "No, your Highness. Of course not. Thank you."

Off with you then, he wanted to say. Instead, "Be ready to head out in the morning." He and Donnelly left her then, and walked on.

The next morning, the bulk of the troops headed northeast toward the Wedge; those that remained headed south for Stonebridge. Corren should have been dreading the journey to Stonebridge after all the traveling he had already done over the last several days, but the truth was, the further away from Tower Hall North he got, the better he felt. The heaviness of his vision released and fell away from him—a few strands remained like a sticky web, but he brushed these off with persistence. He refused to think of it. He refused to let it distract him. He deliberately trained his thoughts on the potion he had to brew and tried to recall as much of it from memory as he could. He mentally ran through the steps of the spell that would create the fiery element they would hide on the ring. He tried to visualize all the troops guarding the Bridge, but only briefly, finding it easier to distract himself with the more magical details of their plan.

He focused on these thoughts as much as he could and ignored the nagging voice telling him he had made a terrible mistake.

Janus rode astride her white mare at the front of her battalion. She was deep in thought and so did not notice Donnelly pull his horse up next to hers. "*Commander* Janus," he said, teasing her.

She startled, then smiled. "So much for being dismissed."

"I don't know how you do it. The prince, of all people."

She shrugged, still smiling. Corren and Nicolai were riding together some distance away. Since they didn't belong to any battalion and therefore had no formation to march in, she noticed they had been sort of floating around. No explanation had been given concerning their presence, which she found maddening. If she knew the prince at all she'd simply march up to him and get her answers. As it was, she had no choice but to stay quiet regarding the mystery. For now.

Not far in front of her was the prince, leading the long line of troops back to Stonebridge. They would be there soon. Janus' stomach contracted nervously at this. She was happy enough to be going south, for several reasons, but Stonebridge was another matter. "Have you been to the castle much?" she asked Donnelly.

"Some."

"Do you see the king there?"

"I have, but not every time. I can arrange for you to meet him if you like."

"No!" she said too quickly to stop herself.

He started at her tone and looked at her in alarm.

She realized there was no undoing her reaction, so she resignedly leaned in to him. "I'd rather he not see me."

Donnelly widened his eyes. "Why?"

"Nothing... I... oh, Donnelly, please don't ask me questions."

Donnelly looked aghast. He leaned in and whispered urgently, "If you don't want the king to see you, you may not want to be encamped at his castle!"

She closed her eyes. A sick feeling of dread filled her. She reached forward and stroked her mare's long, coarse mane, needing a way to soothe her nerves. Lamtarra snorted and bobbed her head in answer.

"It'll be easier to avoid him," Donnelly said, his tone softer as he observed her, "if you're not a commander. Maybe I should recommend someone else."

"No. No. It's fine." She knew she was being foolish, but this was her chance to show what she was capable of, to do something more. Would there be another opportunity? She wanted it too badly to turn down, even though she knew that this time, she may truly live to regret it. She looked at Donnelly and he watched her sternly. She sighed and turned away.

"You don't know when to stop, do you?" he said. "One day, you'll go too far."

"You've been saying that for years," she said, firm now. "I'm still here aren't I? I won the prince's favor didn't I?"

"I doubt your beauty will help you with the king."

"It didn't help me with the prince!" she said. "My strategic knowledge helped me there."

"Yes," he said, looking away.

"It did!"

"I know it did."

"Why did you say that?"

"It was only a jest. Since when does that bother you?"

She looked at him sideways, not sure if she believed him.

They rode on in silence for a while. She firmly told herself not to think about it anymore. There was no sense nursing her worry.

"I don't want you getting into trouble," Donnelly said, interrupting her thoughts.

"I'm not going to get into trouble." She didn't want to talk about this anymore.

"You haven't done anything wrong have you?"

"Of course not!"

"Then what? Does the king know you?"

"Will you please stop?"

"Janus..."

"Donnelly, you don't need to worry. I'm sorry I brought it up."

Donnelly studied her. She pretended not to notice, focusing her attention instead on the horizon, watching for the dip that would indicate their approach to the Rheita Valley and the last crossing of the Big Winding River. He leaned in to her. She tightened her grip on the rough leather of the reins, ready to resist him. He didn't try to learn her secret. He only said, "Stay out of the castle as much as you can. He isn't often on the grounds."

Seven

Thinning clouds streaked across a blazing blue sky from one end of the horizon to the other. The rumbling of thousands of horses' hooves vibrated in Marcellus' chest, pulsing there as if part of his very blood. He topped the crest of the last hill, Rheita Valley opening to his view. Stonebridge and her steady walls capped the massive rise opposite him. Far to his right was Kilona Lake and the dam, with its spinning wheels notched along the top. Below him, the sunlight reflected on the river below, a glittering swathe cut through the green and tender heart of the land.

"There it is," Theo said, just coming up.

Marcellus smiled at his friend. If he could count on Theo for anything, it was this. "Perfect timing."

"Of course."

Marcellus examined the steed Theo was riding as they made their way across the flat top of the hill. It was a finely built horse with a chestnut coat (reminiscent of Theo's red hair) and had a nice, long gait. "Whose mount do you have this time?" Marcellus asked.

"Murray's."

"I thought I recognized him. He looks fast."

Theo grinned but kept his eyes on the valley. "One can only hope."

Marcellus grinned too. "When are you going to stop this foolishness and accept the fact that there is no horse that can beat Kedron?"

At this, Theo dropped the bantering and leaned over. "I actually think I found one that can, but I didn't dare ask to borrow it."

"Why? Whose is it?"

"The lady knight's."

They both turned and found Janus further back atop her white mare. She was talking with Donnelly, an easy smile on her face, the camaraderie between them obvious. She laughed at something he said and Marcellus wondered what they were talking about. A lady knight. What a curiosity. She met Marcellus' eye, suddenly and unexpectedly; he faced forward again. "It's a nice horse," Marcellus said. Theo laughed as if he knew Marcellus hadn't been looking at the horse at all. "Did *you* know about her?" Marcellus asked.

Theo snorted. "I wouldn't keep a secret that good from you."

As they reached the descent, the open valley spread out below them invitingly. Kedron tugged at the reins and cocked his head to one side; he was ready.

"Come on, then," Theo said. "Today's the day I ride to victory and rub your princely nose in it."

Marcellus laughed. "Theo, you've never really grown up, have you?"

"Well, you've never really been a kid," Theo said, "so that evens things out."

Marcellus felt the sting of that comment—he really *hadn't* ever been a kid—but didn't let it show. Instead he settled into the saddle, leaned forward, gripped the reins, kept his eyes on the river. His mind focused and his body drew taut. He was ready too. Behind them, the men slowed their marching and grew quieter. They knew what was coming.

"Glory to the winner?" Theo asked.

"Glory to the winner," Marcellus said.

In an instant, they kicked their horses into a full gallop, leaning forward, urging them on. Marcellus heard the whoops of the men rising up behind them in a roar. Kedron pounded down the hill at a furious pace and Theo thundered along next to him. Marcellus held Kedron back just a bit, keeping Theo close, waiting for the right moment. They shallowed out of the hill and darted for the river, sprinting for the finish line that reared swiftly toward them. The roar of the men fell behind, the water in front of them. Marcellus released Kedron to full speed. He bolted away and Marcellus leaned over his horse, keeping his weight on the stirrups, hovering above Kedron who pounded over the earth like it was the only thing he was built to do. The wind sped past, howling in Marcellus' ears, and his heart flew too.

Theo and his mount fell steadily away. "No," Theo yelled. "Go! Go!" It wasn't enough. Marcellus knew it without even looking back.

317

He entered the river a full length ahead, the water breaking and crashing underneath like applause. He heard the real cheer swelling in the air as the troops celebrated his victory, thrusting swords in the air.

Marcellus slowed, his face flushed hot with the high of triumph. Theo caught up and together they slowed their horses to a trot. They stopped at the bank so their animals could drink.

Marcellus patted Kedron on the neck. "Good boy."

Theo scowled. "Curse that Murray."

Marcellus laughed and clapped him on the shoulder. "One day, my friend. One day."

Aradia walked steadily up the steep, rocky hill, using her new staff as a walking stick. Her gray cloak billowed out behind her in the pressing wind. Stiff shrubs of sage dotted the landscape and the occasional wiry tree twisted out of the ground, pointing to the barren and colorless sky.

When she reached the top of the hill, she looked back the way she'd come. The Norrland hills were a dull yellow straining for green, the grasses parched from lack of rain. Away on the horizon was the edge of this kingdom and the beginning of another; Caedmonia in fact. Arbitrary boundaries, Aradia thought, that would soon perish under her thumb.

She faced forward again and continued on. A path emerged. Not far along, the first guard came into view. An older man with a hard, square face blocked the middle of the path, holding his staff threateningly.

Aradia did not slow, smiled in fact, and merely said: "I am Aradia. Itoh awaits me."

The change of expression on his face, from fierce intimidation to one of fearful meekness, amused her. He stepped aside, as she had been assured he would, and did so quickly so as to avoid slowing her progress. She passed without looking at him and continued along the path, which angled up yet another hill. Large, smooth boulders sprouted out of the hills as if some giant hand had dropped great pebbles from the sky. As she made her way, the great rocks slowly squeezed the path, towering on either side. The direction of the path was now dictated by the location of the boulders.

At the top of this hill were two more guards—which Aradia passed with equal ease—and the first sight of her destination. A wide building appeared before her, low slung to the ground and creeping over the earth like an undesirable growth. The stone was in disrepair and the shape of the building nonsensical, apparently added onto over the ages without plan or thought. The roofline, however, was extraordinary. Made of wood, it sloped up from the bottom and came to soaring peaks at the top, making the whole roof look like the curving waves of the ocean. Aradia had heard of this roof, not so much because of its beauty, but because it was said a great wizard crafted it without laying one hand on a piece of wood or uttering a single word aloud. The truthfulness of this tale was sometimes debated and frequently rejected. True or not, that wizard was long gone. Aradia came to see the latest in the long line of his inferior replacements, Itoh, Lord and Master of the Citadel of Zeverai.

Aradia approached the wrought iron doors of the Citadel. Upon announcing herself the guards flanking either side opened them for her. She stepped inside and the doors closed behind. They escorted her through a long hallway, lit by several torches angled out from the walls. The air was rank and heavy. The burning odor was strong, but did not mask the unpleasant smells underneath. Several doors led off the hallway on either side, but they made straight for the double doors at the end. The other side of these revealed a broad room located under one of the peaks of the sloping roof. The ceiling came to a point high above her. Small groups of witches and wizards watched her suspiciously, some whispering together urgently, others only following her progress in silence as she continued on. She kept her calm demeanor, which was not difficult; she feared no one here.

At the end of the room was a throne, ridiculously tall and elaborately engraved, as if he who sat there were king of the world. *What people won't do to support their illusions,* she thought. Several steps away from the base of the throne and the man sitting atop it, Aradia halted. He was a sallow looking man, with long, dark hair, the ends of which were lost in the many folds of his black and heavy robes. He held a staff in his left hand, a relatively short staff crafted from a single piece of wood, elm from what she could tell.

Neither spoke for a moment. Aradia understood Itoh was waiting for her to bow. She had already condescended to come as his equal; she was not about to pretend he was above her. She waited patiently, knowing it would not take long. In short order he stood, a dark smile stretching his skin as if he were not a person used to smiling. He opened his arms wide. "Our honored guest," he said in a cold voice. "Aradia, Head of the Order of Ceinoth."

There was no reaction to his words from those in the room. They already knew who she was. He lowered his arms, a cool expression on his face, though he still wore the smile.

"It is good that we meet at last," she said calmly. "Itoh, Lord and Master of the Citadel of Zeverai."

"Allow us to prepare a feast to mark this momentous occasion," he said.

Aradia raised her eyebrows slightly. She knew he resented her presence here, a fact that pleased her greatly; she was tempted to accept his offer to prolong his agony.

She smiled. "I have not the time for festivities, Lord, as I will be leaving soon. I trust our time would be better spent discussing the purpose of my visit. A simple meal as we meet will suffice."

He looked both annoyed at her rudeness and relieved to know her visit would be short. His eyes flicked to her staff, not for the first time. "Let us be about it, friend."

They walked together, past pale and somber faces, toward an antechamber to the right. This held just one dark table, and only four chairs though the table was built for many more. The wood was faded and scratched in several places. Without a window, the room's light came from a small chandelier, this missing several candles.

Out of the sight of onlookers, their mannerisms shifted. "You have entered my lair in safety," Itoh said as he sat at the broad table. A poor attempt at a threat.

She sat as well, keeping her staff in plain view for that threat was much more substantial. He studied it warily. She smiled. "I did not expect problems. I am sure I have not entered a lair of fools."

He smiled wryly at this. "You have come as agreed."

By this he meant *alone*. "Yes. And you have behaved as agreed. For this you are about to be richly rewarded."

He smirked, his skin stretching unpleasantly on his face as he did so. "You'll understand if I'm skeptical of this. The Order has never shared magical secrets with us before."

"The Order does not do so now. This comes from me. And it is singular. *One* secret."

He knit his brows together in a scowl. "You promised us much more than one."

"I did no such thing. I promised you a magical secret that would ensure your freedom from the northern territories. That it will. You will no longer be confined by the Guard of the Order and may go where you please. It is you who assumed it would take many magical secrets to accomplish this."

He did not say anything. It was his way of admitting his error. She made no comment on this. It was her way of showing him mercy.

"In exchange," she continued, "you will lend your skills, and that of your members, to me."

He nodded. "Go on."

She smiled amusedly. "I am prepared to arrange an alliance between you and Norrland."

Itoh coughed out a bark of contemptuous laugher. He looked at her incredulously. She waited. "The king will never align himself with us."

"I assure you that will not be a problem. There will be an alliance and it will be by this means that every kingdom known to man will fall to its knees."

Itoh's humor left him and he looked at her aghast. "You are mad. Norrland cannot defeat every kingdom. A small kingdom like Sakkara perhaps, but..."

"*Every* kingdom," she said. "Borders are troublesome to me and I intend to eliminate them. Norrland will soon be perfectly situated to do this. With our help, they will not fail. We begin with Caedmonia."

Itoh was shaking his head. "If we *were* going to attempt such a thing we would not attack Caedmonia, of all countries. We should start with Sakkara. It is small and weak and..."

Aradia was not pleased with this and found it beneficial to make that fact clear. She cut him off sharply. "I came to you because I believed you would be useful to me. If you are so lacking in confidence, perhaps we do not have an arrangement after all."

He straightened nervously, his eyes flicking to her staff. "I do not doubt our *own* abilities."

"What is it you doubt? My power? My ability to teach you what you need to know to accomplish this?"

He hesitated for one awkward moment. His expression relaxed and he cocked his chin. She believed she understood his thoughts. Itoh was treacherous—was famous for it—and was no doubt thinking that once she shared her secret he could use it to resist her, and therefore no "service" to her would be required. She allowed him to pursue this line of thought unchecked, allowed him to continue in his second erroneous assumption. She never said her magical secret would defeat the Guard. It would do nothing of the sort. She merely said the Citadel would no longer be confined by the Guard. Aradia would handle this facet of the plan herself, redirecting their attentions elsewhere as it were, giving the Citadel the freedom of movement she needed them to have.

The magical secret, while more powerful than anything the Citadel now possessed, would merely be enough to alternately subdue and protect non-magical men who had no more strength than a three-foot broadsword lent them. The secret would certainly not be powerful enough for the Citadel to subdue Aradia. She knew Itoh would cause his people to turn on her. She anticipated this with dark delight. Once she taught them her secret, they would strike, she would retaliate in one swift show of force, a certain expendable number of their members would perish, and the obedience of the survivors would thereafter be unquestioned. Itoh would effectively be reduced to a commander of the troops, but she would allow him to continue in his delusion as "Lord" for the time being. His complete removal from power would come at a more convenient date.

Itoh's lips twitched and his false smile wormed onto his face. "Nothing," he said in answer to her challenge. "I doubt nothing."

"Nor should you," she said. "Sakkara is incidental. Caedmonia is her defender and she must go first. You will go straight to Stonebridge. When the city falls, the rest will follow."

Itoh did not argue and Aradia smiled easily, leaning back in her chair. "If you wish to kill your enemy quickly," she said, "go straight for the throat."

Eight

Nicolai reached the king's office first and was greeted by a hearty welcome he could not help but enjoy.

"How good it is to see you," Clement said.

"Thank you," Nicolai said, self-consciously aware that while he was no longer so formal with the king in private, he was unable to bring his mouth to form the word "father" either. He offered a heartfelt smile. "How do you fare?"

"I haven't felt so good in years, Nicolai, thank you." Nicolai nodded, pleased. "I see you've had time to refresh yourself after the long journey home," Clement said as they settled in chairs adjacent to each other. "The clothes fit you well, son."

Nicolai felt himself warm at this. While they were away, Clement had stocked the wardrobe in Nicolai's room with new clothes and, resting on the bottom shelf, a velvet bag full of Caedmonian coins. It was more money than the farm brought in during an entire year, all gathered together in one neat bundle. Nicolai's own clothes had been too torn and blood-stained to salvage. Since he was wearing the borrowed clothes of a knight anyway he felt he may as well accept the gifted clothes for the time being. He had selected the simplest tunic and pants of the lot, though they still felt too fine and conspicuous to suit him. "You are quite generous," Nicolai said, leading up to what he had to say cautiously. "I know you desire to make me feel welcome."

"Indeed, Nicolai."

"The clothes were most needed. I am afraid, however, I cannot accept the coin."

"Why is that?" Clement said lightly, as if not surprised by this at all.

As firmly as he could without sounding rude, Nicolai said, "It is not mine."

324

"No? And what is yours? A lovely farm in Knobby Tree has passed to you, has it not?"

"Yes."

"Have you turned that down, too?"

Nicolai blinked. "No."

"Why not?"

Nicolai realized where Clement had been leading him, but he could not bring himself to answer the question.

Clement smiled and winked. "Fathers hand things down to their sons all the time, Nicolai. I simply choose to do at least some of that while I'm still alive. Now, enough of that. Tell me, what has happened since last I saw you?"

Even if a little reluctantly, Nicolai smiled. Clement had won *that* debate. One result of this was that Clement had relieved Nicolai of a different kind of burden. If this money truly did belong to Nicolai, then surely Clement would have no objection if Nicolai sent it to his mother. He decided to keep this intention to himself, however, just in case.

Nicolai began going over recent events. As Clement listened attentively, Nicolai was glad he had arrived here before the others. It was nice to have his father to himself for a few moments.

When Marcellus entered his father's office, Nicolai was already there. They stood as he entered and Clement gave Marcellus the usual jovial hug. "Home at last," his father said. "Tending to Kedron were you?" Marcellus answered in the affirmative, likewise when his father inquired after Kedron's untarnished racing record. Marcellus' attention was elsewhere. Something was different. It wasn't until Clement starting explaining what Nicolai had told him of current events thus far that Marcellus realized what it was. "Your hands!" Marcellus said without preamble or excuse at the interruption.

His father smiled and held them up. They were steady. His father's hands were steady. Marcellus could hardly believe it. He looked at his father's face and saw a healthy vitality he hadn't seen in years. "What? How?"

Clement gestured to Nicolai, who was standing rather awkwardly nearby, for they had not yet taken their seats again. "Your brother Nicolai is a healer."

"Are you?" Marcellus asked, stunned. "Was it the stone?"

"No, no. An herbal remedy."

"But... the best physicians, they could not heal him."

Nicolai shrugged. "Everyone knows something different."

Marcellus had long forgotten he permanently carried a load of tension on his father's behalf. The release of this was so complete and so sudden he felt dizzy with it. "So it's done then," he said and pulled his father into an embrace. "What a relief!" His father chuckled in his ear. Marcellus felt a sudden lump in his throat and stubbornly blinked back tears. He subdued himself forcefully. "What a relief," he said again, this time in a whisper.

He released his father, who smiled and patted him on the cheek. Marcellus turned to Nicolai. "Praise you, Nicolai," he said, shaking Nicolai's hand with both of his own. "Praise you."

"Not at all," Nicolai said smiling He gave Clement an uneasy glance. "I should tell you..."

"There's Corren," Clement said, interrupting. Indeed, there he was carrying his new staff. Marcellus was too cheered to feel the slightest bit of the stress he often felt in Corren's presence. Too cheered, that is, until he heard his father calling Corren "son," and Corren saying "father" in return. Marcellus' previous elation deflated significantly, but as they settled into chairs to talk he chastised himself for his childishness. *They have every right,* he told himself, even though he didn't truly feel it. He made the conscious decision to hold onto his joy for his father as they commenced the task of filling him in on all that had happened over the last many days. Even though Marcellus had already sent a letter detailing the outcome of the meeting with King Gunderic in Messina and the current movement of Caedmoninan troops into the Wedge, there was still much to tell: Nicolai's journey with Princess Praea, Corren's capture by Aradia, the subsequent encounter at the cave.

They talked for a long time. Though Clement asked a few clarifying questions, he mostly listened with an expression of concern and astonishment. Corren persisted in his annoying habit of addressing Clement as "father." While Marcellus tried to dismiss this, it stabbed at him every time he heard it.

Corren next explained his hidden element plan. "It will take me the next few days to brew the Concealment Potion. We still need to decide how to sneak onto the Bridge so I can use the potion to hide the element on the Gateway. I'd rather no one knows I'm doing this, including the Order. If Aradia finds out it's on there, all she'll have to do is remove it and this plan won't work. We need to give her no reason to suspect anything is different about that ring."

"Meanwhile," Marcellus said, "I'll take a few days to prepare the battalion I'm assigning to guard the Bridge. They'll remain stationed there until this is over."

"How do we handle the Guard?" Corren interrupted, referring to what Marcellus thought of as the Order's army of wizards. "They'll be at the Bridge, too."

Marcellus knew what Corren was suggesting. However, Marcellus had no intention of asking this group of wizards for permission to place his troops anywhere, especially not anywhere within his own city. He looked at Corren pointedly. "They are welcome to stay." Ignoring Corren's raised eyebrows, he turned back to his father and continued. "As we get closer to the Phoenix's regeneration, the three of us will join my battalion at the Bridge. If the only thing Aradia fears is 'the Three as one,' then we need to make sure we're the first ones she sees."

"How long until regeneration?" Clement asked.

"It has been ten days since the Third Song sounded," Corren said. "We have at least eighteen days until the Fourth one sounds. Maybe as long as five and a half weeks. The Fourth Song is key. Once that sounds, we'll hide the element and join the battalion at the Bridge. We'll have about twelve hours until the Phoenix regenerates, the only time it's vulnerable to attack."

"Do we know where Aradia is now?"

Marcellus shook his head. "She could be anywhere. Rather than waste our efforts looking for her, we'll wait for her to come to us. Just in case she is nearby, I think it would be a good idea to have archers on surveillance duty throughout the city, particularly by the gates and the docks. Aradia will be easy to distinguish with that hair of hers. If they see her, they'll have orders to fire."

Clement nodded his head thoughtfully. The afternoon had nearly expired itself. The sunlight was altering from a bright and clear light to a darkening shade of yellow. "Well," Clement said at last. "I think it's a good plan. I have no doubt you will maximize the use of the troops," he said inclining his head to Marcellus. "As for the magic of it all, I trust your knowledge in this area, Corren."

Corren said, "Thank you, Father."

At this Marcellus discreetly took a long, steadying breath, thinking, *Must he say 'father' every time he opens his mouth?*

"Nicolai will continue his training, I hope," Clement went on. "Knight Whittaker had high words of praise for you. I trust you know for yourself how rare a thing that might be."

Nicolai did, in fact, look simultaneously surprised, pleased, and embarrassed. Clement began saying something, as he had twice already, about his gratefulness that Princess Praea was safe. "How fortunate we are that Nicolai found her," he said, offering a sly smile to Marcellus. "Especially considering things."

This was met with confusion and Corren said, "Considering things?"

Marcellus rolled his eyes. He knew exactly where his father was going with this.

"I was quite impressed with the young princess," Clement said, still looking at Marcellus mischievously. "She is a fine young lady with a lovely personality..."

"Father..." Marcellus said, but this was ignored.

"I believe she would make an excellent match for you."

Nicolai straightened in alarm at this. Marcellus was the only one to notice since all attention was on him now.

"Father..."

"After all," Clement continued doggedly, with a playful smile. "Her voice is not too grating and her nose is not too large and she does not find coherent conversation outside the realm of her abilities."

Marcellus smiled reluctantly. Clement was referring to some of Marcellus' complaints about the previous matches his father had tried to arrange. While it was true that Praea was lovely and had demonstrated herself to have an intelligent mind and an admirable sense of duty to her citizens, there was something else. Marcellus glanced at Nicolai who looked like a person trying to conceal his horror, and failing at it.

"I have been in communication with the King of Sakkara..." Clement said.

Marcellus turned serious in an instant, shocked his father would go to such measures without consulting him first. "You have already arranged this?"

"No. King Jareth awaits my reply, pending my discussion with you."

"Good. You can tell him I decline."

Nicolai did not relax at all, only watched the king fervently.

Clement frowned. "Son, the kingdom needs heirs. You are more than old enough."

"It is important that *I* give you heirs?" Marcellus laid stress on the word 'I' delicately, but the reaction to it could be felt nonetheless. Corren shifted uncomfortably and looked down. Marcellus watched his father carefully.

Clement took on a rather regal countenance, not just Marcellus' father now, but the king. "As a prince of Caedmonia, yes, it is important that you give the kingdom heirs."

A prince, Marcellus thought. *Not the Prince, not heir apparent. No, a prince.* "I do not love Princess Praea," Marcellus said, only slightly masking his defiance with a casual air. "Perhaps you should offer her to your oldest son." Nicolai dropped his head in his hands.

"I hardly think I need to be in the middle of this," Corren said.

"You *are* in this Corren," Marcellus said. "You are the eldest son of a king."

"I never said I wanted to be the next king."

Marcellus could see he felt differently. "Are you saying you do *not* want it?"

Corren blinked. His mouth parted but he didn't speak, as if he didn't know what answer to give. Clement and Nicolai both watched Corren intently. Marcellus sat still, but kept the confrontation in his eyes. *Deny your right*, he thought. *Deny it now and see if I don't hold you to it.*

"I..." Corren said, the color rising on his cheeks. "I'm more concerned about Aradia at the moment."

Marcellus narrowed his eyes. He was forbidden a reply by a knock on the door. Clement's eyes, deep and thoughtful, did not leave Corren when he said, "Come!" and a page entered the room. The page delivered messages to Nicolai and Corren. Corren seemed eager to have a distraction. He was not looking at Marcellus at all.

Corren read his message in a room of absolute silence. "It's a summons from the Order," he said. "They want testimony against Aradia. Let me see yours."

As Corren took Nicolai's message to read for him, Marcellus said, "At least you're not in trouble this time." He tried, a little, to keep his tone neutral, but his father caught the bite and shot him a look. Rebuked, Marcellus looked away. If Corren noticed any of this, he did not react to it.

"Nicolai's is the same," he said.

"Why didn't Marcellus get one?" Nicolai asked. He too seemed eager to have the conversation on less dangerous ground. "He saw Aradia too."

"We made that clear to Bellamy didn't we?"

Nicolai nodded.

"I don't know," Corren said, still not looking at Marcellus, "maybe there was some confusion about that, but I think Marcellus should come as well."

There was a pause, heavy and full of all that had been said and gone unsaid. Clement and Nicolai watched Marcellus. Marcellus watched Corren. Corren watched his own hands. Marcellus, long used to balancing the needs of several issues at once, regardless of any needs he himself might have, tucked the disagreement aside for the moment and said at last, "I will go."

Nine

Marcellus decided to escape to the smithy before facing dinner in the Great Hall, glad to be away from Corren for a time. He approached the open-ended low building with its thatched roof and endless stream of smoke rising from the chimney. The heat from the forge reached out past the building and into the open air. Marcellus approached the front worktable and waited. The pinging of metal against metal reverberated with rhythmic predictability. The swordsmith, Gassan, had his back to Marcellus while he worked a long blade of steel on the anvil. The metal shone red hot and answered with a brief, intense glow with each strike of the hammer. Despite the heat and the noise, something about being here served to soothe, rather than agitate, Marcellus' nerves. For the moment, he was content to go unnoticed and let his tension drain away.

His eye roved over the room. Along the far wall was a semi-circular iron rack from which hung the prongs, chisels, and hammers of a swordsmith. Stacks of steel and iron in raw form leaned against the wall. All along the table was evidence of a work in progress: a cup-shaped guard, a round-edged pommel, the uncarved block of a future hilt. All these things awaited the blade Gassan was currently lengthening. Marcellus wondered how his life would have been different if he were a swordsmith instead of a prince. He considered the man in front of him, widely known for his superior craftsmanship and single-minded dedication to his work. He could almost always be found here and seemed to like it that way, moving in his smithy with the same confidence that Marcellus had on the battlefield. He seemed content. Marcellus found himself wondering if he would have been content with a life like Gassan's. Marcellus thought and he wondered, but he had no answer. He had always been a prince of Caedmonia and could not imagine anything different.

He looked over the castle grounds. This was the time of day when people on the grounds were generally moving in the direction of the castle and their evening meal. He saw Janus, the only person going in the opposite direction of everyone else. *It figures,* he thought.

Just as he wondered if she would see him she looked at him, as if she had already known he would be there. She must not have known, though, for she slowed as if in surprise and that strange, confident smile of hers appeared. She veered toward him, as if they were friends about to engage in casual conversation. He couldn't figure her out. He would consider her behavior audacious in anyone else. What was it about her?

Gassan stopped his banging and, turning, saw Marcellus. "Your Highness. I'm sorry, I didn't know you were there."

Marcellus waved his hand. "Not at all."

Gassan put down the peen hammer he was using and hastened to Marcellus at the worktable. "What can I do for you, your Majesty?"

Marcellus placed the hilt of his melted sword on the table as Janus came up next to him.

Gassan's eyes widened in shock and, it seemed, heartbreak at the sight of his handiwork in such a sorry state. He gingerly picked up the stump.

"Can you salvage it?" Marcellus asked. "It is too fine a hilt to lose."

Janus leaned in and Marcellus saw the long, intricate braid trailing down her back to her waist. "What on earth happened to the blade?" she asked.

Marcellus could not say that the blade had disintegrated in a magical barrier put up by a witch trying to kill him and his two secret brothers, so instead he said, "Cracking open too many acorns, I guess."

Janus and Gassan both stared at him a moment and Marcellus was just as taken aback by his own comment as they apparently were. Aside from Theo, he rarely joked with anyone. He was not quite sure what made him say it. It just came out.

Gassan recovered himself immediately, took the hilt and bowed, "I'll do my best, your Majesty." He retreated and Marcellus turned to

Janus regally, intending to recover himself. She smiled at him amusedly. He found it rather disarming.

He began to walk toward the gardens and she walked with him. *Why are you following me?* he wanted to ask. Instead he said, "I wish to meet with you and the other commanders tomorrow, right after breakfast."

"Again?" Janus said, for there had been a meeting just that morning before the troops broke camp for the final leg of their journey. "Commanders have a lot of meetings, don't they?"

He raised his eyebrows and she straightened as if remembering herself. "I'd be delighted to attend, your Highness," she said. He couldn't help but smile.

"You can speak freely, Janus. I encourage my commanders to express their opinions. Even temporary commanders."

She took on an air of sudden seriousness. "That's good to know, your Majesty. My first opinion is you have too many meetings."

Amused, he kept a straight face and nodded. "I see. I shall take that under advisement."

"Very good, your Highness."

They looked at each other sideways, permitting half-smiles to confirm the jest. So strange, a female commander. He realized he had not yet mentioned her to his father and wondered what the King would make of it. Thinking of his father he knew he should get to the Great Hall for dinner. He was tempted to go for a swim, but he had a feeling Janus would follow him all the way there if he let her. If he were going to be followed, he may as well eat.

He switched directions without warning and headed for the castle. He took a few steps before realizing she was no longer beside him. He looked back and saw her standing where he'd left her.

"Dinner's being served," he said.

She nodded. "Um, you know. I'm not terribly hungry. I think I'll tend to my mare."

He watched her for a moment. She seemed uncomfortable, something he had not much seen from her, aside from the night he discovered her among his troops. Well, he wasn't about to persuade her. "Suit yourself," he said easily and walked on alone.

Janus wondered how long she could reasonably stay here, hovering on the periphery of the ever-looming castle as she was. She could not avoid Clement forever. He may not be *often* on the grounds, but he surely ventured out on occasion. The longer she and her battalion stayed here, the more likely she was to be seen. Donnelly had said Stonebridge was typically the temporary stopping place for troop rotation, only a day or two of rest usually. She could hope that was true, but she feared leaving without answers almost as much as she feared getting caught.

She approached the stables and walked past stall after stall until she came to Lamtarra. "I shouldn't be here," Janus said, patting the white mare on her neck. Lamtarra was silent, blinking benignly. "I know, I'm a fool. What can I tell you? It wouldn't be the first time."

Lamtarra snorted.

"Exactly."

Well, if she only had a few days to figure out what was going on then she had better make the best of them. Who knew where she'd be sent to next. Somewhere too far away from here to do her any good, for all she knew.

If she weren't going to eat anyway, there was no time like the present.

"Up for a ride, girl?"

On his way to the Great Hall, Marcellus passed the Haven of Kings and saw Corren in there alone. His agitation at Corren returned instantly. The Haven of Kings was a long, narrow chamber lined on each side by portraits of the past kings of Caedmonia. Corren looked up at one of these now. Marcellus approached slowly and quietly, a habit long borne out of reverence for this room, so he saw the desire burning in Corren's eyes before Corren realized he was not alone. Corren looked at Marcellus with an embarrassed smile, trying to wipe his desire away.

Marcellus edged next to him and looked up too. It was King Dugald the Great, their great-great-grandfather who ruled for over 40 years and restored Caedmonia to a period of peace following a long and painful stretch of war. Marcellus was not really thinking of Dugald the Great. He held in his mind's eye the image of Corren when he had thought he was in here alone. Marcellus knew the look of driving ambition when he saw it.

"Who is this?" Corren asked, trying to keep things light but his very question caused Marcellus to wince. He had known all of Caedmonia's kings from the time he was a young boy, had studied their methods of rule and knew their strengths and weaknesses. It was only the beginning of his training, only the beginning, and here was Corren, the supposed heir, who knew not even the name of the great and legendary king before him. In that moment, the irresolution that had been haunting Marcellus was gone. What Corren wanted didn't matter. Even, for the first time, what the king wanted did not matter. Marcellus made his own decision. Whether the others assented to him or not, he had no intention of yielding.

"This is King Dugald," Marcellus said, not troubling to hide the edge in his voice. "He gave Caedmonia hope at a time when she forgot what hope felt like. He forged her borders in iron, no longer allowing enemies to cross as they wished. Thanks to his skill, his integrity, his strength, his ability to correct the errors of incompetent kings, the people began to trust in peace once more."

Corren was no longer looking at the portrait but at Marcellus, and with no small amount of apprehension. Marcellus, his blood racing hot as if in a battle, stepped to the next portrait and Corren followed cautiously. "This is King Idwallon, King Dugald's uncle and predecessor. He ruled for only three years before being slain on the battlefield. Caedmonia was blessed by his fall." Marcellus looked at Corren briefly, pointedly, and Corren raised his eyebrows. Marcellus looked back to the portrait. "King Idwallon was the son of King Oswald," he said, stepping now to this king's portrait. Corren lagged behind as if pinned to the ground. "King Oswald was responsible for bringing devastation to Caedmonia to begin with. He was slothful and selfish and lived off the spoils of the people while turning away from his responsibilities to keep her borders protected. The citizens fell to poverty, the treasury lay wasted before his lust for the pleasures of the world, and his armies became nothing more than driftwood for the enemy to crush underfoot. King Oswald was not worthy of his charge."

Marcellus turned and faced Corren, who stood still as stone. "King Oswald had no idea what it means to be a king. Being a king is not about sitting on a throne so the masses may adore you. It is not about living amongst fine things and taking whatever your eyes see and your heart desires. It is not about feasting on power. It is about defending a country that has existed long before you and will go on long after you. It is about protecting both land and citizens from whatever malice or evil attempts to descend upon it. Harm can come both over land and over sea. It can come in the form of great armies that outnumber you, or bands of pirates who know how to slip in and out of a village like lightning, leaving only smoke and death in their wake. It can come from floods, from famine, from economic collapse. A king must know how to defend and preserve a country from all these things. Is that something you know how to do?" Corren flinched but Marcellus went on, hardly pausing for breath. "Because being a king is not just about royal blood, Corren. A weak king can bring as much ruin upon a country as any outside foe, maybe more. I have been raised to understand that my role is to protect this country from anything or anyone who could harm her." He stepped closer now and Corren edged slightly away, unable to hold his ground. "Anyone. That is exactly what I intend to do."

Corren said not a word, but he didn't need to. His face said it all. The message had been received.

Marcellus did not wait for a reply, nor did he desire one. He left Corren swiftly, left him to ponder what had been said. Left him alone in the Haven of Kings surrounded by the images of rulers both evil and benign.

The sun had fully set. Only a thin band of dark purple streaked the horizon. The water of the bay was dark and comfortless. Corren sat on the window ledge of his room. His cauldron and supplies for the Concealment potion were laid out on the table behind him. His mind was not on them. Instead he heard a voice, Aradia's voice in fact, over and over again as if it were a hook in his brain as his mind replayed the memories of the past.

If you are to be appointed my apprentice, you must strive to go beyond that of your peers. Who will be worthy to carry on my legacy?

I hope to be, is what he had thought. Had that been so wrong? He had not known what Aradia would become. Yet... why did he somehow feel as if he shared in her guilt?

You thirst for power just as much as I do. He saw her in the carriage, the terrible look on her face as she had said it. As if she knew something. As if Corren could in no way deny it.

The great temptation of an intelligent mind is power. Corren closed his eyes.

Power.

Corren stood, felt to be fleeing. Where could he go? What he fought was within him.

Marcellus' words came to him. *A weak king can bring as much ruin upon a country as any outside foe.*

"Isn't it my right?" Corren said aloud. *Who says I would be a weak king? I am not negligent. Not irresponsible. Not too slow to learn the workings of a kingdom.*

Aradia's words echoed in his mind again. *Power... The great temptation... Power.*

"Not everyone abuses power. Why should I?" The room had no answer. Corren either.

He sat on the ledge again, for he had not moved even one step away from it. He knew Marcellus was raised to rule, that he felt he was losing his birthright; Corren knew this, understood it, but he didn't make up the rules, did he? Thrones go to the eldest. Was it Corren's fault that he was the oldest? Was it his fault that, however unfair, it had been he and not Marcellus who was taken away as a babe? Was that not how the Phoenix wanted it? Wasn't it?

Corren paced to the table and took in his hand the oak leaf that he had picked from the garden. He set it down. He went back to the window and stood, the sky black now, his own haunted reflection the clearest thing he saw. He thought about Marcellus. He grew angry when he thought about the confrontation in the Haven of Kings. Angry with Marcellus. Angry with himself. He was not nearly as angry as he could have been. Something deep within Corren overruled his anger. The truth was he felt more sorrow than anger and the reason was simple. Marcellus was his brother. Corren had desired to have a family for too long—and much too deeply—to dismiss this fact. He could try to be content with the warmth he received from his father and from Nicolai, for they truly filled a need he was eager to have filled. Corren was not content with only this. He wanted Marcellus to feel like a brother too. He did not want a wedge between them. Yet, there *was* a wedge, and Corren struggled with the knowledge that there was a very simple way to remove it. It was completely within his power to do so. Corren could give Marcellus what he wanted, what he maybe even had a right to have, but Corren did not know if he could do it. Even for his brother.

The knock at the door came softly but Corren immediately tensed, on the defensive without thought. The person on the other side turned out to be Nicolai. Corren invited him in, relieved.

"I didn't see you at dinner," Nicolai said.

"Well..." Corren sat on the chair by the table, his word trailing away. He picked up the oak leaf and shrugged. "I thought I'd get started on the potion."

"Can I sit with you?" Corren answered in the affirmative, glad for the company. Nicolai sat on the edge of the bed as Corren settled a stone mortar in front of him. He placed the oak leaf within it and began grinding with the pestle.

"I ran into Marcellus," Nicolai said.

Corren involuntarily stopped for a moment, then started again without looking over. "Oh?"

"He didn't seem to have much of an appetite either."

Corren glanced at Nicolai who had a rather knowing look. "Did he say anything to you?" Corren asked.

Nicolai shook his head. "No." Nicolai had such an easy and sympathetic manner that Corren was tempted to tell him about the confrontation with Marcellus, even tell him about his own doubts about what he should do. This was between Corren and Marcellus though. There was no need to bring Nicolai into the middle of it. Corren went back to grinding. Nicolai, apparently understanding that Corren did not wish to talk, sat and watched patiently. The grinding took a while, for the consistency had to be a uniform paste, as smooth as possible. Between the soothing, repetitive action of the grinding and Nicolai's friendly presence, Corren began to relax and let go, for now, of his worries.

"Why not do that with a spell?" Nicolai asked.

"Magic leaves a residue," Corren said, and dropped the mash into the cauldron. "Sometimes you *want* a magical residue, or can at least tolerate it. Other times not. Some things you have to do by hand."

After that they talked easily, about magic, about farming, a little about the prophecy, but mostly about nothing. Nicolai stayed until late in the night, until the potion reached a stage of simmering and Corren could sleep. Corren knew Nicolai needed to get up early in order to commence his sword training again. Corren knew Nicolai stayed in spite of this because he wanted to be a friend.

For this, Corren was exceedingly grateful.

Janus looked down at the graves in front of her. Five graves, covered in lovely flowers and creeping vines. Such a strange thing to behold here. "You did not tell me there were others," Janus said. The man standing next to her looked at her in his calm way.

"Was I supposed to tell you?"

She turned to him. "Was that the secret? Only that?"

He waited, and she did not think he was going to answer. "No," he said. "That was not the secret."

"So why did you not tell me? How many are there? Surely no more than three."

He shook his head. "There were three."

She paced away. Three. No wonder.

She looked back at the man, who stood still as a tree rooted deep in the earth. He was veiled by sorrow, both of the present and of the past, just as she was.

She had to give it one more try. "You need to tell me what's happening. We all deserve to know."

His face was firm. She knew that look. "I cannot. I..."

"Yes, you can," she said. She was getting nowhere with him. "You won't. That's different."

"You must trust me Janus."

She began for the door, too angry to leave properly. "You've made mistakes before," she said.

"So have you, Janus," he said, but she kept right on going.

Ten

Janus stood next to Lamtarra, who was saddled up for her morning ride, but Janus was too distracted to mount. Instead she lingered on the edge of the training grounds, watching Nicolai work the throwing spears with such dead-on accuracy even she was amazed (in spite of who she knew him to be). Janus pondered his presence here, pondered the five flower-covered graves, pondered her new assignment, and tried to piece it all together.

Marcellus had surprised them all that morning. They were to prepare troops for "guard duty" at the Bridge of a Thousand Ages. And whom were they guarding against? A silver-haired witch named Aradia.

Janus could not help but gape at this. She was not the only one. Whoever heard of troops amassing against a witch? At the Bridge of a Thousand Ages no less. What on earth for? The mystery of it all was maddening.

"This is not a difficult assignment," Marcellus had said as he left them. "After all, it's only one witch."

She realized then this assignment was not his primary concern. She had the distinct impression her troops were a strategic aside in a larger battle she knew nothing about.

She furrowed her brows as she watched Nicolai. She didn't see Corren much, but she knew he was around somewhere. What did they have to do with it? Why did no one wonder more at their presence here? No one seemed to know who they were. Did *they* even know who they were?

Marcellus came alongside her. She looked at him and wondered the same thing. Did he know who he was? If he didn't, shouldn't he? Oh how she wished she could just ask him.

He raised one eyebrow at her and snapped his fingers.

She startled and realized she had been staring at him in a state of complete distraction.

"I apologize, your Highness."

He wore an amused smile. "What could you possibly have been thinking about?"

She wanted to say, *"What do you know of Aradia? What is this really about? What are your real plans?"* For she knew one thing for certain. The troops at the Bridge were useless. He had to know it, too.

"I was only thinking about my assignment," she said.

"Simple enough for you? Can you handle it?" He was jesting with her again. Such a rare side of him, she couldn't help but smile. He was a mystery all by himself, never mind the rest.

"I should hope so," she answered. "If I can't take out a single witch with my own arrow I'll resign my post."

He laughed and so did she. Such bravado.

"That would be one way to get a woman out of my army."

"Hmpf. Again with that?" She mounted her horse, feeling more like herself. "What do I need to do to prove my worthiness, your Highness?"

He ran his eyes over her horse, inspecting the build. "Is she from the king's stock, Janus?"

"No. I brought her with me."

"From Moran?"

Janus of Moran. She flushed warm with guilt. "That's right."

"She is worthy of the king's stable."

Janus straightened. "I should think so. She's completely unbeatable."

He eyed her with those intense blue eyes, apparently getting her meaning. The first hint of a mischievous smile appeared. "I suppose it all depends on who she's racing," Marcellus said.

She took on her best goading expression, "I'm sure she'd be happy to race anyone."

"She looks fast enough," Marcellus said, shrugging, trying to look nonchalant, "but my Kedron has never lost a race and he's raced half the horses in Caedmonia."

"Not Lamtarra."

He shrugged again, but his eyes glittered. "We could fix that."

Janus paused. He reminded her of her old friend, no question about that. She realized she would like to be friends with him, know him for him and not merely the prince as everyone else seemed to know him.

She was taking too long to reply. "You're not afraid to race the prince, are you?"

"I don't know," she said, finding new delight in their conversation. "Are you going to banish me when you lose?"

He laughed. "Kedron is the fastest horse there is," he said. "You won't have to throw the race to prove it."

They looked at one another, playful smiles on their faces. It was her move. "Alright prince," she said. "Go get your pony."

It took them a while to agree on a racing location, though as far as Marcellus could tell, neither one of them seemed to mind the disagreement. He wanted to race through Rheita Valley to the Big Winding River, but when Janus declared that "too easy," well what could he say to that? She picked a stretch along the northwest side of Stonebridge that started low by the sea and climbed the hill to a flat ledge poking away from the castle walls. Quite inviting with its long green grasses and, he knew, a magnificent view of the sea.

From atop Kedron, Marcellus scrutinized the pathway to the top of the hill: narrow in places, rocky in others. "Have you been up that path before?"

"No," she said. "Have you?"

"Yes, and it's no path for racing."

"Well," she said. "If your horse can't handle it, we can take a nice, boring run through the valley. I'm just as content to defeat you that way." Her way of talking to him like that—not like a prince but just as Marcellus—reminded him of Theo. She watched him unguardedly. Behind her stretched the clear, blue water of the bay, the white caps breaking on the surface in reliable intervals. The sound of the water with its rhythmic swells enveloped him; he felt the vastness and power of it moving within him. How he loved the sea.

343

She raised one eyebrow. "Well?"

He remembered she was waiting for a verdict. He glanced between her and the steep climb to the top, thinking. He decided to be blunt. "That's a dangerous path and I take my challenges seriously. If you really want to race me, I'm telling you now to stay out of my way up there."

She smiled at him devilishly. "It'll be easy to stay out of your way. I'll be three lengths in front of you."

He laughed. "Alright then. I gave you fair warning."

"Are you ready?"

He fixed a semi-serious gaze on the hill and said, "If I'm napping at the top when you get there, don't wake me." He did not need to look at her face to know she was smiling, but he looked anyway. Her smile changed however as she grew more serious, more determined. *Competitive*, he thought. She was not the only one.

He turned his attention to the hill, his concentration likewise sharpening. The path, breaking out of the pale sand and rising wild before them, began several strides in front of where they now stood at a halt. Lamtarra shifted slightly closer. Kedron responded by adjusting his stance. "One," Janus said, and Marcellus settled into his saddle, the reins relaxed and sure in his hands. "Two." The wind rushed past him and his heart rushed too, anticipating the race. "Three," and all was still. The wind fell. A lone gull soared away in the distance. Kedron's muscles twitched.

"GO!" They bolted into motion.

The horses flew over the soft earth, the sudden rumbling of sound surrounding them. Marcellus felt the pounding of hooves reverberating through his body. They raced in a straight course for the path at the top of the hill, each jockeying to reach it first, their horses pushing toward it neck and neck.

The opening of the path was wide enough for two and they entered it together. This was all Marcellus needed for he knew the path was about to narrow and he had no intention of yielding to her. The path rose, then leveled, then rose again, their horses gaining the climb in great leaps, slowing only slightly, grasping for the next foothold with all the intensity expected from two horses that had never lost a race.

344

The narrow pass Marcellus knew was coming became visible. Up ahead, the path constricted, hugging next to the side of the hill, a steep drop off on the other side taking a savage bite out of the path before it opened up again.

Marcellus urged Kedron on, communicating his intent not to slow. Janus was still alongside him but Marcellus had the advantage of coming at the narrow pass head on. She would have to slow down or overtake him, but he would not budge. She rode close to him, trying to crowd him, but he held a steady course. His blood pounded through his veins and he felt the first rush of triumph when they reached that moment when he knew she would have no choice but to fall behind and follow him through the narrow pass. It was the advantage he was waiting for.

She did not slow.

There was no time or room to overtake him. He raced toward the path and she toward the drop off with brutal speed. He stole a glance at her. *Did she not see it?* Terror engulfed his exhilaration. "JANUS!"

He pulled on the reins, Kedron's head jerking down but it wasn't enough to get out of her way. She reached the drop off, soared over it as if in slow motion, horse and rider reaching out in one, great slow arc. Horror exploded within him, he may have even reached for her, but she landed solidly on the other side. Kedron's momentum carried him through the pass, Janus now half a length in front of him yelling out victoriously. A series of emotions fired through him: first numb shock, then trembling relief, then amusement at her boldness, and—finally—renewed determination to beat her. He pushed Kedron harder than he had ever pushed him before, but it was no good. She reached the top not quite a full length in front of him, throwing her arms up and whooping delightedly.

They pulled their horses to a stop, needing the length of the ledge to do it. She was smiling brilliantly, her glee evident. He could not help but smile with her. She saw him and tried not to look too happy about her victory. "I've never lost a race before," he said, disgruntled at losing but amused by her failed attempt at modesty. "I thought you were going down that drop off," he continued. "That was quite a jump."

345

"That wasn't very gentlemanlike," she teased, "not letting me pass."

"I wanted to win."

"I'm sorry," she said, and she sort of looked it. The glow of winning was too much for her to seem to regret it very much, though.

"Well," he said, "I suppose it was bound to happen eventually. We shouldn't tell Theo. He'll never forgive you."

She rolled her eyes, smiling. "You just want to keep my victory a secret."

He laughed. "Yes," he said. "That, too."

She leaned over to recognize Lamtarra's good deed. "Good girl," she said, patting her mare on the neck. Lamtarra bobbed her head once, twice. Marcellus sensed this was more than a casual exchange; it was an intimate moment between horse and rider. His favorite thing about her, so far. Janus smiled, patted her horse's neck again and straightened, looking at Marcellus. A slight breeze lifted a stray lock of hair that had escaped from her braid. He watched it rise—and shiver—before fluttering back down to her neck.

He looked out to the sea. It had never looked quite so fine.

Eleven

The journey back down the hill was almost sleepy in its slow pace. Neither one of them seemed to be in any hurry. They talked easily about nothing in particular, so naturally and easily Janus could not help but marvel at it. When they turned to Marcellus' childhood she was amused by his tales of his childhood self. Rambunctious spark he was, full of ambition to be a king until, as a boy of eight, he realized that first his father would have to die.

"I know that should have been obvious to me," he said, "but I hadn't thought of it like that before. The day I realized this was the first day I *didn't* want to be king. I thought, my father can just live forever and I'll live happily under his rule." They followed a curve in the path and he shrugged. "I felt that way for a long time. Actually, I still do. I've just learned to accept things the way they are."

Although apparently he hadn't quite accepted everything the way it was. When the conversation turned to his mother, she discovered a wound that ran deep, along with the answer to at least one of her questions. She found it painful to listen to him speak of it. He confessed he knew little about his mother. Shockingly little. He refused to condemn his father for it. "It's too difficult for him to discuss," he said. "I don't think he's ever stopped grieving her." Janus surmised Clement was not alone, for Marcellus clearly still grieved his mother too. "I only wish he could tell me something. Anything." Janus wished she could help him, comfort him, something.

They came to the narrow pass, stopping their horses. They looked at each other with raised eyebrows and laughed. It was a welcome lightening of their moods. "It's your turn," she said.

"No, no," he said, gesturing. "Please, ladies first."

She walked Lamtarra through and he followed her. She edged back out so he could come up alongside her.

347

"How long since you've been back to Moran?" Marcellus asked.

She truly wished he would stop mentioning Moran. "A long time."

"Is that where you joined the king's army?" She looked at him in surprise, not expecting to have to answer such a question. He smiled slyly. "How *did* that come to be?"

Even Donnelly didn't know the whole truth behind *that* story, though he knew more than anyone. Janus regarded Marcellus. For one wild moment she thought she should tell him the whole thing, all of it, right then. Not for her own selfish reasons, not even for noble reasons. She simply wanted him to know. She imagined his reaction. Her moment of bravery fled her and she knew she could not do it. She would have to settle for getting as close to the truth as she could.

She began. "It wasn't something I had ever seen in my future. Where I come from, people pretty much stay where they are and I thought I would do the same. It never occurred to me that I had a choice in the matter. Then my friend, my best friend actually, just..." Janus sought for the words. "She left one day. Left everything she knew, everything she had ever known, and went off for something I thought..." she stopped, watching Lamtarra's head bob in her rhythmic gait. "Well, to tell the truth, I thought she was crazy."

"Why? What did she leave for?"

Marcellus led Kedron out and around a small boulder in the path before coming back in again. "She was in love," Janus said, avoiding his eyes. "Leaving for that I could see, I suppose, but she was in danger. And she knew it."

"Being in love was dangerous to her?" he asked. She stole a glance at him, in an instant seeing not just the strong countenance of the prince, but the man she was coming to know underneath it all. How ironic for her to be telling him this story.

"Loving this person was dangerous to her." She saw him forming a question, but she went ahead quickly before he could interrupt. "I did my best to talk her out of it. Because of this, we didn't part well." Janus closed her eyes briefly against the memory. It felt terribly fresh still. "For a long time I didn't see her. Then one day, there she was again. Coming home. I thought sure she had come to her senses. When I found out it was just a visit, well, I got angry again." Janus

348

shrugged and smiled. She waved a hand, trying to lighten the weight of the past. "I was being awfully stubborn."

"I'm very surprised to hear that," Marcellus said with mock seriousness and she laughed.

"I'm sure you are," she said and they smiled at each other. "So, yes, thanks to my stubbornness we were in an argument the last time I ever saw her. A really terrible argument, truthfully. We couldn't see eye to eye about things, but it was more than that. I feared for her. She was still in a great deal of danger and really nothing could change that."

"What kind of danger?"

"Well… it's complicated. It doesn't matter anymore because…" and here Janus' voice broke. Unprepared for the sudden surge of emotion, she looked out to sea, forcing the lump in her throat back down. The barren mound of Crescent Island stood as a stark contrast to the golden, glittering surface of the water from the sinking sun's long-reaching rays. She waited until she thought she could continue. "Shortly after I saw her last we heard that she had died, just as I'd feared." She took a deep breath. "After that I tried to go on, but I kept thinking about her and what she had done. Instead of time making it easier to think about, it only became more difficult. Why had she done it? Was it worth it?"

"People risk a lot for love."

"Yes. She did. There was something else; I don't even know what it was. She only hinted at it, the last time I saw her, but I didn't think about it much at the time because I was too angry. Afterward, well, I became fixed on this one comment. It seemed like the missing piece to the puzzle, but I didn't know where it fit. If only I could've asked her. I would've known why she did it. Why she didn't just risk danger, but *pursue* it. I was told I was getting obsessed. Maybe I was. But I needed to know. I needed to understand. Since no one could tell me what I wanted to know, I did the only thing I could think to do."

Marcellus watched her expectantly.

"I left too."

"You joined the army," he said, as if he finally understood where this was going. "Is that what your friend did?"

"Oh no. Her danger was different from mine."

349

He cocked his head, studied her, as if he knew she was being elusive and he sought to open her up, reveal the mystery. "But, Janus. You risk your life too."

Janus nodded.

"*Pursue* danger, you could say."

"I do," she said.

"How is it different? Your cause is noble and hers was not?"

"No. Her cause was noble too, in its way. That's the point. I was completely wrong. My great regret." He furrowed his brows at her, not understanding. How could he? Would he understand even if she told him the whole story, even if he knew what it was really all about? Janus sighed resolutely. She would explain as best she could. "I, too, left my home to see if I could understand what she had given up so much for. I couldn't–wouldn't–duplicate her actions completely, but I followed in her footsteps as much as I could. Truth be told, I expected to come home knowing I had been right, that she should never have left. So out into the world I went, anywhere the wind blew it seemed. After a month went by, when I had thought I would be heading back, I decided to give it just one more month. When that month was over, I decided to give it one more month again. By the time a year had passed, I was finally able to admit to myself that I didn't want to go home. There really was so much in the world that I had been missing and I didn't want to give it up."

Janus smiled inwardly at the rush of memories before her, all the little discoveries that made life vibrant in a way she had never known possible. She had never known the joy to be had in the smell of the salt spray on the beach (because, of course, she wasn't from Moran at all) or the dazzling palette of colors in a sunset or the backbreaking hug from the fisherman's wife who couldn't contain her delight in seeing you. She did not know how high your heart could soar in the naked openness of a never ending prairie or the startling expanse of the night sky unobstructed by a forest of trees. She looked at Marcellus. She had not known a lot of things.

"Was that all it was? Seeing the world? A lot of people do that. Why was that so dangerous?"

"Marcellus, I cannot explain it. I feel so differently about things now. I can only tell you what led me to leave my home, what opened up new opportunities for me."

He continued to study her. She could not bring herself to say anything else to dissipate his curiosity about her vagueness. She had so far lied by omission, which was bad enough, but she could not say anything beyond that. She could have offered explanations to satisfy him, all of them false. She could not commit her tongue to any of them. Not to him. Janus could only look at him resignedly. What more could she say? "Hmm," he said, but his expression lightened and a smile tugged at his lips. "You're a mystery. *Still* I don't know how you came to be the sole woman in an army of men."

She relaxed a little. "You distracted me," she said. "Hush and I'll tell you the rest."

He smiled and she went on. "I ended up living in Braxton. Such a quiet little fishing village. I really liked it there and had gotten to know several of the villagers. I had been there for nearly six months when a band of pirates came." She was sober again. "They stole everything they could. Killed many of the men. Did even worse to the women and children. I'm sure you can imagine. It was chaos. I had never seen anything so horrible." This too brought a rush of memories —it had been so long since she had thought about any of this—and the flash of images of the pirates swarming the city was upsetting. She stopped the horse, almost unconsciously. Marcellus stopped, too. The wind, which had been slightly gusty all day, rushed past her. The sound roared in her ears, magnifying her memory of the raw screams of her friends on that day. She slowly slipped back to the present, was aware of the hill sloping down to the beach, was aware of the little fishing boat bobbing safe and unharmed in the darkening water, was aware of Marcellus watching her... she forced herself to go on.

"I wanted to stop it, but what could I do? There were so many of them. I just kept thinking, this isn't right, this isn't right. Then over the ridge came somebody else. A Caedmonian battalion just happened to be passing by on their way to Welton. If I had known what was going to happen next, I'm sure I would have cried out in relief. But I was just as confused by *their* appearance as that of the pirates. Until I

351

saw what they did." She turned to him earnestly. "They rushed into the village like a storm. I had never seen these men before and yet here they were fighting for us. All the villagers I could see were running gratefully for cover, but all I wanted to do was see better. I tried to stay out of the way, but I did not hide. I watched. If these knights knew any fear, and I later decided that they must have, they did not show it. And they didn't hesitate." Janus paused for breath, then said definitively. "Something in me changed that day."

Marcellus watched her intently, his eyes a more brilliant blue than any sea or mere sky could be. She urged her horse forward. He stayed right with her.

"I knew I wanted to do what those knights had done," Janus said. "I didn't know how I could. I thought my gender would never allow it, but until I found a way to overcome that particular barrier I settled for the next best thing." She smiled mischievously.

Marcellus leaned in. "Yes?"

"I followed the battalion around. I learned as much as I could from a distance. I practiced what I saw them doing on my own. I wasn't sure how I would ever move past that point. I truly feared it would be the most I could ever do, but I kept on anyway. Hoping somehow... I don't even know what. So I made a bow and..."

"You made your own bow?"

"Quite a fine bow it's been, too. So I made a bow and arrows and practiced and followed these poor unsuspecting troops around. Then..." Janus couldn't help but laugh.

"What?" Marcellus was clearly eager to hear it, sensing she was near to his answer at last.

"Fate dropped Donnelly into my lap, and that was my chance."

Marcellus eyed her sideways. "Into your *lap?*"

She shook her head and waved her hands. "No, no. Not like that." She laughed, but she could feel her cheeks getting warm. "No, I ran into Donnelly and persuaded him to give me a try."

"But... how did you do that?"

Janus straightened in mock indignation. "Have you not witnessed my powers of persuasion? Even a man like Donnelly could not argue when I showed him what I could do with a bow."

"You threatened him?"

"Of course not!" This time she really was indignant.

"Then what? For pity's sake."

She laughed. "I gave him a demonstration to prove I was serious. He said I could stay *temporarily*," and here she emphasized the word delicately, but by Marcellus' expression she knew he understood. "I've been with his battalion ever since."

Marcellus was quiet for a moment. He understood well enough how it had all happened, she thought. "Alright then," he said at last with a hint of a smile. They came to the bottom of the hill and descended onto the wide, alabaster shoreline, heading for the north pass leading to the castle. They moved on to safer subjects, much to Janus' relief, and talked contentedly all the way home.

It was dark by the time Marcellus and Janus entered the stables, leading their horses by the reins. Every few stalls a flickering torch penetrated the darkness. Their pace slowed as they walked in silence, their only conversation the soft footfalls on the dirt and their horses' hooves clomping along behind them.

They came to Kedron's stall and Marcellus crossed in front of her to open the gate. She stopped, near to the latch, Marcellus so close he almost touched her as he released the hook. He backed away, let go of the reins, and urged Kedron in. The animal passed between them and Janus cautiously raised her eyes to Marcellus. She found his eyes upon her as well. Kedron's saddle clinked as he shuffled in his stall, eager to be rid of his load. Neither rider moved until, a moment later, a page appeared, swiftly advancing down the length of the stables as one pursued by purpose, as pages so often were.

Some spell over them broken, they each averted their eyes. Marcellus went to Kedron and the offending saddle. Janus stepped back a little, putting her hand under the velvet curve of Lamtarra's neck. *What am I doing?*

The page stopped and bowed to the prince. Janus did not linger. She led Lamtarra toward her stall at the opposite end of the stables.

"You are summoned by the king, your Highness," she heard the page say. "He awaits you in his office."

Marcellus said "Thank you," and the page hastened his retreat, bustling past on his way back to the castle. She could hear the saddle sliding off Kedron and finding its home on the earth with a thud. The chinking of the bit and bridle followed. Only when it was quiet, when she was nearly to Lamtarra's stall, did she look back. There he was, closing the gate, eyes upon her once more.

He offered a tentative smile.

She turned away, but not before she shyly offered one back.

Twelve

Nicolai handed the metal ring to Corren. Nicolai had found it in the smithy; it was thick and heavy, like a horseshoe, only round. Like the Gateway. "Is this good?"

"That's perfect," Corren said, taking it. They were in his room, the finished Concealment Potion still in the cauldron but off the fire. Corren turned the ring over in his hand, examining it. "It looks thick enough. The fiery element is pretty strong. I don't want to break it." He held the ring out in front of him, said "Ett," then let go and dropped his hand. The ring hovered in the air. "What I'm going to do," Corren said, starting back for the table, "is apply the fiery element first, just like I will on the Gateway. Let's make sure this is going to work."

Nicolai glanced at the ring suspended in air, resisting the urge to reach out and touch it. He followed Corren back to the table.

Corren faced the ring and raised his hand, pointing toward it. He opened his mouth, then glanced at Nicolai. "You might not want to get too close."

Nicolai took several steps back, nearer to the bed, but did not sit. He watched intently.

Corren's gaze sharpened, his hand still raised toward the ring. "Sfe kara," he said. Nicolai thought he saw something spark between Corren's fingers. "Bliz ki ett!" A bright orange light swirled around Corren's hand, sparkling and popping. Nicolai squinted his eyes. "Enkumpe!" The orange light sped toward the floating metal ring, a glittering trail of light in its wake. The light collided with the ring in an explosion so bright that Nicolai instinctively flung up his hand to shield his eyes.

In an instant the light was gone. Nicolai blinked rapidly to restore his sight to normal. He exhaled forcefully. Corren walked up to the ring, inspecting it. "Good," Corren said. "It's on there. I can feel it." As far as Nicolai could tell, it looked no different from before.

Corren turned back to the table, this time grabbing his staff. "It's so strong I can almost feel it from here," he said. "That's what we want. It should be able to counteract anything Aradia is intending to use to get through the Gateway. Now let's make sure we can hide it otherwise Aradia will be able to feel it as well as I can."

Nicolai took a deep breath, his heart beginning to race a little in anticipation. He wanted to see Corren shoot that ball of light again, but this would be different. Now Corren needed to apply the Concealment Potion, something Nicolai was curious to see.

Corren backed up a few steps, slowly lowering the tip of his staff, not toward the ring, but toward the potion in the cauldron. "Degass a rowa," he said, and the surface of the potion altered, spun, lifted. Nicolai narrowed his eyes, trying to understand what he was seeing. It seemed the potion was expanding within the cauldron, rising toward the rim, ready to overflow. The liquid lifted past the rim but did not spill over. Rather it held its shape as if there were some invisible barrier around it. There was a gap underneath the liquid; Nicolai could see the rest of the potion still in the cauldron, and he realized what Corren had done. As if it had been a slice of something solid, Corren had simply lifted the top of the potion out of the cauldron. It hovered in the air, its clear liquid form rippling. "Tira met," Corren said. The floating liquid glided toward the ring, guided by Corren's staff, the tip of which was following the path of the liquid.

The shape of the liquid slowly flattened as it neared the ring. Corren said another incantation and the liquid started to glow in soft blues, pinks, and yellows. The shape changed again as it thinned and separated, surrounding the ring both on the inside and without. It stopped, as if waiting, not making contact with the metal yet. Wisps of the liquid curled out of the potion like little claws. When Corren said "Anya vayl immadia," these claws seized the ring and the potion curled together and slammed onto the metal all at once. A blast of energy rushed out in all directions, pushing back Nicolai's hair, blowing the parchment on the table, and shoving the drapery around the window back against the stone wall.

Everything was still.

Corren gradually lowered the point of his staff. Nicolai realized his heart was pounding. Corren approached the ring slowly. He held his hand over it, and closed his eyes. Nicolai waited, his heartbeat returning to normal, but his breath still suspended. Finally Corren dropped his hands, and looked at Nicolai. He nodded soberly. "It worked."

The lanterns in the king's office were lit, the room bright and promising, the fire burning energetically on the grate. Soft, black night draped the glass panes in the balcony doors. Even this cheered Marcellus; after such a relaxing day with Janus, he felt nothing could dampen his mood. "I've been looking for you for hours," Clement said. "I thought maybe you had gone into the city with Corren and Nicolai, but they returned some time ago."

Marcellus raised his eyebrows dismissively, a trace of irritation edging in. The last person he wanted to think about was Corren. "I didn't know they had gone to the city."

"Really?"

Why should his father sound so surprised? What did he expect? "What they do is their own business," Marcellus said.

His father looked at him sympathetically, with a perceptiveness Marcellus did not always enjoy. "Son, are you ready to discuss this?"

Marcellus shook his head. He appreciated his father's concern, but had no desire to discuss it with him. It was easier, for now, for his father's will to remain a mystery. "I have nothing to say."

Clement studied him for a brief moment then nodded, willing to let Marcellus be, or perhaps putting it off in favor of more urgent matters. "I called you here because I have news regarding Norrland. King Gunderic is dead."

"What?" His father held out a piece of parchment and Marcellus took it, reading it through. It was from one of their spies in the north. King Gunderic had passed, but the nature of his death apparently raised suspicions. Now the younger of his two sons was challenging his older brother, Simon (now King Simon) for the throne. The letter

357

briefly outlined some of the infighting and battles that had already taken place. Rebels were the least of their concerns now. The country was dissolving into civil war.

Marcellus shook his head. "This is terrible."

His father nodded his head. "Yes. Their country, once relatively stable, is now in danger of collapse." Marcellus caught the tone of his father's voice—a slight but powerful hint of sternness—and became very still, dropping his eyes again to the parchment in his hands. "Their rule of order, their judicial system, their economy, their citizens all now will be weakened. And what, Marcellus, was the cause of this great injury to their country?"

Marcellus looked at his father. Clement looked back at him directly. Marcellus knew what he was thinking and did not want to pursue it. He looked away.

"Son?" It was not a question, but rather a reminder that he, the king, had asked a question and was waiting for the answer.

Marcellus gathered himself, looked back at his king, subdued the sick feeling in his stomach. *What was the cause of their country's suffering?* With a sedate voice, Marcellus answered, "Her princes are quarrelling."

The king nodded, held his eyes, and said softly. "That's right."

Marcellus looked down and his father said no more. He left the room quietly, but Marcellus remained. He set the parchment on the desk. Behind him the flames of the fire were popping and biting. Marcellus allowed himself to ponder his father's point: when two princes quarreled, it was inevitably their citizens who sustained the wounds.

Marcellus slept in a state of agitation that night, his mind restless with dreams. They were random and scattered: images of war on Caedmonia soil, a startling flash of Corren crowned king, Clement in the Haven of Kings speaking to Marcellus but Marcellus could not hear what he was saying. *What? Father?* Corren patted Marcellus' arm. *It's alright, son.* The dream, nonsensical and thick with unpleasant feelings, lasted a long time. Marcellus woke at last, his mind taking a

358

moment to realize he was no longer asleep but cocooned in his bed, shadowed by tapestries all around, shadowed by his remorse at his father's gentle but pointed rebuke.

He groggily pushed aside the drapes; it was still dark. When he lay back down, he thought of what his father wanted from him. No ruling on the matter of heirs had yet been made, but his father's ruling on Marcellus' attitude was clear, and Marcellus' inherent and deep desire to please him began to hold sway. He tried to remind himself that he could trust his father to make the right decision, that his father had always put the needs of the nation above that of anything else. The only problem was, Marcellus no longer knew what was best for the nation. He only knew what he thought best for him, and this realization shamed him.

He lay restless in bed for a long time, at last deciding that if he were going to go without sleep, he may as well do it while swimming.

Marcellus crossed the grounds in darkness but by the time he got to the vast spring the first sliver of deep purple had appeared on the eastern horizon. He left his clothes on the bench and, bypassing the stairs descending into the pool, strode to a small outcropping of rock. Below him the water was dark and deep; he plunged himself in. His whole body cringed in shock from the freezing water, shivering thoroughly. He swam to the surface, shuddered one last time, then relaxed, the cold no longer unpleasant but invigorating.

Once the temperature of the water was no longer such a preoccupation, he noticed an odd sensation. At first he could not quite identify what it was: a current under the water? his own body still shivering? But he was no longer cold, at least not that cold. This was something else.

The same instant he decided it was like a vibration, a constant vibration humming in the water, he noticed his stone. He had kept his necklace on, unable to leave it unattended even in such a private setting, so his stone was now buried in water. It was not lit. It was not hot. But it felt different. He did not doubt that the vibrations he sensed in the water were coming from his stone. He lifted it out of the water in his cupped hand. The water slipped off its sapphire surface, a few droplets beading up. The vibrations stopped.

His breathing grew shallow. Slowly he submerged the stone and the vibrations started in an instant.

One dolphin swam under him, then the other. He ignored them. He thought of the line in the prophecy, about each stone having secrets only its bearer could unlock. He watched his stone now, dark, alive, quickened. Yet still elusive. What was he supposed to do?

He pulled it in and out of the water, watching the water react, feeling it in his chest, legs, everywhere. He dove under, held it in front of him, completely submerged, dolphins spinning around, his mind spinning too.

Despite that strange but familiar feeling that he could've stayed under water with the dolphins indefinitely, he came up for air and blinked the water out of his eyes. He let his stone hang hard against his chest, warm, vibrating, while he treaded water, trying to think. For lack of knowing what else to do, he pulled the stone up again. The enigma rested in his palm. *Secrets only its bearer can unlock.* "What?" he said aloud.

As if in answer, one of the dolphins sprang out of the water, splashing him, and dove back down. "Not now," he murmured. He dove under the water anyway. If he could've gasped in surprise he would have, for now he saw not two dolphins but six, no seven, no—and he counted again. Ten dolphins, all swimming around him excitedly.

He had never seen more than two in the pool and could not imagine how he had missed them before or from where they had sprung. Small caves retreated here and there on the bottom of the pool. He had never gone into these, for the current at the bottom was strong, but surely these caves weren't big enough to hide eight more dolphins. Why had he never seen them before?

More alarming than their sudden appearance, however, was their behavior. They swam around him almost frantically, closing in on him. Maybe the stone is agitating them, he thought and swam for the surface.

360

They blocked his way, swirling around him like a tempest, rushing through the water quicker than he would have thought they could go. Blood rushing, he maneuvered to get around them. They were everywhere. He could not find a gap. He could not get past them.

A wholly new panic entered him as he remembered his need for air. He slipped into battle mode, making one great effort to break through. This was answered by several dolphins colliding into him with their firm, smooth bodies, pushing him back down, before resuming their circling. He spun, tried again, and again a third time, his arms and legs smarting where he'd collided with them.

A new thought occurred to him so swiftly that he halted his resistance. He floated while they spun around him. He should've needed a breath long ago, but he didn't. He was sustained by something, sustained *by them*. He could still breathe, or rather felt he still had breath in him.

They urged him downward, down to the rocky, shadowy bottom of the pool. At first he did not resist but when the current seized his legs his urgency to reach the top returned.

Two dolphins sped into one of the dark pockets on the bottom and disappeared. The others pressed Marcellus toward it as well. The fact that he could not fight his way through them no longer mattered for the current had him now. The water yanked him feet first not into a cave... but a tunnel.

It careened into a steep descent. He saw nothing but blackness pressing over his open eyes. Marcellus sensed the tunnel walls racing past him. He curved, dipped, spun and more than once his arms scraped the walls, bouncing off stinging and burning. It seemed the watery fall would not end; rushing water roared in his ears, the darkness not relenting even though his eyes strained wide. The tunnel leveled and spit him into calmer waters.

The blackness finally lifted from his sight. He looked around, disoriented. In front of him two dolphins hovered in the water as if waiting. Behind him loomed a massive, rugged wall of rock, softened by patches of swaying seaweed. Out of a black opening came one dolphin, two, three, four, spinning and swimming out in different directions until all eight had joined him. Above, the water lightened just slightly, the rippling surface marred only by the tiny, blurred underbellies of a few boats. The tunnel had led him deep into the bay.

The dolphins surrounded him again, at more of a distance this time. They no longer swam in circles, but seemed only to be waiting. His heart pounded and he waited too, slowly treading water, his chest, arms, and legs throbbing from his collisions with the dolphins and the tunnel.

They all waited, dolphins and man. The stone was silent.

As if time enough had passed, the dolphins came together into two groups, one in front and one behind. Those in front turned their dark, sleek bodies away and swam out into the water. He and the remaining dolphins were still for a moment, then, of his own accord, Marcellus followed. The others came with him. They swam for a long time, deep indigo unbroken in any direction except for the lighter blue of the surface far above. Marcellus swam lighter and swifter than he normally would have; he had the impression the dolphins were helping him do this somehow.

The water lightened as morning advanced. In the distance, something appeared at last, a massive shadowy presence. Its clouded shape gradually sharpened into view. Marcellus realized they were approaching the foundation of Crescent Island.

He followed the dolphins as they swam around the base that was nothing but rock: no seaweed, no coral, no life. Only Marcellus and the dolphins cut through the morbidly still water. Above him, Marcellus could see hints of the surface and the violent waves he knew continuously crashed along the shoreline of the island. Here below, nothing moved.

They overtook the sharp tip of the crescent and swam toward its concave interior. On the other side great heaps of crumbled rock materialized, huge mounds of what looked to be massive boulders, cracked and heaved into pieces. He assumed this to be the remnants of Pearl Island, which had been swallowed by the sea. He looked closer. He halted.

Poking out from the rock, grotesquely pinched at its base and hanging limply, was a hand, or at least the remains of one. Its flesh was gray and peeling, bits of skin lifting up and floating in the water.

362

Marcellus stared at it in horror. *What is this place?* The dolphins urged him on. He swam but his eyes were on Pearl Island. He saw a decaying foot, farther along another hand, only the tips of fingers visible this time. Farther yet was an unrecognizable shape, pale and wasted. Finally he looked away.

The dolphins led him toward the inner circle of Crescent Island. Marcellus was not sure he wanted to follow them anymore. Neither did he believe he had a choice.

In the center of the crescent's cradled shape, deep under the surface of the water, a wide cave gaped open like a mouth in a perpetual scream. The dolphins cut their lithe bodies through the still water, leading him in. They were under the island now, its waters colder, darker, and tinged slightly green. The floor of the cave shallowed below him and the surface of the water drew near. He was in some sort of pool now and could nearly reach the bottom. Ahead were steps made of rock. The dolphin in the front, what little of it he could see through the space made by the other dolphins, seemed to twist and shape into something different. Marcellus thought he saw feet.

His head emerged from the water at last and he saw the dolphins emerging too. Only they weren't dolphins.

They straightened and lengthened into human-like creatures, walking out of the pool on the steps, arms calmly at their sides. They would have seemed graceful in their movements, but their skin was so distorted and misshapen and of such an odd bluish-gray hue that instead of appearing graceful they looked stark and alarming.

One after the other they left the water, both male and female of whatever they were. Hanging from the walls of the cave were what at first appeared to be clumps of wet seaweed, but which turned out to be shiny cloaks that they now wrapped around themselves. A long tunnel retreated behind them, wide enough and tall enough for several of them to walk into it together.

They turned and looked at Marcellus with their odd, haunted faces. His feet were on the bottom; he could stand and emerge from the water if he wanted to. Instead he hunched in the water, only his head above the surface, too stunned to move.

One of them spoke now. "Come," she said. It was a clear, crisp voice, both alluring and rigid.

Marcellus hesitated. He had no weapon, no idea if he would need one.

"Come," she said again.

He began to stand, but stopped. Not only did he have no sword, he had no clothes. The one who had spoken seemed to understand immediately. She retrieved another cloak from the wall. She did not descend the steps to him, but held it out in front of her, offering it to him. He would have to leave the water to get it. Seeing she intended not to move any closer, and realizing with embarrassment that the time for concealing himself had long past, he climbed the rough stone steps swiftly and took the cloak. It was coarse and damp, but he wrapped it around himself anyway. He shuddered involuntarily.

"Come," she said. They turned and began walking down the tunnel.

Marcellus stood there under Crescent Island, with a tunnel full of unknown creatures with unknown intent in front of him. Behind him was a watery pass he knew he could not traverse on his own. Away they went, gliding calmly into the darkness.

There was nothing to do but follow.

Thirteen

Deep into the heart of the island they went. A rhythmic echo resounded through the tunnel as drops of water slipped from the ceiling to the damp floor below. One hit Marcellus on the neck and he brushed it away even though his skin was still damp from the swim through the bay. The air was thick, moist, and smelled of sea salt. Only twice did the tunnel break off toward mazelike rooms, crowded with stalactites and stalagmites like so many pillars. In these rooms, Marcellus sometimes thought he saw other gray, eerie faces peeking at him. Whenever he looked closer, they were gone. There were no torches in the tunnel, no opening to any outside light, but neither was this underground world completely black. A strange, pale blue glow—a mist it felt—hovered in the air, clearing away just enough of the darkness to light the path.

The tunnel narrowed. He and his escorts walked single file, two of the dolphin-humans now behind him, the wet rustling of their strange cloaks sounding ominous. The ground sloped upwards slightly until they came to a large cave, this just as dank as the tunnel had been. The ceiling of this cave hung low, but the room stretched deep into the island, gaping and hollow except for the hundred or so mysterious creatures who were gathered here, still and watching. At the sight of so many, Marcellus felt to hesitate, but he would not allow himself to show fear. If these creatures were his enemies, he would at least keep the advantage of a firm face. Being unarmed, it was the only advantage he had.

Marcellus' eyes were drawn to a somber-looking man, his disturbing face turned toward him. Marcellus sensed he was their leader, though he was not set apart from the rest and there was no difference in his dress. Only his manner distinguished him. He had a regal air of authority that could not be mistaken. Those who had been leading Marcellus stopped, and he with them. The man calmly approached.

He came face to face with Marcellus and dropped his eyes to Marcellus' chest. The drape of the cloak left his stone visible. Marcellus felt a sudden surge of anger, ready to shield the stone from harm with his bare hands if necessary, hardly cognizant of the odds against him, only knowing he had to protect the stone.

The man spoke. "Are you Blue Brother?"

Marcellus' heart pinched in alarm. He didn't answer, trying to think, not wanting to give anything away but his hesitation was revealing in itself.

"You know of what I speak," the man said. "We are enemies of the Cunning One. Are you Blue Brother or no?"

Marcellus blinked. He did not necessarily take this man's declaration of being an "enemy of the Cunning One" at face value, but he saw no advantage to denying who he was since they seemed to know already. "I am," he answered, almost defiant in his tone.

The man in front of him smiled a thin, humorless smile. "Then welcome. I am Danu, King of the Water Faeries."

Again Marcellus could not hide his surprise. He did not think Danu looked like a faerie with his mottled skin and disfigured face. Marcellus had never heard of faeries changing into dolphins. Though, what had he heard about faeries at all, other than songs sung of their myths? Danu made no reaction to Marcellus' surprise and gestured with a sweeping arm, "This way." Watching the other faeries carefully, Marcellus followed Danu to a private room, still just another cave.

They were above the water level now. A tunnel-like opening to the outside let in a narrow shaft of sunlight, cutting through the blue glow and illuminating a rough circle on the stone floor. Through this opening, Marcellus saw a small section of the Bridge of a Thousand Ages and, beyond it, the coast of Stonebridge in the distance. The sun had made its way above the horizon and all outside looked luminous and inviting, particularly when contrasted with the dismal setting he was now in. Marcellus realized the hearing with the Order would be starting soon. He also realized that if he didn't show up, no one would think to look for him here.

366

Danu came near to the opening. The light shone on his stretched, grotesque skin, giving it a silver sheen.

"What is this place?" Marcellus asked but Danu held up a hand without looking, silencing him.

Danu lowered his hand and minutes passed in silence. Finally, he spoke. "For many millennia," he began "water faeries lived in Naida, a beautiful, hidden, underwater realm under the island of Thrayce." He spoke sternly, but a trace of wistfulness lined his words. "Part of our realm was in the water, part above it, hidden within the island itself and marked with magnificent waterfalls, crystalline pools, sparkling coral. Our magic protected us from discovery when we ventured out into the sea or along the shores of humans. Most importantly, it kept humans away from our cherished Naida.

"It was beautiful," Danu said, looking around. "Not like this. And we were beautiful too." He turned back to the sea and said softly, "Not like this."

"Not dolphins?" Marcellus asked.

"Oh no," Danu said. "That was my doing. We shall get to that."

He sighed and continued. "Over the years we noticed from afar the little light in the rock, the Rock of Light you call it. Every several hundred years or so, we saw it fade and diminish before going out, before bursting to life again bigger than before. Each time the flame renewed, the darkness over the land would come. It swallowed the sea too, but we learned not to fear it. The flame was a curiosity to us. No more than that.

"One day, that all changed.

"That day was the day the darkness came, the *last* time the darkness came. This time, something terrifying happened. A great section of earth heaved out of its place and into the sky, surrounded by cliffs such as we had never seen before. The water churned terribly at this and didn't settle for days. Then there was the bridge. The bridge came, too."

"The Bridge of a Thousand Ages," Marcellus said. Danu nodded darkly.

"Yes. We did not know what this was, where it had come from, or why it was there. We could sense the magic supporting it over the water, and the deep magic concentrated at the end. At first, we tried to forget all this. Ignore it. But this was not to be.

"Over the next several hundred years, our curiosity turned to obsession. We studied the Gateway, learned all we could about it. Some of its properties remained a mystery to us. We took to watching the bridge, watching the cliffs, watching the Rock of Light with its little building and people going in and out of it. We became certain those people had the answers we wanted, and our thirst for those answers steadily became desperate."

Here Danu paused, a distant look on his strange face as he gazed toward the sea. Marcellus still didn't know if he should be afraid of this man, this faerie, or not. He felt relatively certain, however, that he would not like whatever Danu had to say next.

"About 500 years ago now, we heard what they call the First Song." Danu stopped again, his face drawn down and full of shadows. "We knew," he said slowly, "the people would come to the Rock of Light. They always come after the songs. We've seen it many times before. It isn't the only time they come, but it is a *certain* time. The song increased our desire for answers, and so..." his voice faltered. In Danu's silence, Marcellus became aware of the sound of waves crashing against the island's base far below. "So," Danu said again, "we made the first of many fatal decisions.

"We came close to the Rock of Light. We allowed our magic that keeps humans away to fade for a moment. We watched and we waited until we saw one of them, a woman, coming to the rock alone."

Danu turned to him, his eyes black, his expression fierce. Marcellus felt a chill seep through him. "We rushed upon her and carried her into the water. We submerged her and her screams ended there." The intensity of his face ebbed as he went on, slowly returning to his former composure. "No one heard us taking her to Naida. Not that she didn't struggle. She had magic, *water* magic we were surprised to discover. But our magic was stronger and there were more of us than her. By the time we reached Naida, she was quite subdued."

Danu's face, blank now, turned away. "Through her, we learned all we wanted to know. All we thought we needed to know. She told us great secrets, though she did not want to."

368

Marcellus dared not ask how they convinced her to tell. He had a sudden vision of Prince Hugh hanging from a tree with his ears cut off. Would faeries stoop to such methods?

"She told us about the Phoenix, the ash, the stones," his eyes flicked down to Marcellus' necklace—exposed, vulnerable, warm—and up again to Marcellus' face, "and about the prophecy. We began to understand the power of the Phoenix, and we wanted it. We made her tell us about the Order. We would go out to the Bridge, examine what she called the Gateway, and come back to ask her more questions. This went on for several weeks. In that short time she began to fade. Our methods were... harsh... but effective. Using what she told us as a guide, we used our magic to learn more about the Gateway, feeling certain we could eventually learn how to get through it.

"This woman, Selene was her name, had a kind of unique magic that we wanted to learn more about. It was her water magic, well, moon magic actually, but the two are very closely related. No matter how we pressed her at first, she would not tell us the secret of this magic. Other secrets, yes. But not this one. As she grew weaker, however, we were convinced we could break her. There was one last property of the Gateway we had not yet discovered how to unlock. We thought her magic might help us understand it." Danu's mouth tightened into a line. "We were not wrong.

"When we at last forced Selene to tell us about her magic, she said, 'This is the last secret you will get from me. I will tell you what you ask me, then I will perish, as will you.' "

Danu smiled sadly. "She was not wrong.

"The secret escaped her lips and she died in an instant. That should have given us pause, but we had already gone well past the point of discretion. We knew she gave us the missing link. We now knew how to get through the Gateway. Still, one problem remained.

"Selene's magic was not something we could duplicate, or even steal. She had a rather unique way of harnessing the power of the moon. Then again, so do we. As I said, water and the moon are very closely linked. So we devised a method we thought cleverly similar. It would be enough, we thought, to get us through the Gateway."

369

Danu turned to Marcellus fully. "We had learned the Realm itself is protected once you get there. You are aware of this?"

Marcellus nodded.

"The Realm is protected against humans who are lesser, weaker beings than faeries. But since no faerie had ever set foot in the Realm, prior to its being lunged into the sky, we could not be certain our magic would protect us. We decided to combine our strength, link ourselves together, certain that this would be enough. Our magic thus joined would overcome the power of the Phoenix, and we could steal its unique abilities.

"That, then, was our intention. We harnessed a magic that is not wise to use. We created two islands in the magical shapes of a pearl and crescent moon. This gave us a place to do our work more convenient to the Gateway, along with a place to gather when the time came to go through. It took several moons, but finally we were ready and prepared the potion that would shatter the magic and carry us through the Gateway. The time had come at last.

"We gathered together under a full moon, a condition we felt important for the magic we were using to replace Selene's magic. We performed the binding ceremony. Our magic, our will, our life force all became fused together magically. We stood on the islands, physically separate but intrinsically bound together, with one faerie assigned the role of Voice and Power." Danu paused. "That was me.

"I alone stood on the Bridge. I alone covered the Gateway with the Breaking Potion. I alone saw what was going wrong. One element was not working. The element—which would have worked if it had been Selene's I'm sure—did not work because our magic was not quite right. I saw as it happened but it was too late. A powerful magic came out of the ring and straight toward me.

"Now," Danu said. "If I had let it hit me, I and all the water faeries connected to me would have died that day. It would have been better. It would have been just. Then maybe we—and you—would not find ourselves in the perilous position we are now in. But I did not let it hit me. I harnessed our magic, and panicked.

"I used the same dark magic, which is better left alone, that we had used to create the islands, and I transformed ourselves into dolphins.

The sudden change of form lessened the blow, so it did not kill us, but it did change us. Our dolphin forms are unmarred, but still only animals. When we transform back into our natural form, however, it is then you see the scarring. It is then you see the mark of evil upon us. Our beauty is gone. Our magic is diminished. We can no longer sustain our beautiful Naida, which beauty was fed by our magic. The waterfalls dried up. The pools grew murky. We could not bear to see it so. We banished ourselves to these underwater caves, fought amongst ourselves, blamed one another, cursed one another, fell to despair and sorrow."

Danu shook his head slowly. "Dark times. Some among us never moved beyond it. Others, myself included, slowly came to feel our fate was just. Our punishment just. Time has evolved our rage into acceptance. We have lived here grateful that at least our evil deed went unnoticed.

"Or so we believed."

Marcellus' skin prickled. He had heard enough. He had been in this place, this terrible, gaping, barren place, long enough. Yet he listened. He had no choice.

"The disappearance of Selene was highly disturbing to the Order. It was a mystery they could not solve. They recorded it in their histories without ever understanding what had happened. Likewise, they recorded the appearance of the islands and the 'disturbance' at the Bridge, again, without understanding at all what had taken place. For half a millennia, no accurate connection between the two was ever made. Until recently.

"Some weeks ago, we saw the second person we had ever seen use the water magic Selene had used. This was also a woman, and she used this magic to come to our islands and discover who lived here. This woman's name is..."

"Aradia." Marcellus was numb and cold. Danu nodded and Marcellus shook his head. "You didn't. You didn't tell her how to get through did you?"

Danu smiled bitterly. "There was a disagreement about that. We told Aradia what we had done, why we are the way we are, not yet realizing who she was. Soon her position as the Cunning One became

371

evident to me and to many others. She confessed her intentions. Once she had the power of the Phoenix, she said, she could heal us. Restore us to our former glory. All she wanted was the recipe for the Breaking Potion. Some were lured by her promise to help us.

"I refused her, not willing to make the same mistake twice. Another faerie stole a copy of the recipe from my chest and gave it to her. When this was discovered, our disagreement soon turned into a fight that ended in the closest I've ever seen faeries come to war. Some were trying to help Aradia escape; others were trying to stop her. It all ended in the water when she deflected our combined magic to Pearl Island, inadvertently killing most of her supporters and collapsing it into the sea. By the time the confusion had passed, she was gone and a third of our number were dead."

Marcellus stood rooted to that damp floor. It wasn't an earthquake that caused Pearl Island to sink into the sea. It was Aradia. *Aradia.* His mind could not quite comprehend it. Marcellus looked out the opening. The water sparkled and shimmered under the full sun, all except a broad line of shadow cast by the Bridge of a Thousand Ages. Its gray stone stood immobile over the surface, unaffected by the movement of the water below. He looked back to Danu, realizing something. "Your potion didn't work. It won't work for her either."

"No," Danu said. "She has the moon magic Selene had. She can do it right."

Marcellus turned, paced to the other side of the empty room and stopped, the rock in front of him pocketed with holes. "Why have you brought me here?"

"To help."

"To help?!" Marcellus spun around. "How much more damage do you want to do?" The cave resonated with Marcellus' voice, fierce in its own right. His heart pumped thickly. Danu did not react to this. He stood there silently, watching the water, his expression patient and calm. Marcellus found this as infuriating as anything else. He paced to the center of the room. Stopped. He went over all Danu had said. Danu let him do this uninterrupted. Marcellus' heartbeat slowed to a normal pace as he cooled, considering things. At last Marcellus sighed and straightened. "How do you want to help?"

Fourteen

Corren checked the door behind him and whispered urgently to Nicolai. "Where's Marcellus?"

"He said he'd be here," Nicolai said lowly.

For the second time in a month, Corren and Nicolai stood side by side, in front of the assembled Order, in the round stone room of the Cloister. As before, seven high-backed chairs perched on a raised platform. As before, three members sat on one side of the central chair, and two members sat on the other with the vacant moon-embroidered chair on the end. Unlike before, the central seat was empty too. The Wysard star embroidered on the back accentuated Aradia's absence.

"Master Corren of Tower Hall South," Bellamy began, the white symbol on the back of his olive hand clearly visible, "and Nicolai of Knobby Tree. You have been called here to bear testimony against Aradia, Head of the Order of Ceinoth."

Corren noticed two of the members eyeing him with suspicion, the same ones, in fact, who had voted for his expulsion. Corren stayed steady under their gazes and addressed Bellamy. "Do you know where Aradia is?"

"You are not to ask us questions," the one named Merhat said. He spoke as harshly as he looked, his thin face with its sagging skin making him all the more off-putting.

Bellamy raised his hand. "It's alright, Sage Merhat." Corren pressed his lips together, gave Merhat a sideways glance. "No, Corren. We do not know where she is. She has not responded to our calls to her."

"That is not information he should be hearing!" Merhat said.

"Why not?" Corren asked, giving Merhat his full attention now.

Merhat eyed him vehemently. "I have a few questions about your story and I'm not the only one."

"Merhat, please." This from Bellamy. "Corren, please tell the Order what you told me."

At this moment, the doors behind them opened and Corren turned, expecting to see Marcellus at last. Instead it was Princess Praea. Nicolai gasped.

"Ah, Princess Praea," Bellamy said. "Thank you for coming."

"I realize I am late," she said, coming to stand next to Corren.

He turned to Nicolai while the princess spoke. "I thought it would be Marcellus," Corren said under his breath. Nicolai looked disconcerted, nodding, eyes flashing to the princess; this increased Corren's anxiety about Marcellus' absence.

"I pray the Order will forgive my tardiness," Praea was saying.

"Not at all, my Lady."

The next several minutes consisted of Corren, Nicolai, and Praea all telling their versions of what happened with Aradia. They did this relatively uninterrupted, for Bellamy asked the Order members to hold their questions until the testimonies were complete. Along with Bellamy, Kai'Enna (the only woman in the Order now) and Kennard (the Head of the Guard who caught Corren on the Bridge to begin with) listened with patience and empathy. Merhat and the other man seemed to be restraining their disdain with difficulty. Through all this, Corren kept checking the door as if that would somehow make Marcellus walk through it. *Where is he?* He and Marcellus hadn't exactly been getting along well lately, but Corren never expected him not to show. Was he doing this to be spiteful, or had something happened? Corren didn't know which he felt more, anger or worry.

When their stories were finished at last, the atmosphere in the room was heavy and grave. Kai'Enna, who had first questioned Corren's character the last time, was the first to speak again. This time her voice was not stern and accusing, but rather quiet and solemn. "It is a terrible thing," she said, her aged face with its beaked nose bleak and sorrowful, "to see such evil among one of our own."

"You're not saying you believe them?" Merhat said.

"Why wouldn't I?" She leaned back heavily in her chair. "There are three witnesses, none of whom have any motivation to lie."

374

"No motivation? No..." Merhat sputtered as if he could not comprehend what he was hearing.

"Do you have a question, Sage Merhat?" Bellamy asked. His hands gripped the chair's arms slightly, his white symbol flashing.

"Yes I do. This young man," Merhat said, pointing a long pale finger in Corren's direction, "has already been found trespassing on the Bridge of a Thousand Ages, using magic against its defenses." Corren noticed the man at the far end, Solesmay, nodding his approval. He had also voted for expulsion.

Here Kennard spoke up. He rubbed his ebony forehead with large hands and held his rather large stature firmly. "Corren has already been cleared of those charges."

"Cleared by whom?" Merhat said, his voice rising. "By Aradia, who has suddenly gone missing! Where is she, I wonder? Has she ever neglected to answer a call before? No. She has not. I say she is not answering because she cannot."

The words hit Corren like a rock. He may have taken a step back.

"What of Nicolai and Princess Praea?" Kai'Enna asked. "They concur with Corren. Their testimonies agree."

"The farmer was on the bridge too," Merhat said. Nicolai straightened at this. His face grew stern. "How do we know they are not all in this together?"

"In on what?" Praea asked, her fair cheeks flashing scarlet. "What, exactly, are you accusing me of?"

"Let's just say I consider your stories to be highly unlikely."

"If they were lying," Kennard said, "their stories would have holes in them. Or inconsistencies. Something. But in all they have said, and it has been much, everything agrees."

"What about the supposed cottage?"

"What about it?" Corren asked.

Merhat sneered. "Bellamy sent Kai'Enna to investigate. It's abandoned. Has been for a long time from the looks of it."

Corren looked in surprise to Kai'Enna, who nodded affirmatively. "She must have emptied it out," Corren said.

Merhat raised his sharp brows mockingly. "Emptied it out?"

"Well how hard would that be?" Now it was Corren's voice that was raised.

"Not hard at all," Kai'Enna said. "I have already expressed my opinion about this. A woman of Aradia's skill would have little difficulty arranging that."

"Then why is she not here?" Merhat said. "Why has she not come?"

The man on the end now spoke. "There are too many questions for us to condemn Aradia," Solesmay said in a strangely lyrical voice. Corren noticed the pewter horn around his neck, strikingly plain compared to Nashua's for this one had no stones gifted by the Phoenix. Corren realized Solesmay must be the Head of the Cantori branch; he was the man who sang the Songs. "We all know Aradia well," Solesmay said. "She has ever been kind and generous, especially toward the young man who now accuses her. She is the reason he was not sent to a life of hard labor and poverty in his youth. In addition to her many responsibilities, even at that time, she took on one more. That was no small thing. Did she have to do this? Did anyone ask this of her? No. She did it of her own free will, demonstrating her superior character. What are we to make of that?"

Corren had asked himself those very questions more than once over the last many days and had never been able to come up with an answer. He looked at Aradia's empty chair and almost saw her perched there, saw her white cloak and silver hair. Why *did* she take him in? He realized Solesmay's question had provided the answer; it was only one more betrayal for Corren to consider. Her act of great charity put her into a different category in the mind of her peers. It demonstrated, as Solesmay said, her superior character. She would have known it would do so. Those around her, including those in a position to advance her career, would forever after view her through rose-colored glasses. And she had put them over their eyes herself.

Corren's anger at her welled up once more. Had she never done anything selflessly? Was he just one more step leading her toward her goal of becoming Head of the Order? Had she not cared for him at all? He shook his head.

"You have no answer to this," Merhat said, satisfied. "Your arrogance cannot save you from facts."

"Arrogance?" Corren could not restrain the anger in his voice.

"I see you have brazenly forged a staff without your sage's assent."

Corren tightened his grip on his staff. "Given that my sage attempted to kill me, I thought her 'assent' to be irrelevant." Corren did not look at Bellamy as he said this, fearing condemnation—or pity—in his gaze.

"You are being foolishly stubborn!" Kai'Enna said to Merhat. "Blind! Three witnesses. You do not see because you do not wish to see!"

"I would like to know," Merhat spat back, "why you are so willing to take the word of three strangers against Aradia. Aradia, of all people."

"What reasons have we to lie?" Corren asked. "You chose not to believe us? That is your right. We came here to warn you and we have. Ignore us at your own peril. You are free to take whatever action suits you. We will take the action that suits us."

"What action might that be?" Bellamy asked, his interest piqued.

Corren and Nicolai exchanged glances. They seemed to understand one another: this situation was far too unstable to bring the Order into their confidence. They would have to be careful. "I assume," Corren said, answering Bellamy now, "that you have assigned the Guard to protect the Bridge from Aradia."

Bellamy glanced at Kennard and nodded. "Yes."

"I trust Prince Marcellus would not mind me telling you that he intends to add his own reinforcements to the Bridge as well." The Order members exchanged surprised glances. "We would like the two groups to work in a spirit of cooperation."

Merhat huffed but Bellamy ignored this. "Sage Kennard, as Head of the Guardian branch, that is your decision."

Kennard nodded thoughtfully. "The more protection at the Bridge, the better."

"Fools!" Merhat again. Corren forced a deep breath, struggling to subdue the hot anger swelling in him. "This boy is looking for a way to get on the Bridge himself. If he makes us think he is helping, then he will hope our guard is down and he will have access to it. Or perhaps he will use the king's army to force his way on."

"Merhat, that's enough," Bellamy said. "Why would Corren have any control over the king's army?"

"He's in league with the prince. He's been staying at the castle."

"You think he's persuaded the prince to help him break onto the Bridge? Think about what you're saying. Why would a non-magical prince try to help a wizard do such a thing?"

"Why is a non-magical prince guarding the Bridge to begin with?"

"Because..." Corren began, but Merhat did not stop.

"We cannot allow anyone on that Bridge, especially not him. I don't like the idea of those troops interfering."

"Like it or not," Nicolai now said, in a gentle yet strong voice reminiscent of the king, "the prince of Caedmonia has every right to place his own troops anywhere he likes in this city." He looked at the Order at large as he continued, "He intends to place troops around the entrance to the Bridge and we tell you this not to gain your permission, but rather as a friendly courtesy so you are not alarmed or taken by surprise. We wish to combine our resources and work together. If the Order," but here Nicolai made a point to look at Merhat, "does not wish to work with us, that is your decision to make. Meanwhile, Corren and I are grateful the prince is willing to grant troops for the Bridge's protection. We will be doing what we can to help ourselves."

Merhat folded his arms. "I find it foolishness."

"That I can see," Nicolai said, much more respectfully than Corren would have. It was all Corren could do, at this point, to keep his mouth shut in order to avoid saying something he might regret. How on earth was he supposed to get the potion on the Gateway with Merhat acting like this?

"You are right," Bellamy said, "that the Order cannot, and will not," another glance at Merhat, "command the prince to do anything. The troops will be most welcome. Please extend our gratitude to the prince."

Nicolai nodded.

Bellamy took a breath, glanced again at Merhat. "If there is nothing further, we thank you for your time and testimonies..."

"You're letting them go?" Merhat asked.

"We have no more reason to keep them here. We have the information we asked for and I'm sure our plans from here on are better discussed privately."

Praea said, "I'll be in Stonebridge if you need me," and excused herself so quickly it was almost rude. Corren was far more interested in what Bellamy had just said to think much about it. Corren wanted to know what the Order's plans were, but he knew they would not tell him. Without good cause, that is. For a brief moment he considered revealing his stone, tucked safely away under his cloak. That would settle, once and for all, the matter about whose side they were on. But Corren didn't trust Merhat and, after Aradia's betrayal, he was not willing to take any risks. Who knew what Merhat's real motivations were? No, he needed to stay silent and they would have to figure out how to get on the Bridge later. They could always come back and talk to the Order again if needed, but clearly now was not the time. Corren looked at Nicolai to see if there was anything else he wanted to say. He was looking at the door after Princess Praea.

Corren nodded to Bellamy. "Thank you for your time." They turned to leave.

Kai'Enna spoke up. "Just a moment, please."

They stopped, waited. Nicolai seemed anxious to leave. She cleared her throat. Another moment passed and Corren furrowed his brows. "Yes?"

She smiled, "Where can we reach you if we need to contact you?"

Corren tried not to stare impolitely at this. The Order knew where he and Nicolai were staying. "At the castle," he said.

Another long pause. She nodded. "Very well. Thank you."

Nicolai and Corren exchanged glances as they left the main room of the Cloister and entered the small room leading to the outside. "What was that all about?" Corren asked, but Nicolai sped up his pace, eager to catch Praea before she left.

"I don't know."

Outside, the wind blew with persistent ferocity. The sky above was a clear, cornflower blue, but that would soon change. Tall, black clouds skated in from the western horizon and the waves along the shore leading away from the Rock of Light were noisy and restless. Nicolai did not see Praea anywhere.

"She left in a hurry," Corren said. Nicolai scanned the ground; he saw no evidence of a carriage, much less the knights who should be escorting her. In fact, he saw what he believed to be Praea's footprints. Prints that stopped and disappeared. Just as she must have.

He realized she must have flown here, and only hoped that didn't mean she had snuck away from her home in Dahlia. But given that two of her brothers had been murdered in the last month, would her father have consented for her to come? Nicolai shuddered at the thought of Praea in Stonebridge alone. Of all places. Nicolai knew Kai'Enna lived somewhere in Stonebridge and wondered if that's where Praea was staying. If she were staying at the castle, Nicolai knew nothing of it. He thought of Kai'Enna's last odd question, and her odd manner. Nicolai suspected Praea's sage had been stalling them so Praea could escape undetected.

He sighed in frustration.

Corren sighed in frustration too, but for a different reason. "How do we get on the Bridge now?"

Nicolai was concerned about this, too. "Is there some way you can sneak on?" They were walking at a quick pace, eager to reach the castle before the storm did.

"Without the Order knowing?" Corren furrowed his brows. "I was looking through my books last night, but I haven't found anything helpful yet. I was hoping the Order would be more cooperative."

"It seems to be just a few who are resistant."

"Those few are more than enough," Corren said, looking toward the approaching sound of horses' hooves.

Nicolai agreed. They had no reason to trust the Order at this point. They would have to find some other way onto the Bridge.

"Well, look who it is," Corren said, his eyes having found the source of the hooves, the sound swelling with each passing second. Tearing down the road on his steed was Marcellus.

"Now he comes," Corren said lowly.

"Hear him out," Nicolai said.

Marcellus dismounted quickly. Though he looked as distinguished and controlled as he ever did, there was something making him anxious. "I'm sorry," he said. "Is it over?"

"Just," Corren said bitingly.

Nicolai filled Marcellus in on the hearing. Though he listened with patience as he led his horse by the reins, there seemed an undercurrent of urgency. When Nicolai was finished they were well into the city and the wind was coming in cold gusts now, the sky above surrendering to gray.

"Alright," Marcellus said. "Not what I'd hoped for, but it is what it is. Now," he said, and whatever earnestness he had been holding back burst forth, "I need to tell you something."

Fifteen

The recipe for the Breeching Potion was not written on the usual parchment. This was dark green, thick, and felt waxy in Corren's hands. The lettering shimmered in silver. As his eyes ran over the ingredients and method, Corren felt his blood drop until he was as cold as the strange material he held. He sat in the chair in his room where they had retreated from both the approaching storm and the listening ears of citizens on the crowded city streets. Marcellus, who had not sat down all throughout his story about his encounter with the faeries, stood by the bed, his arm leaning on the post. "Well?" he asked.

Corren swallowed thickly. His mouth was dry. "This is..." he said, and no more. It explained so much. After Corren had first examined the Gateway at the end of the Bridge, he had come to the conclusion that it would take centuries to figure out how to get through it. He was not wrong. It did take the faeries centuries. They still had to coerce magical secrets from Selene in order to answer their last remaining questions. Aradia didn't have that kind of time to figure it out herself, but she didn't need it. All she had to do was trick them into giving her the recipe. Corren had been wondering how she was planning to get through the Gateway. Now he knew.

"This is what?" Nicolai asked. He sat on the lounge, his elbows on his knees as he leaned forward, watching Corren carefully.

Corren looked at him blankly, the recipe resting on his legs now.

Marcellus furrowed his brows. "Well?"

Corren glanced at the cauldron, neatly put away in the corner of the room. The clay jar filled with the Concealment Potion and the metal ring he had practiced on earlier rested on the table next to it.

"The hidden element is useless," Corren said dully. "A fiery element won't stop her at all. Not at all!" Corren stood. "What a waste of time!"

Nicolai's eyes widened. "What? What are you talking about?"

Corren was reading the parchment again. They watched him, waiting. Corren, yet again, came to the undeniable conclusion. "If this is what Aradia will put on the Gateway," Corren said, "then our hidden element won't stop it. This," he said holding up the green parchment, "is too strong. It will just break right through."

"So we can't stop her?"

"I don't know. Certainly not the way I was planning. We could block her attack, in theory. We could neutralize the effects of this Breeching Potion when she puts it on the ring, but the only way to do that is by making an antipotion designed specifically to stop it. That's what we would have to hide."

Marcellus exhaled, nodded. "That's what Danu said when I told him your plan."

Corren opened his mouth, but halted. He shut his mouth and narrowed his eyes at Marcellus. "Why didn't you tell me that to begin with?"

Marcellus glanced at Nicolai, then looked back at Corren apologetically. He said nothing.

"You were testing me," Corren said.

"I'm sorry." While Marcellus was firm, he said this sincerely. In fact, this entire day he had spoken to Corren without any trace of aggression, a first since their encounter in the Haven of Kings. "We're depending on you quite heavily," he said. "I wanted to see if you could come up with this on your own."

"You don't trust me."

Marcellus lowered his eyes, like he was thinking, or looking for his words. Corren was aware of Nicolai watching the two of them in anticipation. Marcellus looked up. "No, I do trust you."

Corren did not know what to say. Did not even know how to feel. While Marcellus' attitude could not exactly be described as friendly, neither was it cold, and he had certainly never verbally expressed any faith in Corren before. Even though Corren knew the underlying issue of heirs was still unresolved, still simmering under the surface, he could not help being effected by Marcellus' words. Corren was not ready to show it, though. The last few days had been too ugly for him to let it go in an instant. He had bigger problems to worry about anyway. "Well," Corren said, withdrawing his eyes to the cauldron again. "I don't know what we can do about this."

This was met with silence. Corren did not want to look at them. "I thought you said we could block her by hiding the antipotion," Nicolai said.

Corren shook his head. "I said in theory. In reality, it's impossible."

"What? Why?"

"Because," Corren said, sighing now. "The antipotion would require almost all the same ingredients as the original Breeching Potion and some are impossible to get. I mean, most are either hard to come by or expensive or both, but some are... just impossible."

"Like what?"

Corren sighed. Where to begin? "Like the crosshatch petal. These are little plants that grow on the bottom of the seafloor. I've never even seen them. I have no idea where exactly to find one and even if I could find one it would be too deep to..." but a thought struck him mid sentence. He looked at Marcellus. "Unless..."

Marcellus smiled, actually smiled, and pulled a brownish gray petal the size of his palm out of his pocket. It was covered in vein-like crosshatchings and looked distinctly slimy, though, as he dropped it into Corren's hand, merely felt cool to the touch. "Danu thought you might need this."

Corren ran his fingers over it lightly. "Look at that," he said. He stilled his hand, closed his eyes, felt for the elements that made up something so amazing, so rare. His arm tingled. "That's incredible," he whispered, eyes still closed.

"Not impossible?" he heard Marcellus say.

When Corren opened his eyes, he found Marcellus and Nicolai both watching him with patience and trust, like they were convinced he only had to decide to brew the antipotion, and that alone would make him able to do it. It was such a comforting feeling, Corren was reluctant to chase it away. He had no choice.

384

He cleared his throat. "This helps," he began slowly. "This is not the only ingredient that troubles me."

They still watched him, showing almost no reaction to this, as if they didn't quite believe this was a problem. Corren thought maybe he needed to make himself more clear, but he hesitated. Nicolai raised his eyebrows and said, "Well?"

Corren read through the potion again. He decided to start with the small problems, needing time himself to absorb the others. "Alright, well, I would need to go to Furden for the dragon scales."

"Furden?" Marcellus asked. "There's nothing closer?"

"There's a trader there who is the only one I know who will have them. I'm hoping he has koril essence too, or I'll be traveling all the way to Moran. Maybe Welton." He waved a hand. "If he doesn't have these dragon scales I don't know who will. Beyond that," and Corren hesitated again, "it will be expensive."

"We'll come prepared then," Marcellus said.

"Very expensive."

Marcellus paused a beat, and said, "Then we'll come very prepared."

Nicolai smiled. Corren glanced at this before addressing Marcellus again. "We?"

"You don't want to go alone do you?"

He said this so simply, like it would never even occur to him to stay behind. Corren shook his head in answer. What on earth brought about this change, he wondered.

"Okay then," Marcellus said.

"Well," Corren said. He felt the dark pressure of the last several days slowly lifting away, despite the impossible task presented him by the parchment on his lap. "Alright. The bigger problems are Selene's ingredient, the moonlight from the Isle of Iona. And of course this ingredient, which I can't read."

Marcellus furrowed his brows. "Let me see," he said, coming over. Corren held up the green parchment, putting his finger on the place before releasing it into Marcellus' hand. "That's not just illegible," Marcellus said. "It's a different language."

"Yes."

"Maybe this guy in Furden will know what it is," Nicolai suggested.

385

"Maybe," Corren said, taking the parchment back. "We'll certainly ask. I can check through my books too, though I don't think I've ever seen anything like this before." He eyed Marcellus. "You don't have any more tricks in your pocket do you?"

"No," he said, "I don't know what that says either."

Corren read through it again. The others watched him in silence. "I just don't know how to get all this," he said.

"You'll figure it out," Nicolai said reassuringly. "We'll help you."

Corren was only slightly comforted by this. Where before he had felt largely prepared and ready for the Phoenix's regeneration—aside from the problem of how to get onto the Bridge—now the two weeks before the Fourth Song could sound... it suddenly felt very near. The Song could take as long as five weeks, but there were no guarantees and they had to be ready. It wasn't brewing the antipotion he was worried about, that he could handle. Getting these ingredients, that was another matter. He rubbed his thumb along the crosshatch petal, the tingling sensation working up to his elbow as he did so. Something about that leaf, that impossible ingredient, right here in his hands, gave him hope. Maybe... maybe it could be done. Whether it could or not, they at least had to try. Their best hope of protecting the Phoenix was to keep Aradia out of the Realm to begin with. He did not know how else they could do it.

"Let's start by going to Furden," Nicolai said. "Maybe by then you'll know what to do about the rest."

"Wait," Marcellus said. "Will you still be able to conceal the antipotion once it's on the Gateway?"

Corren thought about this, thought about the elements that would be in the antipotion and tried to determine if they—like his fiery element—would be compatible with the Concealment Potion. He looked at the metal ring sitting by the cauldron. "I think so," Corren answered, "but I honestly won't know for sure until I test it."

This was met with sober silence.

"Is this what you want to do?" Marcellus asked.

Corren nodded. "Yes. We'll still guard the Bridge and try to stop her that way but... should we fail, I'd feel better knowing the Gateway is protected. It's still our best hope. Let's start by going to Furden."

"Alright," Nicolai said. "If we're going to do this, I don't think anyone should know anything about it. Not even where we're going. Not your advisors," he said to Marcellus, "not the king. No one."

"Why?" Marcellus asked.

"Because the only way this will work is if Aradia doesn't catch on to what we're doing, right?"

"Right," Corren said.

"If she hears we're on our way to Furden, and that's the only place to get these dragon scales, don't you think she might figure it out?"

"How will she know where we're going?" Corren asked.

"How did she find out who you really are?" Nicolai responded.

Corren's skin pricked. "I'm not sure."

"I've been thinking about this for a while," Nicolai went on. "If Aradia has spies, they could be anywhere. Even here. And," Nicolai said looking directly at Marcellus now, "the Prince of Caedmonia draws too much attention. If we don't want Aradia to know what we're up to then I think we need to travel inconspicuously."

Corren sat back and looked at Marcellus. "I think Nicolai's right. Caution certainly can't hurt us."

Marcellus was nodding slowly. "Yes. But..." he sighed. "Look, I can delegate a great deal. I brought Commander Donnelly with me for just this reason. Anything he can't do, certainly my..." Marcellus closed his eyes briefly, brought his finger to his mouth, then dropped it. He sighed again. "Our father can handle anything else, of course, but I can't cut myself off from him completely. He at least needs to be able to send a message."

Corren and Nicolai had exchanged glances, neither one of them missing Marcellus' self-correction. Since it was said with an undercurrent of frustration, no one seemed eager to comment on the phrase "our father."

"How can he contact you," Nicolai said, "if he doesn't know where you are? Even if we tell him, I wouldn't trust a messenger with our location."

"I have a battalion positioned relatively near Furden and my childhood friend Theo is the commander. No one has to know where we're going. I can pick up messages there. I'll just tell Theo to be discreet. If we end up having to travel further, we'll decide what to do at that time."

"Theo's trustworthy?" Nicolai asked.

"He's a complete scoundrel," Marcellus said, smiling. "But yes, he's trustworthy. We can stop and talk to him on the way."

Nicolai hesitated.

Marcellus got that serious, piercing look of his. "The king may not know where I am," he said, "but he *will* know how to reach me."

"Alright," Nicolai said. "We still need to come up with an explanation for our absences. Something Aradia will believe if she hears about it. Maybe that we're going to Tower Hall North again or something. Just Corren and I. And we can say you're doing something with your troops somewhere else. Somewhere in the opposite direction, like Western Caedmonia."

"I have a problem with one of my judges in the west," Marcellus said.

"Then that's your excuse."

"If Aradia figures out I'm picking up messages at Theo's camp, she'll know I'm not in Western Caedmonia."

"Have the king address the messages to someone else."

Marcellus nodded. "I was just thinking of a code."

Nicolai exhaled, seemed to be satisfied. "That's it then."

Corren couldn't help but be impressed with Nicolai's strategic thinking. No wonder he and Marcellus got along so well. Or perhaps the sword he constantly wore at his side was wearing off on him now.

"When do we leave?" Marcellus asked.

"We've lost a lot of time," Corren said.

Marcellus nodded. Corren was hesitant to say what he was thinking, but said it anyway. "Is there any reason we can't leave today?"

Marcellus raised his eyebrows, but shook his head. "Since it will only be us, it won't take long to get ready."

"I know a place where we can camp south of Landsdowne," Corren said. "We should be able to get at least that far by nightfall."

The storm that had been building had, apparently, arrived, for it announced its presence with a thundering lash of rain against the window. They all looked at the pane, water streaming down the glass, the sky outside dark though it was only midday.

"You're sure you want to leave today?" Nicolai asked.

They looked at one another a moment. The wind howled, whistling through whatever faint gap existed in the window frame. Corren looked over the potion recipe. If his trader didn't have koril essence and they had to go all the way to Moran for it, that was a week's worth of traveling right there. Plus two days to brew the antipotion. They had to beat Aradia to that Gateway, which meant being ready before the Fourth Song sounded. Corren didn't know how Aradia would protect herself from the magic of the Realm once she got there. He couldn't imagine she could endure it very long. He felt reasonably certain Aradia would wait until the Fourth Song before trying to enter the Realm because by then, the regeneration of the Phoenix would only be hours away. Worst case scenario, the Fourth Song was only two weeks away. Corren looked back to the rain-lashed window. Two weeks. That was when they had to be ready. Storm or no storm, there was no time to waste. "Who knows how long the storm will last," Corren said. "I don't think we should wait it out."

The others nodded in agreement, but no one, Corren included, was terribly enthusiastic. They worked out the final details and were ready to go their separate ways to prepare for their departure when Marcellus said, "There's one more thing I haven't shown you yet."

Corren tensed immediately. He didn't need more bad news. Corren's worry turned to curiosity, however, when he saw Marcellus suppressing a smile. "What?"

"Danu gave me a gift."

"A gift?"

"A peace offering. He's feeling guilty, I think. As he should." Marcellus paused, then unsheathed Danu's gift, holding it out for them to inspect. "I wasn't about to refuse."

Nicolai's mouth dropped and he jumped up to examine it closer. Corren rose too, interested, though not with as much enthusiasm. It was a short sword, almost a dagger, with a wavy blade made of the most extraordinary metal. The metal was solid, but with the appearance of liquid moving just beneath the surface.

"That's nice," Corren said. Nicolai looked at him wide-eyed like he didn't think that sufficient praise at all.

Nicolai looked back at the sword with longing. "He only gave you one?"

Marcellus laughed. "Sorry Nicolai. This one's all mine."

The storm lasted through the better part of the day, but the rain finally let up by the time the Three arrived at the lake south of Landsdowne that evening. Corren considered showing them Nashua's cabin. They agreed that would be too risky in case it was being watched. "No fire tonight," Marcellus said once they were by the lake, for though there was plenty of wood around, it was all soaked.

"May I?" Corren asked, gesturing to the ground. Marcellus gave him a confused look, as if to say, *May you what?* Rather than try to explain, Corren simply went to it, thinking no one would mind anyway. He started with the ground first, not wanting to sleep in the mud. In between warming incantations meant to dry the earth, Corren asked them to gather some wood for the fire. Nicolai set to this right away. Marcellus stared at Corren thoughtfully before following Nicolai to retrieve wood as well.

Nicolai soon returned. "You're good to have around, Corren," he said smiling, setting the damp wood on the ground. Once they had a cone built, Corren set it ablaze.

Dinner was simple (stew and hearth biscuits) but satisfying. Afterwards when they were quietly gathered around the fire, Corren noticed Marcellus casting him thoughtful glances. At last, Marcellus spoke up. "How do you do that?"

"Do what?"

"Magic. How do you do it?" He seemed earnest. This combined with his change in dress (simple peasant clothes, on Nicolai's suggestion) made him almost seem a different person than the one Corren had known.

"Well, you have to be able to sense the elements. It's an inborn trait and not everyone has it. But to make it of any use to you, you need to spend years practicing, learning how to control it."

390

"Like harnessing your will?"

Corren nodded. "Something like that."

"Hmm." Marcellus looked back to the fire and said nothing more. His curiosity seemed satisfied, so Corren didn't pursue it.

In silence, they watched the fire and its rhythmic, hypnotic flames. No one seemed eager for sleep. Being here brought back memories of Corren's childhood and on a whim, he started telling them about one. He told about the time he had found a five-legged frog not far from where they were sitting and brought it home to Mother Taiven. She declared it bewitched and chased first the frog, then Corren, outside with the broom and slammed the door. Corren laughed at the memory and they laughed with him. "She hollered at me through the window to go and wash. Even after I did so, she wouldn't let me in until supper." Corren smiled, realizing it had been many years since he had talked about Mother Taiven.

Nicolai shared a story next. He told of an incident involving his mother, an angry goat, and an unfortunate pair of bloomers that had them all roaring with laughter. Once they had recovered, Nicolai pressed Marcellus for a story.

At first he seemed reluctant. Finally he told them about the time when, as children, he and Theo discovered the secret passageway leading from his father's bedroom to his office. They had snuck down that tunnel several times over the course of a week to eavesdrop on private meetings people were having with the king. When the office was empty, and otherwise locked, they would sneak in and play with the swords stored there.

"He caught us just as we were about to try our first duel," Marcellus said smiling. "It was not a happy occasion. It was the only time he ever truly yelled at me. He was furious. I'll never forget it."

Nicolai raised his eyebrows. "That was the only time he ever yelled at you?"

"We were far too young for sparring," Marcellus said lightly. When Nicolai's astonishment did not vanish, Marcellus shrugged and answered the real question. "He's always been gentle and tender-hearted." Marcellus absently twirled the stick he was holding. "You're very like him, actually."

391

Nicolai looked at him in surprise. Marcellus leaned forward and nudged the fire with the stick. Sparks swirled up and flickered out. A log caved into two and the fire crackled and popped in response. Marcellus got up to retrieve another log from the woodpile Corren had made and added it to the fire.

They slipped back into contented silence. Corren looked off toward the mountains. It was a dark, starless night, the sky blanketed with clouds. In such darkness the shadows of the Mountains of Vitra were almost indistinct. He didn't know if he truly saw them, or only the memory of them. He began to look away when something caught his eye and held it there.

Off in the distance, a tiny, familiar flash of orange beckoned at him. It was the same flash of light he had seen here on occasion as a child. It was the same fiery light he had seen in the Labyrinth, the vision of which he had somehow managed to forget. Or nearly forget. Bury. Or try to bury. It all came rushing back to him now and he found himself chilled by sweat.

The light disappeared.

Corren glanced at his staff lying next to him on the ground. It seemed to be mocking him. He looked away.

Marcellus and Nicolai had gotten up and were preparing to practice with swords. They were both pretty well-armed, in Corren's opinion, though when he had declared this earlier Marcellus didn't seem to agree. In any case, Marcellus had brought two swords with him, his usual one and the one Danu had given him. Nicolai brought not just his sword but a few throwing spears he was apparently fond of and kept strapped around his calves. Corren had foregone all these, having only the staff beside him.

He would not look at it again. He turned away, lay on his side, and tried to force himself to go to sleep.

Sixteen

They had been traveling south of the road for two reasons: one was to avoid being seen by Aradia or anyone working for her, and the second was to avoid being seen by Marcellus' own troops. While he didn't know each one personally and his dress may have made him more difficult to recognize, he didn't want to take any chances. There were several knights who patrolled the narrow corridor between the Wilds and the Mountains of Vitra in order to keep bandits at bay. A few small outposts lined the road, but the main camp was nestled into a woody depression at the base of the mountains half way between Landsdowne and Furden. Theo commanded these knights. The Three were perched on a hill overlooking the camp, trying to see Theo and discussing whether they could get his attention without being seen or if Marcellus should just walk into camp, talk with Theo, and be done with it. Marcellus noticed Nicolai keeping a sharp eye around them, watching for scouts, though this was probably overcautious; scouts weren't used here near as often as they were on the border.

"There's Theo," Marcellus said. Theo crossed the camp alone, which was fortunate, but there were several knights milling about. Marcellus couldn't call down to him without drawing their attention as well.

"Now what?" Corren asked.

Marcellus cupped his hands together and whistled a trilling kind of bird call ending with a long *coo*. Theo stopped, looking around. Marcellus smiled.

"What kind of bird is that?" Nicolai asked.

"No kind. We made it up when we were kids." Theo had started walking again and again Marcellus trilled. Now Theo was really looking. "Come on, Theo. Up here."

Theo followed the sound to the bottom of the hill and started looking into the trees but not in their direction. Marcellus took several steps to his right, away from Corren and Nicolai, in an attempt to draw Theo's eye, but to no avail. Marcellus rolled his eyes, then bent down and picked up a small stone and hurled it. It bounced off the top of Theo's skull and he ducked, grabbing the top of his head. Out of the corner of his eye, Marcellus saw Nicolai cringe sympathetically too. But it worked. Theo was now looking right at him. Marcellus raised his arms as if to say "At last!" and waved him up.

Theo's look of confusion stayed painted on his face during his entire climb up the hill.

"Theo," Marcellus said as he drew closer.

Theo nodded in greeting, but his puzzlement only grew as he took in Marcellus' appearance. "What on earth are you doing in those clothes?"

"I'm seeing what it's like to live as a common man."

Theo lifted his eyebrows. "Mm-hmm. And does the common man often take to pelting people with stones?"

"My apologies, but you have all the sense of a tree." Corren and Nicolai, who Theo had not yet noticed, were coming up to them now.

Theo crossed his arms. "At least I'm not hiding in the trees. What's going on?"

"Nothing. I believe you know Corren and Nicolai," Marcellus said, gesturing.

Theo turned and looked at them in surprise. He instantly turned formal. "Yes, your Highness." Theo gave Marcellus an odd glance though, and Marcellus knew what it meant. They had been speaking casually to one another, much more casually than they ever did around other people.

There was no explaining things, so Marcellus got straight to business. "You may be receiving messages for Honnald here," he said.

"Honnald isn't with my troop anymore."

"I know. Just keep them for me and don't tell anyone you have them."

Theo furrowed his brows. "Yes, your Highness."

394

"I'll be by sometime later to check. Don't tell anyone you've seen me. Don't tell anyone I'll be back."

"Is something wrong?"

Marcellus glanced at Corren and Nicolai. "I just don't want to be seen."

Theo seemed to be thinking. "Will you be sending messages out?"

"It depends."

Theo pointed to a tent on the edge of the camp, tucked back into the woods slightly. "When I hear your call again, we can meet in the supply tent. I'll bring parchment in case you want to send out messages. How does that sound?"

"Good idea. Thank you."

Theo looked at Corren and Nicolai curiously, then back to Marcellus. He seemed to be making a decision. He leaned in. "What's going on here?" he asked, and he asked it like a friend.

Marcellus sighed. "Well, if I tell you, you have to keep it to yourself."

"Marcellus!" Corren said sharply, but Marcellus held up his hand.

"It's alright."

"No, it isn't."

Marcellus held up his hand again and Corren glared. Nicolai was not panicked, but rather wary, as if waiting for the catch.

Theo looked at Corren in alarm, amazed anyone would dare speak to the prince in that tone. Marcellus leaned in confidentially. "My father is arranging a union with Princess Praea," he said. "I and my bachelorhood are fleeing into exile."

Theo looked at him for a minute, then rolled his eyes. "Fine," he said turning to leave. "Keep your secrets."

He started down the hill and Marcellus smiled. "Thank you, Theo."

"Hmmpf," he said with a wave of his hand. Through his mock anger, Marcellus could hear his smile.

Marcellus laughed. "Alright, let's go." He turned and saw Corren staring at him in amazement.

"What? You didn't think I would tell?"

"It's not that, it's..." Corren faltered. "You... have a sense of humor."

Marcellus raised his eyebrows. "That's right. Just not with you." He slugged Corren on the arm and walked on, not waiting to see if Corren got the jest.

It was bound to happen eventually.

As Janus made her way to the meeting room by the stables she turned the corner and ran straight into King Clement. She came to a halt. He was looking right at her. He looked confused, like he was trying to place who she was. She had a wild and fleeting hope he may not remember her. After all it was so long ago and she was, without question, in the last place he would ever expect to see her, dressed as a knight no less. Maybe there was a chance he might not suspect anything if she could just pull herself together long enough to wipe away her look of dumb shock.

Recognition swept over his face. Followed by blunt astonishment. It was too late. They stood there, gaping at each other. When his anger appeared next, she shuddered. Donnelly was right. Coming here was a huge mistake.

Something caught the corner of her eye and she jumped. There sat Perkins, watching them in confusion. This was to be a meeting for the new commanders. She looked back to Clement. Surely he would not confront her in front of Perkins.

She tried to look normal, knew she was failing at it, and sat down clumsily on a chair.

She was no longer watching Clement. She was watching the dips and scrapes across the beaten earth floor. The smell of horses was strong here, being so near the stables, which made her think of Marcellus. This in turn brought a fresh wave of guilt. Did Clement see it on her face?

How long did she sit there? How long did time pass without passing? Why couldn't he just execute the terrible scene to come, before Marcellus arrived to witness the whole thing?

At last Clement spoke.

"Let us begin with introductions," he said. Out of the corner of her eye, she saw him gesture to Perkins.

He stood and bowed and Janus numbly stood too. "Perkins of Glenhaven, Sire. It is my pleasure to serve in the king's army."

"We are grateful for your service," Clement said, then turned fully on Janus as she tried not to step away.

She forced herself to look at him. His eyes were like flint. She bowed. "I am Janus, your Grace."

There was a heavy pause.

"From whence do you hail?"

She tried not to get hackled by this. He knew perfectly well where she was from. "Janus of Moran, Sire."

He raised his eyebrows.

He turned to Perkins decisively. "Prince Marcellus informs me you have a good sense of discipline and excel at organization."

"Thank you, Sire."

"I know he has been working with you, but he is unable to be here. I'm sure an assignment from me would please you just as well."

"Yes, Sire. Thank you."

"You will take your battalion to the western shores. You will work with Commanders Lance and Turck there. Prince Marcellus is already on his way, so they will expect you. Can you have your men ready to march in two days?"

Perkins indicated his great pleasure in doing so and Clement dismissed him with all the grace and calmness of a king. Nevertheless, it was an abrupt dismissal, their exchange hardly qualifying as a meeting. Perkins glanced at Janus curiously on his way out. Janus could spare no emotion for him. She did not miss the fact that Clement said Marcellus was away from Stonebridge. Her relief that he would not be here to see her condemnation withered under the heart-sinking revelation that he was gone. She had no time to dwell on this confusing state, for the current situation was about to get worse; she realized she was about to be left alone with Clement. Her instincts to go on the offensive and her desire to seek his forgiveness clashed with one another.

As soon as Perkins was gone, Clement turned to her. "Janus of Moran?" he said in a barely controlled voice.

"What else shall I say?" she said, her defensiveness winning out.

"How on earth did you come to be here? What have you been telling my son?"

"Nothing. Though I think it odd that *you* have not told him anything."

"Do not counsel me!" he said, his anger coming at her in such a blast that she flinched. "You are the last person to have any say in this!"

Janus recoiled at the truth of this. If he was angry at her, it was for good reason. Worse than that, she could see his hurt underneath it all. That was something she could not fight. His pain quenched her hotter instincts. All the regrets of the last many years took hold of her, stole her breath. She suddenly wanted nothing but to make things right. "You are right," she said, her voice breaking. She clutched her shaking hands together. "It is not for me to say. You are right."

He scowled at her.

"I do not wish to fight with you," she said.

"Something new from you."

She cringed, nodded. She deserved that. "I... I'm sorry. I'm sorry for everything."

"I am *not* the one who needed to hear that!"

The truth of that statement was too painful for her to bear. "No, you're not," she whispered. "Clement, please, I'm so sorry. I'm sorry I hurt her and I'm sorry I hurt you, too." He looked surprised by this but she saw his anger persist. She could not blame him for it. "I was so afraid that..." She put the back of her hand to her trembling lips, and he softened, almost as if against his will. She was unable to continue.

She turned away to the wall and leaned her hand against it. She pressed her other hand against her mouth, willing her emotions to retreat.

"You were afraid of the worst happening," he said quietly, "...and it did."

She nodded and turned to him, her raw emotions swelling again. "I made it worse. I know I did. How I've wished I could undo it all. Please believe me. Please forgive me."

He sighed. "Here, sit." He pulled out a chair and she obeyed. "I need to understand how you came to be here," he said.

398

So she told him. She told him almost the exact same story she told Marcellus except that some details did not need to be so cryptic. Others she left out completely because Clement already knew them. She told him in a way that begged understanding. She craved absolution. Although he truly wasn't the person she needed it from, he was as good as it could ever get. There was nothing she wanted more from him or anyone.

By the time she finished, he sat opposite her, his anger gone. All she saw was sorrow, resignation, and gentle compassion. She couldn't help but feel it was more than she deserved.

"You have been serving with my troops all this time?"

"I have served you faithfully, Clement."

"You have served *me?*"

"Yes," she said without hesitation. "You and the place she loved. The place I have come to love."

He shook his head. "Who would have thought it?"

"Certainly not me," she said and he laughed a little. She leaned forward. "You have my unfailing loyalty. Please know that."

He nodded. "I believe you. If nothing else, I always knew you to speak honestly."

She shook her head. "Except for the Moran part."

"Well," he said. "What else are you supposed to say?"

She smiled. "It is nice that at least one person around here knows the truth." He nodded and before she could stop herself, she said, "Don't you think Marcellus has the right to know?"

Clement furrowed his brows and said firmly, "To what purpose?" She saw she had pushed him too far. "How can I... nothing can change what he has had to go without."

Janus waved her hands. "I'm sorry. You don't need to explain." She wanted to argue with him. She wanted to tell him that five of her own were dead. She wanted to know what his sons had to do with it. What they knew of it, if anything. She could not push him about it now.

She watched him struggling to master his own emotions, which were as raw as hers were.

"I'd like to stay, Clement. Please."

"Hmm," he said. It was his turn to stand, pace away, and think apart from her. She waited. Though she wanted to continue in the life she had built for herself, Janus knew he had already shown her more kindness than she deserved. She could not demand any more from him. So she waited, hoping he would allow her to stay but prepared to accept his decision without anger or argument if he wanted her to go. She could not cause him any more pain.

He kept his back to her when he spoke again at last. "You are not to say anything to Marcellus," he said.

"Not without your consent."

He faced her now. "Not at *all*."

Despite her own will in this, she knew it was not her decision. She shook her head and answered, "No."

"I can trust you?"

"I did not tell him when I had the opportunity. I will not tell him if you wish me not to."

"I'm going to encourage him to assign you elsewhere."

She repressed the urge to complain against this. She had wanted to leave before but now that he knew she was here, she felt a strange pain at the thought of leaving. "As you wish."

Clement sighed again. "Well," he said quietly, as if to himself. "Well," and this more firmly, "in the meantime, I may as well pass along your assignment." He did this mechanically, as if falling back on the routine of giving orders to a soldier. She fell back on routine too, standing at attention. When he finished, she bowed her head. "Yes, Sire."

"Very well," he said. She pained at his expression. He was drawn, tired. The shock of it all seemed to be settling in.

She took a risk and put her hand on Clement's arm. His pale blue eyes softened. "I am truly sorry," she said.

He nodded. "I know you are."

"I wish...I wish that..." Her words caught in her throat. So much to say. Too much to say.

"I know," he said. "I wish, too."

Seventeen

Long ago, beneath the earthen blanket of the world, in the green sparkling caverns of Amon Tunde, Janus lay sleeping on a bed of moss. This was thirty years before Marcellus and his brothers were born, but Janus looked much the same as she did now. She looked the same, in fact, as she always had, for faeries were great, immortal, unchanging beings, held still by time that does not seem to pass and does not seem to matter, for time is a resource they never exhaust.

Something pulled her out of her sleep, a nice drowsy nap she was reluctant to abandon. Someone shook her shoulder. She opened one eye and saw Elana leaning near her, her intense green eyes flashing. "Let's go have an explore," she whispered.

Janus smiled, willing to let go of her sleepiness now. She rose from her bed and followed her friend as they headed for the Great Cavern and the Hidden Door that lay beyond. Elana and Janus had known each other from the moment of their creation in a time before memory, but they had only been friends for the last 3,400 years. They were such cherished friends however, so inseparable, that they sometimes talked about how strange it was that they had not become friends sooner. They walked through the long, curving, flower-draped tunnels in a way they hoped looked casual and would not arouse suspicion. Every fifty or sixty years they would leave the earth to explore the above-ground realm of Amon Tunde, sometimes even venturing into those areas of the Wilds not contained by Amon Tunde's boundaries. It was this which earned them the reputation among the earth faeries as restless troublemakers.

Along their way, they were stopped by a group of faeries in the mood for visiting. They tried to escape this conversation with tact, but Janus grew impatient and decided to simply leave. "How lovely speaking with you," she said, in the middle of Iris's sentence, "We must meet again." She grabbed Elana's elbow and urged her along.

"How subtle you are," Elana said when they were out of hearing range.

Janus looked over her shoulder at Iris, her bright orange eyes watching them suspiciously.

The Great Cavern was fortunately deserted, but they sensed faeries coming down Oak Bone tunnel and so broke into a run, trying to get out of feeling range. They crossed the Great Cavern as quickly as they could and bolted down the tunnel leading to the outside. They stopped just short of the Hidden Door, bracing themselves with their arms, laughing and panting. Once outside, they continued running in order to avoid Cyri, one of the sentinels. His vibration was slow and lethargic. He must have fallen asleep at his post again. "Lucky it wasn't Keck," Janus said and Elana laughed.

Thus, their adventure began.

To a human, a faerie's idea of an adventure may not seem like much. For faeries, most of whom were content to spend thousands of years underground with no desire to leave, actually going beyond Amon Tunde's borders and into the Wilds was stretching the limits. Only a few faeries felt comfortable above ground to begin with; these handful acted as sentinels, keeping non-faeries off their hallowed ground. Janus and Elana, with their love for the open earth, would have been well suited for this if they could have been trusted not to leave their posts. They found the forest much too enticing not to explore.

For many of their adventures they were happy to stay in the heart of the forest where the trees were thick, the sun soft, and the sky far above them, always anchored by the eternal boundaries of the trees. They followed squirrels, watched birds, let caterpillars work their furry bodies over their palms. Humans might find this fascination quaint, but animals did not live in Amon Tunde. Janus and Elana found them endlessly captivating.

Other times though, when they were feeling particularly bold, they would sneak almost to the edge of the forest—not all the way—not into the open expanse with no trees and no roots holding the ground

402

steady like it threatened to break off into the sky at any moment. Not that far. Just far enough to see slivers of the curious life that lived in such openness, the human world that seemed so busy and ever changing. Their funny buildings coming and going over time, the people themselves going in and out of existence like so many wildflowers that bloom and are eaten by the wind.

Janus and Elana would crouch on the ground, which was imperfect and brittle here without faeries to tend and soften it with loose dirt or thick moss. Hard lumps would press against their legs and chest. Crickets and little moths would hop and flutter around them. They would be perfectly still, watching humans and their animals going over the land, sometimes using long pieces of wood with shiny objects at the end to tear and churn the earth beneath them. "It's their magic," Elana had said once. "They have no magic," Janus had whispered back, and they went on watching and not speaking.

Sometimes the humans would gather the plants out of the earth and carry them away in huge bundles. The faeries watching this were mesmerized. This was how they sometimes got into trouble, far too distracted to sense the sentinel coming, not noticing him until he was physically behind them, scolding them for leaving Amon Tunde and going dangerously near the humans. They would have to face Salerno then, who would reprimand them in his gentle, resigned way. They would stay underground for a while, not wanting to displease him again. He and they both knew that eventually they'd go back.

The last time they had gone out this is the kind of trouble they had gotten into, so as they now roamed above ground they understood, by unspoken agreement, that they would not leave the upper realm of Amon Tunde or go near the humans. At least, not this time. They decided instead on the next best thing: tormenting pixies.

Faeries had a love-hate relationship with the pixies, impish little creatures no higher than one's ankles (which must be watched near pixies lest they get bitten). On the one hand, pixies' misadventures quite usefully kept the humans fearful of the Wilds and largely out of the way. On the other hand, it was hard to really like such devilish creatures so bent on malice. Most disappearances of humans in the Wilds could be attributed to pixies. The most common way this occurred was via the pixie circle. Humans would become trapped inside and dance to their deaths before they were found, if they were ever found at all.

On this day, one young man would chance to be spared from such a fate. They found him in the little grove they called Acorn Grove due to its abundance of oak trees. He looked like he had already been there some time, days perhaps. All around him the little leaf-like pixies danced and rustled and sang their intoxicating song, sounding like wind rushing through trees. His dance was erratic, he looked about to collapse. Janus knew the pixies would not let him do so until he was dead. At his feet lay a bow and several quivers splayed out from their holder. Janus would later learn he had been hunting deer.

Elana walked quite close to this scene, her eyes wide on the man. Janus grabbed her arm and halted her. She was ready to go back underground where it was safe.

"Let's go."

"What about him?" Elana asked without removing her eyes from him. Her voice sounded high and funny.

"What about him?"

"We can't leave him here."

"Why not?"

"He's too deep in the Wilds. No one will find him." Elana looked deeply saddened. Janus could see no cause for it. "He'll die," she said.

Janus looked at her friend with open curiosity. "They always die. What does it matter if it is today or forty years from now?"

Elana unhooked her arm from Janus' grasp—Janus did not realize until then that she had still been holding on protectively—and took a step forward.

"You cannot let him see you," Janus said. She felt unmistakable panic.

Elana shook her head. "He will be bound to me. I'll not let him go to tell anyone else."

"Elana, no!"

But Elana leaned forward, reached her slender arm toward the man, touched his hand and pulled him out where he collapsed on the ground. The pixies shuddered and instinctively Janus urged them

404

away with her magic. They scattered as if blown by a strong wind, their angry protests whispering fiercely in the air before fading and dying as they fled the scene. Elana knelt next to the human. He roused slightly. Janus stood rooted with fear.

Elana placed her hand on the man's face and Janus clutched her own hands to her chest. "Stop touching him!"

Elana ignored this and put both hands on his forehead. Her healing light went out of her fingers and entered into him. When she was done she sat back on her knees quietly and watched him sit up.

The two looked at one another and seemed to be communicating something. Janus hugged her arms to herself. This was not something that could be undone.

"What is your name?" Elana asked.

He opened his mouth. A kind of grunting sound escaped it. He cleared his throat. "I am Prince Clement, son of Jayron, King of Caedmonia."

Elana stood, calm and composed. Clement and Janus watched her do this with equal awe. "I am Elana, Priestess of the Heart of the Earth, subject of Salerno, King of the Earth Faeries. I have saved you from a terrible fate. You are bound to me and will obey me or suffer instant death. Do you understand human?"

At this no word was spoken. Only the trees rustled far above in the wind and out of the corner of her eye, Janus saw a squirrel scamper across the ground and disappear.

They followed Elana back to Amon Tunde, Clement much too near to them for Janus' comfort. She was in a state of peculiar numbness. What was going to happen to them? It wasn't until they came to the Hidden Door and Elana said the sacred words that Janus shocked out of her stupor, her tongue loosed.

"Elana, what are you doing? You just showed a human the..." she could not even say it.

Elana pointed him in but she was looking at Janus. "There is no harm. He will not be coming out again."

Now he was the one to speak. "You are taking me prisoner?"

"You are bound to me. This is where I live and this is where you will stay."

"No." His voice was firm and Janus shocked at it. Who was he, a human, to tell a faerie no?

Elana clasped her hands in front of her gently and considered him. She looked neither stern nor disapproving, only curious and a little surprised. Neither spoke for a while. Again Janus had the feeling they were communicating something between them and Janus did not know what it was. This angered her for some reason.

"You prefer death?" Elana asked. It was not a threat, only a question.

"I will not abandon my kingdom willingly."

"Your death would not be abandoning it?"

He did not answer this. Firm as before, he refused the Hidden Door with a shake of his head.

Elana turned to Janus. "Go on," she said quietly. "Let me talk to him."

"You cannot let him go."

"I did not say I was going to."

Something about her friend's demeanor was highly disturbing. She did not want to leave Elana alone with him. She wished that they had never found him, that they had never left the earth that morning.

"Go on," Elana said and Janus felt chills on her skin. She did go in and walked three steps before breaking into a run. She sent out a call to Salerno, urgent and silent in that way of the faeries to call without speaking to one they cannot see. She sensed Salerno receiving it, sensed him coming to her, yet she did not slow. She ran past faeries who gaped at her, many glaring disapprovingly. She kept running until Salerno was in her sight.

She bowed hastily before his concerned face and panting said, "It's Elana. Come." Together they hurried back to the Great Cavern, just in time to see Elana entering into it with Clement beside her.

Eighteen

The presence of a human in the depths of the earth was met with no small commotion on the part of the faeries. Disagreements, hostility, and fear all rose and swirled like a tempest in the golden faerie light. Clement looked around in open awe as if he could not look at everything fast enough, though what he found so fascinating Janus did not know.

All faeries had their say about this unprecedented event and how they thought it should be handled. Elana was silent. Salerno, as always, listened without speaking. When it was Janus' turn to speak, loyalty to her friend kept her tongue a little. All she said in a dark and brooding way was, "Humans do not belong here."

Yet the human's bond to Elana was undeniable. Elana had a claim on him and wished him to stay. The fact that he had seen Amon Tunde presented a dilemma. Many expressed their wish that he had perished in the pixie circle, as he ought, but none were willing to assign him that fate now. Neither could they say he should be let go, risking him leading others to their secret home. Others said to let him live the few decades left to him, always guarded underground, and in a short while with his death the problem would thus be expired. Some said the problem would last a bit longer, speculating his closeness with the faeries and their magic would prolong his life unnaturally, though for just how long no one could say. It was no matter; whether he lived fifty years or one hundred more, humans were known to do great damage in time even less than that. When the faeries had worn themselves out with debate, when only a few pockets of argument would swell and fade here and there, that was when Salerno spoke. All knew his words would end the discussion. They listened with uneasiness, though each was prepared to obey.

His voice was grave and his face solemn. "What is done cannot be undone. The human will stay with she to whom he is bound. That is my will for now."

Later, when Janus asked Elana how she persuaded Clement to enter Amon Tunde with her, she only said, "He says he knows I will release him. He intends to wait patiently for it."

"He is trying to trick you!"

"No. He believes it."

"Then he is a fool."

Elana nodded, but only a little. Again Janus felt afraid.

The faeries avoided Clement openly, and avoided Elana too when she was with him. This was nearly all the time. From afar, Janus watched their conversations. Sometimes they were serious and engaged in some heavy topic. Janus tried to imagine what it could be; she feared to ask Elana what they spoke about. Other times they were lively, their laughter floating softly across the cavern to where Janus stood watching. They talked almost constantly, though even when they were quiet they appeared just as content and happy as when they were talking. All of this bothered Janus, but none of it bothered her quite as much as those times when they would be leaning close together, speaking soft and intimately. Janus wanted to thrust both her hands on Clement's chest and shove him all the way out of the earth herself.

When Janus finally managed to get Elana away from him, Elana only talked of Clement and the human world, all the things she found fascinating and Janus now found menacing. "I don't want to hear this!" Janus said one day, shocking Elana into silence. "I do not care about this insignificant human!"

After this, they fought whenever they spoke. After one of these fights, when Janus was alone brooding over it, Clement appeared in Janus' room. She sat up abruptly at his arrival, her hands clutching the soft moss of her bed.

"I am sorry to disturb you," he said, though she thought she heard an edge to his voice.

"Well, you are disturbing me."

"I came to talk to you about Elana." Janus made it clear she was not going to respond to this. She hated this human and wanted nothing to do with him. He went on. "She is quite hurt by you. She believes you to be angry with her."

"No. I am angry with you."

He did not seem surprised by this. "What have I done to anger you?"

"Humans do not belong here with faeries. You should not have come here."

"I did not seek to come here."

"No. She brought you here."

"So you are angry with her?"

"I am not angry with her!"

"But you speak harshly to her. I thought you were her friend."

"We have been friends for three and a half millennia!" she said, standing now. "What do you know of friendship?"

"More, I think, than you."

Janus walked up to him then, directly into his face, only inches from him. He did not move. "You are not worthy to be her friend or anything else! You are wasting away like a flower bloomed and already wilting. Thousands of years from now Elana will still be here and you will be gone and forgotten even among your own kind. You know nothing of the things that last. Do not tell me how to be a friend. I know how to be a friend!"

Clement had narrowed his eyes. "One does not need to be immortal to know how to love and how to hold that love delicately. You say you are her friend but you either cannot see how you hurt her or you do not care. If such is the friendship of immortals, then I want no part of it." With that he left. His words echoed in her head for many days after. She resisted them simply by virtue of their source. She did not want to agree with anything he said or to like anything about him. But she loved Elana, so she grudgingly pondered his words. Inevitably, she felt sorry.

The next time she saw Elana was when she had come to Janus' room alone, something she had not done in a long time, and like a nervous little bird, fluttered down onto Janus' bed. An awkward

409

silence stretched between them as Janus worked to form the words of her apology and Elana worked to say whatever was on her mind. Elana said it first.

"I have something to tell you."

Three thousand years is a long time to know anyone; when Elana said those words, Janus knew what was coming next. Her anger returned in force, her apology forgotten. "I don't want to hear it."

"It's important."

"No!" Janus stood, backing away to the wall, the air feeling to tremble around her. "I don't want to hear what you have to say."

Elana sat there as if there were nothing wrong with what she was doing. Janus wanted to shake her. "No," Elana said. "I suppose you don't. I cannot leave without saying goodbye." A terrible chill ran through Janus and Elana went on. "He desires to be with his people. To serve his kingdom. I want him to be happy."

"You are releasing him?"

"It is already done. He is free to go and I am going with him."

Janus shook her head, almost wildly. "He will harm you. He will harm us. Now that he is free... he will bring destruction to us." She didn't really believe this, but in her desperation the words came out anyway. She almost convinced herself as she said it and felt in a panic all the more.

"He has been free for the past two weeks. He will not harm you."

Janus stared. Elana sat elegantly on the edge of Janus' bed, her long lavender cloak gathering in folds around her feet. She was only two feet away, perhaps three, yet it felt Elana was a great distance from where Janus stood. "But... Salerno... surely he will not agree."

"No. He has forbidden us."

"Then you cannot!"

"Not without consequences. I will not be able to return."

A chill clutched at Janus' heart. "Not... while the human lives?"

"Not ever."

Janus gaped.

"Salerno does not want me to go."

"Neither do I! You cannot do this... this madness!"

Elana stood to leave. "I'm sorry this hurts you."

410

Janus rushed to her, gripping her by both arms. "Please, Elana. Don't go. Not for him. Not for this. It is so fleeting. This is the shortest path to sorrow."

Elana hugged her as Janus clung to her but it was not enough. Elana left anyway and Janus was left alone.

Janus counted the years after that in a way she had not before. They oozed by slowly, like tree sap. She spent a lot of time hovering on the edges of the Wilds, watching the humans, desperate for a glimpse of her friend. No one bothered her when she did this. Always she would return disappointed.

To console herself, Janus decided that when the human was dead, Elana would come back. Salerno would relent and allow her. She dared not suggest such a thing to him yet, waiting until the time was right, but she thought of it so much and so often that she finally convinced herself it was inevitable. Thirty years went by before Janus saw Elana again, coming back through the woods, toward Amon Tunde just as Janus had imagined. Janus had sensed her and ran out the Hidden Door to meet her. Finally the wait was over. Elana could come home!

Elana was not coming home. When Janus saw her stomach, tight, rounded, and huge before her, she stopped short. Elana stopped, too. Faeries rarely married, only half a dozen couples existed in Amon Tunde, but it was even more rare for them to conceive. It was an act of deliberate choice, for faeries had both an awareness of and control over their bodies that humans did not. No faerie took on a child by accident. Elana, by bearing the child of a mortal, had taken within herself a mortal weakness. As long as mortal flesh and blood were in her she, too, was vulnerable to the same perils as a mortal... and there was not much else as perilous to a mortal woman as childbirth.

Janus shook her head at Elana now, willing it not to be so. "Not from him."

"Who else?"

At this Janus could have either wept or raged. She chose to rage. This time, Elana raged back. It was a frightful argument, one beyond

411

which either one knew they were capable. Each was motivated by their own passion: Elana for the man and people and country she had come to love and Janus was driven by her fear that the loss of her friend would truly be permanent.

At last, Elana ended the conversation abruptly and, furious, went in to see Salerno. Apparently this was her purpose in coming. "He will not see you," Janus said, a little spitefully. "You are not allowed."

"He will listen to this," was Elana's reply. Janus watched her disappear through the Hidden Door and did not follow.

Apparently Salerno was willing to listen, because Elana stayed a long while. Janus did not go in to find out for herself. Elana was with child, taken by a mortal. Janus could do nothing but pace among the aspen and oak and elm saplings and listen to her own feet kicking at the dried leaves on the ground.

When Elana emerged, she looked different, calm and at peace. She looked at Janus gently, invitingly, as an opening for them to move past the argument. Janus was still angry enough for both. "You have thrown yourself away," Janus said harshly. "And for what? Humans. Humans who matter not to us and little more to each other. It is like trading the forest for a speck of dirt."

Elana's face grew mournful. "I wish you could be happy for me. But how could you know what I know? How could you understand? You have never loved."

"I loved you," but her voice was still harsh and bitter. Elana only looked more saddened.

"It is not the same. You know that. It matters not to me that he is human, except that I grieve for the loss I know is one day coming. I cannot forever heal a mortal body, chasing away death as he ages and ages. I sustain him as much as I can, but he is still fading. Much slower than the others, yes, but fading. Yet I only love him more and I do not regret at all my life among the humans who you so disdain because you do not understand them. There is passion and feeling and glory among humans that is too great to endure forever. There is evil, too, yes, unlike anything we see in Amon Tunde. But there is something else, far more beautiful than the heart can seem to bear. It must be contained in mortality so it can shine all the more. It is for this I am

412

willing to sacrifice. You, Janus, a faerie living safe in a faerie world, unchanging in both body and mind, will one day owe a debt to these humans who you see as so small. There are those coming who will flicker and vanish like the rest," and here her voice trembled with both sorrow and power, "but within their short existence they will accomplish something so grand it will make it possible for you to go on as you always have, saved from destruction and ruin by a speck of dirt, as you say."

With these words Janus felt so tiny and vulnerable, felt such chills that she held her arms to herself. Her desperation on her friend's behalf overruled any second thoughts, overruled any reason, overruled (for the moment) the sense that she had just been given a glimpse of the future.

Elana took a step toward Janus, her face softened. "Wish me well, Janus. Be my friend."

Janus shook her head and said the last words that she would ever say to the person who, at that point in her life, she loved more than anyone else. "No. Go away."

Before the next new moon, they would learn that Elana had died giving birth to a son. A half faerie.

The greatest thing Janus had feared was Elana's death, so after her death there was nothing left to fear, nothing left to fight. Janus' anger left her; grief swallowed her in its place. Janus mourned. Slowly her grief lessened. She did not become stuck in her grief the way she would later learn Clement had. Instead she became wedged inside the emotion of something else. Elana's last words played over her mind, and two puzzles in particular drove Janus to what the faeries began to call obsession.

The first was this glory of the human world Elana claimed Janus would never understand. This mystery (as Janus had explained to Marcellus on that path by the sea) was what drove her away into the human world, driven by mad curiosity and desperation. Though she wanted to, she could not tell Marcellus about the first time she left the woods and went out into the open air. It was so vast and unsettling, to see the sky unending above her, stretching out toward a distant horizon further away than she had ever seen before. She felt she was about to fly away from the earth and never come back. She retreated to Amon Tunde vowing to forget it all, but she could not forget, nor did she truly want to. She wanted to understand, so she forced herself to brave what Elana had braved and prove that humans were tiny and small and without magic or glory. She needed to know she had been right.

She had been wrong. Janus came to believe that humans made up for their short life span by filling it with as many experiences as possible. They ate hot food, swam in open, crisp water, laughed at the stumbles of their little ones, and lived in a world more immense and varied than anything Janus had ever imagined. The first time she saw the sun rise over the ocean, in blinding, glittering splendor, tears sprang to her eyes. At that moment the true marvel lay within herself. She looked over at the fisherman's wife who had brought her there that morning and saw her smiling with tears in her eyes too. Janus was endeared to the humans forever more.

There were horrors too, theft, violence, filth, poverty, and back-breaking labor for the sustenance Amon Tunde always had in abundance with unconscious effort. In Janus' mind, the evil only made the good shine all the more. She marveled that so much good could still be had among all the bad. For while faeries had wisdom and knowledge of one sort, humans had wisdom and knowledge of another. Their varied experiences, their intense human relationships, all caused them to grow and transform in a way that faeries do not in their great, unchanging world.

As she lived among them, Janus came to change too, to grow more in ten years than she had in ten thousand. Janus came to love humans, understand them, to see them as the odd, bumbling, magnificent beings they were.

The second thing Elana had said to Janus that she puzzled in her mind was this: how could humans save the faeries? What debt could faeries ever owe humans? Elana had said this not with the feeling of vague generalities, but rather as if she had some sort of knowledge about forthcoming events. Recent events only served to reinforce this.

414

Janus would learn that Elana had shared a secret with Salerno on the day of her return. He would never tell her what it was. This is what Janus sought to understand when she visited with him recently, an underground visit she had not paid in years (for unlike Elana, Janus was allowed to return because Salerno, too, had come to wish he had done things differently).

Though she had discovered the existence of three sons—three, not one—by sensing them the way she sensed all faeries, by feeling their connection to Elana, by seeing Nicolai's resemblance to Clement, though she discovered even this still she did not know. Though she knew the faeries truly were in danger, still she did not know. What, *what* was Elana's secret? What did she tell Salerno all those years ago? And why, *why* were two of her three sons hiding their true identities?

These were not the only questions plaguing her. There was one more problem, one more issue, and it weighed as heavily on her heart as anything else. What of Marcellus? She had come to regard him as a friend. A friend unlike any other, for she felt for him as she had never felt for another. She felt connected to him in a way she didn't understand. She would trust him with her secret if she could, but once he knew both the full extent of her deception and how she had hurt his parents, could he possibly forgive her? Would she lose him, too?

Janus could not help but fear the answer to those questions.

Nineteen

The Three spent another day traveling and arrived in Furden late in the afternoon. It was a relatively busy little city that thrived on business from travelers going along the only main road connecting Stonebridge with South Caedmonia. It was a good distance from any other city of size, so many travelers often stopped for food and rest. The market was busy and prone to trading goods more than using currency, but this is not where the Three were heading. Remembering the path well, Corren led the way.

They passed the market and a number of small homes before taking a turn leading up into the foothills. This path was dotted with houses too, but the further along they went and the steeper the climb the fewer dwellings they found.

"There it is," Corren said pointing. Up ahead sat a small three room stone house with a thatched roof, and a low stone wall all around. The garden was overgrown and wild looking, with plants crammed everywhere and no two alike, all growing in whatever scratch of land they had been plunked into.

"This is it?" Marcellus asked.

They went through the garden gate and, on the walk, stepped around some clay pots overflowing with ferns. Corren knocked loudly on the old wooden door, swollen and discolored from wood rot.

They waited.

"It's quiet."

"Maybe he's not home."

"Halloooo!" they heard someone holler, and they all jumped. Up the path came a portly man, heaving himself forward with a tall walking stick, panting and waving. "Hallloooo!" he hollered again.

They drifted back to the gate and waited for him to arrive. He was carrying a brown cloth bag bulging with something unidentified. Corren eyed it warily; it didn't appear to be moving.

"Here I come," he said as he drew near, but still not near enough to avoid shouting. "Here I... Corren!" He laughed. "Ah, my boy! Back again! They come from far and wide to see Twaddle, they do."

Marcellus leaned in to Corren. "Twaddle?"

Corren shrugged.

"Who do you have with you, my boy?" He came through the gate, appraising his potential customers eagerly.

Corren introduced them—Marcellus as a merchant from Furden—but by the time he was done, Twaddle had already accosted Nicolai and was pulling him by the elbow to the side corner of his yard. There was a tree on the outside of the wall, but many of its branches hung over into Twaddle's yard. He was halfway into his bird dropping speech before Corren could do anything about it.

"I can identify every bird in Caedmonia just by the droppings," he said. He swept his hand over the length of the wall and indeed there were a fair amount of white splatters decorating the stones. There were also several clay pots, but Corren already knew the purpose of these. "This is from the speckled hornbill," Twaddle said, jabbing a finger at a spot that had been marked by said bird. "Very common in this area. See the yellow mixed in there?"

Nicolai leaned in, apparently interested. Marcellus rolled his eyes. Corren tried, and failed, to interrupt. "Um..."

"With speckled hornbill droppings you can completely eliminate potato nose. Mix it with two parts dried fern and one part honey. But don't eat it!" He guffawed delightedly at his own joke. "My granddad used it for a year and by the time he was done, his nose was as smooth as a baby's bottom. Has the additional benefit of curing foot rot. But this stuff is no good here," he said indicating the spots on the wall. "You have to catch it in a clay pot soaked in oil or its properties are weakened and useless. These pots are all newly rotated, but I have a pot half full inside if you want to see."

"Um, Twaddle?" Corren said loudly, touching his arm for good measure. "We're here about some dragon scales."

417

"Scales? Hmm. The Yellow-backed Snogroot dragon roosts in the Black Peaks area just over the hill here. Up a ways," he said, swishing his hand out dismissively. "I can give you two scales for three Tridions. A steal!" He jabbed Corren in the chest with his finger to emphasize his generosity.

"No, we..."

"Two Tridions! But I won't go no lower."

"It's not the Snogroot we need. We came for..."

"Ah! A discerning customer! Yes, yes, I remember this about you now. The Snogroot is good for many uses, but you're right, of course. Much too common. You came to the right place. I am widely traveled and highly skilled, as you know. Come inside, come inside."

They followed him into his cabin, the air rank with a ripe smell, every nook imaginable stuffed with the wares of his potion and dragon trade. On a table along the far wall, something either furry or moldy was moving in a way that made it look like it was boiling. Corren decided to stay safely near the center table, the least crowded surface in sight that nevertheless held a healthy collection of knotgrass and stone pine. In a corner, a small cage balanced precariously on a stack of books. In it, a small, white rodent was burrowing into its wood-chip bedding, which flew out in enthusiastic spurts, landing on the floor.

"Stop it! Stop it!" Twaddle said, rapping on the cage. "I'll take your liver out, I will!" The animal ceased its movements and Twaddle went on like there had been no interruption. "I have scales, toenails, dung and even blood. Very precious mind you. Not many dragon trackers get blood. And it's in short supply, believe me. Any dragon you want though. Silver Spikeback. Green Fourtoed. Flying Jasmine. Ooh, they're a tough lot!"

"We need scales from a Scarlet Firebreather," Corren said.

Twaddle's jovial face slackened. "Well," he cast around for his ground. He chuckled uneasily. "Don't be mad, boy. You'd be better off with the Flying Jasmine. Similar properties, only... not so..." he stopped as he considered them, a worried look on his face.

Corren raised his eyebrows.

Twaddle looked about, as if checking that no one would hear. "Dangerous."

"You don't have it?" Marcellus asked.

"Of course I have it!" Twaddle said, sticking out his round chest indignantly. "No one bests Twaddle, the greatest dragon hunter in Caedmonia. I doubt you'll find anyone else with it!"

"Good," Corren said kindly, trying to reassure him. "Then we'll take five."

"Five?!" He looked at each in turn. "You're mad. You can't possibly need more than two. I'd be irresponsible to sell you more than three."

"We need five."

He patted his belly nervously. "Madness," he said to himself. "Are you all potion masters?"

"Do we all need to be?" Corren asked. "You don't need to worry. I understand how these scales work."

Twaddle was shaking his head. "I cannot give one person more than three. Surely three will do. Anyway, you can't possibly afford more than that. They're very expensive, especially this time of year when..." but his sentence caught in his throat.

Marcellus had tossed a leather satchel on the table and it clinked heavily. Twaddle gingerly opened the bag, then gasped and opened it wide, digging in his thick fingers as if in disbelief. The coins jingled together as he probed.

"We want five."

"Five it is," Twaddle said, making his way to another room. "Plenty more where that came from. Take a look at the..." but here his voice faded and muffled as he went deeper into the room, the sound of items being banged and stacked overtaking that of his voice.

His voice emerged ahead of his body: "... can't be too careful, now can we?" (and he came into view) "Here we are," he said, holding out a large bundle wrapped in wool.

"We need koril essence too," Corren said, unwrapping the wool. Twaddle eyed him warily but continued talking nonetheless.

"Yes, yes. Plenty of that. Grab that little bottle there you," he said pointing to Nicolai. "Behind you. No, not the green, the clear. That's right. Now, if you need stripped dog fern I have a new batch dried and ready to go... be careful with that now," he said to Corren.

He had exposed the dragon scales. They clinked together musically,

419

shining bright red, each scale larger than Corren's hands. Corren's heart sped a little as he felt the properties in them, and tried to contain his amazement. He inspected their quality, making sure there were no chips or discoloration. He rewrapped them. Twaddle was in the middle of saying something else, but Corren interrupted him.

"You may be able to make another sale," he said, "if you have this."

Corren dug into the inner pocket of his cloak, felt the odd, waxy parchment containing the potion recipe, felt the small scroll he had stolen from Aradia's office, then found what he was looking for. He pulled out a scrap of parchment, upon which he had earlier written their elusive potion ingredient. He set it on the table and pushed it toward Twaddle who picked it up with a scowl. He eyed Corren. "What is this?"

"You don't know?"

"Is this a trick?"

"No. We need some of whatever it is."

Twaddle looked at him, not moving, his expression hovering on disbelief. Then he laughed uproariously, tossing the parchment back on the table, where Corren snatched it up. "Oh Corren! You thought you could stump old Twaddle. Don't be making things up like that. Ha! Now really, about the stripped dog fern."

Nicolai had hurried them out of Twaddle's home with difficulty. Determined to make another sale, Twaddle was convinced he had *something* else they needed. Finally they were out the door, Nicolai nearly shoving them down the road.

"Nicolai, what...?" Corren started, but Nicolai shushed him. He led them into the trees, off the road. "What's going on?" Corren asked.

"Let me see that parchment."

Corren gave him a confused look, but handed him the parchment anyway.

Nicolai looked at the writing he had only seen a glimpse of when it had made its way across Twaddle's table. It read:

Φύλλο από το δέντρο προέλευσης

420

Nicolai exhaled in relief. "Aradia can't get through the Gateway with this potion."

"Why not?" Corren asked.

"Because there's no way she can get this ingredient."

"You know what this is?"

Nicolai nodded.

Corren and Marcellus both stared at him. "But... I thought you couldn't read," Corren said.

"This I can read. It says 'Leaf from the Tree of Origin.' Even if Aradia knows what this is or where to find it, she wouldn't be able to get to it. It's impossible."

"How do you know?" Corren asked.

"I just know."

"Is this 'impossible' the way Corren thought the crosshatch petal was impossible?" Marcellus asked.

Nicolai paused at this. Corren said, "Would you be able to get to it?"

"Well..." Nicolai tried to think of an answer to that.

"If you can get to it, she can get to it," Corren said.

Nicolai shook his head. "It is well hidden. Aradia cannot reach it."

"How do you know all this?" Marcellus asked.

"Wait a minute," Corren said. "Have you seen it? Do you know what it looks like?"

"I know what it looks like."

"Are its leaves gold? I don't mean do they turn gold in the fall, I mean really gold. Only soft and..." but there was no need to go on for Nicolai's face held the answer already.

"How do you know that?" Nicolai asked.

"I forgot about it until now. When I was in her cottage brewing that base for her, I found an ingredient I had never seen before. I had no idea what it was or why she needed it. It was a gold leaf about this big," he held his hands up to indicate. "Is that it?"

Nicolai could not speak at first. A slow horror crept over him. "She has it already," he said. *She's been there.*

Twenty

They left Furden immediately, heading for a location somewhere in the Wilds that only Nicolai knew to be Amon Tunde. His brothers would go with him as far as they could, then would have to wait. They didn't yet know that he'd be traveling into Amon Tunde alone. And what would he find there? If Aradia had been there, what damage had she done? He imagined Pearl Island sinking into the sea and it pushed him to travel faster. Corren and Marcellus both believed they were on their way to get a leaf from the Tree of Origin, for the antipotion. Nicolai did nothing to discourage this idea. He would try. He would ask. He did not expect Salerno to agree. All this was assuming Salerno was still there... that Amon Tunde was still there. *How did she get that leaf?*

They camped at nightfall—a black, dark night with just a sliver of moon—and began again at dawn. Not far from Theo's post where Marcellus wanted to stop along the way to check for messages, they let the horses drink at a shallow brook and took a drink themselves. This was where Nicolai felt it. On one knee by the water's edge, Nicolai stopped as he was lowering his flask into the stream. The water slid and slipped over the rocks in the creek bed. He stood. A dragonfly hovered near his shoulder. Nicolai cautiously followed what he felt.

Marcellus was the first to notice him. "What is it?" he asked.

A terrible blackness, Nicolai thought, *coming out of the earth itself. Or covering the earth. Or burning it.* "Can you feel that?" Nicolai asked

"What?" Corren now.

Nicolai looked through the trees to his left, saw nothing unusual. Marcellus and Corren approached. "You can't feel it?"

"Feel what?" He heard the concern in Corren's voice. Nicolai knew Corren could not feel it. Marcellus could not feel it.

Nicolai followed it.

He did not have to go far to find the source. Through the trees he saw it; the ground blackened, like flaked coal or burnt wood, shaped in a jagged circle large enough for a man to lie down in. If there had been any plants in that area before it had been touched by evil, there were no traces of them now.

The wind turned. A great stench hit Nicolai and he compulsively covered his nose and mouth. The smell came from piles of what looked to be flesh and intestines, heaped in the middle of the burnt earth. It was as if a person had disintegrated one layer at a time and ended in a sickening heap of slime and odor. "What happened here?"

They slowly circled the area, none of them wanting to touch the area that had been singed. As they circled, another pile became visible behind the first, this of bone. Bone stripped clean. The bones of someone who seemed to have collapsed right where they stood, a jumbled mess.

"It looks," Corren said, "like someone was extracted."

They exchanged dark looks.

"What do you mean, extracted?" Marcellus asked.

Corren turned his back, stepped away; Nicolai and Marcellus followed. He only took a few steps, then stopped. "In certain kinds of dark magic," he said lowly, "you can use spirits to extract the life force from another living thing, but something small like a moth. The largest creature I've ever heard of being extracted is a bat."

"Not a human?"

Corren shook his head, glanced back over his shoulders then closed his eyes and looked away again.

"Why would anyone do that?" Nicolai asked.

"To use the life force. Put it into a potion or harness it in a spell. It's very powerful."

"Very evil," Nicolai said, still feeling the horrible blackness though he was no longer looking at it.

Corren nodded. "Yes. But it can only be done by using a dark spirit as an aide. There are spirits strong enough to extract a human, but there's nothing strong enough to contain those spirits. You can't control them."

"Yet here it is," Marcellus said.

"Yes," Corren said. "Here it is."

"Are you sure that's what it is?" Nicolai asked.

Corren shook his head. "I'm not sure of anything anymore."

They decided the remains of whoever was there should be buried but Corren wouldn't let them touch it. "There's evil still lingering here," he said, and buried it with his staff.

Marcellus waited for the all clear from Theo before descending the hill toward the supply tent. Corren and Nicolai hid with the horses at the top. He worked his way down the hill slowly, being careful not to step on sticks or other debris that would make too much noise and draw attention. Near the bottom he concealed himself behind a large maple, feeling it strange to be sneaking into his own camp like this. He ducked past Theo's horse tied just outside and into the supply tent at last. Theo stood there grinning widely and pulling a leather satchel off his huge shoulders. "Where are your friends?" he asked.

"I am alone," Marcellus said, not wanting to answer questions. "I can't stay long. Have you received any messages?"

"No." At this Marcellus felt relief—everything at home was fine. "I brought you parchment if you have one to send," Theo said pulling it out, along with the ink and quills, and setting it on top of a large crate. "And..." he paused dramatically before revealing a small bottle of wine. "You must be parched."

Marcellus grinned. "Theo, what would I do without you?"

Theo laughed. "If only you knew."

Marcellus pulled down a small, heavy crate and set it next to the larger crate with the parchment. Thus situated at his makeshift table, he picked up the quill and began his letter, already knowing what message to write to let his father know they were safe and well.

Theo put the wine next to him. "You won't insult my good hospitality will you?"

"I was waiting for the goblets."

"No, no. This is for you to take. I have more in my tent."

"In that case." Marcellus grabbed the bottle, pulled the cork—a low *pumm* vibrating the air—and took a long drink. It was a light, sweet wine and made him long for home. "Beats creek water."

"I'm sure. But why does the Prince of Caedmonia find himself drinking creek water in peasant's clothes?"

"Well," Marcellus said shrugging, the tip of the quill scratching along the parchment, "It's a new census on deer... frogs... fish."

"And the crown scares them."

"Precisely." *There is no need for transfers at this time,* Marcellus wrote, and he refreshed his ink, *and by tomorrow...* The lettering blurred. He rubbed his eyes. He must be more tired than he realized; he never did catch up on his lack of sleep the night he ended up swimming out to Crescent Island.

He looked at the letter again. It was still blurry. He rubbed his eyes once more and felt a sudden lurching, as if he were about to fall off the crate. He opened his eyes. Everything swam nauseatingly in front of him.

"Theo?"

"Yes prince?"

"I..." but his tongue was thickening. He saw the bottle of wine swaying in his vision. His body tingled, ached, and sickened all at once. He struggled to focus on the bottle. On the wine.

On Theo's wine.

He sought out Theo, his head aching and his eyes burning now. Finally he saw Theo's face fading in and out of focus. Theo sat with his arms crossed, his face stern.

"What have... you done?" The room reeled and as his body plunged, the floor rushed up to catch him. Blackness crept in on the edge of his vision. Theo knelt next to him, whispering in his ear. "Glory to the winner," he said, and Marcellus knew no more.

Nicolai was not keen on this stop, feeling it overly cautious. How much could happen to a kingdom in just a few days? There was no arguing with Marcellus about it though, so here he sat as time slipped by. Time they could be spending on their way to Amon Tunde. He kept glancing at the supply tent even though he couldn't see the entrance from here; that was on the side facing away from them. All he could see was the twitching tail of a horse tied up outside.

He picked up a dried oak leaf lying nearby. He crumbled it into bits of orange then released the shards onto the ground. Corren sat next to him. He had pulled out the potion instructions, reading through them silently. "If we can get the leaf from the Tree of Origin," Corren said, and Nicolai gave no reaction to this, "that only leaves moonlight from the Isle of Iona."

"I don't understand that," Nicolai said, grabbing another leaf. "What's that supposed to be?"

"I'm not really sure. It's something to do with the Dianese branch of the Order. The more I think about it, the more I fear we're going to have to ask the Order about it. Though, I'm not sure they can help either. The Head of the Dianese branch doesn't answer calls from the Order. She only comes for the Songs and the ash. That's it." Corren rolled up the strange green parchment and tucked it back into his cloak. "They've got to be the most secretive branch, which is saying a lot. The Isle of Iona is where they're located."

Nicolai thought of the Tulaga, and wasn't sure if he could agree. "Will someone in the Order at least know how to find the island?"

"I don't know," Corren said. "But it's not really an island. I had only ever heard it called the Isle of Iona, but that must be some sort of diversion to keep their location a secret. In one of the books I found at Aradia's, I read what it really is. A lake. The Lake of the Moon. If I understand right, only certain people can go there."

"Wait a minute..." Nicolai said. *A lake? The Lake of the Moon?* Corren sat up, looking at something in alarm. Nicolai checked the supply tent but saw nothing, not even the horse's twitching tail.

"Not there," Corren said, standing now and Nicolai stood, too. "There. See it? There."

He pointed through the trees, almost on the opposite side of the camp. Nicolai searched, then saw. He stepped to the side quickly so he could follow the movement better. It was Theo, his distinctive red hair clearly visible, riding away from camp. He was saddled on the horse

426

rather awkwardly for in front of him, draped over the horse's back, was Marcellus.

Nicolai and Corren exchanged glances then bolted to their horses. Nicolai grabbed Kedron's reins along with his own, mounted, and kicked his horse into a run. They took off around the back of the camp, skirting the rim. Theo was out of sight, but once on the other side of camp Nicolai picked up his trail.

"What's going on?" Corren asked as they tore through the woods. "Where's he taking him?"

"I don't know," he said, eyes sharp on the ground. Theo was in a hurry so his trail was heavily marked. They followed the deep hoof marks of Theo's horse and freshly broken branches through thickening trees and increasingly tumultuous ground. Twice Nicolai had to slow to make sure he hadn't lost the path, then they were off again, through a narrow pass, ducking under branches, skirting a fist of brambles. A sudden, small drop off dipped in front of them and they had to pull to a hasty stop.

"We've lost him!" Corren said.

Nicolai was already searching and only said, "No" in response. "That way." They urged the horses into a run again, rushing through the trees to their left, the sound of water approaching just ahead of their coming upon it. It was a wide river, churning violently over rocks and boulders, whose dry heads protruded into the air. It was here that Nicolai lost the trail.

"Here," he said, tossing Kedron's reins to Corren and hopping down from his own horse. He scanned the area quickly. "They went to water," he said, turning his attention to the river now. It wound sharply through the mountains and he could not see very far along its banks, neither upstream nor down. It was possible Theo was traveling in the water, though a horse would have to take it slowly over those rocks. But which way would he have gone?

Nicolai mounted again and said, "Let's hope he only crossed."

427

Twenty-One

Aradia walked down the narrow stone hallway, past gaping doorways leading into ruinous rooms and up to the closed door of the room she sought. She opened it, entered, and nodded her head to indicate that the two men who had been flanking the door should leave her alone. They did so. To her left was the only piece of "furniture" to be found in the square, stone room: a rusted rack that nevertheless held a decent collection of swords and daggers—shiny, new, and comfortingly useful to those with no skills in magic. A crumbling window frame cut a square out of the opposite wall, letting in the biting afternoon sun. Between the window and Aradia was the only thing in the room that truly interested her.

Marcellus lay on the stone floor, still unconscious. She pointed her staff at him and sent two incantations in the following order:

"Revia madi," she said. She watched him stir, scrunch his brow in pain, and glance around confusedly. She waited until he saw her, until the alarm on his face had fully registered, until his arm reached for one of the swords still strapped around his waist. She said the second incantation. "Bindari." His arms pinned to his side, immobile. She didn't bother binding his mouth.

"Welcome," she said.

He grunted something unintelligible, then groaned.

"Hmm," she said. "Not as noble as I pictured you. Of course those terrible clothes aren't helping you." He cleared his throat like he was getting ready to speak, but she went on. "Not in Western Caedmonia at all, are you? What have you been doing, I wonder, sneaking around like this?"

"Looking for you," he said. His voice was gravelly.

"Well," she said, walking smoothly to the rack and withdrawing a dagger, "you've found me."

428

She approached him slowly, her staff in one hand, the dagger in the other. There was fear in his eyes, no question about that, but not nearly as much as there should be. Mixed in with the fear, his luminous blue eyes burned in fury. She smiled. If he did not fear her enough now, that would soon change.

She knelt by his chest, set her staff on the floor and with her free hand grabbed the neck of his tunic. She held the dagger high, its edge glinting, and swung it down in one smooth stroke, slicing the fabric, just missing the skin, revealing his bare chest... and his stone.

She released the dagger where it fell to the floor with a clang; her eyes locked on the stone, the most vivid blue she had ever seen. "There it is," she whispered, not bothering to conceal her raw longing. "This... is *powerful*." She held her hand over the stone, not touching it, not daring, but feeling for its properties. A chill raced up her arm and she shivered. "Worth all the trouble," she said.

She met his gaze, said the incantation to release his arm, and said, "Hand it to me."

"No."

"You don't want to be the second prince to lose his ears do you?" His eyes narrowed, more of that wonderful fury. She smiled again. "Hand me that stone."

"Why don't you just take it?" he said. This was not a question, rather a dare.

She laughed, picked up her staff, bound his arm again, and stood up. "Quite a predicament. If I take it from you, I die. If I kill you, the magic goes with it and it is useless to me."

His surprise was obvious and she laughed at it. "You didn't know the magic is connected to you? I'm not surprised. How unworthy you are to possess such a powerful magical object that you cannot possibly wield. I, on the other hand, am *destined* for it. I cannot do what you would do with it; the prophecy makes that much clear. But I can draw power from it. And I will. When it is mine."

"I'll never give it to you."

She sighed, more for show than anything for she was thoroughly enjoying her victory. "I must say, prince, you do not seem to have the proper appreciation for me. You speak to me with far too much

429

confidence. Too much arrogance. Let's take care of that problem now, shall we?"

Aradia turned to the door, rapped sharply twice, and it opened. "Bring Theo in," she said to the guard. She turned back to Marcellus, a new anger in his eyes now. She lifted her eyebrows. "You know Theo, don't you?" He averted his eyes and she smiled. "Consumed by jealousy, that one. I can honestly say I have no idea what that feels like."

In short order the guard returned with Theo in tow and she indicated, once again, that the guard should wait outside. She brought Theo into the room, closed the door, and addressed him. She noticed he avoided looking at Marcellus. *He is not just a traitor but a coward,* she thought. "Ah Theo," she said smoothly, "Thank you for coming. Your services have been quite useful to me and I am eager to give you your next assignment."

"It is a pleasure to serve you," he said.

Aradia laughed, thinking of the large satchel of money she had paid him with just minutes earlier. "I'm sure."

She walked back to Marcellus and bent down to him slightly. "Pay close attention, please."

With her free hand, she reached into her robe and pulled out a glass ball. The glass reflected tiny slivers of color on its edges, like a rainbow stretched over its translucent surface. "This Ajinn," she said holding it up, "and your friend Theo are going to help me demonstrate what will happen to you if you don't hand over that stone."

She stood and turned to Theo. Theo's falsely obedient face registered concern, but it mattered not.

She drummed her fingers along her staff before grasping it more firmly. Her mind slid into that mode of keen and perfect concentration. Raising the ball in one hand, her staff in the other, Aradia uttered the incantation: "Comessa spitira ret triva a virra." The Ajinn glowed white. Theo only had time to flinch before a white light from the ball and a violet light from her staff shot toward him, merged into one, and struck him on the chest. The rays of light were steady, his screams instant and it was here, always here, that her heart would

430

begin to race. A black scorch mark emerged on his chest and spread out. This became obscured by the white fire now surrounding him. His face, untouched as yet by any scorching or flames, contorted almost unrecognizably as his inhuman screeches reached a piercing volume. Kept alive by her spell, his shrieking would not stop until the end. The white flames concealed his body, but at his feet grew the pile, first of skin, then intestines and other organs, and Theo's raw terror and echoing screams only fed her exhilaration.

"Virra relessa a mi," and the flame rose completely over him. His skeleton collapsed to the floor with a sickening crunch and his screams vanished too. The white light and violet light were still joined, but their new target was the swirling gray mist that had emerged from where Theo had been. She drew it in.

"Enkumpe te," she said, her anticipation spiking, "Penatta! Shelade!" The mist expanded over her, cocooned around her, the lights gone now. The mist touched her skin, where she felt it bleed into her in a warm rush.

Marcellus was shivering. Any anger, any hate Marcellus had felt for Theo was now gone. He could not help but pity any soul for suffering such terrible agony. The floor and wall where Theo had been was blackened and a sickening stench filled the room. Aradia stood with her eyes closed, still and rapturous. Her breathing had been heavy but it quieted now, satisfied. She looked at Marcellus and a chill ran through him. "What a waste," she said. "If Corren had been here instead of you, he would appreciate the brilliance of what you just witnessed. Do you have any idea what I just did? No one else has even *imagined* such a thing." She knelt down to him. He flinched involuntarily. He didn't recall ever doing that before. She smiled at it. "Well, I suppose you appreciate it a little bit, don't you? Now, how about giving me that stone?"

"No." He was surprised at how steady his voice was. "You can kill me first."

She narrowed her eyes. The grip around her staff tightened. "I prefer to torture you," she said.

"I don't give in to torture. You'll only kill me afterwards anyway."

Her face softened. Her lips curled into a smile. "And you'll thank me for it. When I'm through with you, you'll be *begging* for death. Anyone breaks if given enough time. And you will discover that I am a very patient woman."

She walked over to the rack of swords and slowly withdrew one, the metal scraping against the iron of the rack. She turned to face him, raising the blade in front of her. "You men and your weapons. All you know are swords and daggers. Mere playthings when compared to magic. Although..." She ran a finger down the length of the blade, her pale skin glowing against the silver of the metal, "...they do have their uses."

She replaced the sword slowly. She took a deliberate step backwards, aimed her staff at the rack, and said, "Aich nek mayd!"

The swords flung from the wall and shot toward him in a blur of flashing metal. He pinched his eyes closed, his heart racing, bracing for the end, and the fear of death swallowed him for the first time. Moments passed and he felt nothing. Nothing happened. When he opened his eyes, he saw a jungle of swords. They hovered in the air, the points aimed at him, each only a hair away from touching him, the blades and hilts spreading over him like a fan. One was on his forehead, two on his cheeks—the metal bright and looming in the corner of his eyes—others on his shoulders, arms, chest, stomach, legs. They were everywhere. He saw half of Aradia's face, half of her cold smile through the thin space left by the swords. Then he heard her say the word. "Penntah."

The swords lowered minutely. He felt the cool points of the blades on his skin and pressing against his clothes. "Penntah." Slowly, simultaneously, all over his body the pressure increased as the swords lowered, ("Penntah" again) and the pressure exploded into hot pinpricks, this followed by steep pain as the blades pierced his skin, deeper, deeper now ("Penntah") and now he pinched his eyes closed again, gritting his teeth, cringing, straining against the hot pain tearing through him.

"Penntah."

"ARRRGGGHH!" He could not contain it, the swords too deep now to resist crying out. He was aware of nothing but his own screams and the blinding pain searing through him, shaking him, annihilating any sense of time or place, suspended in perfect, wrenching agony.

The pain receded, throbbing, his heart pounding painfully. He realized the swords stopped penetrating, perhaps retreated a little. Dizzy, he opened his eyes. The ceiling blurred above him. The glinting blades near to him pressed against his vision. He was aware of something trickling down the side of his face and again down his wrist, his arm, his bare chest, everywhere it seemed. It was some sort of liquid. Warm. He realized it was his own blood.

Aradia's face swam into view. She was looking at his body, a wild hunger in her eyes. Her hand hovered over him. "You have a strong life force," she said. "A *very* strong life force." When she spoke, her voice sounded disconnected and hollow. This is the way it traveled to him through his pain.

She looked at him. "Do you know why the extraction process is so torturous?"

He could not speak.

"Torture intensifies your life force," she said simply. "Your body's in a panic, every part of your system accelerating. Your heartbeat, your breathing. Your blood races. Extraction involves me magically keeping a person alive through as much of that torture as possible. Your life force is alert and more intensely awakened than at any other time, so when I finally take it from you, it is as powerful as it can be."

She put her face close to his. "It's an amazing rush. Not a bad way to build up one's defenses."

She stood. She seemed to tower far above him, swaying in his distorted vision, arched and ready to pounce. "I'll leave you here to think about giving me what I want." She disappeared from his view.

"Shall I stay?" he heard a male voice ask her.

"Your services are better used elsewhere. He is guarded well enough."

They left and the door slammed shut. All Marcellus could see was the silver blades of the swords and all he could hear was the violent pounding of his own heart.

433

Twenty-Two

Nicolai followed Theo's tracks to what looked like an abandoned village deep in the mountain. The village must have been ancient, for most of the walls of the buildings had crumbled to the ground, their stones worn away by the centuries. The river ran along next to it and, in some parts, water overtook the bank creating a marsh amid the shells of the houses. Other buildings, though on dry ground, had evidence of flooding too, deep green algae identifying the water marks of past floods. Stones lay randomly on the ground, dotting the earth with the remnants of some forgotten history.

Nicolai and Corren hid behind a section of a low stone wall. On the far side of the village and tucked away close to the base of the mountain was a large, though crumbling, two story structure, probably an old manor house. It was the best preserved building in sight, though some rooms were still open to the elements, great sections of their walls having fallen and decayed over time. Guards stood near the entrance. If these men were knights of any particular country, they wore no distinguishing armor. Their weaponry was clearly visible, and Nicolai did not doubt who they were working for.

"There are only three," Corren whispered.

"There may be more inside. Let's see what's around back."

They left their horses tied to a tree and circled the perimeter of the village, ducking behind buildings, shrubbery, and trees. They worked their way around to the opposite side of the guarded building and saw another hole in the lower wall, this one big enough to step through.

They moved closer to the building, carefully so as to not make any noise. As they drew nearer, the opening revealed a large lower room and a wooden table with benches. To the other side they saw just a corner of a room, from which emanated voices, a bang, and the smell of some meal being prepared. Nicolai and Corren halted.

"This is too exposed," Corren said. "What if he isn't even in there?"

"Where else would he be? Theo wouldn't..." then they heard a horrific yell of pain coming from somewhere upstairs in the building.

They froze for a moment, then bolted to the hole in the wall. He was right against the building now, Corren next to him, and could see almost the entire kitchen and the two men working in it.

Nicolai grabbed the throwing spears that were strapped to each calf. He threw one and it hit one of the men dead center in the chest. He stumbled, shocked, dropping to the floor. As the other man cast about for the source, Corren aimed a spell and he fell abruptly to the ground.

They waited to see if anyone else would come or notice the noise. When no one did they climbed through the hole. The two men were sprawled on the floor, above them a large hole in the ceiling leading to whatever decrepit room lay above it.

As quietly as their speed allowed, Corren and Nicolai climbed a flight of stone stairs opposite the kitchen. At the top, the hallway veered off at an angle from the stairs. They followed this. A woman's voice came from up ahead, around the corner. They froze to listen.

"Your services are better used elsewhere." *Aradia.* "He is guarded well enough."

They heard her, and another person, coming toward them. Corren stood swiftly in front of Nicolai, holding out his staff. They silently shuffled backwards, of the same mind that this was not how they wanted to confront Aradia. Nicolai grasped the hilt of his sword. They heard a door open and close. Silence. It sounded like Aradia and her companion went into another room, one very near them.

They glanced at each other wide-eyed. They advanced down the hall again. Corren peaked around the corner, and they rounded it together. It was a long hallway, with rooms leading off each side. A few had doors. Most were in decay and in no condition for a door. Muffled voices came from the room on their left: Aradia and whoever else was with her. They went further down the hall and stopped at a room on the right closed off by a door. A familiar stench penetrated the air.

Nicolai slowly unsheathed his sword. He put his hand on the iron handle, and swung the door open.

Their first vision was that of a body, or what had once been a body and was now piles of flesh and entrails and bone. For one horrifying moment, Corren thought it was Marcellus, but then he saw him further away. He lay on the floor, drenched in sweat, streaked with blood, surrounded by perhaps two dozen floating swords, the tips of which all pierced his body. Marcellus saw them and gave a groan of relief. They stepped inside, closed the door behind them, and rushed forward. His skin was ghastly pale. Small pools of blood were expanding all around him. His tunic was torn and his brilliant blue stone lay exposed.

Nicolai reached to remove one of the swords but Corren seized his wrist. "Don't touch them," he whispered.

Marcellus' eyes widened at this. "Get them off me," he said, gritting his teeth.

Corren held his hand above the hilt of one of the swords and said an incantation. The blade glowed red, then they all glowed red. It trembled violently, then they all did. Marcellus groaned again, this time in pain. "I'm sorry," Corren whispered urgently as the blades returned to their normal color.

Nicolai stared at him wide eyed. "What was that?"

Corren stood with his staff. "Nicolai, you'd better leave."

"What? No!"

"They're all connected by the same spell. I have to remove them all together."

"So do it and let's get him out of here."

Corren shook his head. "I won't be able to control where they go after I remove them. There's too many."

"I'm not leaving."

"Don't be ridiculous. We don't need you hurt too."

Nicolai looked between Corren and the swords, understanding now. "They won't hit you?"

436

"Let's hope not," he said, his voice edgy as he tried not to think of the possibilities.

The sound of voices appeared in the hallway. Corren and Nicolai turned. Corren gripped his staff and Nicolai raised his sword. Aradia was talking with someone, but he could not make out any words. They did not get closer, but rather further away, going down the stairs.

Corren turned to Nicolai. "Quickly. They'll find the others and come looking. Get out."

Nicolai cast a worried look at each of them but left the room hurriedly. Corren pointed his staff at Marcellus, who met his eyes. He had never seen Marcellus look so vulnerable. Corren felt the same.

They didn't have time for hesitation. Corren took aim. "Scoia," and all the blades burned red again, "igroi tath!"

The swords launched out in all directions. Corren had no time to move or duck. The deafening sound of gravelly explosions filled the room as metal sunk deep into the stone walls around them. A sword grazed his upper arm, tearing his cloak and slicing his skin. Another shot by inches from his head. Handles bobbed from every wall, the swords at rest, dust settling in the air. Corren looked down at himself. He was still there.

Corren and Marcellus met each other's eyes as Nicolai shot into the room. "Let's go. They heard you." Corren jumped forward on wobbly legs to help Marcellus to his feet. Corren heard people coming, the pounding of their feet running up the stairs echoing through the halls. *How many are coming?* "This way," Nicolai said.

Shuffling through the door, half carrying Marcellus, they ran down the hallway away from the stairs. Determined to find his feet, Marcellus held his own by the time they reached the room at the end of the hallway, though he was still staggering. As Nicolai and Marcellus ducked into the room—a large hole in the floor opening to the kitchen below—Corren glanced behind them and saw two guards appear at the opposite end of the hallway. Corren aimed a spell at the guards and they both fell to the floor. Behind them, Aradia appeared.

The distance of the long hallway was suddenly short. Their eyes met. Something wild and insensible reared in him at the sight of her. If he had had any sense at all, he would have run into the room with

437

his brothers. He aimed his staff at her, she aimed hers at him, and together they shouted their incantations. A spell so powerful he could nearly see it came from Aradia's staff and collided with the tip of his. The shaft of his staff trembled and shattered beneath his grasp in a violent explosion. Splintered fragments hit his arms, face, cloak and came clattering to the floor around him.

Corren's mind went blank. His body numb. He was defenseless. She raised her staff. He saw it as if in slow motion. He heard the incantation, low, vibrating, slow, inevitable. He was lurched to the side, into the room next to him, and he felt the energy of the spell go past. Bits of stone exploded at the end of the hallway. Nicolai had grabbed him and pulled him into the room. This jolted Corren back to himself. "Get down there!" Nicolai said, jabbing a finger at the hole in the floor.

Below was the kitchen with its fallen guards, Marcellus next to them, his blood-streaked face looking up. "Hurry!"

Corren sat on the edge of the hole then jumped down the rest of the way, landing on one of the guards and stumbling into Marcellus. He heard Aradia's voice and that of more men, coming from the top of the stairs. Nicolai dropped down next to him, landing awkwardly on the guard, where he yanked free the throwing spear that had been stuck in the man's chest. They ran to the hole in the wall leading to the outside, the voices from the stairs rumbling ever closer.

The Three raced through the wall, through the woods, cutting past trees, trying to make it back to the horses, driven west by the sound of guards approaching from their rear and from their left, cutting them off. Corren sent a fiery spell behind them—his best option without his staff—but he couldn't see the guards and had no idea if he hit them or not.

He heard water. They broke through the tree line. A few steps away the river rushed by and Marcellus and Nicolai both dove straight into it. Corren followed, the cold water shocking but not enough to drench his urgency. The current swept them downstream, around the bend. The last thing he saw behind him was the guards appearing out of the woods just as the water swept the Three out of sight.

Aradia came to the river. The men who were supposed to be helping her danced around in indecision, one of them saying, "They crossed to the woods."

"No," another said. "They went to water, follow on the bank." They turned in fear when they saw she had arrived.

She spared no thought for their incompetence at the moment, but instead focused on the situation at hand.

All three of them. In the water.

She walked briskly to the river and put the tip of her staff on the surface of the water. "Fireez ackulay etu crik!"

Every open wound shouted in sharp pain and Marcellus called up the energy to swim only by sheer determination. The water swept them past the abandoned village and around another bend in the river. Here they swam toward the bank. He heard a deep creaking and moaning behind him. He turned in the water to see what it was. At first he saw nothing, only Corren not far behind him, but beyond Corren the noise still came. The moaning increased, gathered an odd shattering quality. Then he saw it.

Advancing toward them was what looked like a wave of ice. The river was freezing into a solid mass, the ice charging toward them.

"Out of the water!" he shouted, swimming frantically toward shore. Nicolai cleared the water first. "Out of the water! Corren!" Marcellus reached the bank and took large heavy steps, his legs weak, willing them to push harder, trying to clear the water completely. Corren trailed behind and Marcellus reached back for him. "Come on!"

The ice sped along the river, its cracking thunderous as it charged. He was finally out of the water, but not Corren. The ice was nearly upon them. Corren took three large leaps and Marcellus grabbed his hand to pull him out but the ice had seized Corren's foot. His hand yanked free of Marcellus' grasp and he fell on his back on the bank. "Burinne" he heard, then Corren was above him, pulling him up.

Automatically they ran again, following Nicolai. Hidden in the trees Marcellus saw the most welcome sight he could wish for: their horses tied and waiting.

Aradia marched along the river, now a jagged sheet of ice, watching for signs that her prey had been caught. As she came around the bend and swept her vision over the length of the river before it disappeared behind another turn, she saw, away in the distance, the Three vanishing between the trees, on galloping horses. No catching them now.

She stopped and fought the urge to hurl something, preferably one of the useless guards, onto the frozen river.

She stood in a kind of tingling shock. Then she roared with fury.

As far away as they were from her, the Three heard it.

Twenty-Three

Once he was on the horse, once it seemed apparent they were not being followed, the intensity of fleeing left him. Marcellus felt his energy drain like a bag slit open. The gouges from the swords began to throb and scream like they were freshly torn. They probably were considering all he had just done.

"We need to stop," Nicolai said, "to look after your wounds."

Nicolai was behind him, but Marcellus did not turn around. He did not slow his horse. "No," he said. "We need to keep going." How far could Aradia's magic reach? How far did they have to go?

His body felt as if on fire, every surface alight, but he pressed on. Awareness of his surroundings shrank. He focused all his thought on fighting against the pain that sliced through him with every jolt in the saddle. They must press on. Their enemy was strong, had forced them into a retreat. He did not know if she was pursuing them or not.

Marcellus was sweating, his skin burning, his mind tripping. The horizon would slip away from him, tip to one side in a slow kind of lurch, then he would shake his head a little and blink his eyes hard and when he opened them the world was straight again but the sun was sharp and blinding. He would squint against it and the earth would start to slide again.

"We are stopping," he heard Nicolai say. Marcellus knew that meant he needed to pull in on the reins but his body would not obey. Nicolai seemed to appear out of nowhere, in front of him, stopping the horse. The world tipped all the way over then and Marcellus dove over after it into blackness.

"He's lost too much blood," Nicolai said urgently. He had caught Marcellus as he fell off his horse and lain him on the ground.

Corren was kneeling at his side. They were all still soaked from their plunge into the river.

"Some of his wounds are still bleeding," Nicolai said. One of these, he noticed, was a cut just below Marcellus' ribs that oozed blood slightly but steadily. "He is feverish too. Can you do something?"

Corren looked in shock too. Nicolai instinctively ran his eyes over him to check for injuries. Other than a shallow cut on his arm, there were none he could see. "I don't have a staff," Corren said. He was looking at Marcellus, but didn't seem to really see him.

"Do you need one?"

Corren said nothing, only stared.

"Corren!"

Corren startled. "No," he said. "No, I don't need one for his cuts. I can heal his cuts. That I can do. I don't need a staff for the cut." As he rambled on Nicolai was reminded of Corren's mood when he had come out of the Labyrinth.

"What about his fever?" he said firmly, interrupting him.

"We'll have to wait out the fever."

Corren began saying incantations, one by one closing the wounds to leave raw, red welts. Marcellus was even more sallow than when they first found him. Nicolai did not think it safe to wait out the fever.

While Corren continued with the wounds, Nicolai hurried to his bag and pulled out what he needed. He retrieved his flask and took a drink until the right amount of water was left inside. He stopped with difficulty, just now realizing how parched he himself was. He added caraway, fennel, and sorrel to the water, keeping his back to Corren to hide the magical techniques he used. He shook the flask rapidly to mix the ingredients.

When he returned to Marcellus, Corren had about half the wounds sealed. Nicolai knelt down and shook Marcellus gently. He called his name once, twice, five times, shaking him firmer now. Marcellus stirred slightly, groaned, grimaced, then stilled, his eyes never opening. Nicolai shook him and said his name again, louder this time.

The grimace returned and Marcellus opened one eye. "I want you to drink some of this." Nicolai lifted Marcellus' head slightly with one hand, holding the flask to his mouth with the other.

He drank very little and made a sound of displeasure. Nicolai did not doubt it tasted very foul.

"A little more."

When Marcellus drank a sufficient amount, Nicolai put his head back down and watched. His face, white and shiny from the fever, began to regain some color. The sweat ran freely now as the fever began to leave him. His grimace slowly melted away. Marcellus opened his eyes, looking up at the blank sky, his mind still evidently inward, focused on his own body.

Corren had stopped. He was watching with a stark, confused look.

"There are more," Nicolai said, pointing to the wounds still open on Marcellus' arm.

Corren returned to these slowly, watching Marcellus' face more than anything else. Marcellus closed his eyes, took a long deep breath. He opened his eyes again. Nicolai saw the pain was mostly gone and the fever had lifted. He would still be tired and weak, there was nothing Nicolai could do about that, but at least he was out of danger.

Relieved, Nicolai set the flask on the ground, stood up, and stretched, his wet clothes hanging heavily on his body. He went to Corren's flask and borrowed a long drink. The river, which they had crossed and traveled down for the better part of their escape, was not far. They could refill their flasks there.

When he turned back, Corren was directly behind him. Nicolai startled. He had not heard Corren approach. "What did you give him?" Corren asked.

"Herbs."

Corren did not seem satisfied with this. He looked at Nicolai as if he had not spoken at all and was still awaiting an answer.

"Just... caraway, fennel...nothing unusual."

Corren gaped openly. "Healing has never been my strong point, but I know caraway and fennel cannot do what you just did."

Nicolai realized Corren probably knew quite well what these plants did, for his own methods. Nicolai's methods were those of the earth faeries. They could harness the power of a little seed or leaf or twig in a way no one else could. Of course, he could say none of this. "There was sorrel, too. That helps."

Corren obviously thought this a non-answer as well, but he did not wait for Nicolai to say any more. He walked over to the flask next to Marcellus and dropped some of its contents into his hand.

He looked at it. He smelled it. He even cocked his ear toward his palm as if listening.

Nicolai grew nervous.

Corren turned to him slowly. "All magic leaves a residue, Nicolai."

Nicolai looked away to Marcellus. He was watching them, fatigued and shivering now. His chest and stone were still exposed. "We need to get him warm."

Corren sighed. "Have it your way." He walked away to Marcellus, knelt next to him, pulled his tunic back over his chest and said, "sulith." The fabric slowly stitched back together, though it left a rather jagged seam. The smaller tears from the swords he left untouched. Corren stood and waved a hand over him, slowly saying another incantation. When he was finished, Marcellus' clothes were dry. Corren turned to Nicolai, looked him in the eye, a knowing look it seemed, then waved his hand again. Nicolai felt surrounded by heat, like a hot blast of summer air. Then it was gone, and he too was dry.

Corren dried himself last. He sat heavily on the ground, a moment later lying all the way down, exhausted.

Nicolai retrieved bread from their packs, along with some dried figs they had purchased in Furden. He walked up to Marcellus.

"Are you hungry?"

Marcellus nodded and took what Nicolai handed to him. "Thank you, Nicolai." Nicolai understood he was thanking him for more than the food. Marcellus wearily reached over and squeezed Corren's forearm, thanking him that way. It seemed enough for both of them.

Corren took food too. When he sat up he had that distant look on his face again.

They ate wearily, their moods weighty and dark. Marcellus looked around slowly. "This is a bad place to stop," he said.

"You picked it," Nicolai said and Marcellus gave a kind of grunting laugh. "You should sleep."

"Not here."

"Are you okay to ride?"

"In a minute."

They finished eating and sat still, needing to rest, needing to go on, watching the area all around and listening for threatening noises. Nicolai voiced a question that had been on his mind. "Who did she extract?"

"Theo," Marcellus said, and took a drink of his water.

Corren turned. "You saw her do it? Did she do it in front of you?"

Marcellus nodded. Corren had not wanted to believe it before. It was too terrible, too evil to consider. He did not realize just how much he was clinging to the slim chance that whoever they found in the woods wasn't extracted by Aradia, until Marcellus confirmed it. In spite of everything Aradia had done, in spite of the evil he knew she was yet planning to do, being confronted with this was too real and immediate. Why? Why was she doing something like this? For what purpose? Tempting as it was to push these questions away, Corren knew they needed to be answered if they could. If Corren and his brothers had any hope of truly defeating her, of protecting the Phoenix and keeping that magic out of her hands, they needed to understand exactly what she was doing.

"Tell me how she did it," Corren said.

Marcellus did not want to at first.

"Please," Corren said. "It's important. We need to know why she's doing this."

Reluctantly, Marcellus described what happened. Corren knew the glass ball was the Ajinn—a spirit contained—and when Marcellus described the colorful quality of the ball, Corren knew then what substance was strong enough to contain a spirit capable of extracting a human. The Murano branch of the Order, the glassblowers, used their ash to craft powerful glass objects useful in the highest levels of magic. The glass was nearly unbreakable. Corren did not stop to explain this.

Corren interrupted with questions, seeking for the details Marcellus would not know to give. What color was the light from the ball? What color was the light from her staff? What did she say? Marcellus did not remember the words of the incantations, but he remembered when

445

she spoke and when she was silent. When he got to the part about the gray mist going into Aradia, Corren cocked his head. "It went into *her?* Are you sure?"

"Yes."

"Are you sure there wasn't some sort of bottle or something she put it in? Something you couldn't see?"

"No. It went into her," Marcellus said, but he was still thinking, as if he were reconsidering. Corren expected Marcellus to remember something she was holding, or maybe a container set near her. *It couldn't have gone into her,* Corren thought. "She said something about building her defenses," Marcellus said at last.

This information processed slowly in Corren's brain, coming together with all he knew about magic, all he knew was possible, and slowly joining with what was impossible. What he *thought* was impossible. "Her defenses," Corren said to himself. He tried to keep his revulsion in check, to see clearly what she was doing. It was difficult not to push it away.

One by one, each thing he had heard clicked into place. Now they knew it all, her complete plan. They already knew she was getting into the Realm by using Danu's potion to open the Gateway, already knew she had the gold leaf she needed and probably everything else too, even the last ingredient—the moonlight from the Isle of Iona—which still eluded Corren. Now they knew how she planned to protect herself from the magic within the Realm itself. With a shield of extracted souls.

The realization pressed him to stand. He walked to the horse. Stopped. He turned and walked away to his left. Stopped.

"Corren?"

Where else could he go?

"Corren?"

He spoke slowly, dully. "She's building a shield." There was no answer to this. He knew they were waiting for him to explain. He didn't want to. He did not want to at all. "Remember when I told you about the magical protection within the Realm itself? That anyone who entered with intent to do harm withered to death on the spot? Well, that's magic Aradia needs to overcome even after going through

446

the Gateway. This is how she's going to do it. She's building a shield so she can stay in the Realm unharmed. The magic of the Realm will still attack her, but she'll be protected by the life forces she has stolen. It's her shield. As the magic attacks her, each life force will be extinguished, one at a time. To be in the Realm even for a little while, she'll need several life forces to protect her. That's why she's done this more than once. She'll need to get out, or kill the Phoenix, before those extra life forces are gone or she will go with them." Corren looked off to the distance. He did not really see what was in front of him. All he saw in his mind's eye was human extraction, at Aradia's hands.

Corren thought about the glass ball, about what Aradia would have had to do to make it into a true Ajinn, to capture the spirit and bring it into submission. He feared his knees would buckle as the thought struck him so terribly that his shoulders hunched with the weight of it. He thought of himself, brewing the Sevenfold Alcalic Base in Aradia's cabin, exhausted, obedient, foolish. He wanted to scream. Before he knew it, he was screaming. It started low in his chest and rose terrible and unstoppable, a roar swelling out of him and shattering the still air, shattering himself. He clenched his fists and spun wildly. "I helped her!" he said, jabbing his chest with his thumb. "I helped her! I brewed the base! Me!"

"The base for what?"

"For that terrible Ajinn! That's what she needed it for! I did it thinking I was helping her stop whoever was after the Phoenix."

Nicolai and Marcellus exchanged glances and he roared again. Nicolai stood abruptly, holding his hand out in a gesture meant to settle him. "You can't take responsibility for this. You didn't know what that base was for."

"No I didn't," Corren said, turning away. Whether he knew or not didn't matter to him. Nothing eased the knowledge that he had helped her to create the most wicked weapon of murder ever conceived. What evil was in her mind to think of it? What evil in her heart to create it?

447

Corren's muscles tensed and his blood raced as determination flooded him. He no longer cared what it took. He no longer cared what was asked of him. This could not go on.

He turned back to Nicolai. "I need to make the right staff."

Nicolai paused, his gaze fixed and penetrating. He seemed to understand exactly what Corren meant, though Corren didn't know how he could. "Was there something wrong with the old one?" This was said in Nicolai's gentle way, as if he already knew the answer.

Corren wanted to apologize. What if it were already too late? What if this had been their chance and he blew it?

"What did you see in that Labyrinth?" Nicolai asked.

It all came back to him in a rush, a flash of images one after the other as if he were going through the Labyrinth all over again: the flash of light in the mountains, the fire door on the ledge of a mountain, forging the staff in a lake of fire, his scarlet stone as a core for his staff... And the final vision: the stone alight followed by his own death. When this rush of images was over he was all the more determined. He did not know the consequences of his actions. He did not know if it was already too late. But he would not hesitate any longer. They were sure to meet Aradia again, one way or another, whether they wanted to or not. Next time he would not be so ill armed.

"I saw what everybody sees," Corren answered. "The pathway to my greatest success. Somewhere in these mountains, there's a ledge with a door of fire. I have to find it. I have to go in it. That's where I will make my staff."

Nicolai waited for a moment. "And you are ready?"

Corren nodded. "I am ready."

Twenty-Four

Near the northern border of Caedmonia, Commander Quinn was suffering an unprecedented defeat at the hands of Norrland troops. Though the Norrland troops numbered only half that of Quinn's knights, and though they were not as skilled or disciplined, they slashed through Caedmonia's knights like scythes taken to wheat. The defeat was baffling, unlike anything even the most seasoned knights had ever seen. No defense raised could quell it. It was nothing Norrland could have accomplished on their own, but the Norrland troops were not on their own, and they were doing more than defeating.

They were exterminating.

Two days later, dawn broke slowly, the sky lightening in sluggish degrees. Nicolai led the Three single-file through the winding pass, with Marcellus following and Corren bringing up the rear. Corren stretched his arms and yawned widely, his third yawn in as many minutes. The mountains worked their way up sharply on either side. In front, all Corren could see were Marcellus and Nicolai rocking evenly in their saddles, and, up ahead in the distance, the mountain peaks they were trying to get to.

"Here we go," Marcellus said. Corren saw the pass widening at last. It looked to be opening into a clearing. "There's grazing for the horses and we can camp under those trees."

Corren couldn't see the trees yet, or much of the clearing either, but he could easily imagine himself lying on the ground—hard or soft, it made no difference—and falling gratefully to sleep. He yawned again.

Nicolai came just into the clearing, then made a sudden stop. "Look," he said dismounting and bending over the ground.

449

Marcellus dismounted too, stretching and grunting. He went up to look. "Rabbit tracks."

"Fresh." Nicolai removed the throwing spears strapped to each calf. "Good. I've had enough of figs."

"I'll take in the mare and be back to help you," Marcellus said, grabbing Kedron's reins and pulling him forward so he could lead Nicolai's horse as well. Nicolai nodded, silently following the rabbit's trail. This was when Corren's first full view of the clearing appeared.

It was a small meadow, luminous green with long grasses bending over the ground. In the center of this stood three trees, massive and aged, like they had existed from the foundation of the earth. There was an oak, an ash, and an elm. Their broad, intertwining crowns dominated everything around them, capturing the fresh light of a new day on their shimmering leaves.

Marcellus released the horses to graze and went off to help Nicolai. Corren dismounted. He approached the trees almost reverently. Stepping into shadow, he came to the oak first and put his hand to the ridged trunk. He looked up at the branches extending out like a fan. He stood rooted there for a moment before repeating the process on the ash, then the elm. He circled the perimeter of all three trees. Off in the distance he heard a whoop of triumph, and made a cursory acknowledgement that rabbit would soon be served. He continued examining the branches; some were too curved for his purposes, or split off to another branch too soon, or angled too sharply away from the main trunk. Others, in spite of having a useable shape, were inadequate due to mottling or scarring on the bark. Corren persisted, however, because he knew there would be at least one branch on each tree that would serve him; he only had to find them.

By the time Nicolai and Marcellus arrived triumphant, with not one but two furry bodies dangling from Nicolai's hand, Corren had found all three branches. He had found the wood for his staff.

That evening, Corren sat with his back against the oak tree, examining the map he had stolen nearly three weeks ago from

Aradia's office. The beginning of Corren's staff—three pieces of slender wood smoothed and bound together in adjoining straight lines—lay by his side. Marcellus and Nicolai were sparring, the sounds of their clashing swords periodically filling the air. They were waiting for nightfall before traveling again, needing the fire door to appear to make sure they were on the right path. The light had been much brighter the last time they saw it; Corren knew they must be getting close. That was good, because they needed to get back to Stonebridge as quickly as possible. While they had been discussing the ingredients they still needed (the leaf from the Tree of Origin and moonlight from the Isle of Iona), Nicolai had remembered something. He recounted how he and Praea had discovered a lake that only Praea could see. A lake bathed in moonlight despite their finding it in the middle of the day.

"The Lake of the Moon," Marcellus had said.

"Praea must be a descendant of Diana," Corren had said, both shocked and excited. "They're the only ones who can see the Lake of the Moon. Or enter it. That's all I know, though, and I only know that much because of the book I saw in Aradia's office." It was decided that as soon as they returned to Stonebridge, which hopefully would not be long, Nicolai would find Praea to see if she could help them. It had been a tremendous relief. For the first time, Corren started to think they might actually be able to do this.

Now Corren read over the map, trying to figure out how long it would take Aradia to travel to the Phoenix once inside the Realm. Of course, he had changed the directions on the copy he had left in her office, but he was not terribly hopeful this would go undiscovered. In any case, she would have planned for a certain amount of time to travel once she got inside the Realm. This was what Corren was most concerned with. Her plans. How much time did she need? How long was she planning on resisting the magic of the Realm?

He tried to determine this by looking at the map. Some directions were easy enough, indicating how far to walk in a certain direction before going on to the next landmark. Other instructions were no help at all. "Follow the White Dry River until you reach the Bones Pit." But how far would that be? Corren had no way to know. He sighed in frustration, lowered the map onto his lap, and watched Nicolai and Marcellus dueling.

Marcellus had expressed his pleasure at Nicolai's progress more than once. Even Corren could see a difference since they first started from Stonebridge six days ago. Currently, they were practicing a certain move, over and over in a predictable rhythm—a technique Marcellus would occasionally employ.

"Step! Swing! Block!" Marcellus would say, and the sound of their blades crossing would accent the word "block." Then they would do it again. And again. The next time they did this, their blades crossed and Marcellus lurched forward and grabbed Nicolai's wrist, holding it there with their swords still locked together. Nicolai's eyes widened and he froze.

"Don't release the pressure here," Marcellus said. "Don't just block me. Push my blade where you want it to go."

Nicolai nodded, his eyes firm with concentration.

"Which way?" Marcellus asked, quizzing him. He let go of Nicolai's wrist but they kept their blades where they were.

"Like this?" Nicolai slowly pushed Marcellus' sword away.

"Yes. Why?"

"Because it weakens your grip and creates an opening."

"That's right. Try again." They resumed their stances, then "Step! Swing! Block!" and the sound of metal exploded in the air.

"Better."

Corren turned back to the map. How long would this take her? How long did she plan on being there? How soon after the Fourth Song sounded could she go in without running out of the souls she was taking into herself for protection? He closed his eyes and repressed a shudder. How many people would she need to extract to give herself enough time?

Corren had no idea how to find the answers to these questions. He sighed and watched Nicolai and Marcellus as darkness slowly fell.

ॐ ॐ ॐ

452

They traveled most of that night, the peak they were aiming for obvious once they saw the fire door again. Dawn came that morning just as they reached the base of the last peak to climb. Here, the mountain rose too steeply for the horses. They left them at the base and climbed on foot, Corren using his unfinished staff as a walking stick.

They neared the top and saw several ledges relatively near one another, any one of which might hold the fire door. Corren wasn't certain which ledge they needed, but he was drawn to one more than the others. They rested there and waited for night to come again. The mountain fell away behind them. In front of them, the rock face sheared up abruptly, presenting an almost perfectly smooth surface. It seemed familiar, like the one he had seen in his vision. There was no mark on the stone. No lettering. Certainly no door. Corren felt with more and more assurance that this was where it would appear.

So they waited on the stony ledge. Despite his exhaustion he slept in fitful stages, awaking frequently as the day slowly advanced. When awake, Corren's eyes rarely left the wall in front of him. He felt strangely comforted by it. Even though he knew nothing would happen until nightfall, he did not want to look away.

On a narrow precipice of an unknown mountain, sleeping near his brothers, Marcellus dreamt an unwanted dream. He was back in the little stone room, with Aradia towering over him. Swords pierced him sharply, and his body's memory of the real wounds lent credence to his dream, bringing genuine pain. Theo was there, pleading for forgiveness, then: "Don't let her do it! Don't let her do it!" Aradia sneered down at Marcellus. "Don't you want to save your friend?" Marcellus tried to speak but she had magically bound his mouth. She turned her staff on Theo. Marcellus saw him screaming, but the sound was fading. Faint. Like it was coming through water.

In the new and thick silence, Theo's face changed and now it was Janus in the white fire. Marcellus' heart jumped, horrified, and he struggled. *No! No!* Whatever was holding back the sound of his dream broke and it rushed to him like a deafening monster: Janus' screams and Aradia's laughter warped together and Marcellus wrenched awake, his heart pounding. He could still hear the scream of his dream and did not know if he himself had screamed. He looked to Nicolai and Corren, expecting them to be watching him. They slept on, unaware of the horror lingering around him.

Light was diminishing, but it was not yet dark. He decided to let them sleep for a while longer. He lay back down, looking at the side of the mountain Corren believed would soon be a door. Marcellus could not see how this would happen, but he was willing to believe it. He was willing to believe almost anything now. Including the one thing he had most wanted not to believe—though he could no longer deny it —and that was just how powerful their enemy was. After seeing what Aradia could do, Marcellus had to agree with Corren: they would defeat her by deceiving her at the Gateway, or not at all.

Marcellus absently thumbed a tear on the arm of his tunic, rubbed the scar it revealed on his arm, and his dream returned to his waking mind. His heart would not still. Was the dream a premonition? Janus' screams echoed in his thoughts. Marcellus wanted to rescue her, pull her away, put his arms around her, shield her, something, anything. He had no power to change the dream. It seemed stuck in his mind, Janus forever screaming, Marcellus forever inert.

They sat in the dark for a long time, Corren holding his partially completed staff as they watched for the door. They did not speak. They moved very little except when an ache in their leg or back would prompt them. The little half wedge of moon dipped down behind the mountain, hidden away.

Finally, Corren stood up. "It is coming," he said and the others stood with him.

There was no sound. No light. He felt it, a vibration somewhere deep within the mountain, deep within him. A hot, fiery glow.

"Get ready," he said.

When the light came, they squinted against it. The door appeared first, an elaborate archway that etched over the stone as if drawn by a great hand. Then came the lettering, just as Corren remembered, flickering like fire, dashing across the top of the door. Nicolai gasped almost inaudibly. Corren knew Nicolai recognized the words for they had the same kind of lettering as the strange ingredient in the potion recipe. Corren whispered, "Read it. Hurry."

Nicolai said the words: "Πυρκαγιά στην καρδιά, πυρκαγιά στο κόκκαλο. Πρώτα του γήινου σταυρού αυτό το κατώτατο όριο της πέτρας." The door began to open. A band of light appeared as Nicolai translated: "Fire in the heart, fire in the bone. First of the earth cross this threshold of stone."

The great stone door slid slowly inward. A bright orange light streamed out, blinding amid the darkness. Corren squinted, stepped into it, and his brothers followed. They found themselves inside a tunnel, glowing in a warm orange hue. The door began to close behind them. Nicolai and Marcellus turned to watch, the deep grinding of stone against stone pressing against their ears. Corren kept his eyes in front of him.

The tunnel was just tall enough to stand in, just wide enough to reach to both sides and brush stone with fingertips. Not far ahead, the tunnel curved to the left and out of sight.

Corren led the way.

He followed the tunnel as it curved. As he came around the turn all he saw was more tunnel. He pursued this until it curved again, this time to the right. He was reminded of the zigzagging path of the Labyrinth. The zigzagging did not continue long. This turn revealed a sharp descent. He had to watch his feet to keep from sliding. The air grew thick and hot. The pale orange light that hovered in the very air of the tunnel brightened considerably at the bottom.

They turned a corner again and a great cavern yawned before them. It stretched far distant in every direction, its edges unseen, consumed by darkness. The ceiling gaped above them, high overhead, the rock glowing and flickering from the orange light reflected from the rumbling fire below. In the center of the cavern, the lake of fire danced and popped and rolled like lava, straining to leap out of its bounds onto the flat stone earth all around it. Despite the heat, tangible and nearly suffocating, Corren felt a chill. This was the third scene of his vision in the Labyrinth. He was halfway to his own death.

Scattered around the cavern were groups of people—at least, they seemed like people. One of these stood very near, alone, as if he had been waiting for them to arrive. His cloak, thin and still in the heavy air, was the color of the mountain. His hair, black as coal, cascaded down his chest. Corren thought he saw smoke swirling in his gray eyes. When he spoke his voice was quiet but deep and penetrating. "I am Taal, King of the Fire Faeries. We have been expecting you."

Corren glanced quickly at the others in the cave—their faces watching—then back to the man in front of him. "I am Corren of Tower Hall South."

The man raised his thin eyebrows. "I know who you are."

Corren subdued his apprehension. Steeled himself. "How did you know I was coming?"

"The fire tells me what I need to know. These are the magical, sacred fires fed by the life force of the Phoenix. Tamed by our magic. You may approach, but your brothers must wait for you." Taal stepped aside and stood still again, his eyes now on the lake. Corren turned to it too. He gripped the wood and walked to the rocky edge of the lake. Around the lake's perimeter, the faeries watched him silently. The fire roared at his feet. The heat beat against his face. He held the wood over the fire with both hands, just as he had seen in his vision. The words came to him. He did not know if this were a memory of his vision or if perhaps the fire was telling him what he needed to know.

He spoke smoothly, rhythmically. "Rikna en emberas lostara." The surface of the lake grew even more tumultuous, heaving itself into great waves. These collapsed in where they had begun, sparks swirling vibrantly before sputtering out of existence. Below his outstretched staff, the fire raised in long, sinewy tendrils, like arms. "Seezth wut," and the fiery tendrils, now claws, grasped the wood, wrapping around it like luminous snakes. The straight rods twisted and spiraled around each other, the wood shifting under his grasp. The color of the wood, before light and varied, now simmered into a deep, smooth brown, coaxed into unity by the flame. The fire danced over his hand, slipped under it, not burning him but sending a jolt through his body each time it touched his skin.

456

Beyond all this, the lake of fire roared. Corren added his own voice to it. "Te virra ke blazia yi obay!" The fire arms plunged deep under the surface of the lake, releasing at Corren's command.

He reached under his cloak, pulled out the necklace, and freed his scarlet stone from its iron casing. He stretched his arms in front of him, gripping his brilliant stone in one hand and the staff bound by fire in the other. The reflection of the flames below winked on the surface of the stone and shone on the smooth surface of the wood.

For the second time in the last month, Corren said the final words to seal together his core of influence and the wood to make his staff complete, to bind it as a force connected to his will. He bellowed these words not out of fear and anger as before, but rather to harness their deep core of power: "ULTIMAH WYSARD BINDARI MAJJICKA!"

The stone broke free of his hand, driven to the edge of the staff that now widened and opened at the tip, ready to claim it. The stone entered in and the tip of the staff twisted around and encased it. The wood arrested its movement, still revealing the blood red slices of what it embraced.

Corren brought his staff close to him, turned, and rested the base on the ground. It was finished. It was ready.

The fire raged behind him. Before him, Marcellus and Nicolai waited at the mouth of the tunnel, watching him fervently. The staff in his hand radiated power in great, slow waves, unseen but not unfelt. He knew that despite their distance from him, his brothers could feel it as well as he could.

PART III

The Gateway

One

There was an urgent rap on the door to Clement's office and he immediately thought of Marcellus. It had been nine days since his sons left Stonebridge and he had not yet received any word of how they fared. He had, however, received word that Commander Theo had gone missing, a fact that raised concerns on many levels.

"Come!"

Through the door came a young man he knew to be one of Marcellus' spies working in the north. Esten was supported on either side by a page. This spy being in Clement's office at all would have been surprising enough, but it was his appearance that made Clement bolt from his desk and rush to his side. He did not look like a spy eager to deliver news and receive his pay; he looked bedraggled and splintered, blood-streaked and weak. In fact, the young man at the door looked nigh unto death.

"Your Grace..." Esten said, attempting a bow, but Clement steered him for the couch where he sat heavily before laying all the way down, unable to stay seated.

"Fetch the physician," Clement said to one of the pages. "Make haste."

The page ran out of the room. "What happened to you?" Clement ran his eyes over the man, inspecting his wounds. Though there were many, he didn't see any that were bleeding badly or in need of instant attention. Nevertheless, Esten's face was pale and clammy. Clement began to fear internal injuries.

"Norrland is advancing on you," Esten said with an urgent, breathless voice. His eyes, however, were alert and burning with intensity. "Their new king was murdered by his brother, who has claimed the throne. He subdued the Norrlanders supporting the rightful heir and has joined with the Citadel of Zeverai in order to attack Caedmonia."

"The Citadel?" Given recent events, this alarmed Clement more than it normally would have. He carefully said, "Even combined with Norrland they surely do not have enough manpower to come against us."

"The wizards number only a few hundred, Sire, but they are powerful and count for many more, ten times as many, at least. I've never heard of them doing anything like they're doing now. They have slain your battalions. Quinn, Orin, Fiesole. Leaving none alive, taking no prisoners." Clement sat back in surprise. The spy's eyes grew wider, his manner more agitated. "They have wizards ahead of them killing anyone they think might be sending messages to you. I barely escaped and I'm sure they believe me to be dead or they would have hunted me, too. They've been advancing for the last four days. They'll be entering the Rheita Valley now if they haven't already."

"Rheita Valley?!" Though he had the map of Caedmonia nearly memorized, Clement looked up at it anyway, his eyes fixed on the specified location. No enemy troop had penetrated that far into Caedmonia in hundreds of years. Clement could see the green valley clearly in his mind. He could not imagine enemy soldiers atop it. "How could they get so far in? What are they doing?"

"I don't know, your Grace. I don't know how they're doing it. It's as if no sword raised can stop them. I don't know how we can defeat them. I don't see how they can be stopped. I don't know. I don't know what we can do."

"Alright," Clement said, "it's alright." He put his hand on the spy's damp forehead, trying to ease his panic, and began to question the accuracy of the man's story. After all, what he said was so unlikely; perhaps his injuries had put him in a state of delirium. But instincts had long served Clement well. Though he knew he needed to verify what he had just been told, he also knew he needed to prepare as if every word of it were true.

The physician rushed in. Before Clement made room he asked, "Is there anything else?"

462

Esten shook his head, but his fear had not left him. "It's alright," Clement said again. "You have done a great service. The enemy will fail now because of your efforts."

Clement was trying to comfort him, but the man's intensity had not left at all. "They're powerful, your Grace," he said, like a man desperate to know that the true gravity of the situation was understood.

Clement met the man's eyes and said soberly, "I know."

He left him and let the physician work. At one point in the next several minutes Esten was moved to another room. This was amidst a flurry of commanders, knights, scribes, and pages all scurrying to meet Clement's commands; Clement saw him go but had no time to bid farewell. He called every battalion in Stonebridge to action and dispatched messages to others nearby. While he sent a unit to confirm the validity of Esten's story, Clement did not really doubt it to be true, no matter how much he wanted to deny it. He glanced at the map again, seeing not just the Rheita Valley, not just the enemy's presence there, but also his own troops moving into position. He imagined the lay of the land, mentally tallying the advantages and disadvantages to every location. The lion within Clement, which had lain dormant for many a year, reared its massive head. His blood began to race hot—an old, familiar feeling. His mind was clear and cool. If ever there was a time when Caedmonia needed someone cunning in war to lead them in battle, that time was now.

The last knight was leaving his office. Clement called to him when he was at the door. The knight stopped, turned, and waited for his king's command. "Dermot," Clement said. "Bring in my armor."

The Three emerged from the woods cautiously as Marcellus took one last look up and down the main road leading to South Caedmonia. It had been two days since Corren forged his staff in fire. The power that Marcellus had only seen in him on occasion before, when casting spells or arguing his point, now seemed to radiate from Corren constantly. He had a new focus, too. Whatever had been holding Corren back before, it was long gone now. It was *that*, as much as anything else, which gave Marcellus growing appreciation and respect for his brother.

Then there was Nicolai, steady as he had ever been. He was the one leading them to their next destination. The only thing Nicolai told them about this was that it was near Knobby Tree and that it contained the Tree of Origin. The fact that this somehow involved yet more faeries was obvious, since the lettering over the fire door and the lettering in the potion were the same. Nicolai did not deny this, but he would say no more. He seemed to be deciding whether or not he could, alluding to a vow he had once made. "But given what has happened..." and Marcellus thought he would reveal more, but Nicolai never finished this sentence. Neither Corren nor Marcellus pressed him to do it. Marcellus had felt Nicolai would tell them whatever his secret was soon. He wanted to give him time to come to it on his own.

They were not too far east of Nicolai's farm and emerged from the forest that lay south of the main road. They had the break they needed—no travelers in sight—and so began crossing. On the other side lay the Wilds. Marcellus' childlike apprehension of the Wilds reappeared as it had when he and Nicolai had gone into them before, looking for Corren. As quickly as it came he banished it. His father's ever-present (and mysterious) admonitions to never enter these woods were deeply ingrained in his heart, but Marcellus would not let the remnants of childhood fear rule him now.

"How much further?" Corren asked Nicolai as they reached the road.

"For you? Not much. Once we're out of sight you can stop and wait for me. I shouldn't be long."

"Wait," Corren said, exchanging a glance with Marcellus. "We're not going with you?"

"No."

A sudden surge of protectiveness came over Marcellus. His concern for Nicolai going anywhere by himself was coupled with Marcellus' feelings about one line of the prophecy that lately seemed to impress him more than any other: *only the Three as one.* "You can't go on alone," Marcellus said.

"I do not think I can take you," Nicolai said simply. He did not slow his pace and spoke with finality, as if it were not a matter up for discussion.

"If we did not split so Corren could forge his staff..." Marcellus began.

Nicolai was already shaking his head. "I cannot take you."

"I'm not letting you go alone," Marcellus said.

"You don't get to decide that."

"Oh no?" Marcellus had raised his voice, angry at Nicolai's refusal to budge. Nicolai brought his horse to a definitive halt. When he faced Marcellus he did so calmly. They were stopped in the middle of the road. Corren looked both ways nervously while Nicolai and Marcellus faced each other.

"No, Marcellus. You do not get to decide. I have brought you as close as I can. I gave my word that I would never reveal this location to anyone. You do not get to say whether or not I'll break it. I will ask if you can come. If you are allowed I'll return for you."

"And if we're not?" Nicolai made no reply so Marcellus continued. "We need to stay together. I thought we all agreed on this."

Nicolai was silent at first. Marcellus thought he had relented. "Then I cannot get the leaf from the Tree of Origin. We'll need another plan."

Marcellus exhaled in frustration. "That's not an option. You know it isn't."

"Can we at least get off the road to discuss this?" Corren asked. Marcellus checked the road. It was still deserted, save one lone figure on horseback, coming out of the Wilds closer to Knobby Tree.

His heart skipped a beat and he looked closer to confirm it. There she was sitting atop her white mare, bow slung over her shoulder, long braid down her back. "Janus!"

She turned. Seeing her face was such a relief that he had difficulty containing his delight at seeing her. Marcellus had not realized how concerned for her his dream had made him. They finished crossing the road and made their way to her, hugging close to the tree line.

She met them half way and greeted him with a smile. "I thought you were still in Western Caed..." she began, then she registered his clothes. When she saw his exposed wounds her amused curiosity turned to deep concern. "What happened?"

His impulse to be frank with her, his feeling he could trust her, made it difficult for him not to give her a straight answer. "Nothing to worry you." This seemed only to aggravate her worries. In fact she now looked at all three of them with concern. "What are you doing here?" he asked as a diversion. "Why aren't you in Stonebridge?"

A shadow passed beneath her face. She put on a curious smile he could not read. "I was visiting a friend," she said but averted her eyes briefly as she said it. He knew instantly that she was hiding something. What this could have meant hit Marcellus with terrible force. The anger he had felt toward Theo, anger temporarily extinguished after watching Aradia torture and kill him, now returned with such strength that he felt his shoulders hunch slightly as he looked at Janus. He remembered Theo, joking and smiling as Marcellus drank the poison. The poison administered by Theo's hand. Theo. The one person with whom Marcellus could always be himself, just like Janus.

But Theo had been hiding a secret.

Just like Janus.

Something in Marcellus snapped. "What friend?" he asked, his voice so hard everyone present reacted to it. He had no emotion to spare for their surprise. Janus' eyes were wide. *Like an animal caught.*

"Just... an old friend," she said. His anger and hurt boiled over into one smooth motion as he gripped the hilt of his sword and drew it with a sharp, metallic ringing. She flinched, her face turning to shock and confusion.

"What are you doing?"

"Your friend wouldn't be Aradia would it?"

"What?!"

"Marcellus!" In his fury, Marcellus did not know if it was Corren or Nicolai who had said it. He plowed on.

"For what price are you selling me to my enemies?" he said, hearing the same hurt in his own voice that he now saw on Janus' face. She looked as pained as if he had already sliced through her with his blade, had recoiled at his words even more than when he drew his sword. Indeed, her eyes were not fixed on the sword but rather on him.

"How can you think that?" This was said in a whisper so soft and heartfelt that he now felt *he* had betrayed *her*.

He looked away, furious with himself, furious that the emotions storming within him were so unchecked that his own voice, face, even his very actions betrayed him. He had sheathed his sword but he didn't know what to think and no longer wanted to look at her. "If my best friend can sell me to my death, why not you? Why not anyone? Who am I to trust? You tell me!"

"What?!" Her voice was angry, protective, and drew his eyes to her. Only one other time had he seen such a look on her face, the time she drew her arrow in a stunning blur at the prisoner who half threatened to slice Marcellus' throat. "Who?" she demanded. If he were going to answer, there was no opportunity. Sounding over the hills, low and startling, were Caedmonia's war horns, coming from the direction of Stonebridge.

Marcellus' anger fled. He felt a sudden chill.

All his life, Marcellus had never heard those horns in this valley, never so close to the capital. He gaped at the horizon, which hid the city from his view. How long did he linger there? Five seconds? Ten? It was the longest he had ever taken to respond to that sound. He bolted his horse and fled for Stonebridge, the rest following him. They flew past Nicolai's farm, the outskirts of Knobby Tree, and through the village itself, people stopping to stare at them as they went. They came over the ridge leading into Rheita Valley. An open view revealed a surprising sight. The southern entry to the city was open, troops marching out the gates at a fast pace. Other battalions were already lined up along the valley, clear to the river crossing and beyond. If these had all come from Stonebridge, Marcellus thought, his father had drained the city of troops.

"What would possess him to do that?" Away to the north, at the head of the valley, Marcellus saw the answer to his question.

A mass of troops—foreign, sinister, deep in the heart of Caedmonia —hovered on a distant rise like a swarm of locusts ready to strike. Though he could only see a small number of troops, he knew there would be more hidden from view behind them. If his father were emptying Stonebridge of all her troops, that number must be very great indeed.

Marcellus processed a series of thoughts very quickly. His body stilled; even the horse underneath him barely moved. He slipped into battle mode, his thoughts turning into commands. Marcellus turned to Corren. "Go to the king and tell him I'm in the valley. You are to stay in the castle with him."

Corren's eyes widened in protest but Marcellus turned to Nicolai and said, "You as well." Even though Marcellus found him to be a natural swordsman, with great strength and determination, nothing could counter the fact that Nicolai had less than one month of training. Neither could anything counter the fact that Nicolai was the only one with information they still needed. Nicolai was disappointed, clearly eager to fight. Marcellus could not help but soften the blow. "We still need you for other things, Nicolai."

Corren spoke up. "We can help."

"Telling the king I'm here is helping. Go on."

"But..."

"I do not wish you to fight!"

"But I..."

Marcellus had neither the time nor the patience to argue. "Who commands the fighting men of this country, Corren?!"

Corren pressed his lips together. "You do, your Highness."

"Deliver the message as ordered."

"As you wish." He turned toward the city. After a moment's hesitation, Nicolai followed.

Marcellus gave no order to Janus, did not even turn in her direction. Yet as he sped away at a full gallop toward the front-most battalion, terribly far in the distance, he was fully aware of the fact that Janus was right there alongside him.

Two

Corren rode through the South Gate, steaming. They would go to the castle and deliver the message to the king, but regardless of what Nicolai was going to do, Corren had no intention of staying there. He wouldn't sit and do nothing with enemy troops so near to the city. How *did* they get so near? His mind was still reeling from it.

The citizens were in a panic, closing up their stores, bringing goods inside and shuttering windows. People from the outlying towns had come into the city and clogged the streets with their carts, piled high with furniture, household goods, and children. Many were heading deeper into the city. Others stopped on the road, looking around as if not sure where to go. People shouted to each other, giving instructions to take down a sign or clear away crates blocking a lane. All around were noise and confusion and very few knights to help maintain order.

Corren heard snippets of conversations his entire ride to the castle, but it wasn't until he was halfway up the hill that one of these conversations brought him to a halt. "But what will keep the wizards out of the shop?"

Corren twisted in the saddle and brought the horse around, barely missing a collision with a cart full of copper pots that went rattling by. Nicolai came up beside him. Two men were bringing their baskets of linen in from the street, moving in a rush, leaning back to balance the weight. They disappeared inside the low stone building and Corren and Nicolai exchanged glances. When the men came out empty handed, Corren said, "What did you say about wizards?"

They both looked startled. The older man took a half step backward toward the door of their shop. The other, who may have been his son, stood still. "We don't want any trouble," the older man said.

"What about the wizards?"

469

"We meant no offense," the younger one said, backing away too, his eyes on Corren's staff now.

"I'm not going to hurt you," Corren said, the frustration in his voice doing nothing to calm them. "Just tell me what's happening." It was not uncommon for wizards to be regarded with suspicion and even fear on occasion, but this kind of open fear—as if he were on the verge of attacking them—was not normal at all.

The younger man said, "We don't know. We only heard a rumor."

"What rumor?"

"That wizards have joined Norrland's army and they're..." but the young man seemed afraid to go on. Now Corren understood why.

Corren pointed his finger to the east, indicating the advancing enemy troops. "Wizards? They have wizards with them? Are you sure?"

Again his agitated manner only served to worry them more. "We don't know," the old man said, backing up and pulling his son with him. "It's just what we heard." Then they were in and the door closed with a bang.

Corren looked at the door for a minute, thinking about what they had said, thinking about what he saw in the valley. He made his decision. "Come if you want," he said to Nicolai. Corren urged his horse into a run, the castle now behind him.

Marcellus and Janus had not gone far when the banner of the front most battalion could be distinguished. "Those are my men!" Janus said and Lamtarra took on a burst of speed as she pulled ahead. Janus' battalion was already in formation, preparing for battle, facing the enemy and waiting. Then their wait was over.

Away on the ridge a distant horn sounded, high and shrill. In answer to the call, the enemy swarmed down the hill. Marcellus would not be able to make it to the front of the line before they clashed, would not even be able to make it to the center of command. He bolted, his eyes firm on the enemy and his own men's responses to them. The movements of his troops were now dependent on the wisdom of their commanders. Marcellus could only hope they would not fail. Janus broke away from him, her course set for her battalion.

The enemy was halfway down the hill now; a gap in the enemy's forces appeared at the top of the hill. This gap widened. Marcellus first counted their poor formation as fortune, an advantage he could use, but the minutes went on and no more enemy troops came over the hill. He pulled Kedron up short. Janus sped away from him.

His body drew tense and alert, his mind sharpened. He saw the field of battle as if from a great distance above. He analyzed what he saw. The enemy had perhaps one fifth the number of troops as Caedmonia, if even that many, with apparently no more behind them. How could they have come so near to Stonebridge with so few? What would drive them to incite battle against so many? If there were so few, why did so many Caedmonian troops come out to meet them? To ensure a clean victory? Marcellus' mind worked rapidly. Ahead of him, the battle converged with a roar that rolled across the valley like thunder, yet Marcellus did not move or respond. He narrowed his eyes. His skin pricked. He looked across his battalions of men and distinctly felt their danger had been increased by the small numbers of the enemy, not lessened by it. His mind could not quite work it out and he sought the answer to it. Though he didn't have it pinned under his finger yet, though it squirmed and writhed away from him, Marcellus watched the almost suicidal attack of so few enemy troops against his own and knew something was wrong.

Janus was still far behind her own battalion, mingled now with another, when she entered the cradle of the valley. The air grew thick with the familiar smells that preceded a battle: horses and dirt freshly kicked up. The low rise of the hill leading to the enemy was covered with troops locked in combat; the fighting had not yet advanced this far back. At first Janus believed the line was being held, but instead of her making progress toward the battle, it made progress toward her. A wedge-shaped mass of enemy troops cut through Caedmonia's ranks like a ship through water. The front lines curled in behind it, pursuing the enemy, but unable to stop or even slow its progress toward the base of the valley where she had just come splashing out of the shallow crossing of the river.

471

Now the enemy troops spread out, the wedge stretching out into a line parallel with the river. As they drew nearer, Janus saw the Caedmonian knights falling, crumpling out of the way almost as if they offered no resistance. She watched this in alarm, not understanding how the enemy was getting through.

They were close. Nearby, she saw the signal to fire and she and those archers around her pulled back their bows and released. She saw the arrows descend upon the enemy like a hailstorm. None of their men fell, nor did their advance slow. In fact they answered so quickly with a rain of arrows she did not even see them draw their bows. With no armor, Janus could only duck and hope. She heard the arrows whizzing by, heard men get hit, looked to her left and saw men falling. A hot flash of pain tore at her shoulder as an arrow grazed her. She compulsively clutched at it to counter the pain. A spark of light bloomed before she even realized what she had done. Now the only evidence of her injury was the blood on her hand and a torn shirt. She glanced around to see if anyone had seen her. Lamtarra reared, screaming. An arrow had plunged into her front quarters. Janus tried to settle her horse, stretching for the arrow, but she could not reach it. A rush of Caedmonian knights were backing up, the enemy visible just beyond them. The battle front was now only feet away from her. She was carried with them back into the shallow crossing of the river. Lamtarra reared again. As Janus hung on, the point of an enemy spear came through Lamtarra's neck, nearly into Janus' chest.

Janus' heart clenched in shock and horror as Lamtarra swayed and veered heavily to her side. Janus jumped off just in time to avoid being crushed as her horse toppled into the water.

Janus caught her feet, the water churning around her calves. She rushed around to her horse's front. Janus would have sent healing light into her horse right then, not caring who saw, but by the time she heaved the spear out of Lamtarra's neck the blood had choked her and she was already gone. "No!" she cried. She would have fallen to her knees but the circumstances allowed no mourning.

Janus turned to face the battle. The only thing standing between her and the enemy line was a Caedmonian pikeman being run through with the blade. She pulled back the bloody spear in her hand and sent it flying at the enemy knight whose dark eyes were upon her. It sailed through the air dead on course. Only moments from him, it jerked to the right as if yanked by an invisible hand and veered past him. She froze, but only for a moment. The man approached, sword raised. She could not hesitate. Still struggling to register what she saw, already doubting her own eyes and wondering what had happened, Janus reached for her arrow. Before she had it cocked in her bow, a deafening crack ripped across the valley as if the earth itself had heaved apart and split into two.

Marcellus had gone down into the valley too, not watching the front but rather scanning the area all around. He was looking for the hole, the weakness, the true intent of attack, and it eluded him. His hairs stood on end and he could not shake the sense that he must uncover their plan, and quickly. Finally, looking up river and following it all the way to its source, he saw what he was looking for. He knew this was the true danger, even though from this distance he could not make out exactly what was happening. He could not see the wizards from the Citadel of Zeverai with the points of their staffs aimed together at the base of the dam. He only saw the unsteady mass of a relatively small group of people next to the dam where it made no sense for people to gather. He saw a flash of violet light all along the base of the dam and in an instant his mind imagined what was coming, registered what it meant, opened his mouth and yelled "RETREAT!" His command was buried by the sound of the dam breaking, great chunks of stone flying, chased by an outpour of debris and water as the lake burst open and rushed its frothing way downstream to where Marcellus and the bulk of his troops stood.

Janus could no longer see the enemy who had been attacking her. She only saw knights dashing about her in confusion, the roar of sound so loud it made listening for orders impossible. She had been pushed back to the center of the wide river now, but that was all she knew of her location. The events of the last few minutes were so

473

disorienting that in her efforts not to get trampled she had lost her bearings. She needed to find her direction, which she did by locating Stonebridge, its massive walls steady in the distance though not where she had expected them to be. Thus straightened, she took hold of her thoughts in the din of sound which surrounded her. She managed to locate the source of the noise. Men and horses rushed by in every direction; what she saw were only angry flashes of the coming flood through random openings to her view. It was enough. She locked eyes on the crushing wave of water barreling toward her. She was in the center of the river, without a horse, without a way to escape the water that was near her; very near. She knew she could not outrun it.

She ran anyway.

She felt as if in a dream, her feet moving yet her body going nowhere. The bank of the river drew no nearer, or so it seemed, as the water came in a rush toward her. She ran, and a swarm of people ran around her, most on horses, gaining ground off and away. Her eyes sought a horse that had perhaps lost a rider, but to no avail. When she looked to the approaching flood that was nearly to her, the sight of the wall of water was so fearsome she could not look away. Her entire awareness dissolved into excruciating terror and she saw she was going to die for no healing light could save her now.

This was her state when she heard her name.

She tore her eyes away, sought behind her, heard it again—"Janus!" —and there was Marcellus racing toward her atop Kedron, his arm stretched out for her, the horse not slowing at all. She turned just as he came to her, reached up her arms and they caught hold of one another. Her body slammed against the hard muscles of the horse, one thigh hit forcefully by the horse's leg, her other leg swinging up and over his back as Marcellus hauled her on top. She seized her arms around his chest and they leaned forward together as Kedron passed the bank, racing beyond it to escape the wide reach of the coming water. It was almost upon them. Kedron ran straight for a ridge. The horse leapt into the air, taking them up the ridge, two great leaps, up again, just above the wall of water as it went screaming underneath them. They climbed another ledge then stopped and turned, watching the flood ravage down river, mercilessly burying knights and steeds, swept away as if mere twigs in the water. Marcellus and Janus stared horrified, breathing heavily, as the river swelled and tumbled and obliterated. All the way down it went, into the fertile valley dotted with homes and villages and crops that crouched helpless and unmoving as the water rolled over all on its unrelenting path to the sea.

The small group of enemy troops had drawn many of Caedmonia's knights into a mass along the river's edge and within the river itself, drawing them into the path of the coming flood. Norrland had sacrificed a few, and by so doing drowned a good portion of Caedmonia's troops and divided the rest. One-third of the remaining Caedmonian host stood on the far side of the water, separated by a river too wide and wild and forbidding to cross. Of the Caedmonian knights left to defend Stonebridge, Marcellus and Janus were among them.

Janus realized she was shaking. She wanted away from that water. Marcellus turned and looked behind him, his eyes fixed on some location behind them. She watched as the color drained out of his face. She looked too. Coming down from the western side of the lake, through the narrow pass between Sheehan and that mass of forest stretching from the Great Gorge to the northern walls of the city, the rest of the enemy came. They had been waiting in ambush, waiting for the flood to divide Caedmonia's troops, creating the perfect opportunity to attack. Janus felt her blood run cold.

"Retreat!" Marcellus boomed to the men in the rear. "Retreat! Back to the city!"

He started to retreat himself. Janus spied a horse that had lost its owner in the battle and quickly dismounted.

"Janus!"

"I'm here!" she yelled back, mounting the horse. She spurred the horse on toward the city, cries of "Retreat!" following her as she went.

Three

Marcellus hastily formed his battalions into formation, constantly checking the advance of the enemy. He had retreated his troops nearer to the city, but stopped them there. He could no longer see the top of the hill from which the enemy had been descending—this being guarded by trees—so he had no idea if there had been a break in their men. He didn't know how many there were. From what he could see their numbers were nearly two-thirds of Caedmonia's now (at least those on this side of the river) with still more coming into his view. The enemy did not slow. He quickly assessed their ranks: footmen followed by archers and light cavalry. There were small units on their flanks that he could not immediately identify. Pikemen, perhaps, but that didn't seem right.

Janus was still near him. "Prince! Your armor!" She had hauled over an armor bearer. Marcellus was too busy calling his men into formation to respond. Under different circumstances he would have pulled all the way back to Stonebridge, lowered the city's gates and let Norrland try, and fail, to take the city by siege. Two hundred years ago the city had withstood a seven month siege and could do so again now except for two problems. The tankers in the castle and city were fed by pipes from the lake, which was now largely drained and certainly below the point where the pipes entered the lake's basin. Without a sufficient water supply, the city could not last. Secondly, if the thick stone dam could be destroyed, so too could the city's walls. Marcellus would have to stop them before they reached the city. He did not know just how he was going to do it. All he knew was he had to keep the enemy away from the city walls.

Arrows went whizzing past. Enemy arrows. One nicked Marcellus on the thigh. He paid it no heed. The line of the enemy was advancing. "Your Highness! Your helmet!" The armor bearer held it up to him. Marcellus' eyes were on the enemy. Their advance was swift and would meet the Caedmonian troops in just minutes. He ordered his archers to fire. Quivers darted out in a series of twangs, vaulting into the air.

"Marcellus!" This caught his attention finally. Janus held up the helmet. "Put it on!"

He grabbed it.

"Take over Murray's battalion," Marcellus said pointing. "He didn't make it." In their retreat he had seen poor Murray's body lying twisted on the ground. Marcellus took the shield the armor bearer held up to him. He looked back up in time to see arrows suddenly very near, heading straight for them. He held up the shield and felt two arrows ping off it. He looked to Janus with concern but she had ducked behind a shield of her own, unhurt, while riding off to Murray's battalion. The armor bearer took an arrow in the neck—his one vulnerability—and fell backwards, wide eyed and sputtering.

Marcellus called for another volley of arrows. This time he did not remove his eyes from their arrows so he saw what he missed before. The arrows changed course, turned back in a high, ferociously fast arc and came streaming down on them. He ducked, understanding it was their own arrows they had dodged earlier. The hairs on the back of his neck pricked as he began to consider what he just saw. The front lines were nearly ready to converge. Marcellus ordered his pikemen to charge, sending his cavalry after them. The archers still stood ready, but Marcellus did not order their fire.

The pikemen ran forward, heads bowed, bodies leaning, long spears in front thrust ahead as a deadly guard. The enemy charged with their footmen bearing broadswords. Marcellus had the advantage here.

Moments before the lines met, his pikemen's spears flew up and back, almost as if they had been jerked out of their hands. The enemies' swords descended upon them without resistance. As the enemy plowed through, Caedmonian spears and swords along the line flew into the air, disarming the knights preparatory to the slaughter. Marcellus' men fell like broken reeds and the knights behind noticed this, faltering in their advance. The men who had not yet been given orders to charge took a step back in surprise. Marcellus yelled to hold the line and they did, but the hesitation in the ranks was everywhere felt. The line was dissolving as enemy troops rushed forward unchecked.

Realizing what was going on, Marcellus sought those who he had seen earlier along the enemy's flanks. These units were closer and he had a better view of their black cloaks and long staffs aimed along the lines. They were using magic against Caedmonia to turn their own weapons against them, to disarm them, and to protect the enemy itself.

"Attack their flanks! Attack their flanks!"

In that instant, the barrier between him and the oncoming foes vanished. Marcellus held his sword and shield at the ready, gripping them as tightly as he could. The enemy was upon him. He raised his sword only to feel it yanked out of his grip—the shield next. An enemy knight near him pulled back on his sword. Marcellus reared Kedron who kicked him blunt on the chest. The man staggered backwards, but did not fall, did not even seem harmed. Marcellus knew the man could not have survived the blow of a trained warhorse without magical protection.

The man gathered his feet and came at Marcellus with his sword again. Marcellus unsheathed his water sword, loathe to have it lost from his grasp too. The enemy raised his sword against Marcellus but the water sword was not wrenched away and he blocked the blow. The man's eyes widened; he froze. Marcellus grunted in satisfaction and went at the enemy with fresh determination. Marcellus' first two blows were blocked, but they were merely intended to guide the man's own sword and shield to where Marcellus could, and did, deliver the third and fatal blow. His knights were having no such success, however. Though Marcellus urged Kedron backwards as quickly as he could, the enemy now came at him from several directions. Three came on him at once. He held them off with difficulty, their apparent lack of training and his skill being the only thing to save him. He knew that without another sword or at least a shield, it would only take one more man to take him down. As soon as Marcellus felled one man, another appeared in his place.

On a nearby ridge, slightly above the battle, he caught a glimpse of Corren. Corren, without armor or sword, stood alone and faced the enemy, his staff in hand.

Marcellus blocked a blow with his sword and reared Kedron again to slow the advance of the others. When he came down his blade tore through the chest of the enemy knight nearest him. Two more replaced him, and it was in slow motion that Marcellus saw these Norrlanders raise their swords against him, one coming from one direction, one from the other. He knew he could block one blade, but not both. He could turn his horse against them, but that would open the way to the enemy on his other side. He could run, but it would not be quick enough. Marcellus raised his sword, the rippling blade thick with blood, its shards of silver flashing in the sun. He raised his sword against one enemy, determined to take down at least that one man before he was struck himself. He saw Corren out of the corner of his eye, lowering his staff at the enemy troops. Even though Marcellus could barely hear the words he bellowed, he felt them as if Corren were right next to him. A field of energy came radiating out of Corren's staff in every direction and hit them all like a blast. Marcellus swayed in the saddle. Men, friend and foe alike, staggered back in one great wave as the spell swept through them all. He looked back to Corren who had lowered his staff, looking frightfully drained. He leaned forward on his staff before falling all the way over and out of sight.

"Corren!"

This call to his brother was swallowed up by the roar of the war cry sent up by his own troops. He looked to his fighting knights. Their weapons stayed in their hands and their blows were sure. The enemy was no longer magically protected. Corren had broken their shield.

The enemy knights around him stumbled, momentarily stunned. Marcellus knew that wouldn't last more than a few seconds and he took full advantage of their shock. He slashed at one, brought Kedron down on another and stole the shield from a third, all the while urgent to get to Corren. By the time two more were dead, his troops had advanced, his own men by his side now. A flash of pale light went past him and Kedron reared. Twenty feet away it exploded in the

479

middle of some of his cavalry and they all flew in every direction, many torn to pieces by the strength of the blast. Limbs and pieces and blood shot out and Marcellus looked away, sickened. When Marcellus sought the source of the light, he was not surprised to find a wizard, with a mad look of concentration, aiming his staff and opening his mouth to say another incantation. Before the wizard could say a word he went limp, eyes closing as he collapsed. Marcellus saw no sword in his body, no arrow, no weapon at all. Behind him, more of his fellow wizards were aiming spells in various directions, but none seemed aimed at their fallen comrade. What had happened?

He looked again to the ridge where Corren had been and still couldn't see him. Marcellus drew back behind the line that advanced steadily now. He fought through trying to get to the ridge. Nearby, another strange explosion tore through a group of his archers and Marcellus grunted. He glanced at the spot where he had last seen the cluster of wizards. They had been pushed back, were retreating steadily despite the spells they cast. Again Marcellus saw one of them fall to the ground with no apparent cause.

Commander Dermot was pushing his battalion forward, saw Marcellus, and shouted. "Do we force a retreat or surround, my Lord?"

Marcellus looked away from Corren's direction and assessed the constricted formation of the enemy's troops due to their descent from the narrow pass. His own troops were starting to surround the enemy's flanks. The tide was turning, there was at least hope now, but it was not over yet. "Stabilize the situation first," he answered Dermot, "then it's kill or capture." He was not willing to let any enemy escape this deep inside the border if he could help it. Even assuming the best outcome of the current battle, they'd be chasing down enemy deserters for days.

"Yes, your Highness," then Dermot went on.

Marcellus sent signals to his battalions on the flanks but continued pushing on to Corren's ridge. Finally he saw him, lying on the ground on top of his staff, his cloak spread out around him. Marcellus leapt off Kedron and knelt at his brother's side. "Corren!" He put his ear to

Corren's mouth, exhaling in relief when he felt Corren's warm breath. He shook him firmly. "Corren!"

Corren stirred only slightly. Marcellus glanced to the city gates. He knew infirmaries would be getting set up just inside the city walls. He would take Corren there. When Marcellus began to lift him, though, Corren groaned and opened his eyes. He made a kind of croak. Not sure if he was trying to speak, Marcellus stopped and bent to him again. "What?"

"Did it light? The stone... did it light?"

Marcellus looked at the stone in his staff. It was the same blood red it always was, grasped by the claws of the wood. "Your stone? No."

Corren was struggling to stand, dipping and swaying on unsteady feet. Marcellus held his arm to steady him.

"Good," Corren said. "I didn't think it time yet."

"What are you talking about?"

Corren shook his head and ran a hand along his moist brow. Sweat pasted his hair to his head. "Nothing. Nothing." He was standing now, though still wavering.

"Are you alright?"

"That spell just... took a little out of me."

Another magical blast erupted nearby and sent bits of earth raining upon them. When the dust cleared Marcellus turned and saw yet another of their wizards fall to the ground. "What's going on?"

"Over there," Corren said, pointing. Mingled deep within his own Caedmonian troops, wizards in dark green cloaks were pointing their staves and saying incantations. These wizards were fighting the wizards among the enemy.

"Who?"

"It's the Guard," Corren said. "As we neared the city we heard rumors that wizards were attacking Caedmonia. We never made it to the castle. We went straight to the Guard instead."

"I'm glad you did," Marcellus said.

"Corren!" Nicolai was running up to them. He was dirty and sweating; a long gash bled freely on his arm.

"Are you alright?" Nicolai asked, concerned eyes on Corren who was still without color though more steady on his feet. "I saw what you did."

"I'm fine," Corren answered.

"What of you?" Marcellus asked. Had they both ignored his orders?

Nicolai absently wiped a trail of blood on his arm. "It's only a scratch." Nicolai was preoccupied with the battle field before him. Marcellus surveyed the valley as well.

Caedmonia, with the help of the Guard, had gained the upper hand. The enemy was in a full retreat, running for the hills. His troops followed, and among these he saw Janus flinging arrows almost without pause. Across the river his separated troops marched north, which would lead them, eventually, to the other side of the lake. If they hurried, they would be able to cut off some of the retreating Norrlanders and pursue the rest.

Far off, someone called "Prince Marcellus!" He searched for the caller, heard his name again, and now he saw. It was Commander Perry, a desperate fear in his eyes, supporting in his arms a fallen knight.

No.

Not a knight. The king.

Four

They rushed Clement to the gatehouse and into a small room just past the portcullis. Marcellus laid his father carefully on a low cot, trying not to feel the horrible dampness of his own tunic, soaked from his father's blood.

He had never felt so close to panic in all his life. He looked at Commander Perry. "Where are Corren and Nicolai? Where've they gone?" Nicolai could heal him. He needed Nicolai.

"They're just here, your Highness."

Corren and Nicolai came through the narrow door, pushing past the grim-faced knights hovering there.

Marcellus' legs went weak with relief; he knelt next to Clement. "Leave us," Marcellus said to the others. They filed out and closed the door as Nicolai and Corren drew near.

As Nicolai rushed up to his father, Clement slowly looked at him, his eyes heavy and dull. His wound ran half an arm's length from Clement's chest to his lower intestines. Nothing inside the gaping wound was recognizable, both because his organs were so badly mutilated and because they were drenched in blood. Nicolai looked at Clement's face, pale and fading. He was hovering over death; Nicolai was amazed he wasn't there already. Nicolai tried to think what he could do, what herb, what seed, what magic. He could think of nothing to stop it.

"Nicolai?" It was a hoarse whisper, coming from Marcellus.

Their eyes met. With that one glance Nicolai's diagnosis was communicated.

Marcellus firmly shook his head no.

483

Nicolai looked to Corren, who had gone around next to Marcellus. He stood over them, his eyes fixed on the fatal wound. It only took one glance for Nicolai to know there was nothing Corren could do either.

"Try!" Marcellus said. "You *try*."

Nicolai did not know what to try, but in the face of Marcellus' desperation he could not say so. He fumbled with his bag, splattered with blood from the earlier battle. He barely felt it in his hands. *What do you give the dying?* He began to prepare a powder to go in the wound. It would go in the wound and then what? Nicolai could not think. He could see his hands working—his own arm seeping blood as well—and he did not know what he was doing. The lights flashed between his fingers as he worked the magic, realizing too late he neglected to hide it. What did it matter? Nicolai felt no hope. A terrible ache in his chest, familiar, much too familiar, grew and grew as he watched his hands making a remedy that would not help. It would not be enough. He dusted the powder over the wound, terrible and gaping and flowing with too much blood that took most of the powder right out with it. "Close it. Close it."

The tip of Corren's staff appeared and he slowly began closing the wound. Nicolai continued adding powder until the wound was sealed and all the death and impotent healing was hidden inside.

Clement groaned.

Through all this, Marcellus stooped over Clement, saying over and over, "You're alright, you're alright."

Clement raised a trembling hand, cupped it over Marcellus' shoulder. "I love you, son." It was not his voice. It was a sigh of a voice, from one sharing a body with death before death took him completely.

"Don't..." but Marcellus' voice broke. Firmer now, "You're not going anywhere."

Clement smiled a ghost of a smile. He lacked strength and it vanished. Clement placed his hand on Marcellus' cheek and let it rest there.

Marcellus shook his head no, willing it not to be. "Please. Stay."

Nicolai felt his father's hand, placed upon his. A weak squeeze. Nicolai beheld his father's face, Clement giving him a tender look of love.

"Father..." Nicolai said, and the rest caught in his heart. Oh, why hadn't he said it sooner? Just one word, but it was more than a word. It was a declaration of love and acceptance; an apology for not having said it freely sooner. It was regret at their relationship being lost so soon; anguish for not being able to heal him. In his father's eyes Nicolai could see he understood it all.

Clement's dry lips trembled. He said, "Son." Nicolai understood that this, too, was more than just a word.

Suddenly, Nicolai could not bear to lose him. He could not bear to lose another father. Corren had knelt down too, opposite him and next to Marcellus. Clement was moving his eyes to him, saying his goodbyes to one last son, but Nicolai was fumbling for his necklace. He pulled it out as Clement said something to Corren that Nicolai could not hear. He took the yellow stone out of the clasp. Clement closed his eyes and let out a long, expiring sigh—the kind of sigh that is one last goodbye to this world and is never breathed in again—and this was when Nicolai put the stone on Clement's chest, just as he had done for Praea all those weeks ago.

Only this time the stone was not lit.

The Three looked at the stone with detained breath; there was not a sound. No sound of their breathing. No sound of Clement breathing. No light. No healing. Nothing.

Someone shifted a foot and it scratched against the floor. Time started again. Nicolai was panting. His father was still gone. Marcellus fell on his father's neck, clutching his shoulders, hiding his face, but Nicolai could hear his repressed cry well enough. Corren turned away, took a few paces, then turned back resignedly, standing like a drained vessel.

Nicolai did not move. His hands, both of them now, were on the stone. His eyes were on the stone. His *will* was on the stone. "COME ON!"

The stone was dark, taunting. Beyond his will. As always.

485

Furious, Nicolai pulled the stone back and hurled it across the room. Corren's hand reached out to catch it, the stone flew past, nearly to the stone wall, then "Ett" and in an instant it froze, hovering in the air. Corren stepped to it slowly and retrieved it. Shocked by himself, Nicolai was truly grateful Corren had stopped it, but he still would have liked the satisfaction of seeing it shattered to bits.

Corren looked at Nicolai. Nicolai felt deathly weary.

Corren slowly circled the bed and held out Nicolai's stone, its bright yellow cradled in Corren's dirt-stained palm. There it was again. He took it, and all the burden it represented. He replaced it in the iron casing and slipped it under his shirt where it fell warm and firm against his chest.

Marcellus had released his father. He closed his father's eyes, straightened his sagging head, lightly brushed the dust off his father's face. Marcellus placed his cheek on his father's chest, looked up at his father. He slowly caressed his hand over Clement's brow and hair. Then again. And again.

Nicolai and Corren retreated to the walls, leaned against them heavily, and waited. It seemed appropriate to give one last private moment between their father and this particular son.

Five

Marcellus stood in the doorway to his father's office when the first toll rang. It was low, long, mournful. A blow. The sound died away completely, then the second toll rang out. There would be twelve in all, the number assigned to the king. With the last bell, every citizen listening would know that King Clement the Beloved was dead.

The doors to the balcony stood open, the sky beyond a heavy, dark blue. The sun had set. Soon, all would be dark. A moment of silence. Marcellus closed his eyes as the third bell tolled. Corren stood on the balcony, his back to Marcellus, his face toward the city, his hand resting on one of the round, stone finials. Marcellus had sent him here earlier, before ordering the ringing of the death tolls. Now Corren waited, and Marcellus was ready.

He crossed the office slowly, past empty chairs, past his father's desk. He came to the balcony doors as the fourth bell rang. A band of purple hung low on the horizon, the last breath of the sun. The water's reflection dutifully joined in the chorus. Corren turned.

The two brothers held eyes, the last sorrowful notes of the bell matching their own expressions. Silence again. Corren turned away. The fifth bell struck. Marcellus joined Corren at the heavy stone railing. Together they waited as the death tolls rolled over the city. They did not speak, only watched as the sky fell to darkness. When the sound of the last bell faded, instead of silence following it, the mournful cries of the citizens rose up in its place. Now they knew. Their beloved king was gone.

Marcellus numbly thought about the rest. The city would mourn for half a fortnight. Age-old rituals of tribute would be observed. Stonebridge would still honor Clement the Beloved as her king, and he truly would still be their king, for during this period of mourning the affairs of the kingdom would be minimally governed by the heir apparent, acting as temporary Lord and Steward of Caedmonia. When the mourning was completed, the Lord and Steward would be crowned king. It was a responsibility that must be borne at the moment of passing, whether stricken by grief or not. It was for this cause that Marcellus came to see Corren now. He knew Corren understood this.

"The kingdom needs a king," Marcellus said, his eyes still on the city.

Corren looked at him. Said nothing. Looked away. "Yes."

"You will not be crowned yet," Marcellus said. Corren turned to him abruptly. Marcellus went on. "However you have certain duties as Lord and Steward that will begin right away. The king is being laid out now and tomorrow at dawn you must open the Throne Room to the citizens so they can pay their last respects."

"Marcellus..."

"It is a simple ceremony, but it is done a certain way. I can show you tonight or beforehand. That is up to you."

"Marcellus..."

"Corren, I..."

"Marcellus."

"What?"

They looked at each other and Marcellus only waited. He could not read Corren's expression, did not know what he was thinking. Marcellus kept his own expression and voice sincere. He held no ill will toward Corren for circumstances. They were what they were, and Marcellus decided he could live with them. He only wanted to do what his father would have him do.

Corren still only stared, his brows furrowed. Whatever he was going to say, it seemed he couldn't say it now.

Marcellus went on. "We need to issue a proclamation tonight, so your presence tomorrow is not a shock."

Corren shook his head. "I don't know anything about ruling a kingdom."

"Maybe not," Marcellus said, wanting to ease Corren's self-doubt, "but you will learn. My service is at your disposal. I will help you with anything you need. If you want my counsel... or if you don't... it's up to you. I will help but I won't interfere with your sovereignty."

Corren shook his head. "You can't be saying this."

"Listen, I... I'm sorry I've..." but Marcellus' words caught in his throat. He began again. "I'm sorry for how I've treated you. I will not see Caedmonia destroyed by rivalry. Also I... I'm willing to serve you. You have proven yourself worthy."

Corren turned away and leaned on the rail again. "That means a great deal to me. Coming from you." Then, "You keep surprising me."

"My loyalty to the crown surprises you?"

"When it's on my head, yes."

Marcellus smiled.

Corren turned back to Marcellus. "I... I appreciate what you've just done. I know what a sacrifice it is for you."

Marcellus acknowledged this by lowering his head in a bow, but Corren reached out and clutched his arm. "Don't."

Marcellus nearly laughed at the reaction. "It is an honor due you as the future king. Get used to it."

"No. I am not the future king. You are."

Now it was Marcellus who stood speechless. He realized Corren must be worried about Marcellus' true intent. "It's alright," Marcellus said.

Corren shook his head again. "It isn't."

"Corren..."

"Please listen to me. I've thought a lot about this and I do not doubt that you were the one left here because the kingdom is meant for you."

Marcellus did not know what to think. Fully ready to serve Corren as the rightful heir, Marcellus was in no way prepared for this. Once again, his view of his future was shifting, as it often had over the last month. He went on, almost numbly, out of dogged persistence. "The law of the land is clear. It is the oldest..."

"No, Marcellus. I no longer desire that which is not mine." Corren's sincerity was evident. "You will be crowned king, and that is how I want it. That is how it should be. Our father knew it too, I'm sure. I think... I think he was just letting us figure this out on our

489

own. Or waiting to see what I would do. If it came to it, I think he would've supported you. The people, too." Corren shrugged and turned back toward the city. "Rightly so."

"You're sure? You're sure you want to renounce your right to the throne?"

"I am the first prince to do so?" Corren smiled, his face still worn from the grief of the last hour. "It can be done. The responsibility goes to you. I do not covet it."

Marcellus could only stare.

Corren shrugged and looked at his hand resting on the stone filial. "My path has led me elsewhere." He ran his hand over the ball, said "scuptath," and the smooth surface altered under his touch. When he removed his hand, the filial had been delicately carved into a gentle swirl. "It is where my heart lies."

Marcellus looked at his brother's face, even more convinced that Corren was worthy to sit on the throne. Yet Marcellus said nothing.

Corren turned to him fully, sighed, and said, "Are you going to keep arguing with me?"

The two stood considering one another, openly and with acceptance, and the mantle of the kingdom descended squarely and heavily into one man's countenance.

Marcellus shook his head no. Corren smiled. "Good."

Corren went to bow, but Marcellus took him by the shoulders, and embraced him instead.

Six

Later that night, Marcellus sat alone in his father's office. His office now, though it didn't feel it. His eyes rested on the parchment in front of him without really seeing it. It was a message from Commander Donnelly saying the enemy had been subdued and they were marching prisoners back to Stonebridge. Most battalions, Donnelly's included, were chasing down stragglers and securing the border. He requested more troops to replace those who had been lost. Marcellus had already sent orders to redistribute his troops hours ago, though some had to come from a distance and it would be days before the defense at the border would be as it should be.

Ultimately, Caedmonia carried the victory, but it was a bitter one. Many men had perished. The land was scarred. Citizens from Knobby Tree and other villages in the valley now huddled within the city, many in hastily arranged shelters while waiting for the flood to subside. Food was being rationed out and the king's treasury would be opened to help rebuild, but the effect of crops lost would be felt by more than just those whose farms had suffered damage. The destruction of the dam (which would take years to rebuild) would soon result in a water shortage, despite Marcellus' order to ration the water left in the cisterns.

Worse than any of this, the king was dead. His father was gone. In the morning he would open the Throne Room and citizens would have seven days to come from near and far to honor their king as he lay in state. He would be buried in a crypt under the Haven of Kings, and that would be that.

Seven days.

The Phoenix could regenerate as early as five. Would he live to bury his father?

491

Marcellus looked at the map on the desk. His father's desk. His father's map. These objects seemed void of life, so insignificant now, tiny things that failed to capture the man Marcellus thought of when he looked at them. What was left of his father now? Only memories... and memories, like people, fade. Marcellus sat in this, the first real moment of silence amidst all the busyness of the last several hours, and could not even summon up the emotion to weep. Weeping did not seem to be enough. What did it matter? He only felt numb sorrow, as if there would never be any more emotion, any more life, any more anything. Only emptiness.

This was his state when he heard his name.

"Marcellus." When he looked up and saw her standing in the doorway, it happened in an instant: the tears fell hot.

Janus came to him, knelt by him, clasped his hand, said nothing. He held her hand tightly. She waited in silence until the emotion drained from him and he slowly came to himself. As he found his voice there was one thing he needed to say, more than anything else. "I'm terribly sorry, Janus."

She knit her brows in confusion. "Sorry? For what?"

"For accusing you." He remembered the look on her face when he had done so.

She shook her head in dismissal. "You were betrayed by your best friend. I understand it made you wary. And I..." She looked at their hands, knit together. "You maybe thought I wasn't telling you something." She nodded as if to confirm it. "I do have something to tell you." She looked at him firmly. "You *can* trust me. I would never hurt you or let anyone else hurt you." She looked back at her hands, soft and warm in his.

He sensed a "but." He grew leery, waiting.

"But," she closed her eyes, sighed, then looked at him directly. "There's something you need to know."

He nodded for her to go on, trying to guess what she would say.

"Marcellus...how do I say this? Your father... he decided to tell you at last but..."

"My father?" Marcellus sat back. This he did not expect. What did she know of his father?

"Marcellus you're... he..." she released him now and dropped her head in her hands. "How am I going to tell you this?"

Marcellus no longer felt this was something between the two of them. "Say it," he said.

She nodded. "Yes. Alright." She closed her eyes again and said, "Your mother was from a place called Amon Tunde. Your father never told you this because his grief was deep, you were right about that, but also because he wasn't sure how to tell you who she really was. Who you really are. Amon Tunde is the realm of the earth faeries."

No sound followed this comment. She watched him hesitantly. He was vaguely aware of her gripping her own hands so tightly on her lap.

"Your mother was an earth faerie."

Marcellus coughed a dry laugh. Then his wisp of humor left him and he scowled.

She stood and paced away from him, toward the sitting area. He did not move.

"I know this," she said, "because I am an earth faerie too."

Faeries. Again with the faeries. All the confusion of the past weeks swirled like a tempest in his mind: the prophecy, Aradia, the potion, faeries, magic all about, and an impending battle for which they seemed so ill prepared. Here it came at him again, but now his father was in the mix and he couldn't even go to him and demand confirmation while hoping for denial.

Janus faced him. "I knew your mother. I was there when she met your father. I saw them falling in love and I'm sorry Marcellus but I hated them both for it. I knew it would be the death of her. It was terrible because I cherished her more than anyone. This was what I could not tell you that day by the sea. My friend was your mother and she left everything she knew to be with your father. For years I didn't understand it. Even after I came to be in the human world and came to love it, love it even more than my own home, I still didn't understand the kind of love Elana felt for your father. Not until..."

She stopped abruptly. She clasped her hands together and stared at him. His heart stopped. He could hardly breathe and couldn't think at all.

493

Her trepidation did not leave her countenance, but her expression softened. "I'm so sorry you didn't know her. I'm sorry you had to hear this from me. I convinced Clement to tell you at last. He would have, but..."

He could not react, could not move, not even a finger. Whatever his expression was, she apparently could not keep looking at him for she took a step back now, her eyes on the floor. "Also I know Corren and Nicolai are your brothers. You should know that, too. I don't know why it's been kept a secret, but I will not tell it. You truly can trust me. Marcellus, I...I'm sorry I deceived you." What could he say or think about that? What she said next she said in a whisper. "Please don't hate me for it."

She left quietly. She left him with his thoughts and everything in his world seemed to be off its hinge.

Slowly, slowly he leaned back in his chair. He slid down until his head rested on the back and he was staring at the ceiling. It was gray, uneven stone, with dark shadows in the dips and yellow light on the ridges from the low-burning lantern on the desk. Every now and then the light would shudder as the flame faltered, then recovered. Marcellus looked at the light. He looked at the shadows. And did not move for a very long time.

Seven

Nicolai did not sleep well that night. At dawn he resignedly watched Marcellus open the Throne Room to mourners in a short and solemn ceremony. Already the line stretched far past the castle grounds, hugging along the city's inner wall and reaching nearly to the southern gate of Stonebridge. As they waited, citizens held their single white flowers, as was the custom, and quietly discussed the many tragedies of the previous day. Despite Marcellus' proclamation assuring them of their safety and the defeat of the enemy, there was still much anxiety to accompany their sorrow.

Marcellus was expected to stand with the casket for the first hour of the viewing, both out of respect for the king and so he could receive condolences from the citizens. After this, the Three would meet in Marcellus' office and prepare to leave again, for despite everything else, the antipotion could not wait. And time was ever running short.

Nicolai spent the time waiting for Marcellus in an urgent search for Praea. He tried the Cloister first, but no one was there. He rode to the Bridge of a Thousand Ages, thinking the Guard of the Order might at least know where Kai'Enna would be. They didn't. Neither did they know where Kennard was, though they suspected he was still out with the troops hunting down wizards from the Citadel of Zeverai. After this, Nicolai didn't know where else to look. He couldn't help it, he began to panic. After everything that had happened, after everything he and his brothers had gone through, would their last two ingredients thwart them after all? For it wasn't just the moonlight from the Isle of Iona that worried him. He still didn't know how he was going to get a leaf from the Tree of Origin.

With his hour nearly gone, he went back to the castle intending to tell Corren and Marcellus they would have to find Praea before they left, for she needed time to travel to the lake. He was hopeful that

Corren might know how to find Kai'Enna; Nicolai wasn't sure how he would explain her connection to Praea, but he would think of something. But what if they couldn't find her? What then? He walked past the line of mourners, through the grand entryway of the castle, and it was here—at last—that he saw her.

There was no preference in the line given to rank or wealth, so like many of the other mourners Praea stood patiently waiting, holding a single white iris. Praea did not see Nicolai; she was visiting quietly with a peasant woman with a round, friendly face. Nicolai had to gently touch her on the elbow to draw her attention.

Praea's eyes flew wide at him. "Nicolai!"

He bowed. "My Lady."

"How good it is to see you, Nicolai." They took a few steps forward as the line advanced. "I'm so sorry about King Clement. It is such a terrible tragedy."

"Thank you, my Lady," he said, finding it difficult to be formal with her when she spoke so warmly to him. He was not the only one who noticed her tone, it seemed, for those near them watched with great interest. "I wonder if I might speak to you," he said.

"Of course."

"I'll wait for you where the line exits," he said gesturing. It would be in poor taste for her to leave the line, so he had no choice but to wait. They took a few more steps forward with the line and she nodded. "I will come to you, Nicolai."

They walked through the castle, seeking seclusion and finding it down a lesser-used, narrow hallway. "I'm glad you are safe," he said as they stopped halfway down the corridor. "When I heard you had been to Tower Hall North..."

She shook her head. "You worry too much. My escort found me eventually."

He checked the hall, still vacant, and took her hand. "And did you come here by escort?"

She shook her head. He knew he had correctly guessed how she had come. "It is so dangerous," he said.

496

"No," she said, a glint in her eye. "It was amazing."

He couldn't help but wonder at this. What would it be like to fly? "I should like to know that feeling."

"I'll take you up with me some time, if you wish."

He looked at her sideways. "You couldn't carry me."

"I'm sure I could carry two of you." He could not tell if she was being serious or not. She had made a similar comment—full of exhaustion and sarcasm—when they had hiked that strenuous climb out of the Great Gorge a few weeks ago. "If it weren't for the horse, I could just fly us out," she had said. Her expression grew more somber now. "It is so terrible about your good King Clement. How does Lord Marcellus fare?"

Nicolai thought of saying something princely, thought maybe he should assure her of the strength of the next king, but he knew she would know that already and his thoughts came out uncensored. "He is grieving."

She nodded. "And how do you fare?"

"I am grieving too, but I'm alright."

She scrutinized him, as if she could know just by seeing him exactly how he felt. Her gaze was questioning, wanting to know how he truly was. "Are you?"

He squeezed her hand. "I will be."

"There has been too much death lately." Though sorrowful, he sensed her anger too. She had lost two brothers and he had lost his father—two fathers, though she did not know this—and one way or another, each death worked its way back to Aradia. And this, after all, was his reason for meeting with her.

"Praea, we need your help."

From the look on her face, he knew she understood his meaning, but she still asked, "Help with what?"

He glanced around to be sure they were not being overheard. "With Aradia."

She straightened. "Tell me."

"Two things. First, are you staying with Kai'Enna?"

Her eyes widened. "How did you know that?"

"You haven't been staying here. Who else do you know in Stonebridge? It wasn't hard to deduce."

"I suppose not," she said. Her eyes darted to something behind him and she released his hand. He turned and saw one of the kitchen staff approaching. They watched in silence, nodded at the man as he went by, and waited until he was gone before resuming their conversation.

"Do you know what the Order is doing to stop Aradia?" he asked.

She shook her head. "No. Kai'Enna and I are looking for her, but we have no idea where she could be. I don't know what everyone else is doing."

"Kai'Enna hasn't said anything to you?"

"No. Do you want me to see if I can find out what else is going on?"

"Not right now. We need you for something more important."

She nodded.

"This may not be easy for you."

She did not flinch. "What do you want me to do?"

"Do you remember the lake we found in the Wilds?"

Her first hesitation appeared. She paused, then nodded.

"I know what it is. It's called the Lake of the Moon, but is often referred to as the Isle of Iona." Her eyes widened in recognition. He realized as a member of one of the branches of the Order, she may have heard about this just as Corren had. "It is hidden from all but those who are descendants of the ancient Sorceress of the Moon, Diana. Female descendants."

Praea blinked. "Are you saying I am a descendent?"

"You must be or you wouldn't be able to see it."

Praea shook her head now like she was trying to clear it. "What does this have to do with Aradia?"

"Aradia must be a descendent too, because she was able to go there and get something she needs in order to reach the Phoenix. If we are to stop her, we need the same thing, and you are the only one who can get it for us."

"You want me to go back?" Praea's fear was transparent now. Nicolai's heart went out to her. What was he asking her to do? But what other way? Praea was right, there had been too much of death

498

lately; if they could not stop Aradia in her plans, it would only be the beginning.

"I wish I did not need to ask you," he said, "but I must."

She considered him and he waited for her answer. Her expression altered; she furrowed her brows. "Something has changed in you."

Did she think he no longer cared for her since he was asking her to do this? He leaned toward her urgently, "I still love you."

Her face softened, moved, and he realized he had never said that before. He could not believe it and wondered what had taken him so long to say what he had felt from the first moment he saw her.

"And I love you, Nicolai." Her voice was thick. "But that is not what I meant. You are different, but I'm not sure how. What puzzles me the most is that even though I have never found anything lacking in you, yet here you are changed for the better."

He smiled and wondered if she did not sense what he had felt all morning. As he had journeyed through the city and saw the mourners and the refugees in shelters, he felt a new responsibility toward them. With his father's passing, being a prince was no longer some vague title, too lofty to seem like anything he would truly be. This city, this land, these people who had suffered... he had an obligation to all of it whether he liked it or not, whether he chose it or not. He now found himself willing to meet that obligation.

"Thank you, Praea," he said, and kissed her gently. "Will you go?"

He saw her resolve strengthen, and he knew before she answered that he could trust her to carry it out. "What do you need me to get?"

Marcellus rubbed the arm of the chair, its dark wood smoothly carved and cool to the touch. He had just come from the Throne Room and they sat in the king's office, ready to leave again. He listened as Nicolai told them about Praea leaving for the Lake of the Moon. It was a relief, no question about that, but again the issue of time came up. "She will have to ride hard to make it there and back in time," Corren said. Nicolai assured them Praea understood the need to make haste and seemed certain she could get there and back quickly.

Meanwhile they still had to get the leaf from the Tree of Origin, which was, at the very least, close by. Even if the river had not subsided enough to cross yet, they could still go north around the lake to reach the Wilds. Nicolai still wasn't saying what this location really was, though Marcellus knew by now. It had to be Amon Tunde. This was what Marcellus was thinking about most, how to tell them what he had found out about their mother. The words eluded him. He had an idea of what Janus had been struggling with. Then there was Janus. That was another issue.

Marcellus leaned forward and sat on the edge of his chair. "I have something to tell you before we go." He launched into it without preamble before he lost his nerve. Like Janus, he barely paused for breath, wanting to get it all out, one startling revelation after another so it could be dealt with as one. When he was finally finished, they sat stunned as he had done. He was prepared to give them time for it to sink in, but Nicolai spoke up immediately.

"Amon Tunde," he said. "Our mother was from Amon Tunde?"

Marcellus nodded.

"So that's why I was allowed."

Corren furrowed his brows but Marcellus understood because he had already been thinking about this. "That's where we're going isn't it?" Marcellus asked. "That's where the Tree of Origin is."

Nicolai nodded. "And if that's why I can go, then that means you can go too."

He stood up abruptly and headed for the door. "Where are you going?" Corren asked a little dazed, still seeming to be taking it all in.

But Nicolai was ready. "To Amon Tunde. Let's go."

Eight

The shallow crossing of the river, while no longer shallow, was at least low enough to cross on horseback. They cautiously negotiated their way through, the water to their mounts' bellies. The valley had not yet recovered from its transformation into a battlefield. The ground was littered with corpses, in the process of being gathered by the many knights scattered about. There would be no secret passage for the Three, but this could not be helped. As they passed, knights watched quietly and the Three nodded somber greetings. Words would have been inadequate, jarring even, so none were spoken.

They crossed to the shelter of the woods quickly. This time, unlike when he had come with Praea, Nicolai made no effort to skirt the erratic borders of Amon Tunde, but entered into the realm freely. Along the way they discussed when Corren should start the antipotion. The Phoenix could regenerate as soon as four days—or as late as three weeks—and herein lay the problem. The antipotion would take two days to brew. If Praea weren't back in the next two days, should they start the potion anyway and hope she returned in time to add her ingredient—which thankfully wasn't needed until near the end of the brewing? If they did this and she did not return in time, the antipotion would be ruined. Or, should they wait for her return before starting to brew, running the risk that the Fourth Song would sound before they were ready? It was a difficult decision to consider and weighed heavily on them. Nicolai was less worried about this, however, than he was about an even bigger question—one none of them seemed willing to verbalize. What would happen if, for some reason, she could not get what they needed? What if they could not? What would they do then?

Nicolai led his brothers down the path to the Hidden Door. As he did so he remembered this pathway was painted on the walls in a

501

humble room of the castle. Was it their mother who had painted them? Clement maybe? They would never know. Along the way, no sentinel approached. As they came to the Hidden Door and stopped, Nicolai saw none now. Without hesitation he said, "Ανοίξτε στον καθαρό στην καρδιά. Γη, αποκαλύψτε την καρδιά διαβίωσής δική σου." *Open to the pure in heart. Oh earth, reveal thy living heart.* The earth hunched open, the green shaft of light piercing the outside world, and the three brothers crossed the threshold into the underground realm of the earth faeries. A realm they lay partial claim to as well.

Nicolai removed his shoes as the earth grumbled closed behind them. His brothers followed his lead. Together they walked barefoot down the long grassy tunnel to the Grand Cavern, glittering and green, its walls a breathtaking display of flowers and weeping vines. It was here, by the sparkling pool, that Salerno stood waiting for them in his long, mossy robe, his wild hair falling past his shoulders.

They approached and stopped. Nicolai felt Salerno's glowing, vibrating presence. He glanced at his brothers and knew they felt it too. Salerno calmly looked at each in turn with his luminous green eyes and said "At last."

Nicolai looked around more closely. Everything looked as it always had, the crystalline water, the sweet, glittering air, the walls draped with soft color from the orchids, lilies, and trumpet bells. All around stood the faeries, slowly gathering, silently watching; perhaps it was in their faces that Nicolai felt something different.

He looked now to Salerno, who watched him knowingly. "What happened here?"

"Evil bled through the earth," Salerno said. "We all felt it."

Salerno led them through Oak Bone Tunnel, just the three of them, and explained what had happened. Though hidden deep at the end of a tunnel known as the Vein of the Earth, the Tree of Origin had been damaged. Salerno, who had always been able to pass through the Vein of the Earth before, was not able to do so now. "The earth forbids it," he said. "I went above ground to where the Tree of Origin grows far below. The ground was black, bleeding evil into the ground, seeping down—I felt—to the Tree of Origin. I cannot erase that evil. I do not know where it came from, but I sense a small part of the tree was carried away. Another part destroyed. That is all I know."

"Maybe it was all destroyed," Corren said.

Salerno looked at him, studied him. "No," he said. "If the tree were gone, we would be gone. We faeries are connected to it, which is why we felt its attack. We are connected to it, and so when part of it was destroyed, five of our number fell with it."

"Fell?" This from Nicolai, not believing.

"Perished." They came to the room known as the Key Chamber. "We have renamed this the Mourning Chamber. The first graveyard of our kind."

The pale faerie light glittered off the bare surface of the walls in this room. It was narrow, and the floor a deep, dark brown from the rich soil. In the center of the room, five mounded graves were laid out in succession. It was only here flowers and vines thickly entwined, covering the dead like a blanket. Dark stone towers, short and stout, rose at the head of each, pulled up out of the earth, Salerno explained, by their magic. The names of the fallen were written in silver. Below each was the phrase: "Of the earth they were born, and the earth takes them again."

Nicolai read the names. These were faeries Nicolai knew and they were dead because Aradia stole from the Tree of Origin.

Nicolai and his brothers had come here for a leaf from that same tree.

They left the Mourning Chamber and Salerno led them solemnly to the Throne room. Here they rested on moss-covered mounds of earth serving as benches. Only hollycrowns grew on the walls here, their golden petals lending a regal feel to the otherwise unadorned room. Only one other tunnel led away from this room: the Vein of the Earth, the tunnel that led to the Tree of Origin. As far as Nicolai knew, Salerno was the only one who had ever been permitted to venture down this tunnel. If he could not get to the tree now, then who could? Even if he could get to it, would removing a leaf add yet another grave to this immortal faerie world?

Salerno studied Nicolai. Nicolai let him do it. Nicolai knew what he needed to do, but he was now in no hurry for it. If he took a leaf,

503

which faerie would suffer as a result? And if Salerno refused to give it to them... Nicolai did not want to consider this, especially since it seemed the most likely answer. What would they do then? Even though they intended to fight Aradia at the Bridge, even though they placed a great, unspoken hope in Corren's staff, there was still that sense that they could not defeat her. It would all come down to the Gateway. If Nicolai could not get the leaf, what hope did they have? Not wanting to hear Salerno tell him no, wanting to delay what he feared a little longer, Nicolai spoke of another matter instead. "Why did you not tell me about my mother?"

Salerno smiled sadly. "It was not the time. I believed Clement would tell you when it was right."

"It was Janus," Marcellus said. Salerno looked at him sharply.

"Janus has revealed herself to you?"

Marcellus nodded and Salerno's gaze became penetrating. If this rankled Marcellus, he didn't show it. Instead he leaned forward. "Did you forbid the union of our parents?"

Nicolai had forgotten all about that line of the prophecy: *From the forbidden union, three defenders will be born.* As soon as Marcellus said it, Nicolai knew that must have been the case. He watched Salerno, who now looked nothing but calm.

He nodded. "I did."

"Why?" Marcellus' tone was almost harsh, causing Nicolai to furrow his brows.

"I believed such a union to be unbalanced and unwise. This would lead to excess hurt for both parties." Marcellus' countenance was dark now. He did not respond. "However..." Salerno said.

Marcellus raised his eyebrows. "Yes?"

"However, I judged in error. Or rather, I overlooked something, for there was indeed a heavy burden of sorrow placed in the heart of your mother and father when they joined their lives together. Your father carried that sorrow to his dying day. There was something else though. Their love for one another was remarkable. It was deep and strong like the waters that flow underground here and give life to everything we see. Their love was like that, too. Unquenchable despite the passage of

504

time, despite any obstacle placed before them. Their love did not spare them of pain. It only made it worth it."

Marcellus was quiet now, his face softened. Salerno smiled kindly and turned to Nicolai.

"You and your brothers will have to return when the circumstances are different. For now, I sense time is precious to you. Tell me, Nicolai, what are you seeking?"

"Harm." He said it automatically.

Salerno raised his eyebrows. "Is that a truthful answer?"

"I fear it to be."

Salerno stood. "Not long ago, your mother stood here in this room. She told me of a prophecy, which I believe you three have been seeking to fulfill. Am I correct?"

The Three exchanged glances, but not ones of surprise. He was not the first faerie king to know more than they had told him. Nicolai should've known Salerno would be no different. He nodded in reply.

Salerno continued. "You are not asking too much of us. A great evil has reached us where no evil has reached before. We cannot keep it from coming again. It must be stopped. Do you know how to do this?"

Nicolai looked again at his brothers and back to Salerno. "We hope so."

"As do I."

Nicolai took a deep breath. The time had come at last. "We need a leaf from the Tree of Origin."

Salerno nodded. He already knew that.

"You may enter the Vein of the Earth."—and Nicolai felt a great rush of relief—"If the earth allows you to proceed, you will find the Tree of Origin at the end. As soon as you see the tree, look to the left hand side. The branch nearest you, farthest to the left and which touches the ground, is mine. If the tree allows you, you may take a leaf from my branch." Nicolai started to protest, but Salerno held up his hand. "It will not kill me. I will be injured, but I would rather it be me than any other. Only, do not cut off the branch," and this he said with a rare, wry smile.

Ready, Nicolai stood, his brothers with him. As he turned to the tunnel Salerno placed his hand on Nicolai's arm. Nicolai halted. He could not ever remember Salerno touching him before. Salerno spoke in a strange tone. Nicolai realized he was worried. "If the earth does not wish you to proceed, it will be dangerous to argue with it."

Nicolai looked at the warm hand on his arm and Salerno removed it.

"We'll be careful."

"Not 'we' Nicolai. You go in alone."

Marcellus stepped forward. "We must stay together."

Salerno shook his head. "I already know the earth will not allow you as it will not allow me. As for Nicolai... I cannot tell."

"But..." Marcellus started to object, but Nicolai turned away from them all and toward the Vein of the Earth. Marcellus saw him, said "Nicolai..." in protest, but Nicolai quickened his pace and plunged past the entrance. He was enveloped in a sudden darkness. He heard nothing. All he saw was a tiny pinpoint of light at the distant end of this tunnel where not even fairy light penetrated.

Nine

Nicolai stopped momentarily. His eyes gaped, straining for any shadowy shape. Nothing came. He could not see the ground before him, or any obstacles that might lay before him, or any pits that might fall out beneath him. He had a sudden thought of plummeting and closed his eyes against it. The darkness did not change. He opened his eyes and reached out both hands to either side of him. He felt rough, cool stone, and began to walk.

He went forward with as much haste as could be allowed while traveling blindly. His eyes fixed on the light that did not seem to be getting any larger. The ground below was, so far, even and steady. When at last the pinpoint ahead began to grow, he picked up a little speed, his confidence growing too.

The width of the tunnel slowly widened until he had to straighten his arms completely to keep his hands on the walls. Soon he could only touch with his fingertips, then had to stretch to do even that. One side fell away, beyond him.

He stopped.

Nicolai leaned to the left and found the wall. He took a few steps, following it. It seemed to be leading further away. He leaned back to the right, touched the other wall, and took a few more steps. It stayed on a straight course for the light, a clear circle of yellow by now. This was the wall he chose to follow. He went on and it led ahead. Occasionally he would reach his left arm out to see if the other wall rejoined him, but it never did. He stubbed his toe unexpectedly and managed to keep from falling forward. He cast his hand about in front of him and discovered a rather large boulder that he had to carefully, blindly climb. Not long after the ground was not where he expected it, but lower, and he had the sensation of falling as his foot found solid ground several inches below where it had been the step before.

Moving along more cautiously now, the wall veered decidedly to the right and fell away as if turning a corner. Nicolai paused but did not stop, deciding to follow the light, not knowing how he would find his way back without a light or wall to guide him, but feeling he mustn't lose sight of his goal. It was then, away from the wall, on uneven ground, watching the light, that Nicolai heard something.

He stopped, halted his breathing, listened. He heard nothing. Then... something. A growl or a rumble. The earth beneath him slid, gave way, and... disappeared. He plummeted and in the darkness reached out. His arms caught and lost a ledge, found another and grasped it, suspending his fall, legs swinging wildly. His chest hung flat now against sheer earth, hard and forbidding. He felt nothing below him. He could no longer see the light.

He heaved himself upward. Bits of earth gave way under his hands and skitted noisily down, and down, until the sound dissipated. If these pebbles had hit bottom, Nicolai couldn't hear it. He continued to lift himself, arms shaking violently, until he was over the ledge. He panted harsh against the earth and the earth answered with biting swirls of dust around his mouth, nose, and eyes. He emerged from the pit and crouched on a narrow strip of ground between it and the wall.

The light appeared ahead of him, right where he left it. Perhaps the earth would not let him reach it. *If the earth does not wish you to proceed, it will be dangerous to argue with it,* Salerno had said. That may be true, but dangerous or no, Nicolai would not be the one to fail at his task.

With one hand on the earth and one hand cupping the lip of the pit, Nicolai advanced forward, urgently now, eyes on the light. He could just make out the stone of the cave all around the opening, its rough surface all shadow and wavy slivers of light. The earth vibrated far below him and he hastened. The pit came to an end, it was all ground in front of him—so far as he knew—and he groped blindly over it on hands and knees toward the light that was widening.

The groan of the earth this time was deafening; all around him came the sound of crushing boulders falling to the earth. Shards of rock pounded the floor and bits of earth stung him and he squinted and coughed against the dust.

Nicolai stood on the grumbling earth and ran.

508

He ran for the light and saw chunks of the ceiling falling in front of him. His feet carried him so fast he nearly flew over the earth despite the odd footing here and the sliding rock there. The ceiling bellowed above him as a massive piece gave way. Nicolai felt it rush down behind him as he ran full on to the light that was near, near now. He could see the ground in front of him, could hear it too, because it was heaving and rippling like the waves of the sea. Nicolai did not slow but pushed himself harder, his legs burning from effort, his lungs straining for air. The earth beneath him bucked and sent him flying. He soared through the door of light, free of the tunnel, and hit grass-covered ground, sliding several feet on his stomach and chest.

The earth was silent. Nicolai gasped for breath, his heart pounding against the ground, and felt the soft grass, wet with dew, against his cheek. His body throbbed, everywhere throbbed, and he forced himself into an aching stand. He looked back at the Vein of the Earth.

It looked innocently back at him.

Nicolai watched for a moment, grunted, then turned and faced it: the Tree of Origin.

It stood in the center of a huge cavern, overtaking nearly all of it. The golden tree was so bright that Nicolai squinted as he looked at it; still his eyes felt the pain of beholding something so glorious. All around the Tree of Origin luminous green grass glittered and shone from the light above. His heart had settled, his breathing calmed, and Nicolai heard only reverent silence, heavy and golden on his body. Gradually adjusting to the light, he felt warmed by it. He felt he could have stood in that reviving glow for the rest of time.

Only one thing marred this magnificent tree. High above, a cluster of branches on the top of the tree's crown were blackened and dead. Directly above these, the ceiling of the cavern was black, so black and so evil it did not even reflect the light from the tree below. This was where Aradia had removed the leaf from above ground, destroying five branches in the process.

Nicolai pulled his eyes from this with difficulty; he had come here for a purpose and set to it now. On the left side of the tree, brushing

509

the ground, was Salerno's branch. Nicolai approached, his feet moist and cool from the dewy grass. When he came to Salerno's branch, he stopped. He could almost feel Salerno in it, that same, glittering, vibrating glow he felt whenever Salerno called to him. Nicolai took a leaf in his hand, wondered how his friend would be hurt when he removed it. Nicolai froze. He frowned.

He released the leaf, a new thought forming. He slowly began to circle the tree. He considered the branches as he passed them, analyzing them not so much with his eyes—for they all looked the same —but rather with his feeling about them. Unfortunately they all felt the same too, all except Salerno's, but Nicolai continued circling anyway. When he reached the back of the tree he began to wonder if he would be able to find what he sought. He wondered if it wasn't higher up. Beyond his reach.

Then he stopped at a branch and at last thought he found what he was looking for. He thought. He did not know. If he were wrong...

He questioned himself then. Perhaps Salerno's was best. Salerno at least offered, was willing to take the hurt upon himself. He was willing.

But Nicolai was not willing to hurt him. He knew the branch now in front of him was the right one.

Nicolai reached out, hovered his hand over first one leaf, then another. Finally deciding it didn't matter, he slowly closed thumb and forefinger around the slight stem of a single golden leaf. He pinched it, pulling slightly downward to remove it. His back cramped, perhaps from his aching trip through the tunnel, perhaps not. The leaf had not come off. Nicolai pulled harder, the branch tipping in toward him as he did so, the leaves tinkling like little bells. Still the leaf would not let go. Not wanting to cause damage, Nicolai released it. The branch recoiled, and Nicolai thought.

He bent down and removed the throwing spear from the holster strapped to his calf. Brilliant yellow light danced on the smooth metal blade of the spear. He held it firmly in one hand and took hold of the leaf with the other, leaving the stem vulnerable. Determined now, his heart clenching, Nicolai sliced at the stem with one swift movement.

It was not the leaf that was cut.

510

The spear's blade split clean in two and the tip fell to the grass with a thud. Nicolai gaped at the leaf, still firmly attached to the tree. He looked back at the ground; the shard of spear was sinking into the earth, or the earth was reaching up and taking it. Soon it winked out of sight and the earth was as smooth and gentle as it had been before, not even a mar in the grass to suggest what was hidden.

Nicolai looked at the spear in his hand. The blade was cut to a stump at a severe angle where the leaf had sliced through it. He looked back to the leaf. It mocked him. Eluded him. After all he had done just to get to it, he couldn't even remove it, the spear weak against such ancient and deep power as this.

Nicolai spun, paced to the outer wall, and stopped, fuming now. He tossed the remnant of the spear on the ground and watched as the earth swallowed this up, too. His anger swelled at this, his mind racing. He closed his eyes. Forced himself to calm. *There must be a way. There must be something I can do.* Nicolai took a deep breath and opened his eyes. He began to think of the faerie magic he knew, looking for something to help him obtain the elusive leaf they needed so badly. He began to see the wall in front of him.

It was elaborately adorned with curious formations of earth. It looked like something patiently carved by water over time, but it was not damp and no water ran here. The ridges, dips, odd shapes, and stunning beauty of it stilled him and he took it in. How few had ever, or would ever, lay eyes on this, a secret beauty the earth keeps for herself?

Nicolai's eyes saw again. A vapor. Or a vision. Directly in front of him, the rock formed something Nicolai recognized but did not expect. He leaned in and raised his hand to confirm what he saw. He ran his fingertips along a point, which widened smoothly and proportionately into a perfectly formed spearhead. His fingers felt the handle next, bringing the vision to reality, for his eyes could not believe without this confirmation of touch. The handle was exquisitely fashioned and, as Nicolai encircled it fully, fit his grasp perfectly. He gave a tug and it came free.

It was a throwing spear, dark like the brown stone of the earth in front of him. It did not shine like a spear made of mere metal. It was

511

heavy and substantial and in the hands of the only one who could have removed it.

Nicolai turned back to the branch. His heartbeat quickened and he took two, three, four purposeful steps toward the tree. He took hold of the leaf, raised the spear of the earth and sliced through the stem. A tearing, hot pain raced across his back and he instantly felt the warm moisture of blood running freely. Nicolai doubled over, his hands bracing himself on his knees. His mind was not on the wound on his back as much as it was on this: the spear of the earth in one hand and in the other, a gold leaf taken from his own branch.

Though painful, the journey back through the Vein of the Earth was smooth and even. There were no pits, no grumblings, nothing to even stumble on. The walls stayed close and steady. The earth had no need to make things difficult. It had already tested him, and he had proven himself worthy.

Salerno tended to his back as his brothers huddled round. "Foolish boy," Salerno said fondly. "This will leave a brutal scar."

Nicolai made no reply as Salerno worked on him, a cooling sensation rolling over the wound. The muscles in Nicolai's body finally relaxed in response.

Marcellus stood nearby. Nicolai tugged on his sleeve. Marcellus bent down, concerned. "What can I do?"

Nicolai only held out the spear for him to admire. In this, Nicolai was not disappointed. He allowed Marcellus to take it covetously, rotate it in his hand, run his fingers over the blade. He glanced at Nicolai, who waited, and put it back on Nicolai's palm reluctantly. "Did Salerno give it to you?"

"No," Nicolai said. "The earth did."

Marcellus looked at him sideways. His face was straight and serious, but there was a familiar light in his eyes.

"Mine's bigger," Marcellus said, and Nicolai smiled.

Ten

Janus lay on the narrow mattress in a stupor, fully clothed though it was well past the midnight hour. She could not sleep. Had barely eaten. Marcellus had not been at the castle all day and no one knew where he was, only that he would return. She never should have left him as she did. Though she had been terrified of hearing condemnation from his lips, she should have stayed with him. Should have comforted him. Should have been there to answer his questions. Anything other than what she did, which was to run.

Janus sighed and sat up. Commanders' rooms in the barracks were simple—only a bed, a wash table, and a wardrobe—but at least they were private, a fact she was exceedingly grateful for now. She could not seem to stay in one position for longer than a few minutes. She glanced out the wooden latticed window and at the empty training grounds two stories below. A page came into view, marching toward the barracks. Janus watched him until he disappeared from sight, wondering what kind of errand he could be about. It was a welcome distraction to her thoughts that lasted all too briefly. Her mind returned to Marcellus once more.

A few minutes passed; a loud knock echoing in the silence caused her to jump. She vaulted from the bed, flew the short distance to the door, and swung it wide to reveal not Marcellus as she'd hoped, but the page she had seen crossing the grounds just a moment earlier. "Oh," she said. *Of course.* "Yes?"

"Commander Janus, Lord Marcellus requests your presence on the training field."

"He's here?" She did not wait for an answer, instead hurried down the hallway, down the wooden stairs, out into the night and the training field, bathed in blue moonlight. Empty. She stopped. In a moment the page exited the barracks and walked past her. She watched him cross the training fields alone. He did not stop, was stopped by no one, and disappeared into the castle at last.

Janus proceeded forward, looking around. Perhaps Marcellus had not come yet, waiting for the page to return. She searched for him, looking off to the shadowy corner of the archery range, scanning the wooden wall separating the grounds from the corral, checking the freestanding rack of swords. Her steps slowed to a halt, and she stood in absolute silence. Alone.

Or so she thought.

She heard it first, the metallic sound of a sword being unsheathed. When she spun toward the rack, there he was, where there had been no one only seconds before. He was removing one of the swords. Her heart skipped a beat, but not from shock or fear—though if he intended on drawing a sword on her it wouldn't be the first time. Rather she felt relief, at finally seeing him in front of her after longing for him all day.

Marcellus turned, faced her. Even in the pale light of the moon, his eyes shone with that magnificent intensity, that one visible mark of his true heritage. He was neither smiling nor scowling. She could not read his expression at all. He came to her with a purposeful stride, neither swift nor tentative. She walked to him too. He was nearly to her before she found her voice.

"Marcellus," she said. He answered by holding out the sword, handle up, blade down. She took hold of it automatically. He released it and turned away. "Marcellus?"

He cleared his throat to silence her. She said nothing more, only watched as he took a few more steps, spun, drew his own sword and said, "I challenge you to a duel."

What? was all she could think. It was the last thing she expected. His expression was serious, but under it she saw a hint of the jest. Janus hardly knew what to say. She could not pretend nothing was wrong. She took half a step forward, the cool hilt of the sword still in her hand. "Marcellus, I'm sorry I left you last night." His expression softened and the blade of the sword dropped slightly. "Are you alright?" she asked.

514

He lowered the sword completely. He looked at her with gentleness. "You're saying it wrong," he said, and raised his eyebrows. "You're supposed to ask me what you get if you win."

Chills ran over her. She felt rooted to the earth. *Had he ever... had he ever seen...?* "What... do I get if I win?"

"What do you want?"

"Oh my."

"Pardon?"

"When did you... when did you ever see me duel?"

"Don't you want to tell me what you want?"

Her hands were shaking now. What did she want?! He was right in front of her! She could not answer him truly and went for a diversion instead. "You don't want to duel me, do you?"

He held his hand up. "I'll make it simple for you. If you win, you can name your prize then."

"*After* I win?"

He nodded.

She laughed. She couldn't help it. "That's terribly brave of you."

At this needling comment he smiled fully, as if this was what he wanted all along. "I have no intention of losing."

Because it was safer to play along, because it felt normal and almost like a judgment in itself, like he was choosing this way to say he wasn't mad at her, she played off his comment. "I remember you said something like that before a certain horse race."

"Anything you want," he said, ignoring the jab. "That's your prize."

He watched her, and waited.

She knew her next line and realized he knew it too. Falling back on this routine no longer comforted her. It terrified her. She gripped the hilt of her sword, felt the moisture on her palms. She said her part. "And you, Marcellus? What do you want?"

If he were trying to keep his expression neutral, if he were trying to keep his voice steady, he failed. For when he spoke, he mirrored some of the terror she felt. "I believe," he said, "that the prize for beating you has already been established."

Forget beating me.

"However," he went on, "the stakes are high. So I ask for one thing more."

"Which is?"

"If I win, you promise no other man will duel you like this again." Her grip on the hilt slackened. He raised his sword, the faintest gleam in his eyes. "Agreed?"

She stood there foolishly, willing her mind to work, her mouth to work. He did not make her stand there long.

"Unless you're too afraid to fight me."

She cocked her head. "I'm not afraid to fight you."

He lifted one shoulder in a casual shrug, his amusement at her evident. "You seem a bit hesitant. Maybe you realize you cannot beat me."

She knew he was goading her, but that didn't stop it from working. "I am not hesitant," she said firmly.

"You deny it but I still see you standing there with a drooping sword. Maybe you have not strength enough to raise it."

She raised it immediately and he laughed. She could not help but smile too. "Alright," she said. "I'll play."

He wagged a finger at her. "Be warned, Janus. I do not intend to go easy on you. We will come out of this knowing it was a real contest."

"Don't worry," she said. "Your defeat will feel real enough."

"This is much better," he said, satisfied with her bantering. "Are you ready?"

She nodded.

He took a step to one side. She instinctively replied with her own step. As before, when they challenged each other their competitive drives took over. They continued to circle each other, his eyes serious now. She grew serious too. Their eyes locked. She sensed his focus sharpen even as her own concentration spiked. Her muscles grew taut, ready to react. They continued to circle, each waiting for the other to make the first move. Finally Marcellus did it, sending the sharp sound of metal singing through the still, night air as their blades met. His attack was easy to block; she knew he did it more to get their swords moving than anything else. It was all she needed. She answered him with a quick series of parries meant to trick him into expecting certain moves; it would allow her an opening later. He blocked these easily, as she knew he would. She altered her approach, attacking him with swiftness. This, too, he blocked.

She backed off, hackled. She remembered what the man in front of her was famous for. She thought she saw a smile in his eyes. It was so handsomely irritating and riled her so completely that she lunged at him again. Any lightness in his eyes was gone, his face firm, his action swift. No matter which way she went, he was there to block her. Her frustration flared. Picking up her speed, she went directly to her best moves, eager now for a sudden victory. Everywhere she sent her blade, his was there to meet it.

She broke the action and they faced one another with ready swords. She glared. "What are you doing?"

"Dueling you."

"No, I mean *what* are you doing? Why are you doing this?"

"I think you know why."

"Marcellus..." but she could not continue. She could not find the source of her own aggravation.

He shook his head. "You hate to lose, don't you?"

She narrowed her eyes, realizing he understood what she was feeling more than she did. But while he may have been blocking her, she had been blocking him, too, and that counted for something. "I am not going to lose," she said, and went at him again with all her speed and strength. As he matched her, the pinging of steel pierced her ears. Her movements became rash, desperate, and she knew she had to stop and not give him that kind of advantage.

When they pulled apart she was panting. He likewise, but he had never looked so serious. "Perhaps we are at an impasse," she said.

He shook his head ever so slightly, his eyes firm. "No. It's time to claim my prize, Janus." The raw power that radiated from him now was so sudden in its appearance that she nearly flinched. He parried his sword so rapidly and with such force that she was forced to grab the hilt with both hands but it was too late. Her sword yanked out of her grasp and soared away from her, landing on the grass with a definitive thud.

She froze, panting, staring at it in disbelief. She gaped at him.

He paused, straightened, and lowered his sword. He took a deep breath. "So long as we're clear about that then."

"Clear about what?" Her shock was still transparent.

"About who's the better swordsman." She furrowed her eyebrows as if to protest and he raised his in challenge, "We could do it again."

"No," she said crossing her arms. "That's fine."

His expression became one she did not expect. He was not smiling, not gloating, not radiating the fierce energy he had when he had disarmed her. He sheathed his sword slowly, the metal singing as it slid into the casing. The look on his face was so intimate that her arms slowly unfolded and fell to her sides.

He approached her unhurriedly. Almost to her, only a breath away, he gently took her hand. His eyes, clear and staggering, never left hers. He raised her hand to his lips and softly placed a kiss on the back of it. She shakily exhaled. He lowered her hand, but did not release it. "Janus?"

She could hardly breathe. "What?"

"I spoke with Salerno today." Her eyes widened. "He told me something."

"He did?"

"He told me the union of my parents was unbalanced and unwise."

She pressed her lips together, fighting against the sting of that comment. She would have agreed with that once. She maybe agreed with it still, but her heart leaned to the man in front of her, and she could not stop it.

"He also said," Marcellus went on quietly, "that their love was enough to make up for it."

He squeezed her hand, and slowly released her. In the absence of his touch, the air felt cold on her skin.

"Do you agree?" he asked. "Was their love enough to make up for it?"

She could only nod. She did not doubt that Elana and Clement would agree.

"Do you think they knew it from the beginning?"

Her emotions stilled. She glanced away, considering his question. Did they know? Could they have truly known what their future

518

together would bring them? "I don't know," she answered honestly. "But..." and here she met his eyes again. He looked at her so deeply that she could not go on.

"But what?" he whispered.

"But," she said slowly, "I think they believed it was worth the risk."

His eyes softened. He hovered there, so close she could almost feel him.

"You never claimed your prize Marcellus," she said in a whisper, for they both knew a kiss on the hand was not what was intended.

He raised his hand to her, fingertips brushing her cheek. He traced along her jaw and gently cupped her chin. "I would not take more than that," he said, his eyes firmly on hers, "unless you gave it to me."

A warm flush rose through her. She paused for just a moment then closed the gap herself. Her lips were on his. The first touch was soft, startling, tentative, then firmer as they pulled each other into a tender embrace. Despite his arms around her she felt she was soaring loose and untethered, just as she had on her first venture into open earth with open sky with no safe roots and no boundaries. Only now he was here with her and the terror she felt was unbelievably sweet; she did not want it to stop. Unguarded, her heart reached for him, calling to him in the vibrant, glowing call of the faeries and he... he answered her in that same shimmering way.

Eleven

The next morning, the Three were in Marcellus' office going over the details of the Bridge defense. Again. With each passing day, they were less able to speak or think of anything else. Discussing the positions of their archers, even if for the fifth time, gave them a sense of control in a situation that ultimately hung on something over which they had no control. Praea still had not returned. Though it had only been a day and they couldn't begin to expect her yet, that didn't keep them from worrying. If she weren't back by tomorrow, they would have to decide whether or not to start the antipotion without her. Corren hoped that was a decision they would not have to make. To distract him from this worry, he found it a relief to focus on the Bridge defense and review troop placements.

A large square of parchment lay open on the desk. It was a hand-drawn map of the buildings located around the entrance to the Bridge. Several buildings were marked to indicate they had a window facing the Bridge. Archers were hiding in these rooms, waiting for Aradia to arrive. If Aradia had a magical shield placed around her, which she surely would, it would fall to Corren to break it. He just had to weaken her defenses enough to make her vulnerable to attack so an arrow could get through, or Nicolai's spear, or Marcellus' sword. Anything. Just something. That was surely where his staff came in.

He began to wonder if that wasn't what his vision in the Labyrinth was all about. He sensed tremendous power deep within his staff, power he had not yet released. There was a reason for this. When he broke the wizards' shields during the battle, he had come dangerously close to releasing it completely. Drawing on the power of the staff in that way had nearly drained him of all his energy. Perhaps against Aradia—when he would need to attack her with all he had, when he would not be able to hold back—his staff would drain him of his very life. Would it be enough to make them victorious? Would he live long enough to find out?

"As soon as the Fourth Song sounds," Marcellus said, "we'll go down to the Bridge so Corren can hide the antipotion." He paused. Corren knew that what Marcellus did not say was, *If it's ready.* "I'll have the area around the Bridge evacuated,"—this was to reduce citizen casualties—"and we'll wait for her here," he placed his finger on the map, "right at the front of the troops."

They were silent for a moment. That was the plan. They all agreed on it. But they did not want to be at the front of the Bridge. They wanted to be in front of the Gateway, as close to it as they could get, in fact. There were two reasons why this should not be. First, the troops guarding the Bridge had no chance against Aradia unless her magical defenses were torn down. Though the Guard would be there too, Corren needed to help. Second, since Corren still had no plan to sneak onto the Bridge in order to hide the antipotion, undetected anyway, he certainly had no plan that would allow them to stand guard for hours right next to the ring.

"So," Marcellus said, and Corren knew by the cautious tone what was coming. "Any ideas yet how to get on the Bridge?"

Corren sighed. "You mean without killing anyone?"

Marcellus did not answer.

"Not yet," Corren said. "I'm working on it."

They were interrupted by a page announcing that Sage Kennard of the Guard of the Order had come to see Lord Marcellus.

Marcellus straightened, turned over the map, and said "Send him in." The page bowed and left. Marcellus asked, "Should we ask him about getting on the Bridge?"

"If he does not agree, that will only cause him to watch us more closely," Corren said, "which will make it that much harder to get on."

Marcellus raised his eyebrows.

"What other plan do we have?" Nicolai asked. "We should ask him while he's here."

The door began to open and Marcellus, seeing Corren's hesitation, said lowly and quickly, "Let's feel him out first." Kennard came in, staff in hand and his forest green cloak billowing behind him. The Three stood to greet him.

"Lord Marcellus," Kennard said bowing respectfully. His face looked worn. "I was so sorry to hear about King Clement."

Marcellus nodded. "Thank you."

"If there's anything I can do."

"I appreciate that."

Kennard greeted Corren and Nicolai. "Thank you for calling upon the Guard when the Citadel was attacking."

"I think we are all grateful for that," Marcellus said. He gestured to the sitting area and they settled into chairs as Kennard explained what was happening with the Citadel now. Most of the wizards had been killed or caught while still in Caedmonian territory, though a few escaped over the border into Norrland. "We normally let them be as long as they are in Norrland," Kennard said, "but now we are actively seeking them. We need to be sure we know their intentions before we let them go in peace. We were concerned they may still be working with Aradia."

Marcellus straightened. "Are you certain they were working with her to begin with?"

Kennard nodded. "For several reasons. Nearer to the border they had a chance to regroup and combine their magic together again. This is not something they used to know how to do. As soon as I saw how they did it I knew Aradia must have taught them this. It is a magical secret known only by the Wysard branch and the Guard. Fortunately, she did not teach them how to keep us from breaking their defenses."

"Like Corren did," Marcellus said.

Kennard turned to Corren very deliberately. "Yes. But it took three of us to break their shield of twenty. You managed to break a shield of hundreds single-handedly."

Marcellus and Nicolai looked at him, astounded. Corren could only shrug. What was he supposed to say? "That is an unusual staff, Corren," Kennard said, inclining his head toward it.

Corren realized Kennard could well see the red stone partially encased in the tip, the main source of this staff's unusual power. He wondered if Kennard knew what that meant. "It has proven useful," Corren said dismissively.

"And powerful."

"Yes."

"It would be, wouldn't it?"

The Three exchanged careful glances. Was Kennard referring to the stone?

"You said there were several reasons you believed Aradia to be involved," Marcellus said. No one missed the fact that he was intentionally changing the subject. "What were the others?"

This redirection did not seem to bother Kennard. "We later captured one wizard who gave us quite a bit of information. First, he confirmed Aradia had been to the Citadel to meet with their leader, Itoh. She taught them how to link their magic, a secret they were eager to learn. Afterwards they turned on her. He said they didn't want to get involved in a war and thought they could get rid of her. Her reaction, with apparently little effort, was to break their shield, killing six of them in the process."

Corren felt his chest constrict and leaned forward. "What do you mean, 'in the process'? Not at the same time? While she was breaking their shield?"

"Apparently."

Corren sat back, his body going numb. If he had needed anything to remind him what they were up against, this was it. Kennard's expression was sober, as if he knew what Corren was thinking. "How does she do those things Kennard?"

"I don't know," he said quietly. "I used to admire her abilities, but now..." he shrugged. "I deeply regret them."

They were silent for a moment.

"There is more," Kennard said

Corren took a deep breath. "Yes?"

"Only about half of the members of the Citadel joined with Norrland's army to fight. The other half went with Aradia."

Corren's eyes widened.

"She won't be coming to the Bridge alone," Marcellus said.

Kennard shook his head. "No."

Corren rubbed his forehead with his hand. They did not need more problems.

Kennard leaned in, catching Corren's eye and holding it. "Do not give up," he said firmly. "We need you."

Something about the way Kennard said it made him think Kennard knew. Knew they were the Three. Kennard was looking between each of them now and Corren narrowed his eyes, trying to decipher Kennard's expression. "There is a resemblance between you," he said softly. "You could almost be brothers."

The Three did not move, nor remove their eyes from the wizard. Corren spoke first, with much more calm than he felt. "You are the first person to say such a thing," he said. "I don't think we look like brothers."

"I suppose not if you don't know what you're looking for." They each straightened, looking at each other with various degrees of concern. Kennard raised his hand to settle them. "It was not hard to figure out, once I stopped listening to Merhat's worries. If Aradia is the Cunning One, then where are the Three? Where our great defenders? When I remembered you were an orphan, Corren, I realized the Three had been right in front of us all along." He smiled at them. "I don't know what I can do, for I have all along felt it would come down to the Three. The prophecy says as much, it seems to me. But if I can help, I want to."

Corren glanced at his brothers, they at him. Could Kennard be trusted? Corren felt he could trust Kennard, who obviously knew who they were anyway, but Corren had learned over the last month that trust was a tricky thing. Corren looked first at Marcellus, then Nicolai with a questioning glance. Nicolai raised his eyebrows as if to say, *We may as well.* Marcellus nodded.

"Have you told anyone else about this?" Corren asked.

"I didn't have the opportunity. I didn't want to suggest such a thing in front of Merhat. Before I could get Kai'Enna and Bellamy alone to share my theory, the only two I could trust, you came with word of the Citadel attacking. I haven't seen them since."

Corren nodded. He didn't know if it would help for Kai'Enna and Bellamy to know or not, but for now he was relieved the secret had not gone any further. "Please don't mention this to anyone else for now."

"Alright."

"Can you tell us what the Order is planning, aside from guarding the Bridge?"

"There has been a lot of speculating. A lot of wondering where the Three are," and here he raised his eyebrows wryly, "and trying to figure out how Aradia plans to get through the Gateway. We have no idea. We've all inspected it and none of us could get through. We wouldn't even know where to begin. I don't know how she plans to do it, but I don't doubt that she will. Aside from this, the main thing we're doing is looking for her, or any sign of her. There are too many places she could be however, and she is very familiar with our methods. We're doing our best, but truthfully, it would not be hard for her to hide from us."

"How many Guard members are at the Bridge?" Marcellus asked.

"Fifty, maybe more. We'll need as many wizards as we can get."

"Yes, we will," Corren said, wondering how many wizards from the Citadel of Zeverai had attacked her at the same time... and unsuccessfully. He took a breath, pondering things. Corren decided to take a chance. "The fact that the Order has restricted our movements is a problem," he said. "If we are to defend the Bridge, we need complete access to it."

Kennard nodded. "I agree. I can arrange that."

"Without letting the Order know?"

He nodded again. "Yes."

Nicolai closed his eyes briefly, obviously relieved, as they all were. None of them overreacted though, not wanting to reveal just how important this was. There was more Corren wanted to ask him. Now that Kennard knew the truth, maybe he could give them information they wouldn't otherwise have. As a member of the Order, he would have access to their archives, access to all the research conducted on the Phoenix back when the Realm was more accessible. Maybe he could answer the question that had been bothering Corren the most.

"If someone with ill-intent entered the Realm," Corren began, "the Phoenix's magic would attack them, correct?"

Kennard nodded. "They would just wilt away."

"How long did that take?"

Kennard raised his eyebrows. "How long? It was almost instantaneous. Just a few minutes."

"How many minutes? Two? Five?"

Kennard furrowed his brows, obviously wondering what would prompt such questions. "Well, I don't know that a time was ever recorded. I have read the accounts of it happening. It was very quick. Maybe..." and he stopped, thinking. "Maybe two, three minutes. I'm sorry, but I don't know for sure."

Corren waved a hand. "It's alright," he said distractedly. It was with a sense of revulsion that he decided to do his calculations based on two minutes first. If it took two minutes for the magic of the Realm to destroy a soul in Aradia's shield, that would be thirty souls an hour. Corren did not doubt Aradia would need at least that much time in the Realm, likely much more. Since he didn't know for sure how much time she needed, he decided to be safe and calculate for twelve hours, the length of time between the Fourth Song and the Phoenix's regeneration. Thirty souls an hour times twelve hours equaled three-hundred sixty souls.

He closed his eyes, his anger spiking. He fought to subdue it. He needed to keep his mind clear. Three-hundred sixty seemed an awful lot of people to kill. If she planned on being in the Realm six hours, that was still one-hundred eighty souls. Was that even possible? Maybe the soul would last longer than two minutes.

He calculated how many people she would need to kill if the magic in the Realm destroyed one soul in her shield every five minutes. That was twelve souls an hour, one-hundred forty-four for twelve hours. Still a sickening number. Half that was still seventy-two souls.

No matter how he looked at it, she would need to murder an unthinkable number of people in order to stay in the Realm for any length of time.

Corren sighed. While the thought of this was nearly unbearable it did give him one comfort. It reinforced his thinking that Aradia would certainly wait for the Fourth Song before going in. He didn't bother to calculate how many souls it would take for her to stay in the

Realm for days or weeks, which is what she would need if she went in before the Fourth Song. Even twelve hours seemed like a long time for which to prepare. But how much time did she need? Six hours? Four? Eight? What? Corren thought again of the map and briefly considered pulling it out of his pocket and showing it to Kennard, but he changed his mind.

"What do you know about the lay of the land in the Realm?"

"Well, it's pretty flat. Only *detanae* trees and a few dry shrubs grow there."

"No. That's not what I mean. Is there anything like a... a map?"

Kennard raised his brows. "Yes. The Realm is quite large. There's a map that tells how to find the Phoenix."

"How long is that journey?"

Kennard exhaled. "I really don't know."

"A day? Two days? Half a day?"

"I don't..." but he stopped. "Well, let me think." The Three waited anxiously. "I don't know for sure. I know the records of the journeys into the Realm seemed to consist of traveling there, studying, and observing the Phoenix, all in the same day. Sometimes people would stay a few days, but not always. Does that help?"

Corren nodded. It wasn't as exact an answer as he would've liked, but it was enough. If a person could travel to the location of the Phoenix and still have time to study it, that meant Aradia definitely wouldn't need the full twelve hours after the Fourth Song sounded. He felt he understood better what kind of time considerations Aradia had to deal with, including the problem of building up her shield. Corren and his brothers planned to go to the Gateway as soon as the Fourth Song sounded. Corren felt more confident about this now. It should give them enough time to get everything in place. Aradia surely would go no sooner.

Early the next day, the Three were gathered in Corren's room, the air thick with the sharp and pungent scent of hyssop. Marcellus was leaning against the window sill, his back to the glass and the sun bright behind him. His countenance was dark with worry, however.

527

Nicolai sat on the bed, anxiously rubbing his thumb along a ridge in the post. It was with a heavy sense of dread that Corren spread out all the potion ingredients on the long table in his room.

All of the ingredients, that is, except one. Praea had not yet returned from the Lake of the Moon. It was Nicolai's agitation at this which caused the most worry. Nicolai clearly expected her back by now. The Three had spent the last hour debating whether or not to start the antipotion. The song could sound in two days. If they wanted to be ready, Corren had to start now and hope Praea got back in time (her ingredient wasn't needed until quite late into the second day of brewing). It was a risk because if she did not return in time the antipotion would be ruined, but so too was it a risk to delay while waiting for Praea's return. What if the Fourth Song sounded right away?

They felt Praea could be back at any time, so it seemed best to start the potion and hope she arrived soon. Feeling this was the right decision did not spare them from their worry. After all they had gone through, this could ruin it.

They did have one small cushion—a very small cushion. Halfway through the brewing, the antipotion would need to simmer for at least six hours, but that simmering could be prolonged for as long as eighteen. After that, though, the rest of the brewing would need to continue on a tight schedule. They could simmer the full eighteen hours if they wanted to, but that, too, would be a risk, pushing them past the time the Fourth Song could sound. This decision was still a day away, however, and one they might not need to make if Praea returned in time.

Corren stood at the table, his hand resting on top of a large hourglass and still wondering if they were making the right decision, when an entirely new thought struck him. He furrowed his brows.

Marcellus noticed this. "What?"

"Well..." The thought was still forming in his mind and he couldn't quite put it to words yet. He lightly touched each ingredient on the table with his fingertips—his compulsive way of taking inventory of what was in front of him—as he struggled to give form to his thoughts.

"It's just that one line of the prophecy. *All four elements must provide their singular powers.*"

"That was the part talking about the balanced potion, right?" Nicolai asked. "The Concealment Potion?"

"Well... maybe."

Nicolai and Marcellus exchanged glances. Marcellus' arms had been folded across his chest but he loosed them now and straightened a bit. "What's wrong?"

"I don't know. Maybe nothing. I was just thinking, what if that line of the prophecy isn't talking about a potion? What if the four elements are something else completely?"

"Like what?" Marcellus asked.

"Like... well..." He paced around the edge of the table and sat at a chair. He rubbed his forehead in thought. "Our stones seem to have bound us to different faeries... different elements of faeries. Earth. Water. Fire."

Marcellus and Nicolai were quiet, but they looked deep in thought now too.

"What if... what if the four elements referred to in the prophecy are us?"

The impact of these words struck Nicolai with peculiar force.

"There are only three of us," Marcellus said, but Nicolai's thoughts were going in a completely different direction.

"Are there air faeries?" he asked.

"I've only heard the myths speak of the three," Corren said. "Earth, water, and fire."

"Could there be others and we just don't know it?" Nicolai had never heard of air faeries either, not even in myths, but he was hopeful anyway. He would rather there be air faeries, than that the fourth element be what he now feared.

"It seems unlikely," Marcellus said, "but that wouldn't be the first unlikely thing to happen. Even so, there are still only three of us. Even if there were such a thing as air faeries, which of us would be bound to them? It doesn't make sense."

Corren nodded reluctantly. "Perhaps not. It was just a thought." He went back to the ingredients on the table.

Nicolai felt compelled to rise from the bed, slowly pace to the other side, and lean against the opposite post, his back to his brothers. He could hear items being moved on the table, heard Corren say an incantation and felt a little rush of energy sweep the room like a breeze.

Nicolai furrowed his brows; his heart was pounding. What if Corren were right? What if the four elements weren't ingredients? What if the four elements were people? There may not be air faeries, but Nicolai knew of someone who could fly, someone who was as bound to the air as he was to the earth. Someone who they needed to complete this potion. Someone who, not insignificantly, had been healed by his stone. Was this why? Nicolai wanted nothing more than to keep Praea away from this, to keep her out of danger. How connected was she? Nicolai slowly sank onto the bed, chills coursing through his body. Was it only her ability to get the ingredient they needed that connected her?

Or was there something more?

Twelve

Praea hovered at the edge of the forest, her hand lingering on the coarse bark of a tall pine. She looked at the lake bathed in moonlight. It was smooth and clear. Not a ripple or fault marred its still surface. She saw no women, but Praea knew they would come once she stepped into their realm. The nearer to the Lake she had come, the more her fear had swelled. Now it threatened to consume her completely. To break its hold she took a deep breath and thrust herself past the boundary of the Wilds and into the Isle of Iona.

A chill slid over her. She wrapped her arms about herself for comfort as much as for warmth. The moonlight was thick and heavy. She nearly felt its silken touch on her skin.

Praea waited. With suspended breath, she listened for the voices. She heard none. As time passed this did not change, and Praea realized she would have to seek them out herself. She dropped her arms to her sides, took a resolute breath, and began walking. The earth beneath was covered with sparse grass that petered out to bare ground—gray and dark—as it tilted toward the water. She followed this and was almost to the water's edge, immobile and sharp as a blade, when at last the whispering appeared. Like a feather of a dream it came to her at first, sound with no shape and no meaning... only a feeling twisting its way toward her. It was only one voice this time, not the mass of voices tumbling over each other as before. It was no less alarming and Praea found that she had stopped moving and held her hands to her stomach. She saw nothing at first, only dark forest and barren shore. Then a black shadow along the trees emerged before being abruptly illuminated by silvery light.

The cloaked woman looked directly at Praea with her large, round, owl-like eyes. The whisper came to language then, and what Praea heard was this: "Praea, daughter of Diana, the great ancient priestess

531

of the moon and mother to us all. I greet thee, dear sister, infant of life. I am Chandra, Queen of the Lake of the Moon, and I come to present your destiny."

All this was said without being said, with Chandra's wide, dark eyes on Praea, approaching in such silence Praea did not even hear her feet on the ground. She came near, and stopped.

Praea answered without speaking. She did not know how she did it. "I greet thee, Queen Chandra," Praea whispered in her thoughts, the words leaving her mind like fragile, wispy vines. She bowed.

Chandra smiled, but it was a dark smile and Praea did not return it.

"You come for secrets," Chandra said.

"Yes, my Lady."

"You are entitled to them, if you agree to guard them well."

Praea wondered if her thoughts were hidden or exposed, worrying about how much Chandra could see. "I come seeking the moonlight," Praea said.

"We all seek the moonlight, but do you know what it is you truly seek?" Chandra continued speaking in the whispering way. It ebbed and flowed in Praea's mind like soft and lulling water. "You come here like one wanting only to leave. You are not the first to do this. Like those before you, you will make an oath. You will be given all. Then you may leave if you choose, though you may no longer want to. Few do. Are you willing to make the oath that assures us of your honor?"

Praea did not know what kind of oath was meant, but she had no hesitation pledging herself honorable. "I am."

"Come then."

Chandra turned and Praea followed her along the water's edge. The silence was absolute. After a short time Chandra came to a stop, turned slowly, and faced the woods. Other women emerged from the tall pines, square lanterns held in front of them, coming in pairs, two lines six women long. They came very near Chandra and Praea, their pale faces glowing in the yellow light. The two lines separated, one going one way, one going the other, until they enclosed Praea and Chandra in a crescent shape against the water.

Chandra turned to the lake, held out her hands, and sent out a vibrating energy with words neither said nor whispered. A small disturbance on the water drew Praea's eye. It was like a little whirlpool, only instead of the water sinking down in the center, it was rising up. This center spun faster and faster, glinting wildly as it lifted above the surface and broke free, a spinning ball of water hovering over the Lake of the Moon, which was still and silent again, as if no thought or breeze had ever touched it.

Without speaking or touching it, Chandra brought the sphere of water, spinning and luminous, over the bank and between them where it now hovered between her outstretched hands.

"If you desire the moonlight," her mind whispered, "you must promise to guard it. The water will hold you to your oath." Chandra's dark eyes flashed in the reflection of the watery sphere between them. "Repeat after me, but take care. Do not speak amiss. Silence is better than an oath spoken falsely. Are you ready, daughter of Diana?"

Praea thought of her brothers, of Nicolai, of Aradia. "I am."

The women in the crescent raised their lanterns, the flickering light casting dancing shadows on their faces. "Hold out your hands," Chandra instructed. "Take the vow I speak into your own mouth." Praea held out her hands, forced her uneasy fingers to still. Chandra led the ball over Praea's hands where it floated in the air above them. From this, a silken ribbon of water let down and slid smoothly over her palms. Chandra spoke aloud for the first time. "As a true daughter of Diana, I freely give this oath," she said.

"As a true daughter of Diana," Praea repeated, "I freely give this oath," and the ribbon of water continued to fall. Where the water went after this, Praea could not tell, for the ground at their feet was dry.

Chandra continued. "The penalty for breaking my oath is instant death."

Startled, Praea widened her eyes. The water ran over her hands. Determined, Praea repeated the words, trying not to falter on the last word.

"By the power of the moon," Chandra went on, "I swear I will never reveal the secrets taught me here."

Praea hesitated. If she could not reveal them, how could she be of any use to Nicolai? But if she did not agree, she would not be able to help then either. Hoping she could find a solution to this dilemma once she had more information, Praea repeated the line.

"The penalty for breaking my oath is instant death," Chandra said again, her dark eyes piercing.

Praea echoed this, and the ball of water thinned, fell, and was gone. Praea's hands were dry, but the sensation of the water lingered. Chandra stepped forward, placed her hands on Praea's shoulders, and pressed two dry kisses onto Praea's cheeks. "All will be revealed."

The crescent of women split into two. Chandra led Praea though the break and toward the trees, the women falling into line behind them. They left the shore and followed a narrow pathway into the forest, the pines towering far above them, their feet quiet on the ground. The path wound softly, then opened onto a wide clearing, likewise veiled in moonlight and nearly as vast as the lake had been. Shimmering, adobe homes, rounded and low to the earth were dotted across the field like hunched wildflowers. Cloaked women, hundreds of them, spread over the clearing. Most were stationary, like carved figures, staring at her from their open thresholds as she passed. Those who moved did so at such a slow, almost lifeless pace that they seemed to be floating. Their skin was colorless as moonlight. Their eyes dark as a starless night.

Chandra led Praea to the center of the clearing. A circle of columns had been erected here, each column at least twenty feet high and three feet in diameter, with massive spheres balancing on top. At first Praea thought these columns were made of marble, but as they drew near she did not know what material they were. Their surface shifted like mist. As they passed between two columns, Praea reached out her hand, brushing her fingertips along the surface. The mist seemed to slide away under her touch. The center of the circle held only soft bluegrass. Chandra and Praea knelt alone. They would not leave for many hours.

Here Chandra explained how they used their magic to capture moonlight, whether in one's hand for small purposes or over the entire expanse of the Isle of Iona. She explained how their magic kept them concealed from all but the daughters of Diana. "Many of the impure bloodline have wandered in," Chandra said, "and drowned in a lake they could not see." Chandra taught Praea many things in the Circle of the Moon, but for last she saved what she called the "Great Secret," the combining of the magic of the moon with the potency of Phoenix ash. Only one fleck of ash was needed to begin the process of harnessing moonlight into oneself. The result, long life.

"How long?" Praea asked.

"I am 638 years old," Chandra said. She smiled her dark smile again.

"Eternal life?" Praea asked in astonishment.

"No. Not eternal. But some daughters have lived close to 900 years. It was not always so, but we have perfected our technique. We are fed by moonlight. As long as we stay in it, it sustains us. Since perfecting our method, we can no longer leave the Isle of Iona once this process has begun, or we will drain and perish rapidly. It is a small price to pay. We have more than tripled our lifespan."

Praea's skin tingled. How would it be to live so long? She looked through the massive columns, considering again the women and their dwellings, wondering what it would be like to live here.

"We live a simple existence," Chandra said, "nourished by our moon, feasting upon the long lives we daughters of Diana claim as our birthright. You can go back, Praea. Back to a world full of fear and violence, with death hovering its grasp over your shoulder. Or you can stay here, beautiful and young for close to a millennia. It is your choice. There is no penalty for leaving, but," and here her dark eyes grew sharp and she leaned forward. "Once you refuse your birthright, there is no reclaiming it."

Praea clutched her hands together on her lap.

Chandra sat back and smiled as if she knew, after hundreds of years of experience, what choice Praea would make. The same choice she herself had made over 600 years ago.

"What say you, daughter of the moon? Do you choose death? Or life?"

Thirteen

"One more hour. That's all I have." Corren sat watching the potion. It was nearing midnight and they were a mere hour away from needing Praea's ingredient.

Nicolai acknowledged Corren with a nod, and paced to the window. Time had passed regardless of their will to stop it. Where was she? What was taking so long? They had let the antipotion simmer the full eighteen hours before proceeding with the brewing; a necessary risk they felt, even though they were now at a point where the Fourth Song could sound at any time. It was a sound they were all dreading, because even if Praea did come within the next hour, the potion still wouldn't be ready for another four. Much longer than they would want to wait if the Fourth Song were to sound. If she did not come in time, all was lost. Their decision now seemed a mistake of horrific proportions.

Nicolai wandered to the cauldron again and looked in. This was part of his nervous pacing that served no purpose other than to give him something to do. He wiped his brow. Ever since Corren had added the dragon scales, the potion radiated an almost unbearable heat despite the fact that the fire under the cauldron burned low. The scales had also changed the formerly yellow potion to a vibrant, glittering red. Every now and then a spark would pop and flash in the air as the surface swirled slowly, still in motion from the last time Corren had stirred it. Nicolai compulsively checked the large hourglass on Corren's table. The sand on the bottom half of the glass had gathered into a daunting pile. A much smaller amount rested on the top, the center of its surface puckered down where the sand was falling, falling...

"Should we send out a search for her?" Marcellus asked, as he had once before.

As before, Nicolai shook his head no. How do you search the skies, and in the dark of night at that? "We can only wait."

Corren stirred the potion, sand fell, and they waited.

Only Nicolai could not wait anymore.

He had earlier shared a theory with his brothers, a theory that had kept him from revealing Praea's secret. The four elements were mentioned in the prophecy, he decided, not because the Concealment Potion was balanced as they originally thought, and certainly not because it represented four actual people, but rather because the antipotion contained highly unusual ingredients from each element: the dragon scales for fire, the crosshatch petal for water, the leaf from the Tree of Origin for earth, and Praea's moonlight for air. Corren and Marcellus had agreed that could well be what that line of the prophecy meant. Nicolai had been relieved by this. It was reasonable, wasn't it? It was the moonlight they needed, not Praea really. She was already as involved as she needed to be. There was no need for Nicolai to reveal her secret to his brothers, nor their secret to her. She was fulfilling the prophecy, even if unknowingly. Did she really need to know more than that? She did not have a stone. The prophecy did not come to her. There was no reason to bring her any more into it.

Still there had been a lingering sense of doubt, and now Nicolai wondered if he had come to the wrong conclusion. Was he just trying to keep Praea out of danger? Nicolai checked the hourglass again and saw time slipping by. He decided he needed to tell his brothers what he knew about her. What if they saw something about Praea's connection that Nicolai could not? What if there was something else they should be doing?

He cleared his throat uneasily. "There's something," he said, "I think I should tell you."

A knock came at the door and all three jumped up. Corren rushed to answer it. It was only a page. Nicolai sat back down, disappointed. "Master Corren, do you know where..." His eyes alighted on Nicolai. "Ah. You are who I seek, sir. Princess Praea of Sakkara requests your presence."

Nicolai bolted from the bed and all three rushed toward the page. He momentarily forgot his training and flinched back a step.

"Where is she?" Nicolai asked.

Gathering his composure, the page said, "In the east anteroom off the entrance hall..." Nicolai flew past him before he even finished speaking. He ran down the hallway, his pounding steps echoing off the stone. He raced in this manner through the nearly deserted castle. Halfway down the final flight of stairs he saw her. Praea exited the anteroom and saw him as well, probably had heard him coming. She rushed to meet him at the bottom. She looked pale, almost silvery pale, and worn. "Praea, you're just in time," he said taking her hand and leading her quickly up the stairs. She sensed his urgency, was not offended by the abrupt greeting, and in fact seemed urgent herself. "Did you get it?" he asked.

"No."

He froze and his heart stopped. "No?"

"It doesn't work that way, Nicolai. I need to know what this is for."

"But if you don't have it..." His mind was spinning. He did not expect this. "Praea, there's no more time."

She put a hand on his arm. "You misunderstand me, Nicolai. What is this for? A potion or something else?"

"A potion," he said distractedly. He had not really believed they would lose the antipotion. He thought somehow everything would work out, but now... "This is the final ingredient and we need it now."

She nodded, tugged on his arm and they began up the stairs again. "I understand. Will anyone be drinking this potion?"

"No."

"Are you sure?"

"Yes. What is this about?"

"I needed to know that your purposes are not the same as their purposes." They came to the top and moved rapidly down the hallway and toward the next flight of stairs. "I cannot give you this ingredient," she said. "But if it is for a potion, I can add it myself."

"But we need it right now. Can you add it now?"

"Yes."

He exhaled in relief and said, "Good. Oh, Praea, that's good. I don't think Corren will let you add it yourself though." Up to this

538

point, Corren had been so particular about method that he had not even let anyone help him stir.

"I have no choice. Before I could learn how to get this ingredient, I had to swear an oath that I would never reveal their secrets. This oath is bound to me magically, and if I break it I will die."

Yet again, Nicolai stopped in alarm.

"When your potion is ready, I will add what you need. I think it will be safe if I do it myself."

"You think! Would that be violating your oath?"

"I am not certain. Please, I don't know how to explain without saying too much."

Nicolai was shaking his head. "Then no. No. Never mind."

"Wait..."

"No. There must be another way. Something... something else we can do." Even as he said it he didn't believe it. There *was* no other way.

"If you thought that you wouldn't have sent me to begin with," Praea said.

He closed his eyes. How much more must he sacrifice? It had been hard enough sending her to the Lake. He had already lost a father. Had lost two of them. His former life was gone. Now Praea too? As much as he had tried to protect her, must she be sacrificed as well?

"Listen to me, Nicolai. I am willing to do my part. It is my risk, and I'm willing to take it. I do not seek to live forever. I have seen the lives of those who do, but theirs is no true life. I fear death, as I suppose everyone does, but even death holds more hope than their numb, desperate existence. You asked me to go to the Isle of Iona for a reason. I went because I am willing. I am still willing. Now, how much time do we have?"

"No time," Nicolai said. He held her to him briefly, urgently, then made himself let go and took her by the hand. "Let's go."

Praea not only had to add the ingredient herself, but insisted she be alone to do it. Corren shook his head adamantly, as Nicolai knew he would. "This is a very sensitive potion, Princess."

"I cannot let you watch me."

"It must go in *precisely* when the sand falls. Not a moment before or after. Then it has to be stirred *immediately*."

"I can do that."

Corren blinked. He had not been trying to tell her how to do it. He had been explaining why he could not leave the potion in her hands.

"There is no margin for error," he said. "This potion cannot be lost."

She looked at the hourglass. "I am going to need the time we have left. I cannot let you stay. This is a magical secret Master Corren."

This silenced him. Nicolai remembered Corren talking about the vigilance with which magical secrets were guarded. He was obviously still struggling to agree.

"Corren, please," Nicolai said firmly. "Just let her do it."

Corren's sigh was almost a growl. "Use this wooden spoon," he said pointing. "The long one, not the short." She nodded. "Stir all the way to the bottom, close to the sides, but do not scrape them. Wide and slow, like this," and he demonstrated. "Exactly like that."

"I understand."

"You will not be able to stop stirring, so you will need to call for us when you are done. We'll be right outside the door. Then I'll take over."

"Yes," she said urgently, eyeing the hourglass. "Please hurry."

They rushed out, with Corren's final words: "We'll be right here."

"I'll call for you. Do not come in too soon." With that, she closed the door, with the Three staring hard at it.

After Nicolai told them what little he knew about Praea's trip to the Lake, and about her oath, nothing more was said. Corren sat on a bench slightly down the hall, his elbows on his knees and his head in his hands. Nicolai could not seem to leave the door and Marcellus waited with him. "How long has it been?" Nicolai asked, for he could not tell. Had it been two minutes? Ten?

Marcellus shrugged.

A minute, or perhaps several, passed in painful silence. Marcellus said, "What if...?" then he said no more.

"What?" Corren asked a little impatiently, raising his head.

"If this breaks her oath... how will we know?"

Nicolai reacted to this by impulsively knocking on the door. "Praea?"

There was no answer and he grabbed the handle. Marcellus grabbed his hand to stop him. "It may not be time."

"She's not answering."

Corren had stood and came now to the door. "If she's in the middle of a spell, she will not be able to. We must wait."

"But what if... what if..." Nicolai could not say it.

"Let's just wait for her call."

They waited, but Nicolai itched to grab the handle again. Images flashed in his mind: of his father dead on the barren earth, of Clement's blank face and Marcellus huddled over him, of Praea's eyes empty and glassy and her lying lifeless on the floor. He closed his eyes and leaned his forehead against the smooth, wooden frame of the door. "How much longer, Corren?" He asked this in a dull, dead voice and did not open his eyes. There was no answer. Nicolai looked over at him.

Corren was studying him, had furrowed his brows, but Marcellus had a knowing expression. It was one of compassion, as if he knew exactly, *exactly* what Nicolai was going through. Perhaps Nicolai was revealing more than he should, but he could not conceal it. He only wanted to know Praea was safe. "How much longer" he asked again, his voice not more than a whisper.

"I don't know," Corren said quietly.

Nicolai straightened and turned away. He clutched at his stone through his shirt. *Maybe for her,* he thought. *It healed her once. Maybe it would do it again.*

Then they heard her, just barely. "Done."

They rushed through the door with one accord. She was stirring as instructed—the potion now crystal clear—but she was even paler than before and looked ready to collapse. Corren took the spoon from her, his arm following her motion and never letting the spoon stop. When

541

she released it, her legs gave way just as Nicolai got to her and he caught her in his arms, his knees bending slightly. "Praea!"

"I'm okay," she whispered, though her eyes were not open.

He lifted her and carried her to the bed, Marcellus gathering near too and Corren, still stirring, kept one eye on the potion and one eye on her. "What's wrong with her?" Nicolai asked.

"It's the magic," Corren said. "It's drained her. She'll be alright."

Nicolai looked at her pale face and she opened her eyes slightly. She whispered something he could not hear and he leaned down. "What, love?" he said gently.

"I just need to rest," she said. As soon as she finished saying it she closed her eyes and slid into sleep.

Nicolai exhaled, relief flooding him. He sat on the edge of the bed. He watched numbly as Marcellus went to the potion, leaning over it. "Is it supposed to look like that?"

"Yes," Corren said. "This is good."

Nicolai looked at the hourglass. Three more hours. They only needed the Fourth Song to wait three more hours.

Two hours later, Corren extinguished the fire burning under the potion with a word.

"It is finished?" Nicolai asked, though he said it softly since Praea was still asleep on the bed.

"It needs to cool and rest." He turned the last hourglass, stretched and yawned. None of them had slept much in the last few days, but Corren had the worst of it. "Just a little longer."

"So that's it then," Nicolai said. He felt almost giddy with relief. They did it. They were nearly ready. He wanted to run down to the Gateway, to put the antipotion on as soon as it was done, but he knew that was not possible. The Fourth Song could sound at any minute, but it could also be another three weeks. Once the antipotion was applied to the Gateway, it would start to lose its potency. A few hours on the ring would be harmless, but weeks could weaken it enough to render it ineffective. They would have to wait. Nicolai, who had been dreading the Fourth Song for the last day, was suddenly ready for it to sound. He was ready to get to the Bridge. Ready to fight. Ready for this to be over.

"Once it's done cooling, I'll make sure the Concealment Potion will work," Corren said, gesturing to the second metal ring they had scrounged from the smithy. "But after..." Praea stirred and they fell silent to watch her. She went on sleeping and Corren spoke again. "After watching these elements work together as I brewed this antipotion, I'm not worried about it anymore. We'll be able to hide it alright. I'm only testing to make sure there are no surprises." He stretched again and gave a huge yawn. "I need to get some sleep but I don't want to move her."

"Go to my room," Nicolai said. "I'll stay here."

Corren and Marcellus exchanged glances. He could guess their thoughts. It wasn't exactly proper for Nicolai to stay here alone with her, but if it was going to be anyone, it was going to be him. Corren seemed too tired to care. He shrugged, waved a hand, and headed for the door. Marcellus still eyed Nicolai however. "She'll be hard to flirt with when she's asleep," he said with a straight face.

Nicolai rolled his eyes and walked to the wardrobe to fetch an extra blanket for the lounge. "Good night, Marcellus."

Marcellus smiled and left, closing the door with a quiet click. Nicolai lay down on the lounge, his body aching with relief. His mind was busy though, and despite his fatigue it took time for him to fall asleep. It was a restless sleep, as if his mind could not completely let go of its awareness of the world. As if even in sleep he could not stop listening and waiting for the Fourth Song to sound.

Fourteen

Despite his exhaustion, Corren did not sleep well and woke at first light. Knowing the Fourth Song could sound at any time caused an eerie kind of restlessness to take hold of him, as if he were afraid he'd sleep through it, somehow miss the whole thing, and Aradia would be victorious. He knew it was a senseless worry, but his heart felt it anyway. In an effort to shake it, he went outside and wandered the grounds. He found a ladder on the far west wall, away from the castle gate and the eyes of its guards, and climbed it easily. Once at the top, he leaned against a broad stone parapet, his staff held loosely in his hand.

The sky in the east was pale by now, reaching for blue, faint streaks of yellow brushing along the horizon in great, broad strokes; a gentle sunrise he could not enjoy. The city, all deep shadows and slumber, sloped away and down to the docks. The sea was a dark mass. Somewhere in that mass lay the Bridge of a Thousand Ages. Corren wondered if that was where it was going to happen. His visions in the Labyrinth made two things clear to him, though he had fought them at first. If he were to fulfill his portion of the prophecy two things had to happen: he had to forge his staff in the fire with his stone as a core, and he had to die. One of those things had already happened. The second, he knew, would happen soon... if they were to succeed. If they did not succeed, it would likely happen anyway. Maybe not for three more weeks. Or maybe today. Today. Before the sun dipped down in the sky again, his life could be over.

A sudden wave of terror rushed over him, smothering him, prompting him to cling to the parapet for relief. None came. He thought it would consume him, take him where he stood. He did not want to die. He thought of all his hopes for himself, everything he had ever wanted in his life. None of it was going to happen. There was nothing left. Only hours, days, weeks at the best and that would be it. He stared wide eyed at the Eternal Flame, as if that would lend some help. He saw only the flame, felt only fear. He held to it with his eyes. He thought of the magic it represented, the magic that gave him his true sense of self. Nothing else gave him such energy, such drive, such satisfaction. Even that had not been enough.

He had needed his family. And he found them. It was this thought —of Clement, of Nicolai, of Marcellus—that gave him joy in the middle of his raw terror, causing it to reluctantly release its bond. It reminded him that if they were victorious, his death would not be for nothing. For them, he would do it. For all of Caedmonia, yes, but mostly for his brothers. His love for them took place in his heart, holding hands with his fear, but his fear was manageable now. Manageable. Slowly he straightened, gathered in his will, held tight to his determination. He firmly pushed his fear away.

Corren watched the sky ease out of darkness. The rooftops of the city slowly brightened with it, touched by the morning light. He could see the Bridge now, its long line, thin from this vantage point, a razor-sharp cut through the water. The Eternal Flame, though small, had been momentarily clear and bright in the darkness of pre-dawn. It slowly began to fade and weaken, nearly consumed by the greater light of the sun that now surrounded it.

Dawn found Nicolai on the grounds as well, walking meditatively through the gardens. He stopped once or twice to help a tentative bud to bloom, but did this almost subconsciously. He was imagining scenarios they might face at the Bridge, as he had often done before. How would Aradia come? How would she attack? Would they get close enough to strike? This was no typical battle and impossible to predict. It was this uncertainty that unsettled him more than anything, more than the danger even. But Nicolai would do his part. To combat the uneasy sense of the unknown, he decided that whether he were waiting for the Fourth Song down at the Bridge or here at the castle, he would be constantly ready. A sword already hung at his side and throwing spears (one born of the earth) were strapped to his calves. He

545

thought then of Corren's staff and, as he always did, felt reassured. It radiated power even when not in use. Corren radiated power too. Nicolai had not met many wizards or witches, though to hear Corren tell it he met the best of them at the Order. Only one person there had radiated the kind of power Corren now had. They would face her soon enough.

Nicolai checked the sky. Dawn seemed to be caught in time, holding its breath. Just like he was. He came to the tree, Praea's tree in his mind, and sat down on the ground where he had first met her a month ago. Only that long? He felt as if he had known her his entire life, as if seeing her for the first time was merely the remembering.

As if his desire had conjured her, he saw her approaching him. When he left Corren's room this morning, she had been sleeping and he didn't have the heart to wake her. He was grateful to see her now. She was the loveliest woman he had ever known, not just for her beauty but for her grace, her determination, her gentle spirit. He smiled as she approached. He could live in this moment for the rest of his life and be satisfied.

He waited until she was nearly to him and made to get up. She held down her hand, offering help and he took it. In that instant he changed his mind, impulsively pulling her down to him instead. She stumbled a little and caught her balance, but smiled and sat close. Her smile faded. "I saw the potion off the fire. I haven't ruined it have I?"

"No, no. You were perfect. It's done."

He saw her relief and put his arm around her. She looked rested and had most of her color back, though she was still a little pale. "Are you feeling better?"

"Yes." She nestled up next to him. He encompassed her gladly, their heads resting together.

"You are dressed like a man of war," she said soberly.

Who would have guessed, he thought. He gathered the curtain of hair off her shoulders, slipping his hand down the length of it. "We need to be ready," he said in answer. She clung to him then, surprising him with her sudden intensity.

"Now I am feeling protective of you," she said, fear in her voice.

546

He sought words to reassure her, to remove her fear. There were none. He only held her tighter and said, "Let's just sit here awhile."

Marcellus had slept on the couch in his office without even changing out of his clothes. He could not go back to his room last night. He had needed his father, and this office was as close as he could get.

He, too, came out of sleep before dawn and watched the room slowly wake with the light. His mind was full of thoughts, so that when he first opened his eyes he did not stretch or move, but instantly furrowed his brows and began to think where he had left off the night before. He was a warrior from a long line of warriors and trying to glean every advantage he could think of against an enemy unlike anyone his family had seen before. There were no historic battles from which to learn or borrow strategy. It was new and uncertain and the cost of losing was unthinkable... to him, to his brothers, to Caedmonia. This was not a battle that could be lost. He determined to beat Aradia and yet, he had no real sense of whether or not their plan would be effective. After seeing how powerful she really was, after seeing how useless weapons were in the battle that killed his father, Marcellus wondered how hard it would really be for Aradia to defend herself against them. Marcellus looked at the water sword, still in its belt and draped over the chair with his other weapons. The water sword had resisted magic once. Maybe it would do so again. So much depended on Corren, Marcellus knew that, but he would not be alone. The Three would stand together. That was how they would live or die. Together.

Marcellus sat up slowly and rubbed his face with his hands. He rose, crossed the room, and washed his face at the basin. He still needed to go to his room and change, but he was not quite ready to do this. He went to the balcony. His eyes leapt to the bay, as they always did. He watched the water lighten with the morning sun. He scanned the water, the horizon, the Bridge, the island, the curving shoreline, all of it, wanting to see all of it. He had seen this view in every kind of weather, in every kind of light, ever since he was a boy. He had seen

547

changes come to the city from this vantage point. He remembered watching the south pier being built and the construction when his father approved building the Far North Quarter on the city's edge. The sight before him now was as familiar to him as anything he had ever known. Yet, it never looked to him as it did now. Lost to him. Like he would never see it again, like it had already gone on belonging to someone else.

That was when he heard it, swelling in his ears, in his chest, in the very air: the Fourth Song. He stilled to listen and knew the entire world stopped to listen with him, caught in that strange sense of calm and immobility each song seemed to bring. His eyes flicked down shore to the Rock of Light, the Eternal Flame at its tip, now just a pinprick, almost indiscernible, even in the weak light of dawn. The haunting notes fell away, he regained his ability to move, and instantly his blood ran hot, his heart pounding. *This is it.*

He noticed something, out in the water and away toward Thrayce Island (though this island was too far to see from here). At first he thought it a trick of the eye, reflections of the sun on the water, perhaps. He could not look away because it kept changing. His heart beat fast with urgency, needing to move, needing to find his brothers and get down to the Bridge, yet he could not look away. He found himself leaning forward a little, trying to pin down what it was. It was moving. Away to the horizon? Toward him? He could not tell.

Then his assessment of it began to solidify. It was a disturbance in the water, moving in a direct course, a little swell on the surface like a watery gopher tunnel. It was moving swiftly, unnaturally swift. He could not think of anything that could move so fast in the water, or go in such a straight path. Marcellus mentally followed its path ahead to find its destination... it was heading straight for the end of the Bridge... straight for the Gateway.

Marcellus leaned far forward now, confirming what he saw. "She's coming," he said lowly. He bolted back into the room, grabbed his swords at a run and tore open the door. "CORREN! NICOLAI!" He raced down the hall and around the corner, strapping on his swords as he ran.

A page came running down the hall toward him, his eyes alarmed. "Your Majes—"

"Get Corren and Nicolai!" he said, not slowing. "Send them to the Bridge! Send them to the Bridge!" He bolted down the steps, three at a time, hollering at every person he saw to get Corren and Nicolai. He thundered through the entrance and flew down the front steps of the castle, out into the thin morning air.

He ran toward the stables, yelling at a knight he saw up ahead. "Get Kedron! Ready Kedron!" The knight's eyes flew wide in alarm and he bolted toward the stables and out of sight. In a matter of minutes Marcellus entered them and spun through the open door to Kedron's stall where the knight was putting on the harness. There was no saddle and Marcellus did not wait for it but heaved himself up onto Kedron's bare back. The horse stomped his hooves in answer to the rough mount. Marcellus leaned over and grabbed the reins, pulling them back over the horse himself. He snapped the reins and Kedron jarred into a full gallop. Marcellus ducked on the way out to avoid a collision with the overhead beam.

He hollered for Corren and Nicolai again, scanning the grounds as he flew past but he didn't see them. Then he was out of the castle gates, pounding through the city streets, the echo of it banging in his ears. "Faster!" He hung on tight with his legs, Kedron's muscles straining underneath him, his breath coming out in hot blasts. "Go! Go! Go!" They raced downhill, skirting the few carts and people out so early in the morning, their shouts swept away before he could hear what was said. His hair beat back, his shirt billowing and flapping. At last they reached the docks. He raced for the Bridge, his eyes searching the water, seeking it. "Where is she?"

The entrance to the Bridge and the troops guarding it came into view. At that moment a huge ball of blue light erupted from the end. From the Gateway. A booming crack like thunder tore through the air and a ring of light flew out, expanding from the ball, rushing toward him. He felt it even at a distance, had just enough time to pull back hard on the reins. The light pummeled him and he flew off his horse, landing hard on his side.

549

As soon as the Fourth Song faded away, Corren descended the ladder of the wall swiftly and noticed the commotion on the castle grounds. He was nearly to the castle when a page spotted him and came running. "Master Corren. Lord Marcellus said to find you and Nicolai and send you to the Bridge."

"To the Bridge? Where is he?"

"Gone, sir. He took his horse without even a saddle and left through the gate at a run."

Corren's heart jolted. *Why did he leave without us?* He ran to the castle, tearing down the halls to retrieve the antipotion. Once in his room, he collected it in a flask with slightly trembling hands, wondering why on earth he hadn't done that last night. He raced back out of the castle, descending the steps. Here he saw Nicolai running up to him.

That was when the blue ring of light reached the castle like the blast of a windstorm. It hit Nicolai first. As Corren caught a glimpse of him being thrust to the ground, he instinctively spun away from the rapidly approaching light. It knocked him forward onto the steps, his chest and forehead crashing painfully on unyielding, sharp edges of chiseled stone.

When the wave of light hit Praea she had just stood—hearing too some sort of shouting on the castle grounds and deciding to investigate despite Nicolai's hasty instructions for her to stay put before he himself had taken off at a run—and it knocked her tumbling to the ground as well. The tree above her, the oldest tree on the grounds, could not withstand the blow. Its thousands of leaves withered and cut loose in a rush, plummeting to the ground like a heavy rain. Bewildered, she swept her arms out, trying to clear away leaves falling all around her, surrounded by a dry crackling uproar in her ears. She stood and the leaves about her came to the knee. She tilted her head back to squint up at the tree. It was skeletal and still swaying from the blast. "What...?"

She pushed through the leaves and hurried for the castle, attempting to control the terrible sense of dread urging her on. Inside she met more confusion: some people still on the ground, others hovering in a daze, others running. Her mind raced, trying to make sense of what just happened. She remembered the image on the cave wall—the blue ball of light at the end of the Bridge of a Thousand Ages. The same blue light she had just seen. Praea sprang into a full run. When she reached the steps she saw Nicolai and Corren (with a bloody gash on his forehead) coming out of the stables on horseback. She watched as they raced out the gates.

They disappeared. She knew full well where they were going. Praea determined that this time, she would not be left behind.

Marcellus rolled onto his back, his head pounding from his collision with the cobblestone street. Sounds crashed in on him, nonsense sounds, jarring and disorienting. They came into focus: he heard shouting and screaming, some from a distance, but one very near.

"Lord Marcellus!"

He squinted his eyes open; a dark face blurred into view.

"Lord Marcellus!"

He blinked hard, twice, and looked again. It was Kennard. "The Gateway," he said urgently.

"I know," Marcellus said, forcing himself to get up, his head and body sharply protesting. "It's Aradia."

Knights rushed into view, those who had been assigned to guard the Bridge.

"We didn't even see her," Kennard said. "How did she get to it?"

Marcellus hobbled toward Kedron who stood nearby, his reins hanging low. Marcellus quickly scanned Kedron's legs for breaks but if his horse had fallen too, he did not appear to be harmed. "She came a different way," Marcellus said, pulling himself up, arms shaking. Once atop Kedron he felt the world spin and dip, his head throbbing. He closed his eyes, willing it to stop, his mind already ahead of him: he had to get to the Gateway.

551

"Can you ride?"

He didn't answer. He opened his eyes and the world stayed steady. He scanned around him. The city was nothing but confusion. He saw no sign of his brothers. He saw a few people still not getting up, all elderly he noticed, and one of these—slumped against a building with a basket of bread spilled out next to him—was being mourned over by a hunched woman, rocking back and forth wailing, "He's dead! He's dead!" It was as if the blast had taken the most aged among them—or perhaps it was just that the aged were too weak to resist it. Marcellus could not tell which it was.

"Send Corren and Nicolai," he said to Kennard. Once more he grabbed the reins, once more pushed Kedron into a roaring gallop. He tore through the troops crammed around the entrance and finally raced down the Bridge of a Thousand Ages. The sea fanned by him impossibly slow, like in a dream where he could never get where he was going. Crescent Island slid by so slowly he wondered if he were passing it at all, then suddenly he saw the end of the Bridge drawing near, the stone walkway curling into a circle, the center of the circle falling to the sea below. Above this hovered the Gateway, a ring just as Corren had described. Except for one difference.

He pulled Kedron to a halt next to the inner circle of the Bridge, the ring level with him now. Marcellus looked hard at the ring. It had been singed. Wisps of steam rose from its blackened surface. Marcellus felt the faint wave of heat coming from it; when he held his hand up close, the heat was bright on his palm. *Maybe it went wrong,* he thought. *Maybe she's in there, but dead.* Somehow Marcellus knew this wasn't true. It wasn't Aradia who had been damaged by her entrance into the Realm, it was the Gateway.

He didn't know if he felt it or thought of it first, but he looked down at his tunic, registered the incredible heat of the stone on his chest, and saw the blue light pressing through the fabric. He scrambled for the stone, brought it out, squinted his eyes at the blinding light. It was the most brilliant blue he had ever seen. Much the same color the ball of light had been when Aradia went through the Gateway.

In fact, exactly the same color.

552

Marcellus looked sharply to the Gateway. "Oh!" He looked down the Bridge for Corren and Nicolai. He saw nothing. He heard nothing. Why weren't they coming?

He removed the stone and dropped the casing back under his shirt, empty. The stone was hot, radiant. His heart was alight too, intense and uncontainable. He looked at the smoking Gateway, back down the barren stretch of Bridge, back to the Gateway where Aradia had gone... how long ago now?

He turned to the Bridge, cupped his hands around his mouth. "CORREN! NICOLAI!" The sea swallowed up his calls. None came back to him. Glancing briefly at the ring, Marcellus tore back down the Bridge, the stone still alight and hot in his hand. "CORREN! NICOLAI!" He saw them racing toward him and he brought Kedron to a forceful halt. "Hurry!"

He sped back to the Gateway, gripping his stone urgently, glancing behind him impatiently to check their progress. "Hurry!" They were next to him at last.

Panting, his face wrought with agony, Corren said, "Aradia's there, isn't... your stone!"

"I know. Are you ready?"

"Ready for what?"

"We're going in after her." Gripping the reins with one hand and the stone with the other, Marcellus stretched over to the Gateway and slid his stone into the ring like a key in a lock.

His hand seized around the stone, a brilliant azure light exploding through the gaps in his fingers. Everything around him blurred and pulled. He felt a sudden jolt, an unmistakable connection to Kedron as if they were magically linked together. His heart leapt in horror as he realized what that meant. "Wait!" Blue light swept around him like a whirlwind and he looked to Corren, reached out for him, yelled "Grab Nicolai too." Corren reached out his hands, one to Nicolai and one to Marcellus. The wind raced past Marcellus in a roar that echoed in his ears and just before he closed his grip around Corren's hand, it disappeared. He held only air. "NO!" Still firmly on Kedron's back, Marcellus felt as if the ground fell away and all that held them was the swirling wind, roaring around them with frightening speed.

553

As suddenly as it had begun, it stopped.

The cool of the sea was replaced by heat so constricting he found it an effort to draw breath. Pinpricks of sweat covered his body. The blinding light was gone and he saw no sea, no water, no Bridge, no one. Only dry ground sparsely scattered with dull green bushes and the occasional tree, though he had never seen trees quite like these before. The sky above was a pale, stark bowl of barren sky, not a cloud to be seen. He was in the Realm of the Phoenix. Alone.

He looked down at his hand. The stone was gone.

All that remained was ash.

Fifteen

The swirling tempest of blue light vanished from within its own center as if sucked into a vortex. When Nicolai saw Marcellus was gone he hunched over as if he had been punched in the chest.

"NO!" Corren said. "He's there without us. He's there alone."

Nicolai looked to the ring. All he saw was empty space where the Gateway had once been. "Where is it? Where's the ring?"

"What?" Corren said looking too, his eyes wide with astonishment. "What... what do we do now?"

"I don't know, but we have to get to him."

"How?" Corren said, his voice a rage. "The Gateway's gone! How are we going to get there now?"

There was no answer, only silence, and Nicolai searched for a solution. He heard someone running up behind them. When he turned and saw it was Praea, everything slid firmly into place. She was running now, but Nicolai knew she had not run all the way.

"That's how," Nicolai said and quickly dismounted.

Corren turned, then gaped at Praea. "How did you get here?"

"She flew," Nicolai said. Now he was the one being gaped at, by them both. "I'm sorry, Praea, but we need you. Can you really carry a man?"

Corren dismounted and came up to them, staff in hand.

"Yes, but..."

"Can you carry two?"

"What's going on?" she asked, glancing at Corren.

"I'd like to know the same thing," Corren said.

"We need to get into the Realm. Aradia is there. Marcellus too. The Gateway is gone and that only leaves the Cliffs." Her eyes widened and she turned to the Cliffs. She followed their sheer edges up to the top. He only allowed her a moment. "Please Praea. We have to get there. We have to stop her."

"Nicolai, what are you talking about?" This from Corren. Nicolai and Praea did not remove their eyes from each other.

"You want me to carry two grown men to the top of those Cliffs?"

"Can't you do it?"

"I…" She faced the Cliffs again. She didn't look at all certain and Nicolai's heart began to pound. *We cannot be stuck here. We can't be.*

Corren stepped in closer. "What's all this about?" he asked firmly.

Praea faced Nicolai fully now, her expression resolute. She took two steps back, raised both arms high, and said an incantation. When she brought them down again, they were massive golden wings beating the air, raising her feathery, shining body, her massive talons curling and tucking up under her.

"A Tulaga!"

Corren and Nicolai watched her lift, their hair and clothes beat back by her flapping wings. "She's… How?" Corren said as she arced over them, then scooped down and took hold of each with an ample clutch of the backs of their tunics.

All at once they were in the air, their shirts tight across their chests and under their arms, legs dangling as the ground fell away at a startling rate. Corren grabbed Nicolai's arm compulsively, holding his staff close to his chest with the other. They flew over water, over the top of Crescent Island, its dark rock protruding from the deep blue of the sea, all the time gaining height. They flew over the city, faces and arms pointing up at them, then that too fell away. They soared over the green and brown spotted land, swathed in the middle by the Big Winding River that seemed small and slight now and continued to shrink beneath them. Nicolai's heart pounded in his ears. The higher they went the more his sensation of falling increased. There was nothing to hang on to or cling to, though Corren was clinging to him. Nicolai had to resist the urge to say he changed his mind and beg her to land. He took his eyes from the ground below and caught the horizon instead. The beauty of what he saw was so stunning that his breath caught in his chest. The horizon stretched far over the earth, the Mountains of Vitra with their endless peaks and the vast heart of the Wilds all gathered together as one. His heart stopped at the stunning beauty of a view as poignant as this.

Praea's flight steepened. The Cliffs reared up ahead of them as she aimed for their pinnacle still far above. The sharpness of the climb caused her speed to slow and it took more effort to fly now. They lost height, falling. Nicolai grabbed Corren's arm too. She recovered, pulling them back up with a tug, her flight slow and laborious. *Maybe this wasn't a good idea after all.* Nicolai did not dare look down but rather locked his eyes on the top, willing them there.

Nicolai heard a ripping sound and he and Corren looked hard at each other.

"What was that?"

They heard it again. Nicolai could see it too, the fabric of Corren's cloak ripping where Praea had grabbed it.

"Praea!"

The fabric let loose, the sound of the rip unending. Corren and Nicolai scrambled, arms and legs flying, to grab a better hold of each other. Corren's cloak broke free of her grasp and he swung in a wide arc below Nicolai, hanging on, Nicolai's arms straining to support him. They dipped wildly again, her wings flapping hard while they sank until she caught the air and brought them back up again.

Nicolai's hold was precarious, Corren's awkward. As they rose, in slow measured rises, Nicolai's muscles began to quake and he strained all the more. He dared not look to see how high they were or how close the top. *Almost there,* he told himself, not knowing if it were true. *Almost there.* He felt a blast of heat and the talon holding Nicolai released. As soon as he realized he was falling... he had stopped. He and Corren landed on hot, blessedly firm ground.

Near them, Praea bent over, panting. Nicolai scrambled off the ground, his bare skin stinging from contact with the searing earth. He went to her. He put his hand on her back as she fought for breath. Here she was, in the middle of it after all. Nicolai didn't know what else would face them today, but he knew one thing. The time had come to tell Praea everything.

৪৫ ৪৫ ৪৫

557

Corren struggled to his feet and looked around. His mind was reeling from the revelation that Praea was a Tulaga, that Nicolai knew this, and that now here they were, in the Realm. This was not how things were supposed to go. Corren tried to think what to do next. In all their planning, in all their scenarios, they never once considered the possibility that *they* would end up here. They looked around. All they saw was desert, dry bushes, a few small rock formations, and the odd *detanae* trees Corren had only read about. Somewhere out there was Marcellus. And Aradia. They had to find them, but how?

"Where do we go?" Nicolai asked.

"I don't..." but Corren's voice caught in his throat. He hastily reached into his cloak pocket and pulled out a small scroll. He unrolled the map he had copied in Aradia's office three weeks before. He had stolen it to keep it out of her hands, never imagining he would need it himself.

He unrolled it quickly. "This is where."

Kedron pranced nervously, snorting. Marcellus patted his neck to calm him. He was not exactly calm himself; Marcellus could only imagine what the horse thought of their sudden change of location. Fighting the dread he felt at the knowledge that he was here on his own, he glanced around, seeking out Aradia. All he saw was more desert, unvarying in its reach to each horizon. He decided to dismount, feeling too easily spotted if she should be near. Once on the ground he had no idea where to go.

He saw no tracks, no sign of Aradia at all. Maybe the Gateway had brought her somewhere different. He scanned the tops of the strange trees. They had wide, tall, unadorned trunks leading straight up to a cluster of branches. These were all short but hung down heavily, the crown of the weeping branches leaving a rather flat looking top. He saw no sign of the Phoenix. *Find the Phoenix and I'll find Aradia,* he thought. He went for the only distinguishable thing in sight, a slight mound to the southeast. It could be where the Phoenix was or it could lead to nothing at all. He headed out, knowing he could just as easily be going further away from Aradia as getting closer to her.

Sixteen

Aradia walked through the Realm of the Phoenix with confidence. Every several minutes, mist expelled from her body before evaporating in the heat. It was the souls of extracted men, vanishing under the power of the Phoenix's magic that tried in vain to reach her. She did not fear it. Her shield of souls was well stocked. She had time enough.

She came to the Stones of Balance and stopped. The rock formation was stout, standing not even as tall as she, a thin protrusion of rock upon which balanced a flat, elongated stone. It was one of the few items of distinction she had seen thus far and she had been walking toward it for the last hour. Aradia reached into her pocket and pulled out the map.

"Turn to the east," it read.

She did thus, began walking, and read on. "Proceed for ten furlongs, turn forty degrees to the north, then follow until you reach the White Dry River."

Here, Aradia stopped.

She looked ahead of her and saw only barren desert, same as always. She looked behind her and saw the same thing. The sun was still high overhead, but dipping in this direction. Dipping toward the west.

Aradia looked back at the map. She searched her memory and found a glitch. She held up the parchment and studied it. She smelled it and found nothing wrong. Only something *was* wrong. This map was not what she remembered.

Again, she thought back to the first time she read this map, shortly after copying it from the original in the Vaults of the Order of Ceinoth. Her memory told her something different from what she now saw. She furrowed her brows. Her memory had never failed her before. Never.

Yet here was the map.

559

She looked to the east. She looked to the west. She looked at the map. Misty bits of someone's soul escaped from her skin.

Aradia made her decision, and began walking.

Marcellus traveled through the same swatch of dry desert over and over again. He knew he must be making progress because the mound ahead of him was slowly getting larger, but it felt he was getting nowhere. It all looked the same, and he couldn't quite fathom the heat. He felt he was walking through the smithy's forge. By the time the sun was high overhead he was parched and drenched with sweat. He felt the heat radiating from the ground like stones warmed in an oven. Kedron felt it too; his pace grew more lethargic, his breath coming in hot gasps on Marcellus' shoulder as he led him along. Marcellus continued, always looking either for signs of Aradia or the Phoenix. What if he came all this way for nothing? He never saw anything else worth following, so he kept going. When, at last the mound was only a few hundred feet away from him, he stopped. It rose perhaps twenty feet in the air. At its pinnacle was a lone tree. Like every other tree in sight, it had a cylinder-type base, weeping branches, and a flat top. This top held something else. As he drew closer, maybe ninety feet away now, he could see what it was: branches and twigs piled neatly into a pyre, and atop this... the Phoenix.

He halted. The Phoenix didn't look how he expected. Though it was the most massive creature he'd ever laid eyes on, and that alone was breathtaking, it was dull in color, its feathers awry, its head drooping. Marcellus remembered it was dying. Corren said it was only vulnerable the minute or two before it regenerated, but looking at it now Marcellus wondered if it weren't vulnerable much sooner. Despite its decrepit appearance, Marcellus felt a bond with it. He could sense its intelligence, its benign character. He wanted to take it somewhere safe, get it out of the open where it sat in plain sight. Even if he could carry such a massive bird, he couldn't reach it. It was high in the tree with only a tall, smooth trunk and no branches for a foothold. No one could climb such a tree. He was not so concerned about climbing; Aradia's staff would have no trouble reaching it.

Marcellus looked around. He saw no sign of her. Maybe she couldn't find her way. Somehow he didn't think so. It had been easy enough for him to find his way and she likely already knew where she was going. "So where is she?"

The hairs on the back of his neck raised and he had the sudden, unpleasant sensation of being watched. He turned. First he felt the bonds, then he saw the person who magically cast them. He fell backwards, unable to catch himself. His head, already sore from that morning's impact, hit the ground again and he moaned.

Aradia swept into his view. Her face wore an expression of raw hatred. She marched up to him, swift and furious, her staff in one hand. With the other, she bent and extracted Marcellus' sword from its sheath, a deathly metallic ringing piercing the air. In a blinding flash she brought it down toward his neck. He saw the sword descend upon him, a slice of white on the blade glaring in the burning sun. Only the bonds restraining him kept him from recoiling but nothing kept him from crying out. In a torrent of images, his mind glimpsed his father, his brothers, Janus, all those he loved then the sword was upon him... and stopped.

His heart beat painfully against his chest. Keeping the blade hard to his neck, Aradia knelt and put her face so close to his so quickly that it felt an attack of itself. Her breathing was short, ragged, fierce, her eyes flashing madly. Her arm, and thus the sword, shook as she trembled with suppressed rage. Marcellus felt the vein in his neck pulsing against the cold, sharp metal of the blade.

"I would cut off your head this instant," she spat, "if it weren't for that stone hanging about your neck!"

His eyes widened in alarm. His necklace—and its empty casing—hid under his shirt. He had a sudden, horrifying vision of her yanking it out with the tip of his sword.

He could not think of anything beyond that.

She stood abruptly, her rage still throbbing on the surface, the sword clutched in her hand. "I will not be denied of it again!" Her voice thundered through the air. She fixed her eyes on him. He could not pull his from hers. Her chest heaved as she fumed at him. It seemed to go on and on, an eternal moment of fear and dread. Slowly

561

something in her changed. It seemed she was looking past him, through him. Her breathing began to settle and her face hardened into a cool mask. Though her eyes had never left him, he felt as if she truly saw him again. She regarded him with a gaze of complete unconcern. When she spoke her voice was even, cold, controlled. "Once the power of the Phoenix is mine, I'll be able to take it from you well enough."

She turned as if to leave, but saw Kedron and stopped. She glanced sideways at Marcellus, and gave him a smile that sent chills into his heart. "Lest there should be any doubt about what fate awaits you..."

In one grand motion she pulled the sword far out to her side and seeing what she was about to do Marcellus fought against his invisible bonds in a panic. "NOOOOO!" She brought it around hard and swift, slashing the sword across Kedron's throat, his blood flying and trailing after it, fanning out in the air. A sickening gurgle came from Kedron's throat as he reeled and arched. He arched onto his side, legs swinging into the air then collapsing back down. His eyes grew glassy, distant. Blood pooled on the dry ground.

Marcellus' wrath, hurt, and terror imploded within him where it raged and came out in a wild and terrible roar. His throat strained and tore and he could not stop, his scream fighting out of him until, breath spent, he gulped in air and coughed out a sob.

"You *suffer*," Aradia said, pointing the sword at him, "because you deserve to suffer! How dare you even *think* to get in my way?"

"I'll kill you!" he said. "I'll kill you!"

She laughed shrilly. "You, little maggot, cannot so much as *spit* on me, let alone kill me." She raised the helm of the sword, its blade—thick with blood—pointing straight down and plunged it into Kedron's belly. The horse's body twitched horribly, even in death, and Marcellus furiously blinked back hot tears.

She watched Marcellus coolly. "Enjoy your last hour of life."

She turned, and with her staff in hand, Aradia walked toward the Phoenix.

562

Seventeen

An hour remained. Aradia stood watching the Glorious Bird patiently, the sun setting in a fiery blaze behind it. The Phoenix's magic attacked her ceaselessly and the mist escaping from her in regular intervals was proof. She stood to the south of the bird, forty feet away, waiting for her moment to come.

Marcellus lay on the ground sixty feet behind her. Immobile. Helpless. Pinned by Aradia's magic that she sent to him each moment. The heat from the ground seeped through his clothes, searing his skin, but he fought to get up for another reason. He strained against his bonds, his anger growing the more time passed and more than once he grunted in frustration. Aradia never turned when he did this.

But she did smile.

When Corren, Nicolai, and Praea first saw the Phoenix, they were coming up to it from the east. Corren felt a rush of relief. They found it. At last. "Now where's..." he began, but was cut off.

The Phoenix raised its head slowly, arched back its long neck, and opened its mouth to the sky. A single note escaped, trembling and mournful. Corren felt a terrible chill.

This was the sign Aradia waited for.

She was hunched forward slightly now, bowed over by the strength of the Phoenix's power pushing on her, for her shield was growing thin. She fixed her eyes on the Phoenix and shook her head. Her fading shield did not matter. "Time's up," she said as the Phoenix's weakening gaze fixed first on her then down to its own pyre. She pulled out the Ajinn and held the cool glass ball directly in front of her. "I win."

She aimed her staff at the Phoenix, another wisp of mist expelling from her skin. Her body ached as she channeled all her magic, all her concentration. She needed every bit of it for her task, but it would be enough. Victory was hers.

"Comessa spitira ret triva a virra!" she shouted. The Ajinn glowed white, emitted a fiery stream of light that entwined with the violet light now streaming from her staff, and shot straight for the Phoenix. The lights hit it on the chest. Aradia shrieked in triumph but no one heard her for the Phoenix's screams ripped through the air as it arched in pain.

Corren—who along with Nicolai and Praea now saw Aradia clearly—said, "No, we're too late!"

Aradia's heart leapt in her throat, her body stinging with excitement, thrilling chills coursing through her. The black scorch mark on the breast of the Glorious Bird spread and the dull red and gold feathers fell on its wooden pyre. The white light surrounded all but the Phoenix's head, the bird still screeching.

"What do we do?!" Nicolai demanded.

"The Ajinn," was all Corren could say. It had to be destroyed, but it could not, just like Aradia could not now be stopped. *We all die today.*

Aradia's staff shuddered. Extracting power required power. Her grip tightened, her will strengthened, and her heart thirsted for what was coming, for she knew she had power enough to take it.

"VIRRA RELESSA A MI!" The purple and white light completely engulfed the Phoenix now. Its body, burnt and spent, fell to the pyre to rise again no more. The gray mist of the Phoenix's spirit now floated above. It held all the Phoenix's magic, all its immortal power, and it was now under Aradia's control. She guided it to her. Her body raced, her grips on the Ajinn and on her staff were firm. The Phoenix's spirit came closer and her enchanted eyes fixed on it, on its glory, on *her* glory.

At the moment the Phoenix died, at the precise moment its body fell from Aradia's extracting hold and crumpled lifeless on the pyre, the stone in Corren's staff lit into a brilliant red. Aradia did not notice this: her eyes were on the Phoenix's spirit. Nicolai did not notice this: his eyes were on the Ajinn. But Corren noticed. And understood.

He turned to Praea, who was staring at the Phoenix's dead body with horrified eyes. He gripped her arm. "I need up there!"

Nicolai did not remove his eyes from the Ajinn. "The Ajinn," was all Corren had said, but it was enough. Nicolai reached down and grasped his throwing spear, made of the earth with more strength than anything made by man, and freed it from its holster. He set his eyes on his target. He brought back his arm, flung it forward, and hurled the spear toward its target. The spear audibly cut through the air, spinning in a tight rotation, dead on course. When the tip pierced the center of the Ajinn, shards of glass flew out in every direction. Aradia recoiled, screamed, and the white light from the Ajinn and the violet light from Aradia's staff vanished with one accord.

The gray mist of the Phoenix's spirit hovered in the air. The great bird lay dead, without power to call its spirit into a new birth. Without the Ajinn, Aradia's staff could no longer control it either. Aradia knew that in just minutes the mist would dissipate, its magic lost to everyone. She screamed with rage that stormed the air, shaking everyone who heard it. Her eyes hunted the source of the spear but what she saw instead was a glittering golden bird carrying Corren to the top of the tree, a red light shining at the tip of his staff held out in front of him. They were aiming for the Phoenix.

Aradia shrieked wildly, took her aim and spoke a deadly incantation: "ANNIHILLIA VIR...rrahhh...!" The incantation sputtered in her mouth and the spell left her staff weakened, aimed in a different direction than Aradia had intended for she had arched her back at that moment too, and froze. Constricting pain shot out from her chest, racing down her arms and thighs and up through her neck. Chasing after this was an icy chill. She jerked her head down a little, again a little more for she could not control her movements as normal. Finally she saw what had pierced her, a blade sticking out of her chest, its metal like flowing water. Blackness stole her vision, from the edges in. Her legs gave out and she collapsed forward in a heap.

Marcellus, who stood behind her, watched her do this. When she had harnessed all her magic to attack the Phoenix, all of her will, she

565

had unwittingly released her hold on Marcellus too. He now put his foot on her back, bent over, and yanked the sword free from her body. Strands of silver hair came up with it, released, and fell back down like the broken remnants of a sticky web.

When they cleared the top of the pyre, the spell Aradia had cast went soaring over Corren's head and hit Praea instead. Her hold on him failed and Corren dropped, catching himself on the edge of the pyre. He fastened his eyes on the Phoenix's body immediately. He was just close enough. He pulled back his staff for the last act he knew he would ever do. Corren plunged the tip of the staff with its glowing red stone under the Phoenix's body. The magic of the stone drained all the strength and life of the wizard wielding it, and his hold on the pyre released.

By the time Nicolai took his eyes from the shattered Ajinn and realized Corren and Praea were gone from his side, they were already at the top of the tree. When he saw the spell hit Praea in the chest, horror propelled him into a run he was not even aware of. "NO!" She arched backwards, transforming out of bird form as she did so, and fell, as if in slow motion, toward the earth. Before she hit the ground, Corren's stone connected with the body of the Phoenix and an eruption of red light flew out in every direction. Corren fell too. The red light reached up and encompassed the gray mist of the Phoenix's spirit, consumed it, swallowed it back into itself as the light crashed in on the Phoenix's body and disappeared. Praea crumpled to the ground, moaning. Corren's dead body fell to the earth next to her with a sickening crunch.

Nicolai fell skidding to his knees, coming between them. "No, no, no." Corren's eyes were blank shells. Praea was shaking, sweating, cringing into a ball, and turning deathly pale.

The Phoenix and the pyre above burst into one great gasp of fire. Nicolai huddled over Praea and Corren protectively when a rush of heat came toward them. The fire, Phoenix, and pyre all disintegrated with one accord. The only thing left was a massive pile of ash.

Nicolai went to Praea and scooped her into his arms, heart aching and mourning for Corren, fearful Praea would soon follow him. Marcellus ran up and Nicolai glanced at him long enough to see him staring at Corren in shock. "No."

Nicolai turned back to Praea, shaking her now, but she would not open her eyes. Her breathing was shallow and strained. She was drenched in sweat and her skin tinged a sickly blue. Nicolai put his hand on her cheek, "What did she do to you?"

"Nicolai." It was Marcellus, but Nicolai could not look at him. "Your stone."

Nicolai pulled back, looked, saw his stone. A yellow light shone gloriously from it. He grabbed it, his heart soaring so quickly it hurt. But it was not Praea he thought of. This stone was lit first for Corren, Nicolai knew it and felt a terrible urgency like he had to do it now before it was too late. He quickly and gently lay Praea down. "Hang on," he said. "You're next." He freed the stone from its casing and with both hands rushed it onto Corren's chest.

The light erupted, blinded him, threw him back. He crashed onto his shoulder. This time he was prepared and scrambled to a sit without so much as a pause, his throbbing shoulder the only acknowledgement of what just happened. He looked to Corren urgently, Marcellus earnestly kneeling and watching too. Corren stirred. Then blinked. Then looked around. Marcellus exclaimed his relief and pulled a bewildered Corren into a hearty embrace.

"What?" Corren said thickly.

Weak with relief, Nicolai searched for the stone. He wouldn't celebrate until Praea was well too, for she was far too still now, her eyes closed, her skin ashen. He didn't see the stone. He scanned the ground again, a sudden panic rising in him. When he glanced at the palms of his hands, Nicolai froze. They were covered in ash. He looked at Corren's chest. His shirt was stained in ash too.

The yellow stone was gone.

Eighteen

Corren stumbled to his feet, still in a daze, not quite believing he was here. He saw Nicolai cradling Praea as if from a distance. Saw Marcellus kneeling on the ground next to them. He saw himself standing, watching it all as if from a great height. He may have turned his head, or the vision may have come to him, but however it happened, the Glorious Bird came now into his view.

This was what brought Corren back to firm reality. The Phoenix had risen from the ashes in stunning splendor, its broad wings flapping, its feathers fiery and glowing as if still ablaze. Its eyes, like embers, fixed on Corren's, and his mind exploded free of its bounds. He felt as if he were on fire. Though there was no pain he felt the fire with such intensity that he thought he must be devoured by it. The windows of his mind were thrust open and he discovered powers and abilities and secrets within himself he did not know he had, the magic of his own mind and heart unveiled, presented to him with such heartbreaking clarity that he felt burst outside of himself. His joy and the fire united as one in their consumption of him as he received this, the last—and greatest—gift of the Phoenix. The fire lessened and the light, in all its array of colors, swirled around him, warmed him, brought him back to his body where he stood transfixed, his eyes on the Glorious Bird once more. His place on the earth was sure. The smoldering Realm of the Phoenix stretched out in every direction.

Then the Song came, the Song of Calling, the clarion call of the Order. The bird lifted off, rising high into the sky. In its massive talons was an egg of ash. It soared away to the north, toward the Order of Ceinoth and the Rock of Light.

The Four Elements were left in the Realm, alone.

ဢ   ဢ   ဢ

Nicolai cradled Praea, rocking her in his arms. "Don't go," he moaned. "Don't go." The spell that would have killed her in an instant had it hit her full force was now slowly draining her life instead.

Corren walked over to his staff. It lay on the ground, not far from where he had fallen when he was dead. He picked it up. The top was not twisted around stone now, but ash, hardened and petrified and, Corren could sense, immensely powerful.

He turned to Praea. She was fading. Nearly gone.

He gently put the tip of his staff on her forehead. He said no words, only called upon his will, focused it, gathered the magic to himself, and gave it to her. A golden light emerged from the staff and swept over her, bathing her in soft, glowing healing. Nicolai sat back, still supporting her in his arms. He watched this in wonder. The light hovered, shimmered, then slowly faded. When it was gone, Praea's eyes were open, bright and alert. She sat up slowly.

Nicolai was not willing to release her. He embraced her, clutched her to him, then kissed her cheeks, her forehead, her nose—she laughed—then he kissed her on the mouth with such passion that Corren was compelled to look away. Marcellus met his eyes, for he had retreated his gaze too.

Marcellus cleared his throat, shuffling his feet slightly. "I'm not going to kiss you," he said, "if it's all the same to you."

Corren smiled, almost laughed at the realization and relief that it was all finally over. And he was here to see it. He felt as if his life was open to him again, clean and fresh, a gift. Marcellus smiled too. Corren took a deep breath. There was only one thing left to do.

With one brief glance at Nicolai and Praea, he turned toward Aradia. Corren approached her body slowly, Marcellus walking along beside him. She lay on the ground, her position awkward and unnatural, her silver hair fanned over her back, concealing part of her pale face. A broad stain of blood marked her back and trickled out from her body below. She seemed diminished, without any of the glory or power Corren always knew her to have, without any fondness that would cause him to mourn her. He had already mourned who he once thought she was, what she could've been. He had already mourned the loss of something that had never been real to begin with. So it was with little regret that he knelt down and brushed her hair away from her neck, revealing the chain of her necklace. He released the clasp and pulled away the silver pendant of the Head of the Order, placing the medallion in his pocket as he stood. Her staff lay by her side, her hand still clutching it. Corren put the tip of his staff to hers and watched as he saw in reality what he willed in his mind: the crumbling of her staff into dust.

"That's that then." Together, he and Marcellus made their way back. Nicolai and Praea had stood and came over to meet them.

"This is yours," Marcellus said and he handed Nicolai his earthen throwing spear. Nicolai took it with the most worry-free smile Corren had ever seen him wear. Marcellus smiled too and looked around. "Now how are we getting home?"

No one answered, for the Phoenix came back over the horizon. It came straight toward them in a glorious vision of flaming red and orange until it was hovering directly above them, flapping its enormous wings, delivering hot blasts of air as it did so. Light surrounded them. It spun like a vortex, windy, bright, hot, swirling and cocooning them. They instinctively huddled together, gripping one another, tucking their heads down as the Phoenix's fire surrounded them.

When the Great Darkness retreated from Stonebridge it revealed not just the sky, ablaze with the setting sun, but the Eternal Flame, so massive and bright that it elicited awe-struck gasps from the citizens still gathered at the docks. Not even the oldest among them had ever seen it so big, not half so big. Janus watched this with wonder, unable for a moment to look away from its brilliant light. Soon she turned and stood with her eyes fixed on the Bridge. This was where she had been led earlier by a tumult of rumors, some that Lord Marcellus had disappeared, some that he had died. This was where she stayed, where she waited along with everyone else to see if the Tulaga would bring back the farmer and the wizard. If their prince would come back from the end of the Bridge. This was what she watched for most. As she looked at the Bridge now, she leapt back.

A pillar of fire shot up from the far end of the Bridge straight into the sky, so high the top could not be seen. It fell back down and flames raced along the Bridge, heading for shore, blackened stone crumbling into the sea behind the advancing wave of flame.

It drew ever nearer, roaring for land. Screams echoed through the air. People ran in terror, but Janus stood transfixed, horrified. There was no way back now. He was gone.

The flames reached the shore and here another huge pillar of flame shot up into the sky. The heat propelled Janus back several steps and she crossed her arms in front of her face for protection from the blast.

The flame whiffed out. She felt before she saw. The white smoke left in the wake of the fire was cleared away by the blowing wind. Four shapes became visible.

There they stood: Corren, Nicolai, Praea, and Marcellus.

Weak with emotion, unable to move, Janus released a gasp of relief. Marcellus saw her, instantly turned to her, approached her quickly. She was vaguely aware of the faces around her, thought she should properly bow to the prince of the land, but bowing was impossible anyway for as soon as he was there he pulled her into in a fierce embrace, whispered her name. She clung to him, too. He took her face in his hands and kissed her firmly.

Despite the extraordinary events of the day, despite everything else that had happened, the citizens watching would not fail to remember —for years after—the first time they saw King Marcellus kiss their future queen.

Corren had been watching this too, but the person he now saw emerging from the excitable crowd surrounding them was Kennard. He looked at them in amazement, his face glowing. He seemed wanting to say something but he spoke no words. Corren smiled and greeted him, but Kennard only replied, "The Phoenix gave us a vision. In the Rock of Light. We saw what happened. We..." and here he looked at them each in turn. "We have not gratitude enough."

571

Corren shook his head, uncomfortable. "No need for that."

Kennard still looked at him with amazement. "Please, we wish you to come." He looked at each of them, Corren, Nicolai, and Praea, but then furrowed his brows, looking around. "But where is Blue Brother?"

Nicolai pointed to where Marcellus and Janus stood and said, "I'll get him."

Kennard watched him go, eager and impatient.

"Kennard?" Corren said softly. Kennard looked at him. Corren withdrew the pendant of the Head of the Order, its silver flame winking orange by the light of the setting sun. "If you would deliver this to the proper person," he said and placed it in Kennard's hand.

Kennard's expression changed. He accepted it with silent, sober acknowledgement. He nodded and tucked it away as Marcellus approached. "Please," Kennard said, "this way."

Corren entered the small round room of the Cloister for the third time—Kennard in front of him, Marcellus, Nicolai, and Praea behind —but now the chairs sat vacant.

"This way," Kennard said before Corren could ask, and led them through the chairs and to a small door in the rear. He opened it to reveal a winding stone stairway leading up from the circular base of the Rock of Light. He climbed. They followed him, spiraling up through the round tower and on uneven stairs made not by man but by the Phoenix's will, until they reached the top. And a door. Kennard went through this as well. Corren thought to himself that he ought not to be in such a guarded place, yet he did not hesitate. He walked through the door as if it were meant to be.

From the center of the round, open room rose a pillar of stone with the enormous Eternal Flame burning within it. Kennard led Corren and the others around it, flames blazing and popping. That was when they saw the rest of the Order. Included among them was a pale-faced woman Corren had never seen before and who he knew must be the Head of the Dianese branch, for they only ever came to retrieve the ash. Six members were here now. They were gathered in a small half circle, waiting for their guests. Kennard approached Bellamy, handed something to him—the pendant Corren guessed—then joined his peers in the circle.

Bellamy stepped forward and addressed his four visitors. "Our eternal gratitude to you, for your selfless defense of the Glorious Bird." Here he bowed and the Order bowed with him.

Corren accepted this with as much grace as he could, resisting the urge to tell them to stop, knowing it would cause offense. When they stood straight again, Corren, Nicolai, Marcellus, and Praea each inclined their head in acknowledgement.

"A change has come to us, we feel," Bellamy now said, "though we do not know what it is. We do know the sacred number of seven must be preserved within the Order. We cannot continue our ceremony without it." Without further explanation he rejoined the circle, the first in the line, and said, "I, Bellamy, Head of the Layrin branch of the Order, elect Master Corren, Red Brother, Head of the Order of Ceinoth." Corren felt a warm rush wash over him. He watched in bewildered silence as Bellamy continued. "He has already passed a Test of Virtue. Members of the Order of Ceinoth, what say you?"

"Corren, Red Brother," Kai'Enna said, managing to convey her faith and conviction in just those three words. Corren's face flushed hot.

"Corren, Red Brother," each said in turn, until six voices were heard. With the last, Corren felt the weight of the mantle their votes placed upon his shoulders. He also felt their gratitude, their confidence, their trust. He could hardly breathe.

Bellamy smiled. "Do you accept, Sage Corren?"

Corren did not answer at first. He felt too keenly aware of the people in front of him and what his responsibilities to them would be. Too keenly aware of the people by his side, knowing that without them Aradia would have been victorious. Without them he would not even be here. The Eternal Flame burned in his side vision; the windows to the Rock of Light opened all around to the outside world as it had since long before him and would continue to do for long after him. One link in the chain; that was his role.

Corren nodded his head. "I accept." His words lingered in the air, giving weight to the silence that followed.

Bellamy stepped forward silently, somberly. From his hands hung the pendant of the Head of the Order. Bellamy raised his hands and brought them behind Corren's neck, securing the clasp. He withdrew his hands and the pendant rested firmly against Corren's chest. Bellamy walked back to the circle, sweeping his arm toward a pillar rising from a raised platform. It was the Pillar of Receiving. Atop it was the massive egg of ash, waiting for the Head of the Order to retrieve it. "Your first task," Bellamy said.

Corren walked forward slowly, his cloak torn, his forehead gashed, and his heart beating with a new sense of purpose, a new understanding. He ascended the steps and stopped at the pinnacle, the egg of ash before him. He placed his hands on its rough surface and lifted the egg he had helped to preserve. With that single movement, Sage Corren ushered in the greatest age of magic yet known to man.

About the Author

DONNA COOK is an Arizona native recently transplanted to Boise, Idaho, where she spends time chasing the kids, exploring delicious eateries downtown, and dancing with her talented husband. She's currently working on the sequel to *Gift of the Phoenix.*

For information about upcoming novels and for fun extras related to the book, visit giftofthephoenix.com.